The Mad Patagonian

Part Two
Into the Abyss and
Back Again

Javier Pedro Zabala

Translated from The Spanish

by

Tomás García Guerrero

Peter Damian Bellis
Editor, English language edition

River Boat Books
St. Paul, MN

You have wakened not out of sleep, but into a prior dream, and that dream lies within another, and so on, to infinity, which is the number of the grains of sand. The path that you are to take is endless, and you will die before you have truly awakened.
—Jorge Luis Borges

I know who I am and who I may be, if I choose.
— Miguel de Cervantes Saavedra

When life seems lunatic, who knows where madness lies? Perhaps to be too practical is madness. To surrender dreams — this may be madness. Too much sanity may be madness — and maddest of all, to see life as it is and not as it should be.
— Miguel de Cervantes Saavedra

Escoraz Family descended from Andres and Ana

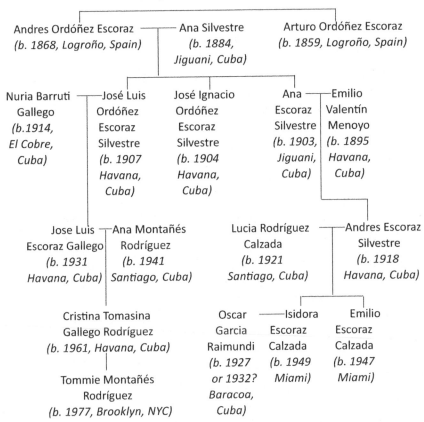

Andres Ordóñez Escoraz ——— Ana Silvestre   Arturo Ordóñez Escoraz
(b. 1868, Logroño, Spain)   (b. 1884,   (b. 1859, Logroño, Spain)
                                 Jiguani, Cuba)

Nuria Barruti ——José Luis   José Ignacio   Ana ——Emilio
Gallego   Ordóñez   Ordóñez   Escoraz Valentín
(b.1914,   Escoraz   Escoraz   Silvestre Menoyo
El Cobre,   Silvestre   Silvestre   (b. 1903, (b. 1895
Cuba)   (b. 1907   (b. 1904   Jiguani,   Havana,
                 Havana,   Havana,   Cuba)   Cuba)
                 Cuba)   Cuba)

Jose Luis ——Ana Montañés   Lucia Rodríguez ——Andres Escoraz
Escoraz Gallego Rodríguez   Calzada   Silvestre
(b. 1931   (b. 1941   (b. 1921   (b. 1918
Havana, Cuba) Santiago, Cuba)   Santiago, Cuba)   Havana, Cuba)

Cristina Tomasina   Oscar ———Isidora   Emilio
Gallego Rodríguez   Garcia   Escoraz   Escoraz
(b. 1961, Havana, Cuba) Raimundi Calzada   Calzada
                         (b. 1927 (b. 1949   (b. 1947
Tommie Montañés   or 1932? Miami)   Miami)
Rodríguez   Baracoa,
(b. 1977, Brooklyn, NYC) Cuba)

Escoraz Family descended from Arturo and Verona

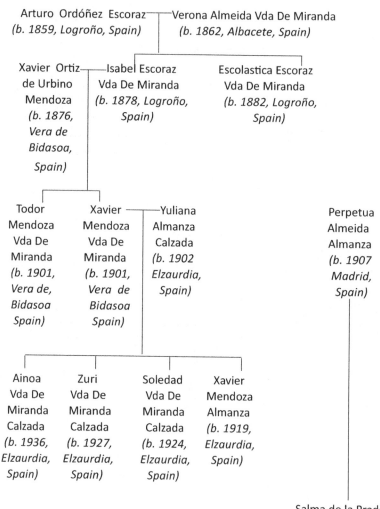

Arturo Ordóñez Escoraz
(b. 1859, Logroño, Spain)

Verona Almeida Vda De Miranda
(b. 1862, Albacete, Spain)

Xavier Ortiz
de Urbino
Mendoza
(b. 1876,
Vera de
Bidasoa,
Spain)

Isabel Escoraz
Vda De Miranda
(b. 1878, Logroño,
Spain)

Escolastica Escoraz
Vda De Miranda
(b. 1882, Logroño,
Spain)

Todor
Mendoza
Vda De
Miranda
(b. 1901,
Vera de,
Bidasoa
Spain)

Xavier
Mendoza
Vda De
Miranda
(b. 1901,
Vera de
Bidasoa
Spain)

Yuliana
Almanza
Calzada
(b. 1902
Elzaurdia,
Spain)

Perpetua
Almeida
Almanza
(b. 1907
Madrid,
Spain)

Ainoa
Vda De
Miranda
Calzada
(b. 1936,
Elzaurdia,
Spain)

Zuri
Vda De
Miranda
Calzada
(b. 1927,
Elzaurdia,
Spain)

Soledad
Vda De
Miranda
Calzada
(b. 1924,
Elzaurdia,
Spain)

Xavier
Mendoza
Almanza
(b. 1919,
Elzaurdia,
Spain)

Salma de la Prada
(b. 1969, Madrid, Spain)

The Mad Patagonian

Part Two
Into the Abyss and
Back Again

L'imagination est l'aiguillon des plaisirs; dans ceux de cette espèce, elle règle tout, elle est le mobile de tout; or, n'est-ce pas par elle que l'on jouit? n'est-ce pas d'elle que viennent les voluptés les plus piquantes?

De Sade, La Philosophie dans le boudoir

BOOK FOUR

the abduction of Escolástica Escoraz Vda De Miranda

Everyone dies, everyone forgets, everyone is forgotten, even God. This is what the great-grandmother of Isidora Escoraz Calzada used to say, a nugget Isidora held close to her heart. Except how did sweet Isidora know her great-grand- mother had said this? She never knew her great-grandmother in the flesh. They had never met. They had exchanged no letters. Isidora's great-grandmother (Ana Silvestre) was born in Jiguani, Cuba in 1884 and died in Havana in 1941 of a broken heart having never left Cuba or seen anything of the world, eight years before Isidora was born, one year after her husband (Andres Ordóñez Escoraz) had been shot and killed tending bar in his own café-turned-nightclub-turned-café at 112 Zulueta Street in downtown Havana, nineteen years after he had first opened the doors to this dream of a lifetime that was destined to become the scene of his death (not realizing that Old Havana was in the throes of perpetual decay even then and he should have opened his new business further west, in Vedado, or perhaps El Cerro, though in subsequent years these neighborhoods would also crumble under the weight of political upheaval and the relentless, turbulent weather and the bitter neglect of the newly impoverished).

The circumstances of Andres' tragic death were suspi- cious to say the least, and therefore quite memorable, at least from Isidora's perspective. A drunken lunatic had burst into his café, a wayward soul who perhaps had been visiting one of the brothels on Xifré Street, one of those stomach-wrenching dives filled with forty-year-old whores where the air inside is a sickly, greenish color from all the cigarette smoke and cigar smoke and the dirty oil lamps and the pestilent stench of semen and body odor and dried urine and the dead fish smell of soaked mattresses; or perhaps he had picked up a beautiful young mulatta girl who lived in the shadows at the end of Calle Galiano in the Plaza del Vapor because she had nowhere else to go. Of course no one knows (or will admit to such knowledge) the precise circumstances. But it is certainly fair to say that this madman reeked of cheap rum and cheap cigars and even cheaper perfume, the kind that smells mostly of dying orchids mixed with the sour citrus smell of lemons. In any event, the moment he entered Andres' café he spied a poster of the Spanish bullfighter Jose Garcia Carranza, alias 'Pepe Algabeño,' hanging on the wall behind the bar. It was from when the bullfighter was just starting out in Madrid. The drunken lunatic studied the poster a moment. Then he pulled a revolver and began firing at the poster and shouting death to the fucking Fascists, though why Fascism sprang to his mind when he saw the poster was not entirely clear.

Perhaps his comments were meant to show support (however misguided or deranged) for Cuba's fifth President, Gerardo Machado y Morales, beloved General of the Cuban War for Independence (which was actually the ninth major conflict in the Cuban struggle for independence descending from a long line of rebellions, revolts and conspiracies that began in 1810), the same Machado who later became an unbearable dictator (or a beacon of progressive hope, it was hard to tell, for such is the fluidity of Cuban politics), and who was toppled in 1933 thanks to a boatload of cash from the United States and would die a few years after that while living in exile in Miami Beach, an ironic twist on many levels, and whose descendants would find refuge in Florida or Panama or far-off Germany under assumed names like Jones or Reyez or Meierhoffer.

Or perhaps the drunken lunatic's comments were directed at the newly victorious Francisco Franco y Bahamonde in Spain, for the bullfighter in the poster had been a staunch Franco supporter and had, the presence of the poster notwithstanding, been killed four years earlier, four days after Christmas, ten days after battling the International Brigades near Boadilla del Monte but then he was sent south, where he had participated without a second thought in the Battle of Lopera under the command of Lieutenant Colonel Eduardo Alvárez Rementería, after which he was shot in the stomach by an unknown gunman on a road heading west near a farmhouse south of Montoro and later died in a provisional Red Cross hospital in Córdoba with the doctors watching helplessly, unable even to provide relief for the pain, for they had run out of morphine and then whiskey and had only

half a bottle of *absenta,* from their personal stock, which they
wanted to preserve for later.

But no matter what the drunken lunatic was ranting
about or railing against, it is also true that Andres had ample
time to duck for cover behind the bar and save his skin, but
according to those drinking in the bar at the time he hesitated,
as if he knew the gunman, and some said he even went so far
as to greet the man by name. There was some debate about
this afterwards among the patrons of the bar. Some thought
he said Beithen or Griffon or Grenfell, though none of these
names rang a bell with anybody. One witness even said he
heard a strange, quivering voice say 'Ah, yes, but not even a
faith as strong as yours can save you from the *otra muerte,'*
but others heard nothing at all. But everyone agreed that no
matter what Andres did or did not say, the unknown gunman
said nothing at all to indicate that he knew Andres; he just
began firing, and Andres fell victim (some would later call it
destiny) to one of the bullets ricocheting carelessly around the
café.

Then again, it was equally plausible that the poster was
not the target. All of the witnesses said the lunatic possessed
notoriously poor aim, for in spite of firing till the gun was
empty, the poster remained in mint condition, as did the
Victorian clock hanging on the wall next to the poster, but
the gilded salon mirror on the other side of the clock, a
showpiece most certainly, had been shattered. Perhaps the
suggestion that the gunman was aiming at the poster was pure
subterfuge on the part of a few unscrupulous individuals, paid
in advance by faceless men hiding in the shadows outside,
hoping to throw truth-seekers off the scent, (as if truth has
a scent), hoping to disguise the fact that Andres had been
methodically assassinated by a team of well-trained assassins
who sowed the tragic seeds of death and confusion wherever
they went, gunned down in cold blood, as it were, for a fistful
of United States dollars, as opposed to the uncertain value
of a few pesos (even those extravagant silver pesos with a
woman beneath a star on one side), but not simply for Andres'
supposed politics, but also because the café-turned-nightclub-
turned-café he had opened in 1922, Casa Oriente, was proving
to be stiff competition for another joint just down the street,

the now famous Sloppy Joe's, owned at that time by Jose
Abeal y Otero and Valentin Garcia, two greasy opportunistic
gamberros with known ties to the Radical Republican Party in
Spain, who had immigrated to Cuba in 1904 but had returned
to Spain on several occasions and had the last time (1931)
supposedly participated in the burning of the convents in
Málaga, though they later claimed to be in Seville at the time,
and who later became good friends with Hemingway, who
also hated the Fascists, real or imagined, no matter where he
found them.

So how was it possible that Isidora could know things
she couldn't possibly know? How is it possible to see the
world through another's eyes, particularly if those eyes are
now closed in the dream of death? Well, perhaps it is best
to be blunt, without any embellishment at all, although it
is fair to say that the various doctors who treated Isidora
when she was fifteen possessed a different (which is to say
scientific) opinion of the nature of her gift. But as far as
Isidora was concerned, she had the blood of two documented
psychics coursing through her veins: Escolástica Escoraz
Vda De Miranda, a niece to Isidora's great-grandfather, who
accompanied him to Cuba in 1899 and who later resettled in
Puerto Rico because the dreams she dreamed in Cuba troubled
her greatly; and Escolástica's sister, Isabel, who remained in
Spain and was later rumored to have predicted the bombing
of Guernica, which in turn led to rumors that she was a spy
fighting with Basque Loyalists in support of the Republic,
and when she was later captured by the Nationalists (some
said she was betrayed), she was tortured for information but
refused to give up a single name, which might have meant
that she had no names in her possession, but the Nationalists
felt she was simply being stubborn and needed to be taught a
lesson, so she was executed with a single shot to her temple.
The Colonel in charge shot her with a 1914 Mauser 6.35 mm
pocket pistol with a blue finish and a walnut grip, and then
with barely a flicker of emotion passing across his Germanic
features, like the shadow of a cloud passing across an out-
cropping of weathered granite, he had her body tossed into
a ravine, where it was said a pack of hungry dogs devoured
everything, even the bones.

But these two sisters were not the only psychics in Isidora's family. Isidora knew without any historical proof whatsoever that she was the last in a long line of psychics (mystics, soothsayers, poets, philosophers) that had dominated her family's bloodline on her father's side for the endless centuries preceding the dawn of the modern age, quite possibly all the way back to the time of the Moors and the conquest of Valencia, but at least as far back as the re-taking of Grenada and the surrender of Boabdil, the last Moorish king, in the year 1492, the same year Columbus set sail for the Americas and eventually discovered the paradise of Cuba.

Isidora could feel the surging power of countless generations of psychic women in her blood, women of great passion and intensity who could bend time and space with their imaginations and send bullets careening across the centuries, women who had never sought the limelight, some who may have been accused of witchcraft and burned at the stake, others who may have worked tirelessly treating victims of the plague and then coming down with the disease themselves and their skin riddled with festering black boils and the boils then exploding, precipitating tragic, agonizing, inevitable deaths (one wonders why they, being psychic, didn't see the tragedy of history as it was about to unfold or would unfold and take appropriate steps, unless you believe as the Greeks did that one can never escape one's destiny), and all of them now existing in a sort of pre-Catholic limbo where they no longer possessed names, probably because the written records of their births and baptisms and inevitable deaths had been lost through fire or water damage or simply the relentless march of time.

This was the wellspring of young Isidora's psychic abilities. She was not perhaps as gifted as some of those who came before her. Her gift was limited to speaking with the recently dead, those wayward souls who could still slip back and forth between this dimension and the next with a story to share or some pertinent advice to give. What is more, she could only speak with those who belonged to her own family. But she accepted these limitations with a grace and wisdom that went beyond her years. She possessed great sensitivity and great compassion, which meant that she could talk with the ghost of her great-grandmother as easily as others might chat with a stranger while waiting for a bus.

-38-

Isidora first stumbled into the lives of the long dead members of her family when she was a small child about the age of three. She was, as you might expect, slightly confused. But she was not frightened. She had no context for fear. She simply thought she was playing with angels, wingless angels, certainly, but angels nevertheless. Isidora took their presence as a matter of course, laughing and clapping her hands in delight as they told their stories, engaging them in all manner of childish games.

She told no one at first, not even her own mother.

She sensed even as a child that her mother would not have appreciated her strange gift, that her mother would have thought she was possessed by demons and quite possibly have taken her to see a priest.

By the time she had turned twelve, she had come to the conclusion that these angels were grandmothers and grandfathers and Great aunts and distant cousins, and that the stories they told were a mythic blend of what had happened to them while they lived, what they had hoped would happen but didn't, and what they saw happening in the future, both their future, which was Isidora's present, and also Isidora's future, which they could barely comprehend.

It was never always clear to Isidora if they were talking about the past, the hoped-for past, or the mysterious, mythic future, which may have had less to do with an understandable desire to pull legs and crack jokes, all with a mischievous tremor in their voices so that Isidora would know she was being kidded, and more to do with their actually being dead and existing outside of time where there was very little to do except bend the meanings of words and play around with the sequence of past events in an attempt to create new memories, which was an impossible task since memories are a purely temporal phenomenon.

It is also important to note that her dead relatives did their best to provide Isidora with specific dates and places when asked, and once or twice they provided extensive genealogies when to withhold such information would surely have caused Isidora great headaches that would have lingered for weeks, an insufferable condition which countless historians have endured in the absence of properly configured genealogy charts.

Then at the age of fifteen, in a bizarre argument she was having with her mother, though what they were arguing about nobody remembers, Isidora said that her great-grandmother, Ana Silvestre from the Isle of Cuba, understood her better than her own mother, who had left Cuba and was therefore without a homeland.

It was an odd thing to say, especially since her great-grandmother had died before Isidora was born, and when Isidora's mother pressed her on this point (only God knows what she was expecting Isidora to say), Isidora said she spoke to her great-grandmother on a regular basis. Instead of a priest, Isidora's suddenly alarmed mother took Isidora to the first of three doctors.

The first doctor, after only three sessions in three days of psychoanalysis, sessions that were held in a dark, windowless, prison cell of a room in which the air conditioning had been deliberately turned off (a diabolical maneuver given that it was the middle of June and the temperature outside was well above ninety-five), declared that Isidora was suffering from a psychotic break with reality precipitated by the lack of a strong father figure (which Isidora's mother agreed with) and the debilitating presence of an overbearing mother, (a claim which Isidora's mother rejected without even a backwards glance at the furrowed brow of the doctor, who wavered at the entrance of his prison-cell office but ultimately retreated into the shadows).

The second doctor, a behaviorist who had written a book with the pompous sounding title *A Re-Evaluation of Auguste Comte and the Prima Facie Paradox of Positivism*, said that Isidora wasn't actually speaking face to face with her great-grand-

mother, or any of her dead relatives for that matter (a statement
that reassured Isidora's mother, naturally), she was simply
making up stories as a way to garner attention, a behavior
she had most certainly learned at home (a purposely vague
statement that infuriated Isidora's mother nonetheless, though
it was true beyond any doubt, and prompted her to seek a third
opinion).

The third doctor, a sort of New-Age Jungian, believed
that Isidora had tapped into the collective unconscious, what
some called the mind of God, a repository, he said, of all of the
stories that have come down to humanity through the ages.
"Yes, yes," he had said with a sudden burst of unrestrained
almost adolescent enthusiasm, "while these stories very well
could be factual accounts of Isidora's actual flesh-and-blood
ancestors, they could also be symbolic stories, in other words,
stories that could be true of any one of the countless souls
that have lived out their lives on this tiny blue dot we call the
earth."

The third doctor suggested that Isidora's mother
ask her daughter to write the stories down, or at the very
least tape-record them, so that he could write a book, yes,
yes, he had always wanted to write a book, and Isidora's
stories might be just the ticket. He would call the book *The
Past Lives of Isidora Escoraz Calzada*, or *The Multiple Lives of
a Spanish Schizophrenic*, or something like that, something
catchy.

"So you think my little Isidora is a radio blasting out
stories from the dead?" Isidora's mother asked. "Is that what
you think?"

"Either that or she has a cochlear implant and is receiving transmissions for unknown reasons from aliens living on a
distant planet," the third doctor joked.

Isidora's mother did not know how to respond to the
third doctor, so she said nothing. But that was the last doctor
Isidora saw. After three months of going to doctors, Isidora's
mother decided that enough was enough. She decided that
if her daughter was cavorting about with her long-dead
great-grandmother and various uncles and aunts and cousins
who perhaps did not yet realize they were ghosts, then so
be it. She would let her daughter find out for herself what a

painful bit of stupidity it was to let the dead get their hooks
into you.

Even if they were family.

Especially if they were family.

And if her daughter were simply telling tales out of
school, submerged in the nostalgia of a lost paradise, then so
be it. She would not bother about any stories that came flowing out of her daughter's mouth. She would let that hopscotch
river run its course.

Isidora never again said a word to her mother about
her strange gift, and by the time Isidora had turned sixteen,
both she and her mother remembered the summer of the three
doctors, as they had both come to think of it, as one remembers a strange, incoherent, improbable dream. Life returned to
normal, or at least to a quasi-normal state.

-39-

Up until Isidora turned eighteen, she was never happier
than when she was listening (usually when there was a bright
full moon in the sky) to her grandmothers and her grandfathers and her Great aunts and her distant cousins telling
their stories. It was a little like owning a museum quality
collection of old photographs, or more precisely, a set of old
photographic glass plates, which were used without a second
thought until the 1920s, but which were slowly abandoned
as less fragile films were introduced into the market place
and after a while were used only by astronomers seeking to
capture the iridescent beauty of the stars.

Many of the stories that Isidora's long-dead relatives
shared with the young and impressionable Isidora were in one
way or another about tragically doomed love affairs, so Isidora
soon found herself hoping to someday fall in love so she could
prove to the bitter and inveterate naysayers of her extended
family that true love was indeed possible, even in an age
that prized brand new linoleum floors above wedding vows.

Naturally by true love she meant a vibrant, passionate, romantic love, the kind that sends a shiver racing like electricity up
your spine and your legs crumble like diseased statuary and
you can barely breathe and you wonder if you will ever walk
again. So she became expert in the nuances of love that most
of us miss, the subtle give-and-take between two consenting
adults at any hour of the day or night; the tragic consequences
of a love that has been forgotten and the resurging hope (more
tentative the second or third time around, which is to be
expected, but no less exciting) that accompanies that very love
when it one day rises up from the cold ashes of forgetfulness;
the quiet fullness of love that descends without warning
upon two aging but once robust lovers who from then on can
only express themselves through the mirror of their eyes, the
lingering, infinitely gentle caress of a familiar, flattering hand.

For Isidora, the expression of love defined all human
activity and the very nature of human existence, at least as
far as she could glimpse from a pseudo-historical, partially
imagined, quasi-psychic perspective.

Love, she decided, was walking along the Malecón on
a summer evening, looking out at the dark blue waters of the
Straits of Florida without a care in the world, the glorious knot
of humanity flowing past, the faces of happy couples glowing
brightly with the pink-glowing evening sky, nobody saying
a single word, a family up ahead buying ice cream from an
ice-cream vendor, and then the light softening, dissolving,
fading into nothingness.

Love, she decided, was a quiet whispering between
two voices that drifted out through an open window on a
dark summer night and the lace curtains billowing in the
breeze and they (the owners of the voices) could smell strange
smells, a mixture of vanilla and cinnamon and tobacco, as if
someone were baking pastries and smoking cigars at the same
time at this very late hour, the smells flowing up from the
Almendares River, originating somewhere on the other side in
Vedado, perhaps a small bakery getting ready for the new day,
and the two voices softly cooing, content whispers they were,
which were soon lost amid the lonely but steady murmuring
of insects.

Love, she decided, was the pattern of raindrops on the

roof and then the sad and yet joyful sound of rainwater rolling
into the tin gutters and then swirling down the drain spouts, a
hollow, metallic echo that drifts across eternity.

Love, she decided, was the last time her great-grandmother had kissed her great-grandfather on the lips. The
morning on that day was dark and moist and a rooster was
crowing in the neighbor's yard. But Andres had to leave every
morning when it was dark because they lived a few miles
west of the old downtown, because Ana did not like the noise
and the congestion of so many smells in such a small space,
because she had grown up in a small nameless village on the
other side of the island, near the El Cobre copper mine with
the smell of sulphur always lingering in the air like bad eggs.
So they lived out past El Carmelo in Miramar, in a small place
near the Almendares River, small when compared to the pala-
tal mansions that once lined the Calzada del Cerro, but gaudy
by any other standard, a two-story neo-classical Baroque style
house with ornate edifices and two inner courtyards and a
brick walkway guarded by two sculpted lions (Andres had
hoped for bronze, but that had proved too expensive).

Andres had built the house for Ana (though he often
joked that he would never finish building this house) because
she had grown up in a palm thatch hut a stone's throw from
El Cobre (figuratively speaking) and knew nothing of the
modern world and modern conveniences and modern thinking, and he wanted her to know these things, though it could
be said that her natural point of view was modern, for she did
point out with some measured irony (and the barest hint of
joyful exuberance) that they were without running water that
first year. But Ana did not mind. She went to the river to fetch
water, even when Andres instructed her to leave the duties of
the household to the mulatta girl he had hired so Ana could
look after the children. But within a year the city planners had
caught up to Miramar and everyone had running water and
electricity and well-kept streets, so the instructions regarding
the hired girl became a moot point.

It was shortly after that, that Andres painted the house
a very bright sunset orange, because Ana liked the color,
but also because it was a modern color, which piqued his
imagination. He was not so imaginative, however, when

it came to the roof. He did not pay any attention to roofs unless they leaked. So the roof was a flat roof made of red Spanish tile. But Andres had quite a good imagination when it came to floors. He had installed solid mahogany floors, dark mahogany, top quality floors he had imported from New Orleans, because the darkness of the dark mahogany wood calmed his spirit and allowed him to read and think with a reflective, contemplative, even creative mind. So there was dark mahogany throughout the house, though Ana had covered up most of the beauty of the floors with Persian rugs. But not in the library. Andres had always craved a library with a dark mahogany floor polished like dark glass so he could see his own reflection staring up at him like the image of God in reverse. There were no rugs in the library. This was the one room in the house that Andres claimed as his own. It was the visible expression of his soul. The shelves contained history books, though most of these were about *The Reconquista*, and volumes of poetry, from the ancient Greeks to the Futurists, in spite of the fact that the Futurists were no longer even read, and scientific journals proclaiming the latest and most astonishing discoveries in astronomy and Egyptology, and dictionaries in several languages (Spanish, English, French, Turkish), and various atlases, and a single shelf set aside for three Cuban philosophers.

The first of these philosophers was Félix Varela y Morales. Andres possessed several issues of a periodical entitled *El Habanero*, which contained treatises on politics and philosophy which Varela had penned, a book entitled *Abridger and Annotator to The Protestant*, which was printed in English, and a three-volume series of essays entitled *Cartes a Elipidio, sobre la Impiedad, la Superstición, y el Fanatismo en sus Relaciones con la Sociedad*. As far as Andres could tell, Varela believed that philosophy and theology were two separate disciplines, which meant that you could believe in God and still work to change the order of things in a country (any country, all countries) that cared little for the welfare of ordinary citizens.

Naturally, Andres applauded this line of thinking on theoretical grounds, although as a practical matter, well, he did not believe that most people thought deeply about such distinctions or even knew they existed, though it should be

noted that his views of 'most people' were shaped to a large
extent by what he read in books. He paid scant attention to the
opinions of those who worked for him at his café or those who
owned the various shops downtown and whom he had talked
with every once in a while when they came into his cafe for
some supper, and not since his first few years in Cuba had he
had any contact whatsoever with the vast, actual majority of
Cubans who lived on the island, the mestizos and the mulattos
and mulattas and the isleños, descendants of slaves and mixed
bloods (who had been born in the dozens of tiny prehistoric
villages that dotted the landscape, such as the village near El
Cobre where his wife had come from), peasants all of them
(with the obvious exception of his wife and her immediate
family) who were now infiltrating the towns and the cities
like a plague of rats. He was convinced that for the majority
of Cubans, the disciplines of philosophy and theology were
identical threads woven into the inarticulate fabric of their
dreams, and so were difficult if next to impossible to untangle.

The second philosopher who captured Andres' fancy
(and who was by far his favorite) was José Cipriano de la Luz
y Caballero. He owned one massive volume entitled *The Works
of don José de la Luz Caballero*, compiled by Alfredo Zayas, no
less, and published in 1890. Andres saw in Luz a kindred
spirit who believed that freedom meant the freedom to think
creatively, without anyone telling you what to think, and
without this freedom, people were no better than zombies,
what space junkies and conspiracy theorists would later call
automatons, though perhaps these words were not in Luz's
dictionary, as they were certainly not in any of the dictionaries
possessed by Andres Ordóñez Escoraz.

The third philosopher to occupy space on the shelf was
Enrique José Varona, who had once come into Andres' café,
before Andres knew who he was, with a group of young men,
students perhaps, or budding revolutionaries. Varona had
looked like a walrus with his thick bushy moustache, or at
least a caricature of a walrus the way he was blustering on
about that damn tyrant Machado and how it was every young
Cuban's duty to take up arms against his regime, and the
young students (or revolutionaries) lapping up every blustery,
walrusey word. Still, Andres didn't know who he was, even

at that point, and then Varona sat down at the bar and the young men spread out among the tables and everyone ordered beers or whiskey, and some ordered cocktails, like Daiquiris or Santiago cocktails, and a few ordered a fancy cocktail called a Cuban President, which Andres did his best to make, though he didn't have any Noilly Prat Vermouth, and he was also out of Curacao, so it didn't really taste like a Cuban, and when he brought out the drinks, the ones who had ordered the Cuban Presidents all held their drinks up in the air in honor of the blustery walrus, who was still talking, and they were calling him don Enrique or El Vicepresidente, and it was only then that Andres realized who this fat walrus actually was. Then Varona saw the poster of Carranza and started talking about the first bullfight he ever saw, the year was 1915, it was when President Menocal had sent him to Mexico City to meet with the new President there, Venustiano Carranza de la Garza, who became President simply by declaring the office was his.

'You would not believe what a stubborn bastard Carranza was,' Varona had said, 'arrogant, sadistic, without any sense of humor or humility, but he was a big man. He towered over the rest of those mealy-mouthed peons, so he could do whatever he wanted, what could they do, there wasn't a thing they could do, so they waited like dead men, fawning over everything Carranza said, shoulders slumped in defeat when he wasn't looking, flattering him when he was with all sorts of mealy-mouthed platitudes. I didn't like the man all that much. I didn't like the rest of them either, but I had to go, you see we were all set to recognize the Carranza government, in spite of the energetic pressure from those who supported Zapata, primarily because Wilson was leaning in Carranza's direction, which you might say had a great impact on the position we took, but you knew that was coming because you knew Wilson didn't like the smell of peasants and you couldn't scrub the peasant smell from Zapata's skin, that was never going to happen.

'So that's how things were, but we didn't talk politics at all. Carranza took us to a bullfight instead. What an extravagant social event that was. We were sitting up in a balcony and just below there was a sea of beautiful, high society women dressed in flowing white dresses and white

lace headpieces, as if they had just come from church. I asked
Carranza why there were so many women at the bullfight,
and he laughed and said because they are all in love with
the matadors, or with him, or both, did I not see they were
all wearing white, it is really too funny, Carranza said, they
are all hoping that the afternoon will end with a marriage
proposal, and then he laughed again. That was the only time
I heard him laugh, although it wasn't much of a laugh. It
sounded more like a bull being run over by a train (the young
men sitting at the tables now laughing). Then Carranza said
the best way to see a bullfight was down close, so we left the
balcony and the sea of hopeful women in white and took seats
down along the rail, where you could smell the heavy horse
smell of the picadores and some of them blinking happily,
lazily, because they were drunk, and you could smell the thin
smell of the alcohol too, like a gauze bandage wrapped around
their faces, because we were close to where they were waiting,
and Carranza said it was going to be a spectacular show,
and it is true our view was unimpeded, but it was a horrible
spectacle, a tragedy, truly.

     'We were sitting in the grey bull ring of dreams with
willows in the barreras, as the poet says. It was all very sad,
but it was also heroic. The bull didn't die the way it was
supposed to. There were maybe half a dozen spears stuck in
its hump and it was wheezing and then its front legs collapsed
and it looked like it was praying. My God it was a sight. Then
the matador came with his sword, but then the bull seemed to
resurrect itself and it stood up and roared like a great wind.
It was very majestic. And then it charged straight through
the matador as easily as charging through a rain cloud and
we all watched as the matador's body flipped up into the air
and came down on top of the bull, and you could see that
one of the bull's horns had caught the man in the stomach,
a terrible, piercing wound on the left side, and then the bull
shook his massive head, which some said was a premeditated
act of murder, but others said it was instead a desperate
apology, like offering up a sacrifice to God in the hopes of a
good harvest, which has always been part of the problem with
religion, if you ask me, the reliance on mystical interpretations
to whitewash simple human depravity, it is our Achilles heel,

though in this case, I am sure you'll agree, the depravity
belonged to the bull, and for a time nobody moved or said a
word, and in the stillness of that moment you could hear the
small, whimpering, plaintive cries of the matador, who was
clinging to this horn of the lily as he was clinging to life, like
the sound of rain falling on water somewhere in the distance,
and then the bull flung the matador to the ground with an
expression that could only be described as one of disgust. We
could all see the matador's intestines spilling out, an absolute
fatal wound if you have ever seen one, a most horrible way
to die, and believe me, I have seen death in all of its forms,
at least on the battlefield, where death is always an intensely
personal, private agony, but this was a thousand times worse,
for we were sitting in a public arena beneath a sky that turned
the color of gangrene and nobody could do a thing to save
the man. Then the bull charged at the picadores and gored a
horse to death, and the sea of women in white were crying
out behind us, above us, like angels desperate to intervene,
praying an endless storm of rosaries and Hail Mary's, evoking
the names of the saints and long dead husbands, a hurricane
of religious despair, and then finally Carranza nodded and
they sent in a handful of soldiers and butchered the beast with
bullets, and the splatter from the bull reached the front row,
where I was sitting with Carranza.'

Then Varona had stopped talking, his voice trailing off,
as if he were trying to remember what time of day the bull
had died, and then he looked at the poster again and laughed
and remarked on the coincidence of the names, 'they are both
Carranza,' he had said, 'so I suppose they are related,' and one
of the young men from the tables laughed and said 'we are all
Spanish, we are all related,' and then the young men laughed,
but Varona wasn't laughing.

After that night, Andres purchased *Estudios literarios y
filosóficos*, the only book by Varona he could find in the book-
shop on the corner, but after reading the book, Andres was not
sure what to make of this man with the walrus moustache. He
seemed to Andres overtly radical, even for a modernist, for he
seemed to believe that knowledge was a tool to be used in the
battle to overthrow mysticism, and Andres was puzzled by the
very notion of doing battle against mysticism, so he poured

over the text again and again and again, but he was never
quite satisfied with any of his conclusions, and he had, in
fact, on the very night before the last time his wife kissed him
on the lips, been re-reading Varona, several lengthy passages
in which Varona claimed that nationalism was essential for
educational reform, looking for things he had missed the
other times and wondering how any of these philosophers
defined knowledge in the first place, for it seemed to him that
mysticism was also a kind of knowledge, though who was he
to say, and before he went to bed that night he went over his
business ledger to determine if he had saved enough money
(a full bank account was also a sort of knowledge, he thought)
to add on to their house that once overlooked the river, for in
the years between the time he had started building the house
and the day he encountered Varona, the city had engulfed
them all around and their view of the river was substantially
diminished.

It was shortly after he had met Varona that he concocted the idea of adding a third story to their neo-classical
Baroque style house and so restore their appreciation of the
Almendares (and also to provide additional bedrooms for their
grandchildren, which is how he had pitched the idea to his
wife). But he did not act on this idea until the spring of 1940,
when he contacted a company in New Orleans that specialized
in decorative elements and ordered two dozen wrought
iron railings for the balcony windows that would adorn the
third-story bedrooms he was going to build, one bedroom
for his grandson, Andres Escoraz Silvestre, who was already
attending law school at the University of Havana, one for his
son José Luis and his wife, Nuria, a beautiful mulatta girl from
Eastern Cuba, who had moved into the house in Miramar
when José Luis had given up playing baseball for Santa Clara,
and a third bedroom for their son, also named José Luis, who
at the age of nine was already a holy terror with a baseball
bat. Of course these mythical rooms did not yet exist, and
now would never exist, because this was Andres' last evening
before his last day, and when he was getting ready to leave
the next morning he was still thinking about the wrought iron
balconies, but also about Enrique José Varona, for the two
seemed somehow connected, as if you could not have one

without the other, at least in Havana, a strange, unsettling
notion at the very least.

Then Ana had kissed him, but it was a short kiss because
she wanted to remind him to come home early for supper,
she was making chicken and tomatoes and rice, but could he
please remember to bring home a jar of peach jam, which was
getting harder and harder to come by, and also that yellow
cheese that came from Miami, she had a hankering for that,
and her words were tumbling out of her mouth even while
he was trying to finish kissing her, and he laughed and said
he would remember, and she was laughing as well, but she
was also deathly serious about the peach jam and the yellow
cheese, and then he gave her a poem he had written that
morning expressing his eternal devotion to her, which she said
she would read later and slipped it into the front pocket of
her apron, and then he left and it was still dark and the sun
wouldn't be up for another twenty minutes.

-40-

After Isidora heard for the first time the story of
the death of her great-grandfather and the last kiss her
great-grandmother gave him that morning, she wept for
three days without stopping. It is fair to say that she felt
the entire story unfold before her fluttering heart more than
heard it being told, as if she were the reincarnation of her
great-grandmother and had simply and without any warning
slipped back into the dream of a forgotten past. She wept
for three days without stopping, without eating, without
sleeping. She simply locked her bedroom door and wept tears
of unending, eternal sadness, and when she finished she saw
that the floor of her bedroom was littered with the fossilized
remains of millions of tiny, dead crustaceans, as if the ocean
of her sadness had caused a second great flood and then,
the waters receding, or perhaps evaporating in the heat of
her exhaustion (for to be caught up in the throes of psychic

despair is to burn with the brilliance of a billion exploding suns), leaving a trail of dead sea creatures to remind her of her great-grandmother's misery. She marveled at the number of tiny dead crustacean bodies that covered her bedroom floor. There were a variety of *Cladocera*, also known as water fleas, which under the microscope resemble tiny seahorse babies frozen inside glass wombs made by Italian glassblowers from the seven islands of Murano, several species of *copepods*, which means "oar feet" in Greek, with delicate tear shaped bodies and several long antennae, which give them the appearance of tiny helicopters or miniature alien spaceships monitoring the background static of the universe, hundreds of species of barnacles, everything from the *Sessilia*, the acorn barnacle, the most common barnacle in the world, to the less common but still plentiful *Pedunculata*, otherwise known as the goose barnacle, and finally a few members of crustacean nobility that had been extinct since the Cambrian Period, the *Canadaspis*, with spikes on its head to keep its vulnerable floating eyes from being eaten so easily, and a bivalved arthropod that went by the name *Perspicaris*, which given the Latinate root would suggest a creature that had greater mental acuity than its peers, but which was most likely a bottom feeder, similar to *Trilobites*, which preceded the *Perspicaris* by roughly fifteen million years. Isidora imagined she had been weeping for eons.

-41-

Now Isidora's favorite story, which she thought of as the story of her origins, and which dazzled her compassionate heart with the brilliance of an intimate confession, was the story of how Escolástica Escoraz Vda De Miranda, who was always for Isidora much more than a distant cousin, came to the Americas from Logroño, Spain, and how without her aid, Isidora's great-grandfather, Andres Ordóñez Escoraz, husband to Ana Silvestre for thirty-eight years, might not have lived to see the dawn of the twentieth century.

The story of Escolástica Escoraz Vda De Miranda while she lived in Logroño, Spain from the time she was born until she began to dream about a white bird trapped in a golden cage:

When Escolástica was born (and before she had been given her name), her father, Arturo Ordóñez Escoraz, thought she looked like a shriveled-up raisin and wondered if she were deformed or perhaps his wife had slept with a pig and what to name such a monstrous looking child and whether or not it was worth the trouble, especially considering that such monstrous babies usually died within three days. But after an hour or two of careful deliberation, which included a brief consultation with Father Mateus Antonio de Nazar, a young Jesuit priest who had been installed in the Church of Santiago only three weeks earlier — they spoke in the shadow of the church tower with the great white storks perched on the top of the tower like sentinel angels who, in spite of their guardian duties, seemed to be eavesdropping on the conversation below — he (meaning Escolástica's father) declared his newborn daughter one of the wisest creatures to ever grace the planet (even wiser than the storks) and decided to name her Escolástica.

According to Father de Nazar, the name Escolástica meant one who possesses a great deal of wisdom, or one who teaches, a meaning which the youngest daughter of Arturo Ordóñez Escoraz and his wife contradicted from the start, at least when one compared her temperament, which was marked by a need to remain in constant motion, to the brooding, taciturn demeanor of the monks who occupied the library in the Monastery of Santa María la Real de Las Huelgas, near the city of Burgos, which don Arturo once visited as a boy, when he was called Pepe, and where he was immediately captivated by the eyes of the monks, which were turned inward in a burning, perpetual gaze that suggested to Pepe some terrible, undecipherable mystery or an unimaginable lament, and from that point forward, Arturo associated great spiritual wisdom with the smell of decaying, leather-bound books, but also the barest hint of manure, for it had been spring when the visit had occurred and the nearby fields had been covered with a mixture of cow shit, horse shit, and dead fish.

It is fair to say that Escolástica was extraordinarily athletic, which explains why she didn't learn to read until the age of ten. By the time she was a year old, she had begun running up and down stairs at breakneck speed and tumbling randomly to the floor at the bottom or the top, sometimes even spinning in the air like a blind circus acrobat, laughing hysterically. By the time she was two, she could be seen all over Logroño riding a small dark horse, a dark chestnut which she rode bareback, her slender, defiant arms raised high above her head and her red hair flowing. She rarely stood still long enough to say good morning to her father or to her sister, Isabel, dark-haired Isabel, who preferred lounging about at the breakfast table, dreaming of marriage even at the age of four, and who, when she (Isabel) started reading at the age of seven, was never seen without a book of poetry, either a collection entitled simply *Rimas*, by Gustavo Adolfo Bécquer (she had memorized over half of the poems by the age of nine, her favorite being a poem about dark swallows who did not return, having feasted their eyes on the beauty and happiness of a young girl, and which after reading, Isabel compared to her own life and her search for happiness and the isolation she felt living, as her father often said, in the shadow of oblivion, so she often looked up at the flat wine colored sky that settled over Logroño on summer evenings like the steady beating of her heart and scanned the horizon for some sign that the swallows were returning), or a slim volume entitled *Cantares gallegos* by María Rosalía Rita de Castro, all because of a single poem, "*¿Como me hei de ir si te quero?*," which left her in a constant state of amazement wondering if she would shed burning tears like glittering beads if her one true love would ever depart, even if only for an afternoon.

But Escolástica had no use for poetry, perhaps because she was poetry in motion. She was a constant blur, the laughter of God burning a hole in the nighttime sky, the music of the heavenly spheres drowning out the anguish of the world, a lightning bolt with the power to illuminate the darkness at the bottom of the sea. Whenever she smiled her smile would linger in the air for hours, sometimes days, the photographic negative of a comet streaking across the icy cold loneliness of space, illuminating even the darkest, loneliest corners of

the universe. Everyone in Logroño was struck with the same
impression because she offered everyone her prettiest, best
most radiant smile. The smile she offered up to her father
and her sister as she headed out the door in the morning was
the same smile she offered up to Father de Nazar, whom she
barely knew, who was either heading to or from the church
sacristy with robes that had just been washed or that needed
washing; just as it was the same smile she offered up to the
chattering old women whom she didn't know at all who were
constantly moving up and down the streets of Logroño in
search of an open church where they could sit down in the
back and rest their feet, for the churches in Logroño were
open only when the presiding priests were actually inside
lighting candles, or hearing confessions, or preparing for Mass
with the church bells ringing (at which point the great sentinel
storks would fly off in lazy, elongated circles until the echo
of the bells would subside and then they would return to
their perches, guardians once again), or any one of a number
of routine, priestly duties; but whenever the priests took
leave of their churches, which was often (and this was true
of Father de Nazar's church as well), they locked the great
church doors, for there had been a string of robberies lately
(the authorities had a fairly good idea of the identity of the
thieves but seemed unwilling to act) so no one wanted to take
a chance with the dozens of gold plates and bejeweled chalices
and silver crucifixes hidden away in unassuming closets or in
cabinets with secret compartments; and sometimes the priests
would stroll along the Ebro River in the morning, looking
across the narrow ribbon of the river and marveling at the
exactitude of God and mumbling incoherent prayers directed
towards Santa María de la Esperanza, the patron saint of
the town, or maybe take a nap beneath the chestnut trees in
the Plaza in the afternoon and the warm breeze that always
blew across, or maybe they would take a stroll along a quiet
street in the early evening (somewhere along Calle Portales,
or perhaps a small section of Calle del Laurel that would
years later be called the path of the elephants to encourage
the *touristas* to forgo San Sebastián and the sea and spend
their vacations instead in Logroño, because Hannibal had set
out from Logroño to sack Rome, as everyone once knew), the

priests looking for a café and a bite to eat, a bit of stew with beans, before returning to their respective rectories for a glass of wine before going to bed, but even the glittering radiance of such a day as this would be easily eclipsed should they, by chance, happen upon Escolástica's smile.

On her third birthday, in an effort to instill in her some appreciation for more contemplative pursuits, her father hired a young maestro to teach her to play the piano and an old courtesan to teach her how to paint. The maestro left after only a single day, claiming that Escolástica was herself the incarnation of music, and one did not need to teach music to play itself, one had only to listen. The courtesan stayed a week, but not because she had any interest in teaching Escolástica how to paint. Indeed, while the courtesan had known a few painters quite intimately, she had no talent for painting herself. One of her coterie of painters, Federico de Madrazo, had remarked years earlier that she was the best pupil he had ever entertained, and though clearly Madrazo meant one thing and not another, the remark encouraged all sorts of wild speculations about her unproclaimed genius and how only the truly great painters abandoned the world stage with such frivolous disdain, and over the years the courtesan herself kept this kind of gossip alive, for she imagined it was far better to be talked about or whispered about than to be forgotten, and in this way she soon became a myth — which perhaps explains Arturo's mistake in hiring her in the first place — and whenever the talk turned towards her perhaps exhibiting what must surely have been a prodigious talent, she remarked with a cavalier laugh that the only painting she did any more was her own face, and again those listening took her meaning one way and not another, and the courtesan's face took on an inscrutable expression with the darkening lines of despair mixing with the blushing smile of giddy deceit, a face that seemed to have been lifted from one of Goya's later paintings.

When don Arturo asked the courtesan to teach his daughter how to paint, she became slightly unsettled, but she could think of no way to properly refuse the don's noble request other than by flinging herself into the dark waters of the Ebro from the newly rebuilt Puente de Piedra bridge,

an act of desperation that would have surely been the end of
the courtesan because the river was moving very fast, partly
because it was spring and the snow melt had filled the smaller
steams to overflowing, but also because at that point in history
no one had dreamed of damming up the river with seven-
ty-four dams, and then one hundred and eight dams, and
then one hundred and twenty. But the moment the courtesan
met the young Escolástica, her fears fled, overwhelmed as
they were by the child's tremendous beauty, which was more
robust and less elegant than the beauty of her sister, Isabel,
and which in time became as legendary as her athleticism.

For one week the courtesan remained in a small sitting
room that opened up to an inner courtyard, seemingly lost in
a trance, as if she had become part of a painting herself, her
eyes locked in a struggle to comprehend the nature of reality
and the immortality of art. Then on the morning of the seventh day it began to rain, a gentle rain that smelled of vanilla
and orange spice and cinnamon pastries and coffee from the
West Indies, and ever so faintly the smell of finely brushed
leather, and which reminded the aging courtesan of an ancient
Basque love song from her youth, "*Chorittua, nurat hua bi
hegalez airian?*" she heard a voice whisper (which translated
means "Oh little bird, where are you going on your two wings
in the air?"), and then another voice said they would go to
Spain together when the snows melted in the pass, at which
point she awoke from her trance and informed don Arturo
Ordóñez Escoraz that his daughter was herself such a work
of art that one could do nothing but stand in front of her and
admire her beauty.

Now by the time Escolástica turned five (or perhaps
seven, or even ten, her precise age is irrelevant), everyone
forgot she was called Escolástica and called her Tiká instead.
It was also at this time that she began dreaming a strange,
recurring dream about a white bird trapped in a golden cage.
The white bird stared out at the world with heavy, sad eyes,
irrevocably sad on a sunny day with a bright blue sky, and
seeming less sad when the world was plagued by the cold
lethargy and gray cloudy skies of rainy days, though perhaps
this was just a trick of the light, and every so often, the door
to the cage was left open, and since the cage was hanging on

a hook near a window, which was also sometimes left open, it
was reasonable to imagine (or hope) that the tiny white bird
might one day escape, but the bird just sat on its perch with
its heavy, sad eyes gazing at the great beyond and did not
move. So Tiká asked her father why the bird didn't fly out
when the door was open, and her father said it was because he
does not see past the bars, he cannot visualize a world without
bars, so he might as well stay put.

In her dream Tiká did not see her father, she only heard
his voice drifting out through the open window or down from
the eaves of the verandah and swirling about her feet with a
few fallen rose petals and dried leaves, and his voice seemed
to her to possess the lilt of cut grass, which is another way of
saying that if one could actually see sounds, which Tiká most
assuredly could, her father's voice was a burnt yellow color,
which was the color of cut grass in Logroño and the surrounding countryside, except sometimes during the hottest part of
the summer when it seemed a burnt orange color. Always the
dream began with Tiká sitting in a wicker chair on the verandah of her father's house, always it was sunset and she was
looking in through the window (usually closed at this point,
but sometimes open) at the tiny white bird in the cage. The
bird was filled with such despair that it rarely sang, though it
sometimes made low, gurgling sounds, as if it were drowning.
On some nights, the door to the cage was always open, and
on other nights the maid (which maid? it was always someone
Tiká had never seen before) came sweeping past with a broom
and stopped and smiled out at Tiká looking in and closed the
small golden door and locked it with a tiny golden key she
kept in a pocket hidden behind the folds of her apron. And
always the dream seemed to possess a haphazard disrespect
for the generally accepted pattern of time, speeding up when
it shouldn't, lingering a little longer at times just for spite,
or perhaps to induce in the dreamer a feeling of melancholy,
and often leaving out whole chunks of time altogether, which
did not always bother Tiká, who assumed they were probably
meaningless chunks anyway, as so much of time seemed to be
whether one was dreaming or not.

In her dream Tiká would be sitting on the verandah,
contemplating the existence (or perhaps simply the presence)

of the bird, and then she would hear the sound of someone shouting down the street; or the old women with their heads covered with shawls chattering their strange foreign language of the fanatically devout as they hurried past her father's house in search of an open church door; or even a church bell ringing in the distance and the shadows of storks floating in the air, or many church bells and many more storks (which was not altogether unreasonable, for there were five churches within the city limits of Logroño, and several more within a mile of the ruins of the old stone wall that marked the original border of the town and had been there in one form or another since the time of the Romans); and every time Tiká looked back at the window and the caged bird, it always seemed to her that years had passed.

Oddly, she never grew any older in her dream, but she knew that many years had passed nevertheless because the tiny white bird looked so very much older, and then when she looked back to the street because of a new voice or the old women making a second or a third pass or another round of church bells and the storks flying off and then returning, she would notice that the weather had changed, the hot winds of summer had vanished and the world had become winter, and the next time the rain had given way to bright sunlight, and so forth. Each time she looked back at the window and the bird, the bird looked older and older, as old as a saint or one of the forgotten immortals. And each time she looked back to the street, the weather had changed, although this was not always so. While the bird always looked older, a feature of her dream that she could always count on, and which, during her waking hours and even years later, was a strange comfort like an unrelenting faith, the weather in her dream did not always change. Some nights in her dream there were no rainstorms at all, it was an endless string of bright, sunny days, and at other times, the landscape of her dream was plagued by a relentless, eternal winter or a creeping, insolent autumn filled with the whirring sounds of flying insects. (All of which seems to suggest, though this intricate thought probably did not occur to Tiká, that the nature of reality is much more fluid than we realize, even when it is constrained by certain seemingly unbreachable parameters.) But in spite of these minor incon-

sistencies, always near the end of the dream Tiká would begin
to worry about the bird and if it had perhaps gone blind, and
always she would ask her father why the bird stayed in the
cage when the door was open, and always she would hear her
father's voice, which sounded like the color yellow, except
when it sounded like the color orange.

Then one night, and it is worth noting that this was the
last time Tiká dreamed of the tiny white bird in the golden
cage, one night the ending of Tiká's dream was different. At
that moment when normally she would notice how very old
the white bird had become (in some versions the bird was
decrepit beyond belief and could barely move or blink an eye),
she saw instead that the door to the golden cage was locked
but that the bird was gone. But instead of calling out to her
father from the verandah (which is the reason she had only
ever heard his voice in her dream), she raced inside and found
him sitting at the dark mahogany roll top desk writing out
long letters or perhaps adding up figures in his ledger.

He was working feverishly to finish his task, a smoky oil
lamp perched precariously on one corner of the roll top, the dim
light from the lamp barely penetrating the shadow he himself
cast over the desk, so he almost didn't see his daughter as she
came running into the room, shouting out her question with
breathless anxiety.

'Papa, papa, the bird is gone. The bird has vanished.
Papa, where did it go?' she said in her dream.

And without even looking up from his work, her father
had said 'It is gone, my little Tiká, because if it did not go
it would have surely died sitting there on that perch. A bird
cannot live long locked up in a cage like that, even if the cage is
unlocked. Nothing can.'

Tiká was too stunned to reply, but later, after she woke
up, and for many years afterwards, quite probably until she
settled (eventually) in Puerto Rico, she wished she had said
something, anything to spur her father into an explanation
of the philosophical implications of the vanished bird, for
as she grew older she spent many weary evenings wrestling
inconclusively with the straightforward and yet exceedingly
complex nature of her father's response as well as the multiple
meanings and shifting realities of the dream itself. But during

those last few moments of the last time she dreamed about the tiny white bird, she stood mute before her father's desk as if he were God himself, listening to the scratching of his pen as he worked at his figures or his letters until the oil lamp gave out and the world was plunged into darkness.

The truth, of course, is that it was unimportant whether or not Tiká understood her dream. Indeed, one could make a case (as a few philosophers and several ancient Greek playwrights have done) that it was best not to understand the meaning of such dreams, presumably because they were prophetic in nature, and if one understood the nature of the prophecy, one might try to alter the course of one's own life, which one could never do, life being a foreordained phenomenon, but one might try nevertheless, which would often result in needless calamity, it would be like dashing one's head against a brick wall until the skull split open, a senseless, bloody diversion from the joy of living one's life with courageous and unquestionably blind faith, so it was best to remain calm in the face of such dreams and plod along without expectation, allowing the folds of life to unfold, and in time the meaning of the dream would become clear because it would reflect the meaning of a life that had been lived.

Such was the case with respect to Tiká's dream, a fact she only truly appreciated one summer afternoon in 1937 while sitting in a rocking chair on a third-floor corner room balcony with an iron railing in a run-down boarding house that had once been a convent for Carmelite nuns on Caleta de las Monjas in San Juan, Puerto Rico. There was still the Latin inscription above the stone archway entrance that no longer possessed any gates. The inscription said "Blessed are those who come in the name of the Lord."

She could not see the sea from where she sat, but she could see the flashing dome of the Cathedral like a great ship riding the waves of a restless ocean and she closed her eyes and breathed in the smell of the sea and the memory of an ocean voyage she had once taken, the only true ocean voyage she had ever taken. Others who had made the same crossing had called it the journey across the gloomy sea, but in her memory it had been a journey bathed in dazzling sunshine, and while she was thinking of that voyage oh so many years ago, she suddenly remembered the dream of the tiny white bird, and she compared it to the dream her life had been and she observed that they were the same dream, and she did not even wonder about this, it was like looking at a sunset, something to be admired from a great distance.

Then the bells of the Cathedral began to ring, a slow, steady, comforting sound, and she found herself thinking back to that moment when the dream of the tiny white bird began to merge with the dream of her life and how very unaware she had been, it had been hidden from her view, this beginning, as so many things are when we are young.

-42-

The story of when Tiká's dream of the tiny white bird began to merge with the dream of her life:

It all began one afternoon when Tiká was seventeen and her sister was twenty-one. Their uncle, Andres Ordóñez Escoraz, who still claimed three rooms near the back of the house as his own but who had left when the girls were six and ten to chase wild geese around the globe, returned suddenly on the heels of a late summer thunderstorm.

The girls thought him a majestic but lunatic sea captain or a deposed and very beautiful Grecian god the way he stood in the doorway, his face covered in shadows, a scene of vigorous, luminous destruction behind him, a theatrical backdrop for his unknown intentions with the rain splatter cascading from the roof of the verandah and the lightning flashing bright green bolts across the sky and smoke rising from the ground like geysers, which was not really smoke but just water vapor rising, and they weren't really geysers either, naturally, but in the minds of the sisters, or perhaps it was just the mind of Isabel, the scene before them had descended from the pages of a great epic tale of madness and love, a tale with the comic vision of *Orlando furioso* (Ariosto, Italian, dozens of characters, a hero who is rejected by a princess and goes mad

and then later flies to the moon to retrieve his sanity, giant sea
monsters and flying horses, Algerian kings who are treated
like deposed gods, sorcerers who build castles of iron to keep
their prisoners from escaping, weeping virgins in search of
true love, Saracen knights with lances that sprout flowers);
or *La Gerusalemme liberata* (Tasso, also Italian, same kinds of
characters but fewer of them, no lances sprouting flowers, as
far as Isabel could recall, but she wasn't sure, the two epics
were kind of merging in her mind); and also a dash of the
brooding melancholy of *The Shipwreck and Demise of Sepúlveda
and Leonor* (Jerónimo Corte-Real, Portuguese, a harrowing tale,
actually, about the death of a sea captain and his family, not
to mention the entire ship's company, who make it ashore
after their ship flounders off the coast of Africa [the captain
had stupidly overloaded the ship with Indian pepper], only
to be duped by a deceitful Bantu chief and then murdered as
they slept).

At first Andres said nothing. He just stood there with his
terrible majesty of a sea captain or a deposed god, and Isabel
almost fainted, but Escolástica, who was now Tiká, recognized
him in spite of the mythology of the rain and the shadows and
the literary grime from ten years of chasing wild geese around
the globe and ran to her prodigal uncle and hugged him
with a wild fury to equal the storm outside, and then Andres
Ordóñez Escoraz, who could not quite believe that the two
little girls he had last seen ten years earlier had become the
two beautiful young ladies he now saw before him, shook the
rain from his shoulders and stepped inside.

Andres stayed at the house for two weeks, regaling his
nieces with stories of Italian excess and Dutch perseverance
and the lingering sadness of the Portuguese, and each night
after the sisters had gone to bed he conversed with his brother
until well into the wee hours of the morning, the two men
dripping with copious amounts of perspiration even though
they were sitting on the verandah and there was a cool breeze
blowing across the valley from the mountains to the north.
Andres spoke with the hushed, courageous, conspiratorial
tone of a revolutionary, because he had nothing to lose but
the future, and his brother responded with the restrained even
timid civility of an overworked postal clerk, for he had given

up on the future when his daughters were born to live in the past, a choice which is often made, as everyone knows, to appease a relentless fear.

The topic of the protracted conversation was a copper mine near Santiago, Cuba. Actually, Andres mentioned a dozen or more now abandoned copper mines with a variety of colorful if somewhat ironic names (La Esperanza, La Independencia, La Union, La Manuela, Kirkappo, El Porvenir, La Caridad, and Maximina, to name a few), one lead mine (Milagro) of dubious quality, three lead and zinc mines (El Angel, Peña Blanca, and Mina Cebrero), one all but exhausted coal mine (La Primera), and several silver mines whose names Andres did not know. The mines had belonged to the Cobre Company, a family-run outfit founded, according to Andres, by an eccentric Welshman named Grenfell with a taste for mulatta girls, but the company had gone out of business because of Cuba Libre and the Ten Years War, which had put a practical end to slavery in Cuba (though slavery in concept was still legal until 1886), and thus abolished the workforce, or most of it, of the Cobre Company.

A petition to officially dissolve the company had been brought before the English Court of Chancery in 1869, but the ultimate ownership and subsequent fate of the mines was never properly determined. Papers had been lost or misfiled, bank receipts had mysteriously disappeared, important letters never sent, the eccentric Welshman who owned the company had been killed in a street brawl in Havana, or perhaps he had been murdered by a man who had been tailing him in the underbelly of Havana for three or four days.

It was almost impossible to believe that such an opportunity existed, said Andres. After the death of the owner, the mines had fallen into the abyss of utter abandonment. But now, over thirty years later, they had miraculously resurfaced under new ownership (a new owner with the same name as the original owner, someone who was related to Grenfell by blood or marriage or who once knew him, or someone who once played cards with him in a back-alley dive somewhere along Calle Galiano, a disreputable street only a few blocks removed from the exact spot where Grenfell was supposedly killed or murdered). The mines were now for sale, singly or

all together, and this is what Andres wished to discuss. But
Arturo was not interested. He had become lost in the labyrinth
of his own mind the moment Andres mentioned mulatta girls,
which was for Arturo a symbol of the future he had once
dreamed of, a future that would have been shaped by a thirst
for adventure aboard a whaling ship and an endless parade of
naked mulatta girls whenever he was in port, a future (or at
least a possible future) he had given up when Isabel was born,
so he paid scant attention to what his brother was saying,
and when it was his turn to speak he lectured his brother on
the value of hard work and the sanctity of matrimonial bliss,
which seemed to him the only thing he could say, and which
he would repeat if pressed, and then he sat back in his wicker
chair and looked at the dark foreboding, vacant sky without
even a star with a blank look of despair. Theirs was the kind
of conversation that would extend indefinitely, a mirror to
the eternity that resides in every man's hopes, a dark glass
of infinite possibility, for neither man was willing to listen
to the other, each waiting only till the other paused to draw
a breath so he could plunge forward with his own reckless,
unvarnished thoughts.

On the last night of the two weeks, Andres was joined
by a shabby looking fellow wearing a heavy longshoreman's
coat, an odd and memorable detail given that it was late
August, who had been spotted skulking about the alleys of
Logroño and had taken up temporary residence near the back
door of The Café with Two Names (for those passing through
it was known as Café la del Oriental, but for those who lived
in Logroño it was known as Café del Fernando and was typical of that part of Spain with dark timbers showing themselves
on the ceiling and plaster walls painted a mauve color because
mauve was becoming popular, and on the wall directly across
from the bar there was a framed copy of an edition of *Le Petit
Journal* dated November 1893, with an artist's depiction of the
explosion of the opera theater of the Liceu of Barcelona by the
anarchist Santiago Salvador Franch, you could even see in the
drawing the bloodied corpses of the victims draped over the
seats like forgotten overcoats).

In truth, as everyone in Logroño knew, it was not all
that unusual to find a few vagrants sleeping in the alleyway

behind The Café with Two Names, in spite of the fact that
the Civil Guard had been charged with cracking down on
vagrancy and robbery or potential robbery, because the Civil
Guard often looked the other way when it came to vagrants
(as it had looked the other way and continued looking the
other way in the matter of the string of robberies that plagued
Logroño's churches and kept their doors closed in the absence
of the priests), particularly if those vagrants had been seen in
the company of a well-known local miscreant named Carabali,
as was the case with the longshoreman in question. The day
after this fellow arrived in Logroño, while taking a stroll along
the Ebro, he had met Carabali. The two men found immediate
refuge in a dimly lit dive and began drinking *absenta* and
sharing intimate secrets, which is how Carabali found out that
the longshoreman and Andres were partners of a sort and that
there was an opportunity to perhaps make some money, not
quite a get-rich-quick scheme, but close enough to appeal to
Carabali's unwavering faith that the world owed him a living.

Later, as they wound their way through the empty
streets, they began singing strange, long-winded, virtually
incoherent songs about priests dying in droves of consumption
and the ancient Romans and their conquest of the Iberian
Peninsula during the two centuries preceding the birth of
Christ. The last song they sang that evening was a once
popular ditty about the defeat of Charlemagne's rear guard at
Roncesvalles in 778.

The following day at four in the afternoon, two members
of the Civil Guard (older men, gray around the temples,
former members of the defeated Carlist party) set off to arrest
the longshoreman for vagrancy and attempted robbery. It
was a dubious charge at best, but understandable. In the
blazing white light of noon that very day, the longshoreman
had suddenly been awakened by church bells going off, and
stumbling from both sleep and the relative obscurity of the
alleyway behind The Café with Two Names, he had burst into
the narrow rough cobblestone of Calle Santiago with a strange,
uncontrollable rage, shouting obscenities at the unseen moon
and shaking his bony fist at the sky and frightening a dozen
or more old women who had just happened by in their eternal
quest for an open church door, and who had thought him a

demon and had pulled their black shawls tightly around their
heads, covering their ears so the demon's curses could not
penetrate the barrier of closed eardrums, and fled into the
white glare of the next street. Fortunately, Carabali intervened
and the longshoreman was spared the indignity of arrest.

As it happened, Carabali was sipping a coffee at Café
Rioja, which was only two blocks away from the alleyway
behind The Café with Two Names, pretending to read a
newspaper and checking his pocket watch every so often.
Then he saw the two guardsmen pass by on their way to arrest
his new friend. He told the boy, Manuela, who was tending
the bar, that he would return shortly, he wanted to see where
these two guardsmen were going in such a hurry, he hoped
his curiosity didn't get the better of him. Then he grabbed
two bottles of wine off the counter, bottles which he had
told the boy, Manuela, to set there some time earlier, smiled
a cavalier smile and said he had a strange and beguiling
premonition that an opportunity to cement a friendship was
at hand. Still smiling, and laughing as well, in spite of the
fact that the guardsmen were no longer in sight, he quickly
made his way to the alleyway behind The Cafe with Two
Names. As the Civil Guard approached the longshoreman,
who had by then resumed his supine position in the alleyway,
Carabali approached the guardsmen and said the unshaven
vagrant before them was a friend and business partner of
Andres Ordóñez Escoraz, the brother of don Arturo Ordóñez
Escoraz. Then he said that in spite of his shabby appearance
he was a man of some stature in Wales and in England, a
compassionate man who for philosophical reasons that could
only be discussed with the clergy preferred the gritty reality of
city streets to the silky, perfumed sheets of the Escoraz house.
Then Carabali handed each of the guardsmen a half-full bottle
of *Crianza*. Without even a wry comment about the nature of
Carabali's gift, they disappeared into the widening glass of the
afternoon sun.

A short digression on Carabali and Lady Luck:
Carabali, it should be said, slept very little, just in case
Lady Luck made a sudden appearance. He was ever
alert, no matter what form she might take. Some days she

arrived in the form of the Egyptian goddess Isis, whose name meant "throne" and who was the patroness of fertility, nature and magic, which is almost like luck, and who according to some zealous believers was actually the first Eve, a genuine and incredibly sexy Mother Earth type goddess who lived on the planet approximately six thousand years ago and whose luck was based on her considerable natural genius, which was twice that of Einstein, which is even better than luck.

On other days she appeared in the form of the Greek goddess Tyche, who may have been from Antioch, and who was the daughter of Zeus and Aphrodite, or, according to some sources, Hermes and Aphrodite, which is incest either way you look at it, and who more than any of the other ladies of luck is associated with the notion of destiny, or at least the destiny of those particular cities where the citizens built temples in her honor, and whose head appeared on many silver coins of the day (and who has not felt lucky upon discovering a few silver coins in a forgotten pocket or stashed away in a hidden drawer), and Tyche was reviled among poets and other intellectuals tit for tat because she despised those who thought they could imagine a better world and so she withheld from them her favor.

Sometimes she (Lady Luck) took the form of the Roman goddess Fortūna, who was the very personification of luck in the Roman world and whose name was forever linked with strength of character and justice (two very Roman virtues, but also German virtues, in a pre-apocalyptic Wagnerian sort of way), and who gave birth (a virgin birth, according to Hesiod) to Pontus, god of the sea, or perhaps, as some said, just the god of seaweed, whose own son, Nereus, was gentle and trustworthy, which was not quite the same thing as seaworthy, though close, which can be confused with luck if you're not paying too much attention to detail; and Fortūna was also called Gaia, at least by Hesiod, and she was also given over to sudden, capricious, even malicious reversals of fortune, like when she claimed the lives of Caesar's grandsons, which might have been a lucky thing for a few aspiring Roman politicians who had no use for the Senate (as was the case with Caligula, and after him, Nero), but it was certainly very unlucky for the grandsons.

On still other occasions, particularly if Carabali were traveling in Northern Spain, she preferred the form of the Basque goddess Mari, who was viewed by those living in that region as a Mother Earth type goddess but may have been just a local enchantress who later became a myth, who lived (lives?) in the Pyrenees mountains and who could take the form of any animal but preferred the form of a goat or a snake, but who became a ball of fire when traveling between various mountains, and who many millennia ago created the moon so that the people of the mountains would not be afraid of the dark, which until the moon had been created the night was very dark and there were all sorts of great thunderous noises, like twenty-megaton nuclear explosions, which the people attributed to dragons or demons, so they were always afraid, but as soon as Mari created the moon, the people abandoned all that superstitious nonsense about dragons, though many still believed in demons for some reason, and Mari was not associated with the idea of luck, per se, for the Basque people thought of luck, which they called *Adur*, as a quality or power used by soothsayers and magicians in both performing simple feats of magic, and in predicting the future, though many of their predictions seemed to unravel even as they were speaking them.

But more and more often she (Lady Luck) took the form of the Virgin Mary herself, who among the Basque people is a curious blend of Mary the mother of Jesus and Mari the mother of us all, and who for the rest of us may or may not be a synthesis of various Sumerian or Assyrian or Babylonian myths, or Roman, if you remember the story of Fortūna and Pontus, but not Buddhist or Hindu or Sikh or Shintoist or Native American, or the resurging Manichaeistic heresy of the Balkan peninsula, which is an off-shoot of Babylonian thinking anyway, or any one of the thousands of different religious perspectives that make up the religious tapestry of the world. It is indeed curious (though certainly Carabali's curiosity never went this far) that in these Western myths we cling to, young goddesses are routinely raped, ravished, seduced, even blessed by some Western god (which is not to say a cowboy or rodeo star) parading about in the form of a bull or an aggressive swan or an untethered angel, and nine months later

they give birth to their very own brown-haired, blue-eyed
god who inevitably must be sacrificed (with the exception of
Pontus, who more or less just vanished from the mythological
record, as if one day after centuries of floating around in a
clump of seaweed he just sort of sank to the bottom of the sea
and dissolved) so that the world may be reborn in spectacular
post-apocalyptic fashion. Or perhaps the change is quieter,
a subtle rendering of reality, like opening a window so
you can watch winter melt away and spring arrive, though
even if you are extremely focused in this regard it is almost
impossible to pinpoint the exact moment when the leaves
appear. And because these earlier mythic stories are, well,
mythic, it is easy (or easier) to see that they are concerned
with a spiritual rebirth, not an actual physical one, but in the
case of the Virgin Mary and her son, Jesus, who have taken
on the dimensions of actual physical, historical personages in
spite of their general absence from the historical record (the
two debatable references in Josephus aside), the implications
are more difficult to assess, for in the minds of the laity (not
to mention certain narcissistic philosophers, misogynist theo-
logians, and the hundreds of television evangelists suffering
from de Clérambault's syndrome), the notion of a spiritual
rebirth has been replaced by the belief in an actual physical
rebirth, which could, of course, be considered extraordinarily
lucky in the sense that you, as an individual, would never
die, but the idea of rebirth here in the West is not imagined in
the sense of emerging a second or a third or tenth time from
some bloody womb, as is the case with the Eastern religions,
but instead refers to simply rising from the grave with your
earthly body restored, which according to the Judeo-Christian
religious tradition means your ideal earthly body, without
blemish, without pain, without the cellular memory of dying,
as opposed to a postmodern vision of the walking dead,
apoplectic zombies with pieces of jagged flesh falling away
as they walk and eyeballs dangling so you wonder how they
can even see where they are going, and still they are somehow
able to take over the world, or at least cable television, all of
which would be extraordinarily unlucky if you were wedded
to the Judeo-Christian view, in which case you might wish to
start completely over as someone brand spanking new.

Now it should also be pointed out that the longshoreman in question possessed a dark, shadowy complexion and
an inscrutable expression, with his hair cropped so close it
seemed he was wearing a skull cap, and a wavering darkness
that surrounded him like a shroud, perhaps because he never
removed his heavy longshoreman's coat, at least not while he
was in Logroño.

He resembled most closely the ghost of an unlucky
and unrepentant Inquisitor from the days of the Spanish
Inquisition who had died a suspicious if not violent death
during the Second Alpujarras revolt in Granada in 1568. And
he somewhat resembled the ghost of a renegade Jesuit priest
who had been lost in the jungles of Venezuela in the 17th century but had been taken in by a tribe of Yanomamo cannibals
who lived along an unexplored tributary of the Oronoco River
and who granted him a special kind of immortality (the kind
reserved for venerable grandfathers or noble enemies), after he
had explained to them with the aid of a mestizo the sacrifice
of Christ and the symbolic meaning of the Communion
wafer, by eating him at a feast in his honor. But he bore little
resemblance at all to the swelling ranks of fat, young Spanish
priests who hoped only for a small parish with plenty to eat
and drink and the chance to die safely in their beds without
being tested by war, famine, pestilence, or the crumbling of
their faith.

He was a man of great courage, willing to take all
sorts of risks, both necessary and unnecessary, but he also
possessed a simmering, calculating maliciousness, which was
fairly easy to see unless you were blinded by his slovenly
charm. He said his name was Grenfell, a Welshman by
birth and a descendent of William Pascoe Grenfell, who
had founded the Cobre Company. He had accompanied the
younger Ordóñez brother from Swansea, Wales, where the
two had met in a brothel overlooking the harbor. Grenfell
was in search of the financial backing to restore what he said
was rightfully his in the first place. He claimed to be a distant

cousin or grandnephew twice removed or a grandson from a second marriage of the eccentric mine owner. Andres was never quite sure he remembered correctly, for the disclosure of the exact nature of the longshoreman's familial connection to the elder Grenfell always and only took place after several pints of warm beer or glasses of wine or bottles of rum had been consumed.

It was Grenfell who suggested that they wait until Andres had assessed his brother's potential as an investor before introducing him to the rightful heir to the mines and the mining company. "He that refuseth instruction despiseth his own soul: but he that heareth reproof getteth understanding," the Welshman was fond of saying. And though Andres did not fully understand the cryptic meaning of the Welshman's words, he did recognize biblical language when he heard it, even biblical language obscured by a thick Welsh accent (not as thick as if Grenfell had come from Bangor, more like he had been born in Cardiff), so he agreed to bring in the Welshman only if absolutely necessary. In truth, Grenfell gave him little choice. Either that or the events that transpired had been decreed since the beginning of time.

-44-

The night before Andres' last day at his brother's house, he and Grenfell talked about Arturo's lack of interest in the copper mines. They were heading to Cuba one way or another. They had already booked passage on a steamer that had been christened with the grand-sounding even mythic name of *Conde Wifredo*, which was leaving from Barcelona in one week, but they needed a small infusion of cash or their plans would surely go for naught. This was Grenfell's position. He spoke with the inflexible conviction of a desert prophet, so there was very little Andres could say to challenge him. Also, for some half-baked and therefore unexpressed and inexpressible reason, possibly because Grenfell wished to repay the debt he owed Carabali for intervening on his behalf with the Civil Guard, but more likely because Carabali now thought of the longshoreman as an investment and wanted to keep tabs on his whereabouts, Carabali accompanied Grenfell and Andres to The Café with Two Names, which is where the conversation noted above took place.

The conversation in The Café with Two Names:
"So that there's the truth of it," said Grenfell.
"What do you mean that there's the truth of it?" said Carabali.
"I mean I know for a fact it was a hell of a lot easier running the mines when we had Negroes working for us," said Grenfell.
"What do you mean you know for a fact?" said Carabali.
"I mean I've heard about it," said Grenfell. "It was easier in all kinds of ways. For one thing, there was no such thing as a strike. They worked when you told them to work, that's one advantage with the darkies, and for as long as you needed them to work, and that's another advantage, and if they didn't you flogged them till they bled or died, not all of them, only the ones that started the trouble. Believe you me, the flogging of Negroes is as cruel and depraved an act as you're likely to see on this earth. I've seen it first hand, so I know. They'd lay the Negroes on the ground, some of them tied to ladders, or some of them held down by two or even three men, and then twenty or thirty lashes with a bullwhip and every blow rattling as loud as a pistol shot."
"What do you mean you've seen it?" said Carabali.
"I mean I've heard about it," said Grenfell.
Carabali blinked stupidly.
"But times change," said Grenfell. "And it's a good thing too. Working them Negroes who came over through the Canaries was like working in a damnable charnal house. It was a slow, withering death to all of us. But now you've got to pay somebody to mine your copper, and that ain't cheap neither, which leaves us where we are."
The men grew silent for a moment, grim.
They were eating black sausage and beans and great chunks of coarse brown bread, and they were sharing what

was left of a bottle of *Crianza*. There were several empty
bottles on the table. All of the men were exceedingly drunk.

Fernando, the owner of the cafe, a beefy man wearing a
butcher's apron stained with the blood of various cuts of meat,
who had no talent for the culinary arts but who had inherited
the café from his father so he had no choice, leaned over the
table with some fresh bread and smiled a butcher's smile
which seemed to slice through the very air, but he only looked
at Andres, the smile becoming an expression of sadness, and
asked how his brother was faring these days, it had been a
month or more since he had seen him. Andres smiled weakly
and said his brother was well, but it was difficult with the two
girls, especially now that the girls were grown up, or almost,
they were too much for his brother to handle, especially without Verona, may God preserve her immortal soul. Fernando
nodded, a slight movement, and said a similar prayer, but
under his breath, as if he were suddenly embarrassed, the
words escaping like steam. Then he said he'd return promptly
with a bottle of *absenta* for later, wiped his great butcher
hands on his apron and grabbed hold of the empties, his great
butcher fingers like fat sausages wrapped around the skinny
glass necks, and returned with a renewed sense of purpose to
the darkness of the bar at the other end of the café.

"Arturo will not help us," said Andres after a prolonged
silence.

"But perhaps he can be made to help us," said Grenfell.

"How is this possible?" said Carabali.

"I don't think it is possible," said Andres.

"He that refuseth instruction despiseth his own soul: but
he that heareth reproof getteth understanding," said Grenfell.

"I have not heard of this," said Carabali. And then to
Andres: "What does he mean?"

But Andres only shook his head.

"It means," said Grenfell, but then he lapsed into silence
and drank some more wine.

Andres ate some more of his stew.

Carabali began to study Grenfell's face, as if closer
scrutiny would reveal some hidden meaning in his silence.

Grenfell seemed to be waiting for something.

Then the door to the café opened and an old man

wearing a wool cap and his capless middle-aged son came
in and they sat down at a table near the only window in the
café. Fernando brought the newcomers two bowls of stew and
a basket of bread and a bottle of *Crianza* and mumbled something and the men mumbled something back and began to eat.
Fernando stood by their table a while, hovering over the father
and the son like the shadow of a church tower, watching the
men eat, then looking out the window and the dark red glow
of the sun washing over the brown cobblestones outside, and
then watching the men some more.

The three men began talking in stark counterpoint to the
conversation at the other end of the café.

It was almost like an operetta. But without the music.

"No one knew the Caribbean would be so much trouble," the old man said.

The middle-aged son laughed but did not look at his
father and his father cuffed him on the side of his head but
still he did not look up.

"Who is going to pay for this war, Lazaro? You?"

"No, I have already paid too much."

"We have all paid too much," said Fernando.

"Yes, it is too much already," said the old man. "What
was the government thinking?"

"Who cares?" said Lazaro. "It is already finished, the
fighting. So who cares? Not even God cares."

The three men started lamenting the useless tragedy of
all the young men who had left Spain to fight the insurgents
and would now never return. Thousands of young men. Tens
of thousands. An entire generation. Someone was to blame
for the terrible embarrassment of losing the war. The army,
perhaps, or the navy, yes, they were certainly to blame. The
navy had been smashed by the Americans. How could that
happen? In what nightmare realm did such things occur?
The heroic pride of Spain had been smashed by farmers and
shopkeepers and maybe a few cowboys. It was a disgrace.
What had happened to the might and indomitable will of the
Spanish Empire? How could one even begin to comprehend
the scope of such a disaster? The government should call for
an investigation. They should hang every Admiral they could
get their hands on, and every Captain too, everyone who

hadn't been killed during the war. Every newspaper in the country said so.

Then it was hard to hear what the three men were saying. The sun had set and the only window in the café had become a dark glass which swallowed everything they said.

Fernando returned to the darkness behind the bar.

On the other side of the café, Andres was still focused on his stew.

Carabali was still scrutinizing Grenfell's face.

"It means," began Grenfell again, as if someone had suddenly pulled a switch, "that every breath draws us one step closer to God, so we all better concede that we are inferior beings and do what God demands of us or we will certainly perish in the fiery pits of Hell, which will be the fate of most of mankind. In Hell the death of the soul is inevitable. That's what it means."

"But who knows what God wants us to do?" said Carabali.

Yes," said Andres. "That is precisely the question I have been asking him the last two weeks."

Grenfell coughed some and spat a wad of phlegm onto the floor. Then he rinsed his mouth with the last of the wine and waved for Fernando, who appeared like a great wind with another bottle and disappeared just as suddenly into the comfortable darkness behind the bar. Then Grenfell smiled and blinked happily, as if he had just arrived at the café. "How much would Arturo pay to preserve the joy of seeing his beautiful daughters each and every morning?" he said. He held up his empty glass in dramatic fashion so that it caught the dim light of the café and sparkled like a diamond. "How much is the joy of beholding such beauty worth?"

"You would hold his eyes for ransom?" said Carabali.

"You are an idiot," said Grenfell. "Not his eyes. We will hold for ransom that which gives his eyes the greatest joy."

"And what is that?" said Carabali.

"We will kidnap his daughters."

"And this is what God wants?" said Carabali.

Grenfell smiled again, a thin, knowing smile this time, like a layer of clouds pressing down upon the horizon, but said nothing. He uncorked the new bottle and poured a glass

for himself and drank it slowly, and then he poured some for
the others and watched them drink.

"It is not so much a question of what God wants," he
said after a while, "but what God will permit."

"Ah, you are a slippery devil," said Carabali. "But what
of this one here?"

Carabali pointed a drunken finger at Andres.

"With Andres' help we will soon have the wind at our
back," said Grenfell. "Is this not true, Andres?"

Andres finished the glass of wine Grenfell had poured
him and poured himself another. It was a full-bodied red with
a hint of smoked something, Andres couldn't quite tell, but it
went down easily. He drank some more and smiled vaguely
at his two companions. He had been trying to follow the
conversation, but he had become uncertain who was talking
at various points so he had given up, focusing on the wine
instead. He could barely see what he was doing. He had the
feeling that he was groping his way through a dense fog.
Then he heard his name and his mind began to clear, and
then he remembered someone had said they were going to
kidnap his nieces and hold them for ransom, or maybe he had
thought this strange thought himself, but Arturo would pay
any price for his daughters, Andres knew this to be true, so
it might work, yes, it was worth thinking about at any rate,
and besides, his nieces would be in no real danger, it would
only be a temporary measure, it would be like a game, and
then his vision returned and he could make out the shadowy,
shimmering figures of Grenfell and Carabali and he nodded
at them ever so slightly and smiled, to assure them not only
that he understood what they were talking about, but that he
was willing to participate in this fantastic scheme of theirs,
and then Carabali gave a nervous, chirpy laugh, because he
wasn't at all sure what Andres meant by nodding, and then
the conversation, which had been put on hold while Andres
regained his composure, resumed, and Andres heard himself
speaking, though he sounded very far away, a trembling,
muffled, hollow sounding voice, almost unrecognizable, like
the sound of church bells under water, as if he had fallen into
a very dark, very deep well. He did not sound like himself at
all.

"You swear the girls will be in no real danger."

"Of course," said Grenfell.

"It will be a ruse, a game, a thing of temporary duration," said Andres.

"Yes, yes, my friend," said Grenfell. And then in a very grave tone: "They are, after all, your very own flesh and blood."

"Precisely," said Andres.

"But all the same, an endeavor such as this will require careful planning," said Grenfell.

"Yes," said Andres. "My brother is most vigilant when it comes to the girls."

"What should we do?" said Carabali.

"I suggest that we kidnap only one of the girls," said Grenfell. "Not both of them, as I first thought. Yes, I think one will be enough. One will be manageable. One will be less complicated."

"Which one?" said Andres.

"That, my friend, I will defer to your judgment."

Andres' eyes glazed over for a moment, as if he were deep in thought, lost in the labyrinth of dark dreaming and parallel universes. He said nothing for a very long time. The voices at the other end of the café filled the seeming void.

"The government knew there was no chance," said Lazaro.

"Why do you say such a thing?" said the old man.

"Because it is true."

"Ah, yes, the truth," said the old man. "But what is the truth, Lazaro?"

"The truth is they sent my brigade south to Tarifa with three Krupp guns to strengthen our defenses along the coast in case the Americans attacked. That is the truth."

"What kind of truth is that? What does it mean?"

"It means they were afraid of the Americans," said Lazaro. "They were afraid the Americans would invade Spain. It means they knew."

The father and the middle-aged son had finished their supper and were savoring the last of their wine.

"Rubbish, rubbish. No one knew. Not even God knew."

"They knew."

"And what happened to these famous guns of yours?"

They set their glasses down.

"I don't know. I suppose they're still there."

"In Tarifa?

"Yes."

"Rubbish. There are no guns in Tarifa."

"There are. We put them there. We started off with three, but the road to Tarifa is not very good, it is very steep and rugged in places and full of holes and we lost one of the guns south of El Bujeo."

They stood up to leave.

"I will say again, there are no guns in Tarifa."

"And I will say again, there are."

"And the Americans, did the Americans invade Spain?"

"No."

"Hah! There is your truth for you, Lazaro."

The door opened and the father and the middle-aged son nodded at Fernando without pausing in their conversation and then stepped through the doorway as if they were stepping into another time, and then the door closed, but you could still hear their voices echoing across the cobblestones as if they were echoing across the centuries.

"When you are as old as I am, you will see things differently."

"They knew, I tell you."

"Rubbish, Lazaro. No one knows."

"You are impossible, old man."

"No one ever knows."

And then the three conspirators at the other end of the café, their voices sounding now like the voices of small birds trapped in a cage.

"Tiká is the one I would choose," said Andres.

"Yes, yes," said Carabali. "She is all adventure, that one."

"Precisely," said Andres. "I think she will run away with us if we ask her."

"Yes," said Carabali, "I think you are correct on this point."

"I think she is eager to leave Logroño," said Andres.

"And what about your brother?" said Grenfell.

"As you said, an endeavor such as this will require careful planning."

"Yes, this is true," said Grenfell.

"What must we do, then?" said Carabali.

"We must make haste slowly," said Grenfell.

"Ah," said Carabali. "That is a good way of putting it. Very poetic.

"Naturally," said Grenfell. "I am Welsh, after all."

The men laughed and drank the rest of their wine, and then they polished off a couple of bottles of Vermouth, which they drank with soda water and some lemon, and all the while they were talking about the journey to Cuba again. Andres and Carabali could barely contain their excitement, even though Carabali had no ticket for the trip to Cuba on board the *Conde Wifredo* or any other steamer, and up until the day before he had never even considered going to Cuba, but there in the dim light of The Café with Two Names he seemed as eager as Andres to walk the streets of Havana, streets they had heard were paved with gold, like the streets of the mythic El Dorado, but Grenfell mocked their ignorance and said they had been misinformed, there were no gold streets in Havana or Cuba or anywhere else in the Americas, there were some cobblestone streets, like anywhere, and many more were just plain dirt, like anywhere, and besides, if the streets had been paved with gold they would have been dug up already because of the expense of the war, the war had been a drain on both sides, and Andres said they were only speaking fig-uratively, they knew gold was not used to build streets, they were not idiots, and they also knew about the expense of the war, but what did that have to do with anything, and Carabali didn't say a word because he had truly believed in streets made of gold and was nursing his disappointment, and yes, yes, he had certainly heard about the war, as everyone had, but everything he had heard had felt like a rumor, and he put little stock in rumors because they were like wisps of smoke, and after that it was very difficult to hear what the three men were saying, it was almost like they had ceased to exist.

It would be safe to say that the democratic approach to planning adopted by the three conspirators was haphazard at best, degenerating at times into crude, even childish debates

or petty tirades that did little to build consensus and which
meant, in all likelihood, that their chances for success were
quite low, better than six to one against.

Andres, Grenfell and Carabali had argued for hours
about the details of how to commit their crime of the century,
long after Fernando himself had locked the front door of the
café and gone to bed, leaving the bottle of *absenta* he had
promised on their table before he went up to his room, which
he shared with a blind parrot who repeated the "Glory Be"
every night while Fernando lay in bed wondering about the
mythological names of the stars until he fell asleep. First they
argued about what they should say to Tiká, the exact language
they were going to use, because Andres felt using precise
language was important, and he had persuaded Carabali on
this point, but Grenfell said that it was preposterous to think
that language might affect the outcome of an endeavor that
was by its very nature brutish and the antithesis to language.
Besides, in most instances action is what was needed, not
language at all, and besides that, he had no flair for using
language, so if that's what they wanted to do, then they had
better count him out. Then they argued about the best time
to plunge into the abyss, this was how Grenfell had put it,
who in spite of his claims to the contrary had a poetic flair
for using language after all. Grenfell's voice took on a dark,
hallucinatory quality and he said early in the morning would
be the most appropriate time, around four, because everyone
would be asleep at that hour, and even those who were awake
would think they were asleep or wish they were, for that has
always been the hour when the boundaries of reality begin
to shift and shimmer and the wrongfully murdered return
to exact their vengeance; and the saints, even those newly
appointed, are able to intercede on behalf of the downtrodden;
and sailors the world over imagine they are making love to
the mermaids of the southern hemisphere (for everyone knows
the mermaids of the northern seas vanished long ago), and in
some cases the union between sailor and mermaid is a tangible
reality, but only if there is sufficient cloud cover; and even the
angels themselves have forgotten where the borders of heaven
end and those of earth begin. Andres, who was less theatrical,
wanted to wait until first light, because most people would

still be sleeping, and those who might be awake wouldn't
know a kidnapping was in progress anyway, they would be
too busy firing up kitchen stoves or brushing the leather of
their saddles before an early morning ride or getting ready to
walk the dusty streets of Logroño in search of an open church.
Carabali suggested they simply hang around Café Rioja
because of the shops across the street and when the girl came
down to buy a new parasol or a new bonnet by Borsalino or a
velveteen toque by Capello or Panizza or a new pair of shoes
or perhaps a pair of Garabaldi boots, they could grab her then
and her father would be none the wiser, but Grenfell said
such an idea could only be the product of a brain overflowing
with the pustulent excrement of disease, had he forgotten that
they had a steamer to catch in one week, well, at least Grenfell
and Andres had a steamer to catch, what was he (Carabali)
thinking, what horribly deficient, idiotic reasoning, who
could say when the girl might head out for an afternoon of
shopping. Carabali said nothing in response. He finished the
last of his Vermouth and turned to the as yet unopened bottle
of *absenta* and vowed silently to refrain from speaking for the
rest of the night, and they (which now meant Grenfell and
Andres) discussed various options for transporting themselves
and the girl first to Zaragoza, where they would collect the
ransom and send the girl home, and then on to Barcelona, just
the two of them at that point, a fact which Grenfell seemed
eager to underscore. Perhaps they needed a fine horse and
carriage befitting the daughter of a gentleman, said Grenfell.
Yes, said Andres, with some measured irony, this would keep
the eyes of the Civil Guard where they belonged, certainly, but
everyone else in town would take note, for carriages had lately
become an uncommon sight, what about a flatbed wagon
instead, the kind used for hauling merchandise. That would
certainly be easy to procure, said Grenfell, but then wouldn't
they have to outfit the wagon with some sort of shipment to
avoid suspicion, wool perhaps, or fresh cut timber, and if they
had the money for such a shipment they wouldn't need to
kidnap the girl in the first place (which was the most salient
point advanced during the course of the whole evening).
Why don't they steal some horses from Arturo's stables, that
would be easy enough, said Carabali (a suggestion which he

offered only tentatively, since he was still partially submerged
in the swill of resentment over Grenfell's earlier remarks but
he couldn't help himself). But the other two just stared at
Carabali as if he had lost his mind, because Arturo did not
possess any stables, and only a single horse, the same dark
chestnut which Tiká had been riding bareback since the age
of two and which Arturo rode only on rare occasions now,
whenever he didn't walk, which he usually did because it was
safer, though sometimes he neither walked nor rode the horse
and rode his bicycle instead, an 1892 black and nickel Elliott
Hickory with pneumatic tires but still using hickory for the
wheels, spokes and rims, hence the name, and which was only
practical around town, where the terrain was relatively flat
and uniform, because you had to get off and push when you
came to a hill, and then going down you were traveling as fast
as a rocket and might crash because the spokes, being made
of wood, might snap from the stress of a rocky road, which
sometimes happened, and which is why Arturo almost never
took the bicycle out, and also because the saddle was rather
inflexible and gave him abrasions, though it should be said
that this contraption had been the last present his wife Verona
had given him before she died and so he sometimes took it
out for a spin around town when he was thinking of her, but
usually not, because he preferred the prestige of the dark
chestnut or the absolute safety of walking even to the memory
of his dead wife, all of which apparently Carabali did not
know. And so it went. By the time the three conspirators left
The Café with Two Names, they had conceived three different
plans, not one, though each instinctively believed that only
one plan existed, and their memories did not improve by
the time they woke up the next day, shortly after one in the
afternoon, for they each still clung to a different idea of the
plan that was the cornerstone of their intentions, and if plan
is not the right word, then perhaps the phrase 'vague assumptions' is more precise, like a child's pure and simple faith,
which is really a patchwork of unexamined hopes and dreams
and unpurged fears, which might be why they didn't stop to
question what they were doing.

Carabali slept that night in a small, whitewashed stone
cottage a mile outside of the original walled borders of the

town, a cottage belonging to a young widow. Presumably her husband had left for Cuba on a merchant vessel years earlier and had never returned and had not even sent a letter, so she had petitioned the Church to annul her marriage, for there were no children, and the Church had been happy to comply. The young widow had been madly in love with Carabali from the very first moment she had laid eyes on him (she had spotted him one warm afternoon peering through the windows of the shops on Calle Ollerías and sighing wistfully), and now she barely gave him time to get his trousers off before she had him in bed ("what is this hiding in your pantaloons," she would say, and then she would give a strange, hypnotic, exotic laugh that sounded like a Bird of Paradise trapped in a sewer). So Carabali had spent the night with the widow, and after he woke, he borrowed a flatbed wagon and two mules from this widow of unflagging desire and gave her a kiss which suggested he would return shortly and with many gifts, and then with a sigh of exhausted relief, which the young widow mistook for a declaration of love, he left his damsel in distress and in less than fifteen minutes found himself sitting inside Café Rioja so he could keep an eye on the shops across the street.

Grenfell slept on the cold stone floor in the back of the Church of Santiago, though how he got there was a mystery, and woke up amid the crazed staring hatred of the old women with their black shawls, who had discovered him on the floor when they arrived just after Father de Nazar had opened the great church doors, and who had poked at him with their canes to see if the white light of Christ had struck him dead upon entering the church, for such was usually the fate of demons, and who had retreated a step towards the shadows, holding up their crosses in the dim church light when he had opened his eyes after their poking, and when he beheld their stark mindless hatred like screaming ghosts, he had fled, clutching at the air as if he were drowning in a sea of incandescent nitrogen, the old women ushering him out with their canes, beating him on the back and on his shoulders and on the backs of his legs, those that could reach, and only after a seeming eternity of running, during which Grenfell became lost in an unexpected maze of cobblestone streets,

did he remember that he was supposed to meet Andres at
his brother's house for dinner and they were going to get
Arturo roaring drunk, a blitzkrieg of drunkenness, and then
shortly after midnight, presumably after Arturo was dead to
the world in a drunken slumber, Carabali would arrive with a
carriage and they would grab the girl and head to Zaragoza,
but not without first stuffing a ransom letter into the pocket
of Arturo's dinner jacket, a letter which Grenfell had already
written at some mysterious point between The Café with
Two Names and the back of the Church of Santiago, but they
wouldn't push the letter all the way down, it would need to
be protruding slightly, like a handkerchief, so Arturo would
be sure not to miss it in the morning when he woke, and then
he would read the letter and he would know what sum to
forward to Zaragoza for the safe return of his daughter.

Andres, for his part, had slept in the suite of three rooms
that had been his childhood bedroom in the back of what was
now his brother's house and had dreamed that the kidnapping
had been abandoned altogether in favor of inviting Escolástica
to join them on their journey to Cuba. They would remain
in Logroño a few more days so Andres could wire ahead
to purchase a first class ticket on the *Conde Wifredo* (Andres
and Grenfell would remain in second class), and while there
was still the thorny problem of Arturo's blessing to consider,
Andres was confident, at least in his dream, that Arturo would
sense in his youngest daughter the same unquenchable thirst
to see the world that his late wife, Verona Almeida Vda De
Miranda, had possessed, and that by permitting his daughter
this chance to escape, he would be honoring the memory
of Verona. What Andres never considered, in his dream or otherwise, was that Arturo had already committed the memory
of his dead wife to the embalming fluid of his despair, and
that if he did see even the glimmer of his wife in the face of
Escolástica, he would never allow his daughter to leave. She
would become a living mummy to ease his pain.

How could Andres have been so unaware of his
brother's grief? The signs were unmistakable. The very suite
of rooms that Andres now slept in had become a shrine to
Verona. The dozens of end tables and side tables and bureaus
and buffets left over from the days of Verona's Saturday night

parties (gala events to which the whole of Logroño had been
invited) were now crammed together in this suite of three
rooms in honor of their former patroness, and while they
seemed carelessly scattered about (so much so that Andres
never took the same route twice on his way from the first
room to the third room and back again), they were precisely
placed so as to remain in the shadows even when the slatted
blinds were raised and the sun was blazing with full force.
They seemed less like end tables and side tables and bureaus
and buffets and more like miniature altars hidden away in the
dark corners of a great cathedral. All of them were covered
with candles and candelabra and tiny ivory statuettes of
Jesus or the Virgin Mary that seemed to weep late at night
(or sometimes in the middle of the afternoon when the *Ábrego*
winds blew in from the south). There were also the relics of a
few saints purchased at the market in Barcelona (when Arturo
took Verona on a tour of Catalonia, which he said was his
ancestral home): a sliver of the left arm of the true cross from
Santo Toribio de Liébana (the vendor had admitted to Arturo
stealing the sliver from the monks at the abbey, which Arturo
took as proof that the relic was a fake, but which Verona said
proved the opposite, though she didn't explain how); the
mummified finger of St. Teresa of Avila (or perhaps it was just
a donkey's tooth wrapped in gauze, which Arturo pointed out
in a half-joking manner, only to have his lack of faith decried
and flung back in his face by his wife); and there were a dozen
or more relics representing saints so famous that Arturo found
it impossible to believe they were genuine (the holy foreskin
of Saint Paul, which came with a tiny jeweled case, and which
more or less resembled a red chickpea; a pile of toenails which
Saint Ignatius of Loyola had one clipped from his Holy toes,
and which had been kept in a small silk pouch thereafter to
prevent their being mistaken for unsanctified toenails and
tossed into the dustbin; a piece of the loincloth of John the
Baptist; an oil lamp that Saint Peter had once touched, the
tongue of Saint Anthony of Padua, and so on), but Arturo had
given up trying to persuade his beloved Verona by then.

So the end tables and side tables and bureaus and
buffets were given over to all manner of Catholic paraphernalia, but the walls were covered with dozens of photographs

depicting the life Arturo and Verona had once lived. There was one of Arturo and Verona attending an operetta in Barcelona; and one of them taking a train to the sea; and then Arturo and Verona on an unknown beach among a crowd of two dozen, all of them fully dressed, the women with parasols, the men wearing top hats or bowlers, all of them milling about, some looking out at the sea, some looking up at a cloudy sky, and a few climbing into an old rowboat pulled up into the sand; and then there was Arturo and Verona standing next to their brand new Hickory bicycles with their house (a Grecian-styled house with Doric columns and a red-tile roof and unrecognizable hanging plants dangling from the railings of the second floor balcony) in the background and storm clouds in the distance; and another of Arturo and Verona standing outside the Church of Santiago for a wedding portrait; and then one of the wedding feast; and then people dancing; and then a separate one of Arturo sitting in dismal repose in a leather chair in the photographer's studio, choking, it seemed, from a collar that was too tight and perhaps also the fumes of the photographic process itself, which had seemed to Arturo to be a deadly mixture of zinc oxide and cyanide; and a matching photograph of Verona in the same chair, smiling an exceedingly photogenic smile for the 19th or any other century, unaware of the deadly fumes produced by photography.

The crowning glory of this shrine to Verona, however, were two portraits done by Joaquín Sorolla y Bastida, either just before he left for Paris in 1885 or just after he returned to Valencia in 1888. The first painting, done in oil, showed Verona wearing a broad-brimmed hat with a green feather to match her green dress and a sad, melancholy expression that gave her face a twisted look, as if she were looking into a dark glass of the future and saw her own death. (She died unexpectedly of an acute attack of neuralgia of the heart, a condition precipitated by the sudden realization that she loved her daughters with an unqualified love that only the poets, the angels, and God himself dared contemplate, but she could not say the same thing for her husband, for in the years since they had been married, her expectations of romantic love had become tangled up with her belief in social etiquette, which Arturo roundly ignored, leaving her breathless with frustra-

tion; so when this realization came upon her, she also realized
that death could not be far behind, for she could not live the
lie of a marriage without love, but at the same time there was
nowhere else for her to go, so she was the only one not taken
by surprise when death came for her one week later, the day
before Palm Sunday, at the tender age of thirty-three, the same
age Christ was when he died, a thought which occurred to
Arturo during her funeral Mass and which immediately struck
him as blasphemous, though he could not have described how,
and he suddenly wanted to hurl himself from the middle of
the Puente de Piedra bridge and drown both his sorrows and
his overwhelming sense of Catholic guilt in the dark waters
of the Ebro river, but then he realized that Christ had died on
a Thursday and his wife on a Saturday, which in his twisted
state of mind brought him some welcome and unanticipated
relief, and so he relented somewhat in his despair.)

The second painting, which hung directly across from
the bed where Andres slept, this one done using a technique
called gouache, which art historians called opaque watercolor,
which gives paintings greater reflective qualities, showed
a naked Verona stretched out on a bed with satin sheets, a
luminescent pink, as if it were late morning or early afternoon
and someone (not Verona) had pulled back the curtains to
let in the sunlight, which was amazingly clean and crisp and
pure, the light washing over Verona, her legs bent at the knees
and her hips turned slightly so that her plush derriere curved
up and out in wanton fashion, and her black hair was curled
tightly and she wore a purple gardenia where it was pulled
up in back. Each morning (by sunlight) and each evening
(by candlelight), Andres explored the contours of Verona's
semblance. He often lingered on the delicate curve of a single
breast pressing down against the satin sheets, and he wished
he could see the expression on Verona's face, which was
turned away, but he could imagine what she was thinking and
feeling. She was holding one hand to her mouth and was staring at the other one stretched out before her, for her lily-white
hand was now a mirror reflecting the luminescence of the pink
satin sheets, her hips, her shoulders, her breasts, all glowing
pink in the late morning or early afternoon light of the painting, a soft light as if filtered through a thin parchment of rose

petals. She was contemplating a future which would involve copious amounts of sex amid the sounds of girlish joy, at least this is what Andres imagined as he looked at the painting of Verona stretched out before him each morning when he woke or each evening before he went to sleep, for he was still a young man who had only been with a woman twice, once with a Carmelite novitiate in Lisieux, France, who wanted to taste sex before her final vows, and once in a brothel in Lisbon, tucked away in the ancient neighborhood of Mouraria with its maze of Moorish streets, with a woman twice his age who said she was a distant cousin of the legendary fado singer and prostitute Maria Severa Onofriana, so he had paid her two times the going rate.

-45-

The abduction of Escolástica Escoraz Vda De Miranda took place in the Year of Our Lord 1899 between the hours of five o'clock in the afternoon on December 8 and two o'clock the following morning, December 9. But the way it began was a surprise to everyone involved, as was the way it proceeded (the middle part), all the way to the getaway (the last part, during which the temperature plummeted to an unusually brisk six degrees Celsius), for it followed none of the details of any of the three plans as imagined or remembered by the three would-be kidnappers.

Andres, who still believed the plot to kidnap his niece had been abandoned altogether, was sitting on the verandah of his brother's house at five o'clock, watching the empty street, waiting for something to happen, a vaguely troubled look on his face, a sense that something was off-kilter but he could not put his finger on it.

Madia, the old battle axe crone who took care of the Escoraz family, had set out an enamel tray with a few empty glasses and a pitcher of sangria on the small wicker table next to Andres, and he was just about to pour himself a glass when he saw Grenfell coming up the street.

Except he did not know it was Grenfell. At first Grenfell was only an unrecognizable shape with the sun casting long shadows and a breeze blowing across the street, kicking up small tornadoes of dust. The figure looked like a vagrant monk trying to swim against the current of religious dissidence, thought Andres, amused by the comparison, or an army deserter from Morocco, perhaps. Andres glanced at the figure with the weary, perfunctory look of forgetfulness and turned to his glass of sangria and wondered what his brother and his two nieces were doing and when they were going to eat, because he hadn't eaten all day. It was very hot and breezy and sangria wasn't enough.

The vague notion that he was forgetting something important flitted across the backs of his eyeballs like ticker tape, but he was too hungry to focus. He looked again at the figure he did not recognize, and then suddenly the figure pushed its way through the front gate and became Grenfell, wearing his heavy longshoreman's coat with its premonitory stench of a perpetual shipwreck. Grenfell started up the stone walk to the house, past the remnants of the flower beds Verona had once labored over and that had contained yellow gazanias and gold and maroon gazanias and white and purple ones, and all manner of daisies, and a few tamarisk with their bright lavender bristles, and geraniums and red carnations and red roses and yellow roses and bluebells and purple gardenias, and row after row of purple heliotropes, which she had first seen in the Parc de la Ciutadella in Barcelona along a path leading to a fantastic waterfall with all manner of vegetative cover and bronze statues of dragons and horses blazing in the white sunlight, which gave just the right Baroque quality to the most elegant gardens she had ever hoped to see but which she knew were an extravagance Arturo would never consider replicating, so she had settled for the heliotropes.

Verona's flowers had been the pride of Logroño and the envy of the priests in every church, even Father de Nazar, for the clergy had always secretly believed, at least in Spain, that the ability to grow beautiful flowers was one of the seven visible manifestations of the mercy of God and a symbol of the relationship between Christ and His flock. As if in response to their unspoken testament, Verona had tended to the needs of her flowers on a daily basis and distributed them freely during festivals to lengthen the joy of the festival goers, and also to those in mourning during those mysterious black days when someone had died an unexpected death, to shorten the agony of their despair, but in the years since Verona herself had died, the flowers had been neglected, so only a few scraggly rose bushes remained, survivors from a time before war and rumors of war and the pestilence that comes with anarchy had infected the mythology of the country, a few red blooms withering away in the dusty summer heat, as fleeting as the smiles of ghosts.

So Grenfell walked past the ruined flower beds, a fitting symbol of the death of Verona, and Andres suddenly wondered if something had gone wrong with the new plan, for he hadn't yet had time to go to the telegraph office and wire for a new ticket. Besides, Grenfell wasn't supposed to show up till later, though in the sudden confusion of trying to recall the details of a dream he mistook for a recent memory, Andres was not certain what they had decided. Immediately he stood up, not knowing what else to do. But Grenfell only inclined his head as he walked up the steps, a subtle gesture of greeting, perhaps, which Andres took to mean that yes, there was a slight change in the new plans, but there was nothing to worry about, everything was proceeding towards a favorable conclusion, they would soon be in Cuba, living in the lap of luxury in spite of the absence of streets paved with gold. Andres felt much better after that. Grenfell would expound upon any changes in the plan at a later point, as warranted, which could certainly wait until after supper, and then Andres felt a surge of unexpected happiness coursing through his veins, an electrifying current. Such is the creative power of the imagination which allows us to believe that anything might be true, even when it is only a phantom, a cinematic flicker, the scent of orchids on an evening breeze. Andres offered his co-conspirator a glass of sangria and the two men sat down in their wicker chairs, a haze of wordless exhaustion descending upon the verandah as they drank. From that point forward, the plans of the two would-be kidnappers on the verandah (and the one waiting in Café Rioja two miles away) unraveled very quickly, and the abduction would have become

a miserable and quite possibly tragic failure, at least as far as
Andres was concerned, had not Tiká realized that her uncle
was teetering on the edge of the abyss, and taken matters into
her own Amazonian hands to save him.

She became a fixed point on the horizon.

She became the mirror to the mirrored face that was
herself.

She became the dream of a small white bird hoping
against hope that one day it would find the courage to fly
beyond the bars of its cage to seek the treasure of countless
nights and days.

She became the dream of her uncle unfolding, a dream
in which she became both the dreamer and the dream itself,
but in much greater detail, for while her uncle's dream had
stopped with his altered memory of the conversation at The
Café with Two Names, Tiká's dream continued until the *Conde
Wifredo* left Barcelona and plunged into the dark, unfathomable waters of the Mediterranean one week later.

In this dream of her first true awakening, she saw her
uncle emerging from The Café with Two Names at a most
ungodly hour, giddy as a delinquent schoolboy, singing
songs of happy revolutions and well-meaning anarchists,
but without understanding the significance of the events the
songs described or the history that had been whitewashed,
the sudden loss of life, the sacrifice of morality, the depths of
human depravity hidden behind the triumphant slogans, the
anguish of mothers who no longer believed in God or in the
saints who were supposed to watch over the helpless world
or even in the priests who tried to bring absolution to their
unrepentant flocks. He sang very loudly, boldly, through
the dark dreaming streets of Logroño, and as he sang Tiká
perceived that every street was lined with the darkly glowing
faces of those who had lived there from the time of the Moors
to the Third Carlist uprising and had witnessed or been
the victims of the countless crimes against humanity which
lay submerged in between the lines of the songs, as if these
faces which bore the lunatic expressions of festival masks
were listening to the words of those songs and remembering
and trying to come to terms with their memories, faces now
suddenly awake, faces appearing in the wavering mirrors of

second floor windows in the rough stone buildings of these
dark dreaming streets of Logroño, looking down in widening
despair at Tiká's uncle walking and singing; faces that had
witnessed the terrible bloodthirsty mysticism of the Moors,
who had turned the surrounding fields red with the blood of
crippled children in the 8th century, tossing the children up
into the air and cutting them in half with exquisitely adorned
swords as the children fell back to the earth, as if they (the
Moors) were slicing melons, and they were laughing all the
while, unaffected by so much blood, believing, as they did,
that deformity was a sign of iniquity before God and so the
death of the crippled children was pleasing in His eyes, an
opinion oddly enough reinforced, though quite unintention-
ally, by later scholars who noted that it was from those very
same fields one century later that the very first red grapes
in La Rioja were grown, which these scholars said was the
first visible manifestation of God's unyielding mercy on that
Iberian plain of sorrows (as if the slate containing the crimes
of the Caliphate had been forever wiped clean), and which
resulted in the very first wine of the region — a fact which
the parsimonious monks of San Andrés de Trepeana noted in
a written receipt they submitted to the Notary of San Millán
de la Cogolla in 873, a receipt for several barrels of wine they
had received from a kindly donor, wine made from the grapes
that sprang from the blood of the murdered children, and after
polishing off all seven barrels in a little under a month, the
monks decided to go into the winemaking business for themselves; or the skeletal faces of refugees from the War of the
Two Peters, who had fled the city of Teruel in 1363 when the
effeminate Peter of Castile — also known as Peter the Cruel,
who was, incidentally, born in the Monastery of Santa María
la Real de Las Huelgas, the very same monastery where years
later Arturo Ordóñez Escoraz first came into contact with the
odor of great wisdom — burned part of the town in search of
a safe place to hide from the treachery of his bastard brother,
Henry of Trastámara, and so the refugees from Teruel had
traveled west from the mountains surrounding Teruel to the
plains of La Rioja, carrying with them the memory of war and
the pestilence of the plague, which swept through the streets
of Logroño like great sheets of lightning, adding many more

faces to the dark dreaming streets in Tiká's dream, perhaps
as many as two-thirds of the town's population had died at
that time, all of them screaming in uncomprehending anguish;
or the faces of the twelve who were burned at the stake for
witchcraft in 1609, a fate which not even Salazar's wisdom
of a young judge of the Inquisition could prevent — eleven
blameless women of the night who were accused of dancing
with the Devil in the meadow of Akelarre (the field of the
He-Goat) and one nameless priest who was accused of healing
the sick with an amulet bearing the image of Saint Raphael,
one of the seven archangels who stand before the throne of
the Lord, defenders night and day against heresy of all kinds,
apoplectic reminders of the wrath of God; or the withering,
perspiring faces of the hundreds of vagabond patriots who
had died at the hands of thirteen-thousand men under the
command of Jean-Antoine Verdier during the invasion of the
First Antichrist in 1808, hundreds of bloody heads rolling
across the cobblestones of Logroño, their headless bodies
later stacked in black heaps like so many forgotten haystacks
dotting the countryside and set on fire, the smoldering ashes
a feeding ground for vultures and crows (and a few wayward
storks); but Tiká's uncle did not see any of the faces Tiká saw,
or he would not see them or he could never see them, trapped
as he was inside a singular vision, oblivious to the lingering
pain of the countless centuries, singing his mindless, happy
tunes while the faces of that pain became heads and the heads
were leaning out of their windows to see who was making all
the racket, accusing, vehement glances because their deaths
had gone unavenged, or perhaps they had accepted the
circumstances of their deaths and were simply miffed because
they had been dragged without mercy from a sound sleep.

And then Tiká saw that not all of the those who had
taken an interest in her uncle had been victims of wars and
plagues and insurrections; she noticed a second group of faces
popping up behind the first group, peering over their shoulders, a tumultuous sea of faces that had never even glimpsed
the abyss while alive and so had not yet accepted the fact that
they were floating about in a sea of death, the faces of simple
peasants who had migrated to Logroño from the surrounding
countryside or came down from the mountains, faces of

shopkeepers and farmers and artisans and minor bureaucrats who had enjoyed the luxury of peace in between the wars and the famines and the raging epidemics, all of them expressing outrage for a thousand imagined slights gone unpunished, or even a few real crimes tossed in (crimes of perjury and slander and petty larceny and adultery, for example, real in the sense that they had in fact occurred, but decidedly unreal in the sense that slander is all but irrelevant when compared to the atrocity of murdering children), and then Tiká perceived that all of the crimes that had been committed, whether crimes of war or crimes of peace, whether real or illusory, crimes against the state, crimes against property, crimes of excessive passion, crimes of omission, crimes of forgetfulness, in every instance they had gone unpunished, every case had been dismissed or delayed, the paperwork misfiled or in some cases destroyed, and now no one even remembered the names of the victims, even the stones had been washed clean, so every death was lost, every name vanished, every criminal had gotten off scot free, but no, the voices cried out in unison, this would not be the case with respect to her uncle, who had roused them all (those who had lived during times of war and those who had lived during times of peace) from a sound sleep, they would remember this one, meaning Tiká's uncle, they would surely send him to the gallows for disturbing the peace and death mask quiet of the dark dreaming streets of Logroño, and Tiká did not understand why the people in her dream were so angry with her uncle, he is not one of them, she said, meaning he should not be grouped with the oppressors, the enslavers, the pseudo-fascist dictators, the tyrannous civil servants, the murderous, degenerate generals, the corrupt kings, he is not someone who deserves abuse, she said, as if anyone knows who deserves abuse and who does not, he is one of us, she said, he is our history, he is a son of Spain, but the tumultuous sea of angry faces had already disappeared by then, the windows of the rough stone buildings clacking shut, though the grumbling and growling of inconvenienced voices lingered on in Tiká's dream for quite a while. So Tiká perceived that her wayward and somewhat naive uncle had become an outsider to Spain and even to the memory of Spain, though he had only been absent from Logroño for ten years, but he was

now in mortal danger nevertheless, and then she perceived
that she was also an outsider, at least as far as the people of
Logroño were concerned, possibly because she possessed the
same gift of second sight that her mother possessed (who,
it was said, had a gaze as penetrating as Toledo steel), but
also certainly, unquestionably, because of her unquenchable
desire to accompany her uncle to Cuba, a paradise on earth
for anyone who could get there, because that was always the
allure of the Americas, the promise and the curse, and so she,
too, was in mortal danger, and then she realized that it was up
to her to save them both.

-46-

When Andres handed Grenfell a sangria and the two
men sat down, Tiká was watching them from the window of
her father's library, standing as silent as crystallized time,
hidden in the folds of the embroidered Chinese draperies
that framed the glass. Had she been reliving the dream of
the white bird she would have been standing next to the tiny
golden cage hanging from a hook, so close she would have
been able to hear the strange, sad gurgling noises it made
as it slept, but as she was in a non-dreaming state, she was
standing next to an Edison home phonograph which Verona
had ordered from New York City the year before the Hickory
bicycles, but which had not arrived until three years after her
death. The phonograph had never been used.

Immediately Tiká recognized her uncle's guest from
her dream the night before. She sent Madia out with a silver
tray, used only during celebrations honoring the memory of
the three kings from the Orient, upon which she had placed
a small white envelope containing a folded note, and she told
Madia to wait while her uncle read her words of warning to
make sure he understood their importance.

What Tiká's note said:
My dearest Uncle, the man next to you is not Grenfell.
He has stolen that name. He is an imposter. I cannot tell you

precisely how I am imbued with this knowledge except to say that I possess the same radiant clarity of vision that my mother, your beloved sister-in-law Verona, possessed even until the day she died. Suffice it to say that this Grenfell has quite nefarious intentions with regards to your ownership of the supposed copper mines in Cuba and we should do our best to utterly disabuse him of the confidence he has heretofore claimed regarding your future as well as mine. Our very lives are at stake in this matter, so please be cautious as you read this note of warning, please do not allow your eyeballs to rotate with nervous agitation as they always do in moments of extreme anxiety, stay calm and calm-hearted, my dear Uncle, for I have matters well in hand. You should say to Grenfell, assuming he has any interest in this note at all, that it concerns a private matter about my father's health, a mysterious disease which has plagued him for years, but which until this very moment you had no prior knowledge of and which, you must stress, has no negative bearing on your current scheme (meaning the scheme concocted by you and Grenfell and your third wheel, who is sitting in Café Rioja waiting until I should decide to purchase a parasol or a pair of boots). You might even suggest that the nature of this illness may prove to be an advantage (you may be as cryptic as you like on this point, for I have no doubt but it will spur the imposter's greedy imagination), and then say no more except that my father, your brother, is returning from a ride on his velocipede, the magnificent Elliott Hickory, which he took for a spin around the whole of Logroño this afternoon, and that he wishes you to meet him at the carriage house upon his return, and from there you will be departing directly to the home of our great and noble friend, don Alfonso Alberto Sebastian Francisco de Hernani y Arredondo de Mariategui y de Esperanza for an extravagant dinner party to commemorate your imminent departure. Father is well aware that you will be bringing a guest and he has made provision for this inconvenience. He knows nothing about the nefarious intentions of this imposter, and I shall keep him in the dark on this matter until you and I have left Logroño for the port of Barcelona and the steamer to Cuba. I will send you more notes as appropriate this evening so you will know what to expect. Again, stay calm and calm-hearted, my dearest Uncle. There is nothing for you to worry about. With the greatest appreciation for your patient indulgence, and with the greatest affection, your niece, Escolástica Escoraz Vda De Miranda.

After reading the note, Andres sank back into his wicker chair and poured what remained of his sangria down his throat and closed his eyes so the world would stop spinning. Then he took Madia's hand (she was still waiting to see if he understood the importance of Tiká's warning) and pressed the note into her palm, looking at her gravely as he did so until she felt a sudden urge to weep. Andres smiled weakly and poured another glass of sangria, which he drank slowly.

Madia disappeared into the house.

"He understands," she said, but in a voice that seemed more like the whispering of insects (which is perhaps what angels sound like) and less a human voice, a surging, insistent echo swirling about the interior of the house, lingering for a moment near the Chinese draperies and then heading down the grand hallway to the back of the house, through the swinging kitchen doors into the kitchen with its red brick walls and terra cotta floor which had been the scene of so much joyous laughter and impromptu parties when Verona had been alive and which now echoed with the silence of her absence, and then into the service closet where the good china was kept on two shelves very high up, and where on the shelves beneath the china Verona had placed dozens of tiny opaque bottles, bottles of blue and green and red glass containing rare herbal extracts from the Orient for promoting good health (extract of Astragalus to prevent aging, extract of wolfberry to improve blood flow, extract of licorice for stomach disorders, extract of Chinese foxglove mixed with the ashes of wormwood to reduce inflammation, extract of gardenias to calm the impatient mind, and so on); and then Madia's voice headed into the grand dining room, now shrouded in the darkness of heavy velvet drapes, and the piano room that was no longer used because the piano, a gilded art-case Bechstein grand piano, had been sold to a lonely German widow who was now living in Madrid and who bought the instrument because it reminded her of her husband, who had died years ago during the Second Danish-German War and was buried with military honors in Berlin; and then Madia's voice took a detour

through the library, which is where Isabel was reading, with
its wall of leather-bound masterpieces slowly disintegrating,
the air thick with the musty odor of ancient wisdom that
lingered like death; and then down a narrow hallway, swirling
past the three rooms that had become Verona's sanctuary, the
insistence of Madia's voice now taking on other qualities, the
trembling, hallucinatory sadness of the lucifugous statuary on
the altars of Arturo's despair, the whispered hopes of the dead
saints that had settled upon those very same altars; and then
Madia's voice poured itself out into the courtyard where years
earlier a courtesan who had once been the mistress of Federico
de Madrazo contemplated the nature of reality and the
immortality of art; and then the voice headed back inside and
the house was suddenly filled with the sweet gardenia smell
of Verona herself, (an intoxicating aroma which most visitors
only noticed upon entering the house and which then seemed
to vanish as they grew accustomed to it, an echo of Verona's
presence embedded in the very brick and mortar of marital
bliss, as if the house could only exist if something of Verona
remained to bind it to this world); and then Madia's voice
headed up the backstairs, which sported a mahogany railing
that Arturo believed was all that remained of a Spanish war
ship that had sunk in a storm along the western coast of Spain
near Cape Finisterre in 1870 but which more likely had been
salvaged from the Church of Santiago in 1795 when a portion
of the church had been torched by French sympathizers during
the War of the Pyrenees; and then the strangely angelic, insect
sound of Madia's voice danced in and out of the various
bedrooms and sitting rooms on the second floor, a labyrinth
of rooms, through keyholes or beneath doors that had been
locked for years and the keys had been lost, bouncing off
mirrors and careening off light fixtures and spinning around
bedposts, an invisible tornado of sound kicking up the dust
of hidden memories and half-suffocated dreams and forgotten
crises of faith, mixing with the dry evening heat and the
reddish light of the sunset streaming in through a few open
windows and the white lace curtains billowing, and then the
sound dissipating, the breathy sound of a warning, a tragedy
to be averted as much as a lament.

The Chinese draperies trembled.

Andres poured himself yet another sangria.

The Chinese draperies stopped trembling.

And Grenfell, who had seemed insensible to the presence of Madia and the silver tray and Andres reading the note, set his now empty glass next to the nearly empty pitcher and eyed his co-conspirator with an expression that seemed mocking and contemptuous as well as reckless and confident.

"What is it you understand, my friend?" he said.

Andres sat up stiffly, his eyes on the open window and the Chinese draperies moving again, but ever so slightly.

"It is my brother," said Andres, watching the draperies as he spoke. "I have been informed that he is suffering from inconsolable grief due to the passing of his wife. In spite of the fact that she died several years ago, his condition has worsened. I only wish that I had known sooner."

"Ah," said Grenfell, his eyes narrowing so that the pupils looked like slits. "Grief is a most treacherous affliction." Then Grenfell smiled the same kind of thin, knowing smile he had tossed about with great frequency the night before at The Café with Two Names. "He that refuseth instruction despiseth his own soul: but he that heareth reproof getteth understanding," he said.

-47-

The home of don Alfonso Alberto Sebastian Francisco de Hernani y Arredondo de Mariategui y de Esperanza was a few blocks from the old town gate on a narrow side street just inside the city limits that ended with the house itself, a magnificent though crumbling Baroque period building with a maze of inner passageways opening up into unexpected courtyards lined with almond trees and orange trees and lush ferns and ivy and gardenias and the shrieks of startled, hidden birds and the mad dash of a few tiny brown lizards and the languid, telescopic eye of a wandering yellow chameleon. In the center of each courtyard there was a small tiled pool (with

aquamarine tiles or teal or deep blue) glittering in the soft
folds of sunlight that drifted down through the branches of
the trees, and there was an elaborately carved fountain in the
middle of each pool and fish swimming about in the froth.
Most of the fountains depicted happy, naïve, fat-cheeked
cherubs blowing ceremonial trumpets, or obscure mythological
animals, or a strange, unsettling mixture of both. But in one
of the courtyards you could gaze upon the supernal beauty of
a dozen or more lascivious marble nymphs cavorting about,
spewing water from their mouths, happy, carefree, uninhibited, suggesting to every man who gazed upon them unending
nights of forbidden pleasure without the unyielding days of
stifling, sun-burnt love that would usually follow.

Laughing with joy, don Alfonso greeted Arturo and
Andres with warm embraces. He acknowledged Grenfell
with a curt nod and took Tiká by the hand. He barely
noticed Madia, who always accompanied Tiká, and he did
not comment on Isabel's absence, who in all probability was
still in the library reading poetry. The don wore the same
suit he had worn for social occasions for twenty-two years, a
Vienna Brocade tailcoat with a gold colored silk vest which
complemented his neatly trimmed red beard but which had
become too tight, a white silk shirt with ivory cufflinks, a silk
puff tie to match the vest, black trousers now held in place by
suspenders, a John Bull top hat, and a gentleman's walking
stick from the age of Napoleon with an ox bone handle carved
to resemble a rose. It was the same outfit he had worn the
day Verona Almeida Vda De Miranda married his childhood
friend Arturo Ordóñez Escoraz. The dazzling brilliance of the
outfit had suggested to some at the time that don Alfonso
was secretly in love with Verona and the only way he could
demonstrate his feelings was to parade about in the uniform
of a courtly peacock in the hopes that she might forget about
her new husband for at least a moment and cast an anguished,
soulful look of regret his way.

They ate in the courtyard containing the fountain with
the nymphs. The household staff had set up a narrow Italian
sideboard covered with steaming hot dishes — a stew of beans
and Botifarra sausage, a stew of meat and vegetables, cooked
snails, a seafood casserole, lamb hooves mixed with turnips,

roasted vegetables bathed in olive oil, small dishes of paella
— and also cod salad with tomatoes and onions and slabs of
bread smeared with tomato paste and garlic, and for dessert
there was mató cheese with honey and peeled pears served
in cream and also almond biscuits and cups of steaming, rich,
frothy Arabic coffee. A barrel of *Crianza* was next to the sideboard.   There was no grand table for dining. Instead, several
chairs were scattered about among the greenery and also a few
small side tables covered in fine Belgian linen for the plates
and glasses and silverware. Don Arturo and don Alfonso sat
in the shadows, surrounded by ferns almost six feet high,
directly across from Andres and Grenfell, who sat directly
beneath the open sky, their skin glowing a soft, dappled red
from the almost vanished sun. Tiká sat nearer the fountain so
she could watch and listen without being noticed. Madia took
on the duties of serving her mistress.

For the longest time nobody said a word. The only
sounds were the tinkling of glasses and the soft scraping of
silverware on plates and the subtle, furtive movements of the
birds hiding in the trees, wings flapping and a few muffled
cries, and the quiet murmuring of the fountain. The sky grew
dark and one of the servants went around the courtyard lighting candles and soon the smoky glow blotted out all but a few
of the very brightest stars. The two dons settled back into the
darkness of their memories and began to talk, though mostly
it was Alfonso. They talked about the tragedy of Verona's
death, and Alfonso acknowledged Arturo's suffering, but then
he said that they had all suffered, the entire town, for she was
the very soul of Logroño, and with her death the town had
become a soulless corpse and they might as well pack up and
leave it to the anarchists, and who knew, perhaps the death of
Verona had signaled the death of other things, the death of the
monarchy, the death of the empire, the death of family, yes,
Arturo, even the death of love, there is nothing left but death
all around this crypt of our ancestors, the modern age has
arrived with a vengeance, the modern world with its modern
thinking will sweep everything else aside, no, Arturo, no,
perhaps it is a question of adaptability, one cannot adapt in a
place where there is so much death, but if one were to pack up
and leave, yes, Arturo, leave Logroño, then perhaps miracles

are indeed possible, yes, Arturo, truly, because the modern age is also an age full of marvels, so perhaps it is all for the best, and all Arturo could manage during this hopeful lament was an occasional cough. Then Alfonso talked about Isabel and Tiká with such effulgent pride that one might have thought they were his own daughters, or nieces at the very least, how they were quite accomplished for young ladies of any age, but how many eligible suitors existed for them here in Logroño, frankly the town was overflowing with louts and vagabonds of every description, no, no, for girls of their bearing, their incredible beauty, Isabel the dark-haired siren with her siren eyes, the spitting image of her mother, Verona, and Tiká with her fiery-read hair that she now wore in a single braid like the warrior goddess of ancient Greece, yes, yes, who in Logroño was worthy of such beauty. One would have to travel all the way to Barcelona, or perhaps further, Monte Carlo, or even Paris, and Arturo agreed with everything Alfonso said and drank his coffee, for by this time the dinner was long finished. Then the two men were laughing, a gruff, chortling kind of laughter that sounded to Tiká like the moaning of lovesick bulls. Then Alfonso said it was time for something stronger than coffee, and a moment later one of the servants brought out a bottle of port wine from Portugal, and then a bottle of Hennessy, and many more bottles appeared after that, but it was hard for Tiká to see what they were. It had grown very dark. Even the few bright stars from before had grown cold and dim, and all that remained of the two dons were two shadows submerged in the sea of ferns, two voices venturing out into the void like the bellowing of two great ships. Only her uncle and the imposter Grenfell were still visible, and even so they were but caricatures, the smoky, dim candlelight dancing across their waxen faces, the angry, inarticulate, ever-present rage of the one and the energetic, irrepressible optimism of the other suspended while they listened to these voices from the darkness.

A short while later Madia presented Andres with two additional notes, the first to be read immediately, the second to be read only after Andres and Tiká were safely on their way. Again Madia waited while Andres read the second note, which took him close to fifteen minutes because he had to read in the dim flickering light of the candles, which meant that the process of reading the note was less like reading and more like deciphering an ancient coded message written in the tongue of the Moors. Grenfell was too busy to notice, for he was drinking from a bottle of brandy that had mysteriously appeared on their tiny side table.

What the second note said:

My dearest Uncle, do not drink the brandy, for it has been laced with an opiate to cause drowsiness and was meant for Grenfell alone. With the help of our very dear friend and our host for the evening, don Alfonso Alberto Sebastian Francisco de Hernani y Arredondo de Mariategui y de Esperanza, whose family aligned itself with ours many generations ago, I have arranged for our departure this very night. The don will permit us the use of his Rochet-Schneider horseless carriage, a two-cylinder contraption he is very proud of because it is modern (he truly appreciates the modern age, in spite of his earlier provocative tone) and it is quite fashionable with its polished brass fittings and patterned leather and handcrafted wooden trim, oh it is quite fashionable. The don is also providing a driver, so we shall be quite snug, as it were, for the vehicle normally seats but two. There is a small trunk in the front which will serve adequately to convey a reasonable number of bags, and we can strap a few more to the back, and then we will be off to Zaragoza, which according to the don is as far as the carriage will carry us before it runs out of fuel, so from there we will travel in luxury by train in a private parlor car, which also belongs to the don, and which he alone occupies when he travels to Barcelona or Madrid or even Seville. The don has notified the railway company to ready the car for our journey. Let me add, my dear Uncle, that the time of our departure is close at hand. Soon Grenfell will fall into a trance-like sleep, at which point several members of the don's household staff will carry him to a small dungeon-like closet in the back of their great stone kitchen, where he will remain asleep among sacks of flour and other vegetable matter until we are well beyond his reach. The don has also wired Barcelona and secured my passage aboard the Conde Wifredo, so there is no need to worry about that. And lastly, the don will put into your capable hands a small purse full of gold coin to meet our needs until

we are properly settled in Cuba. I will explain in greater detail
why don Alfonso is aiding our cause in the third note, which
you must not read until we are away. I will also explain why my
father, your still-grieving and somewhat distant brother, will not
even think to intervene. With the greatest affection, your niece,
Escolástica Escoraz Vda De Miranda.

The moment Andres finished reading the second note,
Madia plucked it from his fingertips and disappeared into
the darkness beyond the ferns. Instinctively he reached for
the brandy but remembered the warning and sat back in his
chair, looking suspiciously at Grenfell, who had stiffened
with Andres' sudden movement towards the bottle but then
relaxed as his one-time companion in crime retreated. Grenfell
chugged what was left of the brandy, which had an exotic
bouquet of dark plums, dark red cherries, pomegranates from
the gardens of Lebanon, and the faintest trace of smoke from
the mountains of Extremadura, where it is said the romantic
poet José de Espronceda wandered aimlessly in the years
before his death from diphtheria lamenting the loss of a
woman he had debased.

For the next several minutes after that Grenfell waved
the empty bottle around in the air as if to ward off insects.
Then he leaned forward and collapsed in a puddle of confusion on the flagstone of the courtyard.

Two servants soon appeared with a small wooden hand-
cart with rusty wheels, which the cook used when she went
to the market to buy vegetables. They loaded Grenfell's body
with delicate intention, folding the top half over the bottom
half, as if he were a dilapidated marionette or a victim of the
plague. With only the sound of the rusty wheels to mark their
departure, they wheeled him away, his arms trailing on the
ground and his legs from the knees down dangling over the
sides.

Andres immediately felt better. He marveled at the
incongruities of life, and though he did not think himself a
superstitious man, he wondered if Lady Luck had perhaps
given him a second chance (without realizing that she had
been his savior on numerous occasions). Then he realized he
was all alone. His brother and don Alfonso had taken their

conversation among the ferns to another part of the house, and Tiká had vanished before the note from Madia had arrived. So he sat in the abandoned courtyard, drinking in the sounds of his solitude. He was almost overwhelmed by the sudden impression that the entire world had been reduced to his immediate surroundings. He wondered if he were dreaming or if he had gone mad. The candles were still burning fiercely, but strangely their light seemed diminished, and then an insomniac bird cried out for relief, wings flapping madly and the branches of one of the almond trees shaking, and then the bird grew still, and for a moment he thought he could hear his blood flowing through his veins, though perhaps it was merely the sound of the fountain and the water splashing on the Arabic tile, singing its happy song of Moorish conquest and the conversion of the world to Islam and the happy faithful entering into paradise. He wondered if he was on the verge of doing great things or if he would have to wait years and years for success to arrive and how long would that be, waiting, waiting, secretly envious of everyone around him, but easy does it, his time would come, perhaps it was already here. Then the silence of his meditation was broken by a gaunt figure wearing riding chaps, riding boots, a suede leather jacket, a tweed cap and goggles.

The figure seemed incapable of speech, and Andres, not knowing what to say, stared mutely at a strangely elongated face with eyes covered by the dark glass of the goggles, which reflected nothing, not even the light from the candles. Then a voice said the Rochet-Schneider was ready and they would be departing within the quarter hour. Then the figure was gone.

-48-

The journey from Logroño to Zaragoza in the Rochet-Schneider was the most exhilarating experience of Andres' life to that point. Their driver, who went by the name of Vicente, had been a fan of automobile racing ever since the Parisian

sports magazine, *Le Petit Journal,* sponsored the first road
race from Paris to Rouen in 1894. There was nothing quite like
feeling the rush of the wind against your face as you roared
across the countryside, that is what Vicente liked to say. He
fancied himself a race driver who had yet to grab a headline,
and so that night he drove like a maniac in spite of the fact
that the road to Zaragoza was not meant for automobiles, and
in spite of the fact that it was the darkest night since anyone
could remember, and a surprisingly cold, almost icy, wind
lashed their faces, Vicente laughing at times with lunatic glee
as the dark landscape flashed by like the churning waters
of a forgotten inland ocean, with only the dim, underwater
glow from two brass lamps to show the way, maintaining
an average speed of twenty-nine miles per hour with bursts
of over forty, a phenomenal achievement in 1899, especially
given the nature of the road, which would have earned
Vicente a place of distinction in automobile racing lore if an
official Marshal had been present to verify his time, but which,
nevertheless, won him the admiration of Andres, who mistook
his recklessness for courage, and their safe arrival as a destiny
achieved rather than what it was, a brazen tempting of the
sisters of fate in which they were lucky to escape with their
lives. Indeed, while the general contours of the land sloped
gradually downhill from west to east, the road itself was steep
in places, jutting up over rocky hills instead of around them,
and there were many places where heavy wagons pulled
by teams of oxen had over many years cut gigantic grooves
into the road, which caused the Rochet-Schneider to bounce
violently at times, and at one point it seemed certain that the
vehicle would topple over in an explosion of twisted metal
and fractured hopes, but the unseen hand of God, the only
power in the universe that could stand against the sisters of
fate if they felt they had been wronged, prevented eternal
disaster, and so the Rochet-Schneider skidded along the edge
of the road instead.

They arrived in Zaragoza at eleven in the morning
and Vicente let them off in front of a small café with a red
awning and a few tables outside on Calle Santa Isabel three
blocks from the Basílica de Nuestra Señora del Pilar. Tiká
was amazed at how suddenly her world had changed, for she

had slept a dreamless, untroubled sleep during the journey
in spite of the cold wind and the rocky road, and then woke
up suddenly to the erratic, trembling, wheezing sound of
the two-cylinder engine like an old man coughing only after
Vicente had come to a final stop. Vicente left the engine
running while he unloaded their suitcases for fear that he
could not get the contraption started again. And all the while
Andres was congratulating him on his magnificent talent
for driving, the precision of his technique, and his uncanny
ability to navigate beneath a cloudy sky, as if he were the
evolutionary equivalent of a human astrolabe, all of which
seemed to Andres irrefutable proof of both the wonders of
technology and the glory of the human race with its limitless
and soul-driven ability to surpass the brilliance of even the
nearest stars, and which fueled from that point on his own
overwhelming even obsessive desire for all things modern.

"You are a force to be reckoned with," said Andres.

"But of course," said Vicente, laughing with great joy as
he climbed back into the Rochet-Schneider and adjusted his
goggles. "I am the greatest driver in the world."

Then with a cloudy burst of city refuse and oil particles,
he left them standing in a pool of sunlight that seemed as
bright and warm as the smile of God.

Two days later, Andres and Tiká boarded the train for
Barcelona, and it was only then that Andres discovered he
had lost the third note, but since Madia was no longer present
to watch him read and digest Tiká's words, and since Tiká
herself had seemingly forgotten the existence of the note, he
never mentioned that it had vanished. Three days after they
arrived in Barcelona, they boarded the steamer *Conde Wifredo*
for Cuba and the everlasting promise of the Americas.

The ship did not depart until an hour after sunset,
two hours later than normal, so those who had come to see
it off had already gone home. It seemed like the world had
become one of Edison's silent movie experiments, the ship
slipping away without the fanfare of brass bands and banners
flying with festival cheer and the popping sound of bottles of
champagne being uncorked and the pealing, joyous laughter
of the city's ancient (some would have said bony-fingered and
decrepit) aristocracy, and then the parting guns sounding out

over the water, and lastly, the handkerchiefs waving goodbye, all of that which usually accompanied such departures on a blameless Saturday afternoon was absent, no, theirs was an unheralded departure that felt as much like going into exile as it did heading off with buoyant spirits on a grand new adventure.

The ship gave only a single, low-humming blast of its great ship horn before it pulled away from the pier. Only the sentinel lights of the old stone wharf seemed to notice, ancient orange globes winking in the dark like dying fireflies, the ship moving slowly through the dark shining waters of the harbor and the warehouse lights and the hazy, distant street lamps reflected there, past the heavy shadow of Mont Montjuïc, which seemed to blot out the nighttime sky, and then out past the breakwater and the gleaming golden brilliance of the lighthouse at Llobregat, and then the glowing magnificence of this great modern city of the modern age that some said existed only in the imagination of poets and philosophers and vagabond kings vanished without a trace, and Andres Ordóñez Escoraz and Escolástica Escoraz Vda De Miranda and everyone aboard the *Conde Wifredo* were swallowed up by the trembling, mythic darkness of the trembling, mythic sea.

-49-

The journey aboard the *Conde Wifredo,* as re-imagined by Isidora many years after the fact:

My great-grandfather never told Tiká that he lost the third note at some point during their journey from Logroño to Barcelona oh so many years ago. Perhaps it had slipped out of his pocket while they were squeezed into the Rochet-Schneider with the mad Vicente at the wheel, that eccentric of mixed Italian and Spanish heritage who was shouting with a maniac race-driver's delight as they sped erratically across the dark, early morning landscape towards Zaragoza. Or perhaps Andres was about to read the note two days later on the train to Barcelona but had become distracted by the scenery flashing by and the stiff comfort of sitting for so many long, unyielding hours and had let it fall from his fingers unread. Who can say? Perhaps if Andres had read Tiká's third and final note, which contained the reason why don Alfonso had helped Andres and Tiká escape to the Americas, as well as the reason why my great-grandfather's lonely, overwrought brother, Arturo, had not tried to stop them, perhaps if Andres had even glanced at the opening lines, a host of future tragedies involving the Escoraz family might have been averted. It is a slippery slope to wonder about such things, let me tell you. But Andres never said a word. He believed it was better to let sleeping dogs sleep, and since Tiká never alluded to the note or what she had written during the several years she lived with my great-grandfather in Cuba, Andres never asked her what revelations and family secrets the note had contained, secrets which remained hidden by their mutual silence until Tiká's last day on the planet when, in the delirium of impending death, she bared her soul to the nurse who was sitting by her bedside.

That is not to say that Andres did not wonder about the note now and then. But he was not overly curious. He was not one to dwell on the past, so he harbored few regrets. But on three occasions during his life, he was overwhelmed suddenly and swiftly by the sense that Tiká's handwritten note from oh so long ago contained advice on how to fulfill his destiny, which, as everyone knows, is the secret to lifelong happiness, and since he had never read the note, he would never know what he was supposed to do and how badly things had gone awry. It was an actual, physical sensation more than a fluttering premonition or a vaguely constituted belief. On each occasion, it was as if a weasel or a hedgehog or a wild rabbit were gnawing on his exposed entrails and all he could do was watch. That's how he had once described it.

The first occasion occurred, as you might expect, aboard the *Conde Wifredo*. The great ship was the pride of the Naviera Pinillos shipping company and had been making the passage from Barcelona to the Americas since 1892. No, it was not a blue-ribbon luxury liner like the *Oceanic* or the *Lusitania*, those grand, gilded ships of yesteryear which carried the intellectual and artistic nobility of Europe and America back and forth across the Atlantic on useless, spendthrift vacations. But the *Conde Wifredo* could accommodate up to eighty first class persons in forty staterooms possessing walnut furniture and Tiffany reading lamps and gilded mirrors (and dinner with the Captain once or twice during the voyage), another two-hundred aspiring souls in second class cabins fitted with American-made quatrefoil iron beds and enough room left over for two or three large steamer trunks, and as many as six-hundred steerage persons crammed into the rat-infested abyss of the cargo holds, depending on how much cargo was on board, where everyone slept three to a bunk, and even the crew would not go below if they could help it, and who could blame them, unless they had first burned away the pestilent stench of the dregs of humanity with a red-hot poker covered in tar and lit with a match, waving the makeshift torch back and forth in the air as they climbed down the ladder, a gesture of fear and loathing. For Tiká, who had never before set foot outside Logroño, life aboard the *Conde Wifredo* was a dazzling display of human frailty. For Andres, who had seen the world but nevertheless suffered from the same chronic idealism that afflicted certain German philosophers of the 19th century, as anyone who knew him in those days could plainly see, the *Conde Wifredo* became a symbol of divine intervention in the face of degenerate, self-absorbed behavior run amok, so Andres retreated to the ship's smoking room or took long, solitary walks along the promenade in the hours between meals to better prepare himself for whatever God had in mind.

The captain of the *Conde Wifredo*, a robust rogue of a man named Ramón Martín Cordero, who had once been arrested for making indecent advances towards a young, wealthy widow and had thereafter harbored treachery in his heart when it came to love, escorted them to their stateroom that very first night, a magnificent suite of three rooms (thanks to the profligate generosity of don Alfonso) with two Tiffany reading lamps, a walnut wardrobe, and a brightly polished Berliner gramophone with a dozen or more discs featuring various operatic pieces that included Tom Bryce singing the English version of 'The Drinking Song' from *Cavalleria rusticana*, Montague Borwell singing the 'Toreador Song,'

and 'Miserere' from Verdi's *Trovatore*. Captain Cordero spoke
eloquently about the various features of the ship as they made
their way down a narrow passage lit only by carbon filament
lamps fixed to the ceiling, which cast an eerie, orangeish,
dancing light upon the newly painted steel walls. He told
them they were always painting the walls somewhere on
the ship. The smells of drying paint and turpentine were a
lingering presence as omnipresent as the breath of God. This
is how the Captain phrased it. He pointed out where the paint
was still wet with an ominous seriousness. He then pointed
out several passageways that were off limits to the passengers.
He asked them if they had ever sailed the clear waters of
Qatar and watched the darkies diving for pearls. He asked
them if they were afraid of barracudas or sea snakes or tiger
sharks. Then he told them a few unpretentious, salty jokes and
laughed uproariously, his face contorting in odd grimaces. He
cautioned them about several members of his crew who had
been seen skulking about the entrance to the grand saloon late
at night, and near the back door to the steerage saloon three
decks below early in the morning. Who knew what nefarious
intentions they possessed? He said if they encountered any
difficulty whatsoever on board his ship they should knock on
his door immediately, for his quarters were directly opposite
their stateroom. Then they neared their destination and his
tone changed abruptly, as if he and Andres were long lost
friends or members of a secret society who were destined to
become mortal enemies. 'Ah yes,' the Captain had said, 'No
one will bother you. You will have all the privacy you need
on this very short journey to the Americas.' And then he had
tossed a cavalier, knowing smile in Tiká's direction. 'Yes, yes,
you and your lovely bride will have nothing to worry about.'
But when Andres had tried to explain that Tiká was his niece,
the Captain only waved his hand in the air with surreptitious
sympathy, his smile widening by several inches, and said 'If
you live among the wolves, my friend, you have to howl like a
wolf,' before disappearing into the cavernous darkness of his
own room.

By the next morning, even before the bugle call to
breakfast, word had spread all over the ship that Andres
possessed a young, fulsome bride and that the happy couple

were on their honeymoon. The men he encountered from
the upper decks all gave him curt, approving, jealous nods,
for clearly Andres was quite a bit older than Tiká, while the
men from the lower decks either gave him idiotic grins or
approached him with a singular familiarity based on too much
alcohol and the universal assumption that all men are pigs and
therefore brothers in arms, asking him unanswerable, predatory questions such as 'how much does she cost?' or 'who
did you have to kill to get your hands on a piece of calico
like that?' or 'how many pups were in that litter' or offering
cryptic advice out of the blue such as 'the wolf always finds a
reason for taking the lamb' or 'never ask forgiveness until the
hangman wraps the noose around your neck,' or 'keep out of
deep water, beauty like that casts a shadowy net,' or veiled
threats such as 'we only own what God gives us,' or 'one day
you will understand the silence of the planets.'

The women of the entire ship quite predictably gave
Andres as wide a berth as was humanly possible given they
were at sea, fluttering about uselessly and nervously like tiny
birds trembling as he passed by, amazed and disgusted and
curious and ashamed all at once, all except a few aimless
looking waifs who trotted after him like lost but streetwise
alley cats trying to play on his sympathies or arouse his
presumed degenerate interest.

Of course Andres said nothing to Tiká, for he did not
wish to unduly alarm his niece, but in truth she only would
have laughed at his suspicions. Besides, what would he have
said? She was immersed in the exhilarating freedom of her
first and only Transatlantic voyage, though it is also true that
this freedom was limited to strolling about the promenade
for the better part of each day with a flock of women from
the upper crust, the wives and daughters and spinster sisters
of newly appointed ambassadors of hope hoping for brand
new verdant pastures to plow; or the wives and daughters of
middle-aged lawyers with strong ties to the Church who were
hoping to take advantage of the provincialism of those living
in the former colonies; or the wives of businessmen who had
lost thousands as a result of the war in Cuba and were now
staking everything they had left on the suddenly resurrected
promise of Latin America. All of the women (except Tiká)

were dressed in black satin or silk dresses with flowing black headdresses, as if they had fallen into the abyss of perpetual mourning, a convocation of black swans gliding this way and that, bemoaning the loss of their ancestral homes.

Truly, the road to everlasting grief is a swift descent. Still, these black swans acted as a buffer against the gossip swirling about the ship, and though the nature of the gossip changed course during the course of the voyage, the nature of their vigilance did not. They became the guardians of Tiká's youthful and exuberant soul and did not let her out of their sight, not even for a minute, not until she rejoined her uncle for dinner each evening, and even then, there was always a black swan ready to alert the others if anyone from the lowliest steward in his white jacket and black cap to the Captain himself so much as winked at her with a lascivious eye. And so it went. Tiká never realized she and her uncle had produced a never-ending radio storm of idle chatter among the crew and those quartered in the lower decks. And she was certainly unaware that she, in all her imagined, naked glory, with tiny diamonds and other jewels flashing out from her braided, fiery-red hair and her lips glistening with the promise of promiscuity, had become a ghostly hologram suspended above the bunks of half the men aboard the mythic *Conde Wifredo* as they plummeted into a sea of turbulent dreams.

It was an impossible situation, to say the least. But what could Andres do? Yes, yes, the sensible course of action would have been to ignore the gossips until the ship reached Havana. Let them have their fun, what harm lay in that? But this was not as easy as it sounds. He who belongs to God speaks the language of heaven. But the reverse is also true, and the *Conde Wifredo* was as godless a ship as there ever was. Everywhere Andres went, night and day, he was bombarded by whispering voices that belonged to men who were clearly up to no good. He thought perhaps he had become the unsus-pecting victim of *aojamiento*, a maleficent eye cast his way. His sanity was teetering on the brink. He spent countless hours in the smoking room smoking an infinity of cigars in a vain attempt to hide behind a protective cloud of smoke and ash, imagining with each puff that he was sitting in the middle of a bonfire dedicated to St. John. He hunted about for a small

cross made from the twigs of the blessed laurel, a cross that
his brother's wife had given him when he had first set off to
see the world, a cross which Verona had said would protect
him against the evils he might encounter, and so he had kept
it on his person ever since, but the cross had mysteriously
vanished. He recited an endless litany of rosaries delivered up
to the hallucination of his growing despair, but he wondered
if perhaps the prayers were themselves forgeries when they
produced no obvious effect. He prayed to St. John of God,
a 16th century Spanish soldier who later became the patron
saint of booksellers, printers, hospitals, the sick, nurses, and
those suffering from heart disease. It did not occur to him to
simply stuff cotton in his ears. On the third night he knocked
on the Captain's door but there was no answer. The barrage
of whispering voices grew steadily more impertinent. They
began gathering outside Andres' stateroom after midnight,
mocking him with their furtive twittering, but whenever he
opened the door he found the corridor empty except for the
shadows produced by the savage flickering of the orange
carbon filament lamps.

Andres soon realized this was part of some strange,
sinister game. But again, I ask you, what could he do? What
else could he have done? The moment he closed the door
and slid the bolt into place the whispering would start up
again and the scenario would repeat itself. He suspected that
the very fabric of reality had come unglued and wondered if
perhaps the ship itself was a conscious entity, an alien being
from another dimension. In a madcap effort to escape himself,
he raced up to the promenade to get a whiff of fresh salt sea
air only to be smacked in the face with the smell of turpentine
from the various ongoing painting projects scattered about the
ship. His tongue seemed to be coated with fur. He leaned over
the rail and watched the ocean swirling past in the moonlight.
The sound of the sea became a siren's melodious song thick
with the syrup of innuendo and a forbidden rendezvous
dangling just out of reach. He began to speak in the language
of barnacles, a panicky, furtive gasping sound tied to the
tidal rhythm of the moon that only made sense under water.
Without showing any evidence of surprise, he wondered at the
strange turn his lunacy had taken. The barnacles on the hull

of the ship began reciting poetry that sounded remarkably
like someone plucking the strings of a mandolin, and Andres
would have liked to stay and listen, for he enjoyed both poetry
and the mandolin (he particularly enjoyed a dazzling aria
written for the mandolin from the middle of Carlo Cecere's *La
tavernola abentorosa*), but he was haunted by the sense that his
future was hunting for him with unassailable determination,
so he kept on moving. He raced back down to his stateroom,
where he sat in the walnut chair next to the silent Berliner
gramophone, sifting gently through the discs of various oper-
ettas with a delicate intensity, as if he could hear the invisible
musicians playing their invisible music of the spheres with
his fingertips. A symphony of competing emotions flashed
across his face: envy, mocking contempt, unashamed even
proud (saucy?) devotion, irrepressible longing, unpretentious
awe, unpurged fear, and so on. He fell asleep in the walnut
chair with the last of the discs in his hands, his hands and lips
quivering slightly.

Later, he woke to a firm but gentle rocking motion, and
the smiling, beaming face of Tiká like a luminous moon crashing into his ominously tragic eyes. She was speaking to him,
but at first he could not catch what she was saying. Her words
were detached from her lips and seemed to be flying about the
stateroom at fantastic speeds, bouncing off the furniture and
the ceiling and the sparkling Tiffany reading lamps, the room
suddenly ablaze with the brilliance of an unseen morning sun
that was somehow able to penetrate even the thickest walls.
'Uncle, dearest Uncle, wake up, wake up,' she said. 'Did you
fall asleep again in that chair? Uncle, whatever is the matter
with you?'

Looking back it is clear that my great-grandfather's
descent into madness was but a prelude to the troubles that
were to plague the entire ship. Four days out of Barcelona
on her way to Santa Cruz de Tenerife, the *Conde Wifredo* was
engulfed by a hurricane of bad luck. There is no other way to
properly describe it. The hurricane began like all hurricanes
with a subtle change in the color of the light. Most people
did not notice the change. Even when someone pointed to the
distant horizon and said 'See how the color has changed from
a calm though hazy blue to a sinister grayish-green,' those

standing within earshot paid no attention to the ominous
nature of the sky along the edge of the world and the changing colors of their destiny, especially since directly above their
down-turned heads the sun was shining brightly. ¡Ay de mí!
We are plagued by lightning that wanders, as the poet says,
and it is true. That night the upper crust dined on beef steak
and oyster pie and sago pudding for dessert. They did not
know the oysters were spoiled. An hour later they were huddled over basins all over the ship, hurling and heaving until
their stomachs were empty. When the ship finally reached
Tenerife the next day, the dysentery had spread to all decks.
The ship reeked with the foul pestilence of rotting vegetation
and sour milk. The ventilator shafts trembled like undersea
reeds.

Naturally, the Captain had no choice but to place the
Conde Wifredo under quarantine for three days until the
sickness had run its course. This almost goes without saying.
But the crew was not happy. Neither were the passengers.
Scuffles broke out on all decks. An engineer, a Bosun's mate,
a stevedore, and a stoker were locked up in a makeshift brig
(the surgeon's office) for cornering a young girl outside the
grand saloon. They were the same ones the Captain had
warned Andres about.

An elderly Canadian passenger, an old man who suffered from mild attacks of dementia brought on by drinking
several cups of black tea in quick succession, chased the black
swans around the promenade with an ivory handled cane,
cursing at them with an anguished, paranoid vehemence,
saying they could all take wing and return to the depths of
Hell for all he cared, he was not yet ready to go, causing one
young woman to fall down a steep flight of stairs, twisting her
knee rather badly in the process.

The smoking room became a seething volcano filled with
baritone puffers talking this and that.

Once the quarantine was lifted, and in spite of the fact
that the confidence of everyone on board had been shattered,
the ship's routine returned to a quasi-normal state.

Fifteen passengers were transferred to a hospital onshore
in a dilapidated goat wagon (which had to make several trips)
that the dock officials had procured at the last minute.

A small group of Jesuits, imbued with the infinite spirit of illumination and progress, departed the ship on their way to the top of Mount Teide, the tallest mountain under the jurisdiction of Spain, so they could make precise astrological observations in the hope of pinpointing God's actual whereabouts.

Seven new passengers were given berths on the first-class deck and paid no attention to the insolent behavior of the bed stewards, who had staunchly refused to turn down the beds of the newcomers as a way of protesting what they felt had been an unjust quarantine.

An additional twenty-two hardy souls followed the seven onto the ship, all of them world travelers who preferred to pay as little as possible for passage, and by sticking to this strategy, they had visited every corner of the globe. All twenty-two found passable (which is not the same as comfortable) bunks in steerage.

The mail bags were delivered.

Coal was brought up in barges and the bunkers were filled.

The ship's vast labyrinth of storerooms was filled with fresh provisions.

Everything seemed to be as it should be.

Everyone believed in their heart of hearts that the worst of the bad luck was over.

Three days later, eight-hundred forty-seven nautical miles due west of the Canary Islands according to the calculations of the ship's Second Officer, the hurricane of bad luck returned with an unrelenting vengeance. Two of the new passengers, a brother and sister, missionaries who were on their way from West Africa to Florida, were clearly suffering from Yellow Fever. The Captain reassigned them to a small closet of a room on the coal deck, and there they remained. He moved them in secret to keep the crew, whose paranoia had become a meteor streaking across the sky, from tossing brother and sister into the sea. Only the Captain and the Chief Steward knew where the missionaries were.

One day later, during the middle of a dreary, drizzly afternoon, the kind of afternoon that is usually quite easy to forget, the ship was struck by a rogue wave that measured seventy feet high, according to a young first mate standing on what a few smart alecks called the Governor's Bridge, a forlorn expression on his face as the wave washed over the deck and the ship teetered ominously on the brink before miraculously righting itself. Three women and one steward were washed overboard from the wave, at least that was the scuttlebutt until a lonely rail of a Presbyterian minister from Boston, who had been on a whirlwind tour of the churches and monasteries in the Catholic countries of Europe to catalogue their theological errors, confessed to inventing the story in the hopes of instilling an appropriate appreciation for the wrath of God in the wayward souls aboard the *Conde Wifredo* and elsewhere, perhaps even his own cornerstone parish back in America. Even so, three women and a steward had, in fact, mysteriously disappeared.

The more superstitious among the crew evoked the name of St. Erasmus of Formia, also known as Saint Elmo, the patron saint of sailors and stomach disorders, who had suffered the tragedy of having his teeth plucked out with hot pincers because his truth was not the truth of the Roman Emperor Diocletian. The crew scanned the ship from bow to stern each evening looking for the bright blue fire of the saint's godly presence as proof that he would stand between them and this earthly hurricane of certain disaster. They were unashamed in their religious devotion.

An enterprising gang of coal-handlers and trimmers (all of them decidedly antireligious by the way they wore their caps) spread the rumor that Saint Elmo's fire was no fire at all but was instead the visible aura of the souls of desperate, degenerate men lost at sea, trapped in the blazing purgatory of their own sinful natures, looking to wreak their vengeance of dissolute lives on the living, and then these same coal-handlers and trimmers (blasphemous, self-indulgent bastards all of them, who would have sold their own grandmothers for a price) passed out tiny amulets they said were made of onyx, though who could say for sure, amulets which would grant their wearers immunity from the pain of a premature death.

The amulets went for three dollars apiece.

Five days out of Tenerife the wireless operator told the Captain he had received a series of staticky messages from

a group of American physicians living in the Dry Tortugas.
The messages were from the future, the wireless operator
said, but not very far ahead, fourteen or fifteen years at most.
They were about various ships in distress. The first was about
the steamer *Olympic* of the Alaska Steamship Company. The
Olympic was apparently wrecked on a reef near Bligh Island,
Alaska. The next was about the steamer *Herman Frasch*, whose
captain was suffering from ptomaine poisoning and on the
verge of death. And so it went, a seemingly endless litany.
The ocean liner *Saturnia* had struck an iceberg 175 miles east
of Belle Island and was taking water. The steamship *Hipplayit
Dumois* had lost its bearing in a sudden fog and had subsequently rammed into the steamship *Madison*. The steamship
Pleiades ran aground in Magdalena Bay. The steamer *Asia*
had suffered a series of mysterious explosions and was now
sinking in the South China Sea. The steamship *Oravia* had
somehow struck the rocks on the Falkland Islands, producing
a great, jagged gash in her hull, and would probably go down
within the hour. The steamship *Alimarante* of the United Fruit
Company was stranded at the entrance to Cartagena Harbor
when she collided with a harbor tug, damaging the blades of
her propeller. The mulatto wheelman of the tug was killed
instantly but no casualties were reported on the *Alimarante*.
The freighter *La Touche* crashed onto a reef off the coast of
Belize and sank within five minutes. The Brazilian freighter
Rio Branco was sunk by a German submersible in the North
Sea. The *RMS Republic* collided with the *SS Florida* and was
subsequently lost at sea. The steamer *Merida*, bound for
Havana with a cargo that included over two million dollars'
worth of Mexican gold, silver and copper, was struck for no
readily apparent reason by the *Admiral Farragut* and sank
before any of the lifeboats could be lowered.

   The Captain did not know what to make of the strange
tale told by the wireless operator, so he sent him to bed. But
he was secretly bothered by the messages of so many ships in
trouble and wondered for a moment about the contentions of
some philosophers that even though most of what goes on in
the world is hidden from our view, everything happens for
a reason. Then without a second thought he took hold of the
wireless, which was still whispering its arcane messages of

death and unavoidable destruction, yanked it (along with its headphones, glowing glass tubes, dials, cords, all of its 20th century paraphernalia) with unceremonious contempt from the operator's table, dashed out of the room and tossed it over the side.

A matronly woman (one of the black swans) two decks below saw the shadow of the plummeting wireless and thought a baby had fallen overboard or been tossed by unscrupulous individuals and screamed and fainted. She spent the next three days searching for some clue as to the identity of the murdered child and the culprits who had committed this most heinous crime, but no one would admit to anything. In a fit of insanity she latched onto the idea that the crew was conspiring against her best detective efforts, nay, the very universe was aligned against her, and when her own husband of twenty-six years, the hopeful Under Secretary to the new Spanish Ambassador to Venezuela, laughed at her suspicions, she took a small penknife that was nevertheless exceedingly sharp, a knife that she had quietly kept in her handbag since her days as a nurse in Madrid oh so many years earlier, and quickly and efficiently sliced her husband's carotid artery just below the ear. Without even a subtle grimace of regret tinged with irrepressible joy, without a flicker of discontent suddenly relieved, she watched him bleed out in a manner of minutes right there in his own stateroom, the sound of an Italian opera echoing from somewhere else in the ship, the wobbly operatic voice (it sounded a little like 'Suvvia, cosi terrible' from Leoncavallo's *Pagliacci*) descending upon this scene of invisible despair with rapacious speed, the husband's eyes blinking stupidly like the eyes of a bull lost in the mechanized labyrinth of a modern day slaughterhouse.

On the ninth day the sun failed to appear.

At first no one knew what to say. It was almost like forgetting how to speak. The ensuing darkness hummed with a cold, crystalline vitality, partially hypnotic, almost mechanical, not unlike the sound of an original DeKleist carousel organ at the epicenter of a whirling carousel. The sound of the darkness was almost soothing.

It soon became apparent that the carbon filament lamps that normally illuminated even the darkest corners of the ship were no longer operating. Everyone on board was reduced to using candles if they wanted to see two steps ahead.

The darkness in the darkest corners of the ship was not as soothing as the darkness that sounded like a DeKleist organ.

After a while the use of language reasserted itself.

The sound of the darkness was soon replaced by a vigorous debate (a dark hurricane of voices, if you will) as people from all walks of life wondered what had happened and why. Battles raged over whether the darkness was God's doing or if demonic forces had extinguished the light of the world. Some said it could be nothing else but a departure from the infinite absolute. Some said the second Antichrist had appeared and that he had gotten hold of Solomon's ring of power. Some denied anything out of the ordinary had taken place at all. Some said the power of God and the power of any and all demonic forces were one and the same.

A naturalist from Glasgow University on his way to search for plant specimens in the Brazilian wilderness said that neither God nor demons were involved. He declared that the ship had simply slipped into a magnetic maelstrom caused by unseasonably warm and therefore turbulent weather over the Canary Islands, it was almost like slipping into a coma, and so the *Conde Wifredo* had been unwittingly and inevitably propelled a cataclysmic number of years either into the mythic future or the symbolic past, he wasn't sure which, but the ship, he added, was most definitely now traveling the waters of the Antarctic. He suspected they were roughly eight-hundred-and-fifty nautical miles southwest of Tierra del Fuego, calculations which he said he based on his innate sense of geography and an appreciation of the laws of physics, especially Bernoulli's equations in fluid dynamics. Of course not all of the passengers were convinced or even believed in science, particularly the hopeful Ambassadors of an aging and fractious Western Europe with their secret financial backers, who believed in the power of paid assassins but preferred to keep this belief hidden, as well as the upper crust lawyers with their secret, religious connections, who believed in a subjective if somewhat unprincipled interpretation of the law, and also the frantic businessmen of a lost generation with no

connections to speak of but with an overwhelming belief in
their own desperate cunning and the naiveté of peasants living
in untapped markets, all of them thought such a turn of events
would have been exceedingly ungenerous at this juncture
in their lives and was therefore an absolute impossibility
(in so far as anything could be called absolute) and so they
dismissed the naturalist's theory as easily and efficiently as
one dismisses a falling star or the whooshing whiz-bang of a
speeding bullet that lodges itself with irreversible authority in
the brain of a retreating enemy.

At the other end of the intellectual spectrum, which
is not as great a distance as one would expect given the
unceasing tug-of-war between the two poles, a few aging and
unheralded poets drifting in and out of senility among the
passengers in steerage penned sonnets evoking the eternal
abyss of the long night.

On the tenth day the sun returned with the same inexplicable suddenness that had accompanied its disappearance.
An incredible (and also inexplicable) wave of heat washed
over the upper decks. Wooden deck chairs all over the ship,
some positioned against the rail, others stacked against various bulkheads, suddenly burst into flames.

The carbon filament lamps were still inoperable.

The passengers did not seem to mind an occasional
descent into darkness now that the sun had returned, but the
crew, who spent a good portion of their working hours in
the suffocating troglodyte atmosphere below decks, became
mutinous in their discontent.

The number of suspicious accidents, none of them as
yet fatal, began to increase. Cause and effect were difficult to
determine. But that was to be expected. The crew had been
growing more and more mutinous with each passing disaster,
and now there was no telling what they might do or when or
to whom.

The whispering outside Andres' stateroom intensified
both in volume and in its sinister tone.

On the eleventh day a young Romanian employed as a
stoker went temporarily insane from the intense heat of his
four furnaces and rushed topside and dove overboard, vanishing beneath the frothy waves in an instant.

The Chief Steward, a pompous man with a rather delicate nose, discovered the dead body of the hopeful Under Secretary to the new Spanish Ambassador to Venezuela. He had been drawn to the stateroom by the faint though unmistakable whiff of human fermentation. He did not wonder who the murdered man was or if perhaps the murderer was still lurking about (he was in no danger on that account, for the wife, after recovering her sense of right and wrong and the glittery decorum of false ethics, had abandoned her upper crust station for the relative safety of the lower decks and hoped to make her way to the New World in disguise). No, his only concern was disposing of the body before the process of fermentation became a public nuisance. Immediately the Chief Steward summoned the ship's Surgeon. Together the two men wrapped the offending corpse in a cream-colored silk sheet, dragged it this way and that through the ship's immense labyrinth of dark, forbidden corridors until they reached the stern, where they joined a gang of unassuming kitchen assistants and anonymous, overburdened stateroom stewards, dark shadows in uniform, wordless exhaustion spreading its wings beneath a star-filled sky, all of them faceless men armed with an endless supply of garbage receptacles, which they were continuously lifting and emptying over the side with robotic precision and then grabbing new receptacles (an endless supply?) off the deck.

With a mighty heave the Surgeon and the Chief Steward hoisted the body of the once hopeful Under Secretary above the rail (exhaling with obvious relief) and dumped it (him, the Under Secretary's putrefied body) into the seaweed covered sea right along with the day's refuse from all quarters. The sharks, a few makos and a few tiger sharks and a few hammerheads illuminated briefly by the soft, trembling light of the untainted stars, came and went and came again, their gray, glistening, humped bodies rolling about like eels.

The Chief Steward and the Surgeon stared for a while in uncomprehending amazement at the row of lowly stateroom stewards and kitchen assistants forever focused on the ceaseless stream of overflowing garbage receptacles.

Then the two bigwigs returned to their own duties.

The wife of the murdered Under Secretary vanished

without a trace. It was if she had never existed.

Of course the same thing could have been said for the Under Secretary.

It was at this point that the crew began to wonder if the Captain knew where they were headed. They wondered if the Second Officer had mislaid the charts or if the Captain himself had decided to assume the duties of navigation using only a 16th century Persian astrolabe.

The grumbling increased with every passing hour. The passage from Tenerife to Cuba had never taken so long.

On the twelfth day the Conde Wifredo passed through the tail of a sudden squall. There were no causalities among the passengers, but three sailors were killed trying to secure the lashings of the starboard anchor.

On the thirteenth day out of Tenerife, power to the carbon filament lamps was restored (good luck), but the ship's propeller shaft fractured (compensating bad luck). No one could say for certain what had caused the damage. Some believed saboteurs were on board. Others believed it was a case of divine retribution. In any event, the fractured propeller shaft was perhaps the last straw as far as the crew was concerned.

At least this was the Captain's impression.

The Conde Wifredo drifted northwest with the Antilles current for several hours until the ship's sails could be properly rigged. Since the Captain had dumped the only wireless on board into the sea, he could not radio for help or even hope that the outside world would know what was happening until it was too late.

How Captain Ramón Martín Cordero prevented a mutiny aboard the Conde Wifredo fourteen days after she had put out from the port of Santa Cruz de Tenerife en route to Havana, Cuba, a mutiny that probably would have been one of history's most unrestrained and notorious affairs, a bloody melee if there ever was one, right up there with the mutiny aboard the Batavia in 1628, which was spurred by the desire for a new life but ended with a shipwreck off the coast of Western Australia and the savage murdering of fully half of the survivors (including a newborn baby who was strangled

with a knotted piece of rope) by the mutineers before they
were rounded up and executed by the government; or the
mutiny that took place on the *HMS Bounty* in 1789, which was
spurred by an understandable desire for a life of unending
sex with pretty Tahitian girls and ended with the unexpected
survival of the *Bounty's* captain, Captain William Bligh, who
was set adrift in the South Pacific, surviving dehydration
and the predatory interest of first cannibals and then sharks
before finally making it to England (a journey of some 3,700
hundred nautical miles that he made in a little over a year
without even a compass), at which point he reported the
mutiny to the British Admiralty, who then chased down the
mutineers and brought them (those that were found) to a
swift and imperious justice; or the mutiny aboard the Mexican
Navy gunboat *Tampico* in 1914, which was in many respects a
bloodless comedy of errors, so it was a far cry from the blood
baths mentioned above, but the *Tampico* mutiny was also the
prelude to the first naval battle of the Mexican Revolution and
therefore a symbol of the discontent of the Mexican people,
which is the main reason it made the list:

Within six or seven hours of the propeller shaft fractur-
ing, the grumbling of the crew became a strong black wind
whipping up and down the corridors of the *Conde Wifredo.*

The more reckless elements of the crew, meaning those
sailors who had narrowly escaped lengthy prison sentences in
Tripoli or Algiers by running off to sea, saw in the growing
chaos a chance to take over the ship and so profit from the
desperate misery of others.

The vast majority of the crew was willing to follow the
reckless elements, partially because they were unwilling or
unable to make any hard decisions for themselves, but mostly
because they knew the reckless elements would find an appropriate scapegoat to take the blame for every disaster that had
occurred during the crossing.

The vast majority believed the *Conde Wifredo* was cursed.

The reckless elements were not limited by such a belief.

The vast majority believed that a curse could generally
be lifted if an appropriate scapegoat was found. If a curse
could not be lifted, there would be hell to pay.

The reckless elements took advantage of these beliefs.

The vast majority believed that the role of the scapegoat was to offer itself up to whatever dark powers had directed the curse in the first place. The scapegoat would be the one to suffer the slings and arrows of outrageous fortune. Everyone else would get off scot free.

The reckless elements were all for someone else suffering the slings and arrows, wherever they came from.

The vast majority believed that God needed a scapegoat as much as they did.

So did the reckless elements.

From this point forward events began to unfold rather rapidly.

The whispering voices that had up till that moment gathered outside Andres' stateroom, now shifted their focus to the Captain's quarters.

The Captain opened his door, armed with a .38 caliber Colt revolver, for he was no fool, and graciously asked the whispering voices to come inside so they could discuss their grievances in private.

The whispering voices became a wavering, etiolated version of themselves and complied.

The Captain offered them a collection of whortleberry tarts, Russian pastries, and tiny glass bowls filled to overflowing with *Pudding a la Republic with Sherry sauce,* all of which had been left over from dinner the previous evening. All of these sumptuous goodies were carefully placed on a silver platter that the Captain held out so all could see and catch a whiff.

The whispering voices accepted the desserts as long as they were accompanied with copious amounts of rum.

The Captain agreed.

The whispering voices stopped whispering long enough to devour the goodies and empty several bottles of rum pinched from the Captain's private stash.

The Captain asked them if they liked the opera, and he had in his hand an unofficial and unauthorized recording of Wagner's *Parsifal* and was heading over to his own Berliner gramophone to put it on when he realized he was the only connoisseur in the room.

The only sounds for a while were the chewing of mouths

and the smacking of lips and the slurping down of drinks.

Then the whispering continued, but the tone was less sinister, more collegial.

The whispering voices said they were tired of all the disasters.

The Captain agreed, he, too, was tired.

The whispering voices wanted to be compensated for the pain and suffering these various disasters had imposed upon the crew. A small bonus, perhaps, a gratuity, if you will, preferably in gold coin, to be shared equally.

The Captain said that could be arranged.

The whispering voices said they wanted fair compensation for the widows of the men who had died. Perhaps a trust fund could be set up, or they themselves could take up a collection from among the passengers and crew.

The Captain said they had his permission to squeeze whatever blood they could out of any turnip they found on the ship.

The whispering voices suddenly realized they had run out of demands, but they also realized they still had the Captain on the hook. They withdrew next to the silent Berliner gramophone and a furious debate ensued. The debate sounded less like a political discussion and more like the furtive, scratchy sounds made by small animals desperately seeking a hole to hide in.

Then the debate was over and the whispering voices resumed their former positions in front of the silver platter with the day-old desserts, but the platter was empty.

The empty platter could have been a problem, but the Captain, ever alert to the vicissitudes of political and social discourse, simply brought out a second platter.

The whispering voices relaxed somewhat. Then they made an additional demand, which was a pretty good indication of the extent of their imagination.

The Captain nodded and smiled to mask his inner insecurities.

The whispering voices wanted some commitment to restoring the peace and tranquility that had been a part of life aboard the *Conde Wifredo* before the disasters had begun.

The Captain thought that was a good idea.

The whispering voices wanted to know how the Captain was going to restore the absent peace and tranquility.

The Captain said he did not know, he had been hoping that things would return to normal on their own.

The whispering voices said such a strategy was unacceptable. They could no longer wait for something so vague and ill-defined as hope to work its magic. They were pretty definite about that. It was too close to religion to suit their tastes. They would be forced to take matters into their own hands if the Captain was unable or unwilling to rise to the occasion.

The Captain suddenly seemed much larger than he actually was. He said of course he would rise to the occasion. That's what made being Captain so much fun.

The whispering voices applauded the Captain's decision. They were amazed at how large the Captain had become.

The Captain said the first order of business would be to draw up a list of suspects, people who were suffering from exotic diseases or who held radical ideas or who had exhibited peculiar, even abnormal behavior, at least when compared to what was generally accepted in polite society. They needed to agree on someone they could blame for the disasters without too much trouble, someone who could rouse the censure, or better yet, even the outright condemnation of the entire ship, but most importantly, someone who could be easily dealt with. In this way, they would appease the gods of the sea and ease their own collective sense of guilt.

'You mean a scapegoat,' the whispering voices cried.

'Exactly!' said the Captain. 'A scapegoat is exactly what we need.'

Two hours later the black gang of whispering voices emerged from the Captain's quarters, all of them giddy as schoolgirls, for they were drunk with the Captain's boisterous self-confidence as much as the Captain's rum. The Captain, for his part, was all business. He waited until the corridor was empty. Only the dancing shadows produced by the flickering carbon filament ceiling lamps remained. Then he took two unhurried steps, stopped, contemplated the mechanical buzzing of the lamps that sounded a little like prehistoric insects, or perhaps it was more like the sound of radiation poisoning, a sort of faint, hissing sound of indeterminate origin, if you can imagine that, a barely heard sound that causes headaches in some individuals but which goes unnoticed by others. The Captain listened carefully to the lamps for a while. It was almost like he was trying to clear his mind of all temporal delusions. Then with delicate precision he pressed his ear against the door to Andres' stateroom and slipped suddenly into eavesdropping mode. Just what he heard is anybody's guess, but after a few moments he seemed satisfied. He retreated into the darkness of his own quarters, a faint smile still on his face, and returned a few moments later with a tiny sliver of paper in his hand, a flash of white, a formal invitation to a tête-à-tête with the Captain in a small vacant cabin adjacent to the smoking room. The tête-à-tête was to take place just after midnight. It was a very serious matter. The invitation said Andres should tell no one where he was going. (If he was pressed he could say that he was going for a late-night smoke.) The invitation also said that Andres' very life depended on his being punctual. That was pretty much it. The Captain peered out from the darkness of the doorway, looking first one way and then the other, as if he wanted to make sure no one was watching. Then he slid the slip of paper beneath Andres' door and vanished into the hazy, orangeish gloom of the corridor as easily as water spiraling down a drain.

The tête-à-tête with the Captain in a small cabin adjacent to the smoking room, just after midnight:
The cabin was decorated with an eye that appreciated scarcity. There was a single narrow oak table in the middle of the room, two chairs positioned on either side, and a small oil lamp hanging from a hook that the Captain carefully manipulated before he sat down. That was it. There was no Berliner gramophone, though the Captain had brought with him his recording of Wagner's *Parsifal*. There was not even a sideboard containing refreshments, though one could almost imagine the smells of whortleberry tarts and Russian pastries if one closed one's eyes. When Andres arrived, with not a second to spare, he was struck briefly by the sensation that he was drowning, he even began to claw at the air, but then the sensation left him and he sat down. The Captain took no notice of Andres'

slapstick antics and was instead scrutinizing the unauthorized Wagner recording, holding the disc up at an odd angle so that what little light there was bleeding out from the oil lamp washed across its surface. Perhaps he was looking for subtle imperfections that would mar the beauty of Wagner's composition. Perhaps he was looking for the name of the orchestra that had brought Wagner's magical music to life. Who can really say? What is important, if only in a vaguely articulated, symbolic sense, is that Andres realized that the Captain held as great an affection for the opera as he did. A bond had been forged, however tentative.

Andres wondered which opera was the Captain's favorite.

The Captain, who instinctively recognized a fellow music lover, passed the recording to Andres, who accepted it without thinking. 'Ah, my young friend,' said the Captain, 'it is a terrible thing to be seduced by beauty, is it not?'

Andres did not know what to say.

'Certainly Wagner knew this truth.'

'Yes, of course.'

'There is a great deal we can learn from Wagner. If only we take a moment to truly listen to his music.'

Andres looked at the disc.

'Yes, Wagner is truly one of the great geniuses of the world. In fact I wouldn't trust a man who said otherwise. But let us get down to brass tacks.'

'. . . .?'

'Needless to say, I am quite disappointed, as I am sure you are. I was expecting you and I would have had an extended heart-to-heart long before this most precipitous moment, a chance to trade assurances, cement a blossoming friendship, pay homage to the competing ideals of liberty and justice, pay a few long-standing debts in the process, everything that your great benefactor, the illustrious don Alfonso, was hoping would transpire . . . .'

It was at this point that Andres forgot where he was. The *Conde Wifredo* did not exist. Neither did Captain Ramón Martín Cordero, except perhaps as the nagging voice of regret, a biting fly lost in the whirlwind of sudden memory. Without any warning whatsoever, Andres found himself once again a

guest of don Alfonso Alberto Sebastian Francisco de Hernani
y Arredondo de Mariategui y de Esperanza, whose family had
befriended the Escoraz family in the days when the Moors
still plagued the Spanish countryside. Andres could hear plain
as day the droning murmur of the don and his own brother.
They were talking about the beauty of Isabel and Tiká and
the lack of suitable suitors in Logroño, which is what they
always talked about. But there was something different about
the conversation as Andres was now reliving it, a subtle
change in the don's tone which Andres had not noticed before
but which he noticed now, a bitterness that could almost be
mistaken for cynicism hidden beneath the don's words, which
leaked out in a syllable here, a phrase there, a bitterness that
masked a deep-seated resentment from years ago, or at least a
lingering regret, and so cast a new light on why the don had
helped Andres and Tiká escape. It was at that precise moment
that Madia had appeared with two notes in her hand, which
Andres knew was coming, for even though he was lost in the
extraordinarily vivid detail of his last night in Logroño, it was
still a memory, after all, which meant that his premonitions
within this dream of the past were foregone conclusions in the
story of the present. So Madia delivered the notes and Andres
read the first, which was in truth the second he had received
that day, and then he pocketed the second, which was in truth
the third, and it was upon pocketing this third note, which
he subsequently lost, that he began to wonder what advice or
explanation this note had contained and if his cause with the
Captain of the *Conde Wifredo* would have been better served if
he had read the third note when it had still been in his possession, and how much, really, did Captain Cordero know about
the circumstances of his hasty departure from Spain, and what
was the Captain's relationship with the don anyway, how
did they know each other, when had they first met and what
were the circumstances, but more importantly, what were the
Captain's true intentions with respect to Andres and Tiká,
what did he really want from them, his affinity for the opera
notwithstanding, and why did Andres get the feeling that all
was not well with the world, a suspicion that both increased
his sense of nervous expectation and affirmed his unvoiced
belief that his hands were tied by Fate so there was nothing he

could do (or could have done) in any case.

By degree, the aura of Andres' out-of-body experience faded and he found himself once again facing the Captain, who had assumed the cloaked shape of a darkly brooding, almost Gothic figure, like a god descending.

'But who can truly prepare for the tragedy of thwarted intentions,' the Captain was saying. 'And now here we are, clinging to the cliff of our illusions. What are we to do?

'Yes,' said Andres, who still had no idea what to say.

He considered for a moment trying to bribe the good Captain with one of the gold coins he kept in the purse don Alfonso had given him, but he was saved from this folly by a flash of insight. Yes, he theorized, if he simply agreed with the Captain, he stood a better chance of surviving the long night.

'What are we to do?' said Andes all of a sudden.

A smile seemed to break across the brooding Captain's face, but it could just as easily have been the crease of a furrowed brow or the light from the oil lamp catching the edge of a suddenly exposed knife.

'Not enough, that's for sure.'

'No, we can never do enough.'

'I'm glad you understand my position.'

'Yes, of course, but . . .?'

'But what else could we have done, eh?'

'Yes, what else could we have done?'

'Not much, I'm afraid. I suppose if you had come to me on your own accord even a week ago, we could have sorted through this mess before it became, well, before everything began to unravel with the speed of light.'

'Yes, I understand, . . .'

'Of course you do. Nothing can beat the speed of light for speed. Except perhaps thought. And maybe the swift wings of death, but that's for another conversation altogether.'

'Yes, certainly, but you see . . ."

'Ah, you want to know when things began to unravel. That is quite a difficult question to answer, my friend. Particularly for a man who sits in the Captain's chair, if you catch my drift.'

'. . . .'

'No, no, I think it is best we move beyond idle conjecture. What would we gain? Let us decide upon a fruitful course of action instead.'

'Yes, but . . .'

'We don't have many options left at this point.'

'. . . .?'

'For one thing, the crew has murderous intentions as far as you and your young bride are concerned.'

'But she's . . . .'

'No, no. There's no use trying to change their minds. Pretty difficult thing to change someone's mind when it's made up. It's like a piece of stone, polished maybe, sculpted, a work of art perhaps, a lonely bust high atop a pedestal, the pride of ancient Greece, but it is still a piece of stone, that's what it's like when a mind's made up. No, the best thing to do is get you and your young bride off the ship as quickly as possible. That's the ticket. Can't think of a better way out of this prickly situation. And believe me when I say that I've been thinking about it for a few hours. Yes, my friend, that's what we're going to do, without a doubt. There's nothing else to do. Absolutely nothing! I know that's not the answer you were looking for. We're still two days from Cuba. You and the little woman will have to hole up for a while, keep out of sight.'

'. . . .'

'No. What I meant was we're two days from Manzanillo. That's on the eastern side. That's the best I can do. I can't take you all the way to Havana. Too risky for that. Even if we made it that far without a suspicious accident, one of the crew is bound to follow you off the ship and give you the 'what for,' if you take my meaning.'

'. . . .'

'No, we don't have an arrangement with the port officials in Santiago. It would be an unscheduled stop and they don't like that. But I can get you into Manzanillo. I know the guy there. Yes, yes, Manzanillo is the place.

'. . . .'

'I knew you would understand, my friend. Besides, you have no other choice.'

¡Ay de mí! Can you imagine the indignity my

great-grandfather and my cousin must have suffered the day
the Captain dropped them ashore? Ah, truly the world is a
dark gallery where the face of betrayal hangs on every wall.
The *Conde Wifredo* did not even put into Manzanillo as the
Captain had said. They plopped a small boat over the side
with my great-grandfather and my cousin in the front with the
few small bags they had brought from Logroño, and then they
were joined by the two missionaries, the brother and sister
suffering from Yellow Fever, who sat in the middle, and a few
others who had come down with either that or some other
ailment, and in the back of the little boat, ranting and raving
and waving his ivory handled cane in the air with a none too
delicate eagerness, was the elderly gentleman from Canada,
still drowning in the wine of his own paranoia, his eyes like
two blood oranges seared by the sun, a blind Homer.

Can you imagine the chaos of such a situation? How
they managed to row ashore I will never know. Lonely
desperate souls crossing the line into a new land in search of
happiness. And there was no telling how far away Manzanillo
was! Who knew where they had been abandoned? There were
no visible landmarks. There were no fishing boats sweeping
this way and that across the waves. No sounds except for
the deep bass horn of the *Conde Wifredo*, which was soon
swallowed by the early morning mist, and the raucous, inhos-
pitable cries of starving seagulls in the distance. The carcass
of a gutted shark floating in the shallows, buffeted by the
carnivorous tide. A trail of blood inking its way out to sea. A
few sun-burnt palm trees scattered along a rocky shoreline. A
few gaunt looking figures wandering about, solitary barefoot
fishermen looking for the best spot to cast their lines. A few
dark clouds on the horizon, the teeth of sudden despair. The
bright heat of the day already begun. Bright white ribbons of
steam rising up from the heavy, scorched earth as if attracted
by the magnetism of the invisible stars. The sun a brilliant,
burnished, quivering red like Quevedo's blood-red moon. This
is how Tiká described it to me. Surely for them the world
had become a bleak and dreadful place. A forbidden realm.
An ancient taboo. An alien planet tucked away in a forgotten
corner of the universe. Surely my great-grandfather and my
cousin found nothing to set their eyes on that did not remind

them of death. If only my great-grandfather had read Tiká's third note. If only, if only, if only.

-50-

A short history of the first three years my great-grandfather spent in Cuba, from the moment he arrived on the island until the moment he met my great-grandmother:

In those early days in Cuba, my great-grandfather had acquired several small plots of overgrown land that were once productive sugarcane farms, several abandoned mills that had been partially destroyed by revolutionaries with torches who were drunk with *aguardiente* and the hope of liberty during the war with Spain, and several broken down, rusted wagons and a few mules suffering from an inexplicable combination of strange necrotic tumors growing out of their legs and necks and random outbursts of paranoia mixed with undeniable rage.

By chance he hired a native *chino*, a thin, wiry man of close to sixty to help him turn a profit on his investments, and within six months the farms were producing sugar cane, the mills had been rebuilt, and the mules had been cured of both their tumors and their paranoid rage with poultices made from the boiled root bark of *negrito* trees found only in hidden valleys high up in the Sierra Maestra mountains. (The mules were later sold to a muleteer newly arrived from Mantanzas who then used them to deliver supplies to the American troops stationed at Palma Soriano and San Luis.)

Only once did my great-grandfather ask about the silver mines that had prompted his initial interest in Cuba. He was chatting idly with a merchant in Bayamo, a man of some wealth and station in life, and the question popped out of his mouth. But the *chino* overheard and burst out laughing. Later he told my great-grandfather that the mines were a myth, a lure to attract the gullible. That was the last my great-grandfather ever mentioned the topic.

The *chino* said his public Spanish name was Nicario
Garro but that his secret, eternal, never-to-be-forgotten name
of the mountains was El Labrao. He wore a ragged white linen
shirt and ragged pants but possessed an otherworldly charm
and a radiant smile featuring three silver teeth that banished
even the shadows of a moonless evening. He was also no fool
and carried upon his person at all hours of the day or night a
rusty sword, a hunting knife tied to his belt, and a heavy club
made of oak, sharpened and scorched on the end. He claimed
to have taken part in the second great anti-colonial uprising
(The Little War, 1879) of Cuban nationalists (those who had
not signed away their freedom by signing the Pact of Zanjón),
yet he took a great interest in Andres' welfare, becoming his
padrino, if you will, in spite of my great-grandfather's obviously unblemished Spanish heritage.

'Blood is an endless sea,' Nicario liked to say. And in a
voice that rang out with the irrepressible purity of lonely high-
ways stretching out towards the horizon and vacant rooms
in cheap hotels and the remorseless, withering decline before
succumbing to death, he suggested that Andres arm himself as
he, Nicario, and all lovers of forbidden freedom were armed.
'The world, my young friend, has in it many *guajiros* who wish
to be ruthless bandits, and many ruthless bandits who wish to
be *guajiros*, and it is difficult to know who is who, so it is best
not to take any chances.'

But my great-grandfather only smiled with the quiet joy
that comes from years of reading dusty books and breathing in
the odor of decay.

He did not believe in weapons, he said.

'Ah, yes,' said Nicario, 'but not even a faith as strong as
yours can save you from the *otra muerte*, the other death.'

My great-grandfather, as you might have guessed, forgot
Nicario's words as soon as they were spoken. He abandoned
all caution to the wind, as they say. On any given day he was
traveling from Manzanillo to Santiago or from Santiago to
Manzanillo. It did not matter which direction he went so long
as he was heading somewhere. Nicario went with him, always
ready with his club to bash in the heads of anyone who mistook my great-grandfather's guileless, unbounded enthusiasm
for something more sinister, but during the first two years

they spent on the road, the need for bashing in heads never arose.

My great-grandfather existed in a bubble of sanctified hope. He spoke openly and honestly about the tragedy of living in a land where you could not buy a box of fancy chocolates to share with small children except in cities like Santiago or Camagüey or Havana.

And the perpetually downtrodden people of the countryside listened to what he had to say.

My great-grandfather expressed heartfelt dismay for the thousands of Cubans reduced to living in the poverty of palm huts because their towns and villages and lonely farms had been burned by the soldiers of the Spanish Monarchy.

And the perpetually downtrodden people of the countryside clutched at their own broken hearts.

He drank *aguardiente* with the villagers wherever he went. (Nicario kept a ready supply of bottles.) And when they were finished the perpetually downtrodden people of the countryside brought out more bottles and they drank long into the night and fell asleep beneath the stars.

My great-grandfather felt at home wherever he went in those days, but he felt most at home in the small colonial towns scattered here and there across Santiago de Cuba province, talking with the old men who gathered every morning in the squares and plazas beneath the branches of *ceiba* trees to consecrate their hearts and souls to the transitory beauty that was and always shall be Cuba

He especially enjoyed walking along the palm lined streets of colonial Bayamo, the cradle of Cuban independence.

He mourned the death of Carlos Manuel de Céspedes, the father of the country, who was killed by a Spanish bullet from the Spanish rifle of Brígido Verdecia, a Cuban by birth who had joined with a company of Spanish soldiers (though to be fair to young Verdecia, the soldiers told him if he did not pull the trigger they would murder his mother and sister). And when my great-grandfather learned that the body of Céspedes had been dumped into a common grave, he wrote a letter to 'All Cubans with Compassionate and Patriotic Hearts' urging that they join together to find the body and bury it in a place of honor.

The letter was published in the newspaper *La Patria*.

(Years later my great-grandfather still received compliments from those who had admired the letter.)

He wept silently for several hours when he learned that Pedro Céspedes, a younger brother to Carlos, had been taken prisoner along with fifty freedom fighters when their ship, the *Virginius*, had been captured twenty-six years earlier off the coast of Jamaica, and that all fifty-one men had then been executed by a Spanish firing squad in front of a slaughterhouse in Santiago, a symbolic gesture, no doubt, meant to communicate to the public at large that every rebel would eventually be rounded up and slaughtered like cattle.

Truly, the wilted light of desperate but undaunted faces is a mirror to our darkest fears, even as it is a beacon of hope for future generations.

My great-grandfather became an advocate of the free press. He became an advocate for civic improvements such as railroads and sewer systems and electric lights and universal suffrage, and libraries with marble steps and dark mahogany floors and mahogany shelves overflowing with books. He could not understand why the only good road in eastern Cuba was the gleaming white road to Boniato Summit, which everyone called the road to nowhere, and longed for the day when he could drive a shiny automobile all the way to Baracoa.

He contracted with a shipping company in New Orleans to deliver gleaming white appliances to the sunny shores of his imagination.

He believed in the paradise of the modern world.

He believed progress was the path to salvation.

But he also had harsh words for those who supported the 'American' interest in Cuba because they believed true democracy was only possible in Cuba with an infusion of yanqui cash every now and then, and a commitment from the Americans to provide rifles and ammunition and military advisors as needed. The United States, he thought, would simply replace the Spanish as the overseers of the country if left unchecked. And yet no matter how much suffocating outrage he felt towards the Americans and their insidious materialistic opportunism disguised as optimism (or towards their predecessors, the Spanish, and their blood-thirsty imperialism disguised as destiny), he also preached an unwavering commitment to peace.

He was a desert prophet living in the wilderness. 'Let rancor and revenge flee far from our hearts,' he would say to anyone who would listen. It was a common enough phrase in those days, a plea from the lips of men who had already lost too much. But whenever Andres uttered this mantra of the hopeless, the words flashed brightly in the air like spinning coins washed in the sunlight of heroism and nostalgia, or like a flock of startled birds taking wing at the sound of distant cannons, before inevitably giving way to the darkness of an uncertain future.

It was at some point after the end of that second year that my great-grandfather succumbed to the cyclone of loneliness that accompanies a life without love. As with all maladies of the heart, it was most pronounced during the wee hours of the morning, and almost invariably vanished with the dawn. But the effects were visible for all to see. My great-grandfather's complexion began to radiate with the pale light of distant planets struggling to maintain their orbits before being swallowed whole by reckless, carnivorous suns. His skin began to bleed with the distinct odor of tobacco mixed with chocolate, and ever so faintly a hint of cherry, a heady perfume which attracted large crowds of young, hopeful widows in town after town, unimaginably beautiful women who bathed twice daily in tubs overflowing with white gardenias so that their skin would be as soft as lambswool. These beauties immediately recognized in my great-grandfather the irresistible vulnerability of a love-sick *torero* and surrounded him with a halo of smiles that promised long, lingering afternoons and tender nights stretching out towards infinity. And so my great-grandfather commandeered the affections of thousands of lonely hearts, but not without incident. In the town of Contramaestre the magistrate declared my great-grandfather's fragrant skin a menace to the purity of marriage and granted everyone with a rifle permission to shoot him on sight. In the town of Yaro, a group of sun-burnt *guajiros* armed with clubs and torches and determined to keep their young widows for themselves, chased my great-grandfather and Nicario up into the Sierra Maestra mountains, where they took refuge for two weeks in the eternal shadow of Pico Turquino, hiding in the 'dark caves and vales, the ancient exile's fate,' as the poet says. Yet my great-grandfather had no interest in any of these women, in spite of their tremendous tragic beauty and their immaculate bathing habits and the persistent echo of their matrimonial desires. He was, he told Nicario, lamenting the absence of his one true love. How could he explain it? He was certain he could feel her somewhere about, somewhere close, feeling in her heart the same tightness he was feeling. He was equally convinced that she knew exactly where he was, but for some strange, mysterious reason she had squirreled herself away. Perhaps she was testing him to see how strong his love truly was, but he banished this thought as soon as it crossed his mind because such behavior made no sense. So her lingering absence was the cause of his monstrous despair, a despair, he told Nicario, that would vanish only when this love of his life actually appeared, or when in a maelstrom of impotent fury his trembling soul would collapse upon itself and so fall effortlessly into the black hole of his own premature death.

Nicario became quite concerned. He had on numerous occasions during those first two years suggested that my great-grandfather find a suitable wife, and so perhaps he felt responsible to some degree for the insufferably melancholic creature my great-grandfather had become. Who can truly say? Nicario had always taken a scientific view of love, which diminished perhaps the romantic notion of two souls becoming one, but it made for a healthier, happier existence. This is what he professed. But my great-grandfather was rooted to his misery and therefore immune to rational arguments. His symptoms worsened. On several occasions his heart stopped beating for a minute or two altogether and Nicario had to give him a quick blow to the chest to get it going again. He began to lose his train of thought in the middle of sentences, going suddenly mute, his eyes fixed on the horizon, a strange, contradictory look of withering compassion mixed with impoverished mirth spreading across his features, as if he were ministering to the solitude of the world.

It was then that Nicario, in a moment of inspiration that could have been mistaken for complete exhaustion, or perhaps a sudden bout of indigestion brought on by too

much Brazilian coffee consumed after midnight, or perhaps
the involuntary paroxysms that accompany a subterfuge
nearing completion, suggested that my great-grandfather try
writing letters to his absent love and perhaps the wind would
carry his words to her ears and she would then know it was
safe to come out of hiding. To Nicario's happy amazement,
my great-grandfather readily agreed. Nicario had expected
some resistance to his suggestion, a long, drawn-out debate
about the difficulties of such a strategy that might possibly
end in fisticuffs, but instead, my great-grandfather smiled
with absent-minded joy and began writing a letter that very
evening. He labored over each word, trying to sift through the
hidden meanings tucked away in the crevices of each phrase,
then each sentence, and finally each paragraph.

The first letter, which took him two weeks to write,
implored his unseen love to smile as he was smiling in anticipation of their first meeting.

The second letter (ten days) inquired after the health of
her parents. (Strangely, my great-grandfather, who seemed to
know even the tiniest details of my great-grandmother's life
before they even met, seemed to know nothing of her father
and his strange, inexplicable death. My great-grandmother's
father had left to join Marti in Florida in 1892 and had never
seen his wife or daughter again, returning to Cuba in 1895 in
the company of relentless Generals hell bent on freeing the
Cuban people, only to die of dysentery while camped along
the Cauto River in May of that year before he had fired a
single shot from his rifle. His body had been found several
yards from the river at dawn on the 18th of May, the new
sunlight creeping through the dense underbrush like snakes
or web-footed reptiles with their tongues flicking at the air,
revealing a poor, disenfranchised soldier with his pants
wrapped around his ankles, face down in the bloody, glistening grass of his own anguish.)

The third letter (one week) promised that she and her
family would be remembered at Mass the very next Sunday at
the Cathedral of the Most Holy Savior. He promised her that
his prayers would be accompanied by a handful of the gold
coins he had carried with him from Spain, and that each coin
was worth one hundred *pesetas*. (Naturally Nicario tried to

dissuade my great-grandfather from this course of action by
reminding him of the parable of the Widow's Offering, but he
was unsuccessful.) He also promised he would say an extra
prayer (and make a second, smaller donation, also opposed by
Nicario) for her cousin, who had suffered from chronic lesions
of the skin for years, though how he knew of the young boy's
shame or that he even existed my great-grandfather was never
able to articulate. (When he met this cousin some months
later, he marveled at the boy's immaculate skin, there wasn't
a single scar from the disease, not a shadow of ill-health, not a
wrinkle of pain, and when my great-grandfather enquired as
to the nature of the miracle that had cured him, the young boy
smiled a bright smile without pretense and said God could
bend the world whenever He chose, but He rarely intervened,
waiting, as He did, until someone requested a miracle on
behalf of another.)

My great-grandfather wrote the fourth and last letter
in a matter of hours. It was a litany of future memories that
flowed from his pen to the paper while he slept in a dream-
like trance at a narrow wooden table inside a small tent
Nicario had set up by the side of the road a mile downwind
of a small town called Jiguani. (They had taken to camping
in the countryside downwind of towns and villages to reduce
the number of young widows who might be attracted by my
great-grandfather's unyielding scent. My great-grandfather
slept inside the tent, though to say he slept is a mischarac-
terization, since on any given night he rarely closed his eyes.
Nicario slept beneath a blanket of starlight without a care in
the world.)

As my great-grandfather wrote the fourth letter, his
memories of the future unfolded with unrehearsed precision
like the three petals of an orchid upon the arrival of the
morning sun. He was amazed at the intense, almost surreal
nature of life. He found himself wondering what was real and
what was not. He wondered if he were a figment of his own
imagination. It was sort of like going to the cinema.

The first petal of the inner whorl:
He and his love-to-be were climbing a steep set of stairs
on a moonlit night. They were heading for an old Spanish fort

at the top of the hill, a gleaming white beacon against the void
and the torrents of discontent. He knelt before his love, who
was wearing a necklace of tiny blue stones like tiny teardrops
and a pair of earrings to match, and without a moment's
thought, the emotions that had been pent up inside his book-
ish heart for oh so many years, all those sleepless nights, came
pouring out like an ocean wave.

They fumbled about for words.

They hesitated.

They smiled and hesitated.

They embraced with a shyness he did not expect, like
two planets crisscrossing open space.

'I am only half-awake, my love,' he said. 'I am still
half-dreaming.'

And then she kissed him.

The second petal of the inner whorl:

It was the middle of the afternoon, a few months after
he had married his one and only love. He saw a river of happy
heads flowing uphill towards the gleaming blood-red domes
of a small-town basilica. The basilica shone brightly beneath
black storm clouds backlit by the sun and dark hills in the distance. Two dark palm trees were swaying this way and that
out front. He saw a lady dressed in flowing blue robes rise up
from the river as it broke against the stone walls of the basilica. She was carrying a golden cross. Then he realized the lady
was not a lady. She was a statue. He realized that she was the
reason for the river. It was a religious procession with the feel
of a carnival. A feast day to honor Our Lady of Charity, a day
filled with the dazzling sunlight of sunflower bouquets, which
erased the darkness of the sky from everyone's mind.

Then he became aware of the sound of many powerful
drums. Soon the drums were inescapable. They were a part of
the air. They were the engine of the river. Then he noticed that
the happy heads were chanting and singing softly, prayerfully,
happily. Or maybe they were singing loudly but his ears were
filled with mud so he could not hear very well. The singing
faded in and out. Then the drumming faded.

He wondered where his wife had gone. Then he realized
she was beside him. She had never left. She was a happy head

the same as all the rest, bobbing up and down. Then he realized that he, too, was a happy, bobbing head. They belonged
to a sea of humanity, a river of bobbing heads like tiny corks
discarded by eager drinkers. They had never been happier.

Somewhere a voice cried out, 'See how she walks on this
road of stormy seas!' Other voices took up the chant. 'See how
she walks, see how she walks,' they cried.

The chanting voices were like a restless wind.

The drumming started up again.

Somehow the happiness of my great-grandfather and
his one true love increased. They knew in their heart of hearts
that it would be an unforgivable sin to take their good fortune
for granted.

The third petal of the inner whorl:

He saw the two of them boarding a train during a
thunderstorm. The railway station looked like it had been
abandoned for years, and yet a train was waiting to depart,
a train that defied all reasonable expectations, a train to take
them west, across a Cuban landscape of palm trees and grazing cattle and coffee plantations and sugar cane all the way to
Havana, which would become the center of their universe. Her
mother and uncle, a thick-shouldered Mambí soldier with very
dark skin who had fought with the Dominicans and then the
Cubans, and several small children were huddled together in
a wet mass on the station platform. Her mother cast one long,
sorrowful look at the train as it pulled away and then bent
her head in arthritic prayer while the children wheeled about
her like small birds, shrieking and laughing with each flash of
lightning. But her uncle neither wept nor shrieked. He stared
after the train with the stone-faced grimace of a revolutionary
on the verge of sacrificing his own life for the liberty of others
who finds himself suddenly betrayed. Then the train rounded
a bend in the terrain and crossed through a field of dripping
palm trees and clumps of giant bamboo and majestic mangoes
and my great-grandfather lost sight of his new wife's family.
He took his new wife in his arms and held her tightly. He
whispered words of soothing love into her ears and her ears
became greedy siphons and she suddenly realized that she
had married a philosopher with the soul of a poet who would

write poetry only for her until the day he died.

'Like sunlight dancing beneath the waves, your lingering kiss,' he said to her.

And she smiled and nestled closer to him.

'Like the deepening shadows of tidal pools, your softly whispered words,' he said to her.

And she put her lips to his ear and said she loved him.

'I am thinking of you always,' he said to her. 'We are like young lovers standing in the shadow of the Eiffel Tower, becoming now the center of creation, the pale blue dust of Orion's nebula spinning across the sky, your soul and mine, breathless.'

Then she kissed him with a sudden wave of compulsion that both excited her and caused her to ache with a cancerous fear. Then the wave subsided and she fell asleep to the gentle rhythm of his breathing, and the silky strumming of his fingertips as he caressed her softly glowing dreaming face, and the distant rumbling of the train as it headed towards the clear skies of the west.

It was an impossible task to capture in a single letter the nuanced and evolving emotions of so many future memories. But my great-grandfather did his best. What else could he have done to purge his body and soul of the negativity of his rootless, romanticized past of a high seas vagabond? And what better way to achieve that inner sanctum of peace and harmony which the eastern mystics have talked about for countless centuries and which is the cornerstone of the love that binds us to each other and to the world. So he poured his heart out.

He was dripping with perspiration when he finished. The night had vanished and a warm breeze blew through the tent, but he did not notice. The warm breeze could have been an Arctic wind or a summer hurricane raging across the Windward Straits, but he would not have noticed those either. He just sat at the narrow table and stared at the fourth letter in his hands. But he did notice the chattering of birds in the fig trees outside the tent. The chattering birds reminded him of a Greek chorus, which in turn led him down into a darkly gleaming labyrinth of stray thoughts about the nature

of Greek tragedy and whether or not a character flaw was a
psychological or even spiritual defect (such as willful pride) or
an error in judgment which could not be avoided, or perhaps
it was simply an untranslatable concept, which meant that
language itself was an imperfect vehicle for thought, not only
between languages, but within the same language, because
you could never be sure what anyone meant, because the act
of using language was in and of itself an act of translation,
which was in fact an act of pure faith, as any linguist or
former priest would tell you, which meant that even something so tangible as visible reality was unknowable, let alone
invisible reality, and what was the nature of reality anyway,
and was the universe full of magical things waiting patiently
for our wits to sharpen, and did the phases of the moon truly
reveal the interconnectedness of the universe, and why did
Plato slam the door on the atomists and their notion of cosmic
pluralism in favor of a singular world view, which really was
the height of egotism, this was my great-grandfather's belief,
but perhaps Plato understood that a singular view of reality
was the only way to preserve at least the illusion that we were
all in the same boat, linguistically speaking, and was there
such a thing as moral evil and did moral evil edify the mind
so we could better comprehend this reality we called life, and
on and on it went, and when my great-grandfather finally
managed to escape this labyrinth of unanswerable questions,
he found himself wondering if the cosmos were trying to tell
him something profound, or if a sinister intelligence was just
having some fun.

Then the birds stopped chattering.

My great-grandfather gathered up all four of his letters
like the four Archangels to oppose the four beasts of the apocalypse and headed out to find Nicario in the silent vacuum of
the world, but he stopped just outside the tent, as if he had
just then noticed the majesty of death descending.

It was precisely at that moment, caught as he was
in the transition between this world and the next, that my
great-grandfather saw a young woman emerging from the
shadows of the fig trees like a nymph from the forgotten
pages of mythology or an alien queen from a spaceship that
had traveled from a distant planet.

The chattering of the Greek chorus resumed.

She was the most beautiful woman in the world.

She had long black hair and olive green eyes.

Her skin was the color of coffee and cream.

She moved with the easy grace of sunlight.

Her smile was a warm ocean.

Everything about the young woman was burned into my great-grandfather's astonished brain that morning, but there was one detail that immediately filled him with an immense and unrestrained joy. She wore a tiny white mariposa flower in her hair, just above her left ear, which gave off an intoxicating though subtle aroma that suggested, among other things, hidden messages and revolutionary songs and the freedom to think creatively and the value of mysticism and the hope of forbidden love. It was a woody scent which shrouded her intentions, but not the bright vulnerability of her feminine spirit, nor the hesitant quality of every breath she took. She was the incarnation of mystery to my great-grandfather, and yet he was not surprised to see her. Without uttering a sound, perhaps because he was suddenly incapable of speech, he handed over the letters.

'I am sorry I kept you waiting so long,' she said.

The young woman's apology had the impact of a revelation. My great-grandfather realized that for uncounted years he had been sharing his body and soul with a monumental sadness which had in all probability crept inside through a break in the skin or had perhaps sailed in through his unguarded airways without his knowledge the day his brother Arturo married Verona, and which had since then altered his perception of reality so much so that sunny days seemed like stormy nights and declarations of love possessed deadly, nocturnal fumes like the cyanide found in the tails of passing comets. But on this day he had been reborn. He later recalled that in those first moments, he had been mesmerized by the haunting insistence of those olive green eyes, and the absolution conferred by the young woman's bright, warm, inviting smile. He remembered her sweetly singing voice mingling with the birdsong of the tiny birds (were they some kind of thrush?) in the fig trees (a fact also confirmed by Nicario, who had been sitting on a small folding chair between two tethered horses, sipping with great restraint a cup of muddy, cold coffee prepared hours earlier, and so had witnessed everything). But still, my great-grandfather had not known what to say. Everything he could have said had been in the letters, but in that moment even the letters had ceased to exist.

'My name is Ana Silvestre,' the young woman said.

My great-grandfather still said nothing. He could only marvel at the beauty of her lips as she spoke.

'I wanted to join you sooner,' she continued. 'I wanted to tell you that I, too, am still half-dreaming. Yes, yes, I wanted to let you know I have been smiling since I first saw you navigating the streets of Jiguani, uncertain which way to turn because you were being pursued by the widows of the war and by the young men of our town who believe the nights of unrelenting sorrow must soon come to an end. In truth I have been smiling since the day you came to Cuba, though I did not see you step from the tiny lifeboat that brought you to paradise, but truly I felt the tremor of your footsteps on the beach that day. Yes, my love, I wanted to thank you for inquiring about the health of my parents and for the heartfelt sincerity of your prayers at the Cathedral. My father thanks you from his precarious perch in heaven, and my mother thanks you from the decrepit misery of premature old age and a life that has been lived in the abyss of perpetual betrayal. No, no, do not be dismayed. She will not thank you in person, she has never been one to embrace social convention, but she bears you no ill will, I can assure you of that. She is suspicious of the world and the ways of the world, just as she is suspicious of me, a suspicion borne of jealousy. Yes, my mother is jealous of her daughter. All of the mothers in my family for the last five-hundred years have been jealous of their daughters. But do not be dismayed. Besides, I am the one you have come for, not her. Yes, my love, yes, I am thinking about you always. I have been thinking about you since the day I came into this carnivorous world. You are the flame that will singe my wings. You are my release, my love, my refuge by the sea.'

My great-grandfather purchases a small farm:

One week after my great-grandparents met by the
fig trees, my great-grandfather stopped traveling the road
between Manzanillo and Santiago. Nicario protested his
decision, for there were many beautiful young war widows
seeking comfort, he said, and besides, he had a wagon load
of unopened bottles of *aguardiente* that needed drinking, but
my great-grandfather, thanks to the luxury of an unexpected
epiphany, was now able to laugh softly at Nicario's ceaseless
quest for the oblivion of pleasure. 'We are but atoms of light,
Nico, seeking only a path to each other.'

Six weeks later, two weeks before my great-grandparents
were married in a wedding to shame all weddings in the
Chapel of Our Lady of Sorrows in the Church of San Salvador
de Bayamo, my great-grandfather purchased a small farm in a
narrow valley for my great-grandmother's family and everyone moved in. Everyone included my great-grandmother's
mother, who was also named Ana, her uncle, Pepe García
Gallego, the brother of her dead father, a small brood of
mangy, naked children always underfoot, sons and daughters
of the García clan, orphans of the war who had nowhere else
to go, and a skinny vagabond of a youth whose tongue had
been cut out by retreating Spanish soldiers, or perhaps this
crime had been committed by overzealous revolutionaries
marching happily to what they assumed would be their
glorious deaths, it was never quite clear. The skinny youth
had been left for dead by the side of the road. Later, my
great-grandmother's uncle had found the boy sifting through
the rubble of an abandoned palm hut in search of something
to eat and had taken him in. No one in Jiguani had ever seen
him before. Everyone assumed he came from the mountains
but no one knew his name. But they could see quite plainly
that the boy was trying to escape from the dead sea of cold
despair. Everyone could see that his life had become an
empty dream.

The day my great-grandmother's family moved into
the small farmhouse (one week before the wedding), my

great-grandmother's uncle gave the boy a tiny closet of a
room that adjoined the kitchen at the back of the house. The
room possessed a single window which looked out on a small
stream traversing a scrubby patch of grass littered with small
white rocks, a home for blue scorpions and crickets and other
phantoms of the twilight, and on the other side of the stream
there was a grove of twisted laurel trees mixed with oak,
and a single Royal Poinciana with its flaming red flowers in
full bloom, a torch to light up the evening sky. The grove
was filled day and night with small restless, relentless birds
singing magical songs about the lingering fever of life and
the joyful purity of giving one's heart and soul to Christ at
the moment of death, which is also the most vulnerable of
moments when we are reborn in all our divine glory. At least
this was the impression you came away with after listening to
that chorus of tiny birds singing. So the room was a sanctuary,
a refuge from the sinister intentions of the world. Why Pepe
García Gallego gave this room to the young vagabond boy
instead of his sister, who had endured the dead sea of cold
despair for many more years, is difficult to say, particularly
since the room was not his to give away. But who can truly
say why anything happens? 'Such gifts in Fortune's hands are
found,' as the poet says.

The instant the young boy knew the room was his, he
broke into a broad grin and pulled out a small golden pocket
watch from the inner waistband of his threadbare pants.
With unguarded enthusiasm, he presented the watch to Pepe
García Gallego, who immediately inspected the artifact with
understandable suspicion. Had the boy become a thief? Had
he descended upon the owners of this elegant golden watch
in the middle of the night and murdered them in their sleep?
Had he discovered the watch while rifling through the pockets
of a rotting corpse? Or was this his only reminder of an idyllic
past followed swiftly by a tragic yet inevitable demise?

The back of the watch contained an appropriately
sentimental expression of great feeling from the 19th century,
written in extravagant floral script that was exceedingly small,
so small that all but those with the keenest eyesight would
require a magnifying glass:

To my beloved son, the last of a noble lineage,

Tomás Francisco Ribeiro y Aguiñiga de la Vega,
And his impossibly lovely bride, AdaNalie Esperanza Barruti,
The brightest star in the heavenly firmament
That adorns the magical Isle of Cuba.
May your faith in each other mirror your faith in God!
Camagüey, 1882

Pepe García Gallego inspected the watch and the writing without the need of a magnifying glass for several long withering minutes before accepting its authenticity, turning it over and over in his hands and then holding it up to the dazzling brightness of the sun and then peering once again at the finely engraved words, as if he half expected the writing to disappear and so reveal a tiny door to a secret compartment. Then he grunted somewhat enigmatically at the boy and the boy shook his head. Then he grunted again and the boy nodded with great vigor as well as visible relief. So Pepe García Gallego returned the watch to the boy and the interrogation was over. The watch became an afterthought, a reliquary of the glorious past, a symbol of doomed love and the inevitability of death, a lament to be whispered on stormy nights beneath the bed covers. How the boy had kept the watch hidden in the years since the war remained a mystery, but no one cared for such trivia. What was important was that the watch had returned the boy to himself and to his now deceased family. From that day forward he was called Tomás Barutti. Such are the vagaries of life.

-52-

The Curse of the Ana Silvestres:
From the day my great-grandmother received her First Communion and was admitted into the realm of reasoning adults by the Church until the day my great-grandfather arrived in Cuba, she was plagued by a recurring dream. She dreamed that she was hiding behind a *moscader*, a fan for flies fashioned from the feathers of a peacock's wing. Where this image came from she did not know, for she and her mother

lived in abject poverty. Neither of them were even aware
of the existence of peacocks until the dream. And when she
asked her mother what it meant, why was she hiding behind
this strange and beautiful fan, her mother said, 'I am so
very, very sorry, my little Ana. I do not know. I am certain
your dream is a reflection of the same lingering curse that
has consumed the hopes of our family since the days of the
conquistadors. But whether the fan in your dream is the curse
itself, or protection from the curse, I do not know. Someday,
perhaps, God will take pity and provide you an answer. All
you can do is wait.'

Centuries earlier the very first Ana Silvestre had fallen
in love with a lonely soldier of fortune. They married in secret,
but then the soldier left with Hernando De Soto in search of
cities of gold in 1539. He never returned. Nine months after
his departure, this very first Ana Silvestre of my family's
mythic past left Havana for the hills near Santiago, where
she herself had been born, to give birth to a daughter. She
gave her own name to the child in the hope that perhaps this
second Ana Silvestre might find the happiness that she herself
had been denied. But this second Ana Silvestre succumbed to
the same misery as the first: a secret lover who went off to war
and never returned, a baby daughter she named Ana Silvestre
in the hope of breaking what was most definitely a curse.

So the die was cast. Every generation thereafter was
compelled to name their first daughter Ana Silvestre because
the previous generation had done so. Naturally there were
subtle variations in how the curse manifested itself. Not every
lover was married in secret. Not every lover died in a war. But
the men always died savage, incomprehensible deaths (even
when they vanished without a trace, the nature of their deaths
was assumed). And the women always gave birth to beautiful
mulatta girls they named Ana Silvestre, hoping against hope
that the curse would miraculously loosen its stranglehold on
the future, at least enough so their daughters might escape the
tragedy of living their mothers' lives.

My great-grandmother dreamed the dream of the *moscader* year after year after year, waiting until the day of God's
revelation. The dream became as familiar to her as the pattern
of her heartbeat or the illusions she fostered in an effort to

escape the tentacles of the curse. Then on the very day my
great-grandfather and my cousin Tiká were abandoned to their
fate by the Captain of the *Conde Wifredo,* this strange, recurring
dream evaporated with the morning mist. What is more, my
great-grandmother knew when she woke up that morning
that she would never dream that dream again. It was for this
reason that her mother decided to lock her away from the
world for almost two-and-a-half years.

'If the dream returns,' her mother said, 'we will know
it is the curse trying to push you back into the world and so
reassert its power over the choices you might make. But if
the dream does not return, then we will know the curse has
finally lost its power, a miracle our family has been imagining
for five hundred years.'

As you might have guessed, my great-grandmother's
mother secretly hoped the dream would return. The mere
possibility that her own daughter might escape the ravages of
a lonely, loveless life that had been the legacy of generations
of Ana Silvestres filled her with a bitter, jealous rage which
she refused to acknowledge even to herself, and which therefore caused her front teeth to blacken and fall out and flaming
boils to appear on her sun-seared neck and the backs of her
fleshy arms. But the dream did not return, so my great-grandmother's mother retreated into the withering silence of an
uninhabitable island. She never spoke to her daughter again.

¡Ay de mí! What can I say? It was many years before my
great-grandmother realized that her very own mother had
become a recluse, a victim of a malignant, desperate, carnivorous envy. Unfortunately, this realization came with the news
of her mother's inexplicable death, so my great-grandmother
was left with the gnawing pangs of a guilt she could not
mollify, though on certain bright, sunny days she was able to
smooth over the rough edges of her anguish by focusing only
on those memories of her mother from the days before the
curse had been defeated.

Two days before her death, my great-grandmother's
mother dreamed that she, not her daughter, was hiding behind
a fan for flies fashioned from the feathers of a peacock's wing.
She did not know exactly where she was in her dream. She
was standing on a deserted, narrow strip of rocky beach with

her back to a series of cliffs made of black volcanic rock that rose quickly from the shoreline. It was late in the day and the wind was beginning to pick up. She thought perhaps she was near Chivirico, but she did not really know. She had never been across the mountains in her life. She had never before come within a mile of the sea. Then a strange, watery voice said she could let go of the fan, so she tossed it into the slowly rolling waves. The iridescent peacock feathers briefly caught the light of the setting sun. Then a backwash of sea-green foam carried the fan out to sea. Then she woke up.

It was at this point, according to my great-grandmother, that her mother left the small farmhouse that had been her refuge for twenty-one years and headed south. She told no one where she was going. The very next day, at seven in the morning, she became the only victim of a small mysterious hurricane that had landed without fanfare somewhere west of Santiago, churning up the coast and depositing sharks and various sea creatures along the rocky shore and then smashing into half-a-dozen rural villages tucked away in the mountains before pushing north across the island and then northeast towards the vast emptiness of the Atlantic Ocean.

Was this eerily prophetic and coercive dream of the fan simply the last gasp of the curse of the Ana Silvestres? Or had the curse reinvented itself and was now capable of attaching itself to whoever was the most vulnerable? Who can truly say? What I can say, and I think everyone would agree, is that it was almost like my great-grandmother's mother knew death was coming and went out to meet him.

-53-

The beginning of Tiká's tale of woe:

Let me first say that Tiká's story is not what you would call a tragedy in the classic sense. A few wild nights, a few erratic outbursts (what some would call temper tantrums), but you must remember that she was very young. And she was a stranger in a strange land, as they say. Her story is only a tiny bit tragic, a demented echo of her life in Spain. But she recovered from her sorrow in a most expeditious manner, which is all anyone can hope for.

My great-grandfather's need to be constantly on the road during his first two years on the island to ease his impossible loneliness, followed so closely by his whirlwind courtship of the second-to-last Ana Silvestre (who was perhaps the most beautiful Ana Silvestre of them all) and their rather extravagant wedding (which will forever be known among the inhabitants of Bayamo as the wedding to shame all weddings), exempted him in some respects from his patriarchal responsibilities towards his niece. At least this is what he would have liked to believe.

But Tiká was still grieving over the loss of the limited freedom she had experienced aboard the *Conde Wifredo*, which meant that in practical terms, my great-grandfather was forced to address her increasingly petulant (which is to say unmanageable) demands with a delicacy that resembled an emerging psychosis.

Initially Tiká's demands seemed insignificant, even reasonable.

She wanted her own horse so she could come and go as she pleased. My great-grandfather sent Nicario west to Pinar del Rió Province and he came back with a dark brown Appaloosa that reminded Tiká of her rambunctious childhood.

She missed the graceful, white storks of Logroño, so my great-grandfather had Nicario take her north to the estuaries of Bahia Naranjo, which were known in those days for their great flocks of whirling birds, where she could reminisce.

She was dismayed that she possessed no books, despite the fact that she preferred riding bareback beneath the Cuban sun to reading. But my great-grandfather acquiesced and gave her his very own bible, a hefty, leather-bound tome gilded with gold leaf which contained a genealogy that went back twenty-seven generations to the last days of the Moorish occupation. He also promised to take her to Manzanillo to see a German bookseller he knew there when she finished reading this magnificent gift of God's Holy word and he would buy her any book on those dust-lacquered shelves that caught her eye. Tiká carted the bible around for a week, glancing at the pages of this moth-eaten heirloom only briefly as she rode from here to there, before she gave it to a startled peasant coffee farmer on his way back from Holguín, a farmer who needed solace after an unexpectedly poor harvest that year.

She complained that her wardrobe had been ruined by the ocean air, which meant that she needed everything from silk blouses to embroidered petticoats to high top Balmoral boots to diamonds and sapphires and imperial topaz and other jewels to decorate her fiery-red braid, to French Aubusson tapestry handbags, to only God knew what else. My great-grandfather asked Nicario to take her shopping in Santiago. Maybe she would find something in one of the various mercantile shops along Enramadas or Marina, and Nicario knew a small French clothier on Calle Trocha, a shop founded at the end of the 18th century by refined émigrés fleeing the bloody excesses of the Haitian revolution.

From that point forward, Tiká's demands only grew more provocative, and her temperament more unstable. One evening she fell in love with the whirling dervish sound of a vagabond group of a voodoo musicians playing *trovas* and salsas and African rumbas and *guaguancós* with a crazy, every-changing assortment of drums and wooden boxes and spoons and even a *corneta china*, but always they sang with their irresistibly sweet voices like the sounds of summer birds taking wing, and so she told her uncle that her excitable soul needed to bathe in this strange Cuban folk music at least twice a day to guarantee her proper spiritual and intellectual development. So my great-grandfather felt he had no choice. He hired the group to follow Tiká wherever she went. She was ecstatic for a month or so, she said, but then her ears grew weary of their unceasing musical zeal, and beneath the cover of a partly cloudy sky, she suddenly and without regret abandoned them to a lonely street corner in Palma Soriano. They did not even notice her hasty departure. Or perhaps they did not really mind.

Two years to the day after arriving in Cuba, she acquired a sudden craving for white clay mixed with coffee grounds, which my great-grandfather mistook for an attack of nostalgia precipitated by the absence of her sister. He was on the verge of sending her to a doctor in Manzanillo to find a cure or to the asylum for the hopelessly insane in Victoria de las Tunas, but Nicario persuaded him that Tiká's desire to devour dirt was merely a symptom of her excessive devotion to the goddess Yemayá, common in women of childbearing age, especially in eastern Cuba, but she was in no real danger as long as she drank plenty of water, it was a fad like all the others that had affected her equilibrium and would pass soon enough, of this Nicario was convinced.

Soon thereafter she refused to accompany my great-grandfather on his travels. She said she had seen all there was to see on the road from Manzanillo to Santiago and vice versa. Then she swore she would slit her own wrists if she were made to live on a farm or in any of the small villages or towns that dotted the landscape like a plague, as they were filled with illiterate, unwashed, *criollos* who had never even heard of the opera. She belonged in Santiago, she said, so she could experience the mystical power of the great composers in the neoclassical elegance of Teatro Reina, where she had already seen *Un ballo in maschera* (the most censured of all of Verdi's operas), as her uncle knew full well because he himself had taken her to see Verdi's masterpiece when they had last abandoned the indignities of the open road for a weekend in the lap of luxury. So she claimed Santiago for her own. She would die in Santiago. There was no force on earth that could break her resolve. Besides, *Rigoletto* was opening in two months.

Tiká's decision to face death rather than submit to her uncle even in the most imaginary of circumstances seemed like an adolescent tantrum. My great-grandfather did not believe her for a minute, but he was also unwilling to take any unnecessary chances, for Tiká still possessed the indefatigable charm of a trained assassin, so it was truly impossible to gauge what she might or might not do. He said that she could stay in Santiago. He gave her a small but sufficient monthly allowance, which, to his credit, he deposited directly into her hands instead of into Nicario's. And he put her up in a posh corner suite on the third floor of the Hotel Venus, with its marble-floored dining room decorated with potted ferns and the portraits of Cuban heroes hanging like trophies on every wall, and a baroque fountain decorated with dancing nymphs (all of them naked) in the middle of the room and a trio of

musicians playing *guarachas* to occupy the lurid imaginations
of the patrons waiting for their dinners. She fell in love with
the hotel at once, especially because she could look out of her
bedroom window and gaze upon the shimmering mystery of
the Cathedral if she felt in need of spiritual reflection, or if she
wanted to connect with her sensual, romanticized view of the
material world, she could cast her eyes upon the European-
style elegance of the Plaza, which during the hot, hazy
afternoons was shaded by old Indian laurels and punctuated
by flowering shrubs — roses and jasmine and oleander set
against a backdrop of pale pink buildings and a bright blue
sky. The view resembled painted porcelain. After the sun set,
however, Tiká's view of the Plaza reflected a darker imagination, illuminated only by the hazy electric glow of evenly
spaced lamplights.

Inevitably, her enchantment with her new surroundings
took on a more passionate color. She became transfixed by the
lingering music of Carnaval, which always seemed to be present, and the indecent laughter of happy tourists ballooning
through the night air, sounds that spoke to an eternal longing
which Tiká had only half-recognized until her first night in the
hotel, and which, now that she was fully aware of what she
had been missing all those years in Spain, would give shape to
the rest of her life. Naturally, my great-grandfather had a few
vague misgivings about Tiká striking out on her own. He was
not so detached from the swirling eddies of human frailty that
he did not suffer from blinding headaches when he thought
about Tiká living a life apart in Santiago. But he could not
quite bring himself to face his own complicity in this tragedy
in the making, so he chose to ignore the obvious. Instead, he
asked Nicario to check in on his niece once a week, just to
make sure she was behaving herself, and in this way he sealed
all of their fates.

-54-

The day that Tiká's fate was revealed for the whole
world to see was the very day my great-grandfather and

great-grandmother were married in the wedding to shame all
weddings in the Chapel of Our Lady of Sorrows in the Church
of San Salvador de Bayamo.

By nine in the morning, a festive, somewhat romantic
spirit had already captured the town, erupting spontaneously
in every one of marriageable age, even those with the most
reclusive temperaments. Secret admirers tied kites to the
balconies of girls they had adored from the shadows for years
in the hope of a single kiss, the kites fluttering about like the
prayers of pilgrims hovering above shrines. And lovers young
and old, inspired by sonnets composed in the fever of true
love, serenaded each other with the irrevocable, unpretentious
joy of small children, their hearts spinning like miniature
cyclones of bright light.

At three in the afternoon the church bells started ringing
and the procession of the priests began. The priests marched
up and down the narrow winding streets of the old part of the
city, following as they always did a wooden cross made from
the beams of an ancient shipwreck bearing the figure of Christ
Our Lord and Savior, and a golden banner with an image of
the Virgin Mary holding her infant Son, the three aging priests
and the two younger ones announcing with solemn ritual,
reverent voices the imminent union between Andres Ordóñez
Escoraz and Ana Silvestre.

Ladies from all over town flocked to their balconies
to watch the procession as it wound its way through the
corridors carved out by the centuries, all of them posing in
staged fashion, their arms and legs positioned at odd angles,
as if they were hoping to catch the passing eye of a promising
young painter, all of them wearing their finest silk dresses
and their hair done up in fancy ringlets that had been all
the rage in Paris a century earlier but which had only made
the crossing to Cuba and the journey to Bayamo in the days
after the great war with Spain had ended, and only when the
procession of the priests had passed by their windows and
their flowing silk dresses were buffeted ever so slightly by the
winds of regret, did they hurry off to the Chapel to cast long,
lingering, wistful looks at the groom, their dark, almond-colored eyes fluttering with unceasing agitation behind vintage
oriental fans.

The Chapel was not large enough to accommodate the entire town, so the men (except for the groom, of course) waited impatiently outside in the sunny, dusty, hazy street, smoking homemade cigars as they talked about this and that.

The men also wore the costumes of a century earlier, embroidered silk shirts and long embroidered coats and short trousers and high-heeled shoes with stockings, costumes that they had retrieved from the long-forgotten trunks of their own great-grandfathers.

At four the ceremony began, filled with the sanctity of incense and tinkling bells and weeping feminine voices.

At six the ceremony was over and the entire town migrated to the Plaza de Armas (which was also known to some as Plaza de Isabel), scattering orange blossoms as they went.

The plaza was illuminated by strings of tiny electric light bulbs that looked like electric eels crisscrossing through dark waters to some, and a brightly lit ocean liner lost in a sudden, evening fog to others.

Dozens of tables, each of them filled with various steaming dishes, were set up along one side. The center table was adorned with a suckling pig that had been skewered and roasted slowly. There were more suckling pigs on the way.

Everyone drank a glass of *agualoja y sangria* (a sweet and spicy water) to start things off.

They drank to the health of the bride and groom.

Then everyone began drinking *aguardiente*.

They drank until every drop had been drunk.

Naturally they ate while they drank.

Everyone had plenty to eat.

After dinner they ate dessert.

Fancy breads were served with thick chocolate syrup, and also guava and orange and lemon preserves.

For the briefest of moments while feeding my great-grandmother a sliver of shredded pork with his fingers, the two of them laughing with unexpected frivolity in the bright bubble of their happiness, my great-grandfather wondered what had become of Tiká. He had not seen her the entire day. Had some mishap befallen her on the road? But he immediately pushed the thought out of his mind. Nicario was with her. Nicario would see that she arrived safely.

Then an eleven-piece orchestra suddenly materialized on the other side of the plaza from the tables. The orchestra was made up of three clarinets, two violins, a bass violin, two peculiar horns known as *trompas*, one guitar, a wooden flute, and a *tambora* drum. Immediately they began to play a *contradanza* from the days of the Haitians, a composition known as *San Pascual Bailón*, a traditional folk song that had been played at every wedding in Bayamo for over one hundred years. This was followed in quick succession by a second *contradanza*, *La nueva cañonera* by Victor Moreno, that filled everyone's aching heart with a mysterious longing for war, and then a popular waltz, and then various rumbas, including a whirlwind *jiribilla* and a more sensuous *resedá*, and then several slow, heart-wrenching songs done in the *trova* style, and then several elegant, lyrical precise *danzones* by that great piano dancer Ignacio Cervantes (the pride of Cuba, who had impressed Franz Liszt one afternoon, it was said, as the great maestro was passing by an apartment on Rue Neuve Coquenard in Paris and heard Cervantes playing the piano, a beautiful melody that brought to mind a crying child and a comforting mother, which tugged at Liszt's romantic heart and he was compelled to knock on Cervantes' door and introduce himself), and then for the rest of the evening the orchestra shifted back and forth between *danzones* from all over Cuba (Valenzuela, Pérez, Arízti) and the heart-thumping, sword-thrusting, indecent rhythm of anonymous *guarachas* from Holguín until everyone in the plaza was twisted up in ribbons of pleasure.

The bride and groom danced several dances by themselves before the jubilant crowd joined in. Then shortly before nine o'clock they abandoned their guests and rode off beneath a star-filled sky on two dark chestnuts. Most of the guests were too busy dancing and drinking and eating fancy desserts to realize the bride and groom had left. A few began to think of their own wedding nights (though their memories were somewhat vague and superficial at first) and what lay in store for the happy young lovers and what a joy it was to be young and naked beneath newly pressed sheets, and then they smiled or frowned or winced with unexpected shame as their own memories took on a more crystalline quality, which magnified either the faith they now possessed in marriage as an institution, or the regrets they felt when they realized they had made a mistake but now it was too late.

The fancy breads with chocolate syrup were the best anyone had ever eaten, by far, everyone said so.

The plaza began to empty out shortly after midnight. The bright moon cast odd shadows from the fluted eaves and the overhanging balconies. Those who were still awake behaved as if the town had indeed mysteriously retreated one hundred years into the past. Or fifty. Or at least ten. It was hard to tell. A wizened voice from the shadows, a friend of Martí and Casal, began reciting revolutionary poetry. '*Iba el negro bayamés sobre el caballo salvaje, sólo jirones por traje y la jáquima de armés.*' Words lost on the wind of a solitary church bell and then returning. And then other voices responding, weaving their way through the darkness, 'Liberty, liberty, liberty,' not as loud as the bell, and then footsteps running, and then a few distant gunshots, as if men with lanterns were chasing after runaway slaves.

When my newly married great-grandparents returned from their romantic sojourn in the mountains, they discovered that Tiká had been granted temporary refuge in the tiny closet of a room adjoining the kitchen, and that the young vagabond Tomás Barutti had been displaced to the cattle barn. No one doubted that Tiká had been lucky to make it as far as she did. She had arrived at the farmhouse outside Jiguani three days earlier on the verge of collapse from an excessive almost supernatural thirst at the exact moment my great-grandparents were trading their eternal vows in the Chapel of Our Lady of Sorrows. While the entire town was migrating to the Plaza de Armas, young Tomás had been dispatched to find help, returning not a moment too soon with a blind midwife from the forest, a peasant woman with an intimate knowledge of herbal remedies who had gained a reputation for suddenly appearing whenever there was need.

The moment the eleven-piece orchestra materialized out of thin air in the plaza, Tiká had gone into labor punctuated by carnivorous screams that clawed at Nicario's bones.

And the moment my great-grandparents arrived at their
honeymoon refuge in the mountains, just as they were slipping off of their dark chestnuts beneath the glistening moon,
Tiká gave birth to a baby girl all balled up and dripping wet,
like a small housecat that had been plucked from a river.
The baby possessed a magnificent head of dark black hair
(dripping wet but strangely luminous), a rarity in any age that
immediately provoked fears of the Devil looking for a few
souls to devour. She did not cry out even when the midwife
cut the cord. She just stared at her surroundings, her eyes like
two blue moons gleaming with awareness.

Needless to say, the birth of the child caused quite a stir,
not so much because the child had been born out of wedlock,
which was a common enough occurrence in that part of Cuba
and elsewhere, but because it was unclear who had fathered
the child and what his intentions had been and if, perhaps, the
birth of a child who did not cry was a sign of the liberating
majesty and unrestrained beneficence of an almighty God, or
if there were demonic forces at work. Given the mysterious
coincidence of the birth taking place in an empty house when
the occupants of that house were that very day attending
the wedding to shame all weddings, these were reasonable
questions as far as the people of Jiguani were concerned.

By the time my great-grandparents rode up to the back
of the farmhouse, it was well after midnight. The sky was
filled with dark, swift moving clouds like the tremors of a
strange dream. They almost didn't recognize where they were,
but then they saw the dark silhouette of the Royal Poinciana
and crossed the shallow stream. The kitchen windows were
bathed in darkness, but this did not seem unusual, given the
hour. But then they noticed the soft whirling lights of many
candles whirling from one window to the next and then
disappearing and then finally reappearing in the window of
the room that had belonged to Tomás.

The lights did not seem like candles. It was as if the
birds that occupied the branches of the twisted laurels and
oaks by day had been transformed into beings of pure energy.

As my great-grandparents entered the kitchen, they were
startled by the hunchbacked shape of my great-grandmother's
mother appearing in the doorway to Tomás' room. She held

a braided candle beneath her chin, which caused shadows to dance across her face with the frenetic, contrapuntal brilliance of newborn sea snakes. The darkness trembled. Ignoring her own flesh-and-blood, she looked instead with luminous rigidity at my great-grandfather and spoke in erratic, dangerous Spanish, but the only words that could be heard clearly made no sense. 'Circulos dentro circulos,' she said. It almost sounded like she was hissing, as if her tongue was a flickering filament. Then she spat on her candle, extinguishing the tenuous flame, and fled as if suddenly galvanized with the fleeing shadows into the interior of the house.

It was at that point that my great-grandparents heard a soft, rhythmic chanting, or perhaps it was someone sighing wistfully because the dawn was so far away, or moaning with the dream-like ardor that usually accompanies great passion. The sound was coming from Tomás' room, but it was difficult to see precisely where. A dozen or so candles were scattered about, their smoky light whirling through the air like incandescent but self-contained bubbles which seemed to obscure rather than illuminate.

The plummeting darkness in between bubbles was an overwhelming ocean of sadness. Then a hand reached out from the darkness in between the bubbles. The hand was somehow attached to the face of Nicario, though the point of attachment seemed to be constantly shifting.

Nicario's face twisted and contorted with radiating concern but did not utter a sound, while his hand made a series of totally unrelated gestures that seemed to say 'Please, my friend, do not disturb this babalawo, he is a master of ancient secrets, yes, yes, do not disturb his concentration, he has almost finished his prayer, yes, it has been a very long and complicated prayer, my friend, yes, I think it would be a good idea to wallow in ignorant silence until he has offered up every last one of his words to the gods and then he can tell us what it means if he chooses, at least that is what we have always been taught,' and then Nicario's face became a mirror of twisted, demented, fragmented chuckling, but again there was no sound.

My great-grandparents struggled to see what was happening. It was almost like being under water. And then it was almost like floating in outer space. The candles became a myriad of stars. The *babalawo* leaned over Tiká and her baby and whispered something only they could hear. The stars began whirling faster and faster. Then the *babalawo* lifted his eyes to the stars and cried out in a voice that seemed too heavy for the air to hold. '*Yemayá okere okún olomí karagbo osa ya bio lewu eyintegbe awa si lekú Yemayá bini ku wa yo kueana o kun iya sa ori ere egba mió o,*' he said.

And then it was suddenly dawn. The bubbles of candlelight had disappeared. Tiká and her baby were resting awkwardly on a narrow wooden bed and a faint beam of sunshine danced on the floor. Every so often Nicario, who was sitting at the foot of the bed, would get up and adjust Tiká's pillows and then slump back down on the mattress.

My great-grandmother was busy at a small cast iron stove in the kitchen.

Her uncle was talking quietly with the *babalawo*.

The *babalawo* had been brought in by the blind midwife because of the child's strangely luminous black hair, and because this child did not cry. It was clear that the *babalawo* and my great-grandmother's uncle had known each other since the ragged days of their boyhood. Pepe García Gallego folded a few *pesetas* into the old man's wizened hands and invited him for a cup of coffee, but the *babalawo* only smiled a curiously detached smile, pocketed the *pesetas*, and skipped out the door into the early morning sunlight and was soon lost among the trees dripping with moisture and the restless but silent birds.

My great-grandfather was sitting at the kitchen table, but he was not hungry. He tried to make sense of what was happening. After the *babalawo* had finished his prayers, Nicario had acted very strangely. He had clapped my great-grand-father on the back, an oddly misshapen look on his face that quickly gave way to a preposterous expression of joy. It had been both a confession and a declaration of his sexual prowess in spite of his age. My great-grandfather had not known what to do. At dawn, he still did not know what to do. Then Pepe García Gallego sat down at the table. He pressed his thick, callused ex-soldier's hands on the rough oak and leaned somberly forward.

'The *babalawo* said your niece was in a very bad way, my friend, but she is much better now.'

My great-grandfather said nothing.

'A very bad way.'

Clouds of black smoke began pouring from the belly of the stove and my great-grandmother raced to open a window and the clouds began to dissipate.

'The *babalawo* said he had never before see someone in such a bad way. She was like an Orisha from the old stories, from before the great crossing, facing the end of the world.'

Suddenly the birds began to sing.

The baby began to gurgle and then cry and Tiká comforted her, but somehow they both remained asleep.

'This is what the *babalawo* said.'

Nicario watched with a restless anticipation, one eye on Tiká and the baby and the other on the clouds of thinning smoke and the conversation taking place in the kitchen. Pepe García Gallego was not affected by the smoke. He said that Tiká had been troubled by dreams from the very first day Nicario had taken her to his bed. The *babalawo* had also told him this. The *babalawo* said he was not sure who had sent her these dreams. At first he had suspected Nicario. Then he had suspected the young boy Tomás, though he quickly abandoned this theory when he learned that the boy had only met Tiká the day her daughter was born. Then he suspected the child itself through the manipulations of Yewa, the true goddess of caves and cemeteries, but what Yewa had in mind and why she would commandeer the spirit of so tiny a child he could not articulate. But then he decided that the dreams were merely the echoes of a future which had yet to unfold and which could possibly be prevented.

The *babalawo* walked with Tiká through the landscape of this future. It was a landscape filled with murder and death and robust but clearly psychotic laughter and families torn apart by a bloody, relentless war, or perhaps several wars, and the sky was black with falling pieces of earth and twisted metal, a very strange sight indeed, perhaps it was her family she saw, or the families of her children's children, but what does that matter, it was a cataclysmic scene beyond belief followed by a swiftly descending eternal night, a spiritual darkness, a billion soulless bodies on the edge of oblivion, gasping for breath like fish drowning in the muck of a newly evaporated sea. This is the way the babalawo had described it. And the longer he and Tiká had wandered through this nightmare landscape, the deeper and more unyielding the darkness had become.

'Yes,' my great-grandmother's uncle said. 'I do not know all the details. Some things it is best not to know. But she was in a very bad way for such a young and beautiful girl. But so long as she follows the *babalawo's* instructions, she will have nothing to worry about.'

The clouds of black smoke were long gone but my great-grandmother had left the window open so she could watch the birds flying this way and that in the light of the setting sun, still singing. Nicario had disappeared. His disappearance had been preceded by an unexpected conversation with Pepe García Gallego beneath the fiery red foliage of the Royal Poinciana. Pepe was wearing a ruffled shirt that looked like a costume from another era. Nicario was wearing the ragged white linen shirt and ragged pants that he always wore. It was a heated conversation full of fiery words like tiny bullets and grand sweeping gestures of immeasurable sadness and forlorn looks aimed at the radiant sky. The two men spoke as if they had been soldiers in arms together and had watched friends die bloody, senseless deaths on the battlefield and elsewhere during the successive wars for Cuban independence.

The highlights of the heated conversation (polished with the stylized, melodramatic flair of a second-rate 19th century Russian dramatist) between Pepe García Gallego and Nicario:

Pepe García Gallego: 'What foolishness have you committed?'

Nicario: 'I could not help myself.'

Pepe García Gallego: 'You are lucky he does not shoot you.'

Nicario: 'Why would he shoot me?'

Pepe García Gallego: 'Because I told him you are no good, that you will abandon his niece and her child at the smallest provocation. I told him you had led a small company

of rebels against the Spanish in 1879. I did not tell him that
you had merely surrounded a small drinking establishment
on the road to Manzanillo and that you had waited in the
dark until the unsuspecting Spanish soldiers left singing
happy songs, and then you mowed them down with ruthless
glee. I told him that General Calixto García himself made you
a Captain in his tiny rebellion, and so you gained a small
reputation as a Lion in War. I should have told him what you
did when General García was captured and sent to prison in
Spain, that you told everyone he had made you a Colonel and
that it was up to you to keep the spirit of revolution alive in
Cuba. I should have told him that. I should have told him
that your words were made of gold but that your heart was a
crumbling mound of earth, a home for glowworms. But I did
tell him that you had stolen the virtue of dozens of hopeful
widows scattered from here to Baracoa, trading upon your
manufactured fame of a shining, heroic warrior, and that only
God and perhaps a few dark angels knew how many sons
and daughters of Cuba were produced by your profligate
indiscretions.'

Nicario: 'Ah, my old friend, I thank you. I could not
have told the story any better.'

(Nicario laughing with unexpected joy, his face bathed
in the reddish, sunlit glow of the Royal Poinciana, but then
growing silent, almost serious, his dark eyes contemplating the
obvious discomfort of Pepe García Gallego, and then Nicario's
eyes relaxing, becoming two red suns in a darkening sky, his
face retracting with a sudden sense of purpose.)

Nicario: 'But what would you have me do? I am too old
for small children. I have always been too old for children.
You know that. Besides, she does not love me. She said she
loves another, but their love can never be. So tell me, my
friend, what should I do?'

Pepe García Gallego: 'I should shoot you myself for the
no-account scoundrel you have always been.'

Nicario: 'Yes, yes, you have said this before, but then
who would remind you of your own indiscretions and the
price we have paid for liberty? Who would share with you the
last of his very last bottle of *aguardiente* and think nothing of
it?'

Pepe García Gallego: '. . . .'

Nicario: 'Who would scour the countryside for men of
good standing, men newly arrived from Spain, perhaps, men
who might make a good match for your own niece and so lift
you and your entire family out of poverty and liberate you
from the shackles of your discontent?'

Pepe García Gallego: '. . . .'

Nicario: 'Who found such a noble Spaniard with a
compassionate and poetic soul and planted the seeds of
romance in his brain and suggested that he write letters to his
unseen love in the hopes of drawing her towards him? Yes,
yes, my friend. What price would you pay for the liberty you
now enjoy?'

After that it was unclear what they were saying. Their
words were laced with hidden meanings that would have
taken years to uncover by even the most astute listener. Then
their mouths became festering, open wounds of uncontrollable
rage. Nicario grabbed Pepe García Gallego by the ruffles of
his ruffled shirt but Pepe knocked his arms away. Both men
took a step back and pulled weapons. Nicario pulled out his
hunting knife, which had not been sharpened in several years,
perhaps decades, which meant that the only effective use of
the weapon required a forward, thrusting, lunging motion that
could be easily turned aside by any experienced adversary,
and Pepe García Gallego pulled out a small flintlock pistol
that had belonged to his grandfather, a pistol that he had fired
only once in his life, and that had been to impress a young girl
whose name he no longer remembered but whose soft, lingering kiss after he had fired the gun was etched in his memory
and had become on certain cloudy afternoons and almost
every night (especially now that he was older) an indelible
reminder of the life he had not chosen.

It was the unexpected appearance of young Tomás
Barutti that prevented a bloody fiasco (or at least a comic
puppet show of wildly errant punches and bloodcurdling cries
of disbelief and heads spinning in exaggerated dismay) and
allowed both aging though determined ex-soldiers a chance
to retreat with their dignity intact. Tomás had been taking
a late afternoon nap in the barn. He woke to the distant,
garbled sounds of the two men quarreling but he did not

realize he was awake. He found himself moving slowly but
inexorably towards the sounds of the quarreling men as if he
were moving under water, so he thought he was immersed in
the depths of a strange, symbolic dream. His actions took on
a life of their own, as if his body were merely responding to
invisible radio waves from outer space targeting his brain. He
watched with unashamed fascination as he slipped on his own
boots and headed for the stall that housed Nicario's horse.
He saddled the horse and then led the animal from the barn.
He noticed that the horse had not been properly brushed for
many days but realized it was too late now. He smiled at Pepe
García Gallego, his benefactor, and Nicario, whom he had
come to regard as a well-meaning but demented cousin.

The quarreling ceased.

The antique weapons were put away.

Dumbfounded, the two men fanned out on either side of
the horse, which suddenly seemed like one of the great steeds
of Etruscan myth instead of the skeletal nag that it was in the
bright and revealing glare of a midday sun.

Tomás gave Nicario the reins and Nicario swung himself
into the saddle with a sudden youthful burst of exuberance, a
temporary gift from the gods for just this moment. The looks
on the faces of both Pepe García Gallego and Nicario had been
transformed from outrage to appreciation. Their eyes were
brimming with nostalgia. You have been my truest friend,
said the eyes of Nicario. And you mine, said the eyes of Pepe
García Gallego. I did not mean to mock the purity of the
marriage between your niece and my friend from Spain. I did
not mean to suggest that their love was a false love based on
pecuniary interests, said the eyes of Nicario. Do not worry, my
friend, I did not tell my niece that you prepared the ground.
She was drawn to her husband by her own heart, said the eyes
of Pepe García Gallego. Then perhaps I am only an instrument
in the hand of God, said the eyes of Nicario. Perhaps that is all
any of us truly are, said the eyes of Pepe García Gallego. Then
the eyes of both men were laughing.

Then Nicario turned the head of his great Etruscan steed
to depart, but he was delayed by Tomás, who was holding
up the gift of his gold watch, his one sole possession and the
symbol of his past as much as a symbol of God's indomitable

will and a reminder that even if true love did exist, it was doomed by its very nature to be short-lived, as are all things of beauty.

Why Tomás gave away his watch he only vaguely understood, but once he did he felt suddenly liberated. (Years later he tried to explain to his youngest daughter, Nuria, who was then barely three years old, that there had been no choice, that it was the price he had to pay to enter his future. But without a tongue he had to resort to making strange gestures with his hands and profound grimaces with his face, and his daughter was unable to grasp his meaning.) Nicario, who suddenly (and secretly) wished to linger, but who firmly believed one must make sacrifices in pursuit of liberty, put the watch in his pocket and vanished in the glare of the setting sun.

-55-

What the *babalawo* told Tiká:

'The world is Ifá and Ifá is the world,' the *babalawo* began. 'But you have forgotten this truth in the crossing to the new world. You have become consumed by the illusion of a singular life, so you are beset by the whirlwind of your own fears and have lost your way. You must conquer your fears to become yourself. *Quienes vencen al enemigo de adentro no tienen nada que temer del enemigo de afuera.*'

Tiká thought about the wisdom of the *babalawo* and the *babalawo* realized he was making headway and smiled, and before his smile had become a memory he launched into a parable about Okana Sode, an oddu with the power to heal the crippling divisions within one's soul.

'One morning, at the bright birth of a new day, Okana Sode was preparing to take a bath in a most luxurious room with a fancy white tiled floor and gleaming white fixtures and mirrors everywhere to dazzle the eye and a pair of French-style doors that opened up onto a patio. Next to the French doors there was a golden birdcage with a white plumed

cockatoo inside. Okana Sode filled her tub almost to the top
with hot water. She mixed in various exotic herbs and potions
and pieces of a coconut shell and the petals of many white
gardenias. The mixture produced a soapy froth that obscured
the depths beneath the surface, and a fragrant aroma that rose
up into the air like an offering to the gods. Then Okana Sode
climbed into the tub and began to soak. She did not mind
that some of the water sloshed onto the floor. She closed her
eyes and hummed a lullaby her mother once sang. Then she
herself began to sing, and the white cockatoo sang along with
her. Okana Sode and the cockatoo passed an hour or two in
noisy contemplation of the wondrous joys of life. But then
the voice of the white cockatoo was replaced by a strange
chewing sound. The serenity of the bath was broken. Okana
Sode wondered what had happened. She could not quite make
out where the sound was coming from, but she could clearly
see that the door to the golden cage was open and the white
cockatoo had vanished. Still, that did not explain the strange
chewing sound. Okana Sode didn't know what to think. The
chewing sound grew louder, and then softer, and then it was
replaced by the slow, slithery scraping sound of claws on tile.
Peering over the edge of the tub, Okana Sode spied the tail of
a crocodile slipping out through the open French doors. She
wondered briefly why she had not noticed a crocodile in any
of the mirrors, but then the thought left her. She got out of the
tub without any hesitation, dripping with the ambrosia-like
fragrance of the white gardenias, and followed the shimmering image of the tail out to the patio, but both the crocodile
and the tail had vanished in the new sunlight as quickly and
as permanently as the white cockatoo. So Okana Sode sighed
an inevitable sigh full of longing and regret and returned to
her bath. It was only after she had settled herself back into
the womb of the tub, with only her head above the water, that
she realized that the petals of the white gardenias had become
long, white feathers, and that she herself had ceased to be
human and had become instead an exact replica of the white
cockatoo she had kept in the cage.'

The instant the *babalawo* finished the parable Tiká felt
like she was drowning.

The *babalawo* said, 'Death is after you in Cuba.'

Tiká began to claw at the air as if battling an unseen enemy.

In a strange, thin, staticky voice, as if it had traveled across the centuries, the *babalawo* said, '*Ifá no se equivoca.*'

Tiká's struggle against her enemy intensified. But then suddenly her strength was gone and she was as weak as any unborn child.

In that same thin, staticky voice, which had a vibrating quality similar to the vibrating quality of radio voices that would take to the airwaves in the 1920s like a flock of excitable birds, the *babalawo* said, '*En Ifá no hay mentiras.*'

Strangely, Tiká's weakness was comforting.

In that same staticky voice as before, the *babalawo* said, '*Ifá habla pasado, presente y futuro.*'

Tiká gave herself over completely to the wisdom of the *babalawo*, and so she was reborn.

Returning to his normal, conversational voice, the *babalawo* said, 'You must continue to feed your faith in Ifá. You must be relentless. To fall into disobedience in this matter would be to hasten the arrival of Death.'

From somewhere there was the sound of distant drumming.

It was a whisper of a sound like the beating wings of tiny birds that filled Tiká's heart with vague premonitions of unrelenting hope.

It was a prayer being answered.

The *babalawo* continued, 'You need not follow my path. You may choose any path you like. But you must choose.'

The fragrance of coconuts filled the lungs of the world.

The *babalawo* smiled again, or perhaps he had been smiling the whole while. 'No one knows what lies at the bottom of the sea, so Olokun will help you cross the waters,' he said. And Tiká understood exactly what he meant.

-56-

¿Adónde te escondiste mi amado? This question is tucked away in the crevices of every soul, is it not? Just the existence

of such a question is why so many of us are drowning in a
sea of sorrow. It is why there are so many counterfeit hearts
of collapsing earth, all of them squirming with glowworms, a
latticework of teardrops tunneling through the shadows of the
long night. Can we not see the truth in the words of Saint John
of the Cross who wrote about the bride alighting on the green
branch? But we cannot help ourselves. How blind we are!
How utterly blind! Ashes and death, ashes and death! This is
all we think about. This is all we see. This is the fate we are
anticipating. But it is not the fate that awaits us. Yes, of course,
the immortal truth of our immortal soul is something we
cannot easily grasp. But it is a permanent reality nevertheless,
a certainty that goes beyond the cycles of the sun and the
moon. It is the one and only truth. Truly the mirror speaks to
all of us sooner or later, if only we know enough to open our
eyes. Happily, my great-grandparents knew enough to open
their eyes on that glorious morning beside the fig trees oh so
many years ago. He was her savior and she was his church.

My great-grandfather later admitted (but only once)
that he had hoped one day to own a colonial hacienda on the
outskirts of Bayamo and a small villa in Santiago with hidden
courtyards and secret doors so that he could come and go as
he pleased without drawing undue attention to any vices he
might acquire, but with the revelation of the scandalous love
affair between Nicario and Tiká and the birth of the dark-
haired, silent child, he felt he had no choice but to abandon
this pipedream and head west to Havana. So he purchased
train tickets for himself and Ana, and then, because his wife
insisted, he purchased a ticket for Tiká and her baby. Unlike
my great-grandfather, who seemed in moments of duress to
think of his family as a means to an end thanks to ten years
of traveling the seven seas in the company of pirates, my
great-grandmother believed with a dogged determination that
bordered on fanaticism in the absolute primacy of patriarchal
obligations, however burdensome.

One month after the wedding to shame all weddings,
they left the eastern shores of paradise for good. Neither my
great-grandfather nor Tiká looked at each other the entire trip.
Tiká was consumed with the haunting beauty of her baby,
though every so often a wave of sudden despair would darken

her face and she would stare out the window at the landscape
flowing past and see a pale, unsteady reflection of herself
looking back with accusing eyes. As for my great-grandfather,
well he was busy trying to assure my great-grandmother
that Havana was the closest thing to paradise on earth, that
in Havana they would drink the ambrosia of the gods, this
was their destiny, she would see, there was nothing to worry
about, the future was a pearl for the plucking, though with
every word that popped out of my great-grandfather's mouth,
my great-grandmother became more and more skeptical.

My great-grandparents spent the rest of their lives in
Havana. First they lived in a small tenement on Esperanza a
short walk from the old Gas Works, where my great-grandfather worked for two years until he became acclimated to life in
the city. Then they moved to a small house on San Nicolas and
my great-grandfather took a position first as a floor supervisor
for Raffloer & Erbsloh Co., a small cordage factory on the
corner of San Pedro and Santa Clara, and then as the manager
of a fancy restaurant somewhere on Trocadero. Two years
later they moved into the two-story, neo-classical, Baroque
style house in Miramar. But Tiká did not move with them.
Tiká said her destiny was to go to Puerto Rico. She had known
this since the *babalawo* had shown her the shining path to her
future. And she had also known that when the time came for
her to leave, she would leave her daughter with her uncle's
family. (This is perhaps why she had named her daughter
Ana.) When Tiká had first arrived in Havana, she could not
bear the thought of leaving her daughter. But now her daughter was now almost five years old. What else was she going
to do? Besides, she was not truly the motherly type. Her aunt,
on the other hand, was by that point a mother of two little
boys, a badly-behaved, dark-haired three-year-old named José
Ignacio, and an infant barely a year old, José Luis. A little girl
was more than welcome. So on a cloudy day in February 1908,
Tiká boarded the *S. S. Saratoga* bound for San Juan, Puerto
Rico. It was a swift farewell, for Tiká could barely look at her
daughter without bursting into tears.

'Please, do not worry Escolástica,' my great-grandmother
suddenly said. 'We will raise your little dark-haired beauty as
our own.' Then she smiled warmly. 'Look, she is already one

of us,' she said. And it was true. Ana Escoraz Silvestre, the
very last Ana Silvestre and my very own future grandmother,
was playing tag with José Ignacio, running up and down
the wharf, disappearing into shadows filled with the heavy,
glistening smoke of ships getting ready to depart, and then
reappearing again, skirting dangerously along the edge
without even a backwards glance at the frothy, brackish black
waters below, which had swallowed many an unsuspecting
child, pushing past the legs of men and women going this way
and that and a few startled seagulls taking to the air and a few
dock workers shouting words of warning followed by a lazy
curse or two, but the children were laughing with too much
rambunctious joy to be bothered by the inconvenient wisdom
of adults.

'Yes,' said Tiká. 'Thank you.'

Then she kissed my great-grandmother on the cheek,
and then my great-grandfather stepped forward, burdened
by a shame which he could not articulate. Tiká kissed him
as well, but he could not look her directly in her eyes, so he
pulled her close and gave her a fatherly embrace and then a
bit of fatherly advice, a few whispered words of encouragement, and though he heard himself speaking, he did not know
precisely what he was saying, for at that very moment the
thought of the long-vanished Third Note flashed a second time
across the dark, foreboding sky of his memory. He wondered
if life would have turned out differently if he had read the
note. He wondered if Tiká would have been leaving for San
Juan that very day. He wondered if they would have been
forced by his own uncertain appreciation of public opinion
to abandon their life in Santiago de Cuba province and move
to Havana. He wondered if that had been a rash decision on
his part. He wondered if Tiká herself might have found love
in the arms of someone other than Nicario. He wondered if
they would have met Nicario in the first place. Then he found
himself wondering why Tiká had left Spain oh so many years
before, what force had sent her spinning erratically across
the globe, what had she been hoping to find, and then he
suddenly realized that she must have fallen in love with a
man she could never marry, yes, that is why she had left, that
was most certainly the reason. He wondered who this man

might have been and if Tiká still thought about him and if she would ever find the peace and serenity that is necessary for true happiness. Then the red tide of his questions receded and he heard his own voice once again, and he was saying 'Do not forget that your family loves you, my little Tiká. Our hearts are spinning like tops.'

Tiká did not know what to say so she said nothing. She pulled away and ran up the gangplank, her fiery red braid trailing behind, fluttering furiously in the air like a burning rope that must be cut out of necessity, or a long-standing faith discarded on a whim, and disappeared into the swirling mass of humanity crowding the upper deck.

-57-

What my great-grandfather was thinking when he died:

Thirty-two years, eight months and ten days after Tiká left for Puerto Rico, on Saturday, October 26, 1940, a fraction of a second before eleven in the evening, the thought of the Third Note once more surfaced in the swirling ocean current of my great-grandfather's brain. He was tending bar that night in Casa Oriente, the café-turned-nightclub-turned-café of his own blood, sweat and tears at 112 Zulueta Street in downtown Havana. He was not thinking much about anything. He was wiping out a few shot glasses, rearranging the bottles beneath the counter, chatting with a few wayward souls.

He had planned to leave that evening by six because my great-grandmother was making chicken with tomatoes and rice. But the young man he had hired to work evenings until the last drink had been served had not shown up to work.

My great-grandfather wondered what had become of this passionate young man with dark Indian eyes and chiseled features that reminded everyone who saw him of Hatuey, the great Taíno chieftain, and who went by the unlikely name of Martín Gutiérrez Reyes, a name which my great-grandfather knew to be false, but he was not one to pry. Besides, he liked Martín very much.

Every so often my great-grandfather glanced at the clock hanging on the wall behind the bar, wondering what was keeping young Martín, if he was okay, for the streets of Havana were nothing if not violent, especially after dark, or if, perhaps, Martín had found a beautiful girl to keep him company and that was why. He hoped the reason was a girl.

And then my great-grandfather's thoughts turned to the clock itself. It was a very beautiful 19th century Junghans German Victorian Walnut Regulator Wall clock that had been delivered by special courier one afternoon from a mysterious, unnamed benefactor. But my great-grandfather had known immediately who had sent this strange, almost symbolic gift. The card that had accompanied the clock had said in precise, typewritten lettering: 'Truly, we are sitting in the grey bull ring of dreams with willows in the barreras,' and below that in a hastily written note: 'Thank you for hosting a most wondrous evening of political discourse and storytelling.'

My great-grandfather had placed the clock on the wall between a gilded French Rococo salon mirror (which he had purchased for a very good price from an antiques dealer who dabbled occasionally in the occult and who had a dozen or more similar salon mirrors in stock which had been gathering dust in his shop since before he was born and which he had been trying to unload for years) and the poster of the Spanish bullfighter Jose Garcia Carranza, alias 'Pepe Algabeño,' from when the bullfighter was just starting out in Madrid.

On the night in question, my great-grandfather had been sending the clock worried looks every so often from about eight o'clock on. The hands were not moving fast enough to suit whatever mood he was in.

Later, one of the regulars at Casa Oriente told the police that my great-grandfather had not been himself the whole evening. 'It was as if he had been waiting for something extraordinary to happen, as if he had glimpsed the end of the world, the destruction of everything we have ever known, but he did not want to share this terrible secret for fear of disturbing the delicate equilibrium of those present' the regular had said in a low, dry whisper, almost inaudible, as if he feared that his words would be taken out of context by an eavesdropping cub reporter seeking to push on the world a lunatic theory about the coming apocalypse and how it would begin in Latin America, supported by American arms dealers, and not in France or the Middle East like everyone supposed, a theory which would inevitably gain a host of followers inhabiting the fringes of society, but which would be largely discredited (also inevitably) by mainstream academia.

At nine o'clock my great-grandfather realized that he had forgotten to pick up the yellow cheese from Miami that my great-grandmother had asked for. He had remembered the jar of peach jam when he had gone out for a mid-morning walk, which hadn't been as hard to find as she had led him to believe, in fact he had purchased three jars, but he was certain beyond any doubt whatsoever that in the absence of the yellow cheese she would not even notice the three jars of jam.

At nine-fifteen he wondered if he could still pick up some cheese, but he was forced to accept the fact that the market had closed hours earlier.

At nine-thirty he shifted his line of thinking from the forgotten cheese to the latest poem he had written for my great-grandmother. He wondered if she had read it. He wished he could see her reaction without her knowing.

At nine-forty-five he was inspired to scribble the poem down on the back of a drink menu he had stolen from Sloppy Joe's. He had stolen the menu only a few days earlier, just to see what kind of drinks Sloppy Joe's was serving. There was a blank space at the bottom of the back page, below an advertisement for Tio Pepe, which seemed the perfect spot for poetry. My great-grandfather was going to pass the drink menu around the bar and see what people thought.

He was very excited as he scribbled. The poem contained the purest expression of love he had ever contemplated. It seemed to capture the unending depth of his emotion, his eternal faith that my great-grandmother was the mirror that reflected back to him the essence of who he truly was. He also felt the poem was utterly modern, utterly original in the way it blended a romantic view of the soul with a current scientific understanding of the cosmos.

(Of course he had forgotten that this poem was word for word a declaration of love he had once uttered to my great-grandmother in a dream, a dream which he had shared

with her before reciting the poem on the night of their first
kiss. But she remembered.)

At nine-forty-five, as he was writing down the words
on the back of the stolen menu, she was reading those same
words by candlelight in the smaller courtyard near the back of
the big house in Miramar.

She had been looking up at the night sky and contemplating the silence of this strangely silent evening (there was
not even the mournful sound of a bolero drifting like a ghost
through the air) when she remembered the poem. She laughed
as she read it, breaking the strange almost supernatural silence
with a sound that could have been mistaken for a handful of
old coins that had been happily tossed into the air so they
could descend swiftly and bounce about on the courtyard
tiles, the echo lingering. Smiling with unrestrained mirth at
his forgetfulness, and wondering if he would remember the
yellow cheese from Miami, she slipped the poem once again
into the front pocket of her apron.

At ten o'clock on the dot my great-grandfather finished
his scribbling. He held up the stolen drink menu so everyone
could see, explained about his poem, and then passed it to the
nearest group of patrons.

Not everyone was interested in reading this poem of
undying love written on the back of a stolen drink menu, but
everyone was interested in seeing what kinds of drinks Sloppy
Joe's was serving.

Those who also appreciated literary endeavors realized
they were being given a glimpse of something beyond their
understanding.

My great-grandfather carefully watched the expressions
on the faces of those who read the poem. Most of them moved
their lips as they read, which he decided was a sign that they
were trying to carefully decipher every nuance. An author
could not ask for anything more.

My great-grandfather spoke the poem to himself as he
watched each set of lips.

I am thinking of you, always,
We are like young lovers standing in the shadow of the Eiffel
    Tower,

Becoming now the center of the Universe,
The pale blue dust of Orion's nebula
Spinning across the sky,
Your soul and mine,
Breathless.

The drink menu took almost fifty minutes to make the circuit. Some of the patrons of Casa Oriente shouted their compliments to the author of the poem as if they were celebrating a great matador (as great as Pepe Algabeño himself, by the sound of it) who had narrowly escaped death while dancing with the most dangerous bull that anyone had ever heard of.

A few mentioned that they had never seen the Eiffel Tower or even thought about going to Paris, but quickly added that this was not a criticism of the poem.

Every so often someone (or an entire table) ordered something from the pages of the stolen menu (Gin Rickeys or Sloe Gin Rickeys or a Raimund's Gin Fizz or a Morning Glory or a Seiberling or an Absinthe Frappe or a Kal Katz or a Mary Pickford or a Paramount or a Happy Night).

My great-grandfather, in spite of the fact that his own drink menu was not as extensive as the one from Sloppy Joe's, did his best to give his patrons what they wanted.

Casa Oriente was filled with the happy glowing faces of drunken men, some with poetic souls, some not, but all of them staunch supporters of each other.

Basking in the glow of these happy, drunken faces, my great-grandfather read the poem once more, savoring each word. It is not certain if he read the words out loud or kept them to himself, but all eyes were upon him in any event. He imagined that my great-grandmother was sitting at one of the tables in Casa Oriente and that she was beaming with great pleasure and noticeable pride.

At ten fifty-five he heard the front door open and close, and then he heard several surreptitious footsteps which then came to an abrupt halt perhaps ten feet from the bar. He looked up, half expecting to see my great-grandmother, and then he laughed at his obvious lunatic state of mind for he knew at that moment she was waiting for him at home.

My great-grandfather saw that a thin, wiry gentleman wearing a plain black bowler had entered Casa Oriente. He noticed that the man possessed a thin moustache in keeping with his emaciated appearance. My great-grandfather had never seen the man before. He wondered why the man was not Martín Gutiérrez Reyes.

Naturally, everyone in the bar had turned their heads when the door opened to see who it was, but to judge from the descriptions they later gave the police, no two witnesses saw the same man. They all agreed, however, that whatever he looked like, he spent a minute or two scrutinizing the poster of Pepe Algabeño before he pulled out a pistol and started firing with indiscriminate glee.

It seemed almost as if he were searching the poster for a hidden message, some of the witnesses said.

Naturally, after the thin, wiry stranger in the plain black bowler (my great-grandfather's singular viewpoint) entered Casa Oriente, events unfolded with a sort of slow-motion, cinematic clarity towards an inevitable end.

At ten fifty-six and ten seconds, my great-grandfather heard my great-grandmother's laughter bouncing all over the tiles of the small courtyard near the back of the house in Miramar. He did not question the suspension of the ordinary laws of physics that permitted this miracle, for in spite of his philosopher's bookshelf and the years he had spent reading this philosopher or that one, he believed in his heart of hearts that through God anything was possible. He listened to the crystalline purity of my great-grandmother's laughter with delicate intensity, as if he could not quite believe such an astonishing sound truly existed.

At ten fifty-six and fifty-five seconds, my great-grandmother's ethereal laughter vanished and my great-grandfather suddenly thought of Grenfell. He started to say the name 'Grenfell' under his breath, but then he quickly swallowed his own voice, as if suddenly realizing that to utter the name of his former adversary would be a fatal mistake. He wondered what had happened to Grenfell and if he had been angry and had vowed revenge.

At ten fifty-seven and twenty seconds he decided that Grenfell must have died years earlier, or if he were still alive he would be well over eighty (or even older) and would pose no real threat to anyone, except perhaps himself.

At ten fifty-seven and forty seconds, an eerie calm settled over Casa Oriente.

At ten fifty-seven and forty-five seconds the stranger in the black bowler pulled out a pistol. No one in Casa Oriente could tell what kind of pistol it was.

At ten fifty-seven and fifty seconds a great booming voice said 'Death to the fucking Fascists!' The voice was coming out of the suddenly and mysteriously enraged mouth of the man in the black bowler. No one could quite believe that a man who was so emaciated could possess such a large voice.

At ten fifty-eight the man in the black bowler began firing.

Everyone in Casa Oriente scrambled to a place of safety, underneath tables, behind chairs, crouching on the floor.

Everyone except my great-grandfather. My great-grand-father seemed strangely disconnected, as if he were lost in the pages of one of his philosophy books. He did not seem to notice the bullets flying about or the crashing sounds they made as they smashed into the French Rococo salon mirror. But he was not thinking about philosophy at all. He was thinking about Nicario. What had become of Nicario, he said to himself. He wondered what Nicario would say if he could see his very own (meaning Nicario's) daughter, little Ana, who was not so little anymore, who was now thirty-seven with a son of her own, little Andres. But what was he thinking? Andres was no longer so little either. Andres was twenty-two and had just graduated from the University of Havana and was going to become a lawyer and work on behalf of the Cuban people. He had grown up just like that! My great-grandfather could not get over how quickly the years had passed. He wondered if Nicario would appreciate the sacrifices they had all made so that his very own (again, meaning Nicario's) grandson could become a shining star of success. Then just like that he could hear Nicario's voice, or some version of it, as if a demented, caricature of Nicario were whispering in his ear. 'Ah, yes,' said the strangely demented, distant voice, a furtive sound like the rustling noise a ferret or

a weasel or a hedgehog makes when it is running away pell
mell beneath the cover of dead leaves, 'but not even a faith as
strong as yours can save you from the *otra muerte.*'

My great-grandfather was just about to respond with a
clever, philosophical remark to this cryptic warning when he
was distracted by the golden, gleaming brilliance of a bullet
speeding with unwavering commitment towards the very spot
where he was standing.

At ten fifty-nine and fifty-nine seconds the thought of
Tiká's long vanished Third Note crossed his mind for the third
and final time. He wondered what wisdom the note contained
that he hadn't acquired over the years. Then he suddenly
decided he was better off not knowing. He was happy with
the way his life had turned out. He wondered what had
happened to Tiká and how she was getting along. He wanted
to tell her he would do it all over again in exactly the same
way if he had a second chance. He had vanquished all of his
doubts.

Then his thoughts returned to my great-grandmother
and the crystalline purity of her ethereal laughter and he
knew no matter what happened they would be together for all
eternity.

And then that was that. At precisely eleven o'clock
on October 26, 1940, during a flurry of erratic gunfire that
according to witnesses barely lasted two minutes, a single
golden, gleaming bullet struck my great-grandfather in the
eye and blew out the back of his skull. The assassin escaped in
the confusion that followed and was never found (or was even
really searched for) and so was never brought to justice. It was
said that my great-grandfather did not even flinch when the
bullet struck.

-58-

The story of Tiká from the day she left Havana, Cuba
until the day she met three ex-poets in San Juan, Puerto Rico:

During the intervening hours between the moment Tiká

left Havana aboard the *S. S. Saratoga* and the moment she
arrived in San Juan with the sky still threatening rain, she
transformed herself, at least superficially, from a deflowered
lady in waiting (though what she was waiting for exactly
she never quite knew) to a young man of vague pedigree. To
be more precise, she abandoned the costume of a weeping,
disconsolate young mother who had just abandoned her only
child to the capricious winds of fate, and adopted instead the
disguise of a young or youngish (closer to thirty than forty)
soldier of fortune in search of a quiet place to recuperate
between forays into the world of war. She cut off her red braid
and tossed it into the sea without the tiniest drop of regret.
Then she flattened her breasts, never that large to begin with
but still sensitive to light and water and cold temperatures,
with the aid of a corset that was two sizes too small, put on an
old army uniform that had belonged to Nicario but which had
seemingly shrunk over the years (either that or the profligate
Nicario had been a much smaller man in his younger days)
and so fit Tiká perfectly, and a pair of boots which were
several sizes too large, so she stuffed the toe sections with old
newspaper.

Why did she feel the need for such a disguise? Who
was going to recognize her in Puerto Rico anyway? Who
cared what sins of the heart she had committed in Cuba
and elsewhere? Was her need perhaps spurred on by some
psychological defect? Was she plagued by a lingering sense
of guilt because of her daughter and so was trying to run
away from her pain? Was she still lamenting the loss of her
one true love back in Spain and thought that by pretending to
be a soldier she might conquer the rebellion of her own inner
turmoil? Was her transformation simply a practical measure
that any woman traveling alone in the world in 1908 might
take? Or had she taken to heart the *babalawo's* warning (obser-
vation? prediction? a charlatan's bold, energetic but ultimately
vague pronouncement that can only be truly appreciated after
the fact?)? Did she believe that a physical incarnation of Death
and not just a mythical, allegorical representation was after
her in Cuba? Was she afraid that Death was still coming for
her, or if not Death, then Death's agents, who probably looked
like skeletons or the shadows of skeletons, dark shadows, the

visible manifestations of Lorca's *duendes*, which should not
be confused with Luther's theological demon of doubt or the
duendes from the folklore of Spain or Portugal or many a Latin
American country, though to be fair, Lorca probably stole his
image of skeletal *duendes* from Cervantes, or if not Cervantes,
then someone further back whose writing was steeped in
images lifted from an oral tradition. Was Tiká afraid that
these *duende*-like agents of Death had slipped on board the
S. S. *Saratoga* in spite of her best efforts to steer clear of their
icy fingertips, and so she had no choice but to embrace this
mummer's pretense? Who can say what was going on in her
mind? What can be said is that Tiká was quite convincing in
her new role. She took the name of Sebastian de Urquiza and
moved into the boarding house on Caleta de las Monjas. And
because of her extraordinary athleticism she was able to best
most of the men she encountered in most feats of physical
skill, including knife throwing, boxing, swimming, archery,
fencing, pistol marksmanship, rifle marksmanship, and horse
riding, but excluding drinking, arm-wrestling and whore-bait-
ing, all for obvious reasons. Her knife-throwing was especially
accurate. From a distance of thirty feet she could pin a man's
jacket to the wall with the man still wearing it and not a
drop of blood would be spilled. She quickly made a name for
herself and was soon accepted as one of the boys wherever she
went. She also made a little money with her knife-throwing
exhibitions, which might take place at any point during the
week, but usually took place on Friday or Saturday nights in
one of the abandoned warehouses on Calle La Puntilla.

In those days, the handful of warehouses on La Puntilla
had become a second home to all manner of adventurers
and mercenaries and defeated soldiers looking to blow off
a little steam. They had come to San Juan from all over the
Caribbean, drawn by a vague, unsettling sense of freedom
like a barely recognizable smell mixed with the more familiar
smells of unrepentant mania and a lingering, desperate futility
descending into fatigue that characterizes many a Latin
American nation (or perhaps all of them). They had infiltrated
every crevice of the island like a seeping poison. Of course
the authorities realized they were sitting on a powder keg (a
cliché, certainly, but a more accurate image, at least in tone,

than that of a 'ticking bomb' or some 'infernal combustible machine' or some more futuristic sounding incendiary device), which is why they turned a blind eye (yes, another cliché, which is meant to suggest a watchful but not too eager to intervene for political reasons kind of eye, so not really blind at all) to whatever crimes were committed in the warehouses on La Puntilla. Better that these men of the shadows should turn upon themselves than upon the decent citizens of San Juan. All of which is to say that Tiká's knife-throwing exhibitions were but one of many impromptu distractions that included various card games, dice games, all sorts of games of chance, occasional boxing matches, wrestling matches, cock fighting, dog-baiting, and so on, each event taking place on a tiny sliver of dimly lit warehouse floor. Money exchanged hands freely at first, and then not so freely as the big winners and the big losers sorted themselves out. Men were killed at the drop of a hat beneath the darkly gleaming rafters and then their bodies were dragged out into the night and dumped without comment into the dark waters of the harbor. Tiká always did quite well in the warehouses on La Puntilla.

During that first year in San Juan she roamed the cobblestone streets of the city at all hours of the day and night, submerged in the abyss of silence and pretense. Her old self disappeared. She acquired a taste for history, which is almost the same thing as acquiring a taste for the truth (which would have been ironic), but not quite. She searched the cafés and bars and seedy restaurants all over San Juan for a history she could claim as her own. Every so often she would stop in at the Army & Navy YMCA on Calle del Sol for an American style sandwich or a bowl of chicken stew and she listened to the stories of the old men while she ate. (Afterwards she might take in a gospel service right across the street, listening to stories of another kind, and reminisce for a moment about her life in Cuba.) Once in a while she found herself in the Plaza de Colón, which was full of orange vendors in brown hats pushing wheelbarrows full of oranges, and white-hatted hat vendors with toothless grins walking with their burros this way and that, bothering the tourists who had come only to look at the statue of Columbus. Or maybe she found herself on Calle de Tetuan, where the roughnecks were always lounging about on the narrow sidewalks in front of various import/export companies until the police chased them away. Or maybe she would head down to the waterfront, where only the heartiest down-and-outers took comfort. She went anywhere that old men, exiles and expatriates and counterfeit soldiers of fortune (mirror images to Tiká herself) gathered to trade stories of forgotten wars on distant shores and the glory of eternal revolution. She adopted the best stories as her own, as every great storyteller does.

One of Tiká's favorite haunts was Café La Ceiba, a café somewhere along Calle de la Luna where it was easy to hide one's face, partly because of the numerous ferns and other potted plants surrounding the tables, but mostly because Café La Ceiba was illuminated (if indeed illumination was the correct word) by a strange bluish light that seemed to distort one's perspective rather than provide any clarity, as if the light were emanating from deep inside a subterranean cavern miles below the surface of the planet (the Devil's abode?) and only occasionally leaked out through a crack in the earth's crust, a crack which was coincidentally just below the rough-hewn floor boards of Café La Ceiba.

In Café La Ceiba, Tiká talked about one of the very first of the Banana Wars, a conflict between Nicaragua and Honduras which had ended in April 1907, though the peace process had dragged on for several more months, and which had been framed by Teddy Roosevelt and the Americans as not so much a war but a policing action to preserve the integrity of the banana trade as well as to keep the ports safe for American *touristas*, but which was in reality an excuse for all-out butchery conceived by Nicaraguan President José Santos Zelaya and later backed by the Americans because they had no other viable choice at that point, because Zelaya believed Manuel Bonilla, the President of Honduras, was working feverishly to undermine the future economic prosperity of Nicaragua.

Tiká talked as if she herself had been one of the defeated captains at the Battle of Namasigüe in March, in which the Americans gave the badly outnumbered Nicaraguan army a dozen Krupp cannons and three or four hundred Maxim machine guns, which the Nicaraguans used to mow down the

hapless Hondurans and their Salvadoran allies without the
tiniest flicker of remorse. Only those who brought up the rear
of Bonilla's freedom fighters stood any chance of surviving the
onslaught.

According to Tiká, who was repeating word for word a
story she had heard from a bearded Guatemalan mercenary
who had survived the massacre and now spent most of his
waking hours in a drunken stupor in El Cielo, a dive on Calle
San José that catered to those who had fought in Central
America, the carnage at Namasigüe was so great that for three
days the sky was black with vultures and other birds drawn
by the festering aroma of rotting meat.

In the more upscale Casa Cataño on Recinto Sur, with
its rich mahogany décor and gilded mirrors, Tiká talked about
the Venezuelan dispute with the Dutch in 1908, a dispute
that began when the president of Venezuela, Cipriano Castro,
asked the Ambassador from the Netherlands, a Monsieur de
Reus, if perhaps he could ask his government to aid Venezuela
in tracking down various defeated revolutionaries who were
nevertheless able to escape to Curacao, a nearby Caribbean
island that belonged to the Dutch, where they (the revolutionaries) would first lick their wounds and then formulate
new strategies for overthrowing the Castro government and
then return to Caracas fully armed and try again, whereupon
M. Reus replied in a published letter that Castro had been
misinformed about any revolutionaries fleeing to Curacao
or any other Dutch colony, which infuriated Castro because
he knew better and so resulted in the expulsion of M. Reus
from Venezuelan soil, which sparked a riot in Curacao against
the Venezuelan consul, so Castro had no choice but to break
diplomatic ties with the Dutch, so the Dutch sent in warships
because things were beginning to escalate, but also because
they didn't like Castro's attitude in the first place, so Castro
initiated an embargo restricting the movement of any person
or persons traveling from Venezuela to any of the Dutch
ports in the Caribbean (or vice versa), because he didn't care
what the Dutch or any other great power thought about him
or his policies and he wanted to show them, so the Dutch
responded by seizing as many Venezuelan ships as they could,
which they did without firing a single shot, which is beside

the point as far as international law was concerned, but was played up pretty big by the newspapers in Europe and the United States as an example of civilized diplomacy in action (as opposed to the ruthless, blood-thirsty approach of every Latin American dictator), but by then Castro had to travel to France because the hospitals in Caracas could no longer help him with his syphilis, which was raging out of control, which the same newspapers mentioned above politely characterized as a kidney ailment even though everyone knew this wasn't true, so Castro left for Paris in the beginning of December, but before his ship had even reached the Greater Antilles, Juan Vincent Gómez, Castro's Vice-President and life-long friend, who had supported Castro's initial grab for power and was in fact his main financial backer in 1899 when Castro and fifty-seven followers slipped across the border of Táchira province, their home province, heading for the capital to launch their *Revolución Restauradora*, this very same Gómez (who later became the most ruthless *caudillo* Venezuela would ever know) had seized control of the country, and so the war with the mighty Netherlands was over.

Tiká talked as if she had been by Castro's side through-out his entire Presidency, even when he contracted syphilis in 1904 from a prostitute on the island of Curacao (the very same island at the center of the controversial events in 1908). She talked as if the only reason she was now in Puerto Rico was because Castro was living in exile in San Juan. She said that she had accompanied him to Paris in November of 1908 in search of a physician who knew what he was doing. 'Who better to cure the French Gout than the French?' Castro had told her.

In all the years she told the story, no one ever brought up the fact that she had actually been in San Juan during those three months from November 1908 to January 1909 when she said she had been with Castro in France. Then again, how would they have known? Her command of the smallest details of the story was quite convincing. She said she had accompa-nied the great dictator to Lariboisière Hospital, though they had spent several unexpected hours traveling the streets of Paris like kidnapped tourists before their driver, as if he had had a change of heart, brought them round to Rue Ambroise

Paré and their destination. They had gone to the hospital to
see Dr. Georges Louis Lemoine, who had written on syphilis
and was in close contact with a Dr. Paul Ehrlich from Austria,
who was close to a breakthrough, but before they went inside,
they stopped at the tomb of the Countess Élisa de Lariboisière,
who upon her death in 1851 left almost three million francs to
the French government to finish building the hospital begun
under Louis Philippe. The monument was very Gothic, very
dramatic, with a black marble façade crowned with black
marble angels and a recessed archway (also black) which
contained a grieving yet strangely serene looking woman
holding a small child with one arm and a dying man with
the other. The trio — pale, ghostly figures carved from white
marble and then painted with pale, dusty colors to suggest,
perhaps, the eternal and yet ennobling sorrow of death — had
been placed on top of a sculpted facsimile of a coffin painted a
copper color. The sculptor, an Italian master without a doubt,
had created the illusion that the coffin was supported by two
facsimile legs sculpted from black marble. Each facsimile
leg featured a lion's face staring out at the public with an
unearthly, inscrutable expression.

    Tiká said that after Castro's treatment had concluded,
she and the deposed dictator stopped for a coffee at Café du
Dôme on Rue de Clignancourt and spoke in furtive whispers
about the rumors that surrounded the life of the Countess.
They marveled at her exquisite passion for life and her indus-
trious courage in the face of a doomed love. In 1814 she had
married Honoré Baston de Lariboisière, an officer who had
served in Napoleon's artillery, a marriage that oddly enough
both families viewed as one of strategic importance, *un mariage
d'opportunité politique*, but Elisa had been secretly in love with
Honoré's brother, Ferdinand. Unfortunately, Ferdinand, the
dashing and beautiful beyond belief younger brother, had
led the charge of the 1st Carabiniers-à-Cheval regiment at the
Battle of Borodino on September 7, 1812 and been mortally
wounded, so his brother was the next best thing. Some said
that Honoré himself had suggested that Ferdinand join the
Carabiniers-à-Cheval regiment because they were always in
the thick of it, which meant that the glory of a noble death
was theirs for the taking.

The only memento of Ferdinand in Elisa's possession, which was an unspoken but tacitly understood point of contention between Elisa and the Count, was a lock of hair which a surgeon named Gudolle had taken from Ferdinand when he (the surgeon) was preparing the body for burial. What Elisa had wanted, however, was Ferdinand's heart, which she secretly and rightly believed belonged to her. But this was not to be. Honoré had instructed Gudolle to extract Ferdinand's heart right there on the battlefield and place it in a small beaker of wine to preserve it. Why Honoré wanted his brother's heart was a mystery, but the gossip in Paris in those days and later was that he had known all along that Elisa had been in love with Ferdinand, and wishing to punish her, but not wishing to provoke further gossip, which would have most certainly made it into the newspapers, which would in turn have made a mockery of his own public declarations of love for his future wife, he thought instead to seek private revenge and take possession of what was for Elisa (and perhaps for Honoré himself) a symbol of unattainable and therefore untainted love.

The couple slept in separate bedrooms from the very first day of their marriage, which explains a lot. What actually happened to the beaker containing Ferdinand's heart is anybody's guess. Some things it is better not to know.

Almost everyone who heard Tiká tell her tale believed that Castro would still be in power if he had remained in Caracas. (A few had forgotten she was talking about Castro and thought her story was about the Countess de Lariboisière and Honoré's excessive jealousy and the gruesome extraction of Ferdinand's heart, but when everyone else began gabbing away about Castro, they realized their mistake and wished they had paid better attention.) Many of the patrons of Casa Cataño tentatively expressed the undying hope that Castro would find the means to regain his Presidency, and then they drained the glasses of fancy tequila they had been drinking, and then someone ordered another round. As if to assure every potential (which is to say drunken) ally who might have been listening that such a destiny was a foregone conclusion, Tiká said that she had been meeting with Castro every few days in secret, hatching plots to overthrow Gómez and return the deposed President to his former glory. Again a few voices expressed their undying hopes, and again the glasses were drained and another round was ordered.

The day that Tiká stopped roaming the cobblestone streets of San Juan at all hours of the day and night, though she was still submerged in the abyss of silence and pretense:

On that day three men arrived at the boarding house on Caleta de las Monjas an hour or so before dawn. They were at the tail end of a passionate conversation about a woman they all seemed to know quite well. The streets were basically deserted at that hour, so their actual arrival was preceded by first their voices, and then the sound of their footsteps (heavy boots on cobblestone, the kind of boots the Conquistadors might have worn, maybe). Their conversation was a mysterious amalgam of innuendo and poetic despair, harboring all sorts of regret tinged with anger, with occasional bursts of rediscovered joy in the spaces in between their words.

Tiká had been listening to the men for at least fifteen minutes from her third-floor corner balcony window. What she was doing awake at that hour she couldn't say. Perhaps she had not been able to sleep at all. Perhaps she had just returned from an evening of conquest at one of the warehouses on La Puntilla. In any event, she had heard the men the moment they turned down Calle San Francisco from Callejon Tamarindo. One moment Tiká had been contemplating the silence of the world, and the next moment she heard three thin, staticky, vibrating voices, as if they had suddenly and irrevocably (this is how Tiká described it to me) emerged from the sewers through a trapdoor.

After a while, the men stopped talking. Tiká heard instead the sounds of metal striking stone, and then slow, furtive scraping sounds, and then the sounds of metal striking stone again, punctuated by strange, unintelligible curses, and then after the curses there was an explosion of weary, ironic laughter that shook the very foundation of the building, and then more scraping sounds, and then more metal striking stone, and more curses, and so on.

Later, after the sun had burned away the night, Tiká felt an overpowering urge to find out what these men were up to. Like a sleepwalker wearing a very thin jacket lined with

the wind, she followed the sounds down a narrow stairway
that led to a part of the boarding house where sunlight did
not penetrate, and soon found herself wandering through
a labyrinth of damp subterranean tunnels and long, dimly
lit hallways that trembled with a faint orangeish glow, and
every so often this glow was fractured by a sudden tremor of
darkness, and then the light returned, like an eye in the throes
of great sorrow closing and then opening again.

It quickly became impossible to distinguish between the
sounds themselves and the echoes produced by the sounds
bouncing off the stone walls of the tunnels and hallways.

Naturally, Tiká became tangled up in the labyrinth, but
she did not mind. She began to listen to the barely audible
currents of sound that lay beneath the sounds of the men,
sounds that had been trapped within the very walls of the
tunnels and hallways, sounds like smoke curling up towards a
stone ceiling and spreading out with an oily consistency after
a torch has been snuffed out, sounds like two hands folded
in perpetual prayer, sounds like a thin smile, with the diffuse
gentleness of lightning on the horizon, escaping into the long
night, sounds like tiny silver bells tied together with a silken
cord and shaken ever so slightly, almost wearily, or the rapid–
fire beating of tiny wings that one might hear just before
falling into a dreamless sleep, sounds that had waited in a
sea of stone, insensible to the passing years, for just the right
person, with just the right mixture of passion and curiosity
and reverence, to wander through this musty labyrinth from
another era with attendant ears. So Tiká abandoned her search
for the three men and followed instead the whispering walls
of the tunnels and hallways beneath the boarding house that
had once been a convent for Carmelite nuns.

The whispering led her to a small chamber some thirty
feet directly beneath a forgotten patio. The patio was in a
small interior courtyard in the dead center of the old convent
and contained the withered remains of various shrubs and
small ornamental trees from Africa or Spain and other
flowering plants, and there was also a single *nispero* tree with
its strangely sweet fruit (like a Flemish pear with a dash of
cinnamon) that had been planted in 1696 and would live for
at least another century. It was a patio where in happier days

two young, seemingly contented Carmelite novitiates tended
the greenery with a delicate but sure touch and, one might
say, a barely suppressed maternal instinct, and each evening
from seven until eight, when it wasn't raining, a handful of
the older ones gathered in silence to contemplate the unknowable mysteries of the universe as much as the lingering pain of
a womb made barren by conscious choice.

The chamber beneath the patio was the source of the
mysterious orange light. Tiká stood for a while at the entrance
to the chamber, contemplating the light, which was emanating
from two perforated brass frame railroad lanterns. She did
not see the owners of the lanterns and wondered if perhaps
she was dreaming. The orangeish glow from the lanterns was
fairly steady, only a slight, sinister flickering, and she wondered what had caused the flashes of darkness from before.
Then a shadow passed in front of the lanterns and there
was another mesmerizing flash of darkness. Tiká must have
said something or somehow drawn attention to her presence
because when the light returned she saw three men standing
motionless in the glare of the lanterns, looking in her direction, their eyes fixed like dead stars or hibernating thoughts,
their faces beaming with comical expressions of paranoia and
autoerotic cunning.

A few minutes later:
'You gave us quite a shock Sebastian de Urquiza,
appearing the way you did on the edge of oblivion, we were
just settling into our labors,' said a dreamily sanguine voice
that belonged to a lanky, dark-complected middle-aged man
wearing corduroy workpants and a cotton shirt. He possessed
finely chiseled features and a shadowy beard like a dusting of
potash. He had one leg and one foot resting on a rather large
piece of stone that seemed to have fallen from the ceiling, and
he was leaning forward slightly, his hands pressing down on
his bent knee. There were various implements scattered about:
shovels, a stone mason's chisel, a few wedges, a pry bar, a
sledge hammer, and several smaller hammers. The man's two
companions were wearing similar costumes. They stood on
either side of him with blank, bewildered looks on their faces.
The flickering of the lanterns bathed the faces of all three men

in a strange, eerie light. It was like there were tattoos dancing
across their skin. 'But what a fine sounding name you have,'
the voice continued. 'Sebastian de Urquiza. What an exceptionally suggestive, and dare I say it, poetic sounding name. It
reminds one of the grand sounding names of Seville the way it
rolls off one's tongue. A name that deserves a page in the
Spanish Book of Heraldry, if there is such a book. But there must
be such a book! My own name, less grand sounding perhaps,
but just as poetic, if you will forgive a little egotism on my
part, the insufferable vanity of wounded pride, my name is
Rodrigo Cabrera Lazar, ex-poet extraordinaire from Carúpano,
Venezuela.' It was hard to tell if ex-poet Rodrigo was actually
speaking, forming words with his lips and sending them out
on their own to cross the void, or if he was communicating
telepathically, as if he were able to express everything he was
thinking with a single, stupefying glance. 'And this affable,
gregarious fellow to my right,' said ex-poet Rodrigo, 'though
you would hardly know this to be true at this curiously
precipitous moment since he seems to have swallowed his
tongue, is Victor Hugo Salmerón la Prieto y Savoix de Pajares,
a truly grand-sounding name if there ever was one, named
after the famous maestro, of course, at least the first part,
probably because his mother had just finished reading *The
Hunchback of Notre Dame*, she was a voracious reader, that
woman, yes she was, as is her son, Victor Hugo, who has been
an ex-poet for longer than he can remember, which might not
be so long if he suffered from amnesia, but I can assure you
that his mind is as sharp this morning as the day he was born,
he hails from the affable seaside community of Santo Tomás
de Castilla, Guatemala and claims to be descended from the
great, or near great, or at least the first Guatemalan poet of
any significant reputation, Rafael Landívar, and get this,
Victor Hugo also claims to have a grandfather from Haiti who
wrote an occasional essay for *L' Observatuer*, the best newspaper in Port-au-Prince (how many literary antecedents can one
man possess and never find a publisher?), and who left Haiti
in 1805, one year after the revolution had ended and the slaves
of Haiti had become ex-slaves (which is pretty close to becoming an ex-poet, let me tell you), which took place over one
hundred years ago, and so naturally, if you stop to think

about what Victor Hugo is saying, you begin to wonder how
old he actually is and how old his father and his grandfather
were and if they are still alive, and if they do indeed all
belong to the race of the immortals, for who else could live so
long, then Victor Hugo has already achieved the immortality
that all poets (and even a few ex-poets) dream about, he will
be alive and kicking when every word any mortal has ever
written, any book ever printed and shared with a small,
well-respected audience, or even the great covetous multi-
tudes, every literary accomplishment will have turned to dust,
but as for me, well I could care less about Victor Hugo's age, I
mean his age as far as I'm concerned can only elevate his
ex-poet's status, which will in turn elevate every ex-poet's
status, if you catch my drift, which brings me to this rigid,
silent monster on my left, Gustav Hermann Metz, who has not
yet decided if he wants to embrace the lifestyle of an ex-poet,
and of course when I use the word monster I do not mean to
suggest that Gustav is a physical monstrosity, for you can
surely see that at five-foot-six he is not so large as all that,
what I mean to say, my dear sweet, perhaps gullible Sebastian
de Urquiza, is that he is a nihilist at heart, a position which I
think it is fair to say the world views as monstrous, or a
monstrosity, or at least the potential is there, and if you were
ever to stare into those icy blue eyes of his for ten minutes, let
alone an eternal-seeming hour, particularly after a good bottle
of Demerara rum, you would see what I mean, yes, you can
see him getting ready to react once he has pulled back from
the darkness of the abyss, yes, I am sure he has a great deal to
say, but as I have already mentioned, Gustav has not yet
decided whether he wants to become an ex-poet like myself
and Victor Hugo, but do not worry my good don, there is no
ill will between us, no hidden animosities, we are friends,
compadres, I do not begrudge Gustav his moment of indeci-
sion, no, I would be the first to admit that the life of an
ex-poet is not for everyone, and if the truth be told, Gustav
may never be able to give up poetry completely, he composes
even as he sleeps, though you would swear he was wide
awake, but every now and then, well, let me just say he seems
to be sleeping peacefully, and then wham, just like that, his
torso springs into action as if he is experiencing the pain of a

sudden cramp, but instead of crying out in agony, he opens
his bloody mouth (he is always chewing his tongue or his lips
while he sleeps so there is always blood collecting in small
pools on his pillow) and the words of a fully articulated,
majestically conceived poem, usually a love sonnet, but occasionally an elegy, come pouring out as from a geyser or an
inverted sewer, unfortunately, if you ask Gustav about his
country of origin he might not tell you, I think he is a little
embarrassed, I think he believes his poetry is no good, I think
he believes his poetry is hampered by the vulgarity of his
native language, which is certainly something a critic might
say, but any poet with a compassionate heart will tell you that
kind of crap is, well, it is utter crap, that's what it is, but we
all believe what we believe, so I will tell you where Gustav is
from, though there's not much to tell, he was born in
Saarbrücken, Germany and he spent a year or two in Munich,
as every good German should, and his family owned some
property just across the border in Behren-lès-Forbach, but
there was some dispute over the title, and after his father died
in 1899 he left Germany for Buenos Aires, where he thought to
make a fresh start, but after ten years he was bored, or he
became the victim of a disastrous love affair with a peasant
girl straight off the Pampas, or perhaps she was an indifferent
socialite who didn't care how she wasted the vanishing days,
or no one would publish his poetry, not even *La Revista*, a
journal with a rather unimaginative name that appeared only
sporadically, it is true, with a few volumes in 1899, and a few
more in 1900, and then they closed down for a few years, but
as soon as they secured additional funding, which was always
a problem, they were back at it in that tiny little office in
Montevideo, which is in Uruguay, not Argentina, as I am sure
you know, and which does not seem all that far from Buenos
Aires if you are looking at a map, but in reality it is a fairly
long journey from one city to the other, you have to take an
overnight steamer across the La Plata river, which they should
really call the La Plata estuary, which perhaps you did not
know, but all that is beside the point, what I was getting at
was that the rents were very high in Buenos Aires in those
days, at least in the neighborhoods the editors of *La Revista*
were looking at, but they were a good deal cheaper in

Montevideo, most likely because Argentina prized liberty and
went on the gold standard and Uruguay prized equality and
the redistribution of wealth, so the editors of *La Revista* went
to Montevideo, not too far from the Fortaleza del Cerro, if I
am remembering correctly, though far enough that you
wouldn't want to walk, yes, yes, a weather-beaten ramshackle
building on the corner of Egipto and Francia that was once a
fish warehouse or a cannery or a repository for abandoned
fishermen's boots, who can truly say, but the smell of fish was
peculiarly strong, almost nauseating, but they had a view of
the harbor and a view of the Isle of Liberty, also known as the
Island of Rats and the Island of Gulls and the Island of Rabbits
and Pigeon Island, and *La Revista* published everybody in
Latin America, José Enrique Rodó they published, and Rubén
Darío, naturally, though he was living in Spain by 1898, so
they probably just lifted a few poems from his first collection,
which came out in '96, and Amado Nervo and Ramón López
Velarde and Julio Flórez and the towering Chocano and
Ricardo Jaimes Freyre, with that sonorous, silky voice that
smothers us all with its beauty, and Luis Lloréns Torres and
Juan Zorrilla de San Martín, that sad, forgotten patriot of tiny,
egalitarian Uruguay, and Federico Bermúdez y Ortega, a poet
with an aristocratic style who nevertheless was able to capture
the undeniable pain of the underdog and so became a voice
against oppression in the Dominican Republic, and Gastón
Fernando Deligne and his decadent visions, and Filinto de
Almeida, an average Parnassian poet who lives, they say, in
the shadow of his wife, and José de Diego and Rafael
Obligado, the old man of Argentine poetry, who strove tirelessly for sober and clean expression, and Carlos Guido y
Spano, who was even older than Obligado, but everyone loved
that crazy old romantic lunatic because he paved the way for
Darío and his disciples, and Manuel González Prada, who was
a philosopher as much as a poet, and Juana Borrero and João
do Rio, that brilliant imposter, and Salvador Díaz Mirón, and
the musical poetry of José María Eguren, and Luisa Pérez de
Zambrana, and perhaps the greatest of the Cuban poets, Julián
del Casal, who died of tuberculosis in 1893 at the age of thirty
but they continued to publish him anyway, how could they
not, and Bernardo Guimarães, who was still going strong even

twenty years after his death, and Luis Muñoz Rivera, whom I
have seen once or twice on the streets of San Juan in the days
since I first arrived, as one sees the fleeing shadow of a startled bird, or the black smoke from a rapidly spreading fire
surging up towards heaven, and Guillermo Valencia, who
didn't write all that much poetry and was perhaps a better
translator than a poet, in fact this was most certainly the case,
and Silva, who cannot die, and so many others, a host of
others we have all forgotten, so it just goes to show, but what
does it matter, that is the question before us, what does any of
it matter, those examples, the boredom, the failed love affair
with the peasant girl or the diffident socialite, the inability to
get published, they are all really just facets of the same nightmarish reality, 'a black sun floating effortlessly across a black
sky,' one of Gustav's images, I think, or maybe he stole it from
a French poet, and so he left Argentina without sadness or
regret, there was nothing left for him there, and now here he
is, newly arrived in San Juan, as we all are, the three of us,
within the last six months.'

-59-

　　How quickly life becomes a knot of tangled strings!
Yes, yes, that is an appropriate metaphor for what happened
next. But to appreciate the nuances of this unfolding tale, the
strange twists and turns, you have to understand why the
three ex-poets had gone down into the small chamber beneath
the patio to begin with, and to place that understanding in its
proper context, you should probably know a little something
about the nuns who had lived in the building that was once
a convent on Caleta de las Monjas. The nuns had been forced
to abandon the convent in 1903. It is a very strange and sad
tale. If I were to give it a title, I would call it *La triste pero
milagroso viaje de las monjas* (The sad but miraculous journey of
the nuns). It is really no different than the journey we are all
taking.

La triste pero milagroso viaje de las Monjas:

The convent had been in pretty bad shape even before
the Carmelites had been forced to move. It had sustained
significant damage from the great earthquake of 1819, damage
that had never been repaired. There was a lingering crack in
the foundation along Caleta de las Monjas, and a section of
the subterranean crypt beneath the interior patio had actually
collapsed as a result of the crack, creating a small antechamber
before the crypt itself. No one from San Juan had offered a
hand to help clear away the rubble, and certainly the nuns
themselves were ill-equipped for such dangerous work.

By the end of the 19th century, the crypt had been all
but forgotten. By 1900, only two nuns among the twenty-three
that remained cloistered within the broken walls of the
convent on Caleta de las Monjas even knew the hidden crypt
had ever existed. The first was Sister María Eugenia Berrios,
an octogenarian who had been in charge of the archives since
before the terrible war with Spain had erupted and so knew as
much as there was to know about the convent's history. The
second was Sister María Amàlia Garrido, who had taken on
the duties of Mother Superior in 1877 with the death of Sister
María Rosalita Perea, who had seen the earthquake of 1819
with her own eyes.

Then in May 1898, tragedy struck again. *¡Ay de mí!*
Truly, our lives can be described as a happiness that becomes
a sadness in search of a happiness. In that month the convent
sustained further damage, some would have said irrevocably
so, during the bombing of San Juan by the Americans. None
of the Sisters were injured, though their sense of serenity
was perhaps bruised beyond repair. But there was no talk of
leaving. The convent was their home. Besides, where would
they go? So the good Sisters simply closed off that part of the
convent which most resembled an ancient ruin and continued
with their daily prayers and spiritual devotion.

In 1903, however, a new Catholic bishop was installed
in the Archdiocese of Puerto Rico, a North American named
Monsignor Blenk. He was neither willing to set aside any
church funds to repair the convent, nor allow the nuns to
remain among the rubble, claiming in a brief meeting with
Sister María Amàlia Garrido and two other nuns held on the

steps of the Cathedral at nine o'clock on a Monday morning
that 'the nuns could not show the proper devotion to God
inside a structure that, because it was crumbling before our
very eyes, no longer afforded its occupants the peace and
serenity that was necessary for contemplative pursuits,' and
then he looked at Sister María Amàlia Garrido with a strange,
quizzical expression on his face, as if he could not quite
remember who she was or why she was bothering him, and
then he said 'God helps those who help themselves,' and that
was that. So the Carmelites were forced into exile, as it were,
but without the means to really go anywhere.

Eventually they made their way to the other side of the
island to the village of San Germán, otherwise known as the
city of hills, where they were forced to beg accommodations
from the villagers, for San Germán was very small. There was
only a small Gothic style church known as The Gate of Heaven
(Porta Coéli) up on a hill that overlooked the main plaza of
the village. Next to the church there were the abandoned
ruins of a 16th century monastery. In other words, there really
wasn't any room in San Germán for nineteen Carmelite sisters
(four had died between 1897 and 1901) and two novices (who
had entered the convent in 1902).

The villagers did their best to make sure every nun had
a roof over her head and a comfortable bed. Most of the Sisters
were afforded the luxury of at least a small closet of a room to
themselves, though several of the younger ones (including the
novices) had to share bunks with the small children of their
hosts. All of which meant that the Carmelites were unable to
live up to their Carmelite vow to abstain from the pleasures
and pains of the world.

It was never clear whose idea it was to journey to San
Germán. Perhaps Monsignor Blenk had simply read over a list
of Puerto Rican towns and villages and picked San Germán
because he liked the sound of it. Most likely because he had
a German relative. Or perhaps it was because San Germán
had been the second city founded in Puerto Rico, and it might
have become a thriving metropolis in its own right, large
enough to rival San Juan, had not repeated attacks by French
raiders in the 16th century slowed its progress, a sequence of
historical events that clearly Monsignor Blenk was ignoring

or had not known. He must have thought that this city that
had become a village had somehow transcended its destiny.
Or perhaps the Sisters themselves chose San Germán because
Carmita Ponce de Leon, a descendent of none other than Juan
Ponce de Leon himself, lived in San Germán, and they (the
Carmelite Sisters) counted among their early benefactors Doña
Ana de Salamanca, who had married a great-grandson of the
great Conquistador, so perhaps they had felt a connection
of some sort, however tenuous, and had written to Carmita
and told her of their desperate circumstances, and she had
written back and invited them to San Germán and said they
were more than welcome, she understood the plight of the
exiled better than most, why her own daughter, the poet
Lola Rodríguez de Tío, had twice been banished from Puerto
Rico, first in 1867 by that idiot stooge of the Spanish, Captain
General José María Marchesi y Oleaga, who had himself been
an exile during the Carlist Wars in Spain so he should have
known better, and again in 1889 by Governor Pedro Ruiz
Dana, another in a long line of Spanish puppets who was
pretty puffed up with his own importance, but now, who even
remembers what he looked like, so, yes, yes, yes, she understood the plight of all exiles and the pain and suffering that
lingers for years and even when you are finally able to return
to your home the pain is still there, that was the way it had
been with her daughter, ¡Qué alegres son las horas! Did they
know that poem? It is an amazing poem. Her daughter had
written that poem. 'How joyful are the hours! Like a flock of
doves wandering across the skies.' Yes, yes, no one understood
their plight better than she did, they were more than welcome,
she would be thankful for the company.

So the Sisters journeyed to San Germán. Naturally, they
prayed in earnest to the Immaculate Virgin to assist them in
their necessity, for they found it quite difficult to maintain a
contemplative focus in such a tiny village, especially when
their prayers were interrupted by clanging pots and screaming
children and the braying of animals at all hours of the night,
and though the Immaculate Virgin did answer their prayers,
she withheld her answer for six years to test the depth of their
need and the sincerity of their devotion.

Then in 1909, precipitated ironically by the sudden

departure of Monsignor Blenk, who was moving on to greener
spiritual pastures (some said Boston, but no one really
knew), the Carmelites returned to San Juan, settling, as was
already mentioned, in Santurce in San Mateo parish. Father
Josef Correa spearheaded a fundraising drive on behalf of
the itinerant nuns. He was the pastor of a small church in
Santurce (Iglesia San Mateo de Cangrejeros, the Church of the
Crab Sellers) on the corner of Calle San Jorge and Avenida
Eduardo Conde. Work soon began on a small three story
convent adjoining Father Correa's church, and a few months
later, on the 14th day of July 1909, two days before the Feast
Day of Our Lady of Mount Carmel, the nuns moved into the
first floor of their new home (it would take another six months
before the rest of the building was finished). Two days after
that, on the Feast Day itself, at approximately eleven-thirty in
the evening with a warm sweet breeze that smelled of almond
trees and mariposa blowing through an open window, the
Immaculate Virgin visited Sister María Amàlia Garrido in a
dream.

The first thing the Immaculate Virgin said in Sister
María Amàlia's dream was that the Carmelite Sisters were to
begin keeping two gardens. One would be an enclosed garden
only for the nuns, in keeping with their vows. But the second
would be a garden for the community of hopeful souls that
had embraced their return. It would be a garden of eternal
gratitude.

The second thing the Immaculate Virgin said was
that the Carmelites needed to restore to their rightful place
everyone who had ever lived and died in the convent on
Caleta de las Monjas. She reminded Sister Amàlia that they
had left much more than a few crumbling walls of stone and
a few fractured memories when they left their historic home.
They had also left behind the remains of their fellow Sisters
who had died in the eternal embrace of their cloister to await
the hope of the Resurrection. She said the Carmelite nuns of
Puerto Rico would never feel completely settled into their new
life until everyone who had joined the Order from the day
the convent first opened its doors in 1651 until the present
day had made the sad but miraculous journey to Santurce.
According to Sister María Eugenia Berrios, who spent several

hours every day buried up to her eyeballs in the archives of
the Order, several documents dating back to the 1600s indicated that there were four burial sites on the property. These
sites contained two-hundred eighty-six Carmelite nuns and
twenty-nine lay persons, but aside from names and dates in
a ledger, there was little information. Sister Eugenia was not
even convinced that the documents were accurate. One of the
burial sites was beneath a tiny church that had been turned
into a small library in the 1780s. A second was apparently
beneath a small chapel that had been given the name The
Chapel of Our Lady of Mercy. A third was beneath the clois-
ters themselves. And the last was beneath the interior patio. Of
course the good Sisters were hardly the sort to wield pickaxes
and shovels and push wheelbarrows about, just as they had
not been the sort to remove rubble after an earthquake. So the
Carmelite nuns turned to Father Correa for assistance.

Father Correa hired the three ex-poets to begin the
delicate process of unearthing the deceased Carmelites and
transporting whatever remained of their earthly bodies from
the purgatory of their abandonment to the cemetery of Villa
Palmeras.

The work began in earnest on November 8, 1909.

Coincidentally, it was on that day that the three ex-poets
first laid eyes upon Tiká, who introduced herself, as you
already know, as a soldier of fortune named Sebastian de
Urquiza, and who, as you have probably guessed, decided to
join this crew of vagabond gravediggers in their impossible
(some would say absurd) quest to reunite two halves of a
broken mirror.

Tiká proved to be quite adept at sifting through the
rubble and locating one gallery after another, each containing
a dozen or more burial niches. She was a virtuoso. The three
ex-poets wondered if all soldiers of fortune could smell out
death as easily, and they were suddenly somewhat afraid
of their new companion, but their fear was tempered by
their growing amazement at the reverence with which Tiká
approached each of the deceased nuns. They had not suspected that soldiers could possess such unrestrained devotion
for the dead. It seemed to be a gift of godlike, perhaps superhuman origins, a concoction of aberrant thinking, no doubt,

which would have been unnerving to say the least, except that
the three ex-poets, being literary men, had long ago accepted
the power of the imagination to reshape reality.

It was actually quite incredible to behold. Tiká would
make the sign of the cross as she knelt down before the skeletal remains of one nun or another, and then she would stare
for a while into the liquid darkness that seemed to shimmer
just above each body, as if she had fallen into a deep well or
was asking for forgiveness. Then the ground would tremble
slightly, as if the universe itself were granting her absolution,
an absolution that was seemingly conferred upon the three
ex-poets as well, indeed, the three ex-poets swore that in those
moments when the ground shook, they could smell the faint
odor of white gardenias and the salty sweetness of the sea, a
miracle which both ex-poet Rodrigo and ex-poet Victor Hugo
believed was a sign of God's infinite grace. Then Tiká would
climb out of her trance and the smells would vanish and she
would say who it was that had been buried in that particular
niche and when she had died, and the three ex-poets would
write down the name and the date and any other information
Tiká might provide. Then the three ex-poets would busy
themselves with wrapping up the remains for transport to the
cemetery, and Tiká would go on to the next burial niche.

Later, well, ex-poet Rodrigo could not help but mention
the miracle of Tiká's bizarre trances to Father Correa.

'Sebastian is like a lightning rod unto God,' ex-poet
Rodrigo said. 'He is like a portal to another realm,' and before
Father Correa could react, ex-poet Rodrigo grabbed him by the
arm, a clinging sort of half-embrace, and began to whisper as
one conspirator to another, 'we cannot do this work without
him, Father Correa, he is indispensable.'

So Tiká was officially hired as a day laborer by Father
Correa on behalf of the Carmelite nuns.

'As long as there are bodies to be discovered, you shall
have employment,' he told her. He did not say anything about
her strange, fantastic ability to decipher the gleaming patterns
of darkness that surrounded each corpse and so divine who
they were. He did not want to know how Tiká was capable of
such magic. Though he was willing to concede the existence
of miracles from a distance, he was not so willing to confront

one face to face. So he let it go. But before he left Tiká to her ongoing work in the crypt beneath the interior patio, he mentioned in an off-hand way that Sister Amàlia wanted to speak with her (meaning Sebastian de Urquiza), partly to express her gratitude in person for doing the work of the Immaculate Virgin, and partly because she always met with those in her employ, but also to discuss what Sister Amàlia said was a transgression of some significance, most likely committed in ignorance, but she (Sister Amàlia) wanted to ascertain that for herself. Father Correa said he would arrange the meeting.

-60-

A list of those who were buried in the first gallery in the crypt beneath the interior patio:

Sister María Rosanna Rivera (d. 1661).
Sister María Inés de Vargas (d. 1663).
Sister María Inés de Maluenda (d. 1664).
Sister María Consuelo Serrata (d. 1665)
Sister María Thérèse Serrata (d. 1665).
Sister María Florentina de Perea (d. 1666).
Sister María Concepción de Guerra (d. 1668).
Sister María Maravillas Cabrera (d. 1669).

Doña Ana de Salamanca (d. 1670), who had married Juan Ponce de León y Loáisa, the great-grandson of the famous conquistador, and was buried as a lay Carmelite because she had always admired the Carmelite Order. After her death, her husband embraced a religious life.

Sister María Luisa de Oviedo (d. 1671), who was uncertain just what to do with herself at first after learning that her husband had died on board a galleon during a naval battle between Spanish and Dutch forces off the coast of Pernambuco, Brasil, but then she realized that her husband's death did not bother her as much as she had thought it would, in fact, she suddenly felt a sense of liberty that had been denied her for oh so many years, and so she took to throwing

wild even extravagant parties, the kind of parties that were
common in San Juan in those days, at least among a certain
portion of the populace, until one night her dead husband
appeared to her in a dream, and he was not angry with her,
for he understood the need to blow off a little steam as well as
any man, but he did observe that she seemed to have lost her
spiritual way through excessive frivolity, and then he said that
if she ever hoped to pass through the Pearly Gates, a destiny
that he himself had not yet achieved, then she might consider
curbing her appetite, and then he suggested that she enter
the new convent in San Juan, that would do the trick, and she
woke up the next morning quite beside herself, for though she
realized everything he had said was true, she could not quite
believe he was the one to speak the words, for he had not been
a religious man, and if he had said anything remotely similar
while he had been alive, she would have laughed in his face,
assuming that he was being sarcastic, but as he had traveled
all the way from his watery grave off the coast of Brasil to the
sunny shores of Puerto Rico on her behalf, she felt obligated
to follow his advice, and so three weeks later she went down
to the convent on Caleta de las Monjas and committed the
remainder of what had been a worldly life to the service of
God.

Sister María Feliche Amarjuelas (d. 1672), who
descended into a life of vagrancy and prostitution after her
husband was killed during a terrible hurricane which struck
San Juan on September 12, 1615 (a hurricane which, incidentally, destroyed part of the roof of the Cathedral), but who
was later redeemed and entered the convent in 1652.

Sister María Isabel Carrizosa (d. 1676), who entered the
convent in 1661 after her husband, a Captain who was part of
the garrison at Fort San Cristóbal, died of an unknown tropical
disease.

Sister María Assunta Luna (d. 1679), who entered the
convent in 1655 after her husband died defending a Franciscan
monk in a street brawl with two Basqueros, a brawl that
occurred just after midnight outside a private gambling house
on Calle Guamani, where the monk was a frequent visitor.

Sister María Catalina Cerralta (d. 1680), who entered
the convent in 1659 after her husband died under violent and

therefore suspicious circumstances upon returning to Spain at the request of the Court of Valladolid.

Sister María Catalina Sarmiento (d. 1681), who lived the life of a lonely widow after her husband died of what was probably Yellow Fever (which he contracted while accompanying Padre Juan Alonso de Solís y Mendoza as he went around the island baptizing Indians), but later, after a great deal of soul-searching, she entered the convent in 1671 with a fully consecrated heart.

Sister María Manrique de Lara (d. 1682), who entered the convent after her husband was lost at sea in a hurricane while traveling to Mexico.

Sister María Clemencia de Girona (d. 1684).

Sister María Inés Figueroa (d. 1684).

Sister María Celestino Collazo (d. 1685).

Doña Ana de Lansos y Menéndez de Valdez (d. 1686), who, after her young husband, Pedro de Villate Escovedo, died in 1625 during the siege of San Juan by the Dutch, devoted the rest of her life in the name of God to ministering to the physical and spiritual needs of the young women of Puerto Rico, who were suffering greatly from the unending wars with France and Holland, and in 1636, at the request of the Immaculate Virgin Herself, who appeared in a halo of light one Sunday morning while doña Ana was praying in the Cathedral, she (doña Ana) asked the Spanish Crown if she could start a Carmelite convent in San Juan, and after her petition was granted, she sold all of her worldly possessions and transformed the very house that she lived in and which had been in her family since the founding of San Juan into the Monastery of Our Lady of Carmel of San José, and in July 1651, she and her sister Antonio and four novices became the first Carmelite nuns to call Puerto Rico their home.

Sister María Antonia Menéndez (d. 1687).

Sister María Isabela de Córdoba (d. 1690).

Sister María Juana de Forera (d. 1691).

Sister María Blanca Estremera (d. 1692), who entered the convent after her husband had left her to go to Chile with Alonso de Sarabia to fight the Indians and subsequently died an unheralded but doubtless heroic death on the plains of Valdivia.

Sister María Margarita Mendoza (d. 1693), who entered the convent in 1657 at the age of twenty-two after her father died of unknown causes.

Sister María Isabel Gudiel de Prado (d. 1693).

Sister María Beatriz de Luna Carrizosa (d. 1694).

Sister María Leonor de Forera (d. 1695).

Sister María Consuela de Prado (d. 1695).

Sister María Beatriz de Cárdenas (d. 1696), who entered the convent in 1674 after her husband was killed in a duel (swords, naturally) by a young nobleman who had recently arrived from Trujillo, Spain.

Sister María Blanca Ayala (d. 1697).

Sister María Teresa de Gonzalez de Oviedo (d. 1698).

Doña María Calderón de la Barca y Quijano (d. 1699), who was buried as a lay Carmelite because of her family's great sacrifice to the glory of God, having sent two sons of Spain (older brothers to doña María) to join with Fathers Andre de Soveral and Ambrosio Francisco Ferror, and twenty-four intrepid soldiers from Portugal, on a journey to bring the Word of God to the native peoples of Brasil, a journey from which they did not return, the entire party being massacred by Indians on the 3rd of October, 1645 in the village of Uruacu.

-61-

Truly, the journey those Puerto Rican nuns took was an incredible journey. But what is more fantastic is that their history is so very fluid. You can look closely at what you think took place, only to find that you have no idea what happened at all. The sad and miraculous journey of those nuns was like that. And it still is. The passing years have transformed their simple journey of weary footsteps into something much more grand. Truly, nothing is ever what it seems to be. I know, for example, that in 1959, Barbara Hutton, the heiress to the Woolworth's fortune, bought the old convent from the Archdiocese and turned it into a fancy hotel called El

Convento, but her interest in the hotel lasted only a few years
and then she sold it to a Mexican hotel chain and then it was
called the Gran Hotel El Convento. But what meaning lies in
these simple facts? I know that the Puerto Rican government
got involved at some point in the years that followed, I guess
because they wanted the convent back from the Mexicans.
But so what? I know that in 1995, a group of San Juan businessmen bought the property and renovated it once more and
they changed the name back to El Convento. I know that these
businessmen wanted a luxury casino, and the government said
okay, so they (the businessmen) brought in all sorts of heavy
construction equipment to begin the casino project, but at this
point, the Carmelite nuns, who had moved into a brand new
monastery in Trujillo Alto some years earlier, they were tired
of all of the rigmarole concerning the ex-convent on Caleta de
las Monjas, they wanted an injunction to stop the casino project because they said there were close to one-hundred nuns
buried beneath the convent and that it would be a disgrace to
their memory to build a casino on top of all those graves with
all those gamblers rolling dice in the bright lights above and
the floozies watching eagerly, and of course they were right
about that, it would have been a disgrace, but it just goes to
show that they had forgotten their own history, they found a
document (a letter? a page from a diary? a bill for services?
an accountant's ledger? an official statement from the bank? a
note from the Bishop? a newspaper article from a now defunct
newspaper?) buried away in their archives that said a partial
exhumation had occurred in 1909, and they took this tidbit to
be the whole truth without realizing that 1909 was simply the
beginning of the delicate process of transporting the remains
of two-hundred eighty-six nuns (not close to one-hundred, like
they thought) and twenty-nine laypersons (which they weren't
even aware of), give or take, from the boarding house that
had once been a convent across town to the cemetery of Villa
Palmeras, yes, yes, they had forgotten their own history, which
I find highly amusing, but in truth it is the same, or will be,
with all of us, so it is probably better to laugh now, if you can,
yes, laughter is wonderfully cleansing, but where was I, oh
yes, so at any rate, despite the best efforts of the Carmelites,
they could not stop the casino project from moving forward,

I think this was in 1996, and according to the newspaper account I read, a construction crew was digging up the interior patio because they were going to put in an elevator shaft for the new luxury casino, and they had only been digging for about an hour when they discovered the ancient crypt that had been there all along, and they were amazed at their discovery and wandered about the crypt for a while with flashlights, but it was still pretty hard to see clearly, so someone set up a halogen floodlight, and then they could see clearly enough, they saw an oval shaped chamber made of stone, and the stone walls were very black from age and dampness and mold, very Spanish looking, which you would expect, but they were kind of out of focus, the walls, because they were glistening in the glare of the halogen lamp, and they (whoever 'they' was, the construction workers, I guess, or the construction workers plus the reporter, the article didn't really say) saw the original underground entrance to the chamber and a narrow stone corridor on the other side, but the light from the lamp didn't carry that far so the corridor disappeared into an inky, shimmery blackness, (this was the reporter talking), as if it were a snake swallowing its own tail, and then they (the same group as before) stood in the center of the crypt and gave it one last look, a dozen heads turning on a swivel, and they counted thirty-three burial niches like the gaping wounds of Christ, all of them glistening (dripping?) with moisture and the bloody memories of another era. Every single burial niche was empty (though nine contained evidence that they had recently been the home of ferrets or weasels or other small creatures that preferred to roam about at night). That is what I know. That is what I once read. But what does any of it mean?

-62-

The meeting between Tiká and Sister María Amàlia Garrido:

On a pleasantly warm afternoon towards the end of November 1909, Tiká and Sister María Amàlia Garrido met in a small garden containing several rose bushes, a layer of Colombian Skullcap, a few coral plants with their tiny red flowers winking with lascivious delight at the sun, a saúco plant without any fruit whatsoever but laden with many clusters of white, star-like flowers, like distant galaxies seen through a telescopic lens, and a single stone bench, slightly curved, with pedestal feet, where Tiká and the good Sister Amàlia sat.

The garden was half a block from the Church of the Crab Sellers and was known to everyone in the neighborhood as the Garden of Eternal Gratitude. There was no fence or barrier of any kind to prevent a single soul from enjoying the peace and serenity offered by those colorful perennials amid the lush greenery of the tropics. It was the very same garden that the Immaculate Virgin had asked the Carmelite nuns to maintain on behalf of the hopeful, kind-hearted citizens of Santurce.

'Ah, my young and enigmatic don Sebastian de Urquiza,' said Sister Amàlia, 'you have made quite an impression on our dear Father Correa. He does not know what to make of you.'

Tiká tried to smile politely and look Sister Amàlia directly in the eyes, but all she could manage was a grimace that looked like she was suffering from a sudden wave of nausea. Her eyes became fixed on Sister Amàlia's hands, which contained a rosary, as you would expect, and a small leather book which was not a bible.

Tiká's mouth was very dry. She tried to say something, or she did say something, but her words were unintelligible to her own ears and fell noisily to the ground like pebbles. Sister Amàlia understood Tiká's meaning nevertheless.

'The good Father is descended from Ponce de León himself, as are many of us in Puerto Rico,' Sister Amàlia said. 'Perhaps all of us,' and she laughed. 'But Father Correa has not yet conquered that absorbing egotism, so deadly to others, that was so much a part of the great conquistador's personality.'

'. . . .'

'Do you see what I am driving at don Sebastian?'

Tiká did not quite understand but Sister Amàlia pressed on.

'There are many soldiers of fortune wandering aimlessly about the streets of San Juan, either by their own misfortune or the design of God, but you are the first to take up residence in the ruins of our convent,' she said. And then: 'In which category do you belong?'

Sister Amàlia's voice was soothing, like honey to coat the throat, so Tiká did not realize she had been asked a direct question. Her eyes remained fixed on Sister Amàlia's hands. The good Sister was silently, methodically, but also absent-mindedly, counting the beads of her rosary with her fingers. She had abandoned the small leather book to her lap.

'What I mean to say, don Sebastian, is that you are a surprise to me,' said Sister Amàlia. 'We may no longer live in that grand colonial building built to withstand Indians and hurricanes and the tropical heat, an amazing structure built by Spanish engineers years ahead in their thinking, but we are very much aware of what goes on behind its walls. And so you are very much a surprise. A puzzle.'

Then Sister Amàlia explained that the Carmelites still owned the ex-convent on Caleta de las Monjas. She said when they had left in 1903, Monsignor Blenk had suggested that they rent the building to help defray the cost of moving to San Germán. The Archdiocese took fiscal responsibility, and for close to a year the ex-convent housed several small retail shops and a barbershop and even a dance studio, but they didn't do very well and so one by one they ceased to exist. She said the building had been completely abandoned since then, and that with the departure of the Monsignor, the Carmelites had once again assumed control. Sister Amàlia said that there had been some talk of turning the building into a boarding house, but they had made no decision as yet.

Tiká said she had not known the history. She said when she first arrived in San Juan she had met two men who had mentioned the possibility of renting a room on the third floor, a room with a balcony view of various rooftops but not much else, though they did say that she would be able to hear the Cathedral bells quite easily. Sister Amàlia wanted to know what men, what did they look like, what were their names, but Tiká did not really remember. Tiká said the two men wore dark jackets and they smelled vaguely of oleander, but she

didn't remember what they looked like. They had become
faceless. Sister Amàlia commented that it was odd they should
smell of oleander, so much like the smell of death, and Tiká
agreed.

Then Sister Amàlia asked where they had met and if
they were still lurking about and what was the nature of
their arrangement with Tiká, and she looked at Tiká with
compassionate (hauntingly compassionate) but also piercingly
determined eyes.

Tiká said they had first met in a seedy waterfront dive
called Casa de las Aguas. She had been in San Juan three
weeks at that point and was beginning to tire of living in one
of those nameless hotels down along the waterfront (in spite
of the fact that such places certainly fit the persona she had
established, though she did not mention this). She knew she
would soon begin looking for a quiet refuge away from the
prying eyes of the world, but at that point she was not looking
to move just yet. Why she had gone into Casa de las Aguas
that particular evening she could not say. Perhaps she had
been thirsty. She did not remember about that either. But she
did remember the two men were sitting at a small table near
the back of Casa de las Aguas and invited her over. They had
been drinking amarettos for several hours and Tiká joined
right in.

Later they took her to the house on Caleta de las Monjas
and Tiká could not have been more delighted. The prayer
she had not yet given voice to had been answered. She gave
the two men a five-peso note on the spot with the promise
of more. She told them she would place the same amount in
an envelope the first Saturday of every month and put the
envelope in the bottom of a small clay pot she had noticed at
the bottom of the stairs leading up to the room. She had been
religious in her diligence with respect to payment. Five pesos
every month, a little high perhaps, San Juan was not Barcelona
or New York City or even Havana, but she very much liked
her third-floor room with a balcony view of various rooftops.

That was the last she had seen of the two men. Every so
often an envelope would linger in the clay pot for two or three
days. But always by the fourth day the pot was empty. Once
she had gone back to Casa de las Aguas to thank the two men

(why she thought they would be there she could not say, but her naiveté was well-intentioned), but the establishment had become a small dry goods shop. Tiká had never once considered the possibility that she was trespassing.

After Tiká had finished with her explanation, Sister Amàlia regarded her with a curious, undecipherable expression on her face. Quite without meaning to, Tiká adopted the same expression. It was almost like two mirrors staring blankly at each other, each mirror reflecting the otherness of a world that is both familiar and unattainable.

Sister Amàlia seemed on the verge of vanishing into herself.

She became a beam of sunlight bending in the wind.

'The stone which the builders rejected is become the cornerstone,' she said.

Tiká wanted to ask Sister Amàlia what she meant by this cryptic pronouncement. (Did she often go about quoting the Scriptures? Or was there a hidden, secondary meaning in her words?) But the good Sister was now wholly preoccupied, as if she had forgotten she was sitting on the pedestal bench in the Garden of Eternal Gratitude and thought she was kneeling instead before the altar in The Chapel of Our Lady of Mercy in the Monastery of the Carmelites in the days before the Americans had arrived, immersed in thoughtful contemplation, remembering, perhaps, the very first conversation she had had with Sister María Rosalita Perea, who had taken her aside one afternoon to reprimand her for the sin of perpetual tardiness and the two nuns ended up talking for several hours about the great earthquake of 1819 and how the pain of that tragedy was still fresh, a burning memory, and so they were both late for Vespers on that day.

Then Sister Amàlia, who in that moment seemed like a crazy person to Tiká, picked up the small leather book she had left in her lap (a very musty smelling book, Tiká thought, like the kind her uncle seemed to enjoy) and looked closely at the first few pages and laughed a meaty, robust laugh, a somewhat unusual laugh for a nun. 'I had wondered why God had placed this tiny gem of a book into my hands this morning,' she said.

The book was called *Historia de la monja alférez doña*

Catalina de Erauso, escrita por ella misma. It had first appeared in 1630, but whatever copies had been printed in those days had long since vanished, a subtle reminder of the transitory nature of all things. The version in Sister Amàlia's hands had been printed in Paris in 1829.

'I suspect this little book has been the source of a great deal of sparkling conversation over the years,' Sister Amàlia said. 'It is the true story of a disenchanted nun who flees her convent in Spain and travels to the New World disguised as a conquistador, if you can imagine that.'

Tiká opened the book and tried to read the first paragraph, but she could not even get past the first sentence.

She began to feel dizzy, even nauseous.

She looked up at the sky and saw a ring of spinning lights.

She felt a searing pain race across her forehead and then she seemed to be falling.

She wasn't sure if she was suffocating or going blind.

Then she heard a voice of honey floating across the void.

'Do not worry don Sebastian de Urquiza, your secrets are safe with me.'

-63-

Tiká remained in the ex-convent on Caleta de las Monjas in her third-floor room with a balcony view of various rooftops for the rest of her life. She began putting the envelopes with the five-peso notes into Sister Amàlia's hand instead of the empty clay pot, until Sister Amàlia herself said payment was no longer necessary. (It is worth noting, by the way, that the building did become a boarding house in 1917, but the Carmelites had not the heart to turn away the indigent, and so by 1923 this vestige of the colonial age was filled to overflowing with tenants without two nickels to rub together, as the saying goes, mostly young widows with scads of children or low-level government workers who could barely make ends meet even with the gift of a rent-free room or disenfranchised veterans of foreign wars who drank away their pensions without regret.)

So she became the wise old man of the boarding house that had once been a convent. She also continued to work for the Carmelites. Long after the last of the remains of the dead nuns had been exhumed and reburied in the cemetery of Villa Palmeras, Tiká began doing odd jobs for the Carmelites in Santurce, sweeping walkways, hauling supplies, repairing windows and replacing roof tiles that had blown away during the many storms that rattled the island, and maintaining the exterior of the new convent as well as the grounds of the Garden of Eternal Gratitude.

Every nun who took refuge behind the walls of the monastery in Santurce knew the name of Sebastian de Urquiza.

There was a great deal of speculation, naturally, about why Sister Amàlia kept Tiká on the payroll. Some of the younger nuns were convinced that the two were secret lovers and that don Sebastian would stop at nothing until he had wooed the good Sister away from a life consecrated to God. The younger nuns thought Sister Amàlia's immortal soul was in danger, for they did not see how anyone could deny themselves the pleasure of don Sebastian's company. They thought Sister Amàlia would willingly and inevitably drown in a sea of licentious depravity in spite of her age. As proof, these believers in every tale of star-crossed lovers ever written would point out that every so often, especially late in the afternoon when the crushing weight of unrequited love in the tropics makes it difficult to breathe, the don could be seen lingering for a bit by the iron gate that forever separated the cloister from the rest of the world.

Others, older nuns who were past the age of menopause and had thus experienced more of the pain and suffering of this life of eternal poverty, were still awed by the otherworldly reverence the good don had shown and continued to show their deceased sisters, who were now resting comfortably in graves shaded from the sun by the leaves of jacaranda trees or laurels. They believed that don Sebastian was or would become a symbol of the transformative power of God's eternal love for us all. This, they said, is why Sister Amàlia had hired him in the first place. She had looked into the darkest recesses of his soul and seen the truth of who he was. As proof, they would remind the younger nuns that the good don Sebastian visited the cemetery of Villa Palmeras every Sunday afternoon to honor the memory of the two-hundred eighty-six Carmelite nuns and twenty-nine lay persons who had made the journey from Caleta de las Monjas. Father Correa had told them so. Father Correa had said that in spite of the internal tragedy of don Sebastian's circumstances, he had been transformed by God's all-consuming love.

What tragic circumstances, the younger nuns cried, though you could clearly see by their body language that they thought they knew the answer.

We asked the very same question of Father Correa, the older nuns said. So we will tell you. Father Correa believed that Sebastian de Urquiza had been born a man by mistake. God meant for don Sebastian to enter into His service as a Sister of the Carmelite Order. 'I do not know how don Sebastian's destiny came to be derailed even before his birth into this lamentable plane of reality,' Father Correa had said, 'but the unexpected, seemingly unnatural, even bizarre reverence don Sebastian had shown your fallen Sisters is, when you look at it through the unblemished reflecting lens of God's giant celestial telescope, simply the reverence of one sister for another. It is tragic even as it is touching.'

-64-

And so we come to the end of Tiká's story.

During the summer of 1937, Tiká became quite ill. Sister Amàlia had died in 1919, taking to her grave the secret she had glimpsed in the Garden of Eternal Gratitude so many years earlier, so it was up to Father Correa to look after the ailing don. Father Correa was in his late seventies and scarcely able to get around himself, so he arranged for a young and very excitable nurse, who worked in a small hospital in Santurce but lived nearby on Calle Fortaleza, to visit the boarding house on Caleta de las Monjas twice a day.

Every morning at six and every evening at four, the excitable
nurse would stop by the don's room and the two would sit
out on the balcony and look at the various rooftops and the
sunlight dancing on the few Spanish tiles that had not been
blown away or shattered by the storms of the preceding three
centuries. The excitable nurse would fix Tiká breakfasts of rice
cereal and tea and late lunches of avocado soup (which had
become Tiká's favorite) and water mixed with a few drops
of lemon juice. Then she would read poetry while Tiká ate,
mostly the poetry of Julia de Burgos, who had become very
popular by 1937, though she had just turned twenty-three; but
also a few neo-romantic poems by Mercedes Negrón Muñoz,
poems which had been published in the newspaper, El Mundo
(Tiká particularly enjoyed a poem called "Arras de Cristal");
and also a few unpublished poems by Colón Pellot, a poet
who attacked the myth of the sexually promiscuous mulatta
and so was somewhat at odds with Muñoz; and every so
often she would read a few poems by Lola Rodríguez de Tío,
which very much touched Tiká's withered, weakened heart.
But Tiká's favorite poem during the two months of her slow
but steady decline was an exceptionally musical poem called
"Festival Song to Be Wept" by the poet Luis Palés Matos.
When she first heard the excitable nurse read this poem she
thought it was about the hypocrisy of not admitting to the
forces that shaped one's destiny. But after two or three read-
ings she began to hear a strain of something else beneath the
words of the poem, something slightly satiric, but also sinister.

The poem moved her in ways she could not
comprehend.

As she listened to the excitable nurse read, she thought
of her shamelessly opportunistic and yet strangely idealistic
lover, Nicario. She thought of her father and the dream of the
white bird. She wondered what had happened to her sister,
Isabel. And what had become of her daughter? Strange as it
may seem, and it certainly seemed strange to Tiká, the poem
reminded her of the feverish twists and turns of her own crazy
life.

Only once, and this occurred just after the last rays of
the sun had vanished, did she share with the excitable nurse
what she thought about the poem. She interrupted the nurse

midway through what might have been the seventeenth reading and said she was overwhelmed by the haunting, lyrical beauty of this poem with its swirling Afro-Caribbean undercurrents of violence and forbidden sexuality and voodoo mysticism and the eternal longing to be liberated from the tangled dreams of others.

Then the nurse continued with the poem in the darkness, reciting from memory. '*Los negros tórtolos bailan cantando salmos oscuros a Bombo, mongo de África*,' she said. Tiká sat back in her balcony chair, closed her eyes and smiled, as if she could hear the dark psalms being sung by black faces illuminated only by firelight, as if she could feel the beating of the mysterious African drums reverberating across the Atlantic.

Death came for Tiká one week later.

The excitable nurse was again reading the poetry of Luis Palés Matos. She read until the sun began to set. She was so intensely focused herself on the strange haunting beauty of the poetry and giving her oral delivery just the right mixture of indignant rage and ironic nostalgia that she did not even notice when the evening Angelus bells of the Cathedral began to ring. Then it was too dark to read without a light so she stopped, and it was only at that point that she realized don Sebastian had fallen into a sort of catatonic delirium. He was staring at the darkening sky with a strange, wild expression plastered across his face, a look of exaggerated mania mixed with the glow of sudden understanding. Only his thin bluish lips were moving. They were forming words at a fantastic rate of speed, yet there was no sound, just a gentle breeze as profound as musty earth blowing out of his mouth. The nurse could also see that the don's breathing pattern had become very shallow, so she leaned over to check for a pulse, even as she realized there was nothing she could do to forestall the inevitable. But as she leaned close, she heard the faint, hoarse whisper that was all that was left of Tiká's voice. She realized at once that the don was baring his mortal soul before God. She grabbed a pad of paper and a fancy fountain pen she kept in her purse to record the details of the don's deteriorating health (temperature, bowel movements, how much he ate while she was there, etc.) and lit a small lantern resting on a heavy mahogany table, salvaged from the halcyon days of the convent, which was set against the wrought iron balcony railing. Don Sebastian de Urquiza was sharing the secrets he had kept locked away in his heart since he had left Spain for the Caribbean oh so many years earlier, and though the excitable nurse had already missed a sizeable portion of what the don had said, she was determined to make up for her lack of vigilance and write down every single word that flew out of his mouth, however bizarre or devoid of meaning, during the few hours that were left.

The deathbed confession of don Sebastian de Urquiza as captured by the excitable nurse between 7:35 and 11:15 in the evening on July 31, 1937, one of the warmest Saturday evenings in years, but without even a hint of rain in the air, a confession which, as it turns out, was identical in every respect to the text of the long-vanished Third Note that Tiká had given her uncle:

My dearest Uncle, first let me thank you for being so patient during this most difficult trial. I did not mean to keep you in the dark for even an hour, but I let my own insecurities dictate my behavior. I told myself our need for secrecy was very great indeed. But it was really my need. I told myself that if your companion, Grenfell, had felt the tiniest pinprick of suspicion, our escape would not have gone as smoothly as it did. But I was not being entirely honest with myself, which means, my dear Uncle, that I was not being entirely honest with you.

So now the hour for secrets is past, and there are two which I must share with you before we go one step further. The first concerns my own reasons for leaving Spain. And the second, which is a tad more complicated, concerns why our good friend don Alfonso Alberto Sebastian Francisco de Hernani y Arredondo de Mariategui y de Esperanza, whose family has aligned itself with ours since the days of the Moorish conquest, has put his own reputation at risk on our behalf.

So let me begin with my first secret, why I left the only home I have ever known. My departure is the inevitable consequence of a shame I have carried with me for years, a shame which has kept me awake and vigilant for countless dark nights. And yet I have only myself to blame, in spite of what my father thought. You see in the summer of my fourteenth year, I began to take long walks with Father Mateus Antonio de Nazar of the Church of Santiago.

These walks were most assuredly innocent enough at first. He explained to me his view of the Scriptures and how they seemed to be losing relevance in an increasingly complex and materialistic modern world. He explained to me that our inability to truly know God was a consequence of this modern world. He explained to me that if we truly wanted to partake in God's bounty, we should look inward and not outward. Everything he said made sense. But what did I know? I was only fourteen. Naturally we began to share our deepest most profound desires, hopes that seemed too fantastic to ever come true. And the sharing of these desires, which had been a sharing only of the mind and the spirit up till that point, led to a sharing of our physical selves.

Yes, I knew even then how malignant and unnatural our behavior was, but I rationalized that every unseemly kiss, every intimate gesture and embrace, however pathetic or perverse to my Catholic understanding, would be seen by God as an act of pure love. I can only say now that a strange mixture of self-loathing and unrestrained lust must have filled my heart in those days. Perhaps that is what love is. I do not know. But whatever emotion I was experiencing, I know now as I suspected then that I was committing an unpardonable sin in the eyes of God.

Can you forgive me, my Uncle, for this monumental disgrace? Please, I beg of you, do not look upon me with disapprobation or reproach, for you are my last hope on this planet.

So to continue my sad, tragic tale.

As fate would have it, my father found out about my illicit liaison with Father Nazar one week ago. He was determined to murder the man on the steps of the Cathedral to show the world what becomes of priests who defile those who are untutored in the ways of men.

Fortunately, don Alfonso intervened and prevented the murder from taking place. He suggested to my father that he send me away to Barcelona and let the whole affair blow over. The don said he would take care of all the arrangements. Besides, he said, no good could possibly come of taking on the Catholic Church.

It was at this point, my dear Uncle, that I became aware

of Grenfell's sinister plot, and that the two of you had booked passage on the Conde Wifredo. Do not ask me how I found out. Let me just say that I realized you were in over your head, as they say, and would need some assistance to extricate yourself, and since the don had already put into motion the deus ex machina of my own escape, it was really quite a simple matter to include you in my plans.

Naturally, the don agreed. What is more, it was don Alfonso himself who suggested that we take advantage of the soon to depart Conde Wifredo to escape Spain entirely. He said there was no telling what fallout might occur should my father forget himself and murder Father Nazar in a last desperate act of revenge. If Father Nazar were murdered, then surely all of the details of our sordid love affair would be revealed during the course of the thorough investigation the Church would initiate, and I myself would most likely be charged as a libertine accomplice and hanged alongside my father. Then he said the fact that the boat you and Grenfell had chosen was the Conde Wifredo was a sign the hand of destiny was guiding events, for he (the don) personally knew the Captain, a seafaring cutpurse named Ramón Martín Cordero. So that is why don Alfonso purchased a stateroom for us on the Conde Wifredo. He was in fact quite delighted with himself.

Of course just because don Alfonso knows the Captain of our ship does not mean our journey will be without peril. We should not put too much faith in any but ourselves. Don Alfonso said Captain Cordero was a born sailor, but he was also an unscrupulous rogue of a man who would sell his own grandmother without regret.

When I asked him how he knew this, he smiled his lazy smile of a man who sits atop a mountain of wealth and said the Captain had been arrested by the authorities in Barcelona in 1892 for making indecent advances towards a young very wealthy widow whose family was distantly related to don Alfonso's wife.

The don said the woman wished to keep the details of the offending behavior from being disclosed in a trial, for then the whole affair would become a matter of public record, so she had asked don Alfonso to seek a more genial solution. I do not know what magic the good don had at his disposal, but apparently he went directly to the examining magistrate in Barcelona and within three hours he was able to secure for Captain Cordero a provisional release from jail so he could return to work for the Naviera Pinillos shipping company as the Captain of the Conde Wifredo, a position which he had recently acquired and for which, also apparently, no other seafaring man of good (or even decent) reputation and family background could be found.

'Better the devil you know, as they say, than the devil you don't know,' which is what don Alfonso said after he told me this tale.

Then he said he would wire ahead to alert Captain Cordero that we would be among his passengers and that we were traveling 'incognito,' as it were, a little subterfuge on don Alfonso's part. He said it is best to let the Captain think one thing and not another. The don has also asked me to tell you that in dealing with the Captain, one must always be cognizant of the fact that his good will almost always fluctuates in relation to the weight of his purse, which is a roundabout way of saying that he will respond to our requests with dramatically admirable speed as long as we pay him a sufficient amount in advance for his services. The don suggests that we allocate no more than five of the gold coins he has put into our hands to purchase the temporary loyalty of Captain Cordero. He says that should be more than enough.

Do you wish I had kept this secret to myself, my dearest Uncle? Can you appreciate why I offered it up to you, on the sacrificial altar of Abraham, if you will, so that we might journey to paradise unencumbered by the past? But before you answer in the affirmative, permit me to share with you my second secret, which is not a secret which belongs to me alone, no, that would be too much for a single soul to bear. It is a family secret that was only revealed to me this past week by none other than don Alfonso (and how don Alfonso came to be in possession of this secret is part of this tale). It is a secret that speaks to the sanctity of marriage and the purity of true love. Moreover, it is a secret that has been hidden all these years, even from you, my dearest Uncle, and perhaps even from my father, though don Alfonso believes in his heart of hearts that my father has suspected all along. Keep in mind that these are not my words. I am simply playing the role of literary amanuensis to capture the voice of the good don himself.

'Ah, yes,' said the don, to tell this tale the way it should be told, I must go back to the days before Arturo married your mother. Your mother's family came from Albacete, a city famous for its daggers, as everyone knows. Indeed, there are no daggers more famous for their bejeweled handles in all the world, with the possible exception of those created by the hand of the great Turkish artisan, Nikola Siyavus Hayreddin Yilmaz, but that is beside the point. Verona's family was of some stature in Albacete, not quite aristocrats, but they had a fashionable address near the Plaza de Toros, or so I was once informed. But I am not certain of this. And my father was certainly not certain. He thought they were gypsies, or dealers in stolen artwork. Perhaps they were.

'My father said they came to Logroño in 1860 in a dilapidated barouche drawn by two diseased chestnuts and then moved into a small second-floor apartment on Calle del Laurel with a vacant shop beneath. They certainly did not seem to be aristocrats. But according to my skeptical father, they arrived with the most tremendous collection of paintings one could imagine in their possession, though again, my father thought the paintings were either stolen or they were clever forgeries. There were some very large paintings by Madrazo, both the father and the eccentric son, and Goya's friend, Brugada, and a few early sketches by Marià Fortuny that had been part of a show in Madrid, and a forgotten painting by José Villegas Cordero from when he was just starting out, and several minor works by Casado and a copy of The Resurrection of Lazarus done in Casado's own hand, and there were dozens of smaller paintings by Pozo and Cancino and Carnicero and Montalvo and a host of others who are now only remembered by historians and aficionados. Verona's father had also acquired a fabulous painting in 1875 by the French painter Jean-Paul Laurens titled "The Excommunication of

Robert the Pious," a king of ancient France whose
piety was well-known but who gave up the hope of
the Resurrection to marry his cousin Bertha.

'So the vacant shop beneath their apartment
became an art shop and art lovers from as far
away as Zaragoza and Madrid came to peruse the
canvasses.   And so it went. Canvasses arrived
and canvasses were sold. Miguel Ramos Almeida
developed a reputation as a ruthless dictator when
it came to pricing art, and for more than a decade,
life was as predictable as clockwork. Even the birth
of Verona in 1862 did little to change this pattern.
But in the summer of 1876, the pattern did change
as if by divine decree. Verona, who had just turned
fourteen, began working in the art shop. She
was a clerk, a salesgirl, the only daughter of the
owner, but she dazzled the eye more than any of
the paintings, and as word of her great beauty got
around, the art-lovers who had before come only to
buy paintings came now just to catch a glimpse of
Verona's smile, for she was always smiling a smile
of honey-colored light.

'In truth, her smile sold more paintings than
the paintings themselves. Yet it is impossible to
describe how beautiful your mother was. Have
you looked carefully at those enchanting portraits
of her done by Joaquín Sorolla, a present from
Arturo in honor of her twenty-fifth birthday. They
are breathtaking, everyone says so, full of mystery
and a sense of wistful playfulness and a haunting,
melancholic vulnerability and yes, even magic. But
they do not come close to capturing your mother's
beauty. The truth of your mother's beauty is
impenetrable. Sorolla's paintings, fabulous and
mythic as they are, are but shadows of a half-
remembered dream. Oh, where is the wine of those
vanished days? Such sweet, sweet memories.

'But please forgive the foolish ramblings of an
old man. I loved your mother dearly. Let me just
say in my defense that it is a terrible tragedy to

look back on a life lived with so much unrewarded enthusiasm, the push and pull of disastrous dichotomies. So naturally I do what anyone would do. I look back with nostalgia to that precipice of a moment before my hopes were fractured.

As you might have guessed, there was a great deal of competition that summer among the boys of Logroño for your mother's attention. If she happened to look your way you counted yourself lucky. If she smiled at you in passing, you believed yourself blessed beyond any reward the priests could promise. And if, miracle of miracles, she happened to speak to you, well, that was too fantastic a possibility to even contemplate. But none of us could predict how she would respond. We became insufferably ludicrous shadows of our favorite Greek heroes. We forgot that we were sons of Spain, and in forgetting we became more ourselves than ever before or since. We were wrapped up in the catastrophe of cold lightning.

'I remember some of the boys brought her baskets of fish they had caught themselves, baskets of black fish and pike and perch and eels, all quite delicious, but she preferred chicken, Catalan style, with sausage and capers and raisins and wild herbs. A few wrote her long, desperate letters which she never opened because they were intercepted by her father, who then tossed them into the nearest roaring fire. Others would try to demonstrate their athletic skill by inviting Verona to that point along the Ebro where the old Puente de Piedra bridge had existed before it collapsed, and these lunatic daredevils would jump into the dark, placid but all-consuming waters and swim to the other side, weaving this way and that way to avoid the rubble that still blocked parts of the river, and when they had reached the opposite bank they would return as quickly as they could in the hope that she might offer them a handkerchief, a laurel to be paraded about as a symbol of their victory, but always by

then Verona had lost interest and abandoned them to an empty afternoon.

'Still others tried to impress her as connoisseurs of music. Every Saturday afternoon she received an elderly maestro for a piano lesson held in the back storeroom of the art shop amongst stacks of canvasses that had not yet been prepared for sale. The piano was one of those gilded, gold-frame affairs with miniature pastoral scenes painted on the panels. It was pushed up against a small oval window, blocking all sunlight. There was a cracked and weather-beaten back door on one side of the piano and a narrow dining room chair on the other. Every Saturday at precisely one o'clock, the elderly maestro would appear with his viola, sit down in the chair and play a squeaky tune on his out-of-tune instrument, and then he would sit back, exhausted from performing, his face glowing with the expectation that Verona would now be able to produce a flawless rendition of the melody after only a single hearing. Of course by then the many adolescent musical connoisseurs of Logroño had gathered in the alleyway dust beneath the storeroom window to dream of Verona's matchless beauty while she played, though on many an occasion they forgot themselves and started playing dice or wrestling with each other, and they would create such an ungodly and combative commotion that the elderly maestro would appear in the doorway like a calamitous wind or a deranged bishop roused from a deep sleep and chase away the dried leaves of their ardor with his precisely aimed bow. Each of those boys, I suppose, thought he was Odysseus trying to wrest free his beloved Penelope from the horde of suitors that had gathered like anarchists on her doorstep. I know that is what I would have thought. My imagination ached with bloodthirsty images. Ah, the stupidity of youth!

'By the next summer, attrition had taken its toll. To be blunt, there were only two competitors

left who stood a chance with this angel from another dimension, myself, and Arturo. We had not approached this adolescent game of love in quite the same way as the others. Instead of chasing after Verona with proof of our passionate intentions, we hung around the shop, sniffing at this painting or that one, feigning an interest in art. But even then we did not speak directly to Verona. We spoke to her father. So by the end of that first year we had acquired a genuine and knowledgeable appreciation for the Spanish masters and were thus able to hold our own in a heated discussion with Verona's father about whether or not Pozo was better than Cancino and whether or not Carnicero was better than both of them, and before we quite realized what had happened, Verona herself was laughing at our untutored naiveté or applauding our inventive, rebellious spirit.

'So it was Arturo and I. All the other boys, your uncle Andres included, who was decidedly younger but smitten nonetheless, all of them had tasted the bitter dust of defeat. Arturo and I felt that we had taken a step towards manhood. But I think what is more significant, at least looking back, is that at the end of that year, Arturo and I also swore to each other that no matter what happened in our heroic pursuit to win the hand of Verona, no matter which one of us should triumph, we would always hold one another in the greatest of esteem, as was befitting the sons of two families that had been aligned for centuries.

'I have to say now that I always felt in the depths of my soul that I was Verona's first choice. I mean no disrespect to Arturo, he is, after all, my truest friend. But in those days I was a dazzling white knight in the chess game of love, which is to say I was ready to take advantage of any opportunity that came my way, and lo and behold, towards the end of that second summer of our pursuit by non-pursuit, an opportunity

presented itself. In late August, as he did every August, Arturo's father headed to the monastery of San Andrés de Trepeana to pick up several barrels of the best wine made in all of La Rioja. Always Arturo's father had made this journey alone, but on this occasion, he took Arturo with him. I could hardly believe my luck. I suspected my future good fortune and happiness lay in Arturo's unexpected departure. I did not waste a moment. The journey to the monastery and back could be accomplished in as little as three or four days, though it would most likely take a full week.

'The art shop featured a storefront window where Verona's father would display paintings he had recently acquired. Beneath the window there was a narrow flower box overflowing with geraniums. Verona would water the geraniums every morning. During that second summer I had taken the bold though predictable step of leaving small notes for Verona in the box. If she spied such a note while watering she would pluck it out with insistent finality, punctuated by a flashing grimace of frustration instead of her honey-colored smile, as if she had discovered a dead mouse (or a not-quite dead mouse, though to be fair, your mother was not particularly squeamish) among the fallen blossoms, but then she would quickly slip the note into her apron pocket.

'When I first beheld that grimace my heart sank, but when she slipped that first note into her pocket and ran back into the shop, I knew that her grimace was a pose so that anyone watching would not guess her true feelings. So I continued leaving her notes. She never spoke about the notes, but I am certain that her heart hummed with anticipation when she saw one among the flowers.

'So the day Arturo left, I left a note in the geranium box. I did not know what romantic magic I might conjure with words, so I did not even try. I simply wrote: "Our friend Arturo has left with his

father. They will be gone a few days. I have little to
do this afternoon. If you are looking for me I will be
wandering through the green labyrinth of Parque del
Espolón. Do you think it will rain? That would be
appropriate. Perhaps I will stop a while and watch
the stone masons working on the monument to
honor Espartero. The masons are exceedingly rough
looking men. I am not sure they would even notice a
thunderstorm."

    'An hour later Verona and I were strolling
along Paseo del Espolón, lingering in the sweet
shadows of the maple trees and a gentle, warm
breeze tickling our secret desires, but only tickling.
We did not speak of love or paintings or anything
that would have ignited the spark of our passions.
We spoke instead of Arturo's absence and this
strange habit he had of whistling when he was
nervous, and why did Arturo reject all visible proof
of God's existence, this attitude really seemed to
bother Verona on that day, he had been raised in a
devout Catholic family as were all the rest of us,
where did such aberrant thinking come from, was
he possessed by some vagabond genie, a demon
spirit that had escaped the destruction of the
Moors, wasn't there anything I could do, I was his
best friend, did I not see what was happening, did
I not see that a great change had come over him,
a dark, foreboding shadow like the sky before a
thunderstorm (not the storm I had imagined), a sky
tinged with green, she had said, she had begun to
fear for the survival of his very soul, and on and on
and on she went.

    'The next day I left a second note and we
found ourselves in the Plaza de San Bernabé. We
walked back and forth past the arcaded shops for a
while, and then we sat on a park bench in the shade
of a few laurels, and next to us there were a few
vendors hiding inside their tents. And then we were
walking again, but our conversation that day was
the same as the one the day before.

'The next day I left another note, and the day after that and the day after that. We walked along the remnants of the old wall and we passed through the Puerta del Camino and we sat in the shadow of the old artillery tower and the rattling echo of those ancient Spanish cannons of death and we listened to the birds singing their dream songs in the trees. We paraded past cathedrals and churches lost in the swirling wake of the old women perpetually in search of an unlocked church door, but we never once thought to go inside ourselves and pray for God's forgiveness and so partake in the dark mysteries of eternal illumination. But everywhere we went we had the same conversation.

'I must confess that by the seventh day of Arturo's absence, I had lost all but the faintest of hopes that Verona would be mine. I do not remember even leaving her a note on that seventh day. All I remember is walking along the gleaming waters of the Ebro, lost in the labyrinth of my own disfiguring despair, wondering how the ghost of Arturo could so completely occupy Verona's mind. Then I was sitting on a bench somewhere, and I heard Verona's voice floating effortlessly across the void. Then I realized she was sitting right next to me. She was resting her head on my shoulder and whispering or sighing or singing softly into my lonely ear.

'At first I took her for an apparition, and I said so in a voice as flimsy as the net of street names and sunny days and lost keys and newspapers we use to wrap our bodies in a second skin in the hope that it will carry us to the shores of paradise, but she just laughed, and suddenly the honey-colored light of her smile outshone the sun with a ferocious intensity that made me tremble, and I looked up at the sky and was momentarily blinded. Then quite without warning, the church bells all over this little city of my tremulous youth began ringing and the sky was filled with so many dazzling *white storks that I could not help thinking (for I was quite superstitious in those days) that surely God was sending me an incontrovertible sign that Verona and I were meant to walk the path of destiny together, and then without reflecting for a moment about what I might say, I started babbling about the storks, I don't know what I said exactly, I was incoherent, I did not possess a scientific mind by any stretch, what did I know of the storks except they filled the sky when the church bells began to ring, but Verona was listening intently to every word I said, yes, the sewer of my stupidity was overflowing, but Verona did not mind, she enfolded me in the honey-colored light of her smile, and when I had finished she kissed me lightly on the cheek and said that no matter what happened, whatever choice she might make or whether her destiny would unfold without her consent, she would always love me for the irresistible, dreamy sweetness that lay hidden several layers deep behind a mask of rigid, calculating, self-indulgent posturing, a mask I no doubt wore because of my family's enviable social position, a mask which she hoped I might one day remove.*

*   'Was Verona, your mother, my one and only love? I will never think or feel otherwise. But the fates that look upon us with whimsical disdain decreed otherwise. In my case, fate took the form of my father. One week after Arturo had returned, my father casually informed me that as far as he was concerned, my childhood had come to an end that very summer and so I should discard all of my childhood infatuations and prepare for the business of life. And if that were not clear enough, he looked at me point blank with his darkly gleaming emotionless eyes — it seemed to me that I was staring at Death himself — and he said I was no longer to wander the streets of Logroño with Verona Almeida Vda de Miranda in search of love. He would not, he said, permit me to cavort with*

gypsies, however beautiful or mesmerizing. And that was that.

'I suspect now that during the single week Verona and I lingered on the lip of eternity, just the two of us, I suspect that Verona had somehow glimpsed the terrible tragedy that would befall our love. She understood better than I the forces that would shape my life. She realized from day one that my father would never allow me to carve out any happiness for myself. I was a prisoner of my family's history, a prisoner of all history. That is why Verona turned every conversation towards the absent Arturo. That is what I believe. And in support of this belief I offer you a summary of the final act of my Shakespearean tale of woe.

'Arturo Ordóñez Escoraz and Verona Almeida Vda De Miranda were married in the Church of Santiago on Saturday the 8th of December in 1877, one of the few days on the Christian calendar that wasn't dedicated to a saint, though it was on that date in 1854 that Pope Pius IX declared the Immaculate Conception a dogma of the Church.

'The wedding arrived with calamitous speed.

'It was as if a great tornado had descended upon Logroño.

'The banns were posted only once. On November 22nd, the feast day of Saint Cecilia the incorruptible, an old priest stood outside the church and announced to those strolling past that a wedding would take place in sixteen days.

'No invitations were sent, but everyone knew the whole town was invited.

'One week before the wedding I purchased a costume for the affair. I pretended I was the one getting married, not Arturo.

'The wedding went off without a hitch.

'Arturo was eighteen and Verona was fifteen, perfect ages for starting out together.

'Six months later, your sister, Isabel, was born.

'I went to Barcelona after that.

I was not happy, My father sent me as an emissary on behalf of his business interests.

'I stayed in Barcelona for three years.

'I did not write to Arturo while I was away, but I missed our friendship, so I went to pay him a visit when I returned.

'Arturo was away for some unknown reason, but Verona invited me in. We sat in the library and she played the same gold-frame, gilded piano that had sat in her father's storeroom for so many years. She said it was a gilded art-case Bechstein grand piano, a very famous piano that had come all the way from Berlin. I don't remember what tune she played, but I do remember I forgot myself while she played. I was transported back to my childhood, to the dust-filled alleyway behind the art shop, an unfractured moment when anything and everything was still possible.

'It was dark when she finished playing. She did not say anything for a moment. She looked at me from the piano bench and the honey-colored light of her smile lit up the room. Then she said she was terribly sorry things had turned out the way they had. She spoke with deliberate, unwavering forethought, as if she had been rehearsing this single line for years. She seemed sincere, but not weepy or sentimental. Then she asked me if I had considered removing my mask. The rest is like a dream. I remember we went upstairs. I remember dozens of various sitting rooms and bedrooms, but this could not have been the case. The house was not that large. I also seem to remember that all of the rooms were locked, but Verona held a key in her hand. I followed her as she went from room to room, unlocking the doors, lighting small table lanterns and then opening the windows to let an insufferably humid breeze swirl about, the white lace curtains billowing, the lantern light flickering. But the last room was not locked and the window *was already open and she did not light the lantern. She took me by the hand and led me to a narrow sea chest of a bed. It was hard to say how old the bed was. I remember thinking it was from the sixteenth century. Then we lay down in the dark and she began whispering softly, her lips grazing my cheek, her words all but unintelligible to my wondering ears for she spoke in the language of flowers or fish, or perhaps she was singing a lullaby her mother had once sung, or perhaps she was sighing one last sigh of eternal regret.*

'Verona and I were never again alone together in the same room. Whenever I paid Arturo a visit on a Thursday or a Sunday afternoon, Verona would mysteriously vanish, though I suspect she had gone no further than her own kitchen to sift through her collection of tiny opaque bottles, which contained rare herbal extracts from all over the world. I suspect she was searching for something, anything she hadn't tried before, to cure the inflammation of an aching heart, but nothing ever worked.

'I have never spoken of that evening in all these years, and I am certain beyond any expressible doubt that Verona kept her tongue as well. All the same, I suspect Arturo knew, as all husbands and wives know when something is amiss. Occasionally, even now, I wake up in the middle of the night, my bed clothes soiled with the sweat of my own stupidity and guilt, convinced that Arturo is trumpeting the truth to the world. Then I take a few short, furtive breaths, the kind a small hunted animal might take when a predator is nearby. Then I get up and head to a small table opposite my bed and fortify myself against the long night with a shot of Demerara rum imported from Venezuela, a habit I had acquired in Barcelona. Then again, perhaps I am mistaken about everything. Perhaps I imagined the two of us lying together in that forgotten sixteenth century bed. Perhaps I imagined those odd moments years later when I would catch Arturo looking at

*me in a certain way, a haunting mixture of disbelief
and vanity that quickly, inevitably, one might say,
hardened into a mask of denial and impenetrable
silence. Such is the way of things. But no matter
which of my memories is now open to dispute, no
matter which truths I have forgotten and which I
have invented, I can say with the unshakable pride
of one who has seen the darkness of the abyss and
lived to tell the tale, that almost nine months to
the day after I had returned from Barcelona in the
spring of 1881, your mother gave birth to a second
child . . .*

It was at that point, a point which to the ears of the
excitable nurse was a stunning but inconclusive climax, that
the death bed confession of don Sebastian de Urquiza ended
because don Sebastian had given up the ghost, as they say. It
was a peaceful death, a gentle but inevitable receding of the
tide. But for the excitable nurse the death of don Sebastian had
come too soon. She stared at the thin, blue, now unmoving
lips for a moment, dumbfounded, even disoriented. Was
the second child don Sebastian? Is that why don Alfonso
purchased a stateroom aboard the *Conde Wifredo*? Or was
the second child simply a half-brother or half-sister to don
Sebastian, in which case the inspiration for don Alfonso's generosity was still a mystery. Or was the story of Verona simply
a fabrication of the lovesick mind of don Alfonso? Or was it
instead a by-product of don Sebastian's addled brain as he
neared the deep waters of death? But if don Alfonso's account
was true, in both the historical details and the pervasive
almost unbearable sense of emotional loss, well, how could
Arturo have remained silent if his wife had loved another man
and had taken that man to bed? Who could stomach the agony
of such knowledge? Indeed, did Arturo really know the truth?
How could he know the truth and still wish to murder Father
Nazar for defiling a child that was not even his to begin with?
And what had become of the execrable Father Nazar anyway?
How could Arturo and don Alfonso consecrate themselves to
the purity of their friendship after all that had happened?
The excitable nurse read over what she had transcribed

again and again, but each reading exposed even more unanswerable questions. She tossed the pad of paper to the floor,
disgusted with her inability to penetrate the elusive mysteries
of this deathbed confession, and stared at the corpse of don
Sebastian. In the dim flickering light of the lantern it seemed
as if the don had simply fallen asleep and was now on the
verge of waking up. But of course this did not happen. The
excitable nurse found herself irrevocably drawn to the face
of the corpse and began assessing its features with greater
discernment. The thin blue lips seemed strangely feminine,
as did the aquiline shape of the nose. Then she noticed the
rounded slope of the shoulders and the slender arms and the
delicate hands (at least when compared to the hands of the
many drunken ex-soldiers that had tried to take advantage
of this dedicated nurse on a Saturday night). Suddenly don
Sebastian's hands seemed incapable of wielding anything
more deadly than a hymnal or rosary beads wrapped between
his fingers. The excitable nurse wondered that she had not
noticed any of this before. She wondered if the don had
undergone a transformation of some sort in death. Then she
recalled the brief conversation she and Father Correa had had
when he first spoke to her about playing nursemaid to a dying
revolutionary. 'You will find don Sebastian a compassionate,
amiable fellow, hardly the gruff, clichéd, explosively violent
sort one usually thinks of when one thinks of an ex-soldier,
and there is a deep sadness about him as well, a sense that his
life was a tragedy that could not be averted, like falling into
an ancient well,' Father Correa had said. 'What happened to
him?' she had asked. 'I do not know precisely. This pervading
sense of sadness is a common enough affliction among those
who have seen war,' he had said, and then his eyes had
narrowed, 'but there is something else as well,' and then his
voice had become almost inaudible, a whisper from beyond
the grave, 'I have said this again and again. I truly believe that
God meant for don Sebastian to enter into His service as a
Sister of the Carmelite Order. That is why the don has worked
these last twenty-eight years on behalf of the good Sisters.
I think don Sebastian was praying for the miracle of God's
transforming grace. I think he wanted the whole world to see
him as he truly was.'

And in that instant, the excitable nurse felt a pricking sensation on the back of her neck and she knew without any doubt whatsoever that the lingering spirit of the don was standing directly behind her, a being of pure energy like a Manichean beam of light, and she was unnerved by this sensation and screamed like a strangled bird, and then she gathered up the confession and the fountain pen and the rest of her belongings and fled, still screaming, from the balcony; and the ghost of don Sebastian de Urquiza, who had in fact been standing behind the excitable nurse for quite a while before she had sensed his presence, remained on the balcony which had become a portal to another dimension, a mute though interested witness whose heart went out to this startled good Samaritan stumbling about in the darkness of the apartment, cursing under her breath at the apparent lack of a telephone in this rundown boarding house on Caleta de las Monjas and then bolting through the door, still screaming as she ran down the two flights of stairs and out into the darkness of the street, still apparently bewildered by the lack of telephones, for she wanted to call Father Correa that very instant and tell him that don Sebastian de Urquiza had died but that his ghost was a terror to behold and that somebody should come and do something quick, never mind the fact that there were very few telephones in that part of San Juan in 1937, and that if the excitable nurse was, say, in her own apartment on Calle Fortaleza and suddenly wished to place a call, she had to go all the way down to the drugstore on Calle Recinto Sur, which is where everyone went in that part of town who wished to use a telephone.

BOOK FIVE

in the shadow of Hotel Milagro

Oscar Garcia Raimundi was a lonely young man with
a restless, lunatic spirit who dreamed of one day opening a
bohemian night club to rival the great dance clubs of Havana
during the Mafia days. But Oscar was not interested in the
glitzy, high-profile Mafia-owned cabarets and touristy clubs
with their palatial extravagance for the movie stars or politicians or socialites from America and their cash cow casinos for
gamblers from the East Coast or the West Coast or businessmen from Chicago or Indianapolis or St. Louis who had flown
in on a whim on Pan American. He wanted to open a club like
the clubs he had frequented when he first arrived in Havana,
the ones where you could find the real Cuba, like the Palermo
Club (always with a nineteen-piece orchestra so you felt like
you were floating in the clouds when you were dancing) or
the Rio Cristal Club or the Jungle Club in Pogolotti or Jiggs
Cabaret and Nightclub on the waterfront, or Oscar's favorite,
the sultry La Campana on the corner of Calzada de Infanta y
San Martin.

The first time he ever went to La Campana, which was
the first time he had been anywhere, was burned into his brain
the way a tattoo is burned into the skin, which is to say that
over time the edges had become blurry, indistinct, the ink had
faded, and yet even until the day he died he could still feel the
thrill of his beating heart on that night, an adrenalin rush like
a midnight hurricane, like fifteen foot waves obliterating the
beach, like falling in love for the first time, the shrill sound of
the women's alto voices shape shifting in the steamy night air,
becoming huskier, rounder, fuller, like a melody, like many
melodies, their laughter becoming boleros and Portuguese
fados and rumbas and sambas and mambos (the forerunner
of the cha-cha-chá), and nimble-fingered, buoyant guarachas
like sun-bright streams flowing fast from the Sierra Maestra
mountains, flooding the valleys below, and a few folksy,
back country Puerto Rican plenas, and a few tangos all the
way from the cobblestone streets of San Telmo, the oldest
neighborhood of Buenos Aires, hips already beginning to
gyrate slowly, legs swiveling around legs, eager, unrestrained,

sexy, passionate, because everyone in Havana was always looking for a place to dance until the sun came up, everyone was hungry to dance, and this dream of dancing through the night, a frenzy of bohemian lust, a madness wild as the sea that gives birth to the future, the feverish sounds of the black nightingales hidden in the waxy leaves of the tamarind trees, this was Oscar's first and only true love, it was his reason for living, it was the joy and burden of his restless soul.

Everything else bored him to tears.

Everything else was blasphemy.

Everything else was a cheat.

But mention night clubs and dancing and a jungle paradise under the stars and his eyes lit up like glittering diamonds.

That first night at La Campana, Oscar was only fourteen years old, or maybe he was nineteen, or maybe twenty-six, because no one ever knew for certain how old he was. When Oscar immigrated to Florida in 1957 he said he was thirty years old, but ten years later when he was running his own version of a bohemian night club between NW 35th Street and NW 31st Street in Miami, he said he was thirty-five, and ten years after that, when he married Isidora Escoraz Calzada in a secret ceremony at ten in the morning, he said he was fifty-seven, and he gave other ages at various times as well, but not to deceive, there was no thought of deception in his mind, no sinister intention, he simply could not remember.

The truth about Oscar's age belonged to a vanished world, a world of fragmented memories and half-remembered dreams like evaporating phantoms. All anyone really knew about Oscar was that he came from the other side of the island, from Baracoa, but rarely did he mention even a morsel about his family. It was as if they no longer existed and perhaps had never existed. Perhaps Oscar had left Baracoa because his uncle had died and what else was he going to do. Or perhaps his uncle had given him a little money, enough for the passage to Havana and a couple of nights to get settled, and his uncle had told him to get out while he could, before he became trapped like his uncle was trapped in a world where time no longer marched forward. Or perhaps his uncle had been arrested and was rotting in jail with only the saltwater smell of the sea floating in through the bars to let him know he was still alive. Or perhaps his uncle had gone up into the mountains in search of gold. Or maybe he had even boarded a steamer bound for Patagonia. Who knew? And who really cared? None of it mattered any more. The past. Oscar no longer cared about the past. He only cared about the future. He had some control over that, like writing his own destiny, and for Oscar the path to that destiny began on a steamy summer night in 1946 when to all discerning eyes he had barely outstripped puberty. On that particular night he stood in the shadows of a tamarind tree outside La Campana for over an hour watching the men and women streaming past, eager to dance to the honey-coated syncopated sound of Orlando Vallejo with a few muted trumpets in the background, or the sweeping, husky sensual squeal of Mayra Freire, who used to wave her arms in the air with balletic precision when she was on stage, or any number of Cuban singers and musicians hovering with delicate hope on the periphery of international fame, the men wearing tuxedos and black ties or white silk dinner jackets and white ties and their hair was slicked back on the sides like Rudy Valentino (this was just before the pompadour became big) and they wore boaters or sleek rimmed Panamas, the kind Humphrey Bogart would wear, and the women wore silk or chiffon dresses, some with ruffles, butterfly sleeves, a little outdated, and some wore bell hats or their hair was curled into a ball on one side. The men smelled of cigar smoke and cheap rum or leather soap or maybe Grant's Whiskey, and the women smelled of vanilla spice or Bergamot oranges and oakmoss or gardenias or lavender or peach. Oscar almost passed out from the heat of standing there in the shadows of the tamarind tree and the heady cloud of all those fragrances mixed together, all of the men and women chatting and laughing as they ran up the steps and rang the bell outside, ring the bell at La Campana from 9 till 4, that was the advertising all over the city on billboards and in the newspapers and even painted on the sides of grocery marts or drugstores, when in Havana ring the bell at La Campana, and there was a little cartoon bell with a smiling face and a dinner platter in one hand, a cocktail in the other, and he (the cartoon bell) was giving you an exaggerated

wink, as if he had just told you a juicy, sexual tidbit about
someone you both knew, and there was a single palm tree in
the background to remind you that this was Havana, Cuba, the
jewel of the Caribbean, the portal to the new world, the very
definition of paradise in the modern industrial age, and there
weren't any stars in these advertisements plastered all over the
city, perhaps because it would have been too expensive to add
stars, or too time consuming, or perhaps because they weren't
necessary, you knew they were there without drawing them,
you could feel them.

In all probability, Oscar would not have found the
courage to duck inside this first cabaret of his imagination had
not a masculine voice like a steam ship called out to him from
a passing bevy of womanly legs. Perhaps they were showgirls.
Hurry boy, the voice said, there are plenty of legs to keep you
snug and warm, to tease the life out of you, to squeeze you
dry, and then a twittering of female laughter billowing out
like white smoke, and he had scrambled to join them.

"Are you following someone or is someone following
you?" said the masculine voice.

"I am following you," said Oscar.

"Hah," cried the masculine voice. "Did you hear that
ladies?"

"Yes, Luis," cried the bevy.

"The boy has wit!"

And then some girlish laughter.

Once inside Oscar forgot about Luis and the showgirls.
Heart pounding, he ordered a bottle of beer and drank it
quickly. Someone tossed him a pack of cigarettes, a pack of
Regalias, and he smoked two or three in quick succession,
though he preferred La Coronas. Hours later he was sitting
at the bar, half a bottle of Ron Bocoy beneath his nose and
the vapors of the dark rum rising up like island gods, an
empty tumbler waiting to be refilled. He remembered he had
been talking with one of Luis' showgirls between numbers,
a long-legged black African with smooth ebony skin, skinny
dark legs like an ibis, and a nose like an Egyptian queen. Her
name was Nerea. For some reason their conversation had
drifted to her parents, descendants of African slaves who were
brought to Cuba near the end of the 18th century to work

the copper mines in the east and whose grandchildren were
freed in the 19th century and called *cobreros* but still worked
in the mines, and after that the great-great-grandchildren of
the grandchildren (her parents) lived on the edge of oblivion
between the murderous, sulphurous darkness of the past and
the cloudy skies of the future, but they had moved inland and
now lived in a small village, Ojo de Agua, in Las Villas, where
the sky was always a deep watery blue like the eyes of God
according to some, and the springs surrounding the village
had strange medicinal properties that some said had been
known since before the Conquistadors and which cured every
ailment from gallstones to malaria, and which in some cases
even extended the natural lifespan of a man (or a woman) by
thirty years or more, but Nerea said she didn't believe in all
that superstitious mumbojumbo, her parents worked in the
cane fields north of there and life didn't seem any easier for
them because of the water from the springs. But then Nerea
also admitted she hadn't seen her parents in years, she didn't
even know if they were still alive. It was easy to forget where
you came from living in Havana, she said. Then they were
talking about Oscar's parents, who had died when he was
very young and so he had been raised by a bachelor uncle
in Baracoa in a small concrete house that looked out at the
sea, but Oscar said very little about his family. All he really
remembered about Baracoa, he said, were the women washing
clothes in the river. Even when their husbands bought them
Bendix washing machines to ease their burden, they washed
their clothes in the river. Perhaps because electricity was an
intermittent novelty in Baracoa, even in the 1940s, and especially in the neighborhoods that stretched out towards the sea.
Or perhaps electricity was simply a myth, something his uncle
prattled on about but which did not yet exist, at least not
in Baracoa during Oscar's childhood, because there were no
roads to Baracoa at that time, it was cut off by the mountains,
so how could electricity have made its way from the rest of
the island when not even a road could get through? Yes, this
is how it was living in Baracoa. This is what Oscar told the
ebony skinned showgirl, whose name was Nerea and who
with her flowing, white-feather dress and her headpiece of a
shining golden sun like a halo and her thick curly black hair

flowing to either side with a single blood-red gardenia pinned
above her right ear suddenly reminded Oscar of the island
goddess Atabey, the Mother of all the Caribbean gods and
goddesses from the days of the first Indians, who was known
by many names, including Apito, Mamona, Guimazoa, and
Ieamaye, which sounded very much like the Orisha Yemaya,
a goddess of Africa who came to Cuba with the first slaves,
and she was known as the goddess of rivers to the Africans,
but after the passage she became the goddess of all the waters
and the Mother of the earth, and she later became the goddess
of all the Catholic saints as well, and sometimes she would
walk among the peoples of the small rural villages of Cuba
in a slave's woven skirt and a turban, her breasts bare, and
she would take the name Cachita Tumbo, and she had the
ability to cause the rivers to overflow their banks and flood
the villages and then the people would have to start all over,
which is, perhaps, what she wanted, and she also possessed
a power over the mystery of electricity, a little known tidbit
about the goddess that perhaps Oscar's uncle had forgotten,
and if she was angry she could be placated with honey and
oranges and eggs and brown sugar and a bottle of champagne
and another one of Anisette liquor.

All this Oscar saw in a flash when he looked at the
beauty named Nerea shining beneath her golden sun, and then
the vision faded and he was telling her about Baracoa. So the
women washed their clothes in the river, he said, and they did
not bother with the modern washing machines their husbands
bought them, which came by a freighter out of New Orleans
that arrived once a month bringing all sorts of merchandise
ordered from various catalogues, and they did not bother with
the electric toasters and radios and alarm clocks that arrived
in the company of the washing machines, yes, said Oscar, that
is how it was, and Nerea was looking at Oscar, at his profile
gleaming in the dim, noisy light of his destiny, at least this is
how it seemed to Nerea, but she said nothing. Oscar stared at
the noisy light reflected in his empty tumbler as he spoke. The
women of Baracoa had no use for the modern world, he said,
and so in fits of enduring madness they dumped their brand
new white washing machines and white alarm clocks and
white radios into a great white pile on the outskirts of the city,

a trash heap gleaming with unwanted appliances like so many sun-bleached skulls staring up at the sky.

That is what he remembered.

That is what he told Nerea.

Then Nerea was dancing with the other showgirls some more, three or four more numbers and their shining golden sun headpieces dazzling the patrons of La Campana with sudden flashes of brilliance in the dim, smoky light. Then the showgirls gave way to three singers with guitars and the cadence of poets, who wore black tuxedos with black ties and burgundy carnations pinned to their lapels, unlike the glitzy mambo groups who played the Tropicana and the Montmartre and wore clownish blue and white striped pantaloons for the tourists and wildly colorful mambo shirts and wide-brimmed Panama hats and wide-brimmed Panama smiles, though it must be said that even this trio later succumbed to the need for glitzy mambo costumes when they grew into their fame and played such venues as The Hotel Nacional de Cuba, where they wore yellow slacks and yellow silk shirts with billowy green and yellow sleeves like folded butterfly wings and orange sashes instead of belts and white Cuban-heeled shoes for keeping time and dancing along the edge of the stage. But here at La Campana this trio of poets dressed in their black tuxedos sang their boleros as if they were dying of unrequited love that very moment, and beneath their lingering, plaintive voices you could hear a habanera bass rhythm (boom — ba-ba-bop) and a trilling sentimental piano that caused the women in the crowd to shiver uncontrollably, and the muffled sound of a conga from the darkness just off stage that reverberated with the languor of eternal hope, and a few muted trumpets shining through the leaves of several fake palm trees, the palm trees glowing with tiny white lights. After the trio with the guitars there were a few more flashy showgirl numbers, and then the guitars and trumpets (and the piano and the bass and the conga) for the rest of the night and the crowd lapping it up, and after a while it was hard to tell how long Nerea had been gone or if in fact she had ever been sitting next to Oscar at the bar, perhaps he had invented their conversation, but it did not matter, he had plenty of rum to drink. Strangely, the more rum he drank — and after he

polished off one bottle another one mysteriously appeared
— the more he became aware of the people sitting at the bar
and those at a few nearby tables. Or at least he became aware
of their conversations, their words swirling about, washing
through him like the vapors of the rum, becoming memories
of a sort, filling the void where no memories existed, giving
shape to a life that he hoped would be his.

First he noticed the two men sitting next to him at the
bar. They smelled of cigars and fancy cologne and faintly
the salt spray of the sea. They spoke of things beyond his
understanding, but the raging passion that filled their voices
filled Oscar with a thrilling rush of adrenalin and the sudden
realization that here in Havana anything was possible.

"It is too late for Carreno," said a thin, whiny voice like
a mosquito. "First he says he knew who killed the Dupotey
boy, and then he says he did not know."

"Headlines, that's what he was after."

"Ah, yes, but that does not excuse the lie.

"Headlines. That's what they're all after!"

"It is like Marti said; the truth wakes up once and never
dies."

"They're all bastards!"

"He is not the man we thought he was. He has become a
caricature of himself, a cartoon. No wonder they have turned
on him. You cannot trust such a man."

"No, I suppose you can't."

"No. Too many lies. Too many unpunished crimes."

"Then it is a good thing they are getting rid of him."

The trio with the guitars ended one number, the angst
of their love lingering even then in the air, and the crowd
broke into a roar like the thunderous sound of the sea. Then
the trio began another number, but Oscar's eyes and ears
were drawn to a table of two men and three girls, all of them
dressed as if they were in dancing costumes, the men wearing
white *pantalones* and blue silk shirts with white ties and white
Cuban-heeled shoes, the girls wearing slinky red dresses with
slits along the sides, black nylons, and high heels that would
show off their legs and their dangerous, bursting at the seams
heart-shaped derrières in any kind of light. The two men
were busy talking, gesticulating wildly, as if they had come to

dance with only their hands. The three girls were trying to get them to stop talking and take them out on the dance floor.

"Grau is no better," said one of the men, a small, brown-skinned man with the long, slender fingers and bright amber-colored eyes of a Chinese merchant of mixed blood. "He says he wants to turn Havana into a refugee camp for suffering souls, a haven for democratic spirits. He says he wants to create a paradise for the poor. He is going all over the country making these speeches, but this makes no sense. He is stepping down. He has already said he wishes Prío to take over. What does he mean by telling such lies at this point? Does he think we are blind? Does he think we are stupid? What unforgivable insolence! We are all suffering."

"But at least he stood up to the Americans. How many Cubans have stood up to the Americans the way Grau did?

"Shit on the Americans. It is because of the Americans that we no longer know what is Cuban and what is not. They are worse than the Communists. They are worse than even the Fascists! Cigars and rum and daiquiris and pineapples and palm trees and sugar cane and the mambo and boleros at midnight and fucking on the beach, this is what the world thinks Cuba is. This is the lie that America has sold to the world. This is the cheap paradise we have become. But we are more than that. We are more than slaves to the greed of America. We have always been more than what America says we are. I say again, shit on the Americans!"

"You are too serious, my friend. Look around you. Look at these beautiful women. Listen to the slow, sexy pull of that bolero. That is the very soul of Cuba. Have another drink, my friend, and let one of these sexy ladies take you to the only Cuban paradise worth dreaming about."

The two men finished their drinks and one of the girls started moving to the bolero, a slow, sexy, uncontrollably sensuous, provocative, hip-swiveling sashay — pa-pa-push-pa-pa-baa-rum-baa, pa-pa-push-pa-pa-baa-rum-baa, pa-pa-push-pa-pa-baa-rum-baa — right there at the table, her eyes half-closed, her lips pursed, a slight puckering, as if she were mocking and teasing the men at the same time, and then everyone laughed and they went out to dance, the women pa-pa-pushing their way into the middle of the dance floor, their eyes now shining with the tiny white lights that illuminated the fake palm trees.

And then a table of three men and one woman, the men wearing silk dinner jackets, borrowed jackets to judge by the way they did not quite fit, their faces unshaven, their white ties already undone, the woman wearing an elegant gold sequined dress with a heart-shaped neckline, staring vacantly in the direction of the trio on stage singing their heart-felt boleros. One of the three men at the table leaned towards the woman, kissing the exposed skin of her shoulders, the nape of her neck, caught up in the rhythm and emotion of the music, but she did not even flinch. The other two were talking in drunken, overly loud whispers that on any given night might carry for miles.

"It is easy money?"

"The easiest."

"And it is lucrative?"

"Yes, it is very lucrative."

"How does it work?"

"Every week there is a steamer from Chile, or sometimes Argentina. You can buy as much as you like. A hundred grams. A thousand grams. It does not matter. They will front you for it. It used to go for $50 a gram on the street but now there is so much of it the price is down to $20."

"U.S. dollars?"

"Of course U.S. dollars."

"What's the catch?"

"There is no catch. Except do not short them on the money. They will kill you if you short them. They do not give second chances when it comes to the money. You come with me tomorrow night and I will set you up."

"Come with you where?"

"The Chinese quarter. A small café on Zanja Street. It is where we always go."

"What about the police?"

"They are already taken care of."

"And the newspapers? Every day they are saying how the police have caught some new drug dealer."

"That is all for show, my friend. A cabaret. Like the show here."

".....?"

"No. No. I mean they are not catching anyone of importance. Only the small fry."

".....?"

"Only those dealing in marijuana."

"You are certain of all this?"

"Do not worry, my friend. We are protected at the highest level."

".....?"

"Alvarez himself. Yes. The Minister of State. It is very funny, no? But he is a coke addict like any other, and he will do anything to keep himself supplied."

The two men laughed.

And then two women talking in the shadows of a giant potted fern near an open window with the blinds pulled up and the candlelight flickering and the moonlight washing across their table, and two empty chairs where their boyfriends had been sitting but they had left to go to their car because they had run out of cigarettes and there were a couple of packs of Regalias stashed in the glove box. In the moonlight coming through the window the two women lost all corporeal substance and seemed instead to be two vanished ghosts from a different time and place.

The women spoke with glittery, moonbeam voices.

"She was sleeping with her brother?"

"Yes, but she did not know that at first."

"How does one not know their own brother? Even if you do not know someone is your brother, you will surely taste it when you kiss him for the very first time."

"Yes. But perhaps that is not always so. At least it was not so in this case."

"She thought they were cousins?"

"Yes."

"And he was very beautiful?"

"Ah, yes, he was very, very beautiful. They said the stars themselves would fall out of the sky if he looked their way."

"Then I can see this happening. Yes, yes, a tragically romantic love, doomed from the start."

"But it was not doomed. That is what I was getting at."

"No?"

"For weeks she cried and cried and her mother and her grandmother tried to console her. Her mother said it was their sin, not hers. They had concealed the truth from her. They had concealed the truth from everyone to hide the fact of the mother's infidelity years ago. And then the grandmother said perhaps it would not be so bad because the boy was only a half-brother. At least it was not as bad as a full brother. God would surely forgive her. God would surely forgive them all. But the girl did not respond to any of their compassionate words or their gestures of kindness. All she did was cry. But the moment they left her alone she stopped crying. It was all subterfuge. The moment they left her bedroom she opened her window and there was a letter waiting for her in a rose bush just below the sill, just as she knew it would be, a letter he had slipped in between two thorny roses to keep it in place."

"¡Ay de mí! This is one who knows how to tangle up your heart. This is one who could be very dangerous."

"Yes, true. But he was deeply in love with her. He wrote to her every night for three weeks and he told her they would slip away from Havana and take a boat to Florida and no one would ever know. They would elope with their forbidden love, that is what he wrote."

". . . ."

"He said their love was the sky and the light. He said their love was the sea without an end."

". . . ."

"He said if they had a child together it would be as beautiful and bright as the children of the moon, their child would be like Hiali from the stories of the first Indians, Hiali the hummingbird, the only son of the moon and his sister who flew off to where the sea meets the sky to start a new life and carve out a new destiny, the first of a new people. That is what he was writing her. So what could she do?"

"Yes, you are right. She could do nothing."

"Her grandmother later found the letters, but it was too late, they were already gone."

"If only I had one such letter. To be loved like that."

"Yes, that is the way love is supposed to be."

"They should make a song about such a love."

"Yes, a steamy bolero, perhaps."

"Why do you suppose she left the letters?"

"Who can say? Perhaps they were in a hurry. Perhaps they could hear the footsteps of the grandmother coming to the door. Perhaps the police had found out about their sin and were coming to arrest them both. Or perhaps she had no need of the letters because she was going to be with him for all of eternity. True love is a mystery, that is all I can say."

The two women sighed long, lingering sighs of regret, almost like they were weeping.

"And to think that we are stuck with these two who do not know how to love, who only know how to smoke their cigarettes and flash their fancy Rolex watches to the world and then we go home and they fuck us quick and hard before the sun comes up, without even a murmur of feeling."

"¡Ay de mí! True love is such a rebellious bird, such a sad, lovely rebellious bird."

Then their boyfriends reappeared and the moonlight dissolved in their presence and they led the two women to the dance floor and all four disappeared into the myth of a new bolero.

-66-

Oscar sat at the bar in La Campana that first night until the early morning sun broke through the slatted blinds of the windows, and the small green lizards which were only ever visible in the twilight just before dawn and which had been snoozing comfortably in the corners, disappeared through a spider web of cracks in the walls. The music had stopped at five in the morning and the only people remaining in the bar other than Oscar were the performers from the night before, their agent (Luis), and the owner of the club. The trio with the guitars and two trumpet players were sitting along the edge of the stage, drinking and trading jokes and laughing, their instruments packed away but within easy reach, as if they were waiting for a train. The bevy of showgirls was scattered about the tables in twos and threes talking with soft, lazy,

murmuring voices, their golden sun headpieces scattered
about the floor, their heads flung back or their legs stretched
out in exaggerated, bathing beauty poses, as if they were
hoping to be discovered by a Hollywood movie director. Luis
and the owner, a fat *pachúco* wearing a bright orange zoot suit
and beige-colored Cuban-heeled shoes and a grimace that contradicted the brightness of the suit, were standing two steps
inside the front door. The owner was counting out a pocketful
of very large bills into Luis' hand. No one seemed to pay any
attention to Oscar, whose head was plastered sideways to the
top of the bar and who seemed to be barely breathing. The
fat *pachúco's* money disappeared into the hazy morning glow
of Luis smiling. Then Luis whistled and everyone started
for the door, grabbing guitar cases and trumpet cases and
golden sun headpieces stuffed under arms. Luis nodded a
quick definitive nod and the two trumpet players broke away
and with their free arms dragged Oscar outside, where Luis
instructed them to deposit the boy into the back of a 1937
Packard for a ten-minute drive to a dump of a hotel called
Hotel Milagro, one block from the Plaza del Vapor. The hotel,
with its Greek pillars and sculpted archways and a first floor
with a fourteen-foot ceiling, had been a bright, eye-catching
teal color years earlier, but the color had faded over time, the
paint flaking away in places, and seemed now a pale reflection
of the pale blue sea on a foggy morning.

Oscar slept the next five hours on a mattress without
a sheet in a room on the fourth floor without even a fan but
which possessed a narrow balcony that loomed precariously
above a hidden courtyard, with a view of dozens of rusty,
wrought iron balcony railings all around, the railings sagging,
a slight bowing in the middle, like ancient hinges beginning
to pull away from the crumbling stucco walls, most of the
railings covered with laundry recently washed by the washday
Madonnas and hung out to dry in the afternoon sun. He
woke to the sound of Nerea singing to herself, though he did
not recognize her voice, and the sound and smell of chorizo
sausage sizzling in a pan. He tried to open his eyes but the
light was too bright and the swarming, pestilent heat was too
heavy, so he just lay there on the mattress, listening to the
sounds of the singing and the sizzling sausage and his head

buzzing. Every once in a while the steam ship voice from the night before interrupted the singing with a question or a pronouncement and then a few words were tossed back and forth, and then a sigh of compliance, and then the singing began again. It went on like that for some time.

In the weeks after that first night, Luis took on the boy as a sort of volunteer charity project. He bought the boy a white linen suit and an immaculate Panama hat for special occasions. He asked Oscar why he had left Baracoa and Oscar said because there was nothing there, and this seemed to satisfy Luis. They talked of the dream of Cuba, Luis' favorite topic, and the fiery spirit of eternal revolution that had consumed the Cuban soul from the very first day Velásquez set foot on the island in 1511 in his costume of a Conquistador with his fierce horses clad in plated armor and his soldiers with their sleeveless chain mail vests, their pikes and swords and halberds and their eager, Pentecostal grins. But even so, Luis said, it took a year to subdue the traitorous blasphemy of Hatuey, the great Taíno chieftain, who had fled Hispaniola, traveling across the Windward Passage with four hundred Indians in canoes, and who upon reaching Cuba had preached insubordination to his Cuban brothers, telling them tales of Spanish greed and treachery and cowardice, atrocities committed by the Spanish in the name of a bloodthirsty god who coveted gold and jewels, as much as the Spanish could haul away in the ships that had arrived on their shores. And more ships were sure to come, Hatuey had said, but the Indians of Cuba did not believe him.

So Hatuey waged war on the Spaniards for a year, just the exiled chieftain and his band of four hundred, hiding in the mountainous jungles on the eastern part of the island and attacking the Spanish at dawn or at midnight or in the middle of the day when the priests or soldiers were sleeping in a haze of wine and sudden sickness. And all the while Velásquez himself was plotting out which new cities of gold he would create and how long before he would conquer the entire island of Cuba and what stood in his way, so he became maniacal in his hatred of Hatuey. When the Spanish finally caught up with this first Cuban insurgent, they bound him to a stake and set him on fire in a soldiers' camp in the shadow of a mountain on the banks of an unnamed waterway that would later be called the Toa River. As the flames began to lick Hatuey's toes, he asked the young priest who had lit the fire if there were many like him in the kingdom of his god, and the priest said there were many, and Hatuey laughed and said then he hoped he never found himself within the borders of such a kingdom, ruled by such a weak, miserly, jealous god who permitted atrocities to be committed in his name. Some of those who were present later said that the priest broke down before the flaming corpse of the great chieftain and wept until the ashes had grown cold. Some said the priest smiled and said there was no danger of that happening, his god had another place specially prepared for the likes of rebels and traitors. But most heard only the spitting hiss of the fire and a couple of popping explosions when the flames reached Hatuey's eyeballs.

Luis said that after the death of this first soldier in the battle for Cuban independence, the priest left Cuba to pursue a more contemplative life for the greater glory of God. But no one knows for certain. Some believed he then returned to Spain to hear the last confession of King Ferdinand the Catholic just before the king died in January 1516. Others believed he made his way to Venezuela in 1520 and later became a Dominican friar. And there were a few who believed he was none other than Bartolomé de las Casas himself, who later became the first resident Bishop of Chiapas, Mexico, and who also wrote passionately about the shameful mistreatment of the natives of the West Indies in his provocative chronicle *Historia de Las Indias*, but who was nevertheless accused of bringing about the slave trade from Africa through the Canaries to the New World because his views spurred the passage of the New Laws of 1542, which made it a crime to turn native Indians into slaves. In the end, said Luis, it didn't matter who the priest was or wasn't because most people soon forgot that chapter of West Indian history altogether.

So Oscar and Luis spent many long afternoons drinking mojitos and Sangria and bottles of cheap red wine, talking about the rebellion of Hatuey and the greed and treachery and cowardice of the Spanish, and the identity of the priest, and what had happened to the four hundred warriors that went with Hatuey, and whether or not they had been burned at the stake as well or maybe they had escaped and intermingled with the Spanish settlers, so perhaps their rebellious blood exists still today in the mixed-blood veins of Cuba's sons and daughters. Oscar wondered if the story was actual history or if it was only a myth, and what was the difference anyway and what did the story mean in either case, but Luis didn't usually weigh in on those more esoteric questions. Once Oscar asked Luis if he thought Cuba had finally achieved the freedom and independence that Hatuey had dreamed of, but Luis only laughed and said the Cuba that Hatuey dreamed of only existed in the imagination and in the heart, it was very much like the Cuba we dream of today, but he did not explain himself.

In addition to these spirited conversations about the revolutionary spirit of Cuba, Luis and Oscar also had many conversations about the future in general and their economic future in particular and how best to profit from everyone's natural desire to carve out a little piece of paradise for themselves. Perhaps Luis was looking to take on a partner in crime, a drinking buddy, a foil for all of his mistakes, for he was only twenty-seven when he met Oscar. Or perhaps he was simply possessed with the vainglorious but altogether accurate assumption that he could shape the course of a young (younger) man's life, particularly an impressionable young man from Baracoa, because he himself was an astute observer of the human condition as well as a man of some wealth and incredible charisma. In any case, he became Oscar's benefactor and encouraged the young man's growth in many ways, or to be more precise, he facilitated, spurred, kindled, rekindled, urged on, not in the sense of pleading with but in the sense of stimulating arousal, an explosion of personal growth, which resulted in Oscar being reborn in the image of Luis.

Luis was a small-time gangster whose passion for music was more of an eccentric hobby than anything else. He approached life with the kind of hard-boiled zeal typical of the characters played by Humphrey Bogart, though with a decidedly more joyful, self-indulgent, even self-deprecating appreciation of the beauty of life. He also possessed a well-honed survival instinct, or perhaps he was just plain paranoid, and so had adopted a professional persona based on those

secondary characters that played opposite the Bogart characters, like those portrayed by the movie star Peter Lorre (who
was born László Löwenstein in the Austrian-Hungarian town
of Ružomberok in 1904 and who fled to Paris when the Nazis
came to power in 1933, and then later to London), particularly
the character of the petty crook Ugarte in *Casablanca* (1942),
but also the insufferably incompetent and thoroughly effeminate (but not flaming) Joel Cairo in *The Maltese Falcon* (1941),
complete with a fancy, perfumed handkerchief that smelled
heavily of citrus and faintly of mint. Luis had more than once
turned the tables on his enemies, both seen and unseen, and
his competitors, both real and imagined, because they had
misjudged the nature of the man they were dealing with. So
Luis felt he had a great deal to teach the young Oscar from
Baracoa, who had only arrived in Havana three days before he
had appeared in the shadows of the tamarind tree outside La
Campana, which was one of several clubs that showcased the
talent Luis routinely discovered.

At some point during those first few months, Luis
suggested that Oscar take Nerea for himself or die trying,
for she was as beautiful and eager to please as any woman
on the face of the earth, and since Oscar was enamored of
this Afro-Cuban goddess, as he would always think of her,
and because Luis spoke with the conviction of a man who
has grappled with the Devil and won, Oscar happily agreed.
Soon, which is to say sometime during that first year, Oscar
and Nerea began strolling about Havana during a lazy
Monday or Tuesday evening (because the clubs were closed
on Mondays and Tuesdays) or on Sunday afternoons (because
what else was there to do), strolling arm in arm down the
Paseo del Prado, the tree-lined soul of the city, a sun-dappled
paradise, strolling for love and pleasure among the happy
promenaders. They passed by busy, bony-limbed men in black
jackets and white slacks and Panama hats or black fedoras
or black-brimmed cane hats and tan suits. They passed by
happy, smiling women who seemed to be floating on clouds of
remembered love in their Parisian dresses with capes or small
lace-covered hats or black hats with flowing silk folds down
the back to cover their necks, looking from a distance like
floating black swans. They passed by adolescent schoolgirls

in school dresses who were tasting for the first time the air of
freedom and dancing for joy because they were old enough
to walk home on their own, beautiful young ladies of the
afternoon who had not yet tasted love except for a love of
music, listening to the music of itinerant musicians as good as
any playing in the clubs but newly arrived, who were tired of
playing in dusty country dance halls and desperate to make
it big in the big city. Of course these ragged, newly arrived
musicians had not known they would have to wait their turn,
for there were thousands of musicians in Havana, so they sat
or stood beneath the sun-washed trees along the Paseo, alone
or in small groups, strumming their guitars and blowing on
their flutes or their horns and the deep rumbling echo of
their congas like summer thunderstorms in the mountains of
the Sierra Maestra, and the rolling flash of their *timbales* like
the sound of small birds learning to fly, their wings beating
furiously against the air until they suddenly whooshed away,
these handsomely decked out musicians in their white linen
slacks and crazy mambo shirts with blue or green or yellow
scarves tied loosely around their necks, making love with their
sexy, soul-thumping boleros and their heart-wrenching ballads
to anyone who would stop and listen and toss a few coins
into a straw hat. Like the schoolgirls already mentioned who
might follow a sweet-faced guitarist anywhere in Havana and
beyond. And all the while the crowd flowing up and down
the Paseo like the rippled beating of a young girl's heart, or a
young woman's heart, or an old woman's heart, except during
the middle of the day when even the pigeons might swoon
from the blazing heat.

     Or sometimes Oscar and Nerea would head down the
narrow streets of the old business district with its electric
street cars running back and forth on black wires like lumbering insects, their antennae extended, past the neon extravagance of restaurants or cafes with names like El Sombreros
or Celia's or Casa Martinez or Café Lafayette, past tall white
buildings from centuries ago with narrow balcony ledges
shaped in the Baroque style and sometimes flags or banners
draped over the wrought-iron railings. And sooner or later
they would find themselves strolling at the pace of a tortoise
(*a paso de jicotea*) along the wider streets like Calle Reina, past

the rows of innumerable shops buried in the cooling shadows of the arcaded walkways, open front shops with painted banners that might say *La Casa de la Suerte* and a painted picture of a cat holding a sword underneath. And always there were the old women in dark dresses with their white hair tied neatly back, survivors of all sorts of deceptions and youthful indiscretions and infidelities and tragically doomed love affairs, buying flowers to put on the tombs of their loved ones, or buying fruit and some plantains and some rice and beans for a little something to eat in the evenings, but no meat, their teeth were too old and brittle for meat, but maybe some sweets to take home for their grandchildren. And where the arcade suddenly vanished, the awnings had been pulled out so only narrow wedges of sunlight would splash across your shoulders.

And always there were trucks from one narrow side street or another trying to squeeze around the corners, some of the trucks carrying merchandise from the harbor to the department stores, like Herman's or Floglar Department Store or *La Época* with its imposing, postmodern, Cathedralesque architecture, or El Encanto with its stunningly elegant window displays of female mannequins dressed in silky black evening dresses with black satin purses or gold lamé gowns with gold lamé capes, the mannequins standing in front of wispy white or gold trees, the branches looking vaguely like ostrich feathers, or the Sears Roebuck where those with money bought refrigerators, or the Ten Cent where everyone else shopped. And some of the trucks were loaded with fish or melons or bananas for the markets, or maybe whitish gray pigs headed to a slaughterhouse, which probably meant the driver had stopped somewhere for a quick drink or maybe to visit a pretty girl with wide open legs in the Tia Nena Club on San Martin, a few blocks from the fancy hotels to the north towards the sea, and almost a mile from La Campana to the west towards the setting sun of Cuba, or maybe he just didn't know his way around Havana because the nearest slaughterhouse was on Calle E a few blocks from the water. And sometimes Oscar and Nerea would stroll past the outdoor beauty parlors with dozens of women lined up to have their nails filed and painted, and sometimes Nerea would join the

line, and sometimes not. And on one street there was a neon
sign that said Optica Nacional fixed to a crumbling façade,
and on another street they sold Florsheim shoes (another neon
sign). On other days they would duck down alleyways and the
smaller side streets and disappear into hidden courtyards and
get lost in an endless labyrinth of crumbling neighborhoods
where the air was filled with the smells of cinnamon and the
soft, sweet buttery smell of baking bread and the spicy tang
of cumin and garlic and orange spice mixed with Mexican
oregano, and the floral bouquet of Chinese wisteria and gardenias and jasmine, and the faint honeysuckle smell of lavender
Bougainvillea and the fruity, woody scent of Mariposa, and
the sweet juicy spray of Spanish limes and the heavy, buttery
butterscotch odor of dark rum and a hint of vanilla, and the
spicy, peppery flavor of Corojo cigars, and a hint of whiskey,
and the fruity, faint raspberry odor of Spanish brandy and
warm beer and fried steaks and sizzling pork chops and coffee
and cheap perfume and the earthy smell of rotting wood from
forgotten Spanish shipwrecks and the crumbling architecture
and the pungent smell of dead and dying fish everywhere
and the salt spray of the ocean that washed everything clean
again. And they could hear men and women shouting at each
other like souls lost at sea. And from somewhere a woman's
voice was saying *'perder guiro, calabaza y miel,'* a very lonely
sound like the tolling of a bell which meant someone had lost
everything. And from somewhere else there was the sound of
laughter, and from somewhere else dishes crashing to the floor
of a kitchen in a third- or fourth-floor apartment. And from
somewhere else the sounds of screeching parrots or white
cockatoos or birds of paradise from the South Pacific that had
been suddenly and inexplicably let out of their cages, and
then doors slamming shut and babies crying and cars starting
up and engines revving and the wheels of the electric cars
whistling, screeching in the distance, and the popping sound
of champagne bottles being uncorked, or perhaps it was the
sound of muffled gunshots, because anything was possible in
Havana, and radios playing ballads and boleros and mambos
and guarachas, and a radio voice selling washing machines,
and another radio voice selling Cannabis oil for rheumatism,
and the crack of several baseball bats all at once, the sounds

swirling about the alleyways and smaller side streets and
hidden courtyards like smoke seeking an escape.

But no matter where Oscar and Nerea walked, they
would always stop at some point in front of El Gallo on
Zulueta Street, a furrier shop that had opened its doors in
1922, and which stood directly across from what was once a
small café, Casa Oriente, which had also opened in 1922, and
which had been the pride and joy of Andres Ordóñez Escoraz
before he was murdered in cold blood, but it had closed the
year of his death and a small bakery now occupied the space
instead, so it was difficult if not impossible to remember what
came before because the smells of sweet breads and fruit-filled
pastelitos and meat-filled *pastelitos* and opera cakes with butter
cream icing wafting through the streets filled everyone's heart
and soul like a benediction. And Oscar and Nerea would
admire the fur coats in the display window of El Gallo,
unburdened by the tragedy of Andres Ordóñez Escoraz, with
Oscar laughing and saying why would anyone want a fur coat
in the tropics, and Nerea frowning and smacking him in the
shoulder or in the chest with her long, graceful fingers balled
up into a tiny, delicate fist and saying a fur coat wasn't a
matter of temperature, and Oscar pretending he had been hurt
but still laughing and then saying yes, yes, some day he would
buy her a fur coat, and Nerea softening, smiling, nestling into
the crook of his arm, asking if it really hurt where she had
smacked him and kissing his shoulder or his chest, and then
a long lingering kiss in front of the window, as if they were
the ones now on display, with her biting his lip, playfully,
passionately, which meant that his lip would be sore for days,
and if he forgot and started chewing on it, it would start to
bleed again. And then the two of them continuing their walk,
barely noticing the station wagon taxis with wooden panels
down the sides and the Packards and the Fords and the
Chevrolets and the Oldsmobile convertibles and the busloads
of tourists motoring past the shops and the fancy hotels, and
some that were not so fancy, and the policemen in bright blue
slickers with the insignia of the Republic on their jackets and
dark blue wide-brimmed hats keeping an eye on the traffic.
But once when they were waiting for the traffic to clear so
they could cross the Paseo del Prado down by the Capitol on

their way to the park, a wine colored Custom Club De Soto convertible passed by, and Oscar stared at the car with mute admiration, and even after the car had vanished he was looking at the spot where he had last seen it, and he told Nerea one day he was going to own a car like that, and for years afterwards he would dream about that car and wonder how he could get his hands on one, and in his dreams he would see the car parked outside nightclubs or cruising along the Malecón or driving out to Playa de Marianao, which is where everyone went to swim or walk along the pier, or heading down Calle Luz towards the harbor and the ferries that went across to Regla. And he would always wake up at this point, suddenly remembering that one afternoon he and Nerea had gone with Luis to Guanabacoa (because Luis had a friend who lived there), taking the ferry across the choppy dark waters of the bay. Luis' friend had sent a wine colored Custom Club De Soto convertible to pick them up from the ferry. Perhaps that had been the one Oscar had first seen. But always in his dreams it was someone else driving and laughing and the car radio blaring, and sometimes he would wake up angry, and always frustrated, his undershirt soaked, sometimes forgetting where he was, even years later when he was in his own apartment in Miami. But when he had first mentioned the car that day, Nerea had laughed and said but not before he bought her a fur coat. She was hoping for a golden-colored ermine, once the fur of European royalty, or sable because it felt like silk, or chinchilla because it was so rare, but any fur would do. And then she had smiled and then the policeman had waved them across and they wouldn't talk about furs again until the next time they stood in front of El Gallo.

They ate when the mood struck them, sitting down at small, sidewalk cafes, the waiters in white jackets and black ties wiping down plates and then setting the table while they read through the menu, the waiters hoping they were big spenders, extravagant tippers. But then they ordered corn tamales and black beans and rice anyway, or maybe paella and pork chops with lemon, and they drank bottles and bottles of cheap Spanish wine and listened to the music of roving troubadours who went table to table singing modern love songs they had written themselves in the hopes of a few dollars before they gave it all up and went back to the farms or the villages where they had been born to descend once again into oblivion. Sometimes after eating they would go to the Rodi and catch a movie, and the best movie they ever saw there, according to Oscar, was *Out of the Past* starring Robert Mitchum, Jane Greer and Kirk Douglas, but according to Nerea it was Gregory Peck and Joan Bennett in *The Macomber Affair*. And sometimes they'd go back to the hotel a stone's throw from the Plaza del Vapor where Oscar had first heard Nerea singing.

And some days Oscar and Nerea would lose themselves in the quiet, ancient, iridescent beauty of the waterfront cafes along the harbor and stop in for a cup of coffee and cheese or pineapple *pastelitos,* if it was early, or if it was later in the evening on a Sunday or a Monday or a Tuesday they would order drinks. And always Nerea wanted Tio Pepe in the evening, because she liked the taste of almond sherry at sunset. Oscar would drink Brandy de Jerez, because it was from Andalusia, Spain, and it was expensive, and Luis was paying him as an assistant stage manager so he now had money in his pocket, and it possessed, as Luis had told him, the magic of the Moors. But most of the time when they walked along the waterfront it was late afternoon and they drank coffee and the pale blue sky was tinted a saffron yellow, and they watched the ocean steamers sailing towards Morro castle and the Straits of Florida, plumes of black smoke trailing, buffeted by the breeze. And only twice during the nearly ten years of their afternoon or evening walks did Oscar tell Nerea that he loved her.

-67-

Of course Oscar did not know that Luis had asked Nerea to attend to his every whim, or that she had agreed only because Luis had asked, which explains a lot, and Oscar never found out she was deceiving him, nor did he ever truly understand the nature of the relationship between Nerea and

Luis, which explains even more.

Luis had discovered Nerea and her pimp in a dance dive on Villegas Street doing an incredibly lewd variation of a Cuban folk dance called "Shoeing the Mare." Nerea was wearing a skimpy, chiffon, see-through top, open in the middle, with bright orange ruffled sleeves, a bodice two sizes too small for her voluptuous chest (which kept popping out that night), black heels and no panties. The audience sat scattered among the tables (covered in stained white linens), which had been pushed out towards the walls as far as possible, forming a roughly circular patch of bare space in the middle of the room so everyone could see what was going on. From somewhere, the kitchen perhaps, there came the slightly distorted, staticky sound of a record (a 78) turned up as loud as it would go, a steamy tango that was popular in 1938 called *Tango Bolero* composed by the Spanish composer Juan Llossas, with an echo of Ravel and a few riffs, perhaps even entire passages, stolen from Bizet's *Carmen*, released by Odeon records and performed with melodramatic, silent-movie precision by the German conductor Bernhard Ette and his Dance Orchestra in The Theatre of the People on Reinhardt Road in Berlin, which was called The Great Theatre before the Nazis took over, (and which was, incidentally, the very same theater which saw the premier of Max Frisch's play *Biedermann und die Brandstifter* in 1958). Nerea was down on all fours in the middle of the dance floor of this dimly lit dive, which seemed bathed in shadows as dark and foreboding as those in any third-rate movie house, except for a narrow spotlight that captured Nerea's radiant smile of an orgasm (obviously fake, but still rooted in a playful, joyful passion for life nevertheless). Nerea's dance partner pimp was going through the motions of shoeing a flirty, rebellious horse, standing with his back to Nerea, his legs straddling hers, wearing the white linen pantalones and white linen shirt of a *campesino* but with the splashy silk elegance of an orange sash looped around his middle and black Cuban-heeled dancing shoes. Hunched over in this pose of a rustic blacksmith, he was pulling at each of Nerea's skinny legs, one at a time (even as she pretended she was trying to squirm free), lifting them up, stroking them to the jerky, staticky, staccato rhythm of the tango with a lascivious grin plastered across his face, and then Nerea finally giving up and her dance partner pimp winking at the bored, sleepy faces of the audience as if he were telling dirty jokes, or trying to, because these bored, sleepy men (and a few women) had seen everything, done everything, like a gang of ancient sailors waiting on the tide, what would it take to wake them up, to get them to crack a smile, to feel the heart-wrenching despair of an unattainable love, one could never be sure, and then Nerea's dance partner pimp spun her around by one leg in a circle, slowly, with a tantalizing, theatrical flourish, as the music came to a crashing end (the entire routine took three minutes and fourteen seconds), so everyone in the audience could see Nerea's bared ass and her juices flowing and catch the scent of her cinnamon perfumed skin.

This is when the magic happened. This is when every man would possess an erection and every woman would feel a sweet moistness gushing between her legs, for Nerea possessed a perfect heart-shaped ass, and the petals of her pussy glowed with the luminescent blush of a pink orchid against the glowing ebony darkness of her perfect curvaceous bottom, a flower from the depths of a jungle paradise to be fondled, to be fingered, to be plucked, to be tasted with the tip of your tongue, a flower dripping with the honeydew promise of eternal mind-numbing pleasure and everlasting youth, and then everyone in the audience, the men and the few women, immediately woke up and began shouting in rhythmic counterpoint to the music that had mysteriously begun again, an endless barrage of '¡Dios mío!' and '¡Mi Vida!' and '¡Ese huevo quiere sal!' and many other emotionally charged and even vulgar expressions of lust and love uttered in the heat of desire and as a prayer to release them from the looming abyss of frustrated dreams, every man (all of them publicly) and every woman (one publicly and the rest privately) in the audience hoping against hope that one day they might find a woman (partner, lover, soulmate) such as Nerea, who could be worshipped as both Madonna and whore, but knowing in their heart of hearts (all of them privately) that such a lucky destiny would never be theirs.

Later, Luis (age nineteen) went up to Nerea's pimp (Joaquin, age thirty-five), a chubby fellow from Pinar del Rio province, where the mountains with their steep limestone sides and lush mountain top jungles look like so many towering haystacks. Joaquin's family lived in the small town of Viñales and worked in the tobacco fields, but he had left there when he was very young. But he would never shake free of his smell of a peasant. He possessed a thick, bristly, over-sized moustache like a horse's grooming brush and eyes burning with the fumes of cocaine and skinny, leathery hands covered in warts. He and Luis spoke in querulous voices for a time, their Cuban passions glowing brightly in the dark, and then Luis put some bills into the man's hands and the man nodded and disappeared through a door that led to the kitchen, where, presumably, he snatched up his record and his Silvertone wind-up portable phonograph and fled into the alley and was never heard from again.

From that point on, Nerea belonged to Luis, which is to say that Luis fucked Nerea pretty much non-stop for the next six years. He danced his own version of "Shoeing the Mare" with her in the kitchen of his seedy hotel apartment in the middle of the night with the lights blazing away and the blinds up, or in the middle of the day with the sun pouring in, or out on the narrow balcony in the pale blue morning light (which required incredible skill and infinite patience on both their parts), so everyone with a view of the inner courtyard could see the flashing ebony brilliance of Nerea's bare ass and Luis spinning her around and then grabbing her ass roughly and sliding her up against the stove or the kitchen table when they were indoors and she would reach back and grab hold of him and his tip would start quivering the moment he felt her fingertips, drops of semen like teardrops would start to bubble out, and then she would pull him inside, all the way up to the hilt, the pink orchid folds of her pussy enveloping him like Chinese silk; or he would push her up against the outer shell of this crumbling hotel of their love when they were on the balcony and the sound of laundry flapping in the breeze from the tiered balconies that surrounded the inner courtyard (and during those moments Luis imagined he was standing before the arched partitions of the Roman Colosseum in its heyday), with Nerea bracing herself against the crumbling rough stone with her forearms, so she couldn't reach back,

and Luis plunging into her and then pulling out slowly, and a
soft moaning prayer escaping her lips, and then Luis plunging
into her again and pulling out again, and more prayers, and
her legs beginning to tremble, and perspiration beading up on
her erect nipples and falling like molten glass drop by drop
by drop to the tiled balcony floor. And then applause of a
sort, a few raucous shouts of '¡Olé!' and '¡Dios mío!' and a few
wolf whistles coming from the shadowy glare of a few half-
open windows and a few clapping hands echoing against the
rough stone, and the rest of the watchers nodding with silent
appreciation. No matter where or when they chose to strut
their stuff, the air would begin to vibrate and even glow with
an intense golden light, or so it seemed to everyone watching
from one of the two dozen balconies with an easy view, as if
the air itself were melting, and Nerea, bathing in the applause
of every invisible or imagined voyeur who had taken in the
show, would squeal and sing and laugh for joy.

Luis told everyone he met that Nerea was as refined and
as sophisticated a *Negro fino* as you would ever want to meet,
as sexy and provocative as the best of the mulattas, he would
say, but she was a pure-blood, and her exceptionally dark skin
gave her a rarefied air, like that of an ancient African queen
or even a goddess, it was hard to put into words, you had to
see her for yourself, he said, in the nude up close to know
precisely what he meant. Luis wanted to show her off in front
of the whole world, though it is also true that in their mad,
public displays of love, he took great pains to keep his own
identity a secret.

Early on they experimented with the standard array of
sexual positions. The Viennese oyster was their favorite. Then
the painter's canvas of their wild and uninhibited fucking
expanded to other parts of the city (which is to say they took
their show on the road), and they invented an erotic cornucopia of new positions for their love-making to accommodate
their changed and ever-changing surroundings, and Luis
began to whisper passionate or tragic love stories into Nerea's
ears to inspire even greater invention and perpetuate their
madness of two dogs howling at the moon.

Sometimes they drove along the lonely coast highway
in search of an appropriate lover's rendezvous, east or west

of the city it made no difference, but always it would be after the sun had set, and as soon as the black rocks and tide pools gave way to sandy patches and palm trees, they parked in the shadows and sprinted to the paradise of their own internal clocks. They made love with a recklessness that shocked even the stars.

Sometimes Nerea would lay her back on the beach, hidden in the shadows of her lover's eyes, and Luis would kneel before her, grabbing hold of her hips and hoisting them up off the ground so that only her shoulders and her head remained in the sand. Nerea would open her legs and Luis would pull her close, slowly maneuvering her soft, pliant body up and down until he slid into her, her inner thighs now pressed against his ribs, her legs bent at the knees, dangling, and sometimes she would even black out because of the blood rushing to her head.

They called this creation The Dolphin in the Sand.

Sometimes they did a variation they called The Mermaid in the Sand, with Nerea on her stomach and her legs pulled up, looking down at the waves washing up along the shore and the foam and a few scattered shells and clumps of seaweed instead of up into Luis' eyes and at the sky above the corona of his glowing head, where she might glimpse for a moment the light from the unreachable stars. Luis liked this position because any time he wanted to he could bend over (he was extraordinarily agile and flexible) and bury his face in Nerea's lush ass and lick the perspiration and the salt spray that had collected in the hidden crevices of his imagination. But she did not like this position.

The only witnesses to these lovemaking sessions by the sea were a few old fishermen. After a long day of fishing they would pull their boats out of the waves, dragging them maybe twenty yards or so, and then flip them turtle-like in the sand. They would clean their catch and then head towards whatever village or town was nearby. Later, some of them would return to smoke and drink and look up at the nighttime sky. A few would crawl beneath their boats and get a few hours' sleep before heading out to sea again.

Sometimes Luis and Nerea made love in the stony, cavernous shadows of the Arco de Belen, a short walk from their

hotel. The arch was part of the northeast corner of the Convent
of Bethlehem, a convalescent home for dying nuns from 1718
to 1842 that was given to the Jesuits in 1854, who then, according to a few nameless Jesuit scholars, turned the small room
above the arch into an observatory (or perhaps they placed
their observatory in the adjacent tower, that would have made
more sense, but who can truly say given the garbled, mythic
texture of most of history) so they could track hurricanes and
dabble in geomagnetism (which some said was the source
of the devil's power) and look at the stars with a refracting
telescope in the hopes of discovering where the angels lived,
which would be scientific proof that God did indeed exist, a
hope that was surely a blasphemy, for if one had faith, one
did not need proof. By 1925 the arch had become a ruin.
During the day it was occupied by beggars who had gambled
away the fillings in their teeth, and mediums who could see
the future if you brought them pieces of fresh fish and a little
rice, and lonely guitarists who came to play because they
liked the way their music bounced off the stones. At night it
was occupied by prostitutes and thieves and drug addicts, by
young mothers who had lost their babies to disease, by jilted
lovers and those who had never been in love, by cripples and
epileptics and the criminally insane, by those suffering from
lockjaw or porphyria, by all those who had been cast away
and were seeking the solace of eternal darkness.
    Some said that in the hours before dawn you could
still hear the plaintive cries of the dying nuns from centuries
ago, as if their lingering, deathbed words were trapped in
the stone itself, leeching out little by little into the future,
prayers asking forgiveness, prayers asking for second chances,
prayers of defiant regret, prayers of contempt, prayers of
wistful vengeance, prayers filled with abject misery and a
longing for even a kind word, some of the nuns wishing they
had taken a different path when they were young, some of
them angry with their fathers or their uncles or their brothers,
some of them wishing they had tasted sex just one more time
before their cunts had become dry (or dozens of times, or too
many times to keep track of, an incalculable number, if they
were truly honest with themselves), some of them laughing a
dry, whispery laughter directed at those who had remained

celibate, a bitter elegy that filled them with sudden remorse as soon as the laughter stopped, but all of them asking Christ to spare them any more pain.

Of the Jesuits only the darkness of their blasphemous souls remained.

Some believed the arch was a gateway to hell. Some believed it was an open doorway to paradise. Some believed it was a tunnel to a parallel universe. Some believed it was just an arch. And some believed it was the only three-centered Baroque-style arch still existing in Havana.

No one gave Luis and Nerea a second glance when they walked into the shadows of the arch that first night. But Luis and Nerea attracted all sorts of attention when they began their lovemaking. Their moans were amplified by the arch itself and sounded as if they had risen from deep within the earth, a heavy, rich, sonorous sound as penetrating as a chill on a moonless night and then the days all jasmine and orange spice. It seemed to those standing in the shadows of the arch that the prayers of the nuns had been answered. It seemed that the sins of the Jesuits had been forgiven. It seemed that a real (which is to say earthy, sensual) and all-too-human paradise was finally within everyone's grasp. Those beneath the arch could not help but breathe in the sounds of ecstasy. And they could not take their eyes off Nerea's beauty, which radiated with an unfathomable light, her pink orchid pulsing (pulsating?) like a neutron star with Luis' every thrust. It was almost like everyone watching had fallen into a trance, and when the show was over and Luis and Nerea had left the shadows for a bite to eat at a little café around the corner from Hotel Milagro, those who remained beneath the arch swore that they had been the ones to fuck Nerea, that no one else had been there, and when they closed their eyes they were fucking Nerea all over again. No one remembered Luis.

This was the beginning of Nerea's fame.

It was beneath the arch that Luis and Nerea created a position they called The Degenerate Nun. Luis would lie down, his back on the cobblestones, but with his legs raised in the air, bent at the knees. Nerea did the rest. She would begin by licking the curve of his muscular ass and the warm moistness of his inner thighs and his overly large bull's balls until he started shuddering slightly (Luis called this part of the program "genuflecting before the altar"), and when he was firm, she would push open his legs and take a seat, her arms holding onto his knees so she could keep her balance, her ass wriggling a bit until she found him and slipped his wriggling eel inside, a bluish tint to her dark ebony breasts like a blue moon eclipsed, though no one was ever sure where the bluish light that illuminated her breasts actually came from, and then she would slide back and forth, sometimes leaning back as far as Luis' legs would go so she could feel him deep inside, her wetness gushing out, spilling across his upended thighs, forming a small pool on the warm cobblestone. The Degenerate Nun was a slow, luxurious fuck, that's what Nerea said. And so it was. Nerea was in absolute control the whole time and enjoyed bringing Luis to the edge and then relaxing and then bringing him to the edge again, and so on. This might go on for thirty minutes. But the audience beneath the arch truly appreciated Nerea's skill and intensity, and they would burst into thunderous applause at the end, and perhaps some lusty, maniacal laughter, and those who were masturbating during the show would gush or explode, and there would be an ocean of juice (the gushing) rolling across the cobblestones and down along Acosta Street towards the harbor, the sewers backing up with froth, and there would be a cloud of spermatozoa (the explosion) hovering in the air for a moment and the lingering taste of salt on everyone's tongues and the hope of nirvana and then the cloud spilling its particles to the ground like so many dead and dying sea creatures.

Then they began to incorporate music into their love-making sessions. On a rainy evening beneath the arch near the end of their first summer, they were joined by a lonely guitar player who played a bouncy, energetic Brazilian samba while they fucked, which Nerea said was a brilliant way to maintain her rhythm. The very next night they arrived at the arch with a brand-new wind-up portable phonograph. In addition to sambas, they experimented with mambos, guarachas, boleros, and even a bachata or two from the Dominican Republic.

It didn't take long (a few months) before Nerea's fame as a sex goddess had spread all over the city. On some

evenings beneath the arch there wasn't enough room to stand
or even breathe. A feeling of claustrophobia would descend.
People would be straining their necks from half a block away
to catch a glimpse of the action. After one such night Luis
said it felt like they were cattle in a cattle car heading for
the slaughterhouse. On another night, he said the stench of
fish and sour wine and rum and blood-filled urine and cigar
smoke and tubercular breath was so thick it blotted out every
sound. So they decided to vary their routine. They decided
to expand their geography even further. They fucked in the
shadows of the great northern gate of the Cementerio de
Cristóbal Colón, with its dozens of whispering statues with
their voices of ecclesiastical poverty trying to undo time, a
spot which Luis had chosen because Candelaria Figueredo, a
hero in the struggle to free Cuba from Spain (she had carried
the Cuban flag into battle at Bayamo in 1868 at the age of
sixteen), was buried there. They fucked beneath the Spanish
lime and fig trees in a small park on San Lazaro Avenue
just east of the University where the ghost of the anarchist
Julio Mella could sometimes be seen. (Nerea had chosen the
park because she had seen an old photograph of Julio Mella
hanging on the wall in the lobby of Hotel Milagro and thought
him quite beautiful for an anarchist with his curly brown hair
and intense, cinematic eyes and pouty lips, but when Luis had
told her that Mella was a dead anarchist, that he had been
murdered in Mexico City at the age of twenty-five-and-a-half
by Stalinist sympathizers because he believed in Trotsky, she
wept at the cruelty of a world that could crush the life of
one so beautiful. Luis had agreed that the world was cruel,
though for different reasons, but she did not care. Fucking in
the park with the ghost of Julio Mella hovering somewhere
nearby was a cathartic release for both of them.) They fucked
on the grassy lawn beneath the walls of La Punta Castle with
those walls in desperate need of repair and two useless canons
guarding the entrance. They fucked while breathing in the
fragrant beauty of the Quinto de Molinos Botanical Gardens
on Zapata Street (a lush estate tucked away inside the city
where stock breeders from all over the world had gathered for
an Agricultural Expo in 1913). They fucked in the shadows of
the arcaded walkway that abutted the Church and convent of

Our Lady of Mount Carmel, once the traffic along Neptuno
Street had thinned, with the lonely sound of a church organ
drifting down from somewhere, and also the baritone elegance
of a priestly voice or several priestly voices singing a once
popular but still sacred baroque cantata. They fucked in every
one of the city father's city parks and across the street from
countless seedy cafes that were open until dawn and in plazas
abandoned at dusk. They even fucked (on three separate occasions) in the Plaza across from the Catedral de la Virgen María
de la Concepción Inmaculada. They fucked to the sounds of
boleros and sambas and tiranas and polos along the Paseo
del Prado. They fucked down along the wharf and up on the
steps of the Capitol. They fucked wherever the city fathers had
erected statues and memorials to honor the hopes of previous
generations, statues and memorials which lay scattered across
the city like so many partisan leaflets.

They fucked wherever people might watch them fucking.

But their favorite place for fucking was along the
Malecón on summer evenings, looking out at the dark blue
waters of the Straits of Florida and dreaming of the future.
They would head to the Malecón whenever they wanted to
escape Nerea's fame. Here they might find some privacy, a
short respite from performing. Their favorite time of day was
as the sun was setting, dissolving into the sea, flashing a soft,
golden white light like the diffuse light of an impressionist
painting against the dark windows of the buildings that
looked out at the Malecón. They would stroll along the old
stone wall across from the buildings, looking for a good place
to climb down to the rocky shoreline below and the frothy,
white foam that came crashing against the wall when the tide
was in, and even when the tide was out their bodies were
covered with a gritty silt and a sticky, salty spray. At this time
of day, the greenish-teal color of the water so close to shore
would turn a deep, invigorating purplish black.

Luis told Nerea that the rocks were volcanic, the remnants of the volcanic activity that had shaped the Caribbean
basin a hundred million years before the birth of mankind,
during the Cretaceous period, part of the Cretaceous volcanic
arc. The rocks were a fitting symbol of everything that had
happened in Cuba since the Spanish arrived, he said, a symbol

of the many fruitless wars for independence and the broken promises and the bald, rippling lies, a symbol of the withering of the Cuban soul, yes, yes, volcanic rock is an appropriate symbol for all of this, he said, for everything we have ever dreamed about, and for everything we will dream about in the future. Naturally, Nerea believed everything Luis said was the truth.

The world whirled with the colors of their love.

They discovered a few narrow sandy patches up close to the wall where they would warm up with either The Mermaid in the Sand or The Dolphin in the Sand, but in time they decided that fucking among the black rocks required greater ingenuity, especially since their sessions along the Malecón were a gift to themselves, one soul merging with another on the edge of the universe, only the darkness to catch them if they fell, so they wanted to create something to equal the great explosion that had created the volcanic rocks oh so many centuries ago, something that would not only shock the stars, but cause them, at least one third of them, to fall out of the sky, a hailstorm of gleaming meteorites.

So they created The Lady of the Sea.

Luis would lean back against the stone wall, his heels digging into the sand for balance (or pushing against the rocks where there was no sand), his legs bent at an impossible forty-five-degree angle zooming up towards a cloudy sky. Nerea would perch upon his straining legs with a casual elegance, her legs straddling his, the pink orchid of her new fame glowing in the half light of sunset or the near dark of after sunset or the pitch-black darkness of an impenetrable midnight sky.

In their young hearts the night was always young.

He would take hold of Nerea's plush ass and move her up and down as he wanted. She could recline on the forty-five-degree angle of his knees, grabbing onto his ankles if she felt herself flying forward, on the verge of being cata-pulted into outer space, but always he had a firm grip, in spite of the strain on his back and legs, always he was in absolute control. Sometimes she would push up on his knees with the palms of her hand, especially if a large wave was coming in. Then she would arch her back as if she were a statue decorating the prow of one of the great, mythic ships of antiquity, a goddess certainly, the salt spray washing over her body.

During these moments she *became* The Lady of the Sea. This was her favorite position. They would fuck among the rocks along the Malecón all night long. In some places the rocks were jagged and they came away with cuts. In other places, they were rounded and even covered with a fine, slippery moss and it was difficult to maintain one's balance. Every night was a testament to their consummate skill. Even so, Luis and Nerea would still sometimes try to come up with a position to eclipse The Lady of the Sea, a new favorite position to fan the flames of their love, but they had already surpassed themselves.

This is when Luis began to tell Nerea stories while he fucked her. He told her all sorts of popular, dimestore novel stories typical of the day, stories of debauchery and murder and swashbuckling mayhem and mulatta damsels in distress and fragile, tragic love affairs with the woman scanning the horizon, waiting for someone who would never return because he had died long ago.

Nerea's favorite story was that of a lovesick soldier of fortune who lost his mind after the death of his one and only love, a beautiful mulatta girl from Santiago de Cuba, a child of one of Velásquez's men who at the age of sixteen had gone off in search of her father but was sidetracked by a soldier's smile. In the version of the story Luis told, the soldier's name was Gonzalo Silvestre. Of course no one knows for certain what his name truly was, for men are always changing their names to suit the changing circumstances of fortune, but it was true, said Luis, that he had come to Cuba with Hernando De Soto in 1538, and it was then that he met the most beautiful mulatta girl that ever graced the island of Cuba. She had been in Havana only a few months when a French corsair sacked the city and so she witnessed great horrors and deprivation, and in the turmoil that always comes with devastation of this kind, she transformed herself into a lady of the night, selling her body to men of fortune so she could escape the withering boredom of starvation. Gonzalo found her wandering the streets along the waterfront when he arrived, and since his was the first honest, friendly face she had encountered since

leaving Santiago, she fell in love with him. He married her
in secret and they spent many nights making wild, lascivious
love beneath the darkly glowing palms along the beach, away
from the bustling commotion of the new town. He told her
their destinies were forever linked because on those nights of
lovemaking it was like she had washed up with a wave, a gift
from the goddess of the sea, a new goddess for a new world,
he said, and so he pledged his eternal love. But he left her to
follow De Soto to Florida and the promise of cities of gold.
She said she would watch the sea until he returned, praying
to their new goddess of the sea that he would not be gone
long, standing there naked on the beach in the enveloping
darkness, waiting to feel his arms around her once again.
So all the while he was gone he held on to this image of her
standing there naked on the beach, the dark palms behind
her mute sentinels of their separation. This image became
the golden cross of his love and his hope for happiness. She
was the only thing worth suffering for, this is what he told
himself. He heard her sweet voice on the wind each night and
imagined that he was holding her, fucking her with the wild
abandon of a Conquistador's lust. Her image obliterated the
misery of sleeping in mosquito infested swamps hundreds of
miles away from the Cuba of his dreams, masturbating to the
rhythmic pulse of six hundred men snoring in the darkness.
She was his salvation. But by the time he returned to Cuba in
1557, she had vanished into the mists of the interior. Or she
had boarded one of the treasure ships loaded with silver that
had stopped on its way from Mexico to the port city of Cádiz
on the southwestern coast of Spain. Or she had given up on
him and married someone else. Or she had died of smallpox.
Or been raped and brutally murdered. Or had died a slow
withering death of starvation anyway. Or she had walked into
the sea in a fit of despair and drowned in the arms of their
new goddess. A new goddess for a new world. No one knew
what had happened. And Gonzalo went mad trying to find
her. He was last seen wandering the beaches, swept now by
only the darkness of her absence, where they had made wild,
uninhibited love. It was said that you could hear his lonely
wail of a cry on nights when the sky was buffeted by clouds. It
is said you can still hear his cry.

Nerea would swoon just thinking about the imagined passion and consequent descent into madness of Gonzalo Silvestre. She wondered that he was so stupid as to head off in search of cities of gold while his one true love waited for him on a beach. Did he not know such love was as rare as an angel's tear? Were all men so stupid? Perhaps he deserved to go mad.

Luis would grow very hard and very thick imagining Nerea waiting for him naked on the beach.

"You are my gift from the goddess of the sea," Luis would say to Nerea.

And Nerea would wiggle her perfect heart-shaped ass, the luminescent petals of her pink orchid glowing in the dark.

"I have been dreaming about you since before you were born," Luis would say.

More wiggling.

"You are my one and only love," Luis would say.

And more wiggling still.

"You are the soul to complement my soul."

And then Nerea: "Would you run off and leave me?"

"I will never leave you."

"Even if there were cities of gold to hunt down?"

"I am through hunting."

Nerea wrapping her arms around Luis, a slow tightening, and then her legs, and then Luis sliding himself into her, a gentle thrusting.

"Would you go mad if I were to die or run away?"

"I am already floundering in a sea of madness."

"Have you always been such a liar? Have your words always been coated with such thick, deceitful honey?"

". . . ."

"Are you not ashamed of yourself?"

". . . ."

"How many other girls have fallen into your trap?"

". . . ."

"It is okay, my love. I forgive you everything. As long as you are good to me."

And Luis would look at her with great emotion in his eyes.

"I will be very good."

And Nerea would smile sadly, as if she had just glimpsed the future.

In time, Luis and Nerea gave up the quixotic thrill of making love all over the city. The image of Nerea and her perfect heart-shaped ass, which had been emblazoned on the hearts and minds of thousands of lonely pilgrims in search of love, faded into myth. Such is the way of things. But Luis and Nerea did not abandon the Malecón, for to do so would have been to abandon each other. Every time they wanted to escape the mundane realities of the world and become invisible to everyone except themselves, that is where they went. And always Luis would heave and grunt and Nerea would gush and moan and her moaning sounds mingled with the crashing sound of the waves and the lonely cry of Gonzalo Silvestre's eternal longing (which may or may not have been the sound of the lonely wind), and these two dogs howling at the moon fell madly in love all over again.

Their ears became their eyes.

Their lips became the lapping of the waves.

Their gaping mouths became mirrors to the nighttime sky.

Their thoughts became the tolling of a distant church bell.

And always the night was young.

But one night while fucking among the rocks along the Malecón they did not fall madly in love all over again. They were like two sailing ships set adrift, though even they did not realize what was happening at the time.

The night in question began as usual with the two of them frolicking among the jagged rocks. But on that particular evening they had misjudged the amount of light left in the sky. They had misjudged who would be traveling along the Malecón and how attentive he might be to the waves crashing against the stone wall, to the shadows dancing beneath the stars.

He was an ice-cream vendor in a white ice-cream shirt and white ice-cream trousers and a white ice-cream hat with a wide brim. His shirt and his trousers were covered in ice-cream stains that looked vaguely reddish in color against the otherwise pristine fabric, a portent of the years to come, perhaps. He was pushing a Guarina ice-cream cart.

The ice-cream vendor's point of view:

The ice-cream vendor saw two dark shadows wrestling against the rocks and the sea rolling in and he thought perhaps someone was drowning. Or perhaps a crime was in progress. This seemed more likely given there were two shadows. The shadows seemed exaggerated in the dimming light. The ice-cream vendor observed that the shadows were zigging and zagging with strangely elongated movements, it was almost like watching an alien couple from another dimension taking pleasure in a simple tango, he thought, although anyone who has ever observed shadows for any length of time will readily agree that this is the normal movement of shadows.

He watched the dancing shadows a moment with a vague look of happiness, as if he were remembering a time when he had danced with a woman, but then his earlier thought that a crime was in progress returned and his vague sense of happiness was crushed. Yes, he said to himself, a woman was being assaulted, a tragic attack that would end badly if someone did not intervene. Yes, he could hear someone groaning, there was no doubt, and without giving a second thought to his own fate (or, incidentally, to the fate of the three half-empty canisters of ice cream that were hidden away in a small compartment in the center of his cart, and which contained strawberry, pineapple and coconut flavored ice cream that had been slowly melting for the last few hours), he got down on his hands and knees on top of the wall, feeling his way towards the wall's edge with a mechanical precision, resembling at that point in the fading light a crab-like creature more than an ice-cream vendor, a crab sporting a white shell with red or reddish-brown markings or blotches, such as the tiny Porcelain Anemone Crab (*Neopetrolisthes ohshimai*) from Indonesia as viewed through the refracting lens of a spotting scope.

He would go over the side of the wall even though he believed he was risking certain death if a crime was actually taking place. He was aware that many such crimes were committed in Havana every day. On numerous occasions as he was pushing his ice-cream cart along the Malecón in the early afternoon light, he had stumbled upon the bloodstains where similar attacks had occurred. He hoped he would get to the woman in time. But in spite of the imagined urgency of the situation, he was excruciatingly careful in his manner of descent. Yes, it is certainly true that he was too portly an ice-cream vendor to take an athletic leap, and old enough, to judge by the gray around his temples, to be suspicious of even the tiniest cracks in the sidewalk. But his girth and his age were not the reasons why he moved so slowly. He simply was not willing to risk a sprained ankle or a broken leg, for then he would be incapable of assisting the woman who was about to become another bloodstain by the sea. This is what he was thinking all in a single moment, a single gasping for breath. This is what he told himself before he grabbed hold of the edge of the wall with a firm yet delicate grip and carefully began the process of lowering his bloated, ice-cream vendor body to the rocky shore below.

A few moments later he dropped without a sound, as silent as memory, without even the tiniest possibility, as far as he could tell, that the motion of his body moving through the air had disturbed the equilibrium of the universe. He looked at the two shadows and breathed in the pure sea air (a gloriously refreshing sensation no matter the circumstances, and which did wonders for his sinuses, which had plagued him since the age of thirty-two). He looked at the two shadows and wondered what was going to happen, and at precisely that moment the two shadows stopped what they were doing and two faces turned to look at the ice-cream vendor. They were huddled together maybe six feet from where the ice-cream vendor stood. There was no judgment in their eyes.

The one face, the face of a man intent on bringing happiness to the world, flashed him a smile full of teeth. The glaring white of the man's teeth in the dimming light was almost painful to behold. The other face, the woman's face, clearly radiated with the happiness that was the cornerstone of her partner's intentions. Her eyes danced about with what the ice-cream vendor assumed was great joy.

If this is not an example of great joy, he thought, then there is no such thing. Indeed, the woman's face, her entire body, glowed with the aura of an undefinable light. The ice-cream vendor's eyes darted this way, then that, as if he were trying to determine if what he saw was real. He seemed to have lost all sense of time. His eyes lingered the longest on the perfectly rounded cheeks of the woman's heart-shaped ass, gleaming like two rounded stones that had been freshly polished.

Then the two faces turned away from the ice-cream vendor and the man and the woman resumed what they had been doing. There was no judgment either in their ignoring the ice-cream vendor. They were simply preoccupied.

Naturally the ice-cream vendor realized his mistake. But he made no move to depart. Any other ice-cream vendor would have returned to his cart and made his way home to wash his ice-cream uniform and prepare for another day. But this particular ice-cream vendor (whose name was Jorge, which you could tell just by looking at him with his wispy beard and his long face of a philosopher) was unable to move an inch. He was, one could say, rooted to the spot, an ironic description given the fact that he was standing in one of the rare sandy patches along the wall, a bit of sand that would disappear with the next great storm. Of course it is also true that the ice-cream vendor, given his portly nature and his advancing years, could not return to his cart above as easily as he had made his descent. He knew there were stairs some- where along the Malecón. He remembered some vagabond boys who smelled of the sea had once jumped up from the other side of the wall and begged for some ice cream, and he had given them some, and then they had disappeared over the wall, and he had wondered how they had accomplished such magic, so he had looked over the edge and there were the stairs and the rocks below and the boys jumping back into the sea. But he couldn't remember where that was, or even, to be honest, if his memory was accurate.

How stupid he had been, he thought. Clearly this amo- rous couple had chosen this precise location among the rocks because who in their right mind would climb down the wall in the dark. They wanted to be alone. The ice-cream vendor stood in mute contemplation of his stupidity, absorbing it, swallowing it, until the burn had dissipated.

But still he did not move.

In all probability, he would not have returned to his cart had there been a set of stairs at his elbow. To be blunt: he could not take his eyes off the luminescent beauty of the woman and every so often her flashing pink orchid winking in the darkness.

And so time passed.

Or time stopped.

It amounts to the same thing.

After a while the two shadows stopped again, but this time they disentangled themselves and approached the ice-cream vendor, who was still unable to move.

No one knew what to say at first.

"You surprised us," said the man after several minutes.

"Yes you did," said the woman.

The ice-cream vendor remained silent.

"But we enjoy surprises," said the man.

"Oh, we do," said the woman. "We are always surprising each other."

The ice-cream vendor shifted uncomfortably.

"Yes," said the man. "We are."

The man and the woman laughed with cryptic pleasure. The sound of their laughter had a muffled, underwater quality about it, as if it were coming from beneath the darkly glowing waves of the Straits of Florida some two miles out instead of from the two happily laughing heads tossed back. The eyes of the ice-cream vendor clouded over with a look of self-deprecating apology. He seemed unable to focus, blinking violently. He seemed incapable of speech. His hands groped wildly at the air as if he were suffering from a raging thirst. One would have thought he had suddenly and quite without warning gone blind. Then the man and the woman invited the ice-cream vendor to join them.

"My name is Luis," said Luis.

"My name is Nerea," said Nerea.

"My name is Jorge," said Jorge.

And with these basic introductions out of the way, Luis and Nerea began to undress the portly ice-cream vendor. From a distance it would have looked like his white trousers and white shirt just melted away, exposing his body to the elements and the darkness and the deft handling of Nerea, whose slender fingers stroked him without mercy while Luis stood back as if he were pretending to be a statue, something iconic, with a hint of history and a sense of purpose, but also possessing an air of whimsy, an appreciation for the absurdity of life, one foot propped up on one of the many black, volcanic rocks that pockmarked the landscape and the surf rolling in slowly, surrounding some of the rocks, Luis watching first with the enthusiasm of an adolescent voyeur, and then forgetting he was a statue and clapping his hands in delight, and then adopting the socially myopic pose of a more reserved movie critic, but still gesticulating with each breath, commenting on everything from Nerea's infallible technique to the ice-cream vendor's overwhelming inexperience (though he was eager to learn, which was a point in his favor) as well as his poor physical condition, which meant in all likelihood that the more challenging positions would forever be out of his reach.

The ice-cream vendor and Nerea attempted The Mermaid in the Sand and The Lady of the Sea, both with the expert assistance of Luis, but the portly vendor began gasping for breath almost immediately and his limbs seemed like they were about to snap from the strain, so Luis and Nerea switched gears.

In the end, and because this was all the poor man was capable of, Nerea allowed the ice-cream vendor to fondle her pussy while she grabbed hold of his balls with one hand and stroked him with the other until he ejaculated all over her arm. Then she licked off the excess and began kissing him on the mouth with a ferocity that surprised even Luis, pushing her gargantuan breasts against the ice-cream vendor's trembling skin, squeezing his fleshy nipples until they bled while she forced her tongue half way down his throat, stroking his shaft with the silk of her fingertips until he was ready once more, at which point she positioned herself against the wall so that he could enter her easily from the rear. He was finished in two minutes and would have keeled over right there had not Luis caught him. Grinning, Luis said: "There, there, my friend, she will take you to a paradise from which there is no return if you let her."

After that they helped the ice-cream vendor back into his clothes, he seemed as feeble and as inarticulate as a stroke victim, and then they helped him find the mythic stairs of his imagination and then they walked him back to his cart. There was a hazy morning glow to the sky, spreading up from the east like a bloodstain, but it was still very dark to the west. They watched as the ice-cream vendor pushed his cart with some unsteadiness towards the darkness, and then he had vanished. Soon after that a soft rain began to fall as softly and as easily as one slips into a coma, and so they decided to go back to Hotel Milagro.

They enjoyed the company of the ice-cream vendor with some degree of regularity over the next several months. In fact, it wasn't too long after they first met Jorge that they headed for the Malecón with the sole purpose of seeking him out. Bit by bit they fell out of love with each other, and in love with this strangely exhilarating ménage à trois.

Always they would find him just before sunset struggling with his cart along the Malecón, whistling a strange sad love song, somewhere between the ravishing, sun-washed brightness of Linea Street, near the park of La Piragua, which became a haven for criminals and reefer heads and vagabond musicians after dark, and the monument to Antonio Maceo y Grajales, a bronze general on a bronze horse leaping up into a very blue Cuban sky, a sky which suggested to Luis the absolute purity of freedom, and to Nerea the peace and quiet of a lazy afternoon in bed, and to the ice-cream vendor a week of bright sunny days when he was sure to sell a great deal of ice cream.

Always Luis and Nerea would lead the ice-cream vendor down to the water and the shadows stretching out along the shore and then night falling.

Always they would nibble away the ice-cream vendor's clothes with their lust for new experiences and their haughty disregard for convention, and always he would react with the unfaltering dignity and unhesitant devotion of a blind man. And always Luis would be there to catch him when he fell.

Then they would help him dress and before he realized where they were they would be walking along the Malecón, his fleshy arms draped across their shoulders, his legs unable to bear his own weight, as if he had been a large fish they had caught, and then all three of them would head back to the ice-cream cart, where they would linger for a while.

Once back at his cart, Jorge would become a new man, suddenly revived, a smile pushing out the pudginess of his cheeks. He would pluck a few ice-cream goblets hanging by their stems from a rack hidden in the canopy of his cart. The goblets were made from cheap spider-web glass, glassware which the Guarina family had purchased by the truckload because they created the impression of elegance for mere pennies. Then he would pour what was left of the melted ice cream (strawberry, pineapple, coconut) and mix in a little rum. He had taken to stashing a bottle of dark rum in his cart for just this purpose. The three of them would toss back ice-cream rum drinks until there was nothing left to toss back.

Sometimes they drank in silence, too exhausted by the night's frolicking to utter even a syllable. On such nights they drank only a glass or two.

But sometimes they entangled themselves in very heated discussions about the improbable relationship between politics as usual and the dream of creating a utopian paradise for the people of Cuba, which is what every politician said they were going to do. The topic was an odd one to follow so much fucking. On such nights they could not get enough to drink.

"It is not as far-fetched as it sounds," said Luis.

They were huddled around Jorge's cart like three conspirators. Luis on one side, his back to the sea, Nerea and Jorge on the other. They were drinking coconut ice cream drinks. They had lost track of how many they had drunk. They seemed to possess an unquenchable thirst.

"Certainly this is easy for you to say," said Jorge. "You come from money. You dabble in this and that and if you lose it is nothing. Your thirst for freedom is a luxury. What do you mean by freedom anyway? Your dreams are a luxury. Your history is a luxury. Your whole life is a luxury that I cannot afford. Even your beautiful Nerea is a luxury."

The streets were mostly deserted, though already there were lights winking on all over the city. A few shadowy figures appeared along the wall. And then a few more. They did not seem interested in the trio by the ice cream cart.

"Did you hear that, Nerea? Jorge said you are a luxury."

"I did hear that!"

Nerea wiggled closer to Jorge. Soon her hips were pressing against his leg and also against the cart, forming a triangle. Jorge was looking vaguely in the direction of the sea, his plump hands and plump arms floundering uselessly by his sides. He was clearly distracted. The sun had inched its way above the horizon and the light was now pouring through the spider web glass of the few goblets still hanging from the rack. Jorge's face was bathed in a soft, rosy glow. The shadowy figures became fishermen casting their lines from the wall or fishermen who had gone over the side and were casting their lines from the rocks. Some of the fishermen were old men. They seemed as old as the rocks. Some of them older. But some were boys no older than ten or eleven.

The sun grew brighter.

Jorge's pudgy pink cheeks resembled the soft underbelly of a sea creature suddenly exposed.

"Do you think I am a luxury?"

Nerea leaned even closer and started nibbling on Jorge's ear as she spoke.

Jorge could hardly breathe. He felt like he was bleeding but he could not tell from where.

Nerea continued nibbling.

Jorge was overwhelmed by the sweet coconut ice cream smell of her breath and almost passed out.

His face had lost all of its color.

"You . . . you are . . . I mean . . ."

It was a rough sea this morning, with tiny, frothy white caps as far as the eye could see. And yet the air was calm and gentle and smelled of lilacs and Chinese wisteria and sweet gardenias and sweet, sun-dried figs.

"Do you think you can so easily do without me?"

"No . . . I didn't mean that . . . I . . ."

"You mean you enjoy fucking me, is that it?"

Luis drained his goblet and fixed himself another drink, watching the scene unfold as if he were watching a movie.

"And you do not want to stop fucking me, yes?"

There was a small tugboat sailing across the horizon, stealing its way into Jorge's line of sight, on its way into the harbor. Jorge wanted to watch the boat, but Nerea took hold of his face with her dark, slender hands and he gave up all pretense and looked into her eyes.

"And when I am gone and you are pushing your cart there is nothing but the silence of your loneliness, yes?"

". . . ."

"And that is why you are always whistling the same sad song. To keep the silence at bay."

"Yes."

"And it is such a lovely, sad song, is it not?"

"Yes."

"So I am a necessity, yes?"

"Yes, yes . . ."

"Mmmmm?"

"I enjoy fucking you and I do not want to stop."

"Mmmmm!" Nerea smiled softly.

From somewhere there was the sound of traffic making its way through city streets, though there were no cars yet driving along the Malecón, just a few trucks.

Nerea kissed Jorge on the mouth, a soft, gentle kiss, like a morning rain shower.

"You are a sweet man," Nerea said.

Nerea cooed some more into Jorge's ear and then kissed him lightly on his blushing check.

Luis laughed, a hearty robust laugh like a thunderclap.

Jorge was trembling from unexpected embarrassment.

"You see, Jorge," said Luis. "Even a luxury can become a necessity."

The three of them tossed back their ice cream drinks and Luis fixed another round. It is hard to say if their drinking took place in the vacuum of absolute silence (even the sounds of the sea and the seagulls and the fishermen along the wall or down on the rocks were muted) or if time simply flowed around them.

And then: "But it is not that way for most," said Jorge.

"No?"

"Most people have no time for necessities of the heart. It is a trap," said Jorge. "Like religion. Or believing in God."

"Be careful, my friend," said Luis. "You are treading on dangerous ground once more."

But Nerea had already stepped around the cart, moving past Luis towards the wall and the sounds of seagulls in the air above and the sunlight washing across her with such brilliance that she seemed naked even though she was wearing a flowery dress from the night before. Luis and Jorge continued their conversation. Nerea stared out at the sea. The wind was picking up. You could hear the wind whistling through a few nearby cracks in the wall. A few fishermen from down along the wall or up along the wall were cursing because their lines had become tangled and then they turned suddenly and their eyes fell upon Nerea and her dazzling beauty and her seeming nakedness and the cursing stopped. Then they untangled their lines and went back to fishing. The wind died down.

"Hah," said Jorge. "Yes, I suppose you are right. But then only the rich can afford to be so romantic. *Dime con quién andas, y te diré quién eres.* One day you and Nerea will pack up and head for only God knows where, and I will still be here pushing my cart along the Malecón, and I will be very much alone, and one day my heart will give out from the heartache of my loneliness, or maybe it will be from the heat, and that will be that."

"But one day life will be different," said Luis. "I have always said . . ."

"Yes, yes, I know, you and your predictions, but it is the same old promise, always dangling there in front of our noses, like a juicy fig and your mouth is watering, but it is always just out of reach. Blanco wanted to give Cuba its freedom if we helped the Spanish in their war with America, but Gómez was against this, and when independence did come, Gómez gave the Americans everything they wanted. He promised us a new paradise but we were still slaves. Nothing changed. And Zayas was not much better. What did he do? He wrote poetry. He possessed a suffering heart. But he couldn't do a damn thing without borrowing money from the Americans. What good was that? Machado, Grau, Mendieta, Brú, how many others were there, I have forgotten, and now we have Batista, the worst of the lot, but it is only a matter of degree, they are all the same, a rotating parade of clowns. A carousel. They will promise anything to get elected and then they suffer from amnesia or worse, they loot the country, they line their own pockets, they line the pockets of a few American Senators, and nothing changes. Nothing ever changes."

"Yes, my friend, but one day, truly, everything will be different."

"You talk like an idealist, but I know you are not. But even if you are right, what of it? When your one day arrives, I will be long gone. I will have exited the planet."

". . . ."

"My poor, sweet, suffering Jorge," said Nerea, and Luis and Jorge turned their attention to the woman of their dreams, an extraordinarily photogenic face that surpassed (they thought) even the fabled beauty of Helen of Troy (for without a photograph, who can be sure?), but Nerea was staring out at the sea once again.

-68-

Time, as the poet once said, murders all things, but especially love. This is one of life's great truths. And so it was with Luis and Nerea. Six years of hard, furious fucking left them lethargic, apathetic, without enough energy even to raise their heads off the pillow when the other entered the room. Dog tired. That is how they felt. He talked about how it would be better to pay for sex. Maybe his tastes had changed. Maybe he was no longer into the exotic. At least he could test the waters if he bought a whore. She talked about selling her own flexible, fluid body for money, like she had done before they met. She craved variety, she said. So perhaps he was right. They talked about separating. She would want for nothing, he said. He would get her an apartment on Zulueta, there was a very nice building just two blocks from El Gallo's, yes, he knew about her love for furs, what woman didn't want a fur, yes, he would buy her one of those as well, sable or chinchilla, whatever she wanted, but Zulueta was too far away from the clubs, she said, and she didn't really like the neighborhood, everything crammed together in such a small space, she was afraid it would give her headaches. He suggested somewhere on Merced, near their favorite church, but she said that would bring back too many memories, she didn't want a head stuffed full of memories, or a heart, for that matter, no, she would rather re-invent herself, start all over, not completely, she would hang on to the parts she liked, anyone would, but she wanted to forget all of the little jokes they used to make and the perverted way he would laugh when he came in her mouth, yes, she wanted to forget things like that, which is why she could never live on Merced. Perhaps she was interested in going to America, to Miami, or Argentina or Chile, or perhaps Mexico City, he had friends all over, he would put her up in a fancy high-rise apartment and she would have a very fine life, but she said she had been born in Cuba and she would die in Cuba. What does she want, Luis asked himself. What is she waiting for? Why won't she tell me what's really on her mind? But he only ever voiced these questions with his eyes, and she no longer responded to his eyes, except to meet them with a determined, probing stare of her own, her face still glowing, always glowing, with an unfathomable light.

Eventually Luis gave up trying to move her out of the hotel and they took to living as brother and sister. She cooked him small meals in their four-room suite plus a bathroom when they didn't go out to eat. She even slept next to him in bed until he asked the hotel manager to bring them a second bed, which he shoved into a fairly large closet they had been using as a pantry. From time to time she took occasional lovers, bringing them back to the apartment at all hours and grunting and moaning in her tiny bed in her tiny bedroom next to the kitchen with the door always open so Luis could watch if he wanted to. And sometimes he did watch, and in the morning after her lover had left they would critique her lover's performance over coffee and pastries, Nerea still wearing the flimsy négligée she had worn to bed, or the lace panties, or sometimes she was in one of Luis' old robes because she had gone to bed naked.

Once, one of Nerea's lovers had a Kongsberg Colt pistol strapped to his leg, which only foreign mercenaries or assassins or anarchists or communists or members of the secret police generally possessed, and when he took off his trousers Nerea squealed. Luis appeared as quickly as a gust of wind and boxed the man's ears, berating him for bringing such a weapon into his home, tossed the gun out the window and the man down the stairs. The hotel staff escorted the boob to the courtyard to retrieve the symbol of his manhood. They swore they never saw him again after that.

Luis was more discreet, as always. He never brought any women home so that Nerea could size them up. He would meet someone at one of the clubs and when she was drunk enough he would drive her out to one of the beaches where he and Nerea used to go to satisfy their voracious appetite.

Or sometimes, if she was a woman of class, he would take her to one of the luxury hotels in old Havana, like Hotel Plaza on Agramonte Street or Hotel Sevilla on Zulueta (just a few blocks from the apartment Nerea had turned down), or Hotel Bristol or Hotel Palace or The Savoy, or once in a while he would be in the mood for the faded elegance of The Gran Inglaterra Hotel on Paseo del Prado, a third-floor balcony room with a view of the harbor entrance and the sea beyond the castle, a narrow wedge of a view, but exhilarating, the same room every time, the very room, the hopeful clerk had told him that first time, where Winston Churchill had stayed when he came to watch the Spanish-Cuban war in 1895.

And on those rare occasions when the woman Luis had discovered radiated with the sweet purity of a country girl (the kind of girl his mother had always hoped her profligate son would marry), he would escort her home, always at her invitation, and make voiceless love to her in a lawn chair or chaise lounge resting partly on a stone patio and partly in the grass, beneath a towering kapok tree, or a multi-stemmed jacaranda with its purples leaves which could be crushed and boiled to extract a cure for syphilis, or perhaps a big yagrumo tree with its white and green leaves (which looked silver and black at night) fluttering like the protest flags of dissident students.

Naturally he would return to Hotel Milagro just before dawn. Nerea would be asleep, her door open, her voice drifting through Luis' addled brain, but he could never make out what she was saying. He would poke his head through the doorway to her room, tentatively, just in case she was with someone, so he could listen to her slow, regular breathing like a clock before he turned in.

It always seemed at that hour that he was trapped in
a strange, black and white movie of a dream. Some place
where time was an endless maze of choices all leading back
to the same pivotal event. There would always be a faint
glow coming from the kitchen window, the soft glow of a
few lights from the other side of the courtyard. A cool breeze
blowing through the window, rustling the newspapers on the
kitchen table. A dog barking somewhere. A few murmuring
voices. Suspiciously secretive voices, Luis would think, but
also weary and skeptical, rising up from the shadows of the
acacia tree that stood in the middle of the courtyard. But then
the voices would sound slightly muffled, as if they had sought
refuge in the narrow, arcaded walkway leading to a rusty
gate and then the street. And then the voices seemed to be
coming from the rooftops. And then it was as if the owners of
the voices had jumped into a passing car. And then they were
back in the courtyard beneath the acacia tree. It was amazing
how strangely sound behaved at night. As if the laws of the
universe no longer applied.

He would listen to Nerea breathing for a few more
moments, her lover too, if there was one, and then step out
onto the balcony for a quick smoke. He would try to zero in
on the voices in the courtyard, but they always behaved with
the uncanny deception described above, as if their owners
were aware he was trying to eavesdrop on their conversation.
Sometimes he would wonder if the owners of the voices had
been sent to spy on him, or to give him a message of some
kind, a proposal, perhaps, or a warning. Then he would laugh
at his paranoia. He didn't have anything to hide, not really.
Perhaps the voices were a trick of his imagination. Or a trick
of God designed to illuminate the depravity in his soul. But
then he would remember that he no longer believed in God.
God didn't exist, so perhaps the voices didn't exist either.
Like so many things he had once been sure of. Then he would
take a last long drag and flick the rest of his cigarette over
the railing, the sparks from the still-glowing ash trailing in
the darkness. Into the abyss, he would think (or sometimes he
would say this out loud, but softly), and then he would sigh.
The barking of the dog had stopped. He would suddenly feel
cold and head back inside and crawl into bed. In the morning,

which is to say just before noon, Nerea would cook him breakfast. He would pretend he had been in all night. And she would let him pretend. That was the state of the relationship between Luis and Nerea when they first met Oscar.

What Luis said to Nerea the night they first met Oscar:

"He is just your type. Or he would be if you admitted to yourself that you had a type."

". . . ."

"Nerea, please. Oh do not be this way Nerea. Not tonight. Have some fun. Dance with the girls on stage. And dance with this boy in between numbers."

". . . ."

"Yes, take him home. Take him home and fuck the hell out of him. I want you to fuck him. It will be good for you to fuck him. No more moping around the hotel at all hours. Even I have begun moping around."

". . . ."

"The hotel staff is beginning to talk."

". . . ."

"You will enjoy yourself, of that I am sure. Yes, I think so. And perhaps he will become a permanent fixture in your life."

". . . ."

"Yes, in my life also. If you want to know the truth, I think this is the very reason I am pointing him out to you."

". . . ."

"I think he and I might become very good friends."

". . . ."

"No, Nerea. I am not being sarcastic. I am speaking from the heart."

". . . ."

"Now you are being a pessimist. A beautiful, pouting pessimist."

". . . ."

"He and I will become good friends. Very good friends. I have already said so. I may even have dreamed it, so it is sure to come true. He has wit, after all. You heard him on the way in."

". . . ."

"Yes? Ah, there is my beautiful Nerea. All smiles and heartache. But he will be good for you. I am sure of it."

". . . ."

"You will attend to his every whim. You will fill his soul with the kind of love that not even the poets dare dream about."

". . . ."

"Why yes, Nerea, you have always been the delight of my soul."

". . . ."

"No, there are no accidents, Nerea. You of all people should know this."

What else could Nerea do but succumb to the pressure of Luis' request? And the boy was quite good looking. He had brown curly hair and pouty lips. He looked a little like Julio Mella. So she attended to Oscar's every whim. Truly she led him across the islands of love, grief by grief. She convinced him that true love existed, but only when he was with her. Sometimes she called him Julio by mistake, but he did not mind, and when she told him why and showed him the photo of Julio in the hotel lobby, he said he was flattered that she thought he looked like the great, mythic anarchist, she could call him Julio whenever she wanted and he would come running. She said Julio was twenty-five-and-a-half when he had been murdered, and she spoke with a very deep sadness that rang out like a bell. But it was not Julio she was weeping for. The moment she started talking about Julio she heard Luis' voice. It sounded like he was standing directly behind her. She could almost feel his arms tying themselves in a knot around her waist, like he used to do on Saturday evenings at the Rio Cristal Club or La Campana when she was adjusting her headpiece in front of a backstage mirror with the glass bulbs of the mirror glowing a hazy, sultry white and Luis nibbling on her neck. But the only mirror in the lobby of Hotel Milagro was on the other side of the room, and when she whirled around there was no Luis. But then she heard him again, only he sounded very far away this second time, as if he were hiding in the mountains, and then she heard him a third time, but this was only an echo of an echo, as if he were

steadily evaporating in the sunlight of a bright Cuban day or
had taken up residence on the moon. Then her field of vision
narrowed and there was a shimmering sensation around the
rim of her eyeballs, and then she was looking down a very
narrow, very long tunnel. It seemed to her that she was looking into a telescope. At the far end she could see Luis waving
at her frantically, a tiny moon dot of a man calling out to her,
but she could not tell where he was, nor could she make out
what he was saying, he was too far away. Then she heard a
gunshot, or several, a barrage of popping noises, she could
not be sure, and then the sound of a great horn, a bellowing
like that of a bull, and she suddenly realized a steamer was
putting out to sea. She found herself wondering where the
boat was going and if her Luis was supposed to be on the boat
and why wasn't he on board, and then the moon dot that had
been Luis became a single drop of blood, and then another
and another, until the telescope was a pipeline filled with
the blood of Francisco de Quevedo's blood-red moon (which
was certainly a bizarre mixing of metaphors), all of it rushing
towards Nerea's blinking eye, and then her eye became her
mouth and she realized with no small degree of horror that
she was sucking on the end of this telescope that was now a
pipe and there was nothing she could do, she could not move,
and in an instant the bloody torrent was upon her, spiraling
into her mouth and down her throat, as if she had become a
sewer gurgling furiously. She did not understand what was
happening to her and squeezed her eyes shut. The gurgling
sound speeded up but at the same time grew more distant.
Then she heard a snapping sound and opened her eyes and
Luis and the blood and the gurgling sound were gone (except
the taste of blood still lingered in her mouth, and also there
was the earthy, metallic taste of iron, presumably from the
pipe, a few flakes of rust that had been swept up in the
torrent). Oscar was now holding onto her arm, but they were
no longer in the lobby of the hotel. They were walking along
the Paseo del Prado in all its springtime glory. She did not
remember leaving the hotel, a fact which vaguely troubled her,
and then she had the sudden feeling that she had been suffering from hallucinations of the sort described above for several
months, maybe longer, but she seemed better now, though

her legs still felt wobbly. "Are you okay?" Oscar asked. "Yes, yes," she said. "I am fine, just a little dizzy from the heat. I didn't know it was so hot." And Oscar seemed satisfied with her answer and smiled, and he saw his smile reflected in her bright, glistening, doleful eyes, and thinking her sadness (for she still seemed incredibly sad) was for Julio Mella, who had died so young, he suddenly said that he was twenty-five-and-a-half years old himself, right at that very moment, the same age as Julio Mella when he died, except that he, Oscar Garcia Raimundi, would not suffer the same fate, he was going to live to a ripe old age. An old mestizo woman who lived in a palm hut on the outskirts of Baracoa had told him so. She said she could read the future as easily as others read the weather in the clouds. She said he was destined to live to be one hundred years old. Oscar seemed very sure of himself. He spoke with a great serious stiffness that bordered on farce. Nerea laughed. (She could not help herself.) And in the very next moment, six months after they had started strolling up and down the Paseo del Prado, Oscar told Nerea he loved her for the first time, and her sadness seemed to disappear. (It was hard to say how deeply she had buried this sadness and if it would one day return, but such are the chances we all take.) "Ours will be the happiest house on earth," she told him. It was the only hope left to her. Naturally, she fell in love.

During those first three years with Oscar, Nerea suffered through countless vulnerable days of transitory hope and unprovoked hallucinations. It was also during this time that Luis set up shop, so to speak, in a small office on the top floor of an ancient three-story building on the corner of San Pedro and Santa Clara, a crumbling shadow of Baroque magnificence across the street from the local ferries with a slightly obstructed view of the harbor. The building had served as a fish market in the days before independence, and then a cordage warehouse until just after the first world war had ended, and it had been abandoned during the frivolous excess of the roaring twenties, and during the death-march insomnia of the threadbare thirties it had become an informal customs house for black market goods and so became the secret home of dozens of corrupt outfits, including a company called Ignazio Tiziano & Sons, an import/export company which occupied the southeast corner of the building (all three floors), and which did a brisk business, or so they claimed, in figs, olive oil, Marsala wine, Spanish brandy, and coffee. At various times during its history the building had been painted ochre, beige, yellow, and white, but the plaster was disintegrating in some places, and in other places the paint had been devoured by the salt air, so now all four colors could be seen.

Luis rarely spent more than two hours in his office on any given day, but he was often there in the evenings, sometimes well into the wee hours of the morning. When Nerea asked him about his late nights he smiled a discreet, crooked smile and said "I shot an ace of spades out of my sleeve during a card game and now I have to pay for getting caught." Nerea didn't understand what he meant, and in all probability neither did he (it was a line he had once heard in a movie, and ever since he had wanted to use it), but she didn't ask him again. But the question lingered in her heart of hearts for many months, a lichen intermingling with her flesh at the cellular level, nourished by heartache, a home for moths and spiders (which suggests that it was most probably a species of red tree lichen, a tropical variety common to the Americas, known in the scientific community as *Cryptothecia rubrocincta*, which resembles nothing so closely as a broken heart even in the brightest sunlight).

What was Luis doing so late in the enveloping darkness (only God knew how late) in a small office looking out on the black, brackish polluted water of the harbor?

It wasn't because of the new women Luis had taken up with. (By Nerea's estimate there had been three dozen since their love affair had ended.) Luis always and only went out to the finest places in town. But Nerea could think of no alternative explanation, and so she descended into a sort of uncontrollable madness, a swift, spiral descent.

She tried to tell herself that his office was a tiny, miserable, hovel of a place with the musty, claustrophobic feel of an ancient prison cell, which was certainly no place for a romantic tryst.

She tried to imagine her Luis spending countless hours poring over the accounts of obscure business ventures. (It was clear to her unconscious mind at least that she would always think of Luis as hers, even if her conscious mind had accepted their changed circumstances.)

Luis had always been secretive about how he made his money. But she had always accepted his secrecy. She had always known that managing musical talent and negotiating contracts with night club owners was little more than an eccentric hobby of his. It was part of Luis' mystique.

Still, no matter how hard Nerea tried, the story of his hovel of an office, a story she had spun out of the golden silk of thin air, because that is something we all do to protect our illusions and soothe our fears, did not give her peace of mind. She could not quite believe her Luis would spend hour after hour in a shabby office looking out on the dullness of the harbor, laboring with the dreary, dogged devotion of a hermetic initiate to earn something so meager as a salary. This image of Luis made no sense to her. For as long as she had known him, he had abhorred actually doing any work. Luis was all appetite. Luis was all frivolity and song. So her madness deepened the way the color of a summer sunset deepens.

-69-

Wounded thus by the treachery of Luis' changed behavior, Nerea suddenly decided one day that he had been going to this office for years, a secret refuge where he had brought all sorts of young, willing women, most of them Asiatic (why they were of Asiatic descent she did not even want to imagine). A room most certainly decorated in the Moorish tradition, for Luis had always said that Islam offered the only version of paradise worthy a man of his appetite. A room always bathed in sunlight and fresh, aromatic breezes even though the slatted blinds were always shut. Thick, plush rugs from Persia scattered across the floor. Several long mahogany sofas along the walls, with elegantly carved legs and plush, brocaded pillows for reclining. Ornately carved tables covered with tiny jeweled artifacts from Morocco or Spain. The window frames and the doorway arch decorated with Tunisian tile work, intricate geometric patterns of blue and aquamarine and teal and gold and white colored tiles that dazzled the eye and inspired thoughts of God and absolute salvation. Elephants carved from onyx or jade or malachite. A great bed to one side covered in satins and silks. Incense burning. Girlish laughter (a soft tinkling sound). The smells of rosewood and balsam and cinnamon swirling with the sunlight. The deeply invigorating smell of the sea. More girlish laughter (more soft tinkling sounds). Three or four girls in silk kimonos or sheer lace or nothing at all, lounging on the sofas or in the great bed, their legs wide open, the women fingering themselves, stroking each other, licking each other, their juices flowing. Luis applying oils to their skin and drinking wine. Luis then pushing himself into each one, taking them one at a time, or two at a time, the others with lingering, approving smiles on their faces and arms outstretched, leaning back against the pillows or in the great bed to catch the sunlight, to bathe in the breeze, waiting to fuck and to be fucked. All of the images, and even the girls themselves, stolen from the paintings of Gyula (Jules) Tornai, the great Hungarian painter (or near great, or at least he painted with great conviction, which is what one reviewer said after a showing of his paintings in London in 1917), who had been born in 1861 in a small village near Presov, Hungary (which was, incidentally, one hundred and sixty kilometers due east of Ružomberok, the village where Peter Lorre was born) and who later traveled the world and spent many years in India and Japan, where he contracted syphilis, and who died alone in a boarding house in Budapest in 1928 (probably from the syphilis) and was buried in a pauper's grave.

    This is the vision of truth Nerea saw when she closed her eyes. A truth about her Luis that she had not known until that very moment. A truth suddenly revealed, the way sunlight reveals itself in the early morning. Or the way a ticking clock reveals itself in the middle of the night. Nerea kept her eyes closed so she could drink in every detail of Luis' culpable depravity. She felt the triumph of finally uncovering his subterfuge. Still, she also felt that in order to be fair, which is to say in order to have a ready response for his every excuse, she needed to document his habits, so she began to

spy on this monstrous shadow of many shadows who had
once destroyed time. Adopting a pose which she believed was
the height of sober disinterest, she listened in on his telephone
conversations, bending her ear around corners and squeezing
it through keyholes. She went through the mail he locked
away in the upper drawer of his desk, a cheap, shabby desk
provided by the hotel so the lock was easy to jimmy, a probing eye looking for the telltale sign of dirt. On rare occasions,
he would mention his plans for the afternoon or evening,
usually in an off-hand, cavalier sort of way, which immediately aroused Nerea's suspicions, so she would later seek him
out in the very parks or cafés or theatres he had mentioned,
reacting with a superior yet bitter nonchalance if she did
indeed run into him. And always she would take note of the
women he danced with or drank with or ate with or fondled
right there in public on Friday and Saturday nights, for she
still danced with the other girls in their rented headpieces at
the Rio Cristal Club or the Jungle Club or Jiggs Cabaret and
Nightclub on the waterfront (she paid special attention there)
or the sultry, lust-filled La Campana.

Of course Luis realized within a few weeks of her
skulking about that Nerea was undone by jealousy. The very
air was charged with the electricity of lovesick despair. Plants
withered as she passed by. Insects and other small creatures
were instantly vaporized whenever she looked their way. The
smallest sound escaping her lips sent shockwaves radiating
out from the epicenter of her grief, causing windows and
crystal vases and bedroom mirrors and glass lamps of all
shapes and sizes within the immediate vicinity to shatter into
clouds of silica and quartz dust, and these same shockwaves
were most probably the cause of an epidemic of burst eardrums that had raced indiscriminately through the population
of Hotel Milagro, and they might have been a contributing
factor in a series of small underwater earthquakes that rattled
the waters of the Gulf some thirty miles out, all striking within
a few days, killing with their deadly, invisible subterranean
vibrations thousands of yellowfin tuna and bluefin and yellow
sea bass and a few lemonfish, and also tens of thousands
of ballyhoo and a few bonito that had lost their way, and
swamping half a dozen small fishing boats besides that were

caught in the aftermath (a forty-foot swell that caused beach erosion as far away as the Bahamas). It seemed to everyone who had occasion to occupy the same physical (and in some cases spiritual) space as Nerea that the fabric of reality was altered. The sole exception was Oscar, for whenever Nerea was with Oscar, even if Oscar was on the other side of the room or across the street, or if she was just thinking about him, she played the part Luis had given her with the aplomb of a silver screen goddess. But for all the rest it was as if the fabric of reality (which certain ancient Chinese philosophers said was made of various strands of silk spun by caterpillars living in the shadows on the moon) had been stretched to the point of breaking, the shimmering celluloid of existence pulled tightly across the gaping hole of the universe, skintight like a drum. So Luis did what any ex-lover driven to the edge of the abyss would do. He invited Nerea to see his office.

Naturally, Nerea wasn't sure how to respond at first. A single, childish voice trapped inside her brain cried out that everything Luis might tell her or show her would be part of an alluring but all-consuming lie, a half-truth to be sure, but also a half-lie and therefore still a lie, but this childish voice was soon lost amid a swirl of eager, self-adulatory adult voices, presumably voices of experience, each with a different theory about what they would see, a different point of view to push on the world, but all of them in general agreement that a half-lie was still half a step closer to the truth, an untutored belief certainly, but quite popular in its day, and then one of the voices rose above the rest with the purity of a dark, starless night and said if Nerea had been wrong about Luis, then she (or they, if you counted each voice) might even forgive him, in fact, she (they) would be forced to forgive him (depending, on how she or they defined truth in the first place). And so Nerea accepted the invitation.

-70-

The next day Luis led a still startled and perhaps sleepy Nerea, who was walking with the paranoid delicacy of a doe, through the lobby of Hotel Milagro to the street outside. It was nine in the morning, a bright, sunny day. They were going to catch a bus, but Nerea suddenly said she wanted to take one of the ancient streetcars that ran along Calle Luz, so they did. It was a short, silent trip, strangely silent, without the thin, metallic rattle that normally accompanies such trips, without the clang of the streetcar bell or the rumbling voices of the passengers, without any sound at all except for an odd whooshing sound as they passed by street corners and people crossing in front or behind or just milling about, as if their streetcar was traveling through an oversized pneumatic air tube.

Nerea wondered if she and Luis had been hypnotized or were going insane, but Luis did not appear to notice the strange silence. The streetcar stopped only once along the way and a few men in suits and Panama hats got on and also a couple of young girls who might have taken the day off from school to go shopping. Nerea saw their mouths moving, the men near the front of the car and the girls at the back, and she tried to listen in on their conversations, but there was nothing to hear. Then Nerea could see the dark gray of the harbor rising up like a great wind and she and Luis got off and Luis pointed to a building and Nerea nodded and followed him but she had no idea where they were. The sunshine was gone. It was now a gray, cloudy day. The air was thick with pestilent heat and the smells of rotting fish and diesel engines and the muffled, groaning sounds of working men. The building Luis had pointed to seemed to blot out the sky.

Nerea felt like she was suffocating.

They headed for the entrance on the northwest side. The entrance was actually two entrances, a heavy, wrought iron gate leading to the market floor, which was usually unlocked at eleven in the morning, but sometimes the gate remained locked until four in the afternoon, and a smaller, narrow wooden door painted a surprisingly bright lime green, leading to the first of a dozen narrow hallways. Those who worked in this massive, colonial-era structure could be seen passing through the lime green door at all hours of the day and night. The plaza leading up to the gate and the door was crammed full of lonely, disheveled men with empty hands and thin-lipped, toothless grins, and fat women with all of their teeth wearing plain cotton dresses and thin rope sandals, and some wearing scarves to cover their heads but all of them holding baskets or containers of some kind. They were all waiting for the gate to open. Nerea felt a sudden urge to weep, but she kept her composure. It was not clear if the men were with the women, or if the men and the women were waiting in the plaza for different reasons.

Luis said it was like that every morning until they opened the gate. Sometimes, he said, the crowd stretched all the way to the Convent of Santa Clara, a distance of four blocks, all the way to a narrow oak door on Calle Cuba that was rarely if ever used. Luis said the nuns who used to use the door with some frequency were long gone. They had sold the building to the government in 1919, and by 1923 the Department of Public Works had moved in and begun the important but enigmatic process of bricking in windows and covering up fancy 17th century archways and nailing shut side doors and back doors in order to limit access to the thousands of confidential documents and bank account ledgers and other official records that should have been kept in an airtight vault three floors underground, but the sealed corridors and locked novitiate cells of an abandoned nunnery were better than nothing. The only people Luis had ever seen even pass by the narrow door on Calle Cuba were faceless, government workers.

Naturally, Nerea wanted to know more about the nuns, but Luis said he had already told her everything he knew. Of course if he had paid any attention at all to the bits and pieces of local legend that float about all historic neighborhoods, he would have known that the convent had once housed a community of Franciscan nuns whose primary purpose was to educate the daughters of wealthy plantation owners and shipping magnates or members of the diplomatic corp. He would have known that those same nuns had counseled those same despairing daughters when those daughters had wished to join the cloister after disastrous love affairs or because their fathers were convinced they would never be able to find suitable husbands. He would have known that the convent had thus become a haven for the victims of unrequited love.

On this the morning of the visit, as if by preternatural or artistic design, the crowd had already reached the door to the convent. Luis said this was unusual for so early in the day. Even the few government workers that passed along Calle Cuba on their way to the convent's main entrance glanced at the crowd with stupefied apprehension. Nerea wanted to know where all the people came from and why there were so many of them, but Luis didn't say a word. Again, Nerea felt like she was suffocating. The crowd became restless, noisy, for they had been waiting since just before sunrise. Nerea almost fainted from the odor of so many unwashed people crammed together in so small a space. Even though they were still outside it seemed to Nerea that they were trapped inside a very small room, part of an underground labyrinth perhaps, or perhaps a gas chamber or an oven or a crypt. She wanted to know what all these people were waiting for.

Luis laughed. Sometimes, he said, it is hard to tell if the crowd is waiting to get inside the market or waiting to get inside the old, abandoned convent. Nerea stopped a moment, wondering if there was any hidden meaning in what Luis had said, but Luis smiled with absent-minded joy and took hold of her arm and ushered her through the crowd. She almost fainted a second time.

Then a breeze swirled around the plaza and the unpleasant smells from the unwashed men and women dissipated. The danger of fainting had passed and the crowd settled down. They were used to waiting. Suddenly they seemed like stones. Patient. Immovable. Unbothered. Suddenly Nerea was aware of thousands of pairs of unblinking eyes staring out at an untroubled sea.

For a moment Nerea became someone else, a woman in the crowd. She was one of the thousand pairs of unblinking eyes. She was holding a basket. She was staring at a man and a woman making their way through the crowd, but she looked at them with weary indifference, as if she were watching the traffic roll by on San Pedro. A gruff, guttural voice from the crowd said something derogatory about the man and the woman, she could tell by the tone, but the only words she could make out were the words: *perro lazarillo*. The phrase was repeated several times, like a chorus, followed by a great deal

of laughter. Then the phrase and the laughter floated away.
Then Nerea was herself again. As Luis guided her through
the lime green door she looked back at the crowd as if to say
either I am completely mad, or you are, but they did not even
flinch.

"Do you think they will storm the gate?" said Nerea.

Luis shook his head, but then he smiled.

"No, no, but perhaps they should."

Nerea didn't know what to say.

She started to tremble.

Or maybe she was perspiring.

She was plagued by all sorts of creeping doubts. She had
a sudden premonition that the world was coming to an end.

Her sense of unreality deepened.

It took them twenty minutes to get to Luis' office. It
took them an eternity. They passed through a series of long
dim hallways and up (and sometimes down) a seemingly
endless latticework of wooden stairs. Occasionally there was a
missing step, but not often. The hallways were lined on both
sides with dozens of heavy wooden doors, also painted lime
green, set at random intervals, one door never directly across
from another, none with any kind of marking whatsoever, not
a sign or a nameplate, not even a number, but each with an
opaque transom window across the top, some of the windows
closed, some of them open. The gloominess of the hallways
grew with every step. Brown glass globes hung from the
ceiling every twenty feet or so, but not all of the globes were
in working order, and those that were cast a weak, syrupy
brownish light that was swallowed up by every passing
shadow. After a while the only sense Nerea trusted was her
sense of sound, but the sounds she heard made no sense to
her at all. Behind some of the doors she could hear quite
distinctly strange gurgling sounds, as if someone were drowning, or possibly conducting arcane experiments to determine
the electromagnetic capabilities of dolphins confined in
saltwater tanks, but who would do such a thing and why
she could not fathom. Behind other doors she could hear the
sounds of machinery humming or furniture being moved or
rifles being fired and the spent casings bouncing on a wooden
floor, or adding machines adding at the speed of light, which

would produce ocular migraines unless you wore underwater
goggles, or laughter followed by heavy banging sounds, and
then light tapping sounds, as if someone were learning to tap
dance, and then the sound of a bottle being uncorked and then
a coughing fit, and then the sounds of someone dreaming,
which sounds a little something like the murmuring of glass
bees hidden in the damp foliage on a foggy summer morning,
and then the click of a movie projector and the whine of a
static-filled screen, and then a radio announcer with a very
staticky voice announcing the results of the last race from
Oriental Park and then a trumpet blaring, or something that
sounded like a trumpet, and the next race getting under way
and the sounds of the horses racing around the track and the
announcer getting very excited, and then the sound of a doctor
quietly talking with a nurse, and then another coughing fit,
and then more laughter. Luis was not bothered by anything
Nerea heard. Then they came to a stretch without any doors
at all and the sounds faded altogether and so they traveled in
complete silence for a while, even the sound of their footsteps
was felt rather than heard, a subtle collapsing sensation, like
one's lungs filling up with blood or seawater, and then Nerea
heard a soft whispering kind of sound, but she could not
determine if it were an actual sound or merely her ears ringing in the absence of any noise. She was about to ask Luis if
he heard this strange ringing sound when they turned a corner
and stumbled into a small group of young men. The men were
wearing overalls and cotton work shirts drenched in sweat
and smoking cigarettes that smelled like burning rubber, cupping the cigarettes carefully with their hands in case a strong
wind should come roaring down the hallway, though such
an event seemed unlikely. Nerea immediately realized that
they were the source of the whispering, their faces contorting
as they spoke a strange, garbled tonal language that seemed
less like a language and more like the warbling, singsong
mimicry of Brazilian parrots. Without warning or any shy
second glances, as if the men were merely slipping revolvers
into shoulder holsters or offering Indian talismans to curious
tourists, they stopped their whispering and then stamped out
their cigarettes and brushed out the wrinkles in their overalls,
straightening themselves against the wall as they did so, and

said "Good morning, El Zayde," all of them in unison, with unapologetic good humor.

By the time Luis and Nerea got to the third floor, the hallways were teeming with all sorts of figures moving back and forth through the brown, syrupy gloom, more young men in overalls and drenched work shirts pushing carts overloaded with boxes of all sorts, older men with satchels or leather briefcases in their hands but without their jackets, nervous men running out of one room or another and then dashing hurriedly down the hall, disappearing into the hazy, brownish soup, the echo of their footfalls diminishing, and young girls in pleasing floral print dresses and red or beige round-toed patent-leather slingbacks, pretty young secretaries perhaps, or mistresses or fiancées or high-class prostitutes who had been up all night, following after the rushing men, waving letters in the air that had never been read or, in some cases, never even mailed, the letters filled with all sorts of personal information, private lies and sexual innuendo, the sordid details of crimes that had been expunged, that sort of thing, the young girls rushing after the rushing men with incredibly light feet, and everywhere in those long hallways traversing the third floor Luis was greeted with warm, friendly grins and happy, approving nods and soft, flirtatious smiles and a few weary but respectful grimaces, and with every grin or nod or smile or grimace there was an appropriate "Good morning, El Zayde" or "Is there anything I can get for you, El Zayde" or "When you have a moment, El Zayde, could you stop by and see so and so, they have a question only you can answer" or "If only you had been here last night, El Zayde, we had a spectacular night last night, we are sorry you missed it."

It was almost too much for Nerea to take in.

Then the voices faded and the hallway was suddenly empty, as if a great wind had indeed come roaring through the building. But the gloominess remained. The gloominess was almost unbearable. "We're almost there," Luis said, but his words had a hollow sound to them, as if he did not quite believe himself. The hallway seemed smaller now and felt more like a tunnel. Nerea wondered if something catastrophic had happened. Perhaps the building had collapsed, she thought. Or perhaps the crowd in the plaza had become a mob and had stormed the gate. Perhaps they had started a revolution. Perhaps people were dying. Or perhaps she had suddenly died. Then Luis laughed as if he were able to read her troubled thoughts. They emerged from the tunnel and the gloom and Luis said, "Here we are."

But they were not yet in Luis' office. They were standing in the middle of a small waiting area, a semi-circular atrium with three office doors, one directly across from the tunnel on a roughly north to south plane, the other two facing each other on an east to west line. The doors were typical of detective agencies and newspaper rooms in the 1930s and 40s, and perhaps even the offices of a few Hollywood movie moguls, with brightly polished mahogany frames and frosted glass windows with fancy curlicue borders and shiny brass door knobs. A few potted ferns and a few dwarf palms filled in the spaces between the doors. The plants were dripping with moisture, as if they had been recently watered. Just this little bit of greenery is a pleasant surprise, Nerea thought.

She listened to the sounds of dripping water for a moment, perhaps to settle her nerves, her face angled slightly up and her eyes closed as if she were waiting for a dream to fall from the sky, and then she felt a drop of water on her skin, and then another, and she opened her eyes and she saw there were great, gaping holes in the ceiling. She could actually see the sky through the holes. It was a blue sky now, the gray clouds were gone, and water was dripping from the holes in the ceiling.

"Here we are," Luis said again, or maybe it was the first time. He pulled Nerea towards the middle door. The door featured shiny black lettering that said Ignazio Tiziano & Sons. It was the same on the other doors. Luis opened the middle door and they went inside.

-71-

Nerea was caught between the involuntary spasms of jealousy and an unwillingness to believe she had been wrong.

The office was like the prison cell of her first imagining, a
vintage oak swivel chair with the heft of a tank and a narrow
desk pushed up against a window with the slatted blinds
closed and barely enough light creeping through to illuminate
the dust particles floating in the air like so many wickedly
capricious spiderlings, dainty harbingers of death, or like so
many jubilant paratroopers descending, as one of the vagabond poets of Mexico City once wrote, as swiftly as clocks.

The desk was overflowing with letters and ledgers and
a few yellowing newspapers, for in spite of his professed
diligence, Luis suffered from poor eyesight late at night and
so had trouble seeing what he was doing. Luis told Nerea
that one of the girls from the steno pool was assigned to his
office and came in twice a week in the evenings to help him
sort through the mess. The seafoam green Optima typewriter
planted squarely on top of the paperwork belonged to her.

Luis flicked on a switch and two brown globes began
to glow near the ceiling, but the darkness in the room only
intensified. A pair of wingback chairs materialized out of the
gloom and also a small side table.

Nerea's mind had been a jumble of contradictory
impressions until she heard about the secretary. She now
stared at Luis with futile pity. Then she began firing questions
at him. To poor Luis the questions seemed random, bizarre,
incoherent, laced with mind-numbing inertia or arsenic or
worse.

"Why do they call you El Zayde?" Nerea said.

Luis didn't respond.

He disappeared into the slatted shadows on the far
side of the room. There were some clinking sounds, spoons
rattling, water fizzing. Then he returned with two high-balls.

"Everywhere we went they were calling you El Zayde."

They sat down in the wingback chairs.

"Yes," he said. "They were."

Luis gave Nerea her drink and then sipped from his own
glass, smiling a slight, satisfied smile

"But why?"

"They always call me that. They think I'm the boss, a fat
fish, the big cheese, the Big Kahuna."

From somewhere outside there was a distant rumbling

sound, like a massive gate being ripped from its hinges and
the earth shuddering and then the sounds of raucous cheering,
or perhaps it was screaming, or perhaps it was the excited,
jittery voices of pilgrims participating in a religious festival for
the very first time.

"It is an honest mistake. They've never seen the Big
Kahuna."

Another sip.

"He doesn't come here at all."

And yet another.

Nerea was watching Luis very carefully, the way his
mouth curled up slightly when he spoke, the way his tongue
rolled effortlessly and casually across his teeth when he
finished a sentence, as if there were some lingering sweetness
to his words that he found immensely satisfying. This was a
Luis that Nerea had never seen before. She wasn't sure she
could believe a word he said.

"I'm the only one who does come here," said Luis. "It is
very ironic."

Nerea wondered who this mythical Big Kahuna was.
She wondered what Luis meant by saying he was the only one
who came here. Where exactly was here and why was Luis the
only one? And how many others might come here but didn't?
What stopped them?

Then Luis laughed a hearty, robust laugh, but it was
laughter also tinged with a philosopher's understanding of the
tragic comedy of life, or perhaps a movie director's take on
things, as if he had just then recognized the tenuous nature of
his own existence and so realized that there was nothing else
to do but laugh in such a strange, uninhibited fashion from his
belly to his heels. In good faith, he tried his best to tell Nerea
everything she wanted to know about his business associates.

-72-

The gist of what Luis told Nerea about his business
associates:

Luis' business associates were all directors of Ignazio
Tiziano & Sons, but they could just as easily have secured starring roles in any number of 1930s Hollywood gangster films,
like *The Public Enemy* (1931) or *Scarface* (1932). They were all
criminals of one sort or another, thugs, killers, disgruntled
bureaucrats with axes to grind, cops on the take, part-time
dock workers, union bosses, drug kingpins, a vagabond collection of second-tier Mafiosi who had been quickly elevated
during the war years to positions of power hidden within
the rat's maze of Cuban politics, a crumbling infrastructure
supported by secret government agencies and high-profile
public officials as well as labor union under-secretaries, media
moguls, and a few well-placed church dignitaries, and so Luis'
business associates (and Luis himself by association) commanded the loyalty of tens of thousands of Cuban souls, and
all because the Americans thought they needed the nefarious
skills of this gang of gangsters during the late 1930s and early
1940s to help keep track of wayward Nazi spies intent on
submarining the industrialized war-waging capability of the
United States.

The American government had been convinced that
the impenetrable shadows of every sleepy, backwater
Caribbean and South American port were infested with all
manner of German and Argentine saboteurs, working in an
obviously clandestine manner for the *Amt Auslands und Abwehr*
(Germany's Foreign Office of Defense, part of the Nazi's
labyrinthine bureaucratic structure), men and women who
would do anything to replace the bald eagle of the United
States with the black eagle of Germany. But the Americans did
not think of Havana as just another backwater port. As late as
1943, the American government clung to the unsubstantiated
belief that the capital city of romantic Cuba was the gateway
through which everything flowing out of the Axis-infested
southern hemisphere on its way north must flow, which meant
it would be the most likely jumping off point for any group
of saboteurs trying to reach the sandy, unpatrolled beaches of
Florida. (Never mind that German spies routinely bypassed
Havana on their way from South America to New York City.)
So they spent a great deal of time and money searching for
Germans in the streets of Havana.

These initial assumptions proved to be incorrect. Perhaps the Americans had intercepted a decoy message and the Germans were laughing their asses off. Perhaps the Americans simply could not swallow the truth that Argentina was too far away to forcefully manipulate and found it easier to chase shadows around the Caribbean and then tell the American public they were fighting the good fight. Or perhaps they believed what they saw in Hollywood movies. In any event, the *Abwehr* sent only one spy to Cuba during the entire war, at least this was the official story, an incompetent boob named Heinz Lüning, who had been given orders to set up a secret wireless station so he could transmit any important military information to agents in Buenos Aires, which is where the real espionage activity was taking place, as everyone knew.

The Argentine agents were a collection of minor German diplomats and Spanish Falangists posing as sailors or businessmen or academics or traveling actors aboard various innocuous-seeming ships, such as the *Sebastian Elcano,* a Spanish school ship out of Barcelona, or the *Cabo de Buena Esperanza,* an ocean liner that was also the maritime home of the actress Lola Membrives (who was, incidentally, one of Franco's favorite spies, though nothing was ever proven) and which ferried her back and forth across the Atlantic once every few months so she could make an announcement on Radio Prieto, encouraging the good citizens of Buenos Aires to come out to the theatre while she was in town, for God only knew when she would return with this terrible war raging across the globe, and after each performance her flunkies would pass out pro-Axis pamphlets to her fans, all of the pamphlets doctored by Doc Goebbels, filled to overflowing with the most insidious manipulations of the truth. Suffice it to say that the agents in Argentina would decide if anything from Lüning was worth reporting to Berlin.

In the end the whole Lüning affair was a rather dark comedy. Lüning was never able to get his radio to work, so he spent most of his time drinking in the various bars and clubs in and around Havana. When he was arrested by Batista's men in 1942, he had yet to send a single message. But Batista and the Allies claimed he was a master spy nevertheless and that he had been an integral component in the web of Nazi submarines operating in the Caribbean, so they had him executed.

As you would expect, the consequences of enlisting
the aid of this nefarious gang of cutthroats was inevitable.
By the 1950s it was next to impossible to curtail the activities
of the gangsters, cutthroats, thieves and assassins that had
been given semi-official permission to set up shop in Havana.
Business had been lucrative, and it appeared, at least on the
surface, that business would continue to be lucrative, for even
though the war was over, neither the rolling succession of
Cuban regimes nor the American CIA was willing to spend the
money "to clean out this nest of Machiavellian vipers," as one
confidential CIA memo had so elegantly put it.

The grandfather of this motley crew was Giuseppe
Federico DiCarla, who had been born in 1881 in the small
seaside village of Scopello in northwestern Sicily. The men in
his family had been tuna fishermen for centuries, but when
he was a small boy his father had gone to work on one of
the great tuna boats out of Castellammare del Golfo, which
translated means Sea Fortress of the Gulf, so they had moved.
Later, Federico had moved to Trapani, a major seaport on the
lip of the Tyrrhenian Sea, a half day's journey from the town
of his childhood, because in those days the roads weren't very
good, a dirt path for ox-carts pretty much, the road crumbling
in places, the hazy shadow of the Zingaro mountains to the
northwest, the humpbacked shadows of peasants plodding
across the plains, the plains dotted with stone farmhouses and
then a village and then nothing except rocky hills and clumps
of twisted fig trees or silvery olive trees (which Federico
said looked as if they were bathed in moonlight even in the
middle of the day), and then another village, and so on like
that, and in every village, along every road, young men in
fustian or velvet jackets, all of them bastard sons of Garibaldi,
all of them wearing skull caps and cartridge belts and muddy
top-boots, all of them with guns, long-barreled rifles, though
mostly for show, except when it came to hunting rabbits. At
least that's how DiCarla remembered it. And that was all Luis
had time to tell Nerea, for the very next instant the door to his
office burst open, shattered into a thousand splinters it seemed
like, and one of Luis' associates or underlings or messenger
boys stood in the doorway, panting and heaving.

At first the messenger boy did not move. He stood in the doorway, still panting and heaving, a dark, vibrating shadow backlit by the sunlight pouring in through the holes in the ceiling. He seemed uncertain if he had come to the right place. He seemed to be wondering if he had burst into a tucked away bathroom where someone was busy in a stall masturbating to beat the band, or else that same someone was reading with an insatiable appetite the mythic though reactionary (and some would say downright sadistic and certainly rightwing) poetry of Silvio Salvático, the mythical Chilean poet and writer and gossip columnist.

"El Zayde?"

"Yes?"

"El Zayde?"

"Yes, yes, what is it? I am right here."

"But I cannot see you."

"Of course not. Your eyes have not yet adjusted. It is very dim in here."

"Yes . . . I guess that makes sense."

The messenger boy removed a pair of black-rimmed eyeglasses and rubbed his eyes. He tried to gain control of his breathing. There was a general noisiness in the air and also the sound of sirens, as if a great hubbub were occurring in the streets of Havana or elsewhere. The messenger boy replaced his glasses. He was a plain, unremarkable fellow with the aura of a befuddled accountant or the likeable but bumbling assistant to a brilliant but emotionally distant and therefore unstable scientist. He was wearing a thin dark cotton shirt and dark pants and rope-soled sandals. Nerea barely gave him a second glance. She thought he made a much better shadow than a messenger boy. He was perspiring heavily. He was not used to excitement. His name was Immanuel.

"The people have stormed the gate," Immanuel said.

"Yes, but what does that mean exactly?"

"It means they have ripped the gate from its hinges and tossed it aside."

"Yes, yes, but what is happening?"

"They are . . . they . . ."

"Yes. Tell me slowly. Leave nothing out."

"They are pouring through . . . they are . . ."

Immanuel gulped a few gulps of air, like people do when they have been buried alive in a coffin and have had to claw their way out, which is no easy task when the coffin is a pine box with several feet of soft, clumpy dirt piled on top, but which is virtually impossible when the coffin features an aluminum shell or some mixture of bronze and copper or some other alloy, so clearly Immanuel was gulping air as if he had just clawed his way out of a pine box that had been recently buried.

"Before that. From the beginning," said Luis.

Immanuel took a few more gulps because you cannot even begin to imagine the stress of being buried in a pine box for even one minute or several minutes until your eyes adjust to absolute darkness, which they might never do, and you are left with the certain knowledge that you are facing eternity all alone without even a chance to say goodbye, unless you get out by some miracle, in which case you have cheated death, so to speak. So Immanuel took a few more gulps, and then he began anyway.

"They were waiting as usual," he said. "The people. But there were many more of them today. No one knows why. It seemed like they were waiting for something to happen. Like a signal, perhaps. Or a sign from God. Leonardo was frightened by so many so he did not open the gate, and we told him that was a mistake but he still refused. The people were clamoring to get in and waving their baskets and bags in the air and he refused. Then there was gunfire from somewhere near the convent and someone said there were soldiers coming or revolutionaries or maybe it was the police, and the people started running away from the convent, but there was nowhere for them to go down that narrow street, there were so many of them, except straight for us. They were heading straight for us like a herd of stampeding bulls. What could we do? Leonardo opened a small porthole window near the gate and started firing his pistol, but he was afraid to look out so his aim was erratic. I think he killed a few pigeons trying to fly away but that was it. The next thing we knew the crowd was surging against the gate, shouting and cheering and laughing and crying. I have never heard so much noise in one tiny space. Then they tore the gate off its hinges, as I said, and this stampede of raging bulls started rampaging all about the marketplace arcade on the first floor, swarming in and out of the various stalls. The vendors had already fled. Did you not feel the building shake? We thought the entire structure would come crashing down on top of our heads with the pounding of so many angry feet. I don't know how many people there were. Several hundred. Maybe more. Angels and demons dancing on the head of a pin. They were racing around, grabbing whatever they could find and stuffing it into their baskets and bags and then running for the plaza, their cups overflowing. And then everything was gone. There wasn't a vegetable or a piece of fruit or a pork chop or a bag of coffee beans or an umbrella or a box of cigars or a bottle of wine or a pair of shoes or a lady's hat or a jar of olive oil or a book of philosophy or a gentleman's serge suit left in the whole place. Everything was gone. Vanished. Vaporized. But then it became clear that only those first few who had led the charge made off with the goods. Everyone else, which is to say hundreds and hundreds of poor, dispossessed, vagrant souls, disillusioned souls, angry and bitter, all of them were still clinging to their empty baskets and their empty bags with the kind of fierce desperation I have only ever read about or seen in the movies. It was worse than any nightmare. They began searching through closets and small storerooms and offices, these vagrants, looking for anything they might steal, anything that would fill up their baskets and their bags and ease their heart-wrenching, raging, insatiable hunger. They spread out into the hallways like a disease. But there was nothing left, El Zayde, and so they fell into a madness, tearing apart entire rooms, dismantling desks and other pieces of furniture, breaking windows and scattering important papers, toppling and then smashing the delicate apparatus and specially designed instruments of various arcane experiments that have been going on for years in secret, heaping together great piles of used tires and other flammable items and lighting small bonfires which soon became big bonfires, setting off small explosions using whatever chemicals were laying

around, most likely anhydrous ammonia or carbon disulfide
or diethyl ether. We thought they would turn upon each other.
We hoped they would. We prayed. But they never did. Did
you not notice the smell of black smoke, El Zayde? Did you
not breathe in the clouds of toxic gas? It was more than we
could stand, we almost passed out, we are not made of sterner
material, El Zayde, I am sorry to say, so we left. But the
hallway to the plaza was blocked, it was covered with heaps
of fallen refuse, bits of the ceiling that had collapsed, broken
lamps, exposed wiring, plumbing fixtures, and everywhere
there was the heavy, black smoke. We could see no way to get
through to the plaza. So we headed up to the second floor and
down the fire escape that we always used when we wanted to
get out of the building without being noticed so we could slip
across San Pedro and take a nice long walk along the water's
edge. But I came up here to find you, El Zayde. There is no
one else on the third floor except the three of us. Everyone
else has escaped safely."

"And the vagrants looking to fill their empty bags and
baskets?"

"I am sure they got out, El Zayde. They seemed, how
shall I say it, very well organized in spite of the chaos. Yes,
there is a meaning behind the madness for any who would
look. But it does not matter. It is a raging inferno down there.
Not even demons would stay in such a place. Not even Lucifer
himself. Even the stone walls are beginning to melt."

A vaguely troubled look came over Luis's face, as if he
were trying to remember what he had eaten for lunch the day
before and was dismayed by his poor memory. He suddenly
felt alternating waves of humiliation and sadness. Then he
heard a snapping, barking sound, which was most likely the
sound of Immanuel saying 'El Zayde, El Zayde, we haven't
much time,' and then he heard a deeper, snapping sound,
more like a deep growl, which was most likely himself saying
'Yes, yes, but we need to proceed deliberately,' and then he
heard a high pitched ringing sound like tiny Christmas bells,
silver Christmas bells which had been fashioned by artisans
living in Mexico City, which was most likely Nerea wondering
what this crazy self-proclaimed messenger boy named
Immanuel meant by saying there wasn't much time and what

were they waiting around for when the world was collapsing, and then Luis noticed that the shadowy appearance of Immanuel was not a result of dim lighting.

Immanuel was black from the smoke and ash that had engulfed the widening apocalypse (the bonfires, the explosions, the raging inferno) of the first floor. It was almost as if Immanuel were wearing a mask, as if the series of explosions and the storming of the gate had been staged for some unknown purpose. Then Luis suddenly smiled as if he had just that moment been raised from the dead.

"Nerea, go with Immanuel, he will get you out of the building. I have to gather up a few things."

Then he laughed a joyful, robust laugh.

"I can't let everything go up in smoke, now can I?"

Immanuel did not laugh at Luis' joke, but he might have been smiling, but it was hard to tell from the smoke and ash that obscured his true appearance. Luis went to his desk and scribbled something on a piece of paper and handed it to Immanuel.

"Call this number and tell whoever answers what happened, just as you told it to me."

". . . ."

"And tell them I'll be along shortly."

". . . ."

"No, don't say anything else. Just hang up after that. They will understand."

Then Immanuel and Nerea headed out through the shattered office door, and it seemed to Luis that they were suddenly swimming in an ocean of blue sky and sunlight and the potted palm trees and ferns were swaying back and forth with a watery gentleness, like strands of seaweed, and Immanuel was no longer a dark shadow with skin the color of smoke and ash, his skin was suddenly and mysteriously washed clean of all grime, his skin was as white as the whitest plume of the whitest bird in paradise, and then Nerea and Immanuel vanished into the darkly glowing wormhole of the hallway on their way to the freedom of a bright sunny day. For a moment Luis stood there, staring after them, as if Immanuel and Nerea were both lifelong friends, though clearly this was not the case. Then he turned to the papers scattered across his small desk and a few files that had been hidden away in a filing cabinet, and he also discovered an old leather briefcase which he had never seen before crammed into the top drawer. Before another thought entered his brain, such as 'Jesus Christ it's hot in here' or 'what the hell happened down there' or 'God damn fucking peasants' or 'I sure hope Nerea gets out okay' or 'who exactly is this Immanuel anyway, I don't remember seeing his face before' or 'what the fuck am I doing, this place is about to go up in smoke,' he began shoving the papers and the files, those that seemed important, into the leather briefcase, and whistling all the while.

-74-

Sometimes it is difficult to know when and where someone's story truly begins, but without this deeper under-standing it is almost impossible to understand why anything happens at all. Understanding the true beginning of any story (yours, mine, anyone's), especially as that story unfolds before our very eyes, gives shape to the entire universe, and it is this shape that gives meaning to our lives. This shape is our collec-tive story, if you will. But nothing is ever what it appears to be. And this is the crux of our dilemma. How far back do we go? Which events do we embrace as absolutely necessary? And which do we dismiss? If we don't go back far enough we will end up in the soup of misunderstanding. If we go back too far we will invariably take a misstep when we start forward again and become tangled up in the labyrinth of everything that never was. Now some will argue that we can never go back far enough, that every story begets another story, and so on, but this kind of thinking doesn't begin with anything we can easily grasp, and it generally leads only to rude awakenings and sudden attacks of vertigo, at least on a personal level, for while the grand narrative extends to infinity, few of us can be certain of our own narrative thread beyond the inevitability of our own deaths. So we do the best we can with the limited information we are given and hope that no one will notice we

haven't a clue, that we have no idea what's going to happen
next because we don't know where we truly came from, so
how could anyone expect us to know where we will end up.
This ignorance, of course, is partially (or wholly, if you do not
believe in God) the cause of what we like to call the tragedy of
life, or the comedy of life if you prescribe to the theories of the
post-apocalyptic romanticists, or the tragicomedy if you are a
dyed-in-the-wool postmodernist. In plain language, we are all
whistling in the dark.

Such was the case with Luis. Why did Luis remain in his
office with the raging inferno raging two floors below? Why
did he suddenly and manically (as opposed to maniacally)
begin stuffing papers into a briefcase when Immanuel had told
him the stone walls were beginning to melt and ten minutes
later or thereabouts, he himself could actually feel the heat
of the stone walls melting? Even Luis, if pressed, would have
had difficulty coming up with a believable answer. And what
about the briefcase? Had Luis simply forgotten he owned a
briefcase or had one mysteriously appeared in the top drawer
of the filing cabinet, as if by destiny's own hand, so that Luis
would use it for precisely that purpose for which it was used?
Who can say? And would Luis have remained in his office if
there had been no briefcase so conveniently placed within his
reach? Why did he stay when all reason and the instinct for
survival must certainly have urged him to flee with Nerea and
Immanuel? And why did he take the time to scribble on a
piece of paper and then give the paper to Immanuel with only
the vaguest of instructions? Such questions are always difficult
to answer and generally require exhaustive, mind-numbing
analysis, which may or may not lead to the overall decay of
civilization, at least as we know it, as a battery of social and
literary critics and numerous television personalities have
suggested, and which is almost certainly the reason that many
books are banned or in some cases even burned during peri-
ods of great social unrest. But we have no business with such
analysis here. Let us simply say that Luis lingered in the dim
light of his office, stuffing papers into a briefcase that seemed
to appear out of nowhere, to honor the wishes of Giuseppe
Federico DiCarla. Which is to say that Federico had once told
Luis that they must never call attention to themselves or their

activities, that if the iron gates to Ignazio Tiziano & Sons were ever breached, if this simple import/export company were suddenly exposed to the probing eyes of the world at large, if their hand was forced and they had to move on and start over, then they should at the very least make absolutely sure they didn't leave a trace. When they were gone, it should be as if they had never existed. So Luis stayed behind for ten minutes or so because of the preemptory wisdom of Giuseppe Federico DiCarla, and wise words they were indeed, because he didn't dare assume that the fire that had swallowed the first floor would effectively erase the existence of Ignazio Tiziano & Sons from the memory of man.

But there was something else that even Luis did not dare admit to himself. Since Federico's natural wisdom sprang from a deeply rooted psychosis which he had nurtured with unfailing vigilance since he was a young man, it is also fair to say that Luis remained in his tiny hovel of a troglodyte's office on the third floor of a burning building because he was afraid of Giuseppe Federico DiCarla. There, it is out in the open. Luis was absolutely terrified of Giuseppe Federico DiCarla. It was a terror, moreover, that had infiltrated every layer of his skin all the way down through the subcutaneous layer. And that is why he asked Immanuel to call the number on the scrap of paper. He needed to get word to Federico as quickly as possible, but he did not want to be the messenger, so why not use Immanuel (particularly since Luis had a sneaking suspicion that Immanuel was more than just the winged harbinger of doom). Luis understood that the moment Immanuel made the call, he, Luis, would be absolved of all responsibility for the storming of the marketplace gate and the apocalypse that followed. Perhaps Immanuel would even take the fall. And at some indeterminate point in the future, he, Luis, would get a note from Federico and there would be a meeting of all of the Directors of Ignazio Tiziano & Sons to discuss what they could salvage from this disaster and how long before they would be up and running again, and he would attend the meeting, and even participate with a few poignant observations, without the fear of reprisal or even reprimand.

Naturally, to those of us who have never been employed by a psychotic Mafia overlord who may or may not have

murdered countless thousands, Luis' fear seems silly. But it is
not for us to judge the nature of Luis' fear. We must simply
acknowledge that this fear exists (or once existed).

-75-

The true story of Giuseppe Federico DiCarla, which is
reason enough to be afraid of him, as Luis was, or at least it
will give you something to chew on, mostly from Federico's
own lips as pieced together by Luis over the years, and which
he was going to share with Nerea word for word but he never
got the chance:

Federico had left Sicily during Mussolini's war against
the Mafia and eventually settled in Havana.

The exact date of his arrival is unknown.

He said he had picked Havana because Moro Castle
reminded him of the medieval castle that guarded the harbor
entrance to Castellammare del Golfo. Sometimes he would
talk about the differences between the two castles. But mostly
he liked to reminisce about his boyhood escapades in Sicily
and his only true love, a girl whose name was sometimes
Maura D'Alessandria, but at other times her name was Mirella
Deodato, and every once in a while, in a fit of unapologetic
nostalgia, her name was Maria D'Angelo.

It was hard to tell how accurate his memory was.

According to Luis, Federico always ate with a knife
hidden in the folds of his napkin.

It was much more than a knife really. A forge-hammered steel blade with diamond cross sections made by an
obscure (which is to say forgotten) artisan in the 17th century.
A leather scabbard with gold plated fittings. A simple,
straightforward, slender blade for thrusting deep into the
belly of an enemy, or a close friend. An assassin's blade, truly.
Federico called it his dagger of mercy.

Always when Federico met someone for the first time
he would mention this knife. Sometimes he would show it to
them with a devilishly deceptive but good-natured charm.

And always, naturally, the same question would follow: why would anyone need to hide a dagger of mercy in the folds of their napkin?

And always, naturally, Federico would smile the polite confessional smile of someone remembering a small transgression from long ago, a childhood sin committed in ignorance, a trivial matter, but very humorous, and then he would oblige the curiosity of anyone who asked with the story of his knife.

It was a very long story.

After a while you would forget it was the story of the knife and you would think it was the story of something else.

But by the end all you could think about was the knife.

I knew nothing of knives when I was a boy, Federico would say. (This is how he would always begin.) Not the kind of knives the Fasci used. Not the knives of the Black Hand dripping with the blood of a thousand bellies ripped wide open and vulnerable widows gnashing their teeth. My father was a fisherman and the only knife he used was for cutting rope and mending nets and gutting fish. But that all changed during the year of Saint Rosalia's Earthquake of Redemption, as it came to be known among the farmers and fisherman and priests of northwestern Sicily. Yes, fisherman who swore they saw the image of the little saint swimming in the waters of the sea even while the stones of ancient buildings were tumbling into the waves. Farmers who saw the shiny gilded patina of her face full of sorrow hiding in the clouds as the earth cracked open and their fields were burned to a crisp by the flames bursting up from below. And the priests were praying to her redemptive spirit, kneeling before a horde of whispering, flickering votive candles like so many dead souls suspended in purgatory, and then they heard a soft and quiet voice, they later said, a voice they knew without a doubt to be her reclusive voice as inaudible as the sound of fluttering eyelids renouncing all temptation; or her firm, incantatory voice ringing out like a sword, praising the boundless, determined mercy of God; or her hopeful, plaintive voice extolling the heroic virtues of a saintly life (virtues now almost only found in the marginalia of ancient Teutonic manuscripts, or in the cryptic dreams of young novitiates after studying the deaths of the Christian martyrs); or her cataclysmic, haranguing voice filled with torrential grace and the musical precision of a chorus of idiot-savants hidden by the clouds; all this they heard even as the leaded glass windows of their churches became a thousand splinters flying through the air like so many daggers. The earthquake was a vision of hell, was it not? Behold the monster with the pointed tail who cleaves the hills and breaketh walls and weapons, the monster of our darkest dreams who infecteth the whole world. Yes. They saw this monster in Caccamo. Yes. In Trabia. Yes, yes. On the other side of Palermo. Yes. You would have thought it could not reach us. You would have thought the distance was too great. But everyone knew something momentous was happening. You could feel the ground move beneath your feet like you were standing in a boat. Even where we lived along the shores of our safe harbor by the sea. A mountain range between us and the source of the earthquake. An entire world between us. A universe.

So the ground rolled and heaved and shuddered for five days and countless buildings cracked and fell apart, and in some places the streets disappeared, great gaping holes opening up and steam rising. In the Cathedral of La Matrici, the altar of the Holy Mary of the Lamp cracked in two, as did the altar dedicated to the Blessed Mary of Carmel. And a crack also appeared in the stone floor in one of the subterranean rooms below the public levels of the church, and there was a slow oozing of spring water from the crack, from a hidden spring beneath the foundation of the church, the water bubbling up, hot and frothy, but this damage was not discovered for many weeks, by which time the paintings that had been stored down there for safekeeping were moldy ruins. And God help the frescoes on the ceiling for the damage they suffered from the intense humidity, which seemed more focused during the five days of the earthquake, attacking only religious artwork and hazy, superstitious thinking, unlike the normally intense humidity of the region which attacked everything with equal fervor.

Every window in the Cathedral shattered and fell to the ground, as did the windows of several smaller churches, but the churches themselves did not fall, which was seen as an example of good triumphing over evil. Some of the jetties

along the waterfront and a few warehouses did collapse and
were washed away with the tide, but this was not seen as
anything except maybe bad luck, or an indictment against
those who had built the jetties or the warehouses in the first
place. Who could imagine such destruction? It was more than
fire and brimstone. We no longer recognized where we lived.
We could see the fierce Erinnys hovering in the smoky air,
three hell-bound Furies stained with blood, their hair a mass
of writhing serpents and horned vipers, their snouts snapping
at us like the snouts of deranged dogs. This is what we saw.
These were the images eating away at our brains. Just like
the priests talked about. Everything they had ever said was
suddenly and irrevocably true. So all the old women were
huddled in churches all over town and beyond even while
the windows were breaking and crucifixes were toppling and
altars were cleaved in two, saying their prayers. *'Aitnê! Aitnê!
Aitnê!'* And who could blame them? It seemed like the end of
the world. Death was everywhere. What else could they do?

But I was not like these old women screaming their
prayers or the priests who pretended they were free of lice
and would not stoop so low as to pluck a louse from the
head of a friend or a penitent. I tried to remain objective.
The earthquake happened in September, two weeks after
the feast day of Saint Rosalia, but only a few days after the
celebration of her feast day had ended. Always with religion
something is happening either just before or just after a feast
day. Soon everyone was calling it the Great Earthquake of
Saint Rosalia's Redemption. But it was mostly the priests
who called it this. Because of all the destruction. Because
now we could rebuild and then we would be redeemed.
Priests will seize on anything. *Ammuccia lu latinu 'gnuranza di
parrinu.* Always religion is giving us some new twist, a way
of remembering the world that would not normally occur to
us. Such was the case here. An earthquake is an earthquake is
an earthquake, I have always said. But what is an earthquake
anyway but a moment in time? A single moment. Looking
back on the earthquake you can see it for what it really was,
a gentle rolling of the ground and a few whitewashed walls
crumbling and a few whitewashed houses falling apart and a
few windows breaking. And then it stopped as suddenly as it

had begun. *Burrasca furiusa prestu passa*, as they say. A furious
storm passes quickly.

Ah Maura, Maura, Maura.

In the days before the earthquake, I mostly ran through
the streets of my town with my only true friend, Ignazio
Tiziano. In those days the streets were covered with a very
fine dust, almost like flour, a mixture of crushed shells from
the sea and tiny grains of wheat and barley from the mills
close to the water. There were always farmers from the plains
with wagons of wheat and barley. We sometimes worked for
the mills, loading sacks of flour onto the cargo ships when
they came in. Ignazio's father was a fisherman like my father,
so we had no desire to make our living in a boat. We were
tired of the stench of fish. Even our sweat smelled of fish, and
always we were coughing up tiny fish bones after we ate or
getting them caught in our teeth. We will die from fish bones,
we used to laugh, but it was happy laughter because we knew
it was not true, even though at the same time it was a laughter
full of despair because we were tired of fish.

We worked in the mills when we could. And we took
to the streets when we weren't working, drinking *assenziu*,
playing *brìscula*, and also a variation of *brìscula* which the
Spanish called *Mano Negra*, which always made me laugh, a
different kind of laughter than with the fish bones, this was a
laughter filled with the passion and great joy of youth, as if I
had discovered a secret joke that no one else knew about, not
even Ignazio.

This is what we would do, and then we would be drunk
and swinging our fists at every shadow, and then later we
would quiet down and the next thing we knew we would hear
women cooing in the darkness of narrow corridors, like the
gnawing, tremulous sounds of dying birds, I used to think,
or the mysterious, mystical, heart-breaking sounds of dying
orchids, their spotted petals drifting slowly, with lazy indifference, to the ground, one by one by one, phppt, phptt, phptt,
phptt, like drops of blood; or sometimes this sound of dying
birds (which was actually the sounds of the women in the
shadows) sounded like the wings of tiny, dark angels beating
in rhythmic counterpoint to the ticking of a clock, which are
all strange, sad thoughts to occupy the empty spaces between

one's ears, I must admit, but that is in effect what these women sounded like, but we were too drunk to know what they were really saying. We would wake up very late the next day with our heads raging and our money gone. *Ah, mi. Di guerra, caccia e amuri, pri un gustu milli duluri.* Which is the Sicilian way of saying that for every solitary pleasure you will suffer a thousand pains.

Oh Maura, my dear sweet Maura.

So the earthquake happened in September, as I have said. By October the west was flooded with refugees from Trabia and Caccamo, even Palermo. Thousands of people had lost their homes. Thousands had also died. My grandmother told us to stay indoors because there were more ghosts walking the roads of Sicily at that time than refugees, more ghosts than the police who were supposed to keep the peace, more ghosts even than the number of words uttered by the priests who were supposed to lead us from despair. Besides, there was nothing we could do. Leave them to the Carmelite nuns, my grandmother hissed, let them sort out who truly deserves help and who is beyond our powers to redeem, let them open their doors, if there are still any nuns left in this part of the world. But we did not listen to my grandmother. And my father had nothing to say except God will provide but we still have to fish, and then he would head down to his boat.

Ignazio and I adopted a different attitude, as you have probably guessed. Our town was not flooded with refugees like so many other towns. It was not an easy place to get to, our town by the sea, unless you took the coast road, and even that was not safe in places where the sea had washed everything away. But a few refugees still came. Refugees always find their way. We welcomed whoever we met, eager for news, but we saw no ghosts. We saw a family with all of their worldly goods piled onto a ramshackle wagon pulled by mule, the dust of the earthquake still plastered to their skin even two months later, eyes staring blankly like enormous black saucers. We saw a young father wearing a white top hat and a torn cloak and a little girl of seven riding piggyback and the memory of a mother crushed to death beneath a collapsing wall, pieces of the wall scattered like seashells across the ground but the mother was nowhere to be seen. We saw an

old woman with trembling hands, sucking on a blood orange
with her trembling gums, asking everyone she met if they
had seen her teeth. Why did they come to our town? Who
knows? Who can say? All of our questions on this matter,
the questions Ignazio and I would ask, were met with angry,
disconsolate stares, which were in turn met with glib remarks,
which were in turn met with puzzled looks, or sometimes an
apologetic glance coupled with a biblical quotation, from one
of the Gospels, usually John, or from the Book of Revelations,
though a few individuals quoted from the Book of Malachi; or
sometimes our glib remarks were met with mute expressions
of outrage, or sometimes vaguely distracted looks, edged with
impatience, as if those we had accosted were now too busy
studying the contours of various clouds passing by to be bothered; all of which were in turn met with further glib remarks
followed by sudden outbursts of laughter, which were in turn
met with burning silences, similar in nature (but not exact by
any stretch) to those burning silences that occur in old movie
houses when the celluloid catches on the bulb, silences which
do in fact produce a sound, a sort of unconscious, staticky
din, like a promise spoken in the wee hours of the morning
between two young lovers too young to know any better,
or a vaguely understood communication from outer space
which sends all of our scientists reeling, silences which are
sometimes so loud as to become deafening, in which case you
are plunged into a more robust kind of silence and your eyes
begin to water and the saliva in your mouth possesses the
distinct taste of burnt hair, a taste which lingers for months
and makes it difficult to swallow food of any kind.

So no one knew what exactly had befallen the refugees.
No one knew why they were here, except for the obvious. At
least Ignazio and I did not know. It was all conjecture. It was
all make-believe. Maybe they had a lonely uncle who lived in
a small house in the shadow of Monte Inici, or a spinster aunt
who liked to wander barefoot on the beach, slipping an occasional mussel like an evening prayer that has been answered
into a basket; or a cousin or a younger brother who had settled here to escape the Carabinieri with their ruthless Madsen
machine guns, which, their reputation notwithstanding, only
mowed down the exceedingly stupid or unaware because the

Carabinieri always set up their machine-gun nests out in the
open, in the middle of a crossroads with the hedges cut back
so you could see who was coming from miles away, and vice
versa, or in front of a stone bridge, the dark, elongated phallus
of the machine gun flashing with the interminable brilliance
of the sun, as if the Carabinieri had spent hours polishing the
dark metal with their sleeves or pieces of fabric torn from their
shirts when they could have been reclining in the shadows
beneath the bridge drinking from their canteens or hidden
away in a clump of trees not too far away with a view of both
the road and the bridge, in which case many more wandering
oblivious peasants and also those with revolutionary intentions would have died. But we did know at least one thing.
We knew the refugees were all looking for someone to take
them in. Or maybe they were looking for a ship to take them
to America. That was a fairly common hope in those days.

October became the month of the refugees. But by
February there were few if any refugees still traveling, and
everywhere the church bells were ringing and the sunlight
was bright and the almond trees were blossoming and people
started to forget about the earthquake in September. But I
did not forget. Just when I thought the earthquake was over,
finished, *finutu*, it started all over again.

(At this point Federico would pause, because always his
listener would gasp in disbelief, but always Federico would
mistake the gasp for laughter, a short, breathy, involuntary
squeal, perhaps, or a belching sound, or a nasally snorting
sound, or a high-pitched twittering capable of causing headaches, but to Federico it was laughter nevertheless.)

You laugh? To laugh is a good thing. Sometimes
laughter is the best way to deal with unexpected tragedy.
And always it is the best way to deal with unexpected good
fortune. *Petra disprizzata, cantunera di muro.* But I am being
figurative here. I am being poetic. Allow me the latitude
of an old man to look back on something that happened a
very long time ago, to reminisce, to remember with a poet's
heart (because Federico had always wanted to be a poet, in
spite of the fact that he didn't learn to read until the age of
seventeen, and in spite of the fact that poetry in general bored
him to tears, unless it was the poetry of a truly great poet like

Angelo Poliziano, who preferred blond-haired boys to girls
and enjoyed kissing fat juicy lips unless those lips had tasted
urine, or Pirandello, because Pirandello was born in southwestern Sicily and he wrote about betrayal and disillusion
and resentment, emotions which always mask a certain degree
of fear, which is amplified when you turn your eye inward,
which you invariably do because the exterior circumstances
are too horrible to behold, but then you realize your interior
self is equally horrible to behold or worse and so you are left
wriggling on the fishhook of despair and self-annihilation, to
use a strange metaphor indeed, not quite a poet's metaphor,
more of a philosopher's attempt at a metaphor, like Mirandola
in his treatises on magic and the dignity of man, Mirandola,
brilliant as he was, a mystic and consummate scholar, who
wished to be a poet but could never quite get the words to
match what he thought was true, which is perhaps why he
destroyed every love-song he ever wrote, a disparity between
language and intent which also troubled the young Federico,
even when he was an illiterate dock worker, and which is
why in his later years, after he had mastered reading to a
degree his fisherman father had never dreamed of (for, in all
honesty, the written word does not even exist for some men),
Federico truly enjoyed Pirandello, in spite of the fact that
Pirandello was devoted to Mussolini, a devotion which was
easy to understand if you understood Pirandello's fears about
chaos and the nature of reality, but which nobody ever really
understood, nor could they be expected to (because the truth
is we can never really understand anybody), and of course
you would immediately forgive Pirandello all of his emotional
and psychological flaws if you ever read the poems in *Mal
giocondo*, which Federico had read on the boat from Palermo to
Naples to Havana, a slim volume of poetry that was published
in 1889, where in one poem a ghost is fleeing from a flatterer,
for such are the deceptions of love that they extend even
beyond death, and love itself is symbolized by green snakes
writhing in agony, or something like that, at least that's how
Federico remembered it, kind of like in Dante, or at least the
corrupt, abridged editions of Dante that Federico had access
to that had been translated from Italian into English and then
back again into Italian).

Yes?

'. . . .'

(Federico is still hoping to be allowed the indulgence of an aging poet.)

Good. It is the same with old men everywhere.

'. . . .'

U Signùri rùna 'u viscuottù a cu nun' avi rienti, as they say.

'. . . .'

Yes, yes. God gives biscuits to those with no teeth.

(Some genuine laughter now. The conversation turning in Federico's favor. Which is to say that his hope of being allowed the indulgence of an aging poet is about to be granted. Some more laughter. It is actually more of a relieved chuckle than genuine laughter, but that's beside the point.)

Yes, yes. I have always thought so.

(A smile and then a pause, or sometimes the other way around, depending upon the nature of the interchange between Federico and the listener.)

So just when I thought the earthquake was over once and for all, I saw Maura D'Alessandria for the first time. I should say that Ignazio also saw her, but when I saw the shimmering mirage of the beauty that was Maura D'Alessandria on that brisk February afternoon with the wind whipping across the harbor and swirling through the narrow streets of the old part of town with such biting fury that I thought I was stranded in the desert, I forgot Ignazio even existed. We had turned down a narrow stone street, Ignazio and I, a hidden street full of the smoke and hubbub of various vendors, a street that in former days had been lined with lime trees, which had later been replaced by almond trees. The street ended at the walls of the castle. It was more an alley than a street and had been given many names over the centuries. The Street of the One-Eyed. Or The Street of the Arabs. Or The Street of the Ostrogoths. Or The Street of the Forgetful Vizier. Or The Street of the Blind Prelate. Or The Street of Adelaide the Malikah of Sicily. Or The Street of Lime Trees. Or the Street of Lemon Trees. Or The Street of Plum Trees. Or The Street of Yellow Plums. Or The Street of Mirabelle Plums. Or The Street of Half-Eaten Fish. Or The Street of Half-Eaten

Tuna. Or The Street of Genoese Silk Merchants. Or The Street
of Apprentice Magicians. Or The Street of Apprentice Fire-
Eaters. Or The Street of the Apprentice Sword-Swallowers. Or
The Street of the Invisible Magistrates. Or The Street of the
Moorish Ciphers. Or The Street of the Dancing Mania. Or The
Street of Toothless Camel Dealers. Or The Street of the Blind
Monks. Or The Street of Fleas. Or The Street of Bedbugs. Or
The Street of Lice. Or The Street of Moonless Nights. Or The
Street of Insufferable Days. Or The Street of Almond Blossoms.
Or The Street of Sour Almonds. Or The Street of Sour Wine.
Or The Street of Vinegar. Or The Street of the Devouring
Sea. Or the Street of the Cleansing Tide. Or The Street of
the Abolishing Wind. Or The Street of Would-Be Assassins.
Or The Street of the Badly Abused. Or The Street of Broken
Knives. Or The Street of the Black Hand.

But it was also known as Via Marianella, because one
day, God only knows how long ago, a struggling merchant
claimed the Mother of Christ had visited his stall, or his tent,
or his cart with a mule standing stiffly in front and mule shit
steaming on the ground and the flies beginning to gather, or
she had visited the rug that he had spread out on the ground
beneath one of the lime trees (and in those days there were
so many lime trees that you could pluck a lime and suck on it
at your leisure and no one would notice and ask you 'Where
did you get that lime?' or wonder out loud 'Why don't I have
a lime to suck on?' and become irritated, because they could
also pluck limes whenever they felt like it) and which (the
rug, an old Persian design) was now covered with trinkets
and fabric from all over the Mediterranean and beyond, and
without the slightest hesitation the Mother of Christ bought
a silk scarf, and after that every merchant on the street had
a similar story, and because the merchants in those ancient
days were all from the land of the Moors, the Madonnas in
their stories were all dark-skinned and slept with goats, not in
the biblical sense of knowing goats, but in the pre-biblical (or
quasi-biblical, or possibly even post-biblical) sense of sleeping
with (near, amongst) animals in a reasonable attempt to keep
warm on a cold night.

Ignazio and I called this dirt alley The Street of Rusty
Swords because of a small tent set up in the shadow of the

castle. The tent was owned by a descendent of one of those
early Arabs. He dressed with the flair of a nocturnal grave
robber. He sold all manner of medieval weaponry used during
the Norman conquest of the castle, or so he claimed, but
mostly he sold small daggers and rusty swords, most likely
the relics of battles from the 19th century from the days of
the Two Sicilies, which he routinely dug out of the stony,
unforgiving ground in the fields surrounding Palermo, usually
after midnight with a lantern perched on a rock, which gave
his face a devilish, greenish tint.

So it was a brisk February afternoon with the wind
whipping up all sorts of dust and the white froth of the waves
and the almond blossoms, as I have already said. With the
smoke from the various smoke shops and the white almond
blossoms falling and more blossoms falling with every gust of
wind, we could barely see. We were guided by our own memories and by the hubbub of voices suggesting we try this or
that. And we were munching on pistachios because you could
not get sweet almonds at that time of year, only sour ones, but
we wanted something sweet. (We were always hankering for
something sweet.) Then we passed by the small piazza to the
Church of the Madonna of the Rosary, though perhaps piazza
is too large a word. It was a very small stone plaza in front
of the church, a plaza rarely occupied by any living creature
save on occasion a few pink seagulls taking refuge from the
sea or a green lizard or two clinging to the pink walls of the
church, trying to escape the sun. But what does it matter such
details? So we walked by the piazza, cherishing thoughts of
medieval knives, wondering what it would feel like to kill
someone with such a knife, but then the wind died down, as
if a great hand had suddenly descended to calm the turbulent
earth, and there she was, Maura D'Alessandria, framed in the
doorway of the church, the trio of sculpted marble figures
in the arch above the door smiling with stern satisfaction, it
seemed, glowing with the joy of certain faith, I might have
said, or at least the absence of any kind of gnawing doubt,
or perhaps gloating, indeed, perhaps they were wallowing
in the self-indulgent, self-satisfied apocryphal mood that
usually accompanies revelations of any kind, as if they had
just witnessed the lights of an alien spaceship speeding across

a winter sky, I might have said all that, except that all of my
words had suddenly vanished. I had fallen into an immense
but exceedingly bright void. I could not tell which way was
up. Conversely, I could not tell which way was down. I did
not know who I was. I could hear myself humming a strange
tune, as if I were someone else. I had never seen such beauty.
Maura D'Alessandria seemed a sister of the Black Madonnas
described by the ancient Arab merchants. I was not sure where
she had come from. It was difficult to tell if she was about to
go inside or if she was just leaving.

In the days that followed, we learned that she had come
from a small farm near Caccamo, she and her uncle. Their
farm had been destroyed by the earthquake. There was no one
else. Her parents died the year she was born.

It is very hard to describe feelings from so long ago.

Suffice it to say that Ignazio and I took Maura everywhere in our small town by the sea. We did not compete for
her affection, nor did she thrust herself in between the love
we had for each other. We became a trinity as holy in our own
minds as the Blessed Trinity the priests always talked about
but which we could never see.

-76-

It was shortly after this that a traveling puppet show
made its way to Castellammare del Golfo. They had come
from Trapani on their way to Palermo, but they had taken the
coast road all the way around, up through Pizzolungo (a small
depression of a seaside village where Adherbal, the great
Carthaginian admiral, spent three weeks with his Nubian mistress of many years, a secret rendezvous by the sea filled with
all of the delectable delights a perverse and fertile imagination
can conjure, after he had defeated Publius Claudius Pulcher
and the Roman fleet in the battle of Drepana two-hundred
and forty-nine years before the birth of Christ, and then after
that Pizzolungo was basically forgotten by the world); and
then on to Bonagia, with its rocky brown hills dripping into a

sea overflowing with tuna (where in 829 the native Sicilians, presumably descended from the refugees of fallen Troy, had erected a Saracen watch tower that didn't resemble a horse in the least at the top of the tallest of the hills to keep a lookout for Saracen raiders coming up from North Africa, but all of their foresight went for naught because on the very morning a Saracen raiding party was in fact heading their way, a shimmering cloud upon the distant horizon like a flock of black seagulls that should have been spotted right off (giving the sons and daughters of Troy ample time to pack up their family heirlooms and their mythology and head for the relative safety of the fortress city of Eryx), the guardian of the watchtower was fast asleep in the arms of two perfumed nymphs, also sleeping, humming with sleep, their naked breasts like bruised plums glowing with a hazy, diffuse, late morning light, as if the curtains were drawn, though of course there were no curtains in the stone tower, unless you can think of a drunken stupor as being curtains, or curtain-like, or having that effect on the light); and then the puppeteers headed up to San Vito Lo Capo (a village that became the final earthly refuge of Saint Vito Martire, a third century saint who was known for healing the blind and the lame and driving away demons and who once called a meteorite out of the sky to punish a village of nonbelievers whose only real crime was that they enjoyed fornicating at all hours of the day and night on the beach in plain sight of the disapproving saint); and after San Vito Lo Capo they headed down along the rocky northern shore where the road disappeared altogether and they found themselves beating their donkeys mercilessly as they traveled along a cobblestone beach and then up a sandy, rocky path through the dense matte of coastal grasses and dwarf palms and the woody shrubs a little higher up and then up along the top of the cliffs, which plunged straight down into the sea, where they stopped for a while to look at the blues and light greens and aquamarines and Arabian turquoises of the Tyrrhenian Sea and the flashing silver like spinning knives of schools of small fish darting back and forth, communicating in a strange semaphore language all their own beneath the bright, fragile surface of the water; and the puppeteers marveled at the deep blue almost Azurite Italian sky studded with swirling

gray clouds like the skies of Titian, for they had never before
witnessed such a view, such colors, which made them want
to weep inconsolably and dance for joy at the same time, and
then a raging storm came along like those legendary storms
of the 15th century that sank boatloads of Algerian pirates,
storms that arrived with fortuitous alacrity, at least from the
perspective of those who lived along the coast in those days in
their God forsaken stone huts and hovels that smelled of dead
sardines and pestilent body odor, and so the puppeteers were
forced to climb down from the top of the cliffs, leaving their
wagons and ragged donkeys exposed, and sought shelter in a
coastal cave.

The storm raged for a day and a night and half a day.
The puppeteers never knew a storm could go on for so long,
at least from personal experience. It was the kind of storm
they thought only happened in epic tales of adventure and in
a few poorly conceived or derivative dime-store novels, storms
which were given symbolic value when in fact no such value
truly existed. Because a storm is just a storm, after all.

By the time the puppeteers reached Castellammare del
Golfo they needed to recover their strength. The process of
recovery required copious amounts of alcohol, wine, beer,
Vermouth, *assenziu*, whatever was available. They stayed for
several weeks, maybe longer, putting on puppet shows in the
plaza in front of the Cathedral whenever they had the energy.
They put on the same puppet show every time the curtain
went up.

They had puppets dressed in peasant dresses whose
heads would twirl with amazement and whose eyelashes
would flutter at the most bizarre moments, giving the impression of uncontrollable coquetry. They had puppets wearing
knightly armor but without weapons and puppets with
swords but dressed like bandits and one puppet seemed to be
a mayor or a councilor with his great floppy hat and broad,
stuffed shirt. They had puppets who were sailors wearing red
caps and merchants with bald heads and moustaches. They
had puppets who were dancing girls and puppets who were
priests and puppets who were matadors and one that was a
bull and a whole chorus of singing nuns, and in addition to
the bull, they had a whole range of animal puppets, mostly of

the farmyard variety, but there was also one Bengal tiger, one lion with ferocious looking teeth and a wild, unmanageable mane, a herd of elephants, a pack of jabbering monkeys, and one White Bird of Paradise from the islands of Bali. They had puppets who were cooks and scullery maids and musicians and a few small children for crowd scenes and also a few British ship captains and sorcerers from far off countries and a contingent of Turkish mercenaries armed only with spears. Most of these puppets also possessed twirling heads. Twirling heads to signify rage, or rejection, or despair, or confusion, or drunkenness, or an insatiable desire for vengeance or sex, or just plain old humorous idiocy.

All of their puppets were approximately one-hundred and twenty centimeters tall and weighed between fifteen and twenty-two kilograms, depending upon accoutrements. Except for the children puppets, which were a bit smaller, not so gaudy.

Naturally not all of their puppets appeared in every show. What a crazy travesty of a show that would be! But for a small fee, a few coins, the puppeteers would let you see all of their puppets, those that would appear in the next performance, and those that were waiting for other shows, perhaps even shows that had not yet been written. No one in Castellammare del Golfo had ever seen such a diverse array of puppets.

The show the puppeteers presented to the citizens of Castellammare del Golfo was called *The Operetta of Turiddu the Wayward Soldier*, which was more or less a bastardized version of the extraordinarily popular Italian operetta, *Cavalleria rusticana*, but if this act of thievery had been pointed out to the puppeteers, they would most certainly have replied with the theatrical swagger of pirates: How else were they to acquire their stories? And then: Everyone else did the same, it was a cutthroat business, after all. And finally: At least they only stole from works exhibiting the highest artistic merit, which is why they stole both their characters and pieces of their plot from Mascagni's version, which premiered in the Teatro Costanzi opera house in Rome in 1890, as everyone knows, as opposed to stealing from Monleone's rip-off version, a sec-ond-rate story if there ever was one, which first appeared in

Amsterdam in 1907 and was understandably banned in Italy, forcing Monleone to rewrite his version if he wanted to make any money from it, which he did, which we are all hoping to do, because if we didn't make any money in this business then what is the point?

-77-

A summary of *The Operetta of Turiddu the Wayward Soldier*, the puppet show which Federico, Ignazio, and Maura D'Alessandria saw at least twelve times, once for each of the Apostles, or once for each of the ancient Tribes of Israel, or once for each of the Twelve Minor Prophets, with the last of those prophets being Malachi, the Messenger of God:

The show began with a puppet soldier riding a puppet donkey. The puppet soldier had just come back from the war (they didn't say which one), and you could see that he hadn't had a good experience because his sword was broken and his armor was missing pieces and he was barefoot to boot. And yet he was as happy as a clam. He was as happy as any number of clams who have not yet been dug out of the sand and boiled in a pot. He was also as happy as any returning soldier should be, or even could be, and he was singing a happy song about the love of his life, a woman named Lola.

The soldier's name was Turiddu, and he used to live with his mother, Lucia, above her wine shop.

The donkey had no name. But then what is a name to a donkey?

Turiddu and the donkey had not been home in twenty years, a fact which Turiddu was singing about in his song about Lola. The donkey did not seem to understand how long twenty years actually was, or at least he gave no indication that he did understand. (Then again, not to belabor the philosophical, but what are twenty years to a donkey?)

The song about Lola went on for a while, and both Turiddu and the donkey did a little jig. Their arms, legs, and heads all whirled in different directions during the jig.

Turiddu sounded a little bit like Enrico Caruso before he
got his big break and became famous and started selling out
concert halls in places like Toledo, Ohio.

The next scene was devoted to Lola, who had married a
local teamster named Alfio while Turiddu was away. Which
is only natural if you think about it. Twenty years is in fact a
very long time, especially when your lover has disappeared.

Twenty years is also a long time when you are deeply in
love. Turiddu had been deeply in love. But as he got closer to
home, the weight of his twenty-year absence began to dimin-
ish, and when he had only a mile to go it vanished entirely.
All of a sudden he could not tell the difference between the
sadness of time passing and the labored, wheezing sound
his donkey made as they plodded across the landscape (or
between the wheezing sound his donkey was making and the
unthinking joyful sound of a pinwheel spinning; or between
the joyful sounds of spinning pinwheels and the hulking shadows of any number of farm implements ruined by humidity
and advances in agricultural science). When Turiddu passed
through the wrought-iron gates of his home town, gates which
served only decorative purposes, like the gates to a cemetery,
and would have therefore been useless against an attack, he
felt he had only been gone a moment.

The only puzzling aspect of the story was that the war
had apparently been over for ten years, a fact which became
clear sooner rather than later. There was no explanation
offered as to what Turiddu and the donkey had been doing
during the intervening ten years, presumably traipsing about
the Mediterranean, what adventures they had survived, what
wonders they had seen, what jokes they had told each other
during the long boring nights of their solitude, assuming that
they had actually been alone.

Ten years is also a long time.

Ten years is almost as long a time as twenty years,
at least as poets reckon time, and one or two English playwrights, and all impressionist painters, and the surrealists,
of course, and also the symbolists, and various estranged
lovers and childhood sweethearts, and all lost children and
most lost pets, and a few doddering grandfathers and a few
grandmothers wearing eyeglasses trying to keep track of their

doddering counterparts, and every pilot of a plane lost in the
Bermuda triangle, and every captain of a treasure ship sunk in
a sudden maelstrom, and every failed critic, and all fictional
characters, and one mathematician of note and several minor
ones, and numerous German philosophers and a couple of
Swedish ones and one who was half-French, and a party of
explorers from 19th century Belgium, and dozens of Cistercian
monks, and twice as many Franciscans, and almost all donkeys, which almost goes without saying.

The audience was left wondering about this discrepancy
of the ten years throughout the action of the show, hoping
against hope that further details were forthcoming.

The next scene was Turiddu's homecoming scene. It
took place in his mother's wine shop. Lola and Alfio were
shopping in Lucia's wine shop when Turiddu arrived. Lucia
was there, but she did not recognize her son at first. Turiddu
could not believe his very own Lola was holding a bottle of
sweet Marsala wine. Neither could the donkey. Lola could not
believe that Lucia did not recognize her own son. Alfio could
not believe that Lucia had a son. Lucia could not believe that
Alfio was so stupid. Lola could not believe that Turiddu did
not remember that she liked a bottle of sweet Marsala wine
every now and then. Lucia agreed with Lola. Alfio could not
believe Turiddu was supposed to know that Lola liked a bottle
of sweet Marsala wine every now and then. Turiddu could not
believe that Alfio was so stupid. Lola agreed with Turiddu.
Alfio grabbed the bottle of sweet Marsala wine from Lola's
hands and shoved it into Turiddu's hands. Lucia was looking
for another bottle of wine because Lola typically bought two
bottles, so her back was turned and she did not see. Lola could
not believe Alfio grabbed the bottle from her hands. Turiddu
was looking at Lola and did not realize Alfio was shoving
the bottle into his hands until it was too late. The bottle of
sweet Marsala wine crashed to the floor and there were bits of
glass everywhere and a puddle of wine in the middle. Lucia
whirled around when she heard the crash and saw the puddle
of wine. Lola still could not believe that Alfio had grabbed the
bottle from her hands. Alfio could not believe that Turiddu
had dropped the bottle. Lucia could not believe there was a
puddle of wine in the middle of the floor of her wine shop.

The donkey didn't know what to believe. Lucia assumed Alfio had hurled the bottle of sweet Marsala wine to the floor. She could not believe he was so stupid. Lola agreed with Lucia. Alfio felt like he was misunderstood. Turiddu could not believe Alfio would say such a thing, for clearly the fault of the broken bottle of wine lay with his impulsive snatching of the bottle from Lola's hands. Lola agreed with Turiddu. Lucia could not believe they were still talking about the first bottle of wine. She shoved the second bottle of wine into Alfio's hands and pushed him rudely out the door. Alfio could not believe he was being treated so rudely. Lola stared at Turiddu for a moment but she didn't know what to say. Turiddu knew what he wanted to say but he didn't know where to begin. Alfio began shouting from the street outside the wine shop. Lola could not believe he was being so obnoxious. Lucia agreed. Lola apologized for the behavior of Alfio and headed out the door. Turiddu could not believe she was leaving. Lucia headed into the back of the wine shop. Or perhaps she headed up the stairs in search of a bed because she was tired and wanted to lie down. Turiddu could not believe what had happened. The donkey sat down in the middle of the wine shop and began lapping up the wine.

There was a great deal of head twirling and arms and legs whirling throughout the entire exchange.

The audience roared.

The next scene took place outside the church, which was across the street from Lucia's wine shop. Lola was walking arm in arm with her best friend, Santuzza. Lola was telling Santuzza about Turiddu's unexpected homecoming and the impact on Alfio. At first Alfio did not know what to believe. Now he believes that Turiddu and Lola have been sleeping together for years, even while Turiddu has been away at war. Alfio did not explain how this feat of magic was accomplished, but it has become for him an unshakeable belief. This is what Lola said. Santuzza suggested they go inside the church and pray and maybe God would provide an answer, but Lola said she wasn't interested in any answer from God. At this point they noticed Turiddu's donkey tied up to a hitching post outside the church. The donkey pretended he wasn't listening to the conversation between Lola and

Santuzza when in fact he was. A group of villagers then came
along singing an Easter hymn about orange blossoms. They
were dancing and twirling while they sang. They danced and
twirled past the church. Lola and Santuzza joined them. The
singing voices faded. The donkey looked out at the audience
with a grave, wise, almost soulful look.

   The next scene was back in the wine shop. Turiddu and
Santuzza were sitting at a small table near the front of the
wine shop. They were drinking wine. It was the middle of a
sunny afternoon. Lucia was somewhere else, but you could
hear her humming the song about the orange blossoms. Lola
and Alfio entered the wine shop. Alfio looked at Turiddu and
gave him an accusatory glance. Lola looked at Santuzza and
gave her an accusatory glance. Turiddu and Santuzza looked
at each other and smiled and their heads twirled with obvious
affection. They gave the impression that they did not care
what anyone else thought. Alfio said something hurtful to
Santuzza and stormed out of the wine shop. It seemed that
he was overcome by jealousy. Lola said something wicked to
Turiddu and followed Alfio. It was not clear what she was
overcome by. Turiddu and Santuzza drank some more wine.
Lucia was still humming from somewhere else. Lola and
Alfio returned with the villagers, including the mayor in his
great floppy hat and broad, stuffed shirt, a few sailors and
merchants, and a priest. The priest said they were going to
excommunicate Santuzza because she had obviously slept with
Turiddu. The priest said the church did not play around when
it came to such matters. Santuzza ran crying from the wine
shop. Then Alfio stepped forward and challenged Turiddu to
a duel. He did not say why. Turiddu agreed. The mayor then
stepped forward and said Turiddu and Alfio would square
off at dawn in the plaza in front of the church. The rest of the
villagers cheered.

   There was a lot of head twirling and arms and legs
whirling.

   The next scene was a banquet held the night before the
duel. All of the puppets were there, drinking and dancing.
The mayor gave a very long speech. Then more dancing and
drinking. Then the priest gave an even longer speech. Then
more dancing and drinking. Then the mayor decided it was

his turn again. This went on for a while. Then Santuzza sang a
tragic love song, but all the while she was singing she seemed
incredibly happy. It was a great number. All the puppets were
spinning and whirling about like whirling dervishes. Everyone
in the audience began to clap and sing and laugh.

The next scene was back in front of the church. Alfio was
standing on one side with a pistol in his hand. Two sailors
were standing behind him. On the other side Turiddu sat on
his donkey. He was holding his broken sword, occasionally
brandishing it in the air. The villagers were huddled in a
clump directly in front of the church. The mayor stepped
forward in his great floppy hat and broad, stuffed shirt and
named both parties in the duel and asked that they proceed
apace so everyone could go back to their breakfasts before
they got cold, and then he stepped back into the clump. It was
still unclear why Alfio had challenged Turiddu to a duel. From
somewhere you could hear a band playing martial music. It
sounded like the music of doom. Alfio twirled around a bit
in time to the music and then stopped and fired his pistol.
There was a loud bang and a puff of smoke and that was it.
The martial music picked up. It now sounded like the music of
doom on donkeyback. Turiddu and his donkey did not waste
any time at all twirling to the music. They simply charged
towards Alfio and the startled sailors. Turiddu was waving his
sword in the air, his head spinning in a way that suggested
bloodthirsty vengeance. The two sailors, who had no pistols,
turned and fled. Alfio, who had a pistol but now no bullets,
also turned and fled. Turiddu chased them off the stage. The
villagers clapped and cheered. The mayor stepped forward
and took off his great floppy hat and made a low sweeping
gesture as he bowed before the audience.

The last scene took place later that day in front of the
church. Turiddu was on his donkey, getting ready to leave.
He was going back to war, any war. He would find a war
somewhere in the world and offer his services to whichever
side would pay him the most. Lucia seemed happy her son
was leaving. She gave him two bottles of wine for the journey.
She told him that his presence was like a calamitous wind
but now that he was leaving, things would settle down a bit.
She told him that Lola and Alfio were no longer together.

She told him that Alfio had forsaken Lola and gone off with
Santuzza. No one knew where they had gone. She told him
that Lola was now working in the wine shop. Turiddu smiled
and said 'We are like so many puppets hung on the wall,
waiting for someone to come and move us or make us talk.'
Lucia smiled back and said 'Such is love.' The donkey seemed
to be grinning like a critic, but he did not say anything. From
somewhere you could hear music playing, but very softly. It
sounded like the orange blossom song from the day before,
but no one was singing. Turiddu and the donkey left. Lucia
went back inside her wine shop. The street was empty. But
from the doorway of the wine shop it looked like Lola was
watching the spot where she had last seen Turiddu. The
audience clapped for twenty minutes every single time and
begged for more.

-78-

        Federico never said if he liked the puppet show. At least
he never said as much to Luis. He did not mention if he even
liked puppetry in general. But he was quite clear about how
he felt about the puppeteers who came to Castellammare del
Golfo.
        I did not like them, he would say. Yes, I was seduced
by their charms at first. We all were, Ignazio and Maura
D'Alessandria and myself. They possessed lively blue gypsy
eyes, the kind that prick you, hook into you, and if you try to
resist them your own eyeballs explode. So you did not resist.
But we were young. What did we know?
        After each puppet show the puppeteers would lock up
their puppet wagon and head around the side of the Cathedral
to a small grove of trees where they had set up camp. It was
a rugged camp with a few tents and a rough wooden table
and a second wagon for sleeping and a third for cooking and
the mules tethered to a picket. But as soon as they started
drinking and ladling out soup and devouring hunks of coarse
brown bread and apples and olives and figs and all kinds of

cheeses, maiorchino and modicano and caciocavallo and persa, well, who could resist? It was Maura D'Alessandria's idea. She was enamored of one of the puppeteers, Luigi Bonanno, thin as a rail, tanned, leathery skin from endless days on the open road, dark blue swirling eyes like a stormy sky, and thick black hair. (Maura said when you buried your face in Luigi's hair and breathed in the smell, which was heavy with salt and rare spices, it was like falling into a nighttime sea.) So they had finished their last show and were packing up their wagons for good and Luigi invited us to join them for a little wine and song, a paean to the beauty of art, he said, which is as much of paradise as we are permitted in this earthly realm, and then he laughed, and it sounded like he was suffering from whooping cough, but it was joyful laughter nevertheless.

So we ate and drank wine and sang, and with all of the commotion in the dim lantern light it seemed that there were more of us sitting there than there actually were, and then one of the men pulled out a mandolin and another started playing a flute and then one of the women puppeteers got up on the table and started dancing, and then another, and the men were grinning with wild teeth and there was no telling what might happen next, and then pretty soon Maura D'Alessandria was up there dancing and laughing at the world with her Black Madonna eyes.

At some point during that last evening someone said we should join them. They were traveling to Palermo in the morning to catch a boat for Naples, and from there they were going to America. We should go with them. All of us. How much fun we would all have in America. And we said we would. Then it was very late. It was after midnight certainly, and the moon had vanished and the stars were obscured by a darkness like a fog. It was one of those nights of oblivion that sometimes descends upon the coast. Ignazio was asleep on the ground and Maura D'Alessandria was sitting on an old woman's sewing stool from one of the wagons, watching Ignazio sleep. It was a hot, steamy night, but just beneath this layer of heat you could feel the ripple of a wind beginning to stir. It was a very strange night. The one lantern still glowing made everything seem steamier, hotter, even darker. You could not even see the features on Ignazio's face. Maura stared at Ignazio's featureless face for a while, and I stared at Maura, whose features drifted back and forth between visible and invisible. We were all perspiring but we did not care. Then Maura said quite suddenly that she had always dreamed of going to America and now she was really going, and I told her that I too had always dreamed of America and that I was sure Ignazio was dreaming then and there about going to America, though I was lying through my teeth on both counts.

Then Maura smiled at me her Black Madonna smile of a saint which ripped through my heart, and I wasn't sure where I was, I had suddenly gone blind except for a halo of light burning brightly on the outer edges of my field of vision, but I heard myself saying that I was going to go back home, there were a few things I needed, a few things I wanted to bring along to America, which was an odd thing to say because I don't recall owning anything of importance, what could I have gone back for, and then Maura laughed, or she must have laughed, for I felt the air vibrating and I was buffeted by a sweet-smelling but violent wind that washed across my face, wave after wave after wave, a ceaseless wave, an eternity, as if a thousand tiny birds were furiously beating their wings in a futile effort to escape this darkness like a fog that had descended upon the world, and then I went home. I do not remember if I made it home that night or not. And again, as I have said, I have no idea what I went back for. I did not own anything of value. And I certainly did not go back to say goodbye to my father. He and I had not spoken in years. But my memory is sometimes not what it was. It is funny how your mind plays tricks on you. My very next memory is standing in the plaza in front of the Cathedral in the quiet moments before dawn and the fog had mysteriously vanished, and so had the puppeteers, and with them Ignazio and Maura D'Alessandria. Perhaps if I had hurried on down the road to Palermo, I might have caught up to them. I might have made the boat. But at that moment I wasn't sure if I even existed, let alone a boat in Palermo. It seems funny now. *Cui lassa la via vecchia pri la nova, li guai ch'un va circannu, ddà li trova*, the old men would say. And it is true. He who leaves the old road for the new will often find himself betrayed. Most people think of a betrayal such as this as the ultimate darkness, but they are mistaken. A betrayal is not a darkness. A betrayal is a glaring bright light. A betrayal burns away the shadows. Before that dark night, Maura D'Alessandria was a changeling who had crept into our bed, mine and Ignazio's, and now I could see her for what she truly was. And Ignazio, too, who had been my constant companion, my lover of moonless nights and the furtive sounds of the sea and the camaraderie of shadows as wistful and improbable as an imagined lover's kiss, he, too, had been a changeling all along, and now he had assumed his true form. This is what I was thinking in the moments just before dawn oh so many years ago, and then I was breathing in the white heat of the Sicilian sun and my lungs had turned black, as if I were a victim of radiation poisoning, and it was very difficult to breathe.

-79-

During the next ten years, I became a different person. I became an expert in the martial art of knife fighting. On the first anniversary of the Great Earthquake of Saint Rosalia's Redemption I found myself once again on The Street of Rusty Swords heading for the tent of the Arab who dressed like a nocturnal grave robber. Before I even knew my own mind, I found myself in a special section of his tent, standing along-side a table devoted to knives of the highest quality, blades of death that had once been owned by nobility. You can be sure that I had no idea what I was looking for, but you can also be sure that every knife I examined, I did so with the eye of vengeance.

The Arab must have sensed my boundless passion for death for he suddenly appeared on the other side of the table. He seemed almost an apparition with his slowly disintegrating gravedigger teeth and his skin stretched tightly across his skull. Then he bowed his head slightly and I felt a wave of nausea and then the nausea passed and he offered me one of his knives for close scrutiny. 'One does not normally speak of knives as possessing a purpose,' he said. 'But then one does not normally come across a knife such as this.'

The knife he held up gleamed in the dim light of the tent
with a supernatural radiance, as if it were a living creature,
or perhaps one of God's fallen angels. The blade was made
of forge-hammered steel with diamond cross sections. The
scabbard was leather with gold plated fittings. The moment
I took hold of it, my hands began to tremble, or perhaps it
was the knife that was trembling. But I could not put the
knife down. The air was suddenly heavy with the earthy, rust
smell of fresh blood, but it was also a sickly-sweet smell, and
as I breathed in this smell of the lingering centuries, I was
suddenly overwhelmed by the knowledge, or the possibility,
or perhaps it was just an inkling of the future, that this knife
had been (or would be) responsible for the deaths of hundreds
perhaps thousands of witless souls.

'Good,' said the Arab. 'You are getting used to each
other.'

I did not know what to say.

'Yes, yes, it will be a good match between the two of
you. It is like true love, yes?'

I wondered where the knife had come from and if it was
truly meant for me or if this Arab with the gravedigger teeth
presented it to everyone, soldier and fanatic and youthful
street ruffians and stravaigers alike, who stumbled into his
tent.

'Yes, the two of you are like young lovers,' he said.
'Anyone can see that.'

He seemed quite sincere, and he was affable enough. He
possessed the hopeful eyes of a hopeless romantic, or a poet
who only wrote love sonnets. But there was also a peculiar
aura about him, a strange, hushed assurance, as if everything
he said or even thought was part of an ancient prophecy that
would bring continents together, or perhaps tear them apart.

'It was fashioned by the great Turkish artisan Nikola
Siyavus Hayreddin Yilmaz,' said the Arab, who seemed to be
somewhere inside my head, squatting inside the cavernous
recesses of my brain, cataloging my secrets so he could one
day use them against me, even though I could plainly see he
was standing just across from me. 'Nikola left Hungary after
the Battle of Saint Gotthard in 1664,' he said, 'which is where
the Duke of Melfi himself commented on Nikola's genius in

making weapons for war, and then Nikola settled in Milan. That is where he fashioned this masterpiece. It is a knife worthy of only the most invisible of assassins.'

And then he laughed and took the knife from my hand with delicate deliberateness and sheathed it and then disappeared into a cloud of darkness, a darkness which most likely was just his gaping, laughing mouth as he walked away, only to reappear moments later with two dusty books, ancient manuscripts which he thrust into my arms along with the still trembling knife. 'To possess such a knife is useless,' he said, 'unless one also possesses the knowledge of how to use it.'

This seemed to me a very logical thing to say, but I still did not know how to respond.

He laughed again, his dark, gaping mouth with its disintegrating teeth like a mirror hanging over the abyss, and then he grew silent, solemn, nodded at the two books. For a moment I thought he was going to take them away. 'But remember,' he said. 'Do not share this knowledge with just anyone. Certainly not men without purpose, for such men are created by God without wit like cows that are born only to carry heavy loads or to be led to the slaughterhouse. Cows without a train.'

Both books were written by the same man, Fiore dei Liberi, who lived in the 15th century, a master of knife fighting and swordplay, and also the use of the spear and the lance. The first was called *Flos Duelatorum* (Flower of Battle), which provided detailed accounts of hundreds of grappling techniques and striking techniques, all useful in hand-to-hand combat, complete with counter for counter maneuvers. The second book, a smaller volume, was called *Dacae Misericordiae* (Daggers of Mercy) and was devoted solely to knife fighting. It was because of these books that I learned to read, first in Latin, because this was the language of the two books the Arab had pushed into my hands, books about the poetry of knife fighting, this is how I felt about them, and then in Italian, because it was an easy jump from Latin to Italian, and besides, Italian was the language of the tuna cannery, where I was now employed.

Very, very soon I had read each volume dozens of times and could demonstrate any technique from any page at the drop of a hat. I became very proficient. In the streets of Castellammare del Golfo I became known as Signore Scurpiuni because of my elegant and thus surprisingly fast and potentially fatal style of knife fighting. I could cut a man to the bone before he could even blink. I could cut out his heart while he was still breathing. I could kill a man before he knew he was dead. My knife had no difficulty finding victims.

Now in those days there was a great deal of knife fighting in the streets of Castellammare del Golfo. I had never paid much attention to the dissolute youths who took to the streets in this fashion when I was with Ignazio, but Ignazio was gone. But it is not what you might think. We were not yet assassins, but there was not a lot for us to do to test our manhood. *Brìscula* was truly an old man's card game, and we were not old men, so we would drink and play cards only until our blood began to boil, and then we would head for the streets, our knives drawn, and commence to fighting. Knife fighting was for us like the Olympics. It was an arena where we tested our courage against each other, our skill, our speed, our passion, sometimes our stupidity, but always our love of life, our *gusto*. Rarely did anyone get killed, though this sometimes happened, as with anything. And yet it was always more than a simple test. For those few moments when we faced a dark shadow with a knife, we transcended ourselves. A knife fight is a complicated dance, some say, but if this is so, then it is a dance that you are not aware of. You do not know you are dancing. You are trying to survive, trying to find the weakness in the other man before he finds your weakness. Yet you are not thinking about any of this. You are simply moving until you are no longer moving.

Our knife fights did not last long. Boom! And this dance of the shadows was over before anyone even heard the music. Boom! And someone lay bleeding in the street, but it was a superficial wound and easily bandaged. Boom! And someone else was trying to hold in his blood but it was too late. Boom! And everyone else ran away. If knife fighting is a dance, it is a dance of death. A single misstep is a tragic thing. But we accepted this. We fought mostly in dark streets after midnight, always in dark streets, and so we had to step out of our daytime selves and assume the shapes and postures of nocturnal creatures. We forgot who we were. Our eyes glowed with the unthinking ferocity of blind angels or caged wolves or gigantic, ravenous bats or black eagles flying down from the mythic mountains to the east. Our nostrils flared, like the nostrils of bulls before they charge. Our hearing was attuned to the slightest whispering of a blade of grass, or the thin, zinging, scorpion flash in the dark of metal on metal, like moonlight catching the wings of a dragonfly, and then Boom! It was over. We were exhausted. So we returned from the edge of oblivion, looking for a bed.

It was at this time of my growing fame as Senor Scorpion that I forgot all about Ignazio and the treachery of his departure with Maura D'Alessandria. It was at this time also that I stopped thinking about Maura D'Alessandria and her beauty. Instead, I sometimes thought about Mirella Deodato, who was a distant cousin of Salvatore Maranzano, one of the young men who was always getting cut up in the knife fights and Mirella would bind his wounds and then cradle him right there in the street and sing to him softly about beauty and love, and the other young men would laugh and walk away and talk about the weakness of Salvatore, but I did not think it weakness so much as he had not yet learned how to commit himself fully to the knife. I would let my eyes linger a while on Mirella singing to Salvatore, and sometimes she would look at me with her eyes brimming with the hope of lost love, and sometimes she would even smile, but it was always a sad smile of infinite patience.

At other times I thought about Maria D'Angelo, who as a young girl in Castellammare del Golfo in 1641 was tending her goats on a hillside covered with rocks and fig trees when a sudden storm blew in from the sea and she and her goats took refuge in a nearby cave, or perhaps it was a hastily dug hole that had been dug out for some reason, and it was very dark in that cave, too dark to see clearly, and there was probably nothing to see anyway but the shapes of the goats moving around and the shape of Maria D'Angelo trying to keep out of their way, but then an exceptionally charged lightning bolt struck the ground outside the cave, illuminating the interior with a sudden brilliance as bright as a billion stars, or so everyone has always said, and during the melee

of departing goats which followed the bolt, Maria D'Angelo
discovered a tarnished copper box. Inside the copper box
there was a smaller silver box, an ancient reliquary, and inside
this reliquary there was a small amulet with a cameo image
of the Virgin Mary and her baby son. Maria D'Angelo forgot
about the raging storm, this is how I had always heard the
story told, and ran breathless to the Cathedral and placed the
dripping boxes and the still fairly dry amulet into the trembling hands of an old priest who immediately proclaimed the
discovery a miracle, partially, perhaps, because of the enigmatic smile you could see quite clearly on the sculpted lips
of the Madonna, and also, perhaps, because of the quizzical
expression on the face of the child, an amazing bit of artistry
in so tiny a sculpture. Soon thereafter they built a church on
the very site of the cave, or close enough to the cave so that it
amounted to the same thing. Such were my thoughts in those
days.

-80-

And then one day Ignazio returned. When I first learned
that Ignazio was returning to Sicily, I was sitting near the
plate glass window of a small café with a view of the tuna
cannery and a triangular blue slice of the bay. It was a café
that I normally never went to. I was surrounded by faces I
did not know or even vaguely recognize. Sometimes I think
I dreamed the entire episode. It was late in the afternoon,
when the shadows were liquid pools. I was drinking amaretto
because someone in the café was getting married. As soon
as I sat down by the window, a hoarse, happy voice started
talking about the happy couple, and shortly after that, the
amarettos started. Amarettos for everyone. The voice said the
couple was planning a four-week trip to Naples and then to
Barcelona on a great white ship with red railings, or maybe
the couple had just returned. So I was drinking them down
one after another and listening to this voice go on and on
about this young couple, these newlyweds, standing at the
railing of this great ship, a bright blue sky in the background

and then the ship pulling away from the wharf (in Palermo? in Trapani? the voice did not say) and the young couple waving energetically at their adoring friends who were waving with an equal amount of energy in return, and some of the friends had brought orange blossoms from the wedding, or some kind of confetti, which they were going to sprinkle on the heads of the young couple as they raced up the gangplank, only they forgot, so now they were sprinkling the heads of everyone standing along the wharf. It was hard to tell if the voice was recounting a memory or projecting his hopes onto the future. Then the sound of the one voice talking was replaced by the sound of many voices, and every so often a hand wearing a white glove would reach past my nose with another amaretto. Violins were playing in the background, or some kind of stringed instruments. People were eating lemon cakes and there was a general hubbub of laughter and small talk and the chomping of teeth to go along with the amarettos. Then I plainly heard a voice say 'A telegraph cable for you,' and then an ungloved hand reached past my nose, and the next thing I knew I was reading a cable that said: 'I am returning August 24. Ignazio.'

After the cable, my imagination took over, though at the time I did not realize that it was my imagination. I thought I had fallen into the abyss of chaotic thinking. Or chaotic perceiving. Sometimes there is no measurable difference between the two. There was no mention of Maura in the cable, so I assumed she had died or run away. The amarettos stopped coming. I realized that the white gloved hand that had been serving the amarettos belonged to the father of the groom, not a waiter, as I had naturally assumed. Someone mentioned something about the famed Bavarian illuminist Jung-Stilling, but I did not hear what exactly. I had never heard of Jung-Stilling. I imagined gutting Ignazio with a knife. The violins or whatever stringed instruments they were sounded louder, as if many more musicians had suddenly arrived. I remembered a diagram from somewhere towards the middle of *Dacae Misericordiae* which clearly demonstrated how to plunge a knife into a man's stomach and then twist it right and left and then up and out so that the man's stomach and bowels would come gushing out. Two men in dark jackets approached my

table and asked if they could sit down opposite from me, for
the chairs were unoccupied. I am sure I said yes. I could not
remember the precise page number with the diagram of
disemboweling a man, but I did not need to remember the
page number. The white gloved hand of the father of the
groom appeared once again with another amaretto. The hand
provided amarettos for the two men in the dark jackets. The
men in the dark jackets said they were Quietists, an obscure
Catholic sect, once all the rage in France, that took a vaguely
more optimistic view of humanity than Pascal, who believed
that human beings were wretched, mindless worms of the
earth, easily deceived automatons with only the horror of
eternal damnation to look forward to, in spite of Christ's
intervention for all of us, except for those lucky few who
received God's grace, which according to Pascal rarely happened. They asked me if I was a Quietist, but I said I had
never heard of the Quietists. The father of the groom-to-be (or
the happy honeymooner) returned again and apologized and
said they had run out of amaretto for the second time and
there was only a very small chance of procuring any more.
Clearly he thought everyone in the café belonged to the party
celebrating the impending marriage of his son (or the return of
his son and daughter-in-law from their honeymoon, if that's
what it was). All of a sudden it smelled of oleander. I looked
at the two men in their dark jackets and they had removed
their jackets, tossing them carelessly over the backs of their
chairs, and had taken out a single bottle of oleander scent and
placed the bottle on the lip of the table. The bottle was precariously perched and looked like it was about to fall to the floor.
The two men were taking turns taking up the bottle and
dabbing themselves all over with the oleander scent and
putting the bottle back down on the lip. The father of the
groom returned, smiling, and said we were in luck, there was
more amaretto on its way. I remembered that Sicily no longer
had any large, predatory animals, except the obvious, but
there were countless hedgehogs and weasels and wild rabbits,
all of which were easy prey if you had a rifle, but hunting
them down was significantly more challenging if you only had
a knife. There were also plenty of hawks and windhovers and
kites, and I always enjoyed an occasional rock partridge or

two. The two men were once again wearing their dark jackets
and the bottle of oleander scent had disappeared. I had not
heard the sound of a bottle crashing so I assumed they had
put it back in a pocket. I remember thinking that Ignazio
would arrive shortly. Perhaps he was heading for that very
café at that very moment. I pulled out my knife, which I
always kept with me, and laid it on the table. I wanted to be
ready. The knife was gleaming. The two men in the dark
jackets were startled by the gleaming brilliance of my knife
and they looked at me with questioning eyes. Then they asked
me some questions that had nothing to do with the knife. They
asked me if I had ever read a book called *Théologie astrale*,
which was sometimes called *La Voie à Dieu*, and was often
confused with a book called *D'un monde à l'autre*. I said I had
not. They asked me if I knew anything about Madam Guyon,
who had written both books, as well as dozens of others. I
said I knew nothing. I assumed by their cryptic questions that
they had forgotten the gleaming knife as soon as they had
seen it. Which was just as well. I waved my hand in the air to
attract the attention of a waiter and the father of the groom
came running. He apologized with red-faced embarrassment
and said the amaretto had not yet arrived, but it was most
definitely coming. He had the assurances of the owner of the
café. I said that was okay but the reason I was waving my
hand in the air was that I was hoping someone would bring
me a white table napkin. The father of the groom smiled, and
his shame at not yet having any more amaretto was replaced
with the unburdened, glowing joy of being of service to
someone in need. He hurried away to find a white table
napkin. The two men in dark jackets, who had never left off
staring at me all the while the father of the groom and I talked
of amaretto and napkins, tried to engage me in a deeper
conversation about the mystical nature of Madame Guyon and
her mysterious mystical dreams of the future, which later
generations would know as the past, assuming her dreams
had been accurately interpreted. The two men explained that
Madame Guyon believed dreams were the way God communi-
cated with the faithful and that the purpose of her dreams was
to bring the lost sheep back to the fold, especially when those
lost sheep were priests and bishops and nuns, and so she had

a spiritual duty to share her dreams with the world. I pretended I didn't hear a word they said, but they persisted. They
said Madame Guyon once had a dream about a beautiful
white bird and when she woke up she yearned for that bird
and spent eight years trying to find it, and she became very
discouraged for a while because she believed that everyone
else in the world was also searching for this bird, she became
discouraged almost to the point of despair, in fact it was
despair, and she did not know what to do with her despair,
and then one day she realized that there was nothing for her
to do, she was the one chosen by God to find this bird, the
white bird of her dream was hers, her will and God's will
were one and the same in this matter, and when she realized
this her despair took wing, as it were, and never came back.
That must have been some bird, I remember saying. It was, the
two men said. What kind was it, I remember saying. We don't
know, said the men. Perhaps it was a cockatoo, I remember
saying. Yes, said the men, or perhaps a cockatiel. Or perhaps a
swan, I remember saying. Or perhaps a dove, the two men
said. But then I couldn't think of another white bird to add to
the list so I didn't say a word, and the two men nodded at
each other and smiled with great satisfaction, as if they had
just disproved Nietzsche's *Doctrine of Eternal Recurrence*. A
silence that was equal parts profound and puerile descended
upon the table where I sat with the two men. They looked out
the window and began trading whispers back and forth. The
father of the groom returned with a napkin. While the two
men were occupied with their whispering I hid my gleaming
knife in the folds of the napkin. A few musicians with flutes
and oboes came into the café and sat with those playing the
stringed instruments. The music swelled as if an entire orchestra was playing. The music seemed to drown out the small
talk from earlier. A few people began to complain about how
loud the music was. The amarettos started appearing once
again. I suddenly remembered that the diagram demonstrating
the proper technique for disemboweling a man was on page
197 of *Dacae Misericordiae*, which was more towards the end
than the middle. The text beneath the diagram also empha-
sized that this particular technique often resulted in a severing
of the aortic artery, which meant that death would follow in a

matter of minutes. I imagined myself plunging the knife into
Ignazio and watching his innards tumble out. I smiled with
great satisfaction at the thought. I let the thought linger. Once
again I was struck by the lack of predatory animals anywhere
in Sicily. The father of the groom took a few of the musicians
aside and spoke to them and the music became more like
background music. The small talk reasserted itself. The two
men in their dark jackets were still trading whispers. I remember asking myself "Who are these two strange men in dark
jackets who wanted to know if I was a Quietist?' I could hear
fragments of their whispering. 'Faith does not consist in seeing
nothing at all,' said one. 'Faith is obscure because it makes us
see and do things that go beyond the scope of natural light,'
said the other. 'Faith is illuminating because it demands that
we sacrifice our reason to a divine authority, which is clearly
above our own weak ability to reason,' said the one. 'Faith is
both obscure and luminous,' said the other. It was hard to tell
what they were talking about. The father of the groom
approached the table with a tray of amarettos, which he
gingerly placed on the table. This is the last of it, he said, and
then he was whisked away by the owner of the cafe. I took up
my last glass of amaretto, as did the two men in the dark
jackets, and we nodded at each other, not quite smiling, in fact
not even close to smiling, we all three possessed looks of
extreme wariness, but then we relaxed because everyone in the
café was holding up their glasses, and then a great booming
voice said 'Salud' and everyone drank and tossed their glasses
to the floor with a mighty smack and many of the glasses
shattered from the impact. Then one of the two strange men
asked me if I had ever read *The Ladder of Paradise* by St. John
Climascus, and I said I had not. Then the other one said *The
Ladder of Paradise* was about how to attain a oneness with God,
and I said I was not sure I wanted to attain a oneness with
God. After that they seemed quite troubled, and soon after
that they left. And then one by one the patrons of the cafe
began to leave, and they were quickly followed by the musicians, for it was well past sunset by then.

I felt suddenly very alone. I could not believe how very
dark it was sitting there inside the café. The café was only
illuminated by two oil lamps hanging above the bar. I was the

only person I could see. I could hear the voice of the father
of the groom, who had remained because he had yet to settle
up with the owner of the café. I could also hear the booming
voice of the owner of the café, who was arguing with the
father about how much was owed. Then the door opened and
there was a rustling, rushing sound, as if a pack of hedgehogs
or weasels or wild rabbits had scurried across the floor, and
then Ignazio sat down across from me. Neither of us spoke.
We had always been able to tell what the other was thinking,
so words seemed unnecessary. Still, Ignazio seemed quite
surprised at the speed of my knife. And he seemed even more
surprised at how quickly his innards fell out of the gaping
hole in his stomach, like animal slop. I don't think he appreciated the depth of his betrayal until that precise moment. His
eyes grew very wide and black and shiny, like two black discs
spinning into space, heading for some unknown destination,
and then his eyes took on a glassy, glazed, distant look, as
if those two black, shiny discs had finished their journey in
record time, and then he slumped forward in his chair and
his head fell like a piece of stone against the table and there
he lay. The father of the groom and the owner of the café
heard the sound and came running to the table. The father of
the groom looked at the pool of blood on the floor and the
collapsing sack that was once Ignazio and then at me, his eyes
brimming brightly in the darkness with the futility of words.
His agitated silence seemed to be saying that a napkin would
not be enough, but perhaps a tablecloth. The owner of the café
seemed little affected by the body. Once he saw that there was
nothing to be done for Ignazio, he turned and went back to the
bar. I realized that he was an old hat when it came to betrayal.
He had probably been betrayed many times in his life. He
would have understood exactly what I felt towards Ignazio
and why killing Ignazio brought me no joy whatsoever. I did
not care that Ignazio and Maura went away to America. That
was not a betrayal by any stretch. That was love. Ignazio's
betrayal was that he did not say goodbye. He left like a thief
in the night, without a word. So when he returned as he did,
I killed him. I really had no choice. That was also love. The
owner of the café would have understood all that. But not the
father of the groom. The father of the groom understood only

that a man had been killed at some point during the party
for his son. He was certain that he was going to be blamed
for the death. He did not know what to do. I wiped the blade
of my knife on the tablecloth and put it away. I told him not
to worry. Then I left. It was late and I was tired, but I didn't
go home right away. It was a strange and beautiful night. It
was a night where there was no joy, but there was no sadness
either. I sat on the old stone wall in the shadow of the castle
and looked out at the darkly glowing sea. From somewhere I
could hear once again the voices of the two men in their dark
coats, but I could not see them. They were nowhere to be seen.
But I could hear their voices clear as a bell. 'But I never said
faith removed reason,' said the one. 'Faith transcends reason,'
said the other. 'Through faith we no longer possess the need
to reason,' said the one. 'Yes, yes,' said the other, 'and then
we see the world through the wisdom of Christ, who becomes
the motor of our soul.' Then there was silence for a while. The
moon had already set. I sat there while the silence absorbed
every last drop of starlight in the sky. Then I went home.

-81-

The murder of Ignazio Tiziano became the crime of the
century and was reported in all the daily rags and scandal
sheets from Trapani to Palermo. Murders were common
enough in the streets of Castellammare del Golfo, but not in
cafés. The police did not know what to do. The owner of the
café came forward and said he did not know who had done
this terrible thing. The police questioned the guests of the
wedding party, but it soon became clear that no one had any
idea what had happened. Most of those in the café at the time
had never heard of Ignazio Tiziano. The fact that the police
even knew his name was sheer luck, but even then it was still
only conjecture based on a card in Ignazio's wallet which
said: 'Ignazio Tiziano, Importer of Sicilian wines, New York City,
America.' The father of the groom, who had brought me an
endless stream of amarettos and had seen me with a bloody

knife in my hand, gave no thought to me at all. All he kept talking about was seeing the body for the first time with its gullet slit all the way from the navel to the sternum and the bloody intestines in a pile on the floor. I became a ghost as far as the death of Ignazio was concerned. The only detail that everyone agreed upon was the fact that two strange men wearing dark jackets had entered the café at some point and had been spotted sitting at the very table where Ignazio's body was later discovered, but the men had mysteriously vanished. The only other pertinent detail was that the men reeked with the odor of oleander. 'They smelled of death,' said one of the wedding guests. 'It should have been obvious what they were planning.' Unfortunately, no one could remember what the men looked like, but their possible existence was all the encouragement the police needed. They immediately began rounding up men of all sorts, mostly transients who happened to be wearing dark jackets, but also a few peasants who had made their way to town the day after the murder and were wearing black fedoras in addition to dark jackets because they had important meetings the next day with bankers or priests and wanted to look nice, and they had come to town a day early so they would be on time the next morning, so they weren't loitering with aimless, suspicious intent, as it certainly seemed to the police, they were simply looking for a room for the night. The police reasoned that the two murderers could very well have possessed black fedoras but had perhaps decided against wearing them when they set out to murder Ignazio. Perhaps they sought to disguise their murderous intentions by abandoning their hats, this is what the police seemed to think. So within three days of one of the most barbarous acts ever committed in Castellammare del Golfo, the city jail and then the public offices of the magistrate (which were both housed on the first floor of a magnificent Baroque mansion with decorative columns and statuary and other sculpted elements clinging to the exterior walls and a heavy oak door with carved panels and heavy iron chains) were overflowing with suspects. It was utter chaos until the magistrate took charge and asked the police if any of the suspects reeked of oleander, which was the only detail of the case he could remember between bites of toast smeared with cheese and honey, which he was enjoying on the second floor of the Baroque mansion with the balcony doors flung wide open but the silk curtains drawn so that his exposure to the sun was somewhat filtered. The police, of course, said 'No, a few smelled of lavender or rosewater, but most had taken on the odor of mules that had been confined in a stable that leaked when it rained,' which was a most appropriate description, since the prisoners had been crammed together for three days in poorly ventilated jail cells or squashed together without mercy in one of the many, damp, foul-smelling waiting rooms or storage rooms or tiny water closets that were part of the magistrate's suite of offices. The magistrate was disgusted. He said the police had bungled the case. The whole building needed to be fumigated and everyone released. The two murderers had certainly escaped to Palermo, and from there they had certainly taken a boat to Naples and only God knew where after that. Four days after the murder all of the men in dark jackets (even the peasants) were sent home. Within a month, the case of the murder of Ignazio Tiziano was abandoned for lack of suspects.

It was at this time that I received a note from Signore Caracciolo. Signore Caracciolo owned a small grocery, which his youngest son managed with quiet almost religious dedication, and a small restaurant on the other side of the plaza from the Cathedral, which his eldest son managed with exquisite theatrical flair. He enjoyed going to Palermo with his mistress for the opera once a month. He had once taken a trip to Rome, where he had met with Pope Pius IX for several hours. It was said that nothing happened in Castellammare del Golfo without his permission.

It wasn't much of a note. Fancy paper and a fancy envelope, but there were very few words, so it was difficult to pin down Signore Caracciolo's intentions. But there was no refusing the note either. The note said: 'Five o'clock. Saturday. The Restaurant.' It was signed Gaetano Caracciolo. Beneath the signature was an image of a black hand holding a bloody knife.

82

Five o'clock. Saturday. The Restaurant:

The restaurant was closed when I arrived and I could
not see in through the windows because the green shutters
were latched tight. I waited around for a while like a criminal
recently released from jail, not certain what to do. The patches
of sunlight and shadow that fell across the cobblestones
reminded me of a Telemaco Signorini painting. I started thinking I had misunderstood the intention of Signore Caracciolo's
note, even though no intention was evident, when his son
emerged from the tiny vestibule between the outer and inner
doors, a big-toothed grin hastily scribbled on his face, and
encouraged me to enter. He offered to take my jacket, but I
was not wearing a jacket, so he begged my pardon and led me
to a small table off in the corner. He hurried away and then
hurried back with a bottle of wine and a glass and a plate of
brown bread and a bowl of stew, an olio filled with chunks of
tuna and shark, carrots and onions and peppers and garlic and
sausage. Then he hurried away again, disappearing through
a shuttered doorway. I don't know how long I sat there. The
bright sunlight outside slipped around the outer edges of the
green shutters and in through invisible cracks in the walls
and underneath the door, but it was still not enough to see
very well. The light inside the restaurant was a hazy, greenish
color, an effect no doubt of the green shutters, but it gave
the interior an alien, underwater feel, as if we (myself and
Signore Caracciolo's son) were trapped at the bottom of the
sea. By the time my eyes adjusted, I had almost finished my
stew. I noticed three darkly glowing figures on the opposite
side of the room, sitting beneath a painting of a street scene,
a street in a small town like Castellammare del Golfo with its
gleaming, whitewashed buildings and the businesses open
and people walking in and out of the shadows on a sunny
day and laughing and carrying on and a couple of children
in the foreground playing with sticks or stick figures or small
hammers or small axes with wooden handles, or perhaps they
were playing with knives. It was still very dark in the restau-

rant so the painting was more an impression of a painting than anything else. I suddenly felt I was a part of the painting, as if I were imprisoned within the canvas of the artist's imagination, a sensation that was strangely liberating, though it was certainly tinged with a sense of melancholy because of the ephemeral nature of existence, even existence granted seeming immortality through art.

The three darkly glowing figures did not say anything or give any indication that they knew about Signore Caracciolo's note. They were also eating soup. The restaurant echoed with the noise of people eating soup. But in the background, I could also hear someone humming. The humming was coming from the kitchen. It had a scratchy sound to it, like it was coming from an old Berliner Gramophone. Sometimes it was louder, though not louder than the noise of people eating soup, sometimes softer, as if someone were playing around with the volume. The three darkly glowing figures seemed also to be humming along with the Gramophone, though whether they had been humming all along or had just started I could not say. But they seemed to be vibrating just the same as they ate their soup, even their bones seemed to be vibrating. Then the humming from the kitchen stopped. One of the figures started to hiccup, perhaps from trying to hum and eat soup at the same time. It was hard to tell which one. Then a gravelly voice broke through the hiccupping.

'Puccio,' said the voice.

Puccio emerged from the kitchen with the same big-toothed grin scribbled across his face.

'Yes Pà?'

'See to our guest. See if he has had enough to eat. And tell him we are having cognac this evening. Ask him if he likes cognac. Cognac and pistachio biscotti. Tell him we have plenty of both.'

'Yes, Pà.'

'And if he does not like cognac and biscotti tell him we have port wine and walnuts. Everyone likes port wine and walnuts.'

'Yes, Pà.'

'But remember to use the small glasses with the port.'

'. . . .'

'And only a small bowl of walnuts.'

'. . . .'

'Too many walnuts are bad for the digestion.'

'Yes, Pà.'

The communication via Puccio went on like this for a while. Then the three shadowy figures turned inward upon themselves, as if they could not wait for the biscotti and were about to devour each other instead, and began discussing what seemed to be topics of great importance and then laughing, and then a few serious gestures and then more laughter, their voices falling and rising with the seriousness or levity of what they were saying. One did not eavesdrop on such a conversation. Still it was difficult to resist the urge. But everything they said seemed to swallow itself. Their words became small silences dropping into an ever-expanding ocean of silence. But occasionally I caught a word here, a joke there.

'U Signùri rùna 'u viscuottù a cu nun' avi rienti,' said the gravelly voice.

And then laughter, and then more murmuring.

'La donna e la gaddina si perdi si troppu cammina,' said the gravelly voice, a little while later.

And then more laughter.

And then 'Puccio!' and Puccio emerging once again.

'Would you please ask our guest to join us. And you may bring out the cognac and the biscotti.'

'. . . .'

'And throw open those shutters. Go on! I can't see a god forsaken thing in here.'

'. . . .'

'It is like trying to see through a bowl of this soup. The absence of light is very disconcerting.'

'Yes, Pà.'

And that was how I met Signore Caracciolo. In the bright sunlight that came pouring through the window I could plainly see that Signore Caracciolo was a man of good humor and good appetite. But I was not sure about the other two. Their faces were obscured by the need to flatter and perhaps succumb to licking boots, like so many wild dogs that follow at the heels of the strongest and the fastest, waiting for the day when the strongest and the fastest stumbles so they can tear him limb from limb. Signore Caracciolo told another joke and the other two laughed, and I tried to laugh, but my heart was not into it, and then Puccio returned and we ate biscotti and drank cognac. After a time, I was numb from the pleasure of the cognac and the pistachio biscotti. Signore Caracciolo continued laughing and drinking and eating, but the other two eyed me up and down. I began to wonder why Signore Caracciolo had summoned me. I wondered how long we were going to sit there eating and drinking. I wondered what I was going to do if I needed to urinate. Then Signore Caracciolo slapped the table very hard and the other two fell back in their seats. It was quite an explosion, like two universes colliding, or perhaps two stars, or at least two automobiles on a dark, lonely road. 'Show me this knife,' Signore Caracciolo roared, and his teeth flashed like tiny silver frogs in the sunlight, silver frogs made from Mexican silver that were once fashionable in Mexico City and perhaps would be again one day.

'Show me the knife,' he roared a second time, and this time the other two joined in.

I laid the knife on the table. It picked up the gleaming brilliance of Signore Caracciolo's teeth and all of us had to shade our eyes.

'It is a beautiful knife," he said. 'It is even more beautiful than I had imagined. You are very lucky to own such a knife.'

Then he took up the knife and slashed at the air.

The other two men began to smile.

'What if I were to keep this knife for my own?' he said.

A dark, knowing look like a lunar eclipse came over the other two men.

'What would you say to that?'

The other two men began to laugh softly, their chests and shoulders rising up and down as if they were in some pain.

'Yes, what would you say to that?'

But I didn't say anything. I just stared at Signore Caracciolo with an involuntary indifference. Perhaps it was because of all the cognac. I was expert when it came to beer and wine and amaretto and *assenziu*, but I had never before tasted cognac. Either that or I was blinded by the dazzling brilliance of my knife twirling about in Signore Caracciolo's hands. Either way the result was the same. But Signore Caracciolo mistook my indifferent stupor for quietly bubbling, murderous rage, and so he smiled a polite smile and slid the knife back across the table.

'I was not serious, of course,' he said. 'Such a knife is a gift from above. It is a matter of destiny.' He paused a moment and looked with great passion into my eyes. 'Yes,' he said. 'It is your destiny.'

Then he leaned closer, turning his head slightly so that I lost sight of his face in the glare of the sunlight pouring in through the window, and in a voice that was less than a whisper, as if he were simply exhaling slowly, the heat of his breath fogging up my mind, he asked if my knife had a name.

I had never thought of a name for my knife before that. Quite without thinking I said 'It is my dagger of mercy. It is called *Daca Misericordia*.' Signore Caracciolo leaned back and his face became visible once again and I could see a look of great satisfaction spreading from one cheek to the other.

'*Daca Misericordia*,' he repeated. 'It is a beautiful name for a beautiful knife.' His voice trailed off, as if he had suddenly remembered the name of a long-lost love. Then his voice began again. 'But do not ever again let another man take hold of it,' he said, 'for the day you do will certainly be your last. Your destiny is bound to this knife like no other.'

Then he shook my hand.

I worked for Signore Caracciolo after that and for a time saw after his interests in Trapani and other places. Whatever needed to get done, I did. But then Signore Caracciolo died and Mussolini began his war on the Mafia. So I left Sicily and came to Cuba. But from that day to this, no man on earth has ever so much as laid a finger on this my dagger of mercy. This knife has been my salvation. It has been my destiny. And no man will ever take hold of it while I still draw breath.

83

The meeting of the Directors of Ignazio Tiziano & Sons
to discuss what they could salvage from the marketplace
disaster and if they perhaps needed to relocate:

The meeting took place in late July in Giuseppe Federico
DiCarla's magnificent colonial home in the hills outside
Guanabacoa. You could not see the house from the road.
All you could see were dense woods filled with yagrumo
and logwood and rosewood and Spanish lime and pine, and
all manner of palm trees. For some reason it was very dark
driving through the woods, even in the middle of the day with
the blue sky and sunlight filtering through the branches. It
was very hot and very dark. Perhaps darkness is not the right
word. Perhaps there is no word that captures the moment, or
even the essence of the moment. It was more like someone
had tried to take a photograph from a speeding car or a spy
plane hurtling through the stratosphere and so everything
had come out blurry and indistinct. In this photograph, which
was in fact reality, the dark shapes of the trees merged with
the shadows and the speckled light so you were never quite
sure where you were in relation to anything else. There were
no recognizable landmarks until you reached the first set of
iron gates, and then two young men wearing caps and holding
long-barreled rifles stepped out of the shadows with thin
faces marked with the stony, implacable seriousness of young
soldiers, and they waved for you to stop and approached
your car, but when they saw who you were, they nodded and
opened the gates and let you pass. And no matter where you
were during that blurry afternoon drive, there were only two
sounds you could distinctly hear, the obvious background
noise of the dozens of automobiles that had made the short
trip from Havana, bypassing the town of Regla with its
unsurpassed view of the city of Havana at night, and then up
through the dusty streets of Guanabacoa itself before heading
into the hills, the automobiles making their slow, meticulous
way through the woods to the mansion, the woods echoing
with their mechanical wheezing and sputtering, the sound of
grinding gears, and from somewhere else, though it sounded

like it was coming from everywhere all at once, leeching out of the very air, as if each individual molecule was a tiny speaker wired directly into the mind of God, you could hear the sound of a fast-moving river, or perhaps many rivers coming together, a deluge. On that particular day, it took very little effort as you were driving through the woods, with your eyes wide open or squeezed shut it did not matter, to imagine that the entire world was covered with water, an ocean deep and dark.

Before the meeting began, before Giuseppe Federico DiCarla emerged from the gloomy interior of the house to greet his friends and business associates, everyone gathered in a grand arcade style patio, Turkish tile on the floor, plaster walls sixteen feet high painted a soft Spanish orange like a distant sunset or the pulsing liquid glow of the street lamps along the Malecón just before dawn, and a dozen or more wicker chairs scattered about with small side tables for drinks and small plates. On either end of the patio a candled chandelier hung from the ceiling. The candles were not lit. A grand archway connected the patio to the foyer and from there to the rest of the house. Along the wall opposite the archway there were half a dozen narrow arched doorways with shuttered panels. The panels were folded back and you could see a lush garden beyond with orange trees glowing with the light of the sun and various shrubs and a small plain fountain in the middle. You could hear the soft sounds of birds calling out to each other from the trees or the shrubs. Or maybe it was your imagination. The fountain was gurgling like a sewer.

There was also a French Provincial table with a rounded mirror of darkly glowing glass. The table was pushed up against the wall next to the grand archway and was covered with all manner of elegant decanters, bottles of expensive liquor, cordials, port wine, anisette, and an assortment of wine glasses and smaller glasses. But the mirror was a very strange mirror indeed. No matter where you stood you could never see yourself. To a normal person, such as those who have no connection with organized crime, the mirror would have seemed very disturbing, but to those seated in the wicker chairs on the patio, it was only mildly disturbing, or even the subject of broad humor. You saw only various darkly glowing shapes reflected in the glass, hunched over shapes or twisted, contorted shapes, whispering and drinking and laughing and gesturing with sly, sinister gestures, pouring more drinks, moving back and forth through the semi-darkness of the patio like demented ghosts.

-84-

The conversation on the patio before the meeting began:

"'You don't get vaccinated for Florida,' I said to her, 'but you do for Mexico and that's a fact.'"

"And what did she say to that?"

"She didn't say anything, she just boarded the bus and sat down."

"A real bitch, huh?"

"In a manner of speaking."

"Sure. So what'd you do?"

"I boarded the bus and sat down right behind her."

"I'll bet she liked that. Deep down I bet she was asking for it!"

"Yeah, sure."

"What'd you do then?"

"I started whistling a little tune I heard once when I was down in Mexico. I don't know where I was exactly. I think I was in Acapulco. A little café called La Mar Azul, as I remember, next to a movie house."

". . . ."

"She didn't like the tune. She acted like she had never heard it before, but it was really quite popular down there. I told her that was no way to treat a fellow traveling companion. I asked if she was going all the way to Miami or if she was getting off at an earlier stop, like Fort Walton Beach or Panama City or Tampa, but she didn't say a word the whole trip down."

"I pretty much keep to myself when I'm traveling."

"To each his own."

"I don't say a word to anybody."

"Of course you don't."

"It's like my tongue is tied into knots."

"You're not the gregarious type, not by a damn sight."

The men laughed.

And two more voices from somewhere else, the voices floating aimlessly about the patio, soaring up towards the darkness of the ceiling and the unlit candled chandeliers.

"Some said it was a group of students angered by this business with the newspapers."

"What business?"

"These kids were waving protest banners and demanding that Grau stop paying off the newspapers."

"Who cares what Grau does with the newspapers? Nobody believes a damn thing they print anyway."

"Yeah, but these students were becoming pretty volatile."

"You mean out of control."

"Exactly!"

"What were they doing on Calle Cuba?"

"I don't think anybody knows. But somebody knew they were going to be there. Somebody called the police, or maybe the police were in on it from the beginning. Either way they were waiting by the Public Works building, and as soon as they saw the students they started firing their guns and everybody started running."

"What about the mob of low-life fuckers that attacked the warehouse?"

"That's the funny part. As soon as the shooting started, the mob rushed the gates and thirty minutes after that the warehouse was burning. You can draw your own conclusions, but it sounds to me like the whole thing was staged."

"You mean some fucker was out to get us from the start."

"That's pretty much the size of it."

And two more voices.

"We need the unions. The Communists can go fuck themselves!"

"As long as Portocarrero is the Minister of Labor, we'll be all right."

"Don't be so sure."

"Portocarrero is reasonable. We can always work with reasonable men."

"Yes, but something happens when these fuckers get a little taste of power. They suddenly become . . . unreasonable."

And then some head nodding, some quiet laughter.

And then all of the voices jumbled together.

"The government denies the police were ever there. But Calle Cuba is stained with blood."

"She actually got off the bus in Tampa, and I almost got off there too, I have to be honest, but the Traficantes wanted me in Miami the next day so I had to give her up."

"Except if the Communists take control we'll have to leave the country."

"You mean head to the States."

"Yeah, sure, America is always an option."

"But nobody wants to give up Latin America."

"Sounds like a good old-fashioned bloodbath!"

"The best kind."

"Where then?"

"Maybe the Dominican Republic.

" . . . ?"

"Why not?"

"You mean as long as Trujillo stays in bed with the Americans."

"Is that what I mean?

"Sure."

"Fuck Trujillo."

"But she sure as hell was stacked. I mean I've never seen a woman that good looking."

"The Communists will never take control."

"You never saw such a beautiful piece of ass in your life. I mean my mouth was watering. I mean her fucking tits were out to here."

"I'd have liked to see that."

"Goddamn fucking tits."

"The street was littered with little green and white flags or banners, so you almost didn't notice all the blood."

"They tried in '26 and look what happened then."

"Those were anarchists.

"It'll start in the east."

"Not Communists."

"Santiago maybe."

"It was one hell of a political statement to make whoever the hell they were."

"It is all the same thing."

"Like it always does."

"It'll never happen."

"Just like in America."

"Yeah, I guess I blew it."

"Well, don't worry about it."

"You wait and see."

"There's a million dames in the world and they all look just like her."

"That's what I keep telling myself."

"America will step in."

"Yeah, just like in America."

"You're God damn right."

-85-

Luis was not participating in any of the conversations floating about the patio. He did not go in for the gossipy prattling of old women. Instead, he and Oscar were off in the corner in two wicker chairs that were partially shrouded by some potted ferns. They were drinking red wine, a Claret, while everyone else was already dipping into the hard stuff. It was Oscar's first time at a Director's meeting. He was wearing the white linen suit and the immaculate Panama hat that Luis had purchased for him when he had first arrived in Havana. He was a gleaming double image of his mentor. Luis was casually pointing out the cast of characters, at least the major players.

The big brute with the truck driver's cap and the broad, flattened nose of a boxer was Johnny 'Big John' DaLuca. He was representing the interests of the Traficante family out of Tampa. He was the one who had teased the girl on the bus. He had flown in just for this meeting.

Big John was chatting away with Antonio Billiteri, a one-time crooner who had ruined his voice smoking cigarettes. They were sitting a few feet from the darkly glowing mirror like two dark saints, occasionally looking at the glass, wondering what had become of their reflections, commenting how easy it is to commit all kinds of atrocities when you are invisible, and then laughing uproariously.

Antonio represented the interests of a money man known cryptically as the Big Jew, which was hardly cryptic at all because there weren't many Jews in Cuba to begin with, and not very many who were called 'Big,' which wouldn't have made literal sense anyway since the Big Jew was only five foot five, so it was clearly a symbolic reference, a healthy sign of respect or fear, and lastly, which is the nail in the coffin (a trite expression, certainly, but appropriate for this crew), there was only one person of Jewish persuasion who worked with the Mafia, who the Mafia were afraid of, who had become his own Mafia.

Big John and Antonio the former crooner had known each other for years. They had had a falling out over a girl some years earlier but they had made amends. They liked to joke about it from time to time, but the truth was neither even remembered the girl's name.

Before he ruined his voice smoking, Antonio had quite a singing career in front of him. He was more promising than Frank Sinatra, even the Big Jew said so.

After the smoking, of course, Sinatra was the man.

The other players on the patio, not including Luis, were as follows:

Eugenio Castellanos, a mixed blood with a flair for making apocalyptic pronouncements (cryptic prophecies written in cantos in the style of Cervantes and pulled out at parties and other gatherings to entertain and provoke wild, pendulum-swinging arguments that would quickly degenerate into fistfights) who had worked in the office of the Mayor of Havana, Manuel Fernandez Supervielle, until the Mayor had put a revolver to his chest and pulled the trigger because he was unable to make good on his campaign promise to supply Havana with an adequate water works. (Oddly enough, the suicide gun was a Kongsberg Colt pistol, which the Mayor's wife was certain did not belong to the Mayor, and the police, after examining the serial number that for some reason had not been filed off, agreed somewhat noncommittally with the wife, sharing with her and with the press only a few pages of their redacted findings, which raised a series of questions that were never answered, at least not satisfactorily, as far as the wife and one or two overly committed and underpaid journalists were concerned, for the gun had been purchased originally in a small gun shop in Hamburg, Germany under the auspices of the German Weapons Act of 1938 by a name-less individual, at least his name had been blacked out on the permit card on file in the government offices in Hamburg, and then the gun appeared to have been registered with the Cuban government as a diplomatic courtesy in the name of another nameless individual, or perhaps the same one (who can truly say?), on behalf of the German Embassy. But what did that prove? We all have our enemies. Even if we are unaware of their existence. Even if they are but shadowy reflections of ourselves.) Eugenio had recently been elected the Treasurer of the Gas Workers Union. He had been involved in organized crime in one way or another since he was fourteen years old.

Ruperto Medino Borges, an expatriate Argentine and former editor of the newspaper *Diario de la Marina*, before Batista put that bastard Ernesto de la Fe in charge of gagging the press. It was rumored that Ruperto was bisexual. It was also rumored that he had fathered progeny with his own daughters, an outlandish thing to say under any circum-stances. Of course every time these rumors surfaced they were met with an icy stare and the threat of bullets, though everyone knew no bullets were forthcoming, and then a front-page story eviscerating the rumormongers before all Havana. Then the rumors would vanish for a year or two. But nothing Ruperto did, no amount of justified outrage he might express, stopped the flurry of sarcastic lyrics (somewhere between letrillas and limericks in terms of form and content) that circulated unpublished for years before they were lost or purposefully abandoned in the forgotten railway station of time, or perhaps they were scribbled on the walls of public bathrooms and later the ink blurred, but which in their heyday exploded with momentary though sophomoric (which is to say moronic) brilliance, no one could deny that, with lines like: There once was a faggot/Ruperto, who was also,/ they said, necrofilico/so they cut off his cock/which they stuffed in a sock/and now he suffers from vertigo.

It was also rumored that Ruperto was losing his eyesight from too many years typesetting (before he became the editor in charge) in that dungeon of a room where the printing presses were kept, presses which needed to be typeset by hand for oh so many mind-numbing years, countless years, centuries, by some accounts, in a room where the only illumination in all that time came from two weakly glowing brown globes, from Edison's original drawings, the editors used to say with charred laughter, set in the ceiling about three feet apart from each other and which resembled nothing if not two enormous eyes of a submerged sea creature from a distant millennium. The rumor of Ruperto's failing eyesight was unsubstantiated.

Eladio de la Campa, a light skinned Cuban of Spanish descent who had recently been elected Secretary of the Electrical Workers Union. Eladio had once worked for Prio, who had gone into exile when Batista took over, and on the surface he said good things about Prio, or most of the time he did, but Eladio had been very young when he first met Prio and it was said that Prio had raped him, that he had two thugs hold Eladio down in a rarely used storage room in the Capitol building, or maybe it was in the back of some café along the harbor or in one of the city father's city parks looking out on the Straits of Florida after midnight, and he had raped Eladio repeatedly, and then he had sworn Eladio to secrecy on pain of death, and not just Eladio's death, but the deaths of his mother and his sister and his sister's small children, and then the incident was all but forgotten. It was if it had never happened. So Eladio secretly hated Prio.

Paolo Cuccia, an attaché at the Italian Consulate who had Sicilian connections and who had handled the deportation paperwork for Lucky Luciano with a skillful white-washing of the most damning details of Luciano's case, which earned him a commendation from his superiors. There was nothing more to say about Paolo.

Various silent, eager, hopeful lieutenants and faithful, diligent soldiers, watchful companions to the men noted above, a few who were heirs apparent, like Oscar, and so were sitting nervously in wicker chairs near their patrons, but the rest spent most of that afternoon leaning up against walls or huddled in the gloomy shadows of the great archway, drinking steadily, seeming complacent, even bored, but watching every movement of every man on the patio, cataloging secret motives and emerging weaknesses with methodical (some would say sadistic) fatalism, their eyes drawn to the smallest of hand gestures, a slightly furrowed brow, a silk handkerchief pulled from a pocket, a fancy, perfumed handkerchief that smelled heavily of citrus and faintly of mint, a pair of legs crossing themselves and uncrossing themselves in quick succession, a crystalline peal of laughter ringing in the semi-darkness and then crashing to the tiled floor, anything that might suggest someone was about to pull a gun.

Oscar was intoxicated with the specter of imminent betrayal and certain violence that hovered in the air above the gossipy men, the noxious fumes of an exploding universe or a hypnotist's trick of the light (a notoriously slippery pair of alternatives that seem on the surface to be mere playful banter but which upon closer examination lie at the very heart of certain philosophical discussions about the meaning of life and the nature of true love, which naturally depends upon one's perspective and the books one has read and whether or not one was abused as a child, as is usually the case, and so is often misinterpreted or overlooked altogether). The last time Luis had attended a meeting, Oscar and Nerea had accompanied him as far as the town of Guanabacoa, and then he had dropped off the lovebirds at a small sunwashed café to eat and pass the time. Naturally, Oscar had been humiliated when Luis left him behind, but Luis had told him he was not yet ready. "These men do not care about your dream to open a nightclub of your own unless you are able to line their own pockets," said Luis. "And if you make such a promise, then you need to be especially careful. They deal in death without acrimony or remorse." So there had been nothing that Oscar could say, not a word of reproach or resignation, not so much because Oscar lacked the social savvy to know when a joke was required or when it would be best to hide in a cloud of silence to elude a bullet, which was certainly true, but because

Oscar was with Nerea that day and she had been wallowing in despair, a pouty expression on her lips which meant she needed considerable attention or she would be a bear for only God knew how long. But all that had been forgotten when Luis announced that Oscar would accompany him into the hills beyond Guanabacoa to attend a meeting of the Directors of Ignazio Tiziano & Sons to discuss their good fortune at living in a world always on the brink of war.

-86-

The meeting of the Directors officially began when Giuseppe Federico DiCarla was wheeled out onto the patio. He was sitting in a rigid, authoritarian pose, defiant but gracious, in a cane-back wheelchair with ivory handles. A young orderly wheeled him towards the second of the six narrow arched doorways. The young orderly was dressed all in white, a gleaming white in contrast to the semi-darkness all around. He positioned the wheelchair so Federico could see both the garden, with its orange glowing orange trees that now seemed like comets that had already struck the earth, and the darkly glowing shadows of the dark men who were sitting in the wicker chairs slowly (or speedily) getting drunk. Federico had a good view of both.

Two young men with long-barreled rifles also accompanied Federico, and he smiled at them, a charming, intelligent, gracious as always but also slightly sinister smile that seemed like the smile of a rebellious Jesuit priest, even though Federico was clearly no Jesuit. The young men slipped into the shadows on either side of the doorway. Soon everyone else forgot they were there.

As soon as the pleasantries were exchanged, which were incoherent and garbled because of alcohol but since everyone knew everyone else it didn't matter, Federico launched into a recitation about a 2nd century Roman philosopher named Celsus, who had accused the early Christians of trying to kidnap the very idea of a Supreme Being and present it as their own. What they wanted, said Federico, assuming the persona if not the ancient voice of Celsus, was an exclusive piece of real estate that only they could claim where they could erect all sorts of luxury accommodations with mini-bars and swimming pools and fancy chocolates and champagne and run about naked day and night (though all of these images, it should be said, came from Federico's febrile imagination, not from the writings of Celsus). The early Christians promised a veritable paradise if you bought their story, said Federico speaking for Celsus, a cornucopia of human delight, if you will, where every desire that went unfulfilled in this miserable plane of reality, every gnawing sacrifice that ate away at your own belief in yourself until there was nothing left, all of this misery would be repleted a thousandfold. That was the story line. But it was a bald-faced lie, an absolute sham, that's what Celsus thought, said Federico. That's what really got him steamed. So he told everyone who would listen that the Christians had created an imaginary world (to say the least) to seduce the masses, and then they were going to steal the actual world when everyone was looking towards the mythic future, and, naturally, the masses were seduced.

Then Federico spoke at great length about a Frenchman who taught philosophy and mathematics at a small private school in Algiers in 1917, and he couldn't remember this Frenchman's name, but he knew that it was not Pascal or Fénelon or Bossuet or Montargis or La Combe, but perhaps it was Renan or Rougier or someone who resembled the figures in the later paintings of Modigliani with their sad eyes and elongated faces and noses like miniature elephant trunks trying to sniff out the truth, but whoever he was, this mad dog of a Frenchman attacked the dogmatic principles not only of the Catholic Church, but of all ideologies that promised liberation but did not deliver (whether it was liberation of the soul, of thought, of the body, of the self, from society, from violence, from hunger, from death, of dreams, it was all the same thing in the end), and then later, and this was always the pattern, those pushing this propaganda would use the gleaming bauble of liberty always just out of reach to stifle liberty itself, and you could hear Federico's rising anger as he spoke, an anger that stretched all the way back to the time of Celsus, an anger that some would call the winds of indignation, the winds which precede the storm.

All this Federico pushed towards his drunken, astonished listeners, and then he sat back in triumph in his ivory handled wheelchair, a ridiculous, aging, infirm Mephistopheles ready to pluck the souls like stone orchids of the already damned from this purgatorial rock garden of existence, where we find ourselves. So Federico sat back in his wheelchair and smiled. He turned one ear towards his own garden and the gurgling fountain and the glowing orange trees like dead or dying comets and the birds calling to each other in their strange, throaty, feathery language of the after-life, and he turned the other ear towards the semi-darkness of the arcade style patio and his stiff, silent listeners, who might have been thinking about Federico's passionate recitation, but they might also have been thinking about how hungry they were even at three in the afternoon because there was nothing to eat on the patio.

There was a strange, noisy crashing sound from the garden, as if an airplane had crashed into the orange trees, or a satellite from the future that had slipped out of its orbit. But it was really the sound of several birds, a flock of birds, starlings perhaps, or some other kind of bird, taking flight. For a moment nobody could see the sun. At least nobody who was looking in the direction of the sun. Which was only Federico.

Antonio Billiteri wondered out loud how much it would cost to get a piece of that prime real estate Federico had been talking about. He did not realize his thoughts had become words. His question unleashed a storm of varying opinions. Big John said he didn't believe in owning property, he believed in hotels, and hotels could get quite pricey, especially if you trashed the room. Eladio wanted to say that Big John was an idiot, but Eladio was always the diplomat and said only that the problem with hotels was that they took advan-tage of the people who worked for them, people who had little or no formal education and could not be expected to stand up to the onslaught of prejudice and racial insults hurled their way for fear of losing their jobs. Paolo said he was staying at The Gran Inglaterra Hotel on Paseo del Prado, in spite of the fact that it was a little run-down, a balcony room with a

view of the sea, the very same room where Winston Churchill
had stayed when he came to watch the Spanish-Cuban war
in 1895, that's what the clerk had said. Paolo said the other
morning when he woke up the prettiest little dark-skinned
maid you ever hoped to see was scrubbing his bathroom
and she was bending over and her skirt was riding up so he,
Paolo, surprised her from behind and carried her back to his
bed. Later they splashed around in the tub and scrubbed each
other with a bar of that black Spanish soap. Then they fucked
some more. Big John and Antonio said they were staying
at the wrong hotel. Paolo invited them to come to a small
party he was throwing the next night. Big John and Antonio
said they would come. Eladio said that was just the kind of
prejudicial attitude he was talking about. No wonder nobody
in Cuba knew where they came from. Ruperto said he agreed
with Eladio from a biological point of view, but intellectually,
now that was a different matter. Ruperto said they were all
descended from the great José Marti, even the poor souls
like himself who had emigrated from Argentina. They (we)
were all his (Marti's) children. Had they (we) not all read and
been amazed by Marti's excellent essays on everything from
when he was in prison in Cuba to his rabble rousing in New
York City as well as the letters he wrote to General Maximo
Gómez? Eladio scoffed at the mere mention of Marti's name.
Eladio said what about Félix Varela y Morales, who wrote that
you could believe in God and still work to change the order of
things in a country like Cuba that cared little for the welfare
of ordinary citizens. Big John said he wasn't Cuban to begin
with so he didn't care about what any of these Cuban writers
had to say. He was Italian. Antonio and Paolo agreed with Big
John. Ruperto was fuming. Eladio said what about Caballero,
for God's sake, or Zayas, or Enrique José Varona, who wrote
for the revolutionary heart in all generations. Where do these
men fit in? What of their patriotism, their dreams for Cuba?
Have you forgotten where we come from? And with that
Ruperto exploded, a rush of words coming directly from
Marti himself: 'A nation is not founded as a military camp is
commanded,' he said. And then: 'The pain of imprisonment
is the harshest, most devastating pain, murdering the mind,
searing the soul, leaving marks that will never be erased.' Of

course nobody knew what Ruperto was trying to say. While
every Cuban boy had learned to quote Marti in grade school,
these particular quotes did not seem to apply to the discussion
at hand. Nevertheless, no one could argue with Ruperto's
passion. He was shouting with such thunderous agitation that
the dust from the ceiling fell like darkness. Or perhaps the
darkness fell like dust. It was hard to tell.

Then there was a lull in the conversation and everyone
calmed down.

Then Eugenio said he was concerned about the attack
on the federal garrison near Santiago. Ruperto asked him
what attack was this. Eugenio said two hundred rebels living
in the Sierra Maestra mountains had attacked the garrison at
Moncada. They had a rented a farmhouse near the barracks,
where they had stashed dozens of light rifles and shotguns
and ammunition and several cartons of old army uniforms to
wear as disguises. They had enough weapons for a small raid,
but not an all-out attack. On the feast day of St. James, the
rebels were to make their way to Santiago, singly or in pairs,
and rent rooms in the various hotels and brothels. A few were
to stay with relatives. They were going to attack at dawn the
next day. Then dawn came, and everything seemed promising.
They met at the farmhouse to get their weapons and to
put on their army uniform disguises. They went over their
plan, the routes the vehicles were to take, the timing of the
assault. They were laughing and joking. They were certain the
soldiers from the barracks would be hung over from a night of
drunken debauchery, the kind of night that went along with
any feast day. They were certain they were going to seize control of the barracks and the weapons that were stored there,
there was a rumor that there were thousands of rifles stored at
Moncada, enough to start a revolution, and they believed that
once they had seized control of all this, thousands of Cubans
would then join their cause. But they were mistaken. They
were mistaken about everything. The attack was a disaster
from the start. Two of the cars loaded with rebels got into
an accident with a bus heading for Bayamo. Another vehicle
got lost in the narrow streets of Santiago, somewhere in the
vicinity of the stairway of Padre Pico. Another ran out of gas.
Only three cars made it to the barracks at all. The first of

these crashed itself through the gate, killing the two guards instantly, but damaging the car to such an extent that it was inoperable. By the time the rebels pushed it from the entrance, which took more time than they had bargained for, they were surprised by a surprise morning patrol making the rounds that had heard the crash and came to investigate. That's when the shooting started. Half of the rebels were killed on the spot. Of those who escaped, all were later caught, and most of these were executed. But some were set free. 'That was a mistake,' said Eugenio.

It was at this point that Ruperto, who knew nothing about this attack on the barracks of Moncada, said 'I know nothing about this attack on the barracks of Moncada,' at which point Eugenio said that was not surprising since the attack had not yet happened, at which point Eladio started to laugh and said, you fooled us, Eugenio, you did not turn this prophecy into poetry as you usually do, so how were we to know you were kidding, and Eladio's laughter rang out with the cruel clarity of a church bell, but Eugenio was not laughing for he truly believed that all of his prophecies were written by the hand of God, this one about the attack on the barracks of Moncada more than any of the others, he was just the mouthpiece reading from a script, an oracle without a political agenda, he was simply the overhead projector projecting God's words written on a celestial transparency, so he said he was not kidding, he did not kid when it came to prophecies, the attack will take place, he said, if not this year then certainly next year, and some of the rebels will be released to appease public opinion, and this will be a mistake, the rebels they release will become dyed–in-the-wool Communists, or close enough that it will make no difference, and so they will try a second time, this is inevitable, and they will succeed, and then Cuba will be saddled with a brilliant, charismatic, but ulti-mately childish dictator who will drive the country towards a host of impossible, absurd agricultural goals, such as trying to improve the production of the nation's dairy cows, pushing the biological limits of the cows in the misguided hope that one day every cow in the country (or even the miracle of just one cow) will be capable of producing an endless stream of milk, an inexhaustible supply, this, said Eugenio, is the nature of the man who will be a dictator like no other, a dictator who will value the dismantling of the tourist trade in the name of social theory more than the welfare of his own people, a dictator who will lead Cuba and the rest of the world to the brink of a third world war, the very edge of the cyclical night, filled with corridors for sleep and nameless fear.

It was at this point that the laughter of Eladio had become the laughter of Eladio and Ruperto and Big John and Antonio and Paolo, and their laughter with its crystalline purity of dozens of very large church bells ringing out from the four corners of the earth turned every single word that fell out of Eugenio's mouth into drops of sea water or translucent pearls that landed harmlessly on the tiled patio floor.

Then the men grew serious and talked about the dangers of Communism for a while. Big John was of the opinion that the only good Communist was a dead Communist. Paolo said he thought that only applied to American Indians or pirates. Big John said what did he (meaning Paolo) think Communists were. Paolo didn't know what to say. Ruperto said the moment the Communists got their hands into the newspapers, the newspapers would be sunk. Eladio said the moment the Communists got their hands into the unions, the unions would be sunk. Let's face it, said Antonio, if the Communists ever take over, we're all sunk. Unless the Americans intervene, said Ruperto. Then Luis said the symbol of Communism should be a sinking ship, and everyone applauded.

Then everyone talked about the possibility of the Americans intervening. Then they talked about the pros and cons of America if you were living in Cuba, and then America if you were living in America, and then they talked about Cuba if you were living in America, but they didn't talk about Cuba if you were living in Cuba because they were already living there, except Big John, who didn't care.

Then Ruperto told a story about a young crippled boy living in Argentina. The boy had spent his life on crutches but he had always wanted to dance with pretty girls and ride horses. He especially wanted to ride the Argentine Criollo because this horse was as rugged as the mountains which the crippled boy could see from his bedroom window and because this horse, which was a little bigger than a Spanish mustang,

could cover astonishingly long distances in a single day. Since
he was a devout Catholic, the crippled boy prayed and prayed
to Saint Antonio for a miracle that would erase his deformity.
He prayed every day. For years and years he prayed every
day. Naturally, no miracle occurred. And after a while, said
Ruperto, the crippled boy became a crippled man, and his
dream of dancing and riding horses began to fade. He felt
betrayed. He cursed the name of Saint Antonio. He thought
about cursing the name of God. And then one day he retracted
his prayer.

The very next morning, said Ruperto, bright and early,
the crippled man's cousin, a long-leagued cattle baron named
Rafael, who owned several ranches near San Cristóbal, arrived
in a gleaming new automobile. The crippled man had not
seen or even heard from his cousin in years and did not know
that Rafael had taken some time off to travel. He was amazed
by his cousin's vehicle, which was a fabulous four-cylinder
Rochet Schneider with a front seat and a back seat. Rafael said
he was on a pilgrimage to the Church of Saint Antonio, which
was only a couple of days by car, and he asked the crippled
man to join him. The crippled man agreed to go, but he did
not say why. He hid his dark purpose even from himself.

That night they camped under the stars, for they found
themselves in a very rural part of Argentina. As they were
settling in for the evening, a bearded man driving a team of
mules appeared out of nowhere. The mule driver asked if
he could share their simple campsite, and the crippled man
and the cousin agreed. Later, all three men were sitting by
the campfire sipping red wine from tin cups, and the mule
driver suddenly began telling them a story about a boy he had
sent to a small Jesuit school in Santa Fe. He was paying for
everything, but the boy was not his. The boy was the son of a
friend from his childhood. His friend had been dead for many
years, but the circumstances of his death were very strange,
some would even say suspicious, so the mule driver had spent
the cascading years that followed describing the details of
that fateful day, which seemed like yesterday, to anyone who
would listen.

On the day of his friend's death, the two of them had
robbed an old priest of a sack of silver, but then his friend had

become suddenly greedy and tried to kill him. Fortunately
for the mule driver, the gun, a pistol typical of men without
integrity, exploded in his friend's hand. The bullet magically
lodged itself in his friend's forehead, killing him instantly.
So with the unlucky death of his friend (but of course lucky
for the mule driver), he found himself in sole possession of
the bag of silver. But later that night he had a strange dream.
Saint Antonio appeared in his dream and told him about
his friend's son. Saint Antonio said the boy was destined to
become a priest. And what was more, the bag of silver was
meant to pay for the boy's education at the Jesuit school in
Santa Fe. That is what Saint Antonio said, and then he disappeared. 'I had never been visited by a Saint before,' said the
mule driver. 'Naturally I went to the village where my friend
had lived with his son. I told the boy his father had died so he
could go to school.'

The next morning the crippled man and his cousin went
one way and the mule driver went another way. The cousin
asked the crippled man what he thought about the mule
driver's story but the crippled man didn't answer, for he was
lost in thought. After a while they came upon a man walking
in the middle of the road. The road was very rough and
made for difficult driving, but it made for even more difficult
walking, so they asked the man if he wanted a ride. The man
accepted and hopped into the back seat. A short while later
he was describing how he had rescued his own soul from
eternal damnation. He said that when he was a young boy, his
father mysteriously died, and a friend of his father magically
appeared with a bag of silver and said the money was to
pay for his schooling. So off he went to the Jesuit school in
Santa Fe, and ten years later he became a priest. It was only
after becoming a priest that he learned that his soul had been
promised to the Devil.

'My father had signed a blood contract with the Devil,'
he said. 'Because he wanted to be a wealthy man. My soul was
part of the price my father had to pay. But he soon regretted
his decision and tried to get out of the contract. After a great
deal of snooping about, he discovered that his contract was
in the possession of an old priest who lived in a small nearby
village where time was measured by the lingering echo of a

single church bell. He discovered that this old priest always prayed in the church of this village until the stroke of midnight, at which point the Devil would appear before the altar with a bag of silver in payment for the old priest's complicity. Then the old priest would return to the rectory for a few hours' sleep. So my father and his friend were waiting for the old priest on the narrow path between the church and the rectory. They were going to rob the old priest and use the bag of silver to buy back my father's contract. But before my father knew what was happening, his friend was waving a gun in the air and the gun went off and my father was killed. The old priest saw the dead body and shoved the bag of silver into the hands of my father's friend and then fled into the darkness.

'The only reason I know about this is because one night, shortly after I had said my final vows, Saint Antonio appeared to me in a dream. He said my soul belonged to the Devil. He told me the story of my father's greed and subsequent death. He said if I wanted to regain possession of my soul I needed to listen to him very carefully. He said I needed to impress upon this priest the error of his ways, and to do this I needed to first accompany him, meaning Saint Antonio himself, on a dark and dangerous journey into the depths of Hell so that I could see the horrors of the eternal pit for myself. As soon as I returned, I was to visit the old priest and describe to him everything that I had seen. You can imagine my despair, but I did exactly as Saint Antonio had commanded and sought out the old priest, and when I finished my tale of horrors, he repented of all his evil deeds, took out a handful of contracts, including mine, which he had been keeping until the Devil called, and burned them right there in front of my eyes. Then he collapsed in a heap, his mortal flesh evaporating like smoke in a matter of seconds.'

By the time the young priest had finished his story, the crippled man and his cousin were nearing the town with the Church of Saint Antonio. The young priest asked to be let off on the outskirts of the town. Then he thanked the men for their hospitality and gave each a gift. To the cousin he gave a small leather Bible with an inscription inside that read 'Nothing is what it appears to be.' To the crippled man he gave a large blue stone, a very deep blue, a lapis lazuli

polished and gleaming, about the size of an ostrich egg, or
even larger, which the young priest said was his only souvenir
from his journey to Hell.

'I shed copious tears on my journey through Hell,' he
said. 'I witnessed unspeakable horrors. But I was there with
the grace of God and under the protection of Saint Antonio
himself, so my tears became this gleaming blue stone. For me
it became a talisman of my great good fortune, a reflection of
my faith, a visible reminder that my salvation is part of God's
divine purpose. But I think you need this reminder more
than I do.' Then the young priest hopped out of the car and
vanished in a swirling nest of dust and pebbles.

When the crippled man and his cousin arrived at the
church it was almost five o'clock in the afternoon, which
meant that most of the votive candles had been lit by pilgrims
seeking miracles. The candles were burning brightly, as
always, though the pilgrims were no longer present, but if you
listened carefully you could still hear the intonation of their
prayers lingering high above in the rafters.

The cousin went immediately to the rail before the altar
and the great statue of Saint Antonio shrouded in perpetual
mystery and lit a candle of his own and knelt down and
prayed, but the crippled man, who was standing near the back
of the church, resting somewhat awkwardly upon his rickety,
wooden crutches, could only stare at the statue of Saint
Antonio with a look of venomous distrust in his eyes.

He began cursing the great saint. 'I prayed to you and
I prayed to you, at all hours, and you did not answer my
prayers,' said the crippled man. Then he reached into his
pocket and pulled out the gleaming blue stone the young
priest had given him. He looked at the stone a moment. Then
he reared back and hurled it at the statue of Saint Antonio
with such force that all of the candles flickered and some went
out. He looked up to see the damage the stone had done, but
instead he saw the statue of Saint Antonio smiling, the blue
stone in the Saint's hand, the Saint rearing back as if to hurl
the stone himself, but the crippled man did not wait to find
out, he was through the church door as fast as his legs could
carry him, and it was only when he was a mile down the
road that he realized he was running without the aid of his

crutches, as nimble and as fleet-footed as any boy who had ever danced with a pretty girl.

No one in the room had ever been to Argentina, except for Ruperto, who said Argentina was a land of romance and lovers of all ages, but also of night terrors and unethical businessmen and Nazi paraphernalia and beautiful movie actresses who did three or four films and became international stars and then went into hiding and were never seen again. Big John was about to say that Argentina was a land of degenerates and whores, worse than the penal colonies of the English or the floating asylums of the French, but quite without warning, Giuseppe Federico DiCarla reinserted himself into the conversation and all thoughts of Argentina ceased.

Within minutes everyone was passionately discussing the storming of the gates of Ignazio Tiziano & Sons. Everyone had an opinion about why the furious mob had stormed the gate, but Federico wasn't interested in opinions. Then Luis said it didn't matter why it happened. What mattered was that it had, in fact, happened, and now they had a choice to make. They had to figure out what they were going to do next. (Luis did not share his suspicions about Immanuel, for that would have needlessly complicated the discussion.) Federico laughed a great thunderous laugh. Or perhaps he was clapping. 'Exactly!' he said, and then he rolled himself over to the French Provincial table and the darkly glowing mirror and spun around to face the darkly glowing eyes (like the eyes of so many rabid hyenas) of the men glued to their wicker chairs.

Federico talked about the vanishing dream of Cuba and how their lives would be forever changed. He talked about the vanishing dream of the Mafia in Sicily during the time of Mussolini and how the lives of the Mafia had changed. He talked about the now vanished dream of his own childhood in Castellammare del Golfo and how his life had never been the same since those bygone days. Then he confessed that he didn't have a clue about what they should do, but he felt deep down in his gut that they had no choice but to abandon their interests in Cuba and head for the sunny shores of Florida. He thought maybe Miami. They had nice clean beaches there and it was a sleepy town compared to Havana so there would be very little competition. He had never been there, but he often imagined what it would be like. The night before his good friend Ignazio had left for America they had talked about places like New York City and Chicago and San Francisco and Miami. Someone had said Miami was the best of the four because it offered a tropical climate. In Miami you could lose yourself in the soothing rhythms of the sea. One of the puppeteers had said this. Yes, he had often imagined what it would be like in Miami. He used to think maybe Ignazio had taken Maura there. That's what he would have done. Life would have turned out much differently if he had gone with Ignazio and Maura.

Federico stopped talking and picked up his knife, which had been hidden from view in the folds of a napkin on his lap. He held up the knife as if he were holding up a sacrificial victim or a rare meteorite from a distant galaxy that had survived the passage through time and the earth's atmosphere. The blade caught the last rays of sunlight filtering in from the garden, the light then bouncing from the knife to the dark glass of the mirror and then folding in upon itself, and suddenly, strangely, it seemed that there were two knives floating in the air. In that moment, it seemed as if Federico had vanished, and all the men still glued to their wicker chairs could see were two gleaming knives. Beyond the knives there was nothing to see except the loss and absence of the world.

-87-

For Oscar, the years following his first meeting with the Directors of Ignazio Tiziano & Sons were a tumultuous dream full of shadowy yet sharply stylized characters, a film noir classic in which two sides were pitted against each other in the eternal struggle for power and the privilege of living beyond the reach of the law. Naturally, there was also a lot of sex and lust (you can't have film noir without eroticism) as well as random acts of cruelty, pre-meditated acts of

cruelty, an atmosphere of all-consuming betrayal, and some
sort of strange, all-encompassing metaphor suggesting that
the reality depicted in this movie was a dream, or conversely,
that the reality depicted in this dream was a movie. To
everyone involved, it was clear beyond the need for words
that the lines for this black and white epic had been drawn
when Federico announced his intention to move operations
to Miami. Antonio, speaking on behalf of the Big Jew, Eladio
and Eugenio, speaking on behalf of the unions and the faceless, downtrodden people of Cuba, perpetually downtrodden,
and Ruperto, speaking for himself, and yet also, in some
strange, vaguely conceived yet symbolic way, for journalists
everywhere engaged in the struggle to preserve the freedom
of the press, were all against the idea. Their opposition was
quite vocal, bordering on belligerent, but what could they do?
Big John didn't care, and neither did Paolo. Only Luis among
the Directors and Oscar among the close associates and other
various hopeful lieutenants stood squarely with Federico.

Ruperto thought the old man had lost his grip. Eladio
thought perhaps he had succumbed to the inertia of an
ever-expanding regimen of medication and old age. Antonio,
again on behalf of the Big Jew (did Antonio ever voice his own
opinion?), assumed that one day they would find the body of
the old man and his shattered cane-back wheelchair with the
ivory handles at the bottom of a ravine or a steep set of stairs
or among the jagged rocks along the Malecón, where the ice-
cream vendors were always pushing their Guarina ice-cream
carts along the wall and the fishermen were always casting
their lines and squinting into the sun (and Antonio could
almost visualize this happening in his mind, not far from the
spot, or one of the many spots, where Luis and Nerea used to
engage in some pretty furious fucking in a doomed effort to
hold on to their disintegrating love). Eugenio was convinced
the end of the world was at hand.

One way or another the world was, in fact, falling apart,
and then, of course, reassembling itself. The salient metaphor
(or perhaps series of metaphors or extended metaphor is more
accurate) for this process, which you have probably already
guessed, was a flaming meteor streaking across the sky and
crashing into the earth, perhaps wiping out a small town,

or even a city if it was large enough, but certainly causing devastation and vast amounts of inky black smoke wherever it landed, and then later, the place where the meteor had struck would experience a rebirth of quasi-religious significance, an elemental Phoenix rising from the ashes, the hope of a new paradise for a new world, but overhead the sky would remain dark and foreboding because you never knew when another meteor might appear. Suffice it to say that everyone knew some kind of change was occurring, they could feel it, each in their own way, but Oscar was perhaps more sensitive to the precise nature of what was happening than the others. Even Eugenio only felt vague tremors, a subtle vibration affecting his inner sense of equilibrium, producing the kind of discomfort, even nausea, usually associated with a wild swing in temperature or a sudden change in pressure after a debilitating descent from a higher altitude.

But with Oscar it was different. From the moment Oscar and Luis had left the meeting, Oscar had felt a strange uneasiness, almost as if he were walking a tightrope with his eyes closed, and this feeling soon developed into a preternatural sense that the malignancy of the world was sprouting like jimson weed before his very eyes. He was not paranoid by nature, but he knew without quite knowing how that he was being watched, spied upon, that someone was listening to his telephone conversations and perhaps recording them, and others were opening his letters with steam and pouring over them with cold, calculating eyes, eyes that also possessed a sadistic glint, looking for some sort of clue about his most recent nightmares or his childhood fears that had ripened into full-blown adult psychoses which they would later use against him without remorse, and then those shadowy someones resealing the letters as best they could, and still others were sifting through his trash, or tailing him in the middle of the night when he was heading back from La Campana or some other club to Hotel Milagro, but whenever he would stop and look around, the rambling echo of their footsteps would fade away. Later he began to notice strangely inarticulate men with rifles or Kongsberg Colt pistols sitting in the worn out leather chairs scattered about the hotel lobby, a dark, jazzy rendition of Gershwin's *Summertime* floating lazily about, reverberating

with the elegance of days gone by, though some would have
said it wasn't Gershwin at all, that it was Sarah Vaughn
singing *Whatever Lola Wants, Lola Gets*, and a few would have
said it was an old Eliseo Grenet song, and Eliseo was singing
as he always did about the suffering of beautiful Cuba (*¡Ay!*
Cuba hermosa, primorosa, ¿por qué sufres hoy tanto quebranto?),
but there was an eerie, mysterious quality about the music
whatever song was playing because no one could tell precisely
where it was coming from, the men peering through the
leafy, vegetative cover provided by various potted shrubs
and withered ferns, also scattered about, seeming little more
than shadows in the dim lobby light (a diffuse, yellowish,
subterranean glow), the men watching his every move with
those same eyes with a sadistic glint mentioned earlier,
strange inarticulate men with a certain gangsterly savoir faire
nevertheless, a polished eagerness otherwise known as the
killer's instinct, the men watching Oscar until he vanished
up the stairs to his room and then chatting amicably with the
hotel desk clerks and bellhops in threadbare jackets and even
other guests, trying to get some information of a personal
nature, what did he eat for breakfast, was he a model of good
hygiene, what was his tolerance for pain, that sort of thing, all
of which Oscar was still somehow able to see and hear down
to the softest decibel of a probing whisper even as he ran up
the stairs in escape mode and squirreled himself away in the
hazy, dreamlike isolation of his fourth floor suite, which he
still shared with Luis and Nerea.

   He became an insomniac roaming the halls of his own
imagination, exhibiting behavior that some would have called
delusional, and that others would have described as a fairly
good textbook example of a psychotic break. While Nerea was
sleeping, he would sit in a chair in the kitchen and look out
through the open balcony doors, staring across the vast dark
expanse of the inner courtyard at dozens of dark shuttered
balconies on the other side, and sometimes he would catch a
glimpse of the moon, but whether it was Quevedo's blood-
stained moon or some other moon symbolizing the future
or the death of enemies he did not know he had or his own
rebirth, he could not tell. Then the moment he would start to
nod off, a door would slam or a car would backfire or there

would be an explosion (whether this was somewhere outside, perhaps even as far away as the distilleries along Infanta, where explosions did occur with some regularity, or in the subterranean recesses of his mind was of little consequence).

So he would jerk back to consciousness and look out the window again, the faint odor of the harbor with its smell of saltwater and raw sewage and dead or dying fish washing through his nostrils (not quite a cleansing, more the opposite of a cleansing), but this time he would see two sets of eyes staring back at him from the darkness outside, bright yellow eyes or bright orange eyes or eyes glowing with a crimson color, boring holes into the fabric of reality. It seemed like the air itself was about to catch fire, but when he would get up for a closer look, the eyes would always speed away like minia-ture spaceships. At times he even thought he could hear the sound of their tiny motors whirring as they headed off into the infinite icy void of outer space, most likely to reconnoiter the planet and then return as soon as he closed his eyes again. This is what he was thinking or mumbling in a barely audible whisper. So he armed himself with a small pocket gun man-ufactured in Spain, a Beistegui Brothers Libia 6.35 mm that Luis had given him, just in case. And he wore his white linen suit and his immaculate Panama hat at all hours of the day or night in the vaguely felt and unexpressed hope that this outfit would protect him from all harm. After a while it became a second skin.

Of course Nerea wondered what was wrong with Oscar. They still fucked as often as she wanted to be fucked, which was once every few days or so. They continued with their long walks for a time, even lingering in front of El Gallo to admire the furs. On occasion they even lost themselves in the quiet, ancient, crumbling beauty of the waterfront cafés along the harbor, drinking coffee and nibbling cheese or pineapple pastelitos while they looked out at the boats, if it was the afternoon, or if it was later in the evening Nerea would be drinking Tio Pepe, as always, because she liked the taste of almond sherry at sunset, and Oscar would be drinking Brandy de Jerez and thinking about the magic of the Moors. But they no longer spoke of love, that rooster that feeds on graveyard weeds, as the poet says. The day Luis had invited Oscar to the Director's meeting, Oscar had told Nerea for the second and last time that he loved her. But after Oscar returned from the hills outside Guanabacoa, he seemed to Nerea like a man who had lost his faith. He barely even said boo to her when he got up in the morning, just enough to be polite. Her early afternoon tirades (justified explosions as far as Nerea was concerned) did not register a blip on his radar. He seemed indifferent to her comings and goings. And when she was squirming beneath his anxious lover's grip, usually just before he fell asleep at two in the morning, she had the distinct impression that she was making love to a ghost.

Then again, nothing is ever what it seems to be. To be fair to Oscar, he thought if he opened his mouth, his odd, altered view of reality would come bubbling out, uncontrollably, like froth, a sewer gurgling furiously, as it were, and then two things would surely happen: one, Nerea's life would somehow be in danger, the tripartite beast would suddenly reveal itself, the lonely clocks ticking away the seconds until forgetfulness, though Oscar wasn't sure if the threat to Nerea had something to do with the strange men sitting in the lobby with their rifles or their pistols or if there were other invisible and more sinister forces at work; and two, Nerea would think he had gone insane. So he kept his mouth shut as much as was possible, and after a time he thought himself heroic for the effort. He was Ariosto's Orlando, whose love for the Saracen princess Angelica caused him to go mad, though Oscar had never read the book. He was Cervantes' don Quixote, trying to wrest free the image of his beautiful and hypnotic Dulcinea from the cauldron of time and truth as the world sees it, though Oscar had only ever heard the story in passing from Luis. But Oscar breathed the same rarefied air as did these two fictional heroes. He was a brother to centuries of wandering champions lost in the pages of crumbling manuscripts, often crushed by worldly forces they did not understand. Like all those who had gone before him, he shared the sultry nights and the beguiling days with lions.

Naturally, with Oscar thoroughly immersed in this mythic cistern of prolonged silence, dressed in the protective armor of his white suit and armed with heroic delusions and the black-handled Libia, Nerea eventually (which is to say after a sufficient number of soul-withering years had passed) turned elsewhere for the simple, unrehearsed joys of conversation with an attentive soul and a few drinks and maybe even a night out on the town. She chose as her escort Immanuel, the messenger boy who had guided Nerea to safety as the warehouse belonging to Ignazio Tiziano & Sons burned to the ground, and who had been rewarded for his heroic initiative two days later with a sinecure in the Gas Worker's Union. Ironically (and this irony exists on many levels), it was Luis who recommended Immanuel for the position, even though he suspected Immanuel was the mastermind behind the destruction of the warehouse. Then again, it was also true that Luis never acted precipitously. He wanted to know why Immanuel had orchestrated the fire. What was the larger purpose? But he needed to proceed carefully because he didn't know who else was involved. This is the only reason Immanuel was still alive. But Nerea did not know about Luis' paranoia, and besides, Immanuel was exceptionally attentive to her flurry of changing moods, the subtle signs of her displeasure (a slightly wrinkled eyebrow, a nervous toe tapping on the tiled floor of a restaurant or café, a hiccup that was meant for a laugh), and he did everything in his power to help her overcome her grief over losing first Luis, and now, seemingly, Oscar, a grief hidden from everyone else, even Nerea, but obvious to Immanuel, who could see quite plainly that Nerea greeted every moment of every day with a stylized, never-changing Kabuki smile.

On the day of the warehouse fire, Immanuel had escorted Nerea all the way back to the hotel. She had thanked him, but not profusely, and then left him in the lobby without even a backward glance. But for the next several months, maybe longer, perhaps it was years, every time she passed through on her way to somewhere or back from somewhere

else, he was waiting for her, trying to catch her eye, his face
glowing with a persistently hopeful smile, his hands holding
a colorful though wilted clump of unrecognizable flowers. She
pretended not to notice him, and in time he became part of the
landscape of the lobby, eternally submerged in the shadows
of Hotel Milagro, a lonely vagrant, forgotten. He always sat
in the same location, in one of two burgundy leather chairs
next to the front desk. Sometimes Immanuel was in one chair,
sometimes the other. The chairs had been positioned for
people waiting for their keys, or perhaps the desk clerk was
retrieving a message or the bellhop was bringing out their
luggage or their coats. But they also provided an excellent,
even intimate view of the photograph of Julio Mella, which
hung on the wall directly behind the chairs, illuminated by
a small brass gallery style lamp fixed to the wall above the
photo, which was framed and encased in glass. Most people
did not recognize Julio Mella, but everyone who sat in those
chairs commented on his incredibly seductive beauty like a
movie star with his curly brown hair and intense, cinematic
eyes and pouty lips. Almost everyone who sat in those chairs
stared at that movie star face for a long time.

 The years passed, the soul-withering years mentioned
above. It is difficult to say if they passed quickly. What
is important is that one night Nerea stopped pretending
that Immanuel wasn't there. She was returning with Luis
and Oscar from an evening of boleros and sambas and the
nineteen-piece orchestra at the Palermo Club. Luis and Oscar
had ignored her for almost the entire evening. The only time
they paid any attention to her at all was when she came
back to the table after her one and only dance number on
stage. She had pushed her way into the line-up with a dozen
girls half her age (or so it seemed to Nerea) because the day
before Luis had said she was getting too old to dance. The
number was incredibly exciting and provocative. It was a new
number, modern in both its sophisticated choreography and
its blend of Latin rhythms, beginning with a fast-paced samba
during which a dozen male dancers in Spanish Conquistador
costumes chased a dozen scantily clad girls around the stage,
but after they caught the girls the music shifted to a very
slow, sensual bolero, and before long the girls had turned the

tables on the now helpless Conquistadors and rode them until they collapsed in a smiling heap. The number was called *The Rape of the Conquistadors*, and was received with a thunderous round of applause and a few passionate wolf whistles mixed in.

When Nerea came back to the table, perspiring heavily but quite happy, she found Luis and Oscar drinking mojitos and submerged up to their eyeballs in a dark, foreboding conversation (at least it seemed dark and foreboding to Nerea). She stood there a moment, expectant, uneasy, and then without even glancing up, Luis said her costume was a little too tight, and then the two men continued talking. They were still talking in fairly animated fashion when they got back to the hotel. They were talking about shipments from Argentina and suitcases full of money and something about Miami, but Nerea really wasn't listening. She was staring at the backs of their heads, trying to erase their heart-wrenching indifference from her memory with laser-like eyes. But Luis and Oscar kept jabbering away, several steps ahead of Nerea, on their way through the dark shadows of the lobby, and they were half-way up the stairs before they realized she was no longer with them, but by then it was very late and neither man wanted to chase after her. Besides, Nerea was a big girl, she could fend for herself. So they went to bed.

But Nerea did not go to bed that night. As she passed by the front desk and the two burgundy leather chairs, she caught a glimpse of the photograph of Julio Mella, and she noticed for the first time all evening how very fast her heart was beating, and fearing it might explode out of her ribcage, she sat down. It was only then that she noticed Immanuel, passed out or sleeping, his hands still holding a withered clump of flowers, his breath coming in steady, rhythmic bursts like the beating wings of a half-drowned bird, the soft light from the gallery style lamp washing across his face like a summer sunset or a midnight comet streaking across the sky. But he was not sleeping. As soon as Nerea noticed him, he sat up, and then Nerea smiled. And it did not matter that she only smiled at him with her unchanging Kabuki smile. The fact that she was sitting in a chair not three feet from where he was sitting and looking at him with vaguely vulnerable eyes

was enough for Immanuel. He sat up and Nerea smiled and he
removed his black-rimmed glasses, blinking rapidly until he
was fully awake, and then put his glasses back on. He blinked
some more. It seemed that his unimaginable patience had
been rewarded. He reached across the empty space between
them with the flowers and then the flowers vanished as if in a
dream.

And then they began to talk.

They talked about that awful and yet strangely glorious
day when Ignazio Tiziano & Sons had burned to the ground
and the thousands and thousands of people who had stormed
the gates, that covetous multitude, had been trampled or lost
in the fire or had run away. They talked about Julio Mella, and
all Nerea could remember was that he had been an anarchist
and that he had died very young, he had been murdered, but
Immanuel knew a great deal more. Immanuel mentioned that
Julio had been a very outspoken student at the University
of Havana and a founding member of the Communist Party
of Cuba. He had been falsely imprisoned by the Machado
government for his participation in a supposed bomb plot,
but there had never been a bomb plot. No bomb had gone off.
There had been no bomb. It had all been a lie. A deception to
preserve a world on its last legs. So the government eventually
released Julio from prison, after sufficient time had elapsed
to avoid embarrassment, and a year later he fled to Mexico,
where they killed him. It was a political assassination, said
Immanuel, and though he did not say who exactly was
responsible, whether it was Machado or those working for him
or some other organization, Nerea could tell by the way that
his eyes flitted back and forth with subliminal anger that he
knew the murderers personally, or at least he knew where to
find them, any that were still alive, and that someday, when
he had planned everything down to the last excruciatingly
complicated detail, they (the survivors) would pay for their
crimes. They talked about the corruption of the current
government. They talked about betrayal. They talked about
the shimmering mirage of hope. Immanuel recited some love
poetry by the Chilean poet and writer and gossip columnist
Silvio Salvático. The poetry was mostly about prostitutes
with hearts of gold, the eternal beauty of the tango and tango

dancers taking to the streets of Buenos Aires at midnight,
and German detectives who were always one step behind the
German criminals they were chasing because they were always
wondering if their girlfriends were sleeping with someone
else, topics which Salvático explored in greater depth in his
second novel, *The French Lady*, which had been published in
1949. They talked about the nature of love and love's transgressions. They talked about death and the mushrooming cost
of funerals and the transmogrification of the human soul and
the overt symbolism of certain Latin-American folkdances like
the plena. They talked about Brazilian crime thrillers. They
talked about avant-garde writers in the Paris of the 1930s,
especially Artaud and his Theatre of Cruelty. They talked
about an obscure book titled *Recopilación de leyes de los reynos
de las Indias*, a compilation of one hundred and sixty-five
years of colonial law enacted in the Spanish colonies between
1512 and 1677, published in Madrid in 1681 by Charles II, a
book which, according to Immanuel, clearly demonstrated
the Spanish philosophical ambivalence towards the law in
general, an ambivalence which suggested an abiding tolerance
for human frailty, assuming that one possessed an acceptable
family lineage, whether actual or purchased, but even the title
of the book bored Nerea almost to the verge of tears, and the
only reason that she didn't fall asleep at this point was that
she had fallen permanently in love with Immanuel's great
passion for explication. They talked of the blossoming science
of bibliography and documentation. They talked of dinner
parties and shopping at El Encanto and beautiful fur coats.
They talked of the majestic beauty of the Paseo del Prado
in the springtime with its lime trees and avocado trees and
deep-green laurels and the tangled knot of humanity walking
to and fro. They talked of Ginés de Pasamonte, a minor fictional character in the novel *El ingenioso hidalgo don Quixote de
la Mancha*, who is sentenced to ten years as a galley slave and
escapes in a mad hurly-burly of a scene in which don Quixote
himself battles the guards for the release of Ginés and the
guards set upon don Quixote with swords and cudgels, and
the other prisoners, dozens of them, start untying themselves,
and Sancho (don Quixote's sidekick) finally frees Ginés and
Ginés runs away. They talked of taking a luxury steamer to

Europe in the spring. They talked of the sorrowful beauty of
the Cementerio de Cristóbal Colón with its dozens of whispering statues that could be heard at all hours of the night. They
talked of the exploding meteorite of time. Immanuel recited
the poetry of another Chilean poet, Pedro González Carrera,
a one-time grammar school teacher and a vociferous Italian
apologist, who, according to Immanuel, straddled the line
between symbolist poetry and sentimental garbage. But without any contempt or literary or political derision whatsoever,
indeed, with the faintest glimmer of exposed pride, which was
surprising, to say the least (but then we all seem to be walking
contradictions at times), Immanuel said Carrera's poetry
seemed to glorify Mussolini and his armies and promised a
complete reversal of history culminating in an ultimate Italian
victory at some point in the future with the aid of a group
of unknown Merovingian Kings who, according to the poet,
had migrated from another dimension or would migrate or
perhaps they were extraterrestrials who had adopted the
form and the mannerisms of the long-dead Merovingians
for unknown spiritual reasons, or perhaps simply to escape
the ravages of the plague or some other virus (it was at this
point Immanuel admitted that he couldn't quite disentangle
the meaning of Carrera's poetry from the poetry itself). They
talked about the withering despair of the nihilists. They talked
about the withering despair of nuns and priests everywhere.
They talked until the dark shadows in the lobby of Hotel
Milagro turned gray.

-89-

In the weeks and months that followed, Nerea and
Immanuel met on a semi-regular basis in the lobby of Hotel
Milagro, always in the same two burgundy leather chairs, their
faces seeming to shine with the dazzling subterranean glow
of Julio Mella's indestructible beauty. They met at all hours of
the day and night, for hours at a time, though they (or at least
Nerea) barely noticed that time was passing. It was Immanuel

who first gave voice to the idea that she would always be in
love with Luis, and so she would always be suffering from a
broken heart, an idea that had been orbiting the sun of Nerea's
despair for quite a while, like a wayward comet.

Nerea decided she could never forgive Luis.

"I want him to suffer as I have suffered," she said.

"We all wish such things from time to time."

"But he is so . . . so . . ."

"Preoccupied?"

"Yes. Preoccupied. I was going to say something else,
something crazy, but . . ."

"But what?"

"It doesn't matter . . . it . . ."

Nerea grew silent. She became absorbed in the beauty
of Julio Mella. Then she heard herself speaking, or more
precisely, she heard her disembodied voice. It sounded like it
was coming out of an old gramophone. It sounded very faint.
And all the while she was listening to her very faint voice she
was looking at the photograph of Julio Mella and thinking
how very beautiful he was.

"Sometimes it's just too complicated to even think
about."

"Yes?"

"I was going to say that he doesn't feel pain like ordinary people do. But that doesn't make any sense, does it? How
do you make people suffer if they don't feel pain?"

" . . . ."

"Oscar is different. Oscar is an open wound. Oscar is a
shooting star in the midnight sky."

" . . . ."

"Oscar is a small but rebellious bird locked in a cage.
He can't breathe without feeling the pain of everyone around
him. But Luis is a different story. Luis is . . ."

"A very carefully cultivated story, if you don't mind my
interjecting," said Immanuel.

The light from the gallery style lamp began to flicker
and then it went out and Nerea suddenly forgot about the
photograph of Julio Mella. She noticed that Immanuel had
somehow slid his burgundy leather chair next to hers. Their
chairs were side by side, but he was sitting on the edge of his

chair, his body turned slightly, leaning into the dark mirror of her thoughts. She wondered if he was going to kiss her. He had one hand on her knee, but this did not seem odd to Nerea. She had become detached from her knee and did not feel the pressure of his hand, but even this lack of sensation did not bother her. It was just something she noticed. Then she realized that their heads were bent towards each other. They had become shadows to each other. They became a single shadow. She closed her eyes and imagined that he was kissing her. The world smelled of mint and rum and vanilla and oleander. 'That is an odd mixture of smells,' she thought. She felt like she was going to pass out. Immanuel's voice did not rise above a whisper. Neither did hers.

"Cultivated?"

"Yes," said Immanuel. "I have been watching Luis for years now. He is a magnificent actor. The outer world sees only a shadowy character with a taste for fine dining and good music. They see Luis wearing exquisitely tailored pinstripe suits and silk socks and sporting perfumed handkerchiefs. They see an educated man, but they forget he carries two pistols and a knife. But this first layer is all a ruse. The world sees a sentimental, effeminate buffoon because that's what Luis wants the world to see. But beneath this layer there exists a hard, merciless opportunist. A man who would kill his own grandmother if there was a profit to be made. But this second layer is also a ruse. It is for his inner circle, his closest friends, his allies, perhaps a few of the Directors, perhaps Federico himself. So beneath this second layer there is another Luis. There is Luis the sensual lover, the sex maniac, the voyeur. Only you, Nerea, have seen this third layer of Luis."

". . . ."

"It is not easily visible, even if you are looking for it. But even this is a ruse."

"How can every layer be a ruse?'

"It is the nature of the world since the beginning of time. What did you expect?"

"I . . . I don't really know.

"I had hoped you would have guessed by now. It is ingenious, really. Luis is truly sentimental at his core. The first layer of Luis is a reflection of his fourth layer. He is a sentimentalist who wears his emotions as a mask to hide a mask of cruelty, which he lets some of the world see, and this mask hides a third mask, the mask of Luis the great lover, and all of these masks hide the real Luis, the Luis who is a weeping sentimentalist, the Luis who feels nostalgia for everyone who ever lived. He is a romantic. When you strip away all the posturing, that is what he is. He has hypnotized the world into believing otherwise. It is absolutely ingenious."

". . . ."

"Yes, as I said, he is a magnificent actor."

Nerea did not know what to say.

The lobby of Hotel Milagro had become a world of enveloping darkness and shifting shadows. She wondered how many people were sitting in the lobby or if she and Immanuel were the only ones. Her only fixed point of reality became the shining, shimmering photograph of Julio Mella, which now seemed to glow with an irrepressible iridescence, in spite of the fact that the bulb to the gallery style lamp had burned out, or perhaps because of this fact. Nerea found herself tracing the contours of Julio's pouty lips with her mind, running imaginary fingers through his curly brown hair, breathing in his imagined masculinity, staring into his cinematic eyes with such cunning intensity that she almost convinced herself that he was truly alive and that he only had eyes for her. Julio, she told herself, was her one true love. Then she sat back in her chair, nestling herself in the corner opposite from Immanuel, confident, if one possessing the pain of an aching heart can be said to be confident, no longer melancholy or dumbfounded or frozen in the moment of her own destruction, her natural animal magnetism beginning to reassert itself. She looked over at Immanuel and smiled a smile that might have seemed frivolous and slightly agitated in direct sunlight, but there in the shadows of the Hotel Milagro lobby it seemed deviant and sinister.

"I want him to suffer as I have suffered," said Nerea.

"You understand what you are asking?"

"Yes. I understand. Whatever you want to know about Luis, I can tell you. I have known Luis for a long time."

Immanuel regarded Nerea carefully for a moment.

"You are certain about all this?"

"Yes."

"I want you to be absolutely sure. Because once we release the hounds, so to speak, there is no stopping. We do not believe in half measures. We will carry through to the end."

Nerea did not even bat an eyelash.

"I just want you to promise me that he will suffer," she said.

Immanuel seemed to disappear into the shadowy gloom of his chair, all except his voice. His voice possessed a radiant clarity, like that of a tiny, silver bell.

"Do not worry. We have eyes and ears everywhere. We will not let him out of our sight for a moment. We will not let him escape. Do not worry. He will suffer greatly. It will be just like in the movies. I promise."

-90-

It was at this point that Nerea gave up all claims to her former self. She found herself spending more and more time in the lobby of Hotel Milagro. She stopped dancing. She stopped going to the clubs at night. She realized her time with Oscar was nearing its end, and she accepted this realization with the stoic fatalism of a religious fanatic, an old-school martyr.

At various random moments Oscar would see her sitting in one of the burgundy leather chairs, her eyes fixed on the photograph of Julio Mella. Usually Oscar was just heading out for a night on the town or he was just returning. Sometimes he was with Luis. They would say 'Hello, Nerea, why don't you join us,' or 'We missed you tonight' or 'Why don't you come up to bed' or 'I can't remember the last time you fixed us some chorizo sausage and eggs' or 'You never sing to us in the mornings any more,' but either Nerea didn't hear them and therefore did not respond, or they were too busy to hear what she might have said.

They walked away quickly. They no longer wondered what Nerea did with her time.

After a while the photograph of Julio Mella took on new dimensions. In the hour just before dawn, Nerea would some-times press her ear to the glass, and she swore to Immanuel that she could hear Julio whispering something, just what she wasn't sure, but it sounded like he was saying 'Las Tunas, Las Tunas,' and then there was the sound of a baseball bat hitting a ball and then the sound of a roaring crowd, a deafening, jubilant roar, and then the nasally voice of an announcer saying the score was three to two, all of this emanating from Julio's mouth as if his mouth were a radio, but that didn't make any sense to Nerea, nor to Immanuel.

Sometimes she could hear Julio whistling.

Sometimes she could hear Julio reciting poetry, but it was always poetry she had never heard before.

Sometimes all she heard was the distant sound of the sea or the sound of boats in the harbor and the sailors shouting or the tolling of a church bell.

Strangely, she never heard him singing a song.

Sometimes his lips were wet, as if he had just licked his lips and was about to give her a gentle, airy kiss. This thought always made her smile.

At other times Julio became eerily silent and detached, as if he were reproaching her for some minor infraction, a small flaw in her personality that she was unaware of. She would sit on the edge of her burgundy leather chair and beg his forgive-ness, but naturally he said nothing. He behaved exactly as a photograph hanging on a wall should behave. Nevertheless, she would implore him to give her some sign of his love, a token of affection, and when he did not respond, she would break down into tears, collapsing on the tiled floor beneath the photograph or draped over the arm of her burgundy leather chair, and then fall asleep. One would think she would have been troubled by strange dreams under the circumstances, but she never dreamed when she slept in the lobby, or if she did she did not remember them. When she woke up she did not know where she was, but she was not afraid of her ignorance. She was like an invisible specter or a newborn child examining the world with attentive eyes, though with some measurable anxiety, in the burgundy leather chair of her choice until she could make sense of her surroundings.

Always the realization that she had fallen asleep in the
hotel lobby took her by surprise. Then her breathing became
relaxed. She became more thoughtful, curious, even reflective.
She began to look more carefully at everything that transpired
in the hotel lobby that had become her entire world, especially
in the wee hours of the morning. She noticed things that
others wished to keep hidden.

For one thing, the dim lighting throughout the lobby
seemed to have changed color from a diffuse, yellowish
subterranean glow to something a little more orangeish, with
a faint blueish tint. It was a devilish glow. She wondered
what might cause the change in color. At times it seemed
otherworldly. At times it seemed as if the color had leaked in
from another dimension.

For another thing, the hotel staff seemed to have
vanished. There was a small placard on the front desk counter
that said 'Ring the bell for service,' and someone had left a
black waiter's jacket and tie hanging on a hook next to the
row of wooden boxes containing abandoned room keys and
messages that had been forgotten years ago and were now
covered with dust.

Nerea had been to the desk several times and had rung
and rung the bell, and she had even called out, but no one
came, and then the last time she had gone to the desk the bell
was gone, and so was the jacket and the tie, though for some
strange reason the placard remained. She wondered if the staff
had gone on strike or been fired or had up and quit and if
they had found other employment or were still looking. She
wondered if there had been a change in management or if the
hotel were closing down. She wondered where she would go
if the hotel closed down.

She didn't remember the last time she saw Oscar or Luis.

She began to wonder if they had ever existed.

She noticed that among the potted ferns and other
withered greenery there were also a few potted foxgloves,
otherwise known as 'The Gloves of the Virgin Mary,' which
according to some botanists and also the purveyors of herbal
remedies contained powerful chemical compounds that could
cure an ailing heart if taken in the right amount, but would
cause certain death if one took too much, which almost

everyone did who turned to foxglove for relief. The foxglove scattered about the lobby were doing quite well. Flashes of purple and crimson and strawberry red in an otherwise dreary landscape.

Nerea also noticed that the lobby was becoming more and more crowded. More and more men wearing fedoras and carrying long-barreled hunting rifles or with bulges in their jacket pockets that looked suspiciously like Kongsberg Colt pistols, the men roaming about, circulating aimlessly among the dilapidated chairs and withered vegetative cover, presumably looking for a place to sit. The men with the Kongsberg Colt pistols would take them out every so often so everyone else could see. They seemed to enjoy the adulation that went with owning such a dependable firearm.

All of the new men seemed to know Immanuel, who went about greeting each new arrival as he would a long-lost cousin or a newly converted radical sympathizer.

After that Nerea noticed a great deal of whispering, which she assumed were private conversations about the sunny weather or the rainy weather and various definitions of paradise and the price of ammunition and the nature of grief and how dangerous it was to travel these days in Mexico, or any of the Latin-American countries for that matter, and how it was only going to get worse.

Most of the conversations were in Italian, which sped by too quickly for Nerea's tiny ears, and the rest were in German, which gave her headaches. But at some point, perhaps because of the verbal impressions left floating in the air by so many whispering men, Nerea found herself swimming in a sea of bizarre, fragmented images, like the amniotic fluid of autoerotic poetry. Naturally, Nerea felt like she was drowning. But she did not drown. Her mind went numb. She felt like she was the victim of an alien abduction experiment, though perhaps this is a bit of a stretch. She felt like she had just been reborn, which is most certainly a cliché, but is perhaps closer to the truth. She took a deep breath and plunged into the impressionistic waves of her insomnia (or the darkly glowing clouds of a coming hailstorm, or the oily, smoky spray that accompanies a hail of bullets, or the roiling mushroom of dust after an asteroid slams into the earth at supersonic speed, it was really quite difficult to label the experience other than to suggest that whatever she plunged into possessed the blurry indistinctness of an old photograph taken in 1930s Germany as the Nazis came to power with crowds of vagrants milling about and coming to blows in the snowy streets in Hamburg or Munich or Berlin). She allowed every word to flow through her. She began to understand what the men were saying. It was easier for her to understand the happy sing-song Italian than the anxious, guttural German. Then the world around her began to coalesce and then disintegrate. She felt like she was sitting in a strange carnival movie house where they were projecting four or five movies onto the screen at the same time. She began to flow back and forth between the images of each movie with extraordinary ease. She felt like she had suddenly mastered the psychic art of telekinesis. As if on cue, the men with their long-barreled hunting rifles or Kongsberg Colt pistols sensed that something had changed. They broke off in the middle of their sentences and stared at Nerea with uneasy awe, as if they suspected she could read their lips. They began to speak with their hands cupped over their mouths. Of course Nerea did not fully appreciate the philosophical nuances and subtle allusions of everything she heard, because all language, as everyone knows, is symbolic in nature and therefore possesses multiple meanings. But she understood enough to realize that Immanuel had set everything in motion and that now there was no turning back.

The words of the whispering men, the grainy, film noir version, as Nerea hears them, which is to say as she perceives them, which provides ample evidence as to her state of mind as well as her emotional state of being:

'It is always sunny in paradise.'

'I beg to differ . . .'

'As do I. Some days it is quite rainy, worse than in Munich.'

'Or in Hamburg!'

'Yes, Schneider. Or in Hamburg.'

'One man's rainy day is another man's pneumonia.'

'There's no such thing as pneumonia in paradise, except for the odd case.'

'But there are plenty of cases in Munich. All over Germany, in fact. Hamburg in particular!'

'Ah, we are intoxicated with death.'

'And tailors.'

'Yes, tailors and death.'

The whispering men laugh.

Their laughter hovers above their heads like rings of smoke or miniature crystal halos and then crashes into the impenetrable darkness hovering above all of them and sends a shower of tiny glass particles to the floor like the crushed remains of saltwater crustaceans from a millennium ago.

The men brush away the flecks of glass that cover their shoulders and their fedoras and the backs of their necks.

The conversation continues.

'It is an old argument.'

'It is the oldest argument.'

'From a time before time.'

'It is not for us to question his reasons. It is simply the way the world is at the moment.'

'Perhaps the world has always been this way. Perhaps the nature of the world remains unchanged.'

'Yes, of course, if by the nature of the world you mean the nature of man.'

'That goes without saying.'

'That would explain why we always do what we are told to do.'

'And why we always will.'

'But not always willingly.'

'No, I suppose not.'

'But then, of course, one has to account for the nature of grief.'

'Ah, grief, the panacea of lost souls.'

'As if a soul can become lost.'

'As if abandoning your beliefs is something to cry about.'

'It is a question for the ages.'

'It is a question for religion.'

'It is a question for science.'

'It is a question for those with good intentions who parade up and down the hospital wards.'

'And then from the hospitals to the cemeteries!'

'It is an endless parade.'

The men are silent for a moment, as if they are contemplating the actual (as opposed to perceived) distance between hospitals and cemeteries.

'Yes, the notion of grief raises many questions.'

'Too many to properly contemplate.'

'It is worse than the riddle of the Sphinx.'

'Decidedly worse.'

'Then again, one can now look at grief as something more than a question. You could, for the sake of argument, look at grief as a question that can now be answered.'

'I'd like to see that.'

'And so you shall, my friend.'

(A few impatient toes beginning to tap, a few impatient fingers fingering the safeties on their pistols.)

'The question of grief, which has troubled mankind since the ancients first scribbled down their thoughts on papyrus, can now be answered through the ingenious application of electromagnetic phase inducers and ultra-high vacuum tunneling microscopes and Boron ion-beam generators.'

'Grief is absolutely meaningless.'

A few obscurantists in the crowd start applauding, but it is difficult to determine why.

'This kind of advanced technology is essential in facilitating a scientific and completely objective way of parsing reality.'

'Is complete objectivity possible?'

A few cheers. A few derisive whistles.

'It certainly is. And on that note, I am here to tell you that the preliminary reports that I have seen state that without any doubt whatsoever the notion of grief is absolutely meaningless.'

More applause from the obscurantists, but again, why.

'Which is something we suspected all along.'

A rhythmic clapping reaching a crescendo.

'Yes, but I already said that.'

A few indignant shouts lost in the growing hubbub.

'But now we have a series of preliminary reports.'

Furious applause. Uproarious laughter.

More brushing away flecks of broken glass.

Then a bit of silence.

But not an awkward, painful silence.

It is actually more like a gentle sigh. Not a pure silence at all.

Then the men suddenly look at Nerea, as if for the first time, as if she has suddenly emerged from a beam of sunlight.

They begin adjusting their fedoras smartly, smoothing out the wrinkles in their shirts, positioning their rifles or their Kongsberg Colt pistols for maximum visual effect.

Nerea pays no attention to their ogling stares. Partly this is because to her the men are featureless. Their heads seem like onions, with dark, rotten spots where their eyes and mouths should be. The smell of onions is everywhere, bouncing off the damp walls, clogging Nerea's eyes, her throat.

She sits back in her chair and closes her eyes and the onions go away. She breathes in slowly and exhales the onion smell of so many men crowded into so small a space.

She becomes a pane of glass through which all light and language flow.

Or she becomes a dark mirror that absorbs everything.

The conversation continues.

'We are little more than tunnels of light burrowing our way through the darkness.'

'That's just one of many possibilities.'

'Okay, quite possibly we are tunnels of light burrowing our way through the darkness.'

'Speeding our way, you mean.'

'Speeding our way, then.'

'That's better.'

'But to what end?'

'To the end of the tunnel?'

'No!'

'To the end of the light?'

'The same thing.'

'Then what is the answer?'

'Yes. That is a fair question. With all of this talk about grief and paradise and summer thunderstorms sweeping across the Cuban landscape, it is worth trying to figure out what it's all for.'

'No one can do that.'

'You mean no one ever has.'

'Or ever will, that's the smart money.'

'Do not be so arrogant. We have men working on it this very minute. Naturally.'

'Men?'

'Yes indeed. We have men tucked away, hidden from view, some observers working apart from the observed, some working in conjunction, an uneasy partnership, some of them closet obscurantists or dabblers in mesmerism or advocates of popular sensualism for all we know, but all of them giving everything they have to solving this thorny problem.'

'Yes, thorny is an apt description.'

'But a bit overused, don't you think, the word thorny.'

'Of course it's overused, that's the tragic consequence of using language to talk about the unknowable.'

'Not as tragic as using bullets.'

'How right you are.'

'And it doesn't matter if the bullets come out of the end of a long-barreled rifle, the kind of weapon that is more appropriate for shooting rabbits and weasels and hedgehogs and the like, like we used to do in Sicily when we were boys dreaming of murder, or one of your fancy Kongsberg Colt pistols, the pride of the Norwegian army, a pistol with extraordinary balance, why with such a pistol you can hit a moving target with ease from three-hundred paces, or even further, and by moving target, of course, I mean . . .'

'Yes . . . you mean . . . (in unison) a man.'

More laughter. Eyes gleaming.

'To the extent that I am able to make myself understood, I am gratified. To the extent that I make any sense at all, I could be anyone.'

A few extra loud guffaws.

'*Quia est in eo virtus dormitiva, cujus est natura sensus assoupire.*'

'Yes, I can see why you say that. We are all of us beginning to fall asleep.'

'Which is why we crave a different kind of buzz.'

'Like the coldest winter chill.'

The laughter swells.

More halos of glass and the glass shattering against the

darkness and falling to the floor. But the glass particles are no longer content to mimic the remains of saltwater crustaceans, a reflection of a lifeless, symbolic past, a calcified moment. No, the glass particles are undergoing a sudden, dramatic transformation. They are becoming the saltwater crustaceans they once merely resembled.

No one knows exactly what is going on. It appears that some sort of conscious (manipulative?) act of creation is taking place. A miracle by any other name. But it all depends upon your point of view. Between consciousness and reality there yawns a veritable abyss of meaning. Then again, one would be hard pressed to deny that something is happening. For one thing, the tiny saltwater crustaceans that were once particles of glass are very much alive, and more and more are joining the ranks of the living with every passing second. Soon the tiled floor of the hotel lobby is covered with what appear to be thousands and thousands of tiny crabs, a swarmy, swarming bubbling froth of freedom and independent spirit, their tiny porcelain-like claws scratching at the tile. It is difficult to tell what kind of crabs they are. They look like ice-cream blotches. They possess white shells with red or reddish-brown markings or blotches. Their shells look like vanilla and strawberry and chocolate ice-cream mixed together. Thousands and thousands of ice-cream blotches. Then it becomes clear what kind of crabs they are. They are tiny Porcelain Anemone Crabs (*Neopetrolisthes ohshimai*) from Indonesia. How they suddenly appear on the floor of the lobby of Hotel Milagro is irrelevant. It is a mystery with a quasi-religious kind of appeal, but it is still irrelevant.

Some of the men armed with long-barreled rifles begin smashing the tiny, helpless crabs. They are marching doggedly around the lobby smashing crabs with their rifle butts, but not so much because they are threatened by the crabs. They are merely repulsed.

The crabs do not scream when they are smashed. They simply disintegrate like a book of abandoned thoughts, a cloud of exploding dust absorbed by the air.

Nerea thinks the men smashing the crabs are quite courageous. She sees in their willingness to face the crab threat an inexorable truth: every destiny would be unfulfilled

if there were no one to do the dirty work. She waves at the
men and two of them see her waving and come over. They
talk briefly, nodding politely and smiling. It is impossible
to hear what they are saying. It is like listening to a strong
wind blowing though the treetops. It is like watching a tunnel
collapsing. It is like they are hatching a plot. Then the men go
back to their work.

Nerea seems quite pleased.

The other crabs continue their aimless scratching until
they too are smashed. They seem unaware of the danger of
the rifle butts. Whether individually or as a whole, there is
no difference in the way they react to the countless deaths
of their comrades. Death is all around them. But they do not
even try to get away, to find some safe, secure hiding place.
Perhaps because there is no place for them to go. There are too
many of them. The tiny, hard-packed bodies of the still living
and the ghost-bodies of the recently smashed (still strangely
present, in as much as some memories are always present). All
of them mixed together. They can barely move against each
other.

Nerea watches the steady destruction of the indifferent
crab colony with great interest, but hers is the self-absorbed
predatory interest of the killer experiencing the thrill (in this
case vicarious) of the hunt, as indifferent towards the crabs as
they are towards themselves, without even a hint of sadness.
The rest of the men have been carrying on with their conversation, unconcerned with the crabs.

'If we possessed spirits that were truly free there would
be no need for war.'

'There he goes again, ranting and raving.'

'Prattling and prating.'

'Stomping about like a raging bull, a mad minotaur.'

'The minotaur of our conscience.'

A burst of overly robust laughter, almost like stage
laughter, as if the men were reading from a script. The sounds
of scattered applause.

'But it is true. We are not free. We are cursed with a
lingering eye that admires everything it sees, that is afraid to
look down lest we become aware of our deformed, crippled
nature, an eye that does not appreciate or even know what

real love is, or beauty. We are blind to the self-erasing, inevitable barbarity of history. We are blind to our own evolving
stupidity.'

'But this is the essence of what it means to be human.'

'The unrelenting darkness of our inner being.'

'A labyrinth which swallows all light.'

'A labyrinth from which we will never escape.'

'Our depravity exposed on the barren sands of eternity.'

'The collective soul of humanity, if you will.'

'And even if you won't.

'It means we are slipping into the abyss, inexorably,
inevitably.'

'Exactly, my friends. Which is why we should always
be prepared to kill and wage war. But always and only in the
name of humanity itself.'

'You mean in the name of an ideal humanity.'

'Perhaps. But it is not so easy to substitute an ideal
humanity for your average, run-of-the-mill humanity. The
goal is to create a world in which everyone faces up to their
responsibility, an ideal world, if you will, as opposed to an
ideal humanity, a world in which there is no room for those
who do not fit in, if you get my meaning. But there is always
resistance to change. I can hear the naysayers even now.
They will argue that the notion of an ideal world is a logical
absurdity because there would be as many versions of this
ideal world as there would be individuals who could imagine
as much, each version competing with every other version,
causing all sorts of difficulties, everything from poverty to
pestilence to despair to corrupt governments to sex maniacs
running rampant through the grade schools to the death by
chemical pollutants of the oceans to rogue black holes invad-
ing our deepest dreams, any disaster you can imagine, all of
it pretty much gumming up the works. It would be practically
impossible to police so many different versions. You would
probably have to lock everybody up, which you could never
do, so you would have no choice but to abandon your own
search for paradise. Everyone would.   There could be no
exceptions. Everyone would be forced to capitulate to some
sort of compromise paradise, a universally acceptable generic
version, just for the sake of keeping the semblance of peace,

which is less than ideal. It is an intriguing critique.'

'And what happens if we fail?'

'We will not fail!'

'But if we do?'

'The alternative is unacceptable.'

'But not unimaginable.'

'No, sadly, not unimaginable. Indeed, it is a horrible thing to contemplate. The gates of Hell would be flung wide open, but not in a symbolic, metaphorical, theoretical way. It would be an actual, physical opening. A tear in the fabric of the universe. The grisly veil torn. A disruption in the space/time continuum that would send us all reeling. Quite probably there would be nothing left at all. Or nothing that we would recognize as something.'

'God forbid.'

'Yes, God forbid."

"Whether he exists or not.'

'A difficult supposition to support.'

'But just as difficult to argue effectively against.'

'Which only proves why the alternative is unacceptable.'

'Absolutely.'

'Then we are all agreed?'

'Yes, in as much as there is very little left to say.'

The lobby is now exploding with the happy, jubilant shouts of happy, jubilant men.

'It is suicide to think otherwise.'

'Or at least a logical fallacy.'

'Or a hopeful implausibility.'

'Or perhaps a fatalism born of an unappeased grief.'

More happy, jubilant shouts.

A few rifles being discharged.

A few Kongsberg Colt pistols.

A few spent cartridges bouncing on the floor.

The last of the crabs have been smashed.

The very last crab is smashed directly beneath Nerea's hovering feet.

Nerea looks from the body of the smashed crab to the photograph of Julio Mella to see what he thinks, but he does not react. He, too, possesses (or seems to possess) an indifferent attitude when it comes to the fate of the crabs.

The men armed with their rifles or their Kongsberg Colt pistols begin filing out of the lobby of Hotel Milagro, with Immanuel in the lead. They are heading out into the shadows of the world at large, a world, shall we say, bathed in streaks of light and dark, a very stylized look, like in the movies, a world possessing a meaning we can only guess at, a world where the gap between consciousness and reality exists only in the imagination, where the freedom of the nihilists (meaning those noble souls that Nietzsche speaks about who live beyond good and evil) is no freedom at all because it is limited by the very change they (the nihilists, wherever they have gone) seek (hope, endeavor) to bring about. Because as everyone discovers sooner or later, our puny brains can only grasp a singular reality in any given moment. By contrast, Nerea's own private world is plunged into absolute darkness.

-91-

The beginning of Oscar's last twenty-four hours in Havana:

The phone rang with merciless rage, but Oscar let it ring. He was sitting in the kitchen, the balcony doors flung wide open, a warm breeze blowing through the room. Luis had predicted that the phone would be ringing off the hook. And he had been right. The phone had been ringing all morning. Luis had said there were a few unnamed, unsavory sorts who were trying to keep tabs on him, and then he had winked at Oscar, but he wasn't going to give them the satisfaction. He wanted to keep them guessing. Did they really think he would slip up so easily, that he would answer the phone and give himself away, that they might trap him in the shadow of Hotel Milagro? If they did, then he still had the edge. He would become a shadow himself, a shadow among the shadows.

Oscar almost laughed out loud at the thought of Eladio and some of the others trying to match wits with Luis. That's the way things were. The spilling of the sand had begun long

ago. From the moment Federico had announced the move to
Miami. Very soon not a single star would be left in the night
sky. And it didn't seem to matter that Cuba was about to
implode and that Miami was a good choice, a logical next step.
What mattered was that the Cuban contingent (this is what
Oscar secretly called them) was relatively young and fearlessly
committed to their own dream of Cuba. What mattered more
was that Federico was no longer as impressively psychotic as
he had been in his younger years. He seemed to be just what
he was: a crippled Italian lost in the loop of memory, one good
shove from the grave. Even his majestic knife seemed merely
a prop. Oscar knew enough to know a coup in the making.
But there was nothing to do at the moment. Luis had said he
would call at one o'clock on the dot, so until then Oscar would
let the phone ring. It was only a quarter past twelve. In the ten
years that Oscar had known Luis, Luis had always done what
he said he would do. He trusted Luis' instincts. Oscar trusted
Luis to get them both safely across the Straits of Florida. They
would vanish into the shadows of a Cuban sunset. What Oscar
did not see, as it turned out, and what he would never see, a
curious blindness, a retreating from metaphor into myth, was
Nerea's role in the whole messy affair. Whether or not Luis
saw it coming was another matter.

The phone stopped ringing. Then it started again.

"Only twelve-thirty," Oscar said to himself. "Fuck."

He heard some shouting from out in the courtyard
and moved to the balcony for a better look. He could see a
washday Madonna on the other side, a corner suite one floor
down, a beautiful bombshell in a pair of tight-fitting jeans and
a flimsy, cotton blouse and her hair pulled back. The smell
of gardenias drifting from somewhere. The smell of lemons.
The sea. The smell of gunpowder. The woman was leaning
out across her balcony, the laundry she had just laid across
the railing fluttering in the breeze. The way she was leaning,
Oscar could see the roundness of her breasts all the way to her
nipples. She was glistening in the steamy, tropical sunlight.

Oscar smiled and let himself get hard. The woman was
shouting at a young man who was sitting on a bench beneath
the leafy branches of the acacia tree that occupied the middle
of the courtyard. Behind the bench there was a small patch of

garden that had been neglected for years and the weathered remnants of what was once a glowing golden trellis. Oscar could not quite see who the young man was because of the branches, but he seemed very young. The woman was letting him have it pretty good. She was very passionate in her displeasure. But the young man didn't say anything. He continued sitting on the bench, smoking a cigarette, the smoke swirling up through the branches of the acacia tree and dissolving in the air above. The shouting reached a crescendo and then mysteriously plunged into a vacuum of nothingness. For the briefest of moments, Oscar could not hear a single sound, no woman shouting, no insects buzzing, no music drifting through the air from another apartment, no cars motoring on the street beyond the courtyard, no mysterious gunman sliding the bolt of a long-barreled rifle into place.

Then a cacophony of sound returned and all of the aforementioned sounds came tumbling past Oscar's ears. He jerked back, as if he had been struck. But whatever had struck him was only a figment of his imagination. He leaned forward again, his hands resting on the balcony railing. He was still very hard. The woman was dripping with perspiration. It almost seemed that her blouse had dissolved. Then she picked up a second basket full of wet clothes. She had already emptied the first so there was no more room on the railing. She lifted the second basket and dumped it over the side. 'Take care of your own fucking laundry,' she shouted, and then she disappeared, all except the image of her beautiful brown bouncing breasts and her dark erect nipples.

Oscar went back inside, got a Coke from the fridge, popped the top and guzzled half the bottle.

The phone had stopped ringing.

It was ten minutes to one.

'Fucking bastards,' Oscar thought.

He drank some more Coke.

Luis had told him this day would come. He had been saying as much for years. Then two days ago he had told Oscar to pack a suitcase. But not just any suitcase. Luis had pulled out a Platt Guardsman leather suitcase with brass hardware that he kept under his bed. It was a medium-sized suitcase, elegant, just right for traveling, and roomy enough for a few shirts, a few pairs of slacks, an extra pair of shoes, socks, various sundry items, and half a million dollars in cold, hard cash (fifty stacks of unmarked one-hundred dollar bills, naturally, the easiest way for revolutionaries, international spies, embezzlers of all sorts, Mafiosi bagmen, and high-rolling casino whales to carry obscene amounts of money from point A to point B). Luis had opened the suitcase and showed Oscar the false bottom, which popped up when you pushed down on the two opposite corners simultaneously. 'It is a smuggler's dream,' Luis had said with his customary bravado, but for a moment Oscar had been able to detect just the slightest hint of anxiety in Luis' booming baritone voice of a steamship, the thin wavering vibrato of a man pushed to the breaking point, but then the vibrato had vanished, or Oscar had ignored it, or by then the air itself had been vibrating so intensely that Oscar could not tell the difference, and so Luis had once again seemed to be his happy-go-lucky, charismatic self.

They were sitting in the kitchen at that point. There was a soft, fragrant breeze that smelled vaguely of gardenias and lemons and the sea. The suitcase was back under Luis' bed. They had been drinking mojitos, or perhaps it was beers. Oscar didn't remember. Luis had said the timing couldn't be any better with the Feast Day of Saint Christopher on Saturday, the whole week would be a beautiful chaos which they could take advantage of. Oscar hadn't been quite sure he understood what Luis was talking about, so he had started to ask why he needed a suitcase, but Luis had cut him off with a slicing gesture and then went over and shut the balcony doors and then sat back down. His voice had become a whisper. He had then instructed Oscar to pick up a second suitcase, identical in all respects to the first one. Oscar was to fill the false bottom of this second suitcase with various tourist pamphlets and brochures from the nightclubs and the restaurants and cafes in Vedado along La Rampa and elsewhere. The kind of places that were fun but not too expensive. He was to pack the rest of the suitcase as if he were going away for a week. Then he was to sit by the phone and wait for Luis to call. That was all Luis had said. Then he had opened the balcony doors and the soft, fragrant breeze from before filled the kitchen. The two men had finished their mojitos or their beers in absolute silence.

The very next morning, Oscar took care of everything Luis had asked. Right down to the letter.

He picked up a Platt Guardsman suitcase from Herman's Department Store, a mirror image to the one Luis owned.

He packed it just like Luis had said.

He wanted to show Luis but Luis was not around.

The day after that, Luis and the original suitcase were gone by the time Oscar woke up, but there was a note on the kitchen table that said Luis would call at one in the afternoon.

So Oscar was waiting for Luis to call.

The new suitcase was on the floor beneath the kitchen table.

It was hot and he was very thirsty. Oscar finished his Coke and got up to fish another one out of the fridge.

At precisely one o'clock, the phone rang.

"Are you alone?" a voice said.

The voice sounded vaguely like Luis, but it also sounded vaguely like any number of haunted, desperate, faceless men anywhere in the world. Oscar felt like he was trapped inside the labyrinth of a dream.

"Yes," said Oscar.

"Did you get the suitcase?"

"Yes," said Oscar.

He started to relax a bit. Only Luis knew about the suitcase.

"Is it packed? Are you ready?"

"I'm ready."

Then Oscar let the words of Luis wash through him unimpeded by questions or affirmations. He could feel his brain spinning and clicking as the images of the future Luis described whirred past at record speed. It was a movie unfolding. But it was also a clock unwinding, the mechanical parts beginning to separate and fly off into space, a collection of seemingly useless gears and wheels lost in a vacuum, a spinning, whirling, chaotic cloud reflecting the light from random stars, but then the mechanical parts reassembling themselves, seemingly without a clockmaker, fitting together in ways that had been previously unknown.

"Go down to the front desk. Take your suitcase with you. And make sure you take your Beistegui Brothers Libia with you. At least keep it in a pocket so you can get at it if you need to."

". . . ."

"When you get to the desk, give your key to the clerk and tell him you will be gone for a week. Say it loud enough so anyone who is listening will hear, but not so loud as to draw attention to yourself."

". . . ."

"The clerk will pass you an envelope with a hastily scribbled note inside, but do not open the envelope or read the note. Slip it into your pocket and ask the clerk to call you a taxi."

". . . ."

"Sit down in one of the leather chairs near the revolving doors. Place the suitcase on the floor squarely between your legs."

". . . ."

"Do not sit in one of the chairs by the front desk, the ones near the photograph of Julio Mella. In all probability they will be occupied. But even if they are vacant, do not sit in them. The chairs are a trap."

". . . ."

"While you are waiting for the taxi, study the men in the lobby. There will be many men. All of them will be carrying guns. Study them carefully. These are the men who wish to do us harm."

". . . ."

"There's no need to worry. They will not try anything in the lobby during the middle of the afternoon. They are men of the shadows, not sunlight."

". . . ."

"I am not saying this to make you feel better. I could give a crap about how you feel. I am saying this to help you stay alive. Study the men carefully. File away their faces. But above all, keep your wits about you."

". . . ."

"When the taxi arrives, a fat, stubby man will go to the front desk and make a phone call. Do not worry about him.

Keep your eyes on the taxi driver. He will be a thin, hooked-nose fellow standing just inside the revolving doors, scanning the sea of men occupying every chair in the lobby."

". . . ."

"He will seem less like a taxi driver and more like an elderly concentration camp survivor who has been doing quite well since the war. He will be well-groomed, his hands neatly manicured. He will be exceptionally well-dressed."

". . . ."

"He will take his time surveying the lobby. Then he will notice your suitcase. Or more precisely, he will notice the position of your suitcase."

". . . ."

"He will approach you with a broad smile, and you will smile back. He will ask you if you need help with your suitcase."

". . . ."

"If he is wearing a dark brown Mallory hat with a red feather in the hatband, then you are to say 'No, thank you, I can manage,' and then he will lead you to the taxi.

". . . ."

"If there is no red feather or he is wearing a different kind of hat or no hat at all, then you are to say 'No thank you, I have only just arrived,' and then return to the front desk, quickly but not too quickly, and retrieve your key, head back to the apartment and wait for me to call again."

". . . ."

"We will not have too many cracks at this, so let us hope he is wearing the dark brown Mallory with the red feather."

". . . ."

"You must understand that nothing is what it appears to be. Your life depends upon understanding this."

". . . ."

"Once you are inside the taxi, read the note."

". . . ."

"The note explains in detail what we are up against."

". . . ."

"Do not worry about where the taxi driver is taking you. He knows where he is going. And do not worry about the two or three taxis that pull out to follow you. The taxi driver will

lose them along the Malecón, or if that does not work, he will
lose them in some of the smaller side streets in Vedado before
doubling back."

"...."

"The taxi driver will drop you at the corner of Aguiar
and Obispo. You are looking for an office building of sorts in
the 200 block of Calle Obispo. It is a magnificent pale yellow
building, a beautiful baroque structure, especially when the
sunlight bounces off the gilded cornices. But do not get caught
up in admiring the architecture. Head up to the third floor."

"...."

"Do not take the elevator. Take the stairs, and when you
get to the third floor, take a left and go to the end of the hall."

"...."

"Remember to take your suitcase with you."

"...."

"When you get to the end of the hall you will see a
single frosted glass door with the name Ignazio Tiziano &
Sons, International Office in black lettering. The office is
normally closed on Wednesday afternoons. If you can see the
faint yellow glow of a lamp coming through the frosted glass,
knock twice. A small but gruff voice will ask who is there. You
must respond by saying 'the bull, like a castle under siege, has
been eaten.'"

"...."

"If you happen to forget this colorful phrase just look at
the note from earlier."

"...."

"A moment later the outer door will open, but only a
crack. Do not go in right away. You will hear the sound of a
second door, an interior door, opening and closing. You are to
go inside the office only after you hear the second door close."

"...."

"If the outer door does not open, or you do not hear the
sound of the second door closing, return to the taxi and head
back to the hotel and wait for me to call. Same as before."

"...."

"Let's just be clear, if for any reason at any point along
the way something goes wrong, head back to the hotel and
wait for me to call."

". . . ."

"Once you are inside the International Office, you must once again repeat the phrase from the note for the man behind the counter, but very slowly, as if you are speaking to a deaf person and he can only read your lips."

". . . ."

"The man will study your lips for a moment. Then he will open the top drawer of a steel filing cabinet and remove a narrow envelope containing an American passport and a ticket, your ticket on the *S. S. City of Havana*, which will be heading to Key West on Thursday. The passport is a forgery. But it will get you through U. S. Customs."

". . . ."

"Do not ask the man about your ticket. He will give you the envelope with no knowledge of what is inside. Then he will smile, a flat bland smile, an inscrutable smile that will suggest that nothing is ever what it appears to be. Then he will retreat into the dark interior of the office and turn out the lights."

". . . ."

"At this point you will return to the taxi. You will notice that the taxi waiting for you will be a different taxi with a different driver. Do not worry about this change. Your new taxi driver will be a recent immigrant from Africa. Or quite possibly he will be a student from the University who grew up in the mountains in the east. It really does not matter which one. Whichever one it is, he will be very enthusiastic. He will ask you where you wish to go and you will say you have a ferry to catch, but not until the next morning."

". . . ."

"The ferry leaves at ten-thirty in the morning. But you do not need to worry about that just yet."

". . . ."

"The new taxi driver will repeat his question. But he will not seem confused. He is just looking for confirmation. Then you will say 'It is a long time between now and then. Why don't you take me down to the nightlife on La Rampa?' He will smile a dazzling bright smile and say 'Okay, boss,' and off you will go."

". . . ."

"It does not matter precisely where you go. A café, a restaurant, a nightclub. Go to the Tia Nena Club on San Martin if you like. But keep your suitcase with you at all times."

". . . ."

"The new taxi driver will stay with you the entire night."

". . . ."

"At five in the morning, tell the taxi driver to take you out to Playa de Marianao. He will pull into a small parking lot in the shadows of the yacht club. The yacht club is hidden by trees."

". . . ."

"You are not to go down to the beach. You are to wait there until the sun rises."

". . . ."

"Do not get out of the car under any circumstances."

". . . ."

"There is nothing to do at that hour anyway."

". . . ."

"As the sun rises, you will notice a second car parked in the lot. It will be a wine-colored Custom Club De Soto convertible."

". . . ."

"It will be Federico's De Soto. But Federico will not be there. A fat, stubby man will get out of the De Soto."

". . . ."

"You will recognize the fat, stubby man as the same one who made the phone call in the lobby of the hotel. He will approach the taxi cab, but he will be surveying the landscape as he approaches to make sure there is no one else in the vicinity. When he is satisfied there is no one else, he will motion for you to roll down your window."

". . . ."

"You will roll down your window and say 'the bull, like a castle under siege, has been eaten.'"

". . . ."

"Yes, yes, if you need to look at the note then by all means look at the note."

". . . ."

"The fat man will roar with laughter, a great belly laugh, and then he will hand you a set of car keys."

". . . ."

"The keys to the De Soto. A second set. For later."

". . . ."

"You are to stay in the taxi. The fat man will return to the De Soto and drive away. You will wait ten minutes and then tell the taxi driver to take you to the ferry. But tell him to take his time. You are in no hurry. With any luck you will arrive at the wharf at nine o'clock."

". . . ."

"You are not to get on the ferry at this point. There is a small café near the wharf. Café Paraiso. The taxi driver will know.

". . . ."

"You cannot see the ferry from this café. But that does not matter."

". . . ."

"Go into this café and sit down. Take the second table from the door next to the windows."

". . . ."

"It is unlikely the table will be occupied. The regulars all sit at the counter."

". . . ."

"The café will be overflowing with regulars, but there will be no one else. Order a coffee and a small breakfast. Make sure you set your suitcase on the floor beneath the window sill. And make sure you take your time with your breakfast. Sip your coffee slowly. Read the paper. But do not talk to anyone. Not even the waitress, except to order your food and pay your bill. If someone happens to ask if you are traveling on the ferry, give a noncommittal shrug and look out the window."

". . . ."

"I will arrive at the café at nine-thirty."

". . . ."

"I will sit at the table next to yours. The third one from the door. I will be carrying my own Platt Guardsman suitcase, which I will set down next to yours."

". . . ."

"I will not stay long. I will order a cup of coffee and I will drink it quickly. At nine-forty-five I will leave the café, but I will be taking your suitcase. You will take mine."

". . . ."

"At ten o'clock you will pay your bill and leave the café. Leave a decent tip, not too generous, but don't be miserly."

". . . ."

"At that point you are to board the *S. S. City of Havana*."

". . . ."

"Leave the café through the front door. There's no need to be melodramatic."

". . . ."

"Once you are on board the ferry, head down to the automobile deck. Put the suitcase in the trunk of the De Soto. The car will be waiting for you, naturally."

". . . ."

"Make sure the car is secure. Then head back up to the passenger lounge. Grab a drink. Sit down. Look out at the water. Try to relax. You will just be killing time at that point."

". . . ."

"I will join you soon after that, as soon as I can."

And just like that the line went dead. The voice of Luis disintegrated into a blur of static. Oscar sat for a while trying to absorb everything Luis had told him. It seemed very hot and his head was swimming. He did not know what to think of it all. He finished his Coke. He put on his white linen suit and his immaculate Panama hat. Then he got up, plucked his suitcase from the floor, and headed down to the lobby.

-92-

Where Luis went that morning after he left Hotel Milagro with his Platt Guardsman suitcase:

Luis left the apartment at eight in the morning. He stopped briefly at the front desk and chatted with the clerk. They talked in deliberate monotones. They talked about American baseball. The clerk was a big fan (though you could not tell this by his tone). They talked about Joe DiMaggio. The clerk thought DiMaggio had a goofy grin but he had never seen someone swing the bat with such ease. His brother had seen DiMaggio play in an exhibition game in Havana in the spring of 1947 between the Yankees and the Dodgers, but he (the clerk) did not get to go. He had never seen DiMaggio in person and now he never would. But he had seen a few clips in the newsreels at the movies. The clips showed DiMaggio in his heyday.

The sounds of dark jazz floated lazily about the lobby. They floated about like clouds.

It was almost like being somewhere else.

Luis and the clerk talked for fifteen minutes or so and then the phone rang and the clerk turned his back to Luis and answered it. When the phone call was over he turned back around and leaned over the counter and whispered something into Luis' ear. After that Luis asked the clerk for some paper and an envelope. The next thing anyone who might have been watching would have seen was Luis handing the envelope back to the clerk and then heading out through the revolving doors. But this happened very quickly. If they (the watchers) had so much as blinked they would have missed the inherent subtleties of this carefully scripted cloak and dagger moment. Where the clerk stashed the envelope was anybody's guess. Probably one of the wooden boxes containing abandoned room keys and dusty messages.

On his way to the revolving doors, Luis walked right by Nerea, who was watching him very carefully from the gloomy obscurity of one of the burgundy leather chairs with the pouty cinematic beauty of Julio Mella hovering above. Luis and Nerea did not make eye contact, but Luis had the strangest feeling that someone other than Nerea was watching him. He had the impression that Julio Mella was watching him. It seemed like Julio wanted to either warn him or absolve him.

The men in their fedoras who had taken over the lobby allowed Luis to leave without incident.

The revolving doors whooshed with unexpected ferocity and a blast of sunlight roared through the lobby, illuminating even the darkness beneath the chairs furthest away from any kind of electric light. For a moment the only sounds were the

whooshing of the doors and the roaring sunlight. Then the
sunlight dissipated and everything returned to normal. The
men began grumbling to themselves but they did not get up
from their chairs. Dark jazz echoed throughout the lobby once
again.

After Luis left Hotel Milagro he hopped into a taxi
and told the driver to take him to the corner of Empedrado
and Mercaderes, a stone's throw from the Cathedral of San
Cristóbal. It was normally a ten-minute ride, but traffic was
heavier than usual this morning because of the upcoming feast
day celebration. Vendors were already setting up in the Plaza
across from the Cathedral in anticipation of the crowds filling
the city. Even though the actual feast day was Saturday, the
party was already starting.

Luis said something funny to the driver as he paid
the man and the two of them laughed like old friends. The
two men talked about how hot it was, unusually hot for
November.

Then Luis walked half a block and stopped in the Plaza
to admire the Cathedral, marveling at its majestic, starkly
white luminescence beneath the bright blue sky. It was like
a white-hot coal that had slipped outside of the furnace of
time. This is the impression the Cathedral made on Luis,
though not perhaps in those exact words. But the feeling was
similar. The Cathedral seemed to be glowing with acquired
heat. Luis could feel the steady, rhythmic pulsing heat of
a nearby star. Then he could feel the music of an aspiring
humanity set in stone, which resonated with a different kind
of heat. Then Luis realized he had never seen the Cathedral
look so alive, which was a different kind of heat yet again.
Luis stood marveling at the Cathedral for quite some time. He
had not been inside since he was a small boy. He remembered
orange-glowing walls inside when the sun poured in through
the windows and polished marble columns, an earthy, beige
color, like the legs of giant elephants. He remembered a choir
singing various dusty cantatas and the nuns weeping their
silent, deadly tears and the smell of incense clogging his
throat, but that was all.

Then Luis bought a lemon-filled *pastelito* from a vendor
in the Plaza. He stood very still while he ate his *pastelito,*

observing the other vendors who were still setting up their booths or their carts in the Plaza, and the snappily dressed early risers who were sitting outside a small café with a postcard view of the Cathedral and its ancient Baroque façade of a religious relic, the early risers sitting eagerly at a few outdoor tables with the white umbrellas open, waiting for this vendor or that one (because it was still early) so they could buy something, and chatting happily and pointing in random, unpredictable fashion at the pure blue of the sky or the bell tower on one side of the Cathedral or the clock tower on the other side or at the pigeons scattered about. Sometimes the pigeons were spooked and there was a flurry of wings and a small cloud billowing up into the air and then settling down again. From a distance it was hard to tell if they were pigeons or white doves sent by the Holy Spirit.

One of the vendors was selling fireworks. He was already doing a brisk business among a group of small boys who would normally have been in school but school for the week had been cancelled because of the celebration. Some of the boys were wearing white shirts but the others were shirtless, because it was so hot.

The figure of a priest in a white cassock and a black sash emerged from the Cathedral and hurried down the steps and the boys scattered, as did the pigeons, and one got the distinct impression that the priest disapproved of the vendor selling his fireworks to the small boys and was about to say something but changed his mind at the last second and then disappeared around the corner as if he were seeking pardon or revenge.

All of a sudden Luis decided he had seen enough and he headed away from the Cathedral, west along Empedrado. He finished the last of his *pastelito* while he walked, smacking his lips with great satisfaction. He walked with such carefree abandon that you would not have noticed the suitcase in his hand unless you looked very long and hard. If anyone had been following him at that point they wouldn't have known what to think.

Two blocks from the Cathedral Luis suddenly ducked into a small park and disappeared in a cloud of green. The cloud of green was actually a small grove of tamarind with deep-green laurels and several other varieties mixed in. The waxy leaves of the tamarinds reflected the bright pure sunlight. The air itself seemed to be shimmering.

Luis walked to the other side of the tamarind grove and sat down on a bench in the middle of the park. He set his suitcase on the stone walkway by his feet and looked across at a towering marble statue of Miguel de Cervantes Saavedra. He had always admired Cervantes and came to the park often to look at this statue. Sometimes it seemed less a statue and more like a ridiculously expensive adornment for a ridiculously expensive sarcophagus. Because we have to believe that something survives death, even if it is only a piece of stone. Luis did not agree one hundred percent with how the sculptor had portrayed Cervantes. The great writer seemed half asleep sitting in his marble Renaissance chair. Perhaps it was the moment just before the idea of *Don Quixote* had occurred to him. Or perhaps he had just finished writing the first few chapters. Or perhaps he was trying to remember some trivial event from when he was a boy. Or perhaps he had just finished a very large meal. It was hard to tell.

Luis sat on the bench for a while until it seemed that he had become part of the bench, one stone statue gazing upon another. Church bells rang out at regular intervals but he appeared not to notice. He was not annoyed. He did not even flinch. Then, inexplicably, which is to say just like that, Luis left the bench.

To all outward appearances he seemed to be in no hurry, and yet there was a sense of urgency with every step. He cut back across the park and then headed south on Aguiar until he came to Obispo. He stopped at the corner, looking in both directions several times, back and forth and back and forth again, as if he could not make up his mind where exactly he wanted to go, as if he were peering into the future and he wasn't sure he liked what he saw, as if he wished he had more choices in front of him, which is, of course, what we all wish.

He stood very still for a while.

He stood very still and thought he could hear music drifting over the rooftops and swirling down the streets. Perhaps a few musicians had set up in the Plaza near the Cathedral and were entertaining the growing crowd.

Then he turned abruptly and headed up the 200 block of Calle Obispo. He walked without even looking at the numbers on the buildings and then went inside a pale yellow office building. He did not pause to admire the architecture, which was yet another magnificent example of the Spanish Baroque style. He did not even bother to look up at the gleaming brilliance of the gold gleaming cornices. He climbed the stairs two at a time in spite of the suitcase.

When he got to the third floor he headed down the hall, all the way to the end, and went through a frosted glass door.

There was a bald-headed clerk sitting at a counter who looked up as Luis entered. The clerk smiled a thin, bleak smile and disappeared into the dark interior of the office. He did not seem to be feeling all that well. He seemed to be suffering from a stomach condition of some sort. A few minutes later a different man emerged from the darkness. For some reason it was difficult to tell what this second man looked like. He seemed devoid of any distinguishing features, almost faceless. He looked vaguely Spanish, which is not all that surprising in Havana, but that was all anyone might remember.

Luis and the second man carried on a wordless conversation. It was almost like they could communicate telepathically. Luis looked past the man and the man followed Luis's gaze and then hurried away and shut a door and locked it and returned, and then Luis gave the man a strange, grave look, which seemed to say that he hoped the man was better prepared for what was to come, and with that the man gave Luis a nervous look and laughed a thin, shallow whistling laugh like light swirling down a long dark tunnel and disappearing forever, but Luis made a calming gesture and then pulled out a narrow, almond-colored envelope and gave it to the man and the man seemed relieved and put the envelope in a steel filing cabinet that was plainly visible behind the counter. Then the second man returned to the interior and the bald-headed clerk reappeared and sat down and Luis left. The bald-headed clerk did not seem to be feeling any better.

After he left the pale yellow office building, Luis headed to a small café he knew. The café was only a short walk away. Luis went inside and took a seat near the back, near a narrow row of telephone booths. It was very dark near the back, but

Luis needed a little respite from the bright sunny day.

He ordered a flatbread sandwich with a bit ham and pork and a hint of orange sauce, garlic, peppers, and mustard. It was a working man's lunch, even though Luis was clearly not a working man.

When the waitress brought the sandwich she smiled at Luis, a gentle, hopeful, flirtatious gleam in her eye, but Luis did not return the smile.

He did not even notice the waitress.

She stared at him a moment and then left quickly.

He ate his sandwich. He drank two beers.

From where he was sitting, the people passing by the front of the café looked like glimmering shadows gliding back and forth across the two-dimensional brightness of the sunlit window.

After he finished eating he disappeared into one of the phone booths. It was a tight fit with his Platt Guardsman suitcase, but he made it work. He chose the one all the way in the back, so he could see anything coming his way. He sat in the phone booth for a while but he did not call anyone.

At least not right away.

Nobody in the café seemed to care that Luis had taken over a phone booth. It was almost like the phone booths did not even exist. Then at precisely one o'clock Luis picked up the phone and made a call. Even if you had been sitting inside the phone booth with Luis, you would have been hard pressed to understand what he said. He spoke very fast, pausing just long enough between thoughts to catch his breath. If you had been standing outside the phone booth it would have sounded like waves crashing at the beach. It was also hard to say who he called. Some would have said impossible. At times it seemed that there was no one on the other end, just a gnawing, protracted silence waiting for more.

Then Luis hung up and dialed a second number. This second phone call was very short, no more than ten seconds.

Then Luis flung open the folding door, headed outside and hopped into another taxi. He told the taxi driver to drop him at the wharf, he needed to catch the ferry to Regla, and the driver nodded and off they went. If Luis noticed the two taxis that seemed to be following his taxi, he gave no indication. Perhaps he did not care. Perhaps he thought they were simply reflections of the taxi he had chosen, ghostly double (or triple) images dancing in the dark windows of the shops and cafes along the streets and that once they had stopped moving these ghost images would catch up, all of the images coalescing into a single taxi. Or perhaps he had anticipated that no matter where he went, he would be followed. In any event, he didn't bother with the two taxis that were following close behind, even when his own taxi driver said he could lose them if Luis wanted. Luis only laughed and said it wasn't anything to worry about, nothing was what it appeared to be. It was sunny outside and he could hear church bells ringing, a gentle ringing in his ears. Luis sat back and enjoyed the ride, short as it was.

-93-

Escaping on the ferry to Regla:
The two taxis following Luis had been delayed in an unexpected bottleneck on Calle Cuba, just before the old convent, and Luis' driver commented on this and then spun the wheel and they sped down Luz towards the ferries. By the time the other two taxis had disentangled themselves, Luis had already paid his fare and disappeared into the tunnel-like darkness of the ferry building, emerging only briefly into the sunlight on the other side before he boarded a small blue passenger ferry. As the small boat pulled away from the wharf, Luis could see the other two taxis shuddering to a stop just inches before they would have smashed into a few parked cars. Several dark figures popped out of the taxis and raced after the ferry, but they were too late. Luis watched them on the wharf staring mutely at the dozens of boats that were motoring this way and that across the harbor and the seagulls hovering in the air above.

Briefly he wondered how they had picked up his scent and if they knew where he was going, but then these thoughts left him. Another ferry would leave shortly, but it didn't matter. By the time it arrived in Regla, Luis would have melted into the background.

Luis sat in the middle of the boat, not because he was afraid of the water, but because he wanted to stay in the shadows as much as possible.

It was a pretty short trip. When he got to the other side of the bay he looked back to see if the next ferry had started across, but he could not tell. Then he headed out towards the street and a wine-colored De Soto convertible pulled up and Luis climbed into the back seat. The driver did not look at Luis and Luis did not say a word.

A few minutes later they were lost in a labyrinth of narrow winding streets south and slightly east of the warehouses and the refineries and the two grain towers and the new thermoelectric plant and the chemical plants along the water and the green fumes boiling up into the air. A working-class neighborhood filled with a mix of narrow but brightly painted wooden houses that might be swept away with the next great storm, and a few crumbling stone buildings, colonial ruins trembling with the majesty of the past. Narrow balcony railings covered in flowers and vines. Black Madonnas were everywhere leaning out over the railings, three-foot statues precariously perched, calling out to those below in the stony, silent language of salvation, but when you looked up you lost all perspective. The Black Madonnas seemed to be suspended by wires in a bright blue liquid sky. And no matter where you were you could hear a strange, drumming music and muffled, chanting voices. When you tried to focus on the drumming sounds or the voices they vanished as easily and as quickly as a misplaced hope, only to be resurrected as soon as your mind became absorbed (inebriated, sidetracked) by something else.

After a while the De Soto stopped in front of a small neighborhood café, a nameless establishment, a narrow, triangular building at the corner of three streets, a series of narrow wooden panels folded back on themselves and the ground floor exposed, a hot, dusty breeze blowing through the open space, a long counter where dozens of patrons stood and ate long, lazy lunches and drank beer and laughed and chatted and drank some more. Most of the patrons were the descendants of African slaves. They did not give Luis and the wine-colored De Soto convertible a second glance.

Two young men wearing fedoras and holding long-barreled rifles (not unlike some of the men occupying the lobby of Hotel Milagro) appeared out of nowhere and ushered Luis into the café. They led him around to the side of the counter and a small table tucked away in a dark corner behind a mahogany screen.

Federico sat on the far side of the table submerged in the grainy subterranean light of the corner. At first he seemed only a featureless dark hole, a blind beggar. Only the ivory handles of his cane-back wheelchair and the ghostly impression of his orderly dressed in white and standing up against a closed side door gave away his identity.

The two men sat at the table for a very long time. They made their thoughts known by using cryptic hand gestures that bordered on farce, uttering strangely garbled phrases, descending into sudden, protracted silences, and then trading happy, beguiling smiles. They drank mojitos the whole time. The mojitos were not part of the regular menu and were instead prepared especially for Federico by the owner herself whenever Federico happened by. The owner was a heavy-set woman with thick, bushy hair and elephantine legs. Her eyes glowed with a disturbing brilliance like Quevedo's blood-stained moon. She wore dark glasses so she wouldn't frighten her customers. Her only name was Jaqueline. Federico had known her for years.

Luis and Federico seemed little concerned with the world around them, and yet there was an anxiety in the way they were communicating, a sense that time was running out and that they better do something before the last grains of sand had slipped through the neck. Of course they also realized that whatever plans they concocted would make no difference. Instinctively they realized there was only one end in sight. But this was the life they had chosen. At times they seemed on the verge of giving up completely. But then their passions were reignited and they seemed more determined than ever. They relished the fact that this was their last hurrah.

Highlights of the conversation between Federico and
Luis:

"It is not hard to know God, my friend, provided you do
not force yourself to define Him."

"I would not say God is the problem."

"No, no, I suppose not."

The two men laughing softly, some murmuring, the
older one descending into a state of mental detachment, as
if he is suffering from a series of strange premonitions, the
younger one suddenly thankful that he possesses all of his
faculties. Then a loud burst from the other side of the mahogany screen and then the clinking of beer bottles.

And then a few minutes later:

"It is the same as with everything else. First we dream a
dream. Then we are seduced by the dream. And then we are
sacrificed in the name of the dream."

". . . ."

"It is the old, old story."

"I am not sure there is any other way."

"No, of course not."

". . . ."

"Our options are limited."

"I have arranged everything."

"Good, good. "

"At least we'll give them something to think about."

"Perhaps."

Silence. The orderly moving from the door to the other
side of the screen and then returning with a tray of mojitos.
The two young men with their long-barreled rifles standing
alertly in the dark, listening intently for anything out of the
ordinary, watching intently, their eyes glowing with a peculiar
reddish glow, like the landing lights of an alien spacecraft, the
young men ready to pull the trigger if and when such action
becomes necessary.

And then: "Where did this Immanuel come from?"

"I do not know. I suspect he came up with the boys
from the unions. Eladio and Eugenio were sending us all
sorts. I don't know how we managed to use them all, but we
did. It is just like these union fucks to get in bed with the
Communists."

"Is that what is happening?"

"What else could it be?"

"*Ah, mi. Di guerra, caccia e amuri, pri un gustu milli duluri.*"

"The Communists are everywhere. I am sure Eladio sees it as a matter of survival. He doesn't know what else to do. But I am surprised about Eugenio. He has been speaking out against the Communists for years."

"Perhaps he has been lying all along."

"Yes, perhaps."

"You are sure Eladio and Eugenio are working with this Immanuel?"

"I am sure."

". . . ."

"They want to demonstrate their solidarity with every-thing Cuban, with Cuba's future."

"And they are willing to destroy everything we've built?"

"It would seem so."

"Then perhaps they are not Communists at all. Perhaps they are simply anarchists left over from the war. Or maybe ex-Nazis filled with rage and frustration with nothing better to do. Perhaps this is all just an accident of timing."

"It is a thought."

"And what about Ruperto?"

"No, I don't think Ruperto is involved. He has his own reasons for wanting to keep things as they are. But they are personal."

". . . ."

"I think they have been planning this for a very long time."

"How long?"

"At least since the storming of the warehouse. I am certain they were behind it. Just as I am certain that they knew you would suggest we move to Miami. Yes, they have been lurking in the shadows for a very long time indeed, plotting, planning, moves and countermoves. Communists, anarchists, ex-Nazis, it does not matter. I did not realize Eladio and Eugenio were revolutionaries at heart. They are ticking time bombs."

". . . ."

"You must admit as adversaries they have proved themselves to be quite formidable."

"But what is their goal? What do they want?"

"But Federico, you surely must know what they want. They want to explode. That is what ticking time bombs do."

But Federico does not understand.

Luis smiles at his friend and drinks some of his mojito. 'Yes,' he thinks, 'all this must be quite a shock to the old man. It is a wonder he doesn't just keel over.'

And then, still smiling, a soft almost apologetic smile:

"What they want is to take over. They want to be in charge. It is like you said, the old, old story."

Silence.

The two men look at each other for a moment, at least they are looking at the dark shadowy holes their faces have become.

"I cannot believe we didn't see this coming."

"Yes, but we can see it coming now."

And back and forth they go, assigning blame where no blame should be assigned. Wishing they could undo time but knowing that such wishes never come true. Their words take on a harder edge. Their words are lacerating the air. They wonder if they could pull back the shredded folds of reality and peer through to the other side. Then they begin to laugh at the absurdity of it all. The naiveté of long-cherished assumptions. The landscape of a world that has suddenly become the landscape of a cartoon. They feel like they have flown to the moon and back. They congratulate themselves on maintaining a purity of heart and mind and soul.

And then:

"You are sure this will work?"

"Yes, Oscar will be able to slip through. I will divert their attention."

"This is a dangerous game you play, my friend."

"Ah, yes, but it is just as dangerous for them."

The older man suddenly looks over at the orderly, and the orderly, who has been waiting for this sudden look, slips out through the side door and returns a moment later with a leather satchel, which he hands to Federico.

The two young men with their long-barreled rifles flashing darkly from the shadows seem amused. Federico unbuckles the satchel and peers inside, then sets it on the table and pushes it across towards Luis.

"Let us hope everything will work out as you say."

Moments later the satchel is empty and Luis snaps shut the Platt Guardsman suitcase. The additional weight is barely noticeable.

"You will be needing the keys."

Federico and Luis trade cinematic smiles, though in a world plunged into a perpetual film noir darkness, their smiles could just as easily be expressions of deep sorrow. The orderly dressed all in white produces two sets of keys and hands them to Luis.

"The De Soto?"

"Yes."

The long lingering lunch in the café is over and most of the patrons have gone home or back to work. In the distance you can hear drunken men singing. It almost sounds like the tolling of bells from distant churches. A young boy is unfolding the narrow wooden panels that are never noticed when the café is open. He is closing off the open space. It is tedious work for the boy, but there is no one else to help him. Then the café is officially closed until the sun sets. The orderly opens the side door and a narrow rectangle of afternoon sunlight slashes through the interior darkness. Luis pauses in the sunlight, and for a moment he seems trapped between two competing versions of reality. He looks at Federico, who is not moving, who suddenly looks like a skeleton in the glaring, sacrificial light of the open door with his pale, parchment skin stretched tightly across his forehead and two gaping black holes where his eyeballs should be. He no longer recognizes his friend.

"Are you staying then?"

"Yes, I think I shall stay a while. It has been years since I've had a good talk with my friend Jaqueline. It has been too long. We sometimes forget what is important. I do not even know if she still considers me a friend. One should never be so presumptuous."

94

What Luis did with the wine-colored De Soto convertible:

The drive back to Havana was uneventful. But Luis did not head back right away. He parked the De Soto (with the top closed) in a narrow side street in the shadow of a chemical plant and a green haze all around. With the heat and the haze, he could barely breathe, but he waited in the car until the sun began to set and then he could breathe more easily. Then he turned the key. The men who had most certainly jumped on the next ferry and followed him to Regla had just as certainly given up by now. The long shadows of the evening sliced through the landscape and it was becoming difficult if not impossible to see what was what with any degree of confidence. As Luis drove along the water he had the distinct impression that he was looking at a painting but the colors had started to run together. His eyes were glued to this painting, which was the world, oh, not the entire world perhaps, but certainly his world, a world that had once been surprisingly clear with sharply drawn lines and vivid Technicolor colors, but which was now beginning to disintegrate, the lines blurring, the images crumbling into black and white apparitions, and then just a black nothingness sliding off the page, the sludge of human memory, but if he closed his eyes (which he tried for a few seconds at a time while driving, just for a kick), he could once again see the world as it was, as he knew it to be, every moment of his life up until that point radiating with an explosion of minute detail, sharply rendered, the kind of detail that gives life to life, but then as soon as he opened his eyes that world would vanish as completely as if it had never existed, as if the lunatic painter (for who else but a lunatic would dare take such liberties with the world?) was trying to suggest that objective reality was beyond our grasp and that we needed to live our lives with our eyes closed or we would end up stark raving mad.

This is what Luis was thinking as he drove along the water and the night sky was descending.

At nine o'clock he drove into a small garage on a name-less street in Vedado, a nameless garage, practically invisible to the naked eye, and yet everyone in the neighborhood knew it was there. The garage appeared to be closed, but as Luis drove around the corner, a light in the garage office began to flicker, and then a steady, yellowish glow began to radiate outward, as if the office had suddenly caught fire, and then a pair of shutters were pulled shut, though the yellowish glow was still seeping through the slats, and a shadow rushed out to the sidewalk and a metal gate was pulled back and Luis drove in.

The humming of the engine echoed off the walls of the garage for a moment and then Luis cut the engine.

The gate was pulled shut.

"You are late," said a slightly puzzled voice, a deep masculine voice, but not as deep as the baritone steamship voice of Luis.

The voice was barely a whisper.

It was barely a fragrant breeze and the waxy leaves of a tamarind tree trembling slightly.

"I'll only be getting a few hours of sleep as it is."

"Yes," said Luis. "But it could not be helped."

"If you say so."

The two men stepped towards the garage office, but only a step. They remained safely ensconced within the shadows of the interior of the garage. There was plenty of light for their purposes. They were backlit by the soft yellow glow still seeping through the shuttered window of the garage office. They became two darkly glowing silhouettes, the fat stubby outline of the one, the square-shouldered and crisply manicured outline of the other with the triangular corner of a suitcase protruding.

There was just enough light to swear by.

"Did he get off okay?"

"He did. But he didn't look too happy about it."

"I suspected he wouldn't."

"You didn't tell him a damn thing, did you?"

"I told him enough."

"You mean enough to keep him away from trouble. But not enough if trouble came looking for him."

"Something like that."

The two silhouettes laughed. The yellow glow from the office seemed to glow more intensely with their laughter, as if the mania of their innermost impulses was directly connected to the electric grid.

"I don't owe you any more favors after this."

"Agreed."

"Good."

"So he got off okay?"

"I already said."

"A dark brown Mallory hat with a red feather in the hatband?"

"I told you."

"Yes, I know. I was just checking."

"You're a god damn lunatic Luis."

"And where is he now?"

"I guess he's probably in the second taxi."

"You guess?"

"Okay, that's exactly where he is. He's in the god damn second taxi. Except if he's already at one of those fucking nightclubs you suggested."

". . . ."

"One last fling in Havana before he goes, is that what you were thinking?"

"Sure."

"I hope he gets himself as much pussy as he can handle."

". . . ."

"What if he skips out on you?"

"He won't do that."

"Yeah, well, if you say so."

"Who's driving the second taxi? The immigrant from Africa or the student from the University?"

"Neither."

". . . ."

"We had to make a change."

". . . ."

"He's a good man. He used to play baseball but now he's mostly a drunk. But he's a good man."

"Was that wise making a change like that?"

"I said he's a good man."

"Yes, but I don't like unexpected changes."

"I know you don't. But it could not be helped."

"I see."

"I'm telling you it will be fine. He's a good man."

"Let's hope so."

"God damn it Luis! I'm doing the best I can! What the hell do you want from me?"

"The bull, like a castle under siege, has been eaten."

And it was only then that the fat, stubby man realized that Luis had been teasing him about the new taxi driver.

The two silhouettes broke into a relaxed, carefree, shining example of unrehearsed laughter.

They laughed for a very long time.

Once again the yellow glow from the office seemed to glow with greater intensity.

It seemed like the window was about to burst.

Quite probably there was a sudden surge on the electrical grid that caused minor blackouts all over town.

"I'll say it again, Luis. You're a god damn lunatic."

"I know it."

"It's like you think we're all characters in a god damn Hollywood movie."

"But we are, my friend, we are."

And then there was nothing more to say. Luis handed the fat stubby man the two sets of keys to the De Soto. He stood on the cement pavement of the garage ramp and watched the fat man disappear into his office and the light went out. Then he looked back at the De Soto. The De Soto was still warm from the drive. It still seemed to be vibrating slightly. Luis stared at the car until he could no longer distinguish the car from anything else in the garage. Then he headed for a narrow archway next to the gate. There was no door, just an opening. He swung his Platt Guardsman suitcase through the opening with a carelessness that could only have been caused by giddy euphoria and headed out into the Cuban night.

95

The men in dark fedoras with their long-barreled rifles
or their Kongsberg Colt pistols chase Luis through the darkly
gleaming streets of Havana:

The webbed darkness of Berkeley's God, this chaos of
the soul, was riddled with the streaking meteorites of festival
rockets, though who was lighting them and from where it
was impossible to say. Music filled every corner of every
street, every nook and cranny. Thousands of musicians had
descended upon the city, as they always did during times of
celebration, many having arrived by bus from as far away as
Oriente province. But this particular celebration was unlike
any other festival that anyone ever remembered or would
remember. It was an anomaly, never to be repeated. It was
like Carnival and Christmas mixed together. On the feast day
itself, the faithful would be forced to sit in silence inside the
Cathedral while they prayed to the wooden statue of Saint
Christopher for his blessing. But the days and nights leading
up to that Saturday of their repressed, penitent fears would be
filled with a more raucous, rumbling kind of energy.

That first night set the tone for everything that followed.
The clang of a siren or two went by. The happiness swelled.
A woman screamed. But it was not clear if it was a scream of
terror or a scream of passion. Elongated shadows appeared,
like the shadows of alien creatures that had taken refuge on
the earth. Then another festival rocket went up into the air
and these strange shadows evaporated or were forgotten
and when they returned in the light of a passing car or some
other source of illumination it was clear they were only tree
branches swaying in a gentle breeze. The happiness spread
like a disease. So did the laughter. And the church bells
ringing. Thousands of unseen men and women were singing
songs of happy-go-lucky joy or drunken, melancholic love
or blasphemous frivolity. Each song a vision of happiness
unto itself. Happiness any way you sliced it. Amnesic voices
emanating from distant radios (as if from distant stars); or
sex-starved voices emanating from dozens of third-rate movie

houses that littered the landscape like limping (clubfooted) degenerate uncles, the willing, willful, festival-going throng mesmerized by the flashing pockmarked light of crumbling movie house marquees, each marquee with an incalculable number of missing bulbs that would never be replaced, or ruptured bulbs still implanted in their sockets with jagged edges that might cause injury, each marquee flashing incessantly, as long as there was darkness to flash against, or absorb, the marquees more darkness than light really, symbols of eternal night; or implacable, unforgiving voices (happy in their eternal, dogmatic pain) emanating from those forgotten churches on that godforsaken strip south of Zanja with their slowly disintegrating stone walls that still reverberated with recriminations from centuries ago; or lingering, lecherous, satisfied voices emanating from the interior darkness of posh nightclubs with their hollow happy men, and women's eyes dripping rouge; all of these happy, effervescent voices (and many more besides) mixing together in the stratosphere, as close to heaven as was physically possible, the currents of the upper winds swirling the voices about, mixing them together so you could barely tell one from another, and then the voices somehow separating, reforming, reshaping the world in ways that only the infinite logic of music can express, a billion permutations.

So no one paid any attention to Luis. Even if they (whoever might have been looking for Luis) had known where Luis was going to be at any given moment, they would have had difficulty pointing him out because there were hundreds like Luis roaming the streets, jostling each other in this horde of happy pedestrians, without apology, without awareness, some of them looking for a place to stay for the night, and for the next several nights after that, but many more were content to roam the streets until they collapsed from exhaustion or were lucky enough to find a seat at an outdoor café, where they drank a beer or two and then nodded off.

By midnight most of those who were still awake seemed to be reveling in the peculiar synchronicities of earthly existence. Quite a few were wearing bizarrely painted masks: animal masks, bird masks, Conquistador masks, priestly masks, prison inmate masks, masks of the Inquisition, masks of the Devil, masks of crippled angels and hallucinating saints, gas masks with elephantine rubber attachments, ski masks with no attachments at all, aviator caps with goggles, which were not masks precisely but worked well enough, masks of indifference, masks of vengeance, masks of annihilation, masks of incompetence, masks of craven betrayal, masks of insensitive lovers, masks of night terrors, masks of greedy politicians, masks of blood-thirsty generals, masks of demons from the pit, masks to protect you from the horrors of radiation sickness (though it should be pointed out that these masks, while cleverly decorated, were not even close to the real thing and would never work), masks that were realistic down to the tiniest imperfection, masks that were clearly abstract representations, all done in wild, vibrant colors that were only visible if they caught the glow of a festival rocket or a flash from a passing headlight or the dim reflection of a street lamp bouncing off one of the darkened storefront windows; the masked revelers cavorting about, grunting and gurgling and grinding their teeth, making obscene gestures as they danced through the darkly glowing subterranean shadows. Wild dogs howling at the moon. Some were wearing only their masks and had painted their bodies to match, accentuating their good points, hiding their deformities. Some of these bodies were elaborate works of art. Surrealist expressions of the soul of the individual, however demented. And this is how it was all over Havana. One wondered how the remaining nights could hope to surpass this first night celebrating the Feast Day of Saint Christopher. It beggared the imagination.

Luis walked from the nameless garage to Linea and waved for a taxi. He was certain no one was following him. But he was also certain that dark men wearing fedoras and sporting long-barreled rifles or Kongsberg Colt pistols were scattered all over the city on the chance that he might stumble by. So he told the taxi driver to drive around for a while, Vedado, Miramar, Cerro, it did not matter. He wanted to think through what was left to do. He cracked his window because it was stuffy inside the cab.

Once or twice he thought he saw the darkly gleaming barrels of long-barreled rifles sticking out from the tangled knot of humanity walking to and fro along the sidewalks. But

the taxi was going by too fast to be sure. On several occasions
while the taxi waited at a stoplight, Luis heard snippets of
conversations drifting in through the window as the pedestrians passed in front. All of the snippets seemed to carry savage,
sinister, even desperate overtones.

At one stoplight Luis heard:

"Are you sure you know the way?"

"Yes, of course, but that doesn't mean much tonight."

"And you're sure he'll be the only one there."

"I'm not sure of anything. But it doesn't matter to me."

And at another stoplight:

"I don't care about any of that. All I want is my money."

"That's what I told him."

"Yeah, well, there's no telling what I might do if I don't
get my money."

"I told him that as well."

And at a third:

"So I told her I didn't give a fuck, and do you know
what she said? She said go ahead. You're a big boy. Do something stupid."

"So what did you do?"

"What do you think I did?"

"That's what I'm afraid of."

And at a fourth:

"We'll leave in the morning."

"Do you think we'll get away with it?"

"I'll guess we'll find out."

"Yeah, I guess we will."

Shortly before midnight, Luis told the taxi driver to drop
him at a small apartment building he knew on Calle Crista
in the old part of town. He knew a woman that lived there,
and he was fairly certain that he had never mentioned her
name to Nerea. It was far enough away from the glamour and
excitement of the celebration that he might actually get some
sleep. It would be the perfect spot to hole up for the rest of the
night. But the traffic was worse than before. The police had
closed off half a dozen streets, which is to say they had set up
a series of impenetrable barricades, and at each barricade there
were a couple of overly friendly officers in their bright blue
slickers, in case it rained, joking with those heading up to the

Plaza, laughing without remorse, encouraging those who were
already drunk to find some quiet corner to sleep it off before
they got into real trouble, giving any students that passed by
a real hard time, because these officers were real hard cases,
all of them filled to the brim with a brutal, lacerating rage that
needed to be purged from time to time in small manageable
bursts, like bleeding a radiator, or God only knew what
unforgivable crimes might occur. You knew they were armed
and would pull out their guns at the drop of a hat. You could
hear the rattle of death in their laughter.

The barricades and the police made it impossible for
Luis to get where he wanted to go, at least by taxi, and so
quite without meaning to, Luis found himself for the second
time that day in front of the ferry building. The taxi made a
u-turn and sped off into the darkness. Luis grit his teeth. He
did not like unexpected coincidences. He did not believe in
them. The last ferry had left hours earlier, so there was no one
there, but all the same, Luis felt like he was being watched the
moment he stepped out onto the pavement.

Already there was a taste of rain in the air and somewhere offshore in the dark waters to the southwest there was
the rumbling of a storm in its infant stage. Luis heard the
rumble of the storm without hearing it. He was looking at
the black hole across the street where Ignazio Tiziano & Sons
had once stood. The ruins of the once magnificent colonial
structure still remained, a charred reminder of earlier days.
Luis smiled a grim, resigned smile. He could not say at that
moment precisely how long ago the warehouse had burned to
the ground. Standing there in the darkness of his imagination
he felt as if he were looking across centuries. Then he noticed
movement near one of the gated archways of the ferry
building. Two shadows emerged, or partially emerged, then
a pinprick of light, as if someone had lit a cigarette, and then
another pinprick, and then a dry, barely audible murmuring,
more a sensation of vertigo than a sound, the darkness swirling, becoming darker.

Luis turned up his collar as if signaling an unseen
partner that now would be as good a time as any to intervene
on his behalf, but there was no one to notice this subtle and
yet strangely comic gesture (when viewed from afar) except

the two shadowy figures already noted. Still, Luis did not panic. His manner was immaculate. He was wearing a beige herringbone blazer, which he often wore when he went out, no matter the temperature, a crisply ironed white shirt and a chartreuse tie and brown and beige saddle shoes to match the blazer. Nodding politely but casually (what some would interpret as blatant mockery) in the direction of the ferry building, Luis adjusted his grip on the Platt Guardsman suitcase and crossed San Pedro, heading down Santa Clara towards the old convent that had been converted into the Department of Public Works in the 1920s. He moved with the kind of athletic nonchalance that was a trademark of certain Hollywood heroes. The two shadows seemed to watch his crossing with great interest. Perhaps they were watching the suitcase, which was strangely visible in the darkness, as if it were glowing from within, as if it contained a fully operational miniature nuclear reactor or a laser-driven electromagnetic plasma gun capable of vaporizing a city block in seconds, a prototype in either case, naturally, developed by the Nazi's during the war and stolen in 1944 and smuggled out of Germany before it could be tested and turned into a secret weapon. Perhaps the dark men in their dark fedoras who were scattered all over the city were really after the suitcase. Who can say? Then without any warning at all (which is to say without taking one last long drag of their cigarettes and flicking the stubs to the pavement with anxious disgust, or shouting with indignant reproach and flashing their long-barreled rifles or Kongsberg Colt pistols in the air in dramatic fashion as they raced across the street, narrowly avoiding the oncoming traffic, as if guided by fate) the two shadows filled in behind Luis. They were perhaps thirty yards away, a distance they maintained with calm but rigid vigilance, neither gaining nor losing ground, no matter how slowly or quickly Luis walked.

On two occasions Luis stopped and turned around to look at them, partly to test their resolve, but also to make a show of his own cavalier indifference, a pose certainly, but only Luis knew this for a fact, and the two shadowy figures also stopped, but they turned towards each other, looking away from Luis as if they didn't care whether he existed or not, still smoking their cigarettes, chatting amiably in German, probably about Juan Manuel Fangio, the great Argentine automobile racer, who had won the German Grand Prix in August of that year, the climax of a distinguished career, and what a disappointing finish for Barth (who would win a few championships for Porsche in the years to come, but nothing like Fangio), good old Barth, the only German to finish in the top twelve, or perhaps they were talking about the lack of good German food in Havana, particularly Labskaus (a plate of mashed potatoes, beets, and corned beef, served with a fried egg, pickles, and pickled herring), which they sorely missed, or the diminishing prestige of owning a Jules Jürgensen watch, or how long before they could go home.

As Luis neared the convent it seemed less like the government building it had become and more like the convent it once was. Luis heard a strange sound, like water rushing from an exposed pipe or the furious beating of wings against the bars of a golden cage, but he could not tell where the sound came from. It seemed to be everywhere. And then it was nowhere, as if a spigot had been suddenly turned off or the caged bird had escaped and flown away or died trying. In the night sky above distant buildings Luis could see the streaming rockets and the smaller firecrackers and clouds of smoke, and from somewhere he could hear music. Then a crowd of students rushed past. Heading down Calle Cuba, away from the celebration, they talked of the vengeance of young love and bruised egos, their young voices draining away like molten lead across the cobblestones, dripping into the sewers, but Luis had already turned the corner. Then he stopped for a moment, why he could not say, and stared at the one-time convent on the other side of the street and the narrow oak door that had been closed off for years. Leaning back against a rough stone wall on his side of the street, Luis closed his eyes and listened to the rhythm of countless centuries flowing past. He did not hear anything remarkable, the music from the celebration, the distant fireworks like exploding suns, the young voices, yes, but no heavy footsteps echoing in the night, no German voices. He stood very still, listening intently, his breath coming in short, raspy bursts. He wondered if there were indeed two men following him, shadowing his every movement, or if he were trapped inside the hallucination of death. He could almost hear the blood rushing in his veins. Then the sounds of rushing water or flapping wings returned, but very faintly, an imperfect duplicate. He heard the weary voice of an old woman and the sobs of a young girl. He heard the sounds of a door opening and closing and light footsteps scurrying down the street in one direction and then a bevy of light footsteps rattling along in the other direction.

Luis realized he hadn't eaten anything in hours. He felt dizzy. A gnawing unease gripped him. He opened his eyes, half-expecting to see two shadowy figures with guns drawn, waiting for him to make a move, happy, remorseless grins plastered across their faces. But there were no shadowy figures, no guns. Instead he seemed to have wandered into a Clovis Trouille painting (*Dialogue au Carmel*, 1944). A huge group of revelers dressed as Carmelite nuns (except you could see they were wearing racy black nylons and no panties beneath cream-colored petticoats) were milling about the street, smoking cigarettes in erotic fashion and blowing steamy kisses to unseen lovers, as if they had been posing for a playfully sadistic painter for several hours and needed desperately to satisfy their animal urges, which had been restrained for far too long. Luis and all the other voyeurs of our collective imagination, all those trapped in the oblong shadows of time where pale fear dwells, were sly-nun-ogling and ding-dong-dangling. It was a worthy attempt to revive flagging spirits. Then all of a sudden, the nuns stopped blowing kisses and made their way en masse to the narrow oak door. One by one they slipped inside. There was a small iron lantern hanging just above the door, the lantern glowing orange against the apocryphal night and all human hate. Luis had never noticed the lantern before, but this was true of most who passed by the convent on their way to somewhere else. A couple of rockets tore across the sky. This was followed by the faint buzz of a tumultuous crowd cheering with great passion. He heard a rustling sound as if papers were being shuffled, and then the sounds of nuns saying their evening prayers (but whether these voices belonged to the costumed revelers he had just seen or were actual nuns he did not know). The light above the narrow oak door went out but immediately someone

opened a window in the second-floor room above the door
and turned on a small lamp.

From where Luis stood he could see a French Rococo
salon mirror in the room, an odd fixture in an abandoned
nunnery, the mirror oddly angled, gleaming with the opaque
brilliance of another dimension. He could see a young girl
reflected in the mirror. She was clearly experiencing some
sort of unabated, emotional distress. Luis wondered if the two
shadowy figures that had been following him were waiting
for him to begin moving again or if he had somehow given
them the slip when he turned the corner. Then the voices
of the praying nuns faded into nothingness and the sound
of the young girl sobbing, which had been humming along
in the background the whole time, somewhat subdued, like
static, became for the briefest of moments the only sound Luis
heard or even remembered hearing. He could only see the
young girl's passing reflection in her room above the door
as she danced back and forth past the mirror of her grief,
pouring forth her breathless lament because no one inside the
abandoned convent heard her anguish, or if they did they did
not know how to respond. Luis, who knew the language of
tears better than most men, was immobilized by the crystalline
purity of the girl's sad story even more than by her radiant,
vulnerable beauty. She wept as we will all weep when the
world splits in two and the end has finally arrived. Because
love is the saddest thing when it goes away. Because love is
unfathomable when one is wounded so deeply. Because in
such moments love does not even truly exist.

The girl was wearing a plain white sleeveless dress
trimmed with a bit of yellow lace, or perhaps it was an
undergarment of some kind. Her darkly glowing hair was
curled about her shoulders and she wore a peacock feather
above her left ear. She had fallen in love with a young man
who hailed from a great aristocratic family that had at some
point acquired the shield of the Marquisate de Cañada. They
had supposedly arrived in Cuba in 1746 when Diego Peñalosa
was the acting governor (the very same year, coincidently, that
the salon mirror described above had arrived in a shipment of
goods from Barcelona but which had then disappeared from
history until it was purchased in the Plaza del Vapor in 1841

by a Santería mystic, a friend of the young girl's grandmother, who lived outside of time and who believed that every mirror is a window to past lives and an oracle with the power to ease all pain). The young girl was herself the daughter of a slave and an unknown Spanish naval officer, at least this was the story her grandmother had told her time and again. But the young man did not care about her lack of pedigree and had pledged his eternal love one evening beneath the shimmering glow of a cloudless sky. They had taken a lover's stroll in the labyrinth of fragrant cobblestone pathways that was always and forever the Quinto de Molinos Botanical Gardens, unconcerned with any watchful eye that might be following their every movement. Believing in their heart of hearts that this was their wedding night, they slept in each other's arms in the soft darkness of a tamarind grove, though in truth they got very little sleep.

The next morning the young man told his new wife to hurry home and pack her things and he would call on her later that afternoon and they would take a boat to Spain and so begin their new life. And she did hurry home, to a small hovel of an apartment in a collapsing tenement building on Cardenas, where her grandmother looked after her. But she never saw the young man again. At four in the afternoon an elegant but funereal black barouche with the hood pulled all the way forward arrived out front, the four black horses gleaming proudly in the sunlight, and a gaunt looking gentleman emerged and went inside. His driver waited. The young girl had been watching from the window and knew something was terribly wrong. When her grandmother opened the door, the old don motioned for her to fetch the young girl for he had something important if not profound to say, and then he pushed past the grandmother and sat down in a small rattan chair. But the grandmother did not move. She could not move. She collapsed in a puddle of anxiety and called out to her granddaughter to come quickly, and the young girl rushed to her grandmother and looked up at the gentleman, her eyes flashing with rage, for she assumed he had struck her grandmother with his ivory handled cane without even taking off his gloves, though why he would do this she did not know. (Of course in a symbolic sense the gaunt gentleman had indeed struck the old woman, but the blow had occurred years earlier.) Impatient to say what he had to say, he stood up and was about to open his mouth, but then the grandmother started wheezing and he was obliged to bring her a glass of water. She could barely hold the glass, and when she had finished, her wheezing had not improved, but she had enough strength left to embrace her granddaughter and whisper into her ear. 'This man is not to blame,' she said. 'Except in the way that all cruel and heartless men are to blame. He is your father. And he is also the father of this young man you have been seeing, your half-brother, by a woman born in Barcelona, not Cuba. Do not expect your father to help you.' And then the grandmother died and the old gentleman left in his elegant but funereal black barouche and the young girl knew she would never know love again. That was why she had sought refuge at the Convent of Santa Clara. She did not know where else to go. Then there was a flash in the mirror, the image of a fiery comet descending upon a doomed planet, and Luis saw the face of a world-weary nun appear in the window. Their eyes met and Luis felt a shuddering sense of shame and despair, though precisely why he only vaguely understood, so he looked away and the world began to spin and he felt he was spiraling down into the depths of the earth, but then almost immediately he looked back at the window, only it was now boarded up, just as it had been boarded up for years. The bout of vertigo had passed.

"Are you okay?" said a voice.

Luis blinked back a few tears and straightened himself against the stone wall that had been there for centuries. The stone was very rough. Luis had been leaning at an odd angle and his shoulder was numb.

"Yes, yes, I am fine."

"You are sure?"

The voice belonged to a woman dressed as a flamingo. She was with two young men, one dressed as a Jesuit priest and the other as a Taíno chieftain, perhaps the great Hatuey himself. They all seemed genuinely concerned. But Luis was looking past the woman and her companions to the corner where Santa Clara intersected Calle Cuba, and sure enough,

the two shadowy figures who had been on his tail since the
ferry building were rounding the corner that very instant.
They were waving Kongsberg Colt pistols in the air in dis-
jointed fashion and running pell-mell, as if they had thought
Luis was trying to escape, but when they rounded the corner
and saw Luis surrounded by the three festival-goers, they
abruptly but smoothly changed gears, slipping their guns into
their coat pockets and walking quickly to the other side of
the street. They stopped in a pool of darkness in front of the
narrow oak door and the lantern that hadn't been lit for more
than thirty years. They stared mutely at Luis but with unwavering intensity, as if daring him to abandon the relative safety
of his side of the street. They were also most likely trying to
assess if the flamingo and the other two were a chance meeting or if they perhaps worked for Luis. If you didn't know
they were there you would have seen nothing but a gleaming,
glowing fluid darkness. If you didn't know they were there
you might have thought a black hole had begun eating away
at the fading dream that was Cuba.

"So you are heading to the Plaza?" said Luis.

But there was now boyish laughter in his voice, as if
he had acquired a second wind. Or the notion of destiny
was a mere word and so was easily discarded. Or history
was repeating itself so he knew what to expect. Or Luis was
perhaps one of those rare individuals who could laugh in the
face of certain death, which was not as far-fetched as it might
have seemed to those who knew him. For what is death really
but one more mask?

"Yes we are," said the flamingo. She stepped closer to
Luis, smiling a fluid, flirtatious smile. "Can't you tell?"

She twirled around for show, an extravagant pirouette,
her feathers fluttering in the sudden breeze and the flashing
curve of plush brown cheeks.

The Jesuit priest and the Taíno chieftain said nothing. It
was not clear if this was because they had nothing to add or if
they now perceived Luis as a rival.

"Let's go," said the flamingo.

She grabbed hold of Luis' free arm, laughing and
twittering with coquettish delight, her flamingo feathers
fluttering some more as they headed towards the sounds of

the celebration. The Jesuit priest and the Taíno chieftain fell in step directly behind.

Once again the two shadowy figures on the other side of the street followed their quarry with rigid vigilance. But they were not as calm as before, not as symmetric in their stubbornness, not as sure of themselves, so they kept chattering back and forth in guttural whispers, two wayward Teutonic knights on the edge of an underwater forest, stifling the urge to run away because it suddenly felt like they were out of their element, their hands ready to plunge into their coat pockets and pull out their pistols if need be and to hell if there were any witnesses. But they did not pull out their guns.

The streets became more crowded and there was a great deal of jostling elbows in every direction but no punches were thrown.

Luis and the others passed by a police barricade without incident. The flamingo was laughing uproariously. She could not help herself she was so happy. Her happiness seemed to infect everyone around her, the Jesuit priest, the Taíno chieftain, even Luis. Then a few voices cried out from the other side of the street, but they were not the voices of the two shadowy figures, who were still traveling in liquid darkness, slipping in and out of the shadowy cracks between buildings. The owners of the new voices were friends of the flamingo (who quite honestly was very well known and had a good word for everyone, even the police).

"You had already left," they said.

"We started out early," said the flamingo.

"But we didn't wait around," they said. "We knew where you were going."

Laughter. Hugs. Warm embraces. A soft cushy squeeze.

"We brought wine," they said.

They held up bags presumably containing wine.

"But we didn't bring any glasses."

"We don't need glasses," said the flamingo. "We can pass around the bottles. Just like old times."

"Ah, but can we do that at our age?"

"Speak for yourself Valerio!"

"Yes, Valerio. Tonight we will live only in the moment!"

"Is there any other way to live?"

"Tonight age does not matter."

"Bravo, bravo!"

"Tonight time itself will stand still."

"Yes, time is an illusion."

"At least until the morning."

"And then we will pay for it," said Valerio.

"Yes," said the flamingo. "Just like old times."

More laughter. It was almost like singing.

No one noticed that Luis was clutching a Platt Guardsman suitcase, or if they did they didn't care.

The newcomers were also dressed in a variety of exotic costumes; a black jaguar, even though there were no jaguars in Cuba, two devils with twitching tails and pitchforks (plenty of those), a Spanish Conquistador, the great goddess Atabey, a dark serpent with the crest of an iguana, and several unknown or forgotten or perhaps extinct species of plumed birds. Everyone drank wine while they walked. They crumpled up the empty bags and tossed them to the ground. They tossed the empty bottles into the gutters and the bottles broke and they laughed and their laughter sounded like breaking glass. They were only a block from the Plaza. They passed by jugglers and acrobats. They passed by a second police barricade but the officers were busy listening to a musical trio on the corner — the beating of a conga drum and the strumming of a guitar and husky voices singing. It was becoming more and more difficult to communicate, unless one could do so telepathically. The music of the trio on the corner was replaced by another group of musicians standing beneath the awning of a small café further up the street. As if they were all reading from the same script (even Luis), they became a conga line, weaving their way from side to side, the glow of the festival now lighting up the sky, a great golden bubble of light coloring the buildings and the cobblestone streets and the great stone Cathedral itself, as if Havana truly was and always had been the fabled city of gold that the Spanish and those who believed in the dream of the Americas were always seeking.

Luis could no longer see the two men from the ferry building so he hoped for the best.

They entered the Plaza and were immediately consumed by the happy, restless crowd. The music of dozens of competing groups was swirling above their heads like a cloud. It became difficult to breath. It became difficult to see. No one was sure what they were looking at. Luis scanned the sea of bobbing heads. Here and there he spotted men wearing dark fedoras. Their long-barreled rifles sticking up out of this mass of humanity were a dead giveaway. The men were gliding back and forth in seemingly random fashion. Luis counted half a dozen. That made at least eight if you counted the other two.

The impromptu conga line disintegrated, pushed apart by the swelling, surging, shimmering crowd. Luis felt the hand of the woman dressed as a flamingo slip from his fingers. The flamingo and the Jesuit priest and the Taíno chieftain went in one direction, towards the south end of the Plaza, the black jaguar and the Conquistador and the others were pushed towards the Cathedral steps. They were all calling out to one another but their voices were lost in the festival din. Luis somehow remained in the center of this swirling circle. The flamingo called out to him and waved, a tiny dot in the distance. She blew Luis a kiss, and then she was swallowed whole.

Luis noticed that the seemingly random movements of the men in dark fedoras, who held their rifles in a rigid upright position at all times, were not so random. They were methodically canvassing the Plaza, crisscrossing this sea of restless, costumed faces, an invisible net, a tightening noose. Every once in a while they looked up at each other and nodded and smiled savage, sinister smiles. They no longer needed to use language to communicate. They seemed to be part of an alien race dedicated to crushing all hope, especially hope in the hereafter. They seemed to be tuned to the same radio frequency and thus moved about with mechanical, robotic precision. They were not about to squander this night's opportunity.

Luis kept his eyes focused on his own emerging path across the Plaza. A rocket tore across the sky and the crowd cheered and the men in dark fedoras looked up at the sky for a moment, a look of sudden surprise registering in their collective eyes, giving Luis a chance to slip through. But it didn't matter. He was hoping to head along Empedrado towards the park and the tamarind grove, but there were several men in fedoras closing in from the west, cutting across the Plaza with an unexpected urgency, cutting off his path of escape. They did not see him, but surely they sensed he was close by.

Luis turned on his heels and quite by accident found himself heading straight for the very same cart where he had bought a lemon-filled *pastelito* oh so many hours before. Of course Luis noticed this second unexpected coincidence, how could he not, but there was nothing to be done about it.

The cart with its white umbrella rising up towards the stars which were barely visible seemed like a small boat riding a rough sea, an oasis on the waves.

The man who had sold Luis the pastelito was gone. A young woman had replaced him, his wife perhaps, or perhaps his daughter. Luis thought this was a lucky break. The woman was very pretty. She was prettier than she had a right to be. "We have nothing left," she said, and she smiled at Luis, an apologetic smile that was also very becoming.

-96-

The tiny trap doors and sliding panels on the top and the sides of the vending cart had been closed and secured. Luis laid his suitcase on top and put his arms around the young woman. He began whispering into her ear and she giggled and laughed and blushed as appropriate and pretended to push Luis away. The intimate secrets they shared during this initial conversation were immediately forgotten, but the emotions roused by the sharing of those secrets remained, at least as far as the young woman was concerned, an eternal flame bubbling erratically but with miraculous persistence in the midst of a strong wind.

"Perhaps you wish to take me to the movies?" she said.

"Yes," Luis said. "That would be nice. But it is too late for that."

"Perhaps it is," she said.

And then: "But perhaps not. Come with me. I know a place. I will show you."

Together they took hold of the handles of the cart, the young woman gingerly but hopefully, Luis full of purpose but seemingly without hope, and pushed their way slowly through the cheering, swirling, mesmerized crowd. They left the white umbrella in its upright position, but slightly tilted, so they could move without being seen, except for their hips and their legs, which were clearly visible beneath the umbrella fringe.

Under any other circumstances, the fact that the umbrella remained in its upright position would have aroused suspicion, but on this, the first night of the celebration in honor of the Feast Day of Saint Christopher, it went unnoticed, except as one might notice the changing configurations of a cloud or a flock of birds suddenly taking wing or a tiny boat floundering on the horizon.

Beneath the umbrella, Luis heard the song of an empty heart beating. He was convinced that each pair of footsteps that went rushing past were the footsteps of the men wearing dark fedoras. He expected that at any moment these men would descend upon the cart, toppling their chances, and both he and the young woman would die in a hail of bullets. But this did not happen.

Luis was able to keep the cart moving (a minor miracle) because he was somewhat detached from what was happening, a spectator to the movie of his life unfolding, or at least this most recent portion of his life. It was not perhaps the movie the young woman had alluded to. Then again, perhaps it was. For Luis, this thrilling escape sequence began with a spectacular wide angle camera shot, a dramatic, heart-pounding aerial view, as if he were hovering in the darkly glowing stratosphere just above the Cathedral clock tower, suspended by wires he had never noticed before and that one never notices except during times of great duress.

He saw a small white umbrella floating casually, precipitously, in the sea of dark bobbing heads. The umbrella was moving slowly towards the shadows south of the Plaza.

The dark bobbing heads were illuminated at various times by sulphurous streaking rockets and exploding firecrackers, or by the irresistible golden bubble glow of the festival lights that had been strung this way and that, random, crisscrossing patterns, or by the blazing air-raid searchlights that swept back and forth across the facade of the Cathedral instead of the dark (and also darkening) skies above, the light bouncing off the Cathedral and descending upon the crowd, wave after wave after wave.

The umbrella, by way of contrast, was a constant luminous death-mask white.

Luis saw the men in their fedoras rushing all around the white umbrella, but always on their way to some other part of the Plaza. Never once did they think to look beneath the umbrella. From somewhere Luis heard the dark exotic timbre of Dizzy Gillespie's *Night in Tunisia* (the 1942 version), a fast-paced yet soulful romp — bass strings plucking, discordant, surreal, muted horns blaring, ringing bells, snare drums rattling, the haunting clarity of a lonely saxophone, an inevitable, inexorable, mythic movement that seemed to lift you up suddenly and swiftly from the shadows of an alleyway into the bright glaring neon blues and greens and purples of a busy city boulevard and the nightlife hissing and crackling, and then just as swiftly depositing you back in the shadows, the tension mounting with every passing second — all of which matched the relentless, frenetic mood of the dozens of men in their dark fedoras chasing after their own tails, all of them looking to clean someone's clock, eager to display their killer's instinct for all to see, and the joyful fatalism of a seemingly invulnerable Luis, who with each step became more and more convinced that he and the girl were about to slip away clean, their clocks intact.

Then Luis saw the white umbrella reaching the edge of the Plaza and the heaving darkness just beyond the glow of the festival lights, the crowd thinning at that point, less exuberant, the dark jazz of Dizzy Gillespie fading to nothingness, the immediate danger of the men in their dark fedoras receding like the blood-filled tide of an ancient sea, the kind of tide that might leave behind the bodies of countless dead sea creatures. And then the danger was gone, the grace of God fully implemented, as far as anyone could reasonably infer, a temporary fix most assuredly, but sufficient for the time being.

The luminous white umbrella slowly disintegrated, vanishing into the grainy haze of a dimly lit street, though precisely which street and which direction the umbrella went

Luis was unable to say, for he was suffering once again from the sensation of vertigo, perhaps from looking down from so great a height.

It is also worth noting that the entire time Luis and the young woman were huddled beneath the white umbrella, pushing the cart through the crowd, the young woman was chattering away. She did not fully appreciate the danger they were in, which annoyed Luis to no end, and which probably added to his returning sense of vertigo. But she was young and her brain was as empty as the eternal sky except for the words that came bubbling up out of her mouth. She said her name was Elisa and she lived with her brother. He had given her the cart for the evening because he wanted to enjoy the festivities, a sinful, profligate brother if there ever was one, she said, a dark, wayward soul. Then she looked at Luis and giggled but Luis wasn't paying any attention to her. She said her brother wouldn't be home until well after daylight broke, if he came home at all. And this thought did register with Luis, but only as a distant blip, a vague memory.

Then she said she had seen Luis before. She mentioned the names of some of the clubs she frequented and how she had always admired Luis, who was not like the rest of the men she saw at the clubs. "Those boorish louts," she called them, as if she had lifted the words from a cheap romance novel. But all Luis could think at that moment was how could this girl have spotted him in any club, he was never spotted, no one ever knew where he was or where he was going. But then he laughed to himself, a soft, grave, rolling laughter, thoughtful laughter, almost inaudible. Because that was obviously not true. Because someone had known where he was going to be at various points throughout the entire day. Some strange, unfathomable clairvoyant had been able to sneak a peek inside the dark corridors of his imagination, his unvarnished soul, if you will, and lay traps for him.

Now his fate and the fate of the Platt Guardsman suitcase depended upon the good will and naiveté of a beautiful young woman who couldn't shut up and who was leading him only God knew where. And in that very moment the young woman said "We're here," and 'here' turned out to be a narrow art deco tenement that was blue or aquamarine where

the street lamps cast their beaded raindrops of light, but a
shimmering dark gray everywhere else, except for the heavy
black translucence of a series of porthole windows rising
up towards the clouds, and a darkly gleaming bronze panel
directly above the polished front steps with a series of smaller
oblong panels protruding from either side, one on top of the
other, a singular work of art that seemed like some weird
insignia (sinister, ominous, prophetic, otherworldly, vaguely
Egyptian), a symbolic (coded?) representation of eagle's wings
or some other large bird of prey. A warning perhaps to future
generations. A prophecy once known to only a few now
visible for the whole world to see. Unrestrained in its daring.
But who can say?

Luis and the young woman pushed the cart through
a small archway along the side of the building and down
a narrow path and stopped before an iron gate and a few
bicycles shoved against the wall. The gate was unlocked and
led to a set of stairs and the dim almost subterranean glow
of a single lantern hanging from a chain. The young woman
trembled, an involuntary betrayal of her wild and uninhibited
imagination, and a glimpse of those lurid and generally
unattainable delights which are the spur to oh so many
unsolved crimes. Her breathless anticipation was a warm
breeze blowing through Luis' empty heart. So he accepted his
destiny, whatever lay in store. The two of them left the cart
with the bicycles and pushed their way through the gate and
hurried inside.

-97-

Inside the art deco tenement:

The building had been newly restored, the suites newly
refurbished. Polished marble floors. Newly painted plaster
walls that seemed to glow in the dark, a soft golden glow. The
walls had been seemingly painted by a victim of dementia.
They were a blank canvass that had been filled with unsettling
geometric patterns from the fifth dimension, a nightmare

landscape that may or may not have been designed by the
Dutch painter Piet Mondrian (or perhaps a deranged disciple)
in a last ditch effort to imprison God before he died (or keep
Him out), a landscape without any meaningful narrative
whatsoever composed entirely of rectangular staircase patterns
(patterns which had in fact never shown up in a Mondrian
painting) collapsing inward towards nonexistence or expanding outward towards infinity, patterns which would bring
about intolerable headaches if you stared at them in bright
sunlight. Opaque crystal wall lamps clinging like ice gave off
a cool, blue liquid light like music (no doubt to mitigate the
impact of the fifth-dimension geometry). The doors to each
room or suite of rooms were made of a rich, dark mahogany.
The rooms themselves featured mahogany furniture to match
the doors and were decorated with cool crisp greens and blues
and deep dark browns and other earth tones. Narrow, frost-
ed-glass, floor-to-ceiling windows in thin mahogany frames
opened up onto narrow balcony ledges with freshly painted
railings. The balconies were too narrow to stand on. If you
opened a window the smell of fresh mint instantly filled the
room, even on a rainy, alcoholic day

The luxurious though decidedly futuristic atmosphere
appealed to Luis' sense of vanity, his secret belief that not
only did he deserve a better fate than the plebian masses, but
that he was destined to live forever. But how was it that an
obscure, nameless vendor and his sister could afford to live in
such a place? Luis did not seem even remotely concerned with
this anomaly or the sinister implications it exposed.

Fast forward a few frames:
Luis and the young woman had been fucking for hours
but they were finished. The young woman was sprawled
across a king-sized bed (also mahogany), the satin sheets
in a rumpled mess on the floor revealing the bare mattress,
a ceiling fan rotating above her with mind-numbing, cruel
regularity. She was in a semi-comatose state, snoring softly,
her naked body gleaming in the darkness, almost cadaver-like.

Luis was sitting up against the headboard, contemplating her nakedness, her ghostly pale elastic whiteness.
She seemed less beautiful than she did before. Not just

because they had had sex. Her loss of beauty went deeper than that. Luis crawled closer and examined her with clinical detachment. She was far skinnier than she had appeared at the festival, thin-boned like a bird, and she had no hips to speak of, no curves of any kind. Her dark hair framed her face nicely, and her pouty lips suggested a fullness of spirit that was exceptionally erotic. But her teeth were crooked and her eyes seemed like sunken craters in the dim light. Without her clothes to hide her obvious deformities, she resembled an abused corpse that had been tossed into a narrow ditch with a jumble of bodies all twisted and broken and covered with lime and then earth and then recently dug up, or someone who had barely escaped death in a Nazi concentration camp, or a strangled marionette, any one of these more than a warm-blooded girl. She was a withering, shredded, fragment of a ghost wandering through the neon blue corridors of time, that was how Luis suddenly perceived her.

He went over to the portable record player on the small unadorned mahogany table opposite the giant bed. The girl had put on a record when they first arrived, before they started tearing off each other's clothes in the diffuse, bluish light. The music had stopped a while ago but the record was still spinning, the steady mechanical whirring of static to match the rotation of the ceiling fan. Luis flipped the record over and jazz like a swelling sea filled the room, a sound both familiar and otherworldly, as if it were originating in an underwater cavern and slowly bubbling up to the surface.

He listened to the jazz for a while.

He stood before the record player, watching the disc spin, listening to the jazz, still partially erect, thinking about the girl on the bed. In spite of her now withered, skeletal appearance, the memory of the young woman as a beautiful sex goddess lingered in his imagination. The sex had been quite good, nothing like making love to Nerea, but it had been good sex nevertheless, full of acrobatic maneuvers and back-wrenching explosions.

Luis felt no guilt over his lack of genuine human compassion for the girl. Instead he felt a degree of calm he had not experienced in quite a while. He felt more in control, even though he knew being in control was a placebo one offered oneself, an illusion. Like religion. Like God. Yes, he thought, the sex had been quite good. He could still taste the girl on the tip of his tongue. What had excited him the most was that she had totally surrendered her body to his every whim. She had been his to command, a rag doll he could break again and again if he chose and she wouldn't cry out, not even a whimper, as if she had been placed under hypnosis by German mesmerists so they could conduct strange experiments in a basement laboratory. So Luis had not noticed her thin, shapeless ass, her pale almost translucent skin like fine parchment. He had been blind to her flaws (as he had been blind to other things). His freedom to do with her as he wished had become the ultimate aphrodisiac.

But something had happened between then and now. The dark mirror had once again been placed over the open grave. The portals to the other dimensions had been smashed. And in the vacuum of his utter isolation, Luis realized he had fucked this woman because of Nerea. Because he had abandoned Nerea only because he had become bored, and Nerea had abandoned him in return. Because the hopes of earlier days had become a meteorite exploding in the upper stratosphere, which is what happens to everyone's hopes, eventually, and now there was no going back. This is what he was thinking as he looked at the young woman sprawled across the bed, the sound of the jazz shape-shifting, becoming a slow, mournful sound now, a lazy current, a quiet bleeding out of all emotion, the light from the unreachable stars now speeding away at a fantastic rate towards nothingness. Then the young woman stirred. She sighed and rolled over but did not wake up. The bluish light from the wall lamps washed over her skin and gave her a slightly scaly, reptilian sheen that was repulsive to look at, and yet for a fleeting moment she became beautiful again, strangely beautiful, an alien beauty.

Luis could not get over her strange, alien beauty.

He went over to the window and opened it a crack and looked down at the street. He breathed in the smell of fresh mint. It had begun to rain so it was difficult to see. The world outside had become distorted, a weaving blur of background noise, the moisture of the storm spurting through the crack in short bursts, a spitting cannonade of moisture, and Luis was about to close the window when he caught a shadow of movement beneath a dimly glowing streetlamp on the other side of the street. He could see the outlines of two men staring up at the window, as if they had been waiting for the window to open since before the rain had started.

Luis stared at the two shadowy outlines, the men all but obscured by the rain and the darkness. It seemed for a moment like they were taking a shower together, and Luis was struck by the absurdity of the image. Then one of the shadows seemed to incline his head, a nod of understanding, perhaps, or one of futile apology, but the gesture seemed out of place, absurd, sinister and yet friendly, a scripted bit of irony. Then the two men retreated from the light and there was a sharp popping sound and the streetlamp went out. But Luis knew they were still there, waiting patiently in the darkness.

The sound of the jazz had become static again.

The rain was coming down much harder than before and the darkness was trembling. It hadn't rained this hard in months. Luis closed the window and took a few steps towards the record player, the fresh mint smell still lingering in the air, and it was only then that he realized the girl was no longer on the bed. She was standing beside the bed now. She had placed his suitcase on the bare mattress and had rifled through its contents, discovering in the process the false bottom. Dozens of one-hundred dollar bills were scattered about, spilling out of the suitcase, dripping down the side of the bed towards the polished mahogany floor, but the young woman was not interested in the money. She was pointing a gun directly at Luis, her eyes fixed on his, relentless, probing eyes without even a glimmer of paranoia or artificial kindness, as if she were trying to catch a glimpse of his soul, as if she were trying to decide if he was the reincarnation of the Egyptian god Amun-Ra, or just another parasitic, sex-starved bum she had pulled off the street who deserved to die a brutal and ignominious death, but she needed to look into the depraved, neon glare of his soul to be sure. But the gun was not hers. The gun, a single action Modèle 1935 pistol, belonged to Luis. It was an elegant weapon, mostly for show, a relic, a curio, which Luis carried in a shoulder holster whenever he went out to the clubs. He did not remember bringing the gun along that day. But there was his empty shoulder holster draped over his beige herringbone blazer, which was draped over a lonely looking chair pulled out from the wall. And there was his gun.

Fortunately for Luis, the young woman was unfamiliar with the Modèle 1935 pistol. Or at least she was unfamiliar with the drawbacks of a slide mounted safety. Or maybe her thumb just wasn't long enough. Or she was still half asleep and didn't realize the safety was engaged. At any rate, when she flexed her firing hand and pulled the trigger, nothing happened. Which is to say that the gun did not fire as she had expected (hoped? prayed?). Naturally she looked at the disobedient (unresponsive? malfunctioning?) pistol as if it had violated the laws of physics. It was only for a split second, mind you, an involuntary reaction to be sure, and quite understandable. But a split second can be an eternity. Plenty of time for Luis to turn the tables. Immediately he disappeared, a chameleon becoming one with the dappled blue darkness, his image reappearing for the briefest of moments in first one window and then another, and so on down the line, a shimmering, passing reflection with no substance, like an echo. Then he disappeared altogether.

She whirled her shooting arm first one way and then another, trying to anticipate his next move, but she could not locate him. She felt the universe collapsing, her universe anyway. She did, however, manage to release the safety. After all, she only needed one clear shot. Then she felt his breath on her neck and she realized it was too late. He had grabbed hold of her from behind, a wrestler's embrace, with one arm reaching across her neck, pulling her close, and the other slipping around her waist, his hand twisting up towards her face and then latching on to the gun. She had tried to slip away. She had spun the moment she felt his body press against hers. But she would not let go of the pistol and so her movement was checked.

If one did not know any better, one might have thought they were engaged in a strange, primitive, ritualistic mating dance. Every step seemed carefully choreographed. Faces glowing like deranged but easily manipulated puppets. Hands folded as if in prayer, the barrel of the pistol pointing skywards. Lips almost touching, scarcely a whisper apart. Luis looked at her, his eyes burrowing deeply into hers, as if to ask her what did she think she was doing, and her eyes flickered in response, a sultry, haughty reply, did he think she was a flower that would simply bend in the breeze, the two of them spinning around the gun in stark counterpoint to the spinning ceiling fan above, their hips swiveling in the dim bluish light, their eyes locked in telepathic misery, their faces contorting wildly, passionately, in weird angst-ridden grimaces, their thoughts an incomprehensible mishmash of clichéd phrases from old movies, if you needed some money all you had to was ask, don't do me any favors big boy I can take of myself, if it's not the money then what is it you want, did I ask you what you wanted big boy, no you didn't, then you can wipe that smug look off your face, look I'm sorry, it's too late for that big boy, if you want me to go I'll go, it's too late for that either, but it doesn't have to be that way, sure it does big boy, but why, because we do not believe in half measures, sure baby, because once we release the hounds there is no stopping us, and with a violent upsurge of rage and self-loathing she tried to jerk free the pistol, but she did not realize that they had danced themselves into the corner near the row of windows. She jerked back but immediately convulsed forwards and the gun went off, a straight clean shot soaring up through the pale white elasticity of her chin, through the arched roof of her mouth and out the back of her skull.

It was hard to say who had pulled the trigger, but the trigger had been pulled nevertheless.

Her fingers slid back, releasing the gun. A few drops of blood gurgled down her neck, a faint blush of color dripping down, spreading across her breasts. Then she slid down along the wall, withdrawing into herself, no longer impatient, a white ribbon crumpling to the floor, a flash of light vanishing in the darkness. There was blood splatter on the wall and bits of skull. Luis was surprised by how much blood there was. She had seemed so pale, so drained of blood. But there she was now, a crumpled-up white ribbon floating in a pool of darkly gleaming molten lead.

He lingered over the dead body only a moment. All of his senses were keenly alert. He stepped to one side of the nearest window and opened it a crack to see if anyone

had heard the shot. It was the same window he had opened
earlier. Once again he breathed in the smell of fresh mint. He
wondered how the smell could be so powerful with all of this
rain, this endless, merciless rain. He wondered if he had ever
felt so alive, but he could not remember a time. He scanned
up and down the street but saw nothing. Then a car turned
the corner, moving past the row of darkened tenements, its
headlights glowing with underwater brilliance, and stopped
roughly parallel to the dead streetlamp. Luis thought the car
resembled a 1937 Packard and laughed, a slight, incredulous
laugh, but he could not be sure. The car seemed to generate a
small bubble of light with just its presence, but it was a hazy,
diffuse light which made it virtually impossible to determine
the car's precise make and model. All one could do was guess.

The car's engine hummed for a while but nobody got
out. Then it flicked its headlights twice and the two shadowy
outlines from before emerged from the absolute darkness of a
hidden doorway. Someone rolled down a window and the two
shadowy heads leaned into the car. One of the shadowy heads
kept popping back up. The head seemed to be looking straight
at Luis every time, as if he (it?) needed to make sure that Luis
was still there. Then the head would pop back down.

Most men would have been desperate to escape. They
would have grown weary of peering into the darkness, trying
to eavesdrop on a conversation that never took place because
these people did not exist. The streaming rain would have
taken on the quality of prison bars. Panic would have ensued.
Fatal mistakes would have been committed. But Luis was
not given over to such mundane emotions. He stood at the
window a while longer, watching, waiting. The one shadowy
outline popped up again and again, almost with the regularity
of a clock. Then Luis noticed a steady parade of shadowy
figures emerging from other hidden doorways, all of them
drawn to the 1937 Packard idling in the middle of the rain-
drenched street.

Then the other shadowy figure, the one who had been
leaning his head inside the car window the whole time,
popped up and glanced at the encroaching shadows. It might
have been a glance of warning. But more likely it was a glance
which meant: 'hold on, be patient, there's nothing anyone can

do in a rain like this, back to your doorways, we'll take care
of things in the morning, he isn't going anywhere.' Given the
intensity of the rain it was only natural that the message was
slightly garbled. Some of the ones who were nearer the car
tapped their ears as if to clear away the static of the universe
and then they understood and returned to their hiding places.
But those who were further away tapped their ears inconclusively and shook their heads, as if to say whatever listening
devices that had been implanted near their cochleas were not
working (presumably these were strange, futuristic devices
that had been implanted by an aging French physician,
originally from the town of Villefranche-sur-Saône, who had
had his license revoked years earlier for undisclosed crimes
and so was now living on the outskirts of Algiers, where he
would perform any operation you wanted for a small sum, no
questions asked).

    The other shadowy figure, who seemed to be more or
less in charge of everything on the street, began making a
series of bizarre, convoluted gestures with his hands, a sort
of impromptu sign language spurred on by the necessity of
instructing those with the possibly defective implants to try
a different frequency. One by one those furthest away began
turning the dials of electro-magnetic frequency modulators
hidden away in semi-secret, interior pockets in the lining of
their jackets. One by one they found the correct frequency
and then they understood what was expected of them. One
by one they tapped their ears or gave the thumbs up sign and
retreated into the shadows. All in all, Luis counted two dozen
pairs of shadowy figures taking refuge in dark doorways
along the street and in narrow crevices that had sprouted up
between various buildings over time. This was not counting
the two original shadowy figures or the mysterious occupants
of the car, who remained hidden from view.

    Luis was always a fascinating enigma. He never did
what others would do. Satisfied that he was in no danger
until the morning, he retreated from the window. But danger
of a sort still lurked within the dark cavities of this luxury
apartment on the top floor of this unnamed art deco tenement
hidden away in the crumbling eternal poverty of Old Havana,

somewhere close to the harbor, on a small mostly deserted side-street that did not exist on any map and had never existed as far as the city fathers were concerned.

Quite all of a sudden, Luis noticed a steady, shallow rustling-slash-clicking sound, as if some animal were trapped inside the walls. He crawled back onto the bed, and for the first time he noticed a rounded aperture directly above the headboard. The aperture contained a rounded lens like a glass bauble which resembled upon first glance a recessed light of some sort. But it was not a light. Luis put his eye to the lens and the rustling-slash-clicking sound stopped. The dark, gleaming curvature of the lens made it impossible to see what lay behind it. All Luis could see was a circle of glassy darkness and in the center of the circle there was a faint, opaque glow, like a supernova from a galaxy a billion light years away, and then the galaxy became a giant, expanding eyeball that pushed itself to the edges of the glass, swallowing all light, and then the giant eyeball disappeared and there was a sudden explosion of light from the lens, a blinding flash that sent Luis reeling backwards onto the mattress, momentarily blind but otherwise unharmed, and though he wasn't certain what had happened, he still had the presence of mind to roll off the bed, landing on his feet, his gun ready.

Even as Luis rolled off the bed, the strange sound started up again, only it was louder, and it had become more of a sliding-slash-banging-slash-thudding sound now, as if the weasel or hedgehog or whatever it was trapped within the walls had given up all pretense of hiding and was now, in a fit of madness, making a break for it. Luis followed this new sound out of the bedroom and down a long hallway that opened up into a rounded foyer with additional hallways jutting off in all directions.

Without warning, a narrow mahogany door that Luis had not noticed before burst open. It seemed like a door to a coat closet, or maybe to one of those secret wine rooms you always hear about, or maybe to a set of stairs that led to the roof. A wiry, bluish shadow rushed out into the foyer. That was pretty much all Luis could see, for his eyesight had not yet returned to normal. But he could see well enough to coldcock whatever it was, which he did using his pistol. The wiry, bluish shadow tumbled to the floor without resistance and did not move.

Luis pulled up a chair and sat down, one eye on the unmoving shape at his feet, the other on the open door, just in case there were any more surprises. He started humming a few bars of one of the jazz songs from before to amuse himself. It was a popular tune, but he couldn't quite remember the rest so he gave up.

He stared at the darkly gleaming passage beyond the open door for a while, how long he could not say. It seemed to him a passageway to an unimaginable dimension, or alternately, the long-forgotten entrance to the tombs of the Hetaerae, those concubines of ancient Greece who had once been riverbeds teeming with life.

-98-

An hour or so before dawn:

Everything in the room was the same, except Luis was dressed, immaculate as always, his Platt Guardsman suitcase on the floor next to the chair, and the wiry bluish shadow had become a middle-aged man wearing a pair of pleated dress pants with no belt, a pair of cheap rope sandals, and a wrinkled orange-colored sports shirt, a pastel orange like those painted sunsets you see decorating the stages of those nameless, cheesy cabarets along San Martin.

Luis recognized him as the man who had sold him the lemon-filled pastelito in the Plaza. He was the older brother of the dead girl in the bedroom. Yes, that made sense. It was obvious now that he had been posing as a vendor. He had dark, sullen eyes and dark, leathery skin from too much time in the Cuban sun and a matte of stringy blond hair streaked with gray. He wore some sort of medallion around his neck that gleamed a cold, dark blue, as if it were the underbelly of an alien spacecraft lifting off from the earth.

"It hurts, doesn't it," said Luis.

The man didn't respond. He was half-crouching on the polished mahogany floor, leaning forward on his knees as if immersed in prayerful mediation, rocking slowly side to side, not really chanting, it was more of a steady moaning sound, his hands cupping the back of his head, the pose of someone who has recently found God, laying bare the sins of a lifetime.

"That sharp, spine-shattering pain will go away in a little while," said Luis. "But you'll probably be sore for days."

The man rolled and sat back on his haunches and looked up at Luis with a well-worn expression of incredulity, shading his eyes with his hands as if he were suddenly sitting in a pool of bright searing sunshine instead of the blue dappled darkness where he found himself.

Luis started to chuckle.

He could hardly contain himself.

"Of course a blow like that sometimes affects the memory. I've known guys who couldn't remember a thing for weeks. I'm not saying that's what going on with you. In fact for your sake I sincerely hope that's not the case."

Luis was motioning with his gun while he talked. The casual, charming indifference with which he carried on seemed to magnify his sinister intentions. All the middle-aged brother could do was stare at the gun. Then Luis grew very serious and leaned forward slightly as if he had a great secret he wished to share.

"Do you believe in the law of seriality?" he said after a while.

The middle-aged brother said nothing. The look of incredulity on his face had been replaced with a look of pious despair that could just as easily have been mistaken for the unbidden fear that accompanies a sudden flash of debilitating and previously unknown pain.

"I have been reading a slim book by a forgotten intellectual named Paul Kammerer. He is German, like yourself, though he lived in Austria. The book is called *Das Gesetz der Serie*. My German is not so good, so it has been taking me a long time. But the book was published in 1919, the same year I was born, so I just had to read it, you understand. Besides, it is not without merit. Kammerer believed that there was no such thing as coincidences, that hidden beneath the surface of everyday occurrences there existed a pattern which could be deciphered. He would stand on a street corner taking note of

what people were carrying, and from these simple observations he said he could deduce the mechanics of the Universe.
Naturally I had to test out his theory. Why just the other day
I was taking note of how many pedestrians were carrying
umbrellas and how many were carrying walking sticks with
fancy brass ornamental heads and how many were wearing
Tyrolean hats. I was standing on a random street corner the
way Kammerer himself used to do, keeping a tally of every
umbrella and every walking stick and every hat I saw, and
there weren't any umbrellas, it was a very hot, sunny day, so
why would there be any umbrellas. And there weren't any
Tyrolean hats either. But there were seventeen men walking
around with fancy walking sticks with ornamental brass
heads. The next day I went back to the same street corner and
there were two dozen pedestrians wearing Tyrolean hats, what
you and I would naturally call fedoras. And there were two
dozen more carrying umbrellas, which was absurd because
that particular day was just as bright and sunny and hot as the
day before, yet two dozen people were scurrying about with
umbrellas. The walking sticks, of course, had vanished. There
were no walking sticks at all. There were men with umbrellas,
and men wearing hats, and some of the men wearing the hats
were also carrying umbrellas, which I found suspicious. And
that brings me to the present. Today I have been seeing men
in fedoras everywhere I have gone, but the walking sticks
they were carrying that first day and the umbrellas they
were carrying that second day have been transformed. They
have metamorphosed into long-barreled rifles. And tonight
it is raining and there is not a single umbrella to be seen
anywhere. Say what you will, but this all seems odd to me.
Doesn't it seem odd to you? Tonight it is raining. All hell has
broken lose, you could say. And everywhere you look, all over
Havana, no matter where you go in this wretched garden of
good and evil, there are men in fedoras with long-barreled
rifles scrambling about like rats in a maze. But no umbrellas.
No doubt all of this would seem to the untrained observer to
be the very definition of chaos. But to the trained scientific
eye, it is not chaos at all, it was all mapped out eons ago. That
is what Kammerer would have said. It is what he did say. All
history is the serial repetition of a singular event which gives

birth to a future version of itself, and this process is repeated again and again, endlessly, until the clocks break down. That is a fairly good paraphrase. So all of these men in their fedoras rushing about in a thunderstorm, why all of that is just the latest event in a long invisible thread of interconnected events that stretch back to those long-ago days when we still lived in caves."

". . . ."

"Yes," Luis said thoughtfully. "It is history with topical alterations repeating itself. Assuming you also believe in history. So maybe there is something to seriality after all.

". . . ."

"I like to think there is. But it is not a theory that appeals to everyone."

And then Luis stood up quickly, abruptly, as if he were late for a train, and motioned for the middle-aged brother to join him. The man was still groggy from before and begged for Luis to leave him alone, so Luis had to grab hold of him by an armpit with his free hand and help the poor sot to his feet. Then he shoved him into the glowing darkness beyond the open door. It was very dark in this tunnel in between the walls. There was a faint glow at the opposite end, but it was a long way away and didn't provide any illumination at all. They had only taken a step or two into the darkness when the middle-aged brother tripped over something and fell with a great clanging commotion to the floor. He became a dark shadow swimming in an even darker ocean of darkness.

Luis fumbled along the wall until he found a switch and flicked it on and a row of tiny yellow lights like tiny submarine portholes started to hum with electricity. The man was lying in the middle of a pile of gray metal canisters that had been knocked off a shelf, film canisters, evidently, for the long narrow room seemed to be a repository for all sorts of paraphernalia associated with the movie industry.

Luis helped the man to his feet.

From somewhere Luis could hear a strange, insistent clicking sound, but he could not pinpoint its location.

There was a row of shelving along one side of the room with dozens of additional film canisters stacked chaotically, carelessly strewn about the shelves, some bearing neatly printed labels, others without any identifying mark at all. Tucked away on the lowest shelf, obscured by the shadow of the shelves above, were a dozen mason jars containing various unknown liquids and gels and colored dyes, and a few larger containers made from dark brown glass, each with a label that had the image of a skull and crossbones and the name of a chemical compound (silver halide, Sulphur, Selenium, a name derived from Selene, the Greek word for the moon, because like the moon, Selenium radiates electricity in direct proportion to the amount of light that falls upon its surface, and trichloroethane, otherwise known as chloroform, which was often used to clean photographic negative plates and reels of film, but had other, darker uses as well).

Further down the tunnel there was a dazzling display of vintage movie cameras and other apparatus. A shelf of cast-offs from the silent days of Hollywood. A 1929 Kodak. A 1936 Revere. Dozens of movie projectors of all shapes and sizes. And a 1924 Moviola editing machine that had originally been purchased by the Douglas Fairbanks Studios for $125.

There were also various work tables and a few narrow benches and three dusty filing cabinets pushed together and a stone sink with two basins. The work tables and the benches were covered with a thin film of dust which was oily to the touch, possibly from the residue of various lubricants used to keep the cameras and projectors and other equipment in mint condition. There were also a few tools left on the tables, tiny pliers and screwdrivers, a pair of scissors, and several pairs of tongs. Swirling piles of discarded, exposed film and worn projector belts and oily rags were scattered here and there on the floor like abandoned nests.

The strange room seemed like the lair of a deviant nocturnal creature with exotic tastes and imperfect morals. At the far end, roughly parallel to the small aperture in the bedroom wall above the headboard, there was a small camera that rested on a rolling wooden platform that had been pulled away from the wall, but one could see quite clearly that the camera lens fit perfectly into the aperture. When the platform was pushed flush against the wall one could film the occu-pants of the bed without their being aware, as long as there was music playing and they had been drinking.

Across from the aperture there was a small table with a vintage movie projector clicking away mindlessly, the wheel turning without regret, projecting a silent movie onto the wall. It was like watching ghosts suspended in the hollow darkness of the abyss, Luis thought, surreal figures dancing with carefree, liquid abandon, their world disintegrating around the edges, a flickering, entertaining show of light and shadow collapsing inward upon itself, and then oblivion.

The movie projector was on the same circuit as the lights. The star of the film was the dead woman. The film seemed to be a collage of dozens of skillfully spliced together random encounters with various men, all of the encounters taking place in the bedroom on the other side of the wall. The woman was always wearing a flimsy, swirling silk robe that was designed, admittedly, so one need not guess what was underneath. It was also easy to tear off, after which the men were always trying to scramble on top of the woman, her nakedness a luminescent white light bulb in the blue-tinged darkness. She would welcome them with open legs at first, scattering the pillows about with subtle, theatrical expertise so they neatly framed her face for the camera. But somehow by the end of each scene she was always able to flip the men onto their backs, framing their faces with the pillows instead and laughing with self-indulgent, almost demonic joy, and then she would ride them till they disappeared within themselves, becoming puddles of wordless ecstasy, drifting off into an easy, dreamless sleep.

Naturally, there were a few obligatory shots of the men nibbling on the woman's pussy and her arms writhing about in the air like burning snakes. A few shots of the men taking her from behind and squeezing her breasts (about the size of small lemons or limes cut in half) while they pumped away furiously, their scrawny, hair-covered legs soon quivering with fatigue. And a few shots of the woman taking their greasy cocks into her mouth and the men closing their eyes, begging for more, until they creamed into her smiling face. All of these shots were clichés, of course, but it was precisely because they were clichés that they would arouse the prurient interest of countless disenfranchised voyeurs, recovering alcoholics, recovering drug addicts, defrocked priests, sodomized altar boys, raging, salivating pedophiles, crippled necrophiliacs, and other sexual deviants, all of them male, who lived in the marginalia of history.

Next to the table, presumably so one could enjoy the silent film, there was a glowing golden chair like an ancient throne with Egyptian figures cut into the panels on the sides and in the center. This center panel featured two seated individuals facing opposite directions, each holding an oblong scepter like Braun's original cathode ray tube, each with a crown of flowers growing out of his or her head. They were flanked on both sides by a long procession of smaller individuals, servants and other flatterers, wearing small wrinkled hats, or possibly they were wigs, and bearing gleaming trays filled with delectable things to eat or drink. There was a row of hieroglyphics above the two kings (or queens, or one of each), presumably describing the scene below. Above the hieroglyphics there flew a symbolic eagle. The eagle possessed a giant eye like a glowing lens that looked down upon everything else in the center panel (and beyond?) but which would have looked directly into the middle of the back of anyone sitting in the chair, somewhere about the fifth thoracic vertebrae of the spine, which is that part of the spine most prone to injury.

The chair was in fact a replica of a royal throne from the second millennium before the common era. The original had been discovered in 1905, almost by accident, by Theodore M. Davis, an American lawyer turned amateur archeologist who sponsored the excavation of thirty tombs in the Valley of the Kings from 1902 until 1915 and who was the most famous archaeologist in the world until Howard Carter discovered King Tut's tomb in 1922. The replica that Luis had stumbled upon in this mysterious art deco tenement on the edge of nowhere had been manufactured in Paris shortly after the existence of the original had been proclaimed to the world. This proclamation had set off a boom in chair making. Hundreds of replica chairs were manufactured from 1906 to 1908, for the Egyptian motif was quite popular at that time. Replicas of the golden throne became all the rage among the hot-to-trot set in Europe and elsewhere. The chairs became symbols of status. But by 1955, most of them had been lost or stolen or destroyed in suspicious fires. The presence of such a chair in Havana was an anomaly to say the least.

Luis told the middle-aged brother to take a seat and pointed at the replica chair with his gun.

The man obliged him without any fuss.

The last scene of the silent film made its way through the rotating sprockets and then vanished in the blazing glare of a white-hot flickering spotlight. The thin, celluloid filament continued to flap uselessly as the wheel turned. The white light would blaze until either someone flicked off the switch or the bulb burned out.

"Do you smoke?" said Luis.

Luis was sitting a few feet away on a narrow bench pushed up against the wall opposite the shelves. He had set his gun on the bench so he could roll two cigarettes. The man looked at the gun but decided against making any sudden moves.

"Yes," said the man.

And then he gave Luis a strange look of warning.

"But not in here."

Luis nodded absently, measuring the tobacco, licking the papers and rolling them shut. He lit the cigarettes, tossing the burnt match to the floor.

"The chemicals," said the man.

"Yes, yes," said Luis.

He handed the man one of the cigarettes.

"But what does it really matter?"

They smoked their cigarettes for a while in silence, breathing in the nicotine without regret, but with a longing for better days.

"You have been making films for a long time?"

"Yes," said the man.

And then he paused as if he were struggling to breathe.

And then: "For ten years here in Havana. And for seventeen years before that in Germany. Stuttgart. Berlin. St. Moritz. Nuremberg. Lübeck."

"You worked for the Nazis?"

"Of course. Who didn't?"

Luis savored a long drag on his cigarette and blew smoke into the air.

"I see," he said.

The man began to squirm in the gleaming golden replica chair.

His breathing difficulties intensified.

"I worked on some very important films. I worked with Werner Klingler. I worked with Leni Riefenstahl. I worked with Reinhold Schünzel. And before the Nazis I worked with Fred Sauer."

"And who are you working with now?"

The man grew silent. Luis was waving his gun in the air once again as he spoke. The man had not seen Luis pick it up from the bench. A look of grim uncertainty spread across his features.

"I suppose it doesn't matter," said Luis. "You are working with the same men. You are working with different men. In the end, it is all about the work, isn't that what you believe?"

"Yes, yes, something like that."

"It is only your body of work that remains."

"Yes," said the man. "One can hope."

"And your filmmaking is quite good," said Luis. "What little I have seen of it."

The man began to eye Luis carefully but did not respond.

"Yes, you are quite good, aren't you."

". . . ."

"You and your sister. You are quite a pair!"

Slowly the man sitting in the gleaming golden chair had begun to look less like a man and more like a sceptered corpse, all the blood draining from his face, rushing to his toes. The tremendous weight in his blood-laden toes held him in place.

"It is not quite as you think," he said.

"No? What do I think?"

"She was not supposed to shoot you. I do not know why she took out your gun."

". . . ."

"Perhaps it was because of all the money. We did not expect so much money."

". . . ."

"It was a stupid thing to do. She was only supposed to detain you. Keep you interested."

"And you? What was your role?"

"To. . . to . . . in case she failed."

"I see."

Luis took out his perfumed handkerchief. The claustrophobic smell of this tomb in between the walls was washed clean with the invigorating cent of citrus mixed with mint. Luis handed the man his handkerchief and the man nodded and dabbed his forehead, which had begun to perspire heavily. Then he handed it back.

"Thank you," the man said. "One does not normally expect to receive such kindness under circumstances like these."

Luis repocketed his handkerchief. The scent of citrus vanished while the scent of mint still lingered.

"Yes, you were both quite good," said Luis after a while.

Luis smiled a strangely tender smile.

"And yet the general public has never heard of you, have they."

". . . ."

"Not here. Not in Germany. But then that's the point, isn't it. You make films that do not exist. You make films that no one is supposed to see."

". . . ."

"No one except those poor sots caught by the camera. What did your sister call them? 'Boorish louts,' that was the phrase she used."

". . . ."

"And you have been making these films for ten years? You must have been an extremely valuable asset."

". . . ."

"Did you ever have any trouble?"

Luis took one last long drag on his cigarette and sent the stub spinning through the air.

It landed in one of the sink basins.

Then he stood up with a renewed sense of purpose, as if he had suddenly realized that all of his doubts were a smokescreen.

"I mean did anyone ever refuse to pay?"

His gun gleamed in the flickering darkness.

"Did anyone ever refuse to give up the goods?"

"Yes . . . well . . ."

The man wasn't sure what to say or what to do. His mind was full of the terror that comes from unanswered questions. He looked past Luis to the shimmering, bluish light of the open door so very far away. Perhaps he was hoping that someone, anyone, his dead sister, or the men with the long-barreled rifles waiting outside in the rain, or even God himself, would materialize out of thin air to help him out of his predicament. But there was no one there.

"One time, yes, of course," said the man. "There are always one or two rotten apples."

Luis took a single step towards the man and stopped. He was smiling with the same charming indifference as always, waiting for the man to finish.

The man looked Luis squarely in the eyes and continued speaking, though his voice seemed now slightly agitated, his breathing a little bit faster, the veins in his neck beginning to throb uncontrollably, which probably indicated a condition of some kind.

"Please! Please! It was back when we first started," he said. "It was during our first year. I had no interest in which clubs Elisa went to. That was up to her. My interest was later, but it varied, as with anything. And then one night she came home with a very big fish. She came home with Manuel Fernandez Supervielle, the Mayor of Havana, and I was very much interested. He did not look much like a mayor when he removed his white jacket and his white Panama hat and his alligator shoes. He looked like any other flabby, blubbering fuck you might see on any street corner. But I made him look good with my camera. When I was finished editing that piece of film he looked like don Juan himself. Yes? It was hard to believe. I could hardly believe it myself. So we watched the film together. Don Juan was fucking my sister. We were sitting right here watching those images dancing on the wall and it was don Juan we were watching, not the Mayor of Havana. It was a triumph. But Supervielle did not appreciate my artistry. He said he would not pay for a romp in the sack with a two-bit German whore. Love is a peculiar thing, I said to him.

Love is a burning acid that scars your throat. What audacity,
he said to me. Excuse me please, I said to him. And then he
said he would not pay. He would not do it. Who the fuck
did we think we were? This is what he was saying. He would
have us both deported. He said he knew Ramón Grau. With
just one phone call he would have us sent back to Germany.
Yes, yes!! And if we made any fuss we could go back in a
box. Or maybe he would ring up the secret police. What did
he mean by that? I was not afraid. I told him that I had had
run-ins with the secret police before. Back in Germany. *Die
Geheime Staatspolize*. Hah! But he appeared not to hear me.
He said they would take us away in the middle of the night,
and we would never be heard from again. Rubbish! Rubbish!
Everyone knew the secret police were corrupt, like anywhere,
but especially in Havana. We would simply have paid them
off and they would have been satisfied. Ah, yes, yes, we
all know it is the way of the world. *Ungesellige Geselligkeit!*
Everywhere this is how it is. Naturally, I followed him home
that very morning and shot him point blank in the chest. I
emptied the gun. Seven shots point blank. The next day the
papers said he had shot himself in the chest because he was
unable to make good on a campaign promise. They did not
bother to say how many times he had shot himself. They just
said it was suicide. How could they think that? Besides, who
would kill themselves over such a small thing? And who puts
a gun to their chest to commit suicide? No one does this. And
why not? Because it is too sloppy. And because there is no
guarantee that you will succeed in killing yourself that way.
Maybe the bullet goes clean through. Maybe it misses the
heart, the lungs. Maybe all the vital organs are left unharmed.
Maybe it is a magic bullet. Who can say? A miss is as good
as a mile, as the Americans say. Hah! All I know is that those
who are seeking calm passage across many a bad night want
the certainty of a single clean shot. Is not life a lingering fever?
Is this not the experience of everyone? Is not . . . is not . . . ?
What is the phrase? *Der tod ist der seligste traum.* Yes, that is
it. But who does not know this? No, no, those who choose to
commit suicide with a revolver almost always put the barrel
of the gun into their own mouths. Or up against their temples.
Then there is no doubt. Death is inevitable. It is just a matter

of squeezing the trigger. A reflex. An instinct. All the learning in the world cannot replace instinct, that's what we were told. Are you not prepared for victory at any cost? *Totaler Krieg! Kürzester Krieg!* Now folk rise up and storm break loose! *Achtung! Aufgepasst!* Who were we to say any different? (Silence. A sigh. A sad, forlorn smile.) Yes, it was all a great joke, was it not? (A short pause.) But truly, it is not hard to pull a trigger when you want to taste a bullet. And then lights out, as they say in the movies. But this was not the case with Supervielle. But this did not matter. The papers said it was a suicide. And why would you not believe what you read in the papers? Supervielle, they said, had shot himself in the chest, a fatal wound. They did not say how many times he was shot. They did not say how long he took to die. And that was that. There was no investigation. No one seemed to care. Which was okay by us anyway. We couldn't have planned it any better. That was the only time we ever had any trouble."

The two men were still looking directly at each other, each with an unflinching gaze, but each gaze suggested different things. In the background you could hear the faint mechanical whirring of the projector and the steady hum of electricity, and beneath that, as if it were an echo of an echo, you could hear the hypnotic lull of falling rain.

"What is your name?" said Luis.

The man blinked but did not reply.

"My name is Luis," said Luis.

Again silence. And then: "My name is Georg."

Luis glanced down at his pistol, checked it to make sure it was loaded, and then he held his hands ready. The gun was beautiful to behold, as is the case with many instruments for evil. Especially those which are sometimes used for a greater good.

"You will make it quick?" said the man.

Luis smiled.

"I will make it quick."

The man gave Luis a long hard look. It was almost like he was whistling in disbelief, the way people do when something unexpected happens and they don't know how to react. But there was no sound.

"You know it will make no difference."

"I know."

"You can't evade them forever."

"Yes, of course."

"They know what you are thinking before you even think it. They will get you in the end, you can be sure of that."

"Yes. Perhaps you are right."

Luis smiled a dazzling, mischievous, boyish smile that was as bright as any sun that ever shone above the shores of any paradise.

"But you will never know one way or the other."

He raised his arm in a motion so fluid and effortless that it seemed like a current of air and pulled the trigger. There was a flash and his smile faded and the brightness that had lit up the room a moment earlier faded and a bullet hole appeared in the man's forehead, dead center, the hole filling with blood, the blood swirling around, steadily expanding beyond the boundaries of the hole, a strangely dark burgundy flower unfurling, like a rare Brazilian orchid, perhaps, or a genetically altered rose. The man dropped without batting an eye.

Luis did not even bother to look down. He fairly zoomed past the row of tiny yellow lights like tiny submarine port holes that illuminated the tunnel, however poorly, and then he was back in the foyer. His gun was already back in its holster. He seemed indifferent to the virtual certainty that the men waiting for him outside in the rain might have heard this second shot. He knew they would wait until just after sunrise before moving in, whether it was raining or not. So he would have a thirty-minute jump on them, or close enough, which would give him just enough time.

He picked up his Platt Guardsman suitcase and gave one last look around the foyer and the several hallways jutting off like spokes into the gleaming obscurity of multiple universes. 'What a shame,' he thought. 'They had a pretty good setup here.' Then he slipped out through the front door into a pool of blue dappled darkness and vanished like starlight falling.

Nerea was sitting in the back seat of the 1937 Packard which Luis used to drive, and which she had appropriated no questions asked at the beginning of their separation on that night so very long ago when Luis had said her costume was a little too tight. The engine hummed with rhythmic infallibility. It was not yet raining, but there was rain on the horizon. The car was moving slowly through the narrow, winding streets of Regla. At times it would stop for a while, as if sniffing at the air, and then it would suddenly roar down the street, a strange, lumbering tracking animal that had once again caught the scent. The dozens of Black Madonnas perched in hidden recesses and on balcony ledges above the streets seemed to be watching the predatory vehicle with vengeful eyes.

After a while it seemed like the Packard was lost.

It drifted down the same streets several times.

It drifted through the indifferent shadow of a chemical plant and the green haze all around, but there was no obvious reason to stop so the car kept moving. Twice it drifted right past the narrow side street where Luis was asleep in the De Soto, but the darkening green haze that surrounded the De Soto was all but impenetrable.

Nerea was wedged in between Immanuel, who was fidgeting with the safety on his Kongsberg Colt pistol, and Julio Mella, who had returned from the dead just this once because Nerea loved him desperately and because she was desperately in need of his assistance (practical advice? psychic protection? his revolutionary charisma? his vigorous lyricism? his visionary spirit?). It was this double dose of desperation that had called him back. Julio had always been a sucker for a desperate woman who was desperately in love with him. And always these women were extraordinarily beautiful.

Of course Immanuel could not see Julio. All he could see was an empty space on the right side of the Packard and Nerea making strange gestures and cooing sounds and moving her lips as if she were involved in an intimate conversation. At one point Immanuel tried to get Nerea's attention, he had something to say, or perhaps a question that needed to be answered immediately, but Nerea didn't even look his way. She simply shifted her shoulders and her hips, as if to block out any further intrusion, and continued chatting with her invisible companion. Immanuel hardly had any room for his elbows. His growing sense of frustration with Nerea and the natural hostility that accompanies such feelings was only kept in check by Nerea's incredible, intoxicating beauty, and the hope of a little intimacy all his own a little later on.

The conversation between Nerea and Julio Mella while they were driving around Regla:

'Yes, of course my dearest Nerea. I have been in love before.'

'. . . .'

'We took turns cooking. How I loved her delicious pasta. We were like two sweethearts.'

'. . . .'

'No. I don't remember the details. It has been a long time. And I have not been paying all that much attention to the world as it has become.'

'. . . .'

'I remember one evening she invited some friends over . . . no, not friends . . . well, friends also, but it was a Party meeting. She was rushing around, all excited, and I said to her "Tina, my love, I will arrange for dinner," and I did, and she was so pleased.'

'. . . .'

'She went to pick up something or other and when she got back the dinner was all laid out. Flowers on the table. Fruit in a bowl. Something like that. Like a painting.'

'. . . .'

'I remember taking care of dinner like that on numerous occasions. Or perhaps it was only a few times. And each time I left her a little note that said how much I loved her.'

'. . . .'

'Ah, do not be jealous, my dearest Nerea. *Mas que nada.* Remember, that was all before I met you.'

'. . . .'

'I know you have been hurt. I know you have been crying out. That is why I am here. Because of your tears.'

'. . . .'

'Yes, but you will have to trust me.'

'. . . .'

'Good, good. Now the first thing to keep in mind is that
you are in extreme danger. Yes. These men, this Immanuel,
they are not fooling around. I have seen this type before. They
are desperate men. Very desperate. They are jackals in thin
disguise. They will stop at nothing. You must believe me.'

'. . . .'

'Yes. Once they were idealists. They were desperate in
their idealism. But then they forgot themselves. Now all that is
left is their desperation.'

'. . . .'

'Yes, Nerea, you are beautiful, but that will not be
enough. You must hone the edge of your beauty until it is
razor sharp. They must always be afraid that you will cut their
throats without a second backwards glance. They will kill you
without hesitation the moment they think otherwise.'

The 1937 Packard slowed and then stopped. The sun had
set and there was only a faint reddish glimmer in the gaps
between buildings. Where the streets dipped down towards
the harbor you could see the dark, frothy water bubbling up
beneath the fading light. But it was very dark inside the car,
and Nerea lost sight of Julio in the darkness and began to
panic, but his reassuring voice was still hovering somewhere
nearby. 'Stay strong, my love' the voice said. 'I am right here.
I have not gone anywhere. Remember: keep the edge of your
beauty razor sharp.'

Nerea's panic dissolved. Her once gushing heart once
again hardened, became a bulwark against excessive emotion.
Julio's calm voice of honeyed death was replaced by the
stringent, Germanic urgency of Immanuel's desperate need to
shoot someone.

"We are here Nerea. They must be still inside. We have
had men watching this place for over an hour and no one has
left."

Immanuel stopped talking and put the fingertips of one
hand up to the side of his head, cocking his head slightly and
exerting a small pressure on his mastoid process, the posterior

portion of the temporal bone just behind the ear. He seemed
to be listening intently to some inner voice. Nerea peered
out through Immanuel's window. They had stopped in front
of a small café on the ground floor of a narrow, triangular
building at the corner of three streets. A young boy was sitting
up against a series of narrow wooden panels that served as
a temporary wall when the café was closed. He seemed to be
asleep, but when he saw the car he got up and disappeared
into the darkness of the streets and did not return.

The café had seemed deserted, except for the boy. But
from somewhere there was the laughter of voices and the
tinkling of glasses and more laughter. Nerea also noticed a
faint glow from one of the narrow windows near the back of
the café. There was also the dark shadow of a car parked in a
narrow slit of an alley that ran between the triangular building
and a row of tenements. The car was partially obscured by the
deepening shadows that existed between the two buildings.
There was only one car.

"Yes," said Nerea. "I am sure no one has left during the
past hour."

Immanuel began to get out but Nerea put her hand on
his shoulder.

"I will take care of this," she said. "I also have had men
watching this place. But my men are on the inside."

Immanuel started to protest, but Nerea quieted him with
a brief but gentle kiss. She grabbed hold of his pistol and slid
it back into his coat pocket.

"I will take care of this," she said again.

Nerea slipped out of the car.

Immanuel neither saw nor heard the door open or close.
He watched her shadow dance past the glare of the headlights
and then he lost sight of her in the shadows between the café
and the tenement and could only imagine her dark purpose.
The doubts he had harbored about her resolve gave way to a
shuddering fear for his own well-being. He knew Nerea was
certainly worth keeping. But he began to wonder if perhaps
she was also worth losing.

The evening air hummed with dark energy.

The side door leading from the café to the alley opened
and the hospital orderly employed by Federico emerged. He

seemed like a gleaming ghost in his white orderly uniform.
As Nerea approached, he lit a cigarette and took three long
drags and tossed the glowing stump to the ground. They
spoke in low murmurs and then Nerea went into the café. The
orderly closed the door and got into the front seat of the 1956
Chevrolet Bel Air four-door hardtop that had been parked in
the alley for most of the day.

It was very hot inside the car so he rolled down the
window. Then he settled himself into the seat and jiggled the
key until he found the sweet spot somewhere between the 'off'
and 'on' positions so he could listen to the radio. There was
a ballgame on. Every now and then there was the crack of a
bat and you could hear the crowd roaring with delight and
then the static charge of a lightning bolt somewhere else and
then the announcers cooing in amazement at what they had
just seen. After a while the orderly leaned his head back so
he was resting against the door frame, his left arm hanging
limply across the lip of the window, and closed his eyes. He
disappeared into the sounds of the ballgame. It was like being
in a different universe.

Inside the café it was another story.

The lighting was very poor, a single orangeish lamp
hanging over the center of the counter, a small table lantern
also glowing with a diffuse orange light in the center of the
table which had been Federico's home for the last several
hours. It was the kind of subterranean light that seemed to be
mostly darkness until your eyes got used to it.

Federico did not notice Nerea at first. He was slumped
to one side of his cane-back wheelchair with the ivory handles,
his eyes half-closed, humming softly to the sounds of dark
jazz emanating from two speakers perched on a shelf behind
the café counter. His face of a skeletal corpse was streaked
with orange light, a strange, otherworldly glow. The speakers
were invisible in the dim interior light.

Two young men wearing fedoras sat in the darkness
behind Federico. The light from the lamp and the lantern
did not reach where they were, so they seemed a part of the
surrounding darkness. They were sitting on tall stools pushed
up against the wall. Their long-barreled rifles were leaning

against the same wall but within easy reach. They were also
listening to the music, their bodies swaying slightly, as if
buffeted by a gentle breeze, their eyes also half-closed. It was
hard not to close your eyes listening to such music. A steady,
sensuous syncopated drum beat (bump, bi-ba-bi bump, bump,
bi-ba-bi bump, bump, bi-ba-bi bump, baaa baaa baa-bi bump),
sweeping strings, a tinkling bell sound falling away, a little
piano, a little vibraphone, and a mournful, hesitant trumpet
alternating with a mellow, hopeful saxophone.

Nerea stood for a moment looking at Federico. The two
men in fedoras realized Nerea was not the orderly and they
stiffened slightly, reflexively, but they did not open their
eyes. It was almost as if they were not quite prepared for
the moment at hand. Then they each took a deep breath and
opened their eyes. They saw Nerea in the flesh and nodded,
quick, staccato nods, as men will do when their nerves have
been rubbed raw from waiting, and exhaled slowly, steadily,
the balloon of the universe collapsing, all light and oxygen
disappearing through a tiny pinprick.

Federico felt the stiffening of the two young men and
opened his eyes and saw Nerea looking at him. They smiled
politely at each other, though in the dim light it was hard to
say how their smiles might be interpreted.

"He is not here," said Federico after a moment.

"I know that," said Nerea.

The dim orange light seemed to burn more brightly,
more intensely. Federico motioned for the two young men in
fedoras to come into the light, but they spread out along the
back wall like shadows on either side instead. Only their faces
caught the light, but only intermittently, and at odd angles.
Their faces resembled two theatre masks floating in the blackness that eventually envelopes everything. Federico realized
they were no longer his to command. It was one of those rare
moments that become etched in the memories of everyone
who takes part.

The jazz flowing from the speakers shifted gears, became
less sensual and more refined, elegant, noncommittal, a couple
of guitars flowing up and down the octaves, a harp plucking,
a light snare drum rapping away, hidden beneath the artistry
of the guitars.

Federico pulled out his knife while they listened to the jazz. He offered the knife to the all-consuming darkness, the lamp light and the orange lantern light glinting off the diamond cross-sections of the blade, as if he were offering one of God's fallen angels back to God. Then he laid the knife on the table with sudden assurance and sat back in his cane-back wheel chair, turning to the young man nearest the café counter, a calculated turning. "Arnaldo, would you kindly see to our hostess for this evening?"

Arnaldo shook his head as if emerging from a trance. He had been staring at the terrible beauty of the knife and had forgotten where he was.

"Signore?" he said.

"Yes, Arnaldo, the proprietress of this fine establishment, my friend Jaqueline. I did not realize we were still friends until today. It has been a very long time. One should never be so presumptuous when it comes to friendship."

And then: "Please see to her."

Arnaldo looked over at Nerea to see what he should do. Nerea gave a slight nod of her head, almost imperceptible. She was captivated by the old man's insistence, his romanticized sense of order, his perverse gallantry.

"And please be swift, Arnaldo. Do not let her linger."

Federico raised a glass to Nerea and drank the last of it.

Arnaldo vanished in the gloomy obscurity behind the café counter. A narrow doorway that led to a series of smaller rooms, perhaps, or to a set of stairs that led to a second-floor apartment, where a heavy-set woman with thick, bushy hair and elephantine legs was changing into a lace négligée, a gift from long ago, the woman singing softly to herself while she changed, her eyes glowing with the disturbing (prophetic?) brilliance of Quevedo's blood-stained moon.

"It is a shame that our friend Luis was not here to share one last drink."

Nerea did not say a word. She remained standing, almost invisible in the orangeish gloom, two cat's eyes glowing in the dark.

They heard a single shot from somewhere above them and then the gentle thud of a woman in a lace négligée now free of memory. No one flinched.

It was as if no one had even fired a rifle.

Arnaldo returned.

The two young men slid around the table and joined Nerea standing in the darkness. A pair of gleaming cat's eyes flanked by two golden glowing theatre masks.

"The waves are glowing like lava," said Federico. "But not for you. You do not need to be afraid, not yet."

"Afraid?"

"We all must face our fears sooner or later."

Federico smiled a jubilant smile that left the others wondering. Then the two young men raised their rifles and fired. They did not miss.

-100-

Oscar did just as Luis had suggested and spent his last night in Havana soaking up the nightlife on La Rampa. He got roaring drunk, for how else did you say goodbye to Cuba. By midnight he could not tell one nightclub from another. By two in the morning he was suspended in the semi-lucid state of an eternal dream. He imagined that he was trapped between two panes of glass, a specimen beneath the indifferent eye of a polarized light microscope. Sometimes his dream flowed in one direction, sometimes in another, as if someone had simply flipped the two panes of glass for a look at the other side. Or perhaps the eye of the microscope was rotating. Oscar had no control over which direction his dream was taking, but his constantly changing perspective gave him a new appreciation for the subversive nature of reality.

The beginning of this dream seemed strange indeed. He felt like his life was repeating itself, but he could not be sure. He was looking out on the world with an atrociously puffed eye, a bruised face. He could not tell precisely where he was. He had fallen down somewhere among some tables and men in tuxedos were rushing about and there was a line of dancing girls hovering in the spaces between the lights. The girls were wearing ruffled headpieces. They seemed genuinely concerned for his well-being. He was trying to speak to them but every-thing was upside down. The girls resembled weirdly beautiful plumed birds with painted beaks and exposed somewhat vulnerable breasts. Their feathers barely covered their naked hips. They were flapping their wings, jiggling their hips so you could glimpse their plush, juicy curves, their bodies circling this way and that in the smoke-filled gloom, calling out to each other in their strange, throaty bird language. It was quite erotic. Or perhaps he had tripped on the steps going into this last nightclub on his last night in Havana. Or going out. Some of the nightclubs on La Rampa were treacherous indeed with their crumbling steps of bygone elegance. Or perhaps someone had tripped him on purpose, just for a laugh. The circle of whirling birds disappeared. The circle was replaced by the hyena teeth of a doorman laughing. The teeth were very close to Oscar's face. He wasn't sure if the doorman was trying to communicate some words of wisdom or making a derogatory comment at Oscar's expense. The doorman had recently been drinking Danziger Goldwasser, a bittersweet liqueur containing tiny gold flakes and a heady aroma of juniper, cinnamon, licorice, and a hint of menthol. Oscar was immobilized by the man's breath. He wondered how long the doorman had been drinking, that's how strong his breath was. It was almost like chloroform.

Then Oscar's taxi driver rushed into the nightclub, grabbing him by the armpits, helping him to his feet. The plumed birds returned, but they were now shrieking. The laughing hyena face of the doorman becoming a pack of rabid hyenas. Teeth flashing in the semi-darkness. Snapping at the air. The terrifying sensation of being dependent upon someone else. Perhaps he should go to a hospital. No, no, no hospitals. No doctors. It's just a case of nerves. A little too much to drink. He slipped and fell and hit his eye on the corner of a table. Clumsy, stupid, drunken fool! The hyenas chasing them down the steps of bygone elegance but the taxi cab waiting, the engine humming. The hyenas vanishing, dematerializing as easily as they had materialized. Out of thin air back into thin air. But still we better get the hell out of here. You never know who might be watching. Tires screeching and then a series of hairpin turns. He could feel the blood oozing down

his face. No. No longer oozing. The blood had dried. A mask
of blood concealing his confusion. He could not see because
of his eye. Except he could see a little bit. A sliver of light
and shadow penetrating the dark veil. The taxi turned down
a side street. Row after row of tenements flashed by. Slices of
time. Thin sections to place on a microscope slide. The liquid
gold of streetlamps. Men hiding in the darkness of doorways.
Stepping out briefly only to retreat after a few seconds, a crazy
dance. Or perhaps that was later. Or perhaps he had imagined
everything. Bruised ego as much as a bruised face. Then the
sound of the sea and the streetlamps vanished. The taxi shuddered to a stop and a door opened and the taxi started moving
again. 'He isn't hurt that bad,' said a voice. 'But bad enough.'
It was a gruff, raspy masculine voice. It sounded vaguely like
the voice of a cancer-stricken parrot. He recognized the voice
but could not place how. Perhaps it was just from earlier in
the evening. Then he heard a woman's voice and he forgot the
first voice even existed. He had never heard the voice of this
woman before, but it was a soothing voice, a tranquil voice, a
cajoling presence absolving him of all worldly responsibility,
like a burial at sea. 'I'll do what I can,' the woman said. He
tried to focus on what he was supposed to be doing. He
suddenly remembered about the suitcase and wondered what
had become of it. He did not realize that he was clutching the
handle of the suitcase until the woman tried to loosen his grip.
'He won't let go,' she said. But that was all she said. There
were no other voices after that. The woman started dabbing
at his face, dabbing at the dried blood. He assumed it was a
woman. The same woman who owned the soothing, cajoling
voice. At any rate, it was a slender, gentle, penetrating hand.
A provocative hand. It reminded him of something else but he
could not remember. Something from when he was a boy in
Baracoa, perhaps. Or when he had first arrived in Havana. Or
something that had not yet happened but which had become a
part of his memories just the same. He felt like he was moving
back and forth through time. Then the taxi stopped again and
the woman rolled down the window and the smell of the sea
surged through the interior. The woman poured some powder
into a small flask and shook it. Then she brought the flask to
his lips and forced him to drink. It tasted like Brandy de Jerez.

He couldn't remember the last time he had tasted anything so
fine. He felt revived, but whether it was the smell of the sea or
the warmth of the brandy he did not know. His eye began to
feel better and he tried to sit up but slid back down.

-101-

Looking into a mirror hanging above a gaping black
hole:
Oscar is drifting in and out of consciousness. He is
clinging like a crab to the underbelly of a strangely glowing
yet invisible cloud that passes overhead, over the roof of the
taxi. It is a hardtop vehicle, but the roof has been peeled back.
He is west of the city floating east. He can see the bubble of
golden light that is the Cathedral. His eardrums are bursting
with the swirl of music from the Plaza and the strained voices
of people enjoying themselves and church bells chipping away
at the night and footsteps running in circles and clocks ticking
away like time bombs and rockets singing their siren songs,
the sounds winging their way back and forth across the landscape like a flock of panicky, deranged geese. He has become
impaled on the sounds from below. He has lost sight of his
actual body languishing in the taxi cab so many miles away.
He is certainly too far away to know if he is still breathing or
not, but he does not really care. The boundary between the
golden light of the celebration and the darkness beyond is
constantly shifting. He recognizes that he is undergoing some
sort of strange, virtually impossible metamorphosis, but he is
not afraid. What a spectacular view, he thinks. He absorbs the
view for a while. It has his complete attention until he notices
a strange clacking noise. The clacking noise is very close by.
He wonders if he should be alarmed, but then he realizes that
he is the source of the clacking noise. He is making the sound
with one of his claws. He is unable to determine which claw,
perhaps because he is new to his crab body and does not yet
know how to exert any control over it. Briefly he wonders
what his crab self is doing. Why is he making such an irritat-

ing sound? How long will the sound continue? Is it possible to
regulate unconscious, automatic bodily functions with conscious effort? Or is all this just an illusion anyway, an intellectual game? He wonders if there are others floating about like
himself, engaged in similarly puzzling behaviors, pondering
similar, unanswerable questions. 'Certainly there are others,'
he thinks to himself. 'I see them every time I close my eyes.'
But this statement of a pure and simple faith is not a convincing argument. His nerves are tingling. Weird burning sensa-
tions are creeping along, neuron to neuron, a webbed pathway
stretching to infinity. Smoke is rising from the surface of his
body. Short bursts of intense pain. Splinters of light. The pain
is coming from the interlocking segments of his exoskeleton.
He can feel the blood rushing to his crab head and then down
to his crab legs and then back up to his crab head. A sense of
vertigo. He is spinning like a disc. He seems to be suspended
in space and rushing through space at the same time, a crab
on the end of a skewer, but he does not understand how this
is possible. Then he gives up trying to understand. Once again
he is enamored of the view. He is very high up now. His crab
self dissolves and he is absorbed into the sky. He becomes the
sky looking down, the sky listening, the sky remembering. All
human experience is written on the glistening membrane of
his memory. He is now the dark sky over Regla. He is hovering just above a small café on the ground floor of a building
where three streets come together. He is changing again, a
changeling, collapsing inward upon himself, drawing himself
together, then descending slowly, uncertainly, like an alien
spacecraft on its first interstellar voyage. The doorway to a
parallel universe opens and then closes. The flash of a blue
underbelly. Or white. Or something metallic. There is a man
dressed in white sitting in the front seat of a 1956 Chevrolet
Bel Air four-door hardtop. The Chevrolet is parked in the alley
that separates the café from a tenement building. The man is
listening to a baseball game on the radio. The man is leaning
back against the doorframe on the driver's side, staring
vacantly at the radio dial. 'I have seen this man before,' Oscar
thinks, but he cannot pinpoint when and where. He tries to
get the man's attention, banging on the car door, shouting
through the open window into the man's ear, jiggling the door

handle with visible agitation, but the man does not respond.
Oscar suddenly realizes that he is invisible. He exists in
another dimension. The rest of humanity is insensible (as in
unaware of, existing in a comatose state) to his presence. This
is why the man does not respond. He realizes that the world is
a holographic image, a movie projected onto the screen of
history. He tries to wrap his mind around the implications of
this thought, but implications are slippery things. He is not up
to the task. The implications are slipping in and out of the
shadows, the starlight, the moonlight, the diffuse orange glow
emanating from the windows of the café, the shimmering fish
scale light reflected off the distant sea, the afterglow of a
supernova a billion light years away, and then one last gulp of
oxygen and they (these oh so slippery implications) are gone
forever, descending to depths where we cannot follow, depths
which we do not even truly believe exist. The announcers
announcing the game are very excited. Oscar is in the process
of forgetting himself. He is standing just outside the car,
listening to the game. It has been a long time since he has
listened to a ballgame, but the radio reception is marred by
staticky bursts of lightning bolts from somewhere else. It
sounds like it is a game from years ago. Every few minutes
there is a lightning bolt but the time between bursts is diminishing. The storm is getting closer. At least it is getting closer
to the radio station. Oscar forgets where he is. Then he hears a
single gunshot. The man in the car does not notice. Perhaps it
wasn't a gunshot. Perhaps it was just another staticky burst of
lightning. Then a few moments later he hears two more gunshots, the second one a hairsplitting echo of the first. The man
in the Chevrolet has heard them too. The man leans forward,
peers out of the passenger side window in the direction of the
gunshots, but with visible disappointment, as if he had
expected something with a little more punch to it, like the
spine-shattering power of a twenty-megaton nuclear explosion.
Of course everything is relative. The man acts as if the two
gunshots are anticlimactic. Then there is a tumultuous roar
from the radio and the man is transported to a universe all his
own. It sounds like someone has hit a homerun with the bases
loaded. It is a tremendous smash. A rocket. The man looks to
the radio in disbelief. The team with the homerun was not his

team. The man does not remember the last time a player on his team pounded the ball with such hellacious force. He wonders if any of the players on his team ever will. He is beginning to lose his faith in the future. Then the door to the café opens and three figures rush out into the alley and the man is sucked back into the universe of the gunshots. This is precisely as it should be. No one can escape where they are. The first figure to emerge from the café is a long-legged woman with the headpiece of a shining golden sun like a halo upon her head and thick curly black hair flowing to either side and a single blood-red gardenia pinned above her right ear. She resembles an exquisitely carved voodoo statue of the goddess Atabey, but perhaps she is the sinister alter ego of Atabey because her face is contorted, twisted in a grimace of vengeance, impending death, not glowing with the promise of new life. She is not at all like Oscar has always imagined her to be. She rushes out into the alley and heads around the front of the Chevrolet. She is followed by two men with long-barreled rifles. The first man follows closely behind this darkly gleaming apparition of Atabey. The second goes around the back of the car. The man inside the car opens the door and gets out. He is smiling a flattering, congratulatory smile. All the same, he looks less like a man in his gleaming white uniform of a hospital orderly than a ghost hovering between this world and the next. He waves at the woman, who stops directly in front of the car and stares at him with cold, blank, uncomprehending eyes. He does not see the second man who comes up behind him. He is puzzling over the woman's cold, blank eyes. He is baffled. He has never seen such eyes before and is not sure what to make of them. 'Cat's eyes,' he thinks, but precisely what it means to have cat's eyes he is unable to articulate to himself. He does not yet have an inkling of something more ominous. The second man raises his rifle and pulls the trigger. The head of the man dressed in white explodes in slow motion. It is a singular moment. A singularity. Without a center. Particles of brain and blood are spinning through the air, but their trajectory is unlike the normal trajectory of explosions. It is as if space itself has exploded. It is like the moment of creation, an infinite jest exposed. 'Just a few more loose ends' the woman says, and then she is

absorbed by a 1937 Packard that has been waiting in the
darkness at the mouth of the alley. The Packard speeds away.
The two men with long-barreled rifles get into the Chevrolet.
They have been given the night off. They listen to the end of
the ballgame, cracking jokes like brothers and arguing about
which is the better team before driving away.

-102-

From the replacement taxi driver's point of view:
This was the first time the replacement taxi driver had
driven for the fat stubby man. It was his fourth taxi company
in three years. His full name was Miguel Valentín Hidalgo
Lazaro Montes de Oca Fleitas y Pertierra, but he went by
Jabuco, a nickname that had been given to his grandfather.
Jabuco said he had enjoyed a remarkable ten-year baseball
career. He said he had played for the Petroleros de Cienfuegos
club from 1942-1945. This last part might have been true. He
said he had been an acrobatic outfielder known for his blazing
speed and for making leaping, twirling, game-saving circus
catches down the alley on the first-base line or in the center-
field gap near the fence. The fans would toss coins of varying
value onto the grass in appreciation. But the replacement taxi
driver also claimed to have been part of the Almendares club
team that won the Cuban League championship in the 1946-47
season, defeating Habana in a clean sweep. This was probably
not true, given the roster of that squad was very well known.
At other times, usually after one too many warm beers, he
changed his story completely. He said his name was Eusebio
Miguel González López and that he had played on Club Fé
in the years before the Great War with the likes of Cyclone
Joe Williams (who had come over from the Negro League),
Dolf Luque, Alejandro Oms, Valentín González (an outfielder
who later became a popular umpire at Almendares Park and
could be seen puffing away on a cigar and chatting with fans
behind home plate at the end of every game), Pelayo Chacón,
Torriente, Esteban Montalvo, Perico el Mono (who, as it
turned out, was a wiry, Old World monkey, just like his name

suggested, who wore a red costume and was employed for many years as the mascot for the Habana club and wasn't a ballplayer at all), and José de la Caridad Méndez, also known as the Black Diamond, arguably the greatest Cuban pitcher (right-handed) in the history of Cuba, to name just a few of the players the replacement taxi driver said he had rubbed shoulders with. In his darker moods, he said he was Antonio Susini and had once killed a teammate with a 1912 Spalding Gold Medal baseball bat. He did not say why. Jabuco was a harmless enough character for the most part, but one never knew if he was joking or not.

The fat stubby man had given Jabuco very precise instructions. He was going to fill in for a very important fare that evening. The two drivers that normally handled such fares had mysteriously disappeared. No, there was no cause for alarm, the fat stubby man had said. People disappeared in Havana all the time, only to reappear a few days later no worse for the wear. Jabuco's eyes had narrowed with understandable suspicion at that point. He knew the first part about Havana was true, but not the second part. He knew of many people who had disappeared and had never reappeared, except, on occasion, as barely recognizable corpses. Yes, it was certainly true that such disappearances did not happen as frequently as they had in the days of Machado. In those days the newspapers were filled with stories of people vanishing and then two or three days later their bodies would be found dumped by the side of a road or mangled and stuffed into trash cans or burned beyond belief from unexpected explosions and flash fires or floating face down in the Almendares River. And who really knew how many people Machado had shackled with weights and tossed into the sea? Once a couple of fishermen had pulled a gigantic shark out of the waters of the harbor and when they cut open its stomach they discovered the partially digested body of a University professor, José Marinello Menoyo, who had been missing for a week. There had been some debate at the time as to the true identity of the victim. An unnamed journalist had claimed it was the professor because the belly of the shark also contained a ring that Marinello had purchased while on a trip to Mexico City in 1929, a ring bearing a strange insignia: a tiny eye of Horis at

the center of a tiny triangle made up of three swords. The ring
had not been on the professor's dead hand when the fishermen discovered the body, but who can say what happens in
the confusion and terror that reigns inside a shark's stomach.
But no one came forward to say the ring did not belong to the
professor, and that had settled the matter.

Naturally the fat stubby man was not dismayed by
such stories. He had laughed at Jabuco's misgivings. Such
ominous fabrications are worse than old wives' tales, he had
said. Then he had become deadly serious. He told Jabuco he
was to pick up a young man in the 200 block of Calle Obispo.
At five in the evening he was to pull up to a magnificent pale
yellow building, a beautiful baroque structure like they have
in Barcelona, and wait for a young man with a suitcase. He
was to drive the young man to the various clubs on La Rampa
or elsewhere, but he was to steer clear of all the nonsense near
the Cathedral. What crazy instructions! Jabuco had started to
chuckle at that but the fat stubby man had cut him off with a
look. He was to see to the welfare of the young man. Under no
circumstances was he to pick up another fare or call a friend.
This young man was too important to fuck with. He was
connected. He worked for Giuseppe Federico DiCarla. Enough
said. More than enough. Jabuco would be well compensated
if everything went as planned. So he would stay with the
young man throughout the evening. Yes, a bodyguard of sorts.
Then at five in the morning he was to drive the young man
out to Playa de Marianao, a small, tucked-away parking lot
near the yacht club. 'I will meet you there,' the fat stubby man
had said. 'Make sure you are not followed. And do not let
anything happen to this young man. It is worth much more
than your life. It is worth my life. Do not be late.'

So Jabuco made sure he followed the fat stubby man's
directions to the letter, though at various times throughout
the evening he wondered just what he had gotten involved
in. The young man was wearing a very white, very bright
linen suit and a shabby Panama hat. The suit was outdated
and the hat had seen too many years as well, as if both items
had belonged to the young man's father. The replacement
taxi driver thought the young man looked ridiculous, but he
didn't say anything. He had taken the young man to half a

dozen clubs, but all they did was sit at tables in the shadows
and watch the dancing girls and drink beer and then maybe
a couple of mojitos, and always there was a young girl or an
older woman popping by, seeking them out, as if the young
man were a beacon in the obscurity of each dimly lit corner,
the women wanting to sit down and chat and drink and join
the party, or maybe take the young man to the dance floor for
a quick samba, but he always refused. He wanted to be alone.
He wouldn't leave the table. He clung to his suitcase while
he drank. It was idiotic the way he held on to the handle. The
women were all very good looking. They were all of them
worth a few minutes on the dance floor. They were all of
them worth much more than a few minutes. At the very least
the young man could have taken them one by one into the
back seat of the taxi. He could have fucked them until they
squealed. You could tell that they all wanted to be fucked by
the way they approached the table with their tits popping
out of their skimpy tops and their hips swiveling back and
forth in lazy gyrations as they talked and smiled and smoked
their cigarettes and blew smoke rings like soft kisses. But the
young man was not interested. He made love to his suitcase
instead. And the women slipped away in the dark, searching
for willing lovers at other tables. The replacement taxi driver
did not understand. It was like the young man was saving
himself for another the way they do in cheap romance novels
or Hollywood movies. But the young man was a good tipper.
Every time they got back into the taxi, the young man forked
over a crisp, cool Benjamin. 'For your trouble,' he would say,
and then he would toss off a curt nod, a thin-lipped smile, as
if he were in fact suffering the eternal gnawing despair of a
long-lost love, and they would climb into the taxi and head
off to the next joint. So the replacement taxi driver didn't say
anything critical.

It was after midnight that the scripted predictability of
their routine began to fall apart. The dancing girls no longer
seemed so friendly. The waiters seemed almost sinister. And
it seemed to the replacement taxi driver that everyone was
packing a gun. At one club, a glitzy pleasure palace on San
Rafael, they downed an entire bottle of tequila after one of the
dance numbers with the help of a skinny, red-haired dancer

with a grayish complexion and corrupt green eyes implanted
in an innocent-looking face. The red-head seemed to know the
young man, but he didn't seem to remember, and this infuriated the red-head. She started a row, shouting and screaming.
She tossed a drink in the young man's face, an overly theatrical gesture, and a few nearby customers started to complain
and you could hear the sounds of a few chairs being pushed
back. The manager came running, and also a few waiters. One
of the waiters grabbed the red-head from behind and held on
to her shoulders while the manager talked quietly with the
young man. The manager was dabbing at his forehead where
the perspiration was beading up. He and the young man were
standing to one side of the table, their faces illuminated every
now and then by the flashing, pulsating lights from the stage.
The one waiter seemed to be whispering words of love to the
red-head, trying to calm her down, soothe her irritated soul.
He was standing very close to her. She was wriggling, trying
to squirm herself free, or at least pretending to. Her green eyes
glowed with unadulterated pleasure. Then the young man
gave the manager two-hundred dollars and the manager, the
waiters, and the slightly squirming red-head vanished in the
pulsating, semi-darkness as quietly as they had appeared.

      Needless to say, all hell broke loose at the last club of
the night, Cabaret Conchita, a den of thieves if there ever
was one on Zapata, which was known for its risqué shows,
and which offered private rooms in the back for viewing
pornographic films. The replacement taxi driver had warned
the young man. The young man said he had been there
many times before. They stopped out front, the engine of the
taxi humming. They could see the purple neon lights of the
club flashing with mindless, mind-numbing gaiety. 'See you
inside,' the young man said, and then he got out of the taxi
and disappeared almost instantly beneath the hazy obscurity
of a long, tunnel-like awning, except for a pair of legs going
up a set of steps, and then the legs were gone and there was
the sound of a padded black door opening and then closing.
The replacement taxi driver parked the car up the street, about
half a block, but he did not get out right away. He sat there
a while, smoking a cigarette. It was only two in the morning.
Three hours to go. He sat in the car longer than he had

intended, staring blankly at the rearview mirror, dispassion-
ately, drunkenly, watching the shimmering, refracted images
of the patrons of Cabaret Conchita going in and out.

At some point later on, a series of yellow cabs pulled
up to the awning and a dozen or more costumed revelers
emerged. They hovered just beneath the awning for a minute
or two but seemed uncertain where they were or what they
should do. It was hard to tell what they were dressed like,
for they were all missing pieces from their costumes and
had filled in the various odd gaps with pieces from other
costumes, so they resembled the fragmentary unreality of
a world that had come unglued, the demons and demigods
and nightmare tropes of a troubled mind. Some of them wore
shining silver Conquistador helmets and capes made from
the plumage of rare, Caribbean birds. Some of them wore
the white cassocks of priests but carried swords dripping
with blood instead of golden crucifixes. Some wore masks
resembling diseased or deranged tropical animals (monkeys,
jaguars, alligators, iguanas with spiked jowls). There were
insects with the heads of cats and sphinxes with the wings of
beetles. There were skeletons wearing tuxedo jackets and black
ties, brightly colored tights and dancing shoes. There were
ghosts dressed as baseball players (or baseball players dressed
as ghosts). Some looked like Cuban tobacco farmers from
the waist up, complete with ragged straw hats and bushy,
broom-bristle moustaches, but they were goats or some other
cloven-hoofed creature from the waist down. Some possessed
pitchfork tails that were twitching uncontrollably. They were
all chatting away nervously.

Then a towering black brute emerged from the last taxi.
He was wearing a black tunic and white pantaloons decorated
with black roses. He wore black knee-stockings and black
shoes with glorious golden buckles and sported a black cane
with an ivory handle carved to resemble the head of a jackal.
He wore a white powdered wig from the 17th century. His
teeth were painted black.

The towering black brute greeted the demons and demigods hovering beneath the awning with a sweeping flourish
of his caneless hand followed by a great crackling laugh, and
then the group vanished through the padded black door as if

by magic. The replacement taxi driver thought he had seen fire coming out of the black behemoth's mouth as he laughed and smoke curling about his head, so he sat up abruptly, keenly alert, as if someone had shaved the scales from his eyeballs, and turned in his seat for a better look, but there was no one there. Even the several taxis that had deposited the demons and demigods at the door of Cabaret Conchita had mysteriously vanished. He decided he must have been dreaming.

It had begun raining, so he started the car and backed up to the awning and then raced inside.

At first he did not know where to go. Everything seemed closed. A bony misshapen dwarf of a man was rummaging around in the coat check closet. The dwarf had not yet found what he wanted and seemed on the verge of giving up when he noticed the replacement taxi driver.

"It is always by way of pain that one arrives at pleasure," he said.

The replacement taxi driver nodded in a vague, noncommittal way.

"If it's after hours you want you've come in through the wrong door," he said.

The dwarf disentangled himself from the lifeless arms of a few forgotten dinner jackets and overcoats and rain slickers and stepped away from the closet. The replacement taxi driver could see that the dwarf had also painted his teeth black. The dwarf smiled a grim, knowing, caricature of a smile. It was an ungodly smile.

"You're picking up?"

"Yes."

"Then you'll have to go this way."

The dwarf led the replacement taxi driver down a long narrow corridor that glowed with an eerie blue light. They passed by a dozen numbered doors. One could only guess what was going on behind the doors. Behind one they could hear the sounds of a man and a woman arguing and then a smack as if someone had been slapped, and then more arguing followed by more slapping sounds. Ah, yes, the brutality of love. Behind another there was the sound of heavy breathing. Behind another the incessant clacking sound of a movie projector projecting a third-rate movie. Behind another the tinkling of small bells (wedding bells, perhaps, or the bells of altar boys, or just a ringing in one's ears). Behind another the soothing tremors of jazz. Once again the replacement taxi driver heard the crackling laugh of the towering black brute and the nervous jabbering of the demons and demigods from his dream. Behind the remaining doors there was nothing except the unfaltering sibilant echo of God whispering to Himself. At the end of the corridor they came to a set of double doors.

The dwarf smiled his ungodly smile again. "Just head right through there," he said. "That's the only way in or out at this hour."

The scene inside Cabaret Conchita:

A wide-angle movie camera view of the nightclub stage and the tables staggered on two tiers so every customer has a good view of the dancers. A set of double doors up front, close to the stage, but also close to a narrow door with a porthole window that leads to the kitchen.

A young man is sitting awkwardly in the middle of the floor, his legs splayed out in front of him, absorbing the darkness. A table nearby is turned over on its side. There are a few pieces of broken glass on the floor, a candle still glowing, puddles of water or gin reflecting the stage lights. The young man's white linen suit is stained with the overindulgence of the evening, of many evenings. But strangely, his Panama hat once again seems immaculate. Perhaps this is simply a trick of the shadowy, subterranean light in the club. The young man is clutching a suitcase and pointing a small black-handled Beistegui Brothers Libia pistol with feverish intensity at the surprised knot of thieves and cutthroats and naked showgirls that have made Cabaret Conchita their midnight home.

No one moves for fear of the first bullet. After that, of course, they will tear the young man to shreds.

"Stay away," says the young man. "Stay away."

"Sure kid," says a beleaguered, garbled voice.

And then: "But you can't get all of us."

The thieves and cutthroats, who are all wearing black tuxedos instead of festival costumes, start a round of chuckling that races about the room like a brisk wind.

It is at this point that the replacement taxi driver bursts through the set of double doors, as if he has been sprinting downhill, a dramatic, improbable entrance. The doors bang open with a great booming sound. It almost sounds like a gunshot. The young man swings his arm wildly but relaxes when he sees who it is.

"I wondered where you were," he says.

The young man waves his gun at the crowd as if he were acknowledging old friends.

"We've been having a hell of a time."

The replacement taxi driver reaches the young man and pockets the black-handled Libia. The young man watches the gun until it vanishes, and then becomes suddenly silent, absorbed by the moment, a blank, untroubled look on his face.

"Sorry about my friend here," says the replacement taxi driver. "He didn't mean anything."

"Sure," says a voice from the darkness.

"Keep him on a leash the next time," says another voice.

The knot of thieves and cutthroats begins to untangle, disperse, but the bevy of naked showgirls is still hovering about the stage, looking on with thoughtful, concerned, compassionate expressions on what are normally vacant, stylized faces.

The replacement taxi driver tries to hoist the young man to his feet, gripping him beneath the armpits, but he didn't bargain for so much dead weight. The young man seems aware of his surroundings, but he is very drunk, a fact which seems to work against the replacement taxi driver's best efforts.

"Need some help?"

A man from the dispersing crowd steps near. He has a leering horse face, the face of an out-of-work doorman. He leans over for a closer look at the young man's bruised eye.

"That's going to be one hell of a shiner," he says. "Hell, it already is!"

There is a snapping sound like a lever being pulled and the stage lights go out, and very faintly, as if there is a radio on in another room, you can hear the crackling laughter of the black brute from the replacement taxi driver's dream. A few of the showgirls squeal, and then one by one they vanish into the darkness backstage. The only illumination in the room comes from the blue emergency lighting near the double doors. It is hard to say who is controlling this puppet show.

"What the hell happened?" says the replacement taxi driver.

"You got me. One minute your friend here is just like any other square Joe. He's ogling the girls and chatting them up between numbers and they're slapping his hand away but it's all in good fun. Then the last number is over and everyone heads for the door and Whamo! Your friend here crashes into that table. Plants his eye right on the corner."

". . . ."

"The next thing anybody knows he pulls out a gun and is waving it in the air. Naturally everyone freezes. You can't be too careful in a place like this."

". . . ."

"Pretty much everyone in this joint is packing some kind of pistol."

". . . ."

"I mean you knew someone was just about to plug the poor sap. You could feel it in the air. Like electricity or something."

". . . ."

"Like a goddamn bolt of lightning!"

". . . ."

"That's when you waltzed in through those double doors. A regular twinkle toes. Right on cue!"

The horse-faced man and the replacement taxi driver half-carried, half-dragged the young man and his suitcase (which he refused to give up even in his battered, drunken state) out of the club and laid him in the back seat of the waiting taxi. The rain was coming down harder than ever. It seemed as if the world was being washed away as fast as it could reassemble itself. Even the furiously beating wipers made no difference.

The replacement taxi driver shifted into gear and released the clutch slowly as he pulled away from the curb.

He was pretty sure the kid's eye needed medical atten-tion, but hospitals were out. You didn't take some kid who worked for Giuseppe Federico DiCarla to a hospital. He knew that much. You had to be discreet. You had to keep a tight lip. And that made it simple. He only knew one place to go. So that's where he went. But all the way there he wondered what he had gotten himself into. He couldn't shake the notion that the entire planet was off its axis. Everything was spinning out of control. And as he drove through the wet, darkly gleaming streets of Havana at three in the morning, he couldn't shake himself free from the memory of that black behemoth and his great crackling laugh.

He had no doubt that he would be haunted by the sound of that laughter for the rest of his life, however short or long the rest of his life might be.

-103-

The replacement taxi driver believed only an ex-nurse named Ismene could save the kid's eye. She lived in a crumbling tenement building on a street without a name somewhere in the labyrinth of streets and side streets and hidden alleyways east and southeast of Infanta. He always had trouble finding her place and usually ended up at a small all-night drugstore on Zequera. There was a weather-beaten wooden phone booth just outside the drugstore where he would dial her up, and ten minutes later she would be sitting next to him, a small brown satchel in her lap. The satchel contained a variety of pills and powders which were easily administered to passengers too drunk to notice. Just mix up a little potion in a flask, slip into the back seat and force it down their throats. It didn't matter if they struggled or not. They wouldn't remember a thing later. Then the replacement taxi driver and the ex-nurse would head to a secluded spot along the Almendares River and rob their victims blind. The crimes were never reported. The victims would wake up a few hours later, sitting half naked on a park bench or wandering around the Cementerio de Cristóbal Colón like some kind of resurrected zombie or shivering with embarrassment in the

waiting room at the train station, but they couldn't remember
a thing. The replacement taxi driver had not seen the ex-nurse
for several months. With the rain beating down as it was,
he drove around for thirty minutes before he found the
drugstore.

    The call from the phone booth:
    "Ismene?"
    Silence. The sound of the rain.
    "Ismene?"
    A furtive movement at the other end.
    The replacement taxi driver was looking through the
rain-streaked glass of the phone booth. He was looking at
his taxi. His eyes didn't waver. He didn't bother about the
people going in and out of the drugstore, the light from
the interior spreading out, a small golden bubble against
the darkness. Nor did he care about the clerk sitting by the
register, who kept looking out through the plate glass window
with the frosted drugstore lettering as if a crime were taking
place. Because crimes were always taking place outside this
drugstore. The taxi started vibrating, the engine sputtering,
coughing. Then it was running normally again. He usually left
the car running, but this neighborhood made him nervous.
He knew he was being watched. He could feel eyes all around,
hidden in the crevices between buildings, in the shadowy
darkness of doorways, watching everything that happened on
this rainy night. This is how it seemed. He tried to make sure
he did nothing that would call attention to itself.
    "Ismene?"
    A slightly cranky feminine voice cursing under her
breath.
    "Ismene? Are you there?"
    "Of course I'm here. Who else would be here? Do you
know how late it is?"
    "Yeah, I'm sorry, but it's sort of an emergency."
    "An emergency, huh. Is that what you're calling it these
days?"
    The sound of a chair being pulled out from a kitchen
table.
    And then: "Okay, so what is it?"

"I've got this young kid. He smacked his eye pretty good on the corner of a table. I need you to take a look at it."

"You do, huh. Why don't you try the hospital?"

"I can't do that Ismene. A hospital's no good. Not with this guy."

A long silence, except for the rain, and the glass paneled doors to the drugstore whooshing open and then whooshing closed in the background, and a few people blabbering away, incoherent, oblivious, thinking themselves the only souls wracked with pain on the entire planet. Then there was a tiny explosion of sound spiraling out from the receiver, or a series of tiny explosions: the sounds of a chair being pushed back, and then footsteps walking away, and then footsteps returning and the chair sliding back up to the table and someone rifling through the contents of a small leather bag or satchel, and then a sigh of satisfaction, or if not satisfaction, then perhaps hopeful resignation.

"Ismene?"

The rustling sound of someone pickling up the receiver.

"You're in luck. I've got everything we need."

"But Ismene . . ."

"Shshshsh. I'll be down in a few minutes."

The line went dead.

The replacement taxi driver put the phone on the hook and slipped out through the folding door. The people were still going in and out. Their faces glowed with an eerie dead light, as if their faces were not flesh-and-blood faces at all but were instead bronze or gold masks that could only reflect whatever illumination came their way. The clerk was still looking out through the plate glass window every now and then. Nobody paid any attention to the phone booth. The replacement taxi driver slid into the front seat and waited. The young man had not moved an inch. Twenty minutes later the curbside door opened and Ismene plopped herself next to the replacement taxi driver. She was wearing an elegant gold sequined dress with a heart-shaped neckline and gold high heels to match. She had been holding a flimsy silk jacket over her head to keep the rain off. With her hair dyed a platinum blonde and standing barely five feet tall, she gave Veronica Lake a run for her money.

"You're late."

"I know it."

Ismene removed a small brown shoulder bag from her shoulder and placed it in her lap. Then she leaned towards the replacement taxi driver and flashed a smile dripping with love and sarcasm. Her right eye disappeared behind a veil of blonde hair. "Come on sweetie," she said. "We can't stay here."

The replacement taxi driver nodded without returning the smile and they pulled away from the curb.

In a vacant lot somewhere along the Almendares River on the Vedado side, unidentifiable lights bobbing in the darkness, a few moss-covered trees clinging to the edge of the riverbank, the feeling of being submerged in a rising tide of insect sound (the deep-bellied thrumming of cicadas, the whir of mosquitoes), the tang of the not-so-distant sea lingering in the air, the rain beginning to subside:

"He isn't hurt that bad. But bad enough."

"Sure. I'll do what I can."

"He's a pretty important fish, I have to tell you."

"Why do you have to tell me anything?"

"I don't know. I just thought you should know."

"Sure, sweetie, sure."

The ex-nurse was already in the backseat. She reached over to the front and grabbed her bag. The replacement taxi driver didn't remember her getting out of the car. He shrugged a blasé shrug, indifferent to the possibility of miracles, however minor, and flicked on the radio. Maybe the kid's eye wasn't all that bad, but it sure as hell looked bad. Better to be safe than sorry. Besides, he was tired of skipping around from cab company to cab company. The ex-nurse flicked the switch of a small pocket flashlight. The dim yellow light barely pierced the darkness, at least this was the replacement taxi driver's opinion, but it was more than enough for the ex-nurse. He watched her searching her bag for a moment, and then he settled back in his seat and closed his eyes. The sounds of a vibrant, bluesy jazz number filled the interior of the car.

And then a few moments later: "He won't let go."

The replacement taxi driver cracked an eye but did not turn his head.

"Of what?"

"Of the suitcase."

"Don't worry about the suitcase. He hasn't let go of the suitcase the whole damn night."

The replacement taxi driver descended back into the jazz. A vague premonition washed over him. Or perhaps it was the repetition of once familiar sounds. The ex-nurse pulled a flask from her bag and a small pouch containing a white powdery substance. She carefully measured out a spoonful of the powder and poured it into the flask. She shook the flask, and before the replacement taxi driver realized what the repetition of those familiar sounds meant, the ex-nurse was cradling the young man's head and helping him to drink. He swallowed every last drop. She let his head sag back against the seat.

"Ismene, what the hell are you doing?"

"Giving him the dope."

"What the hell for? I wanted you to look at his eye."

"Is that what you wanted."

It wasn't really a question.

She reached over towards the young man's bruised eye, peeled back the eyelid and flashed the flashlight at the pupil. Then she did the same to his unbruised eye. Then she sat back smiling that same smile of love and sarcasm.

"Tell me you didn't get me out of bed at 3:30 in the morning just because some drunk got a black eye. Tell me you were thinking how much you missed me. Tell me you wanted to see me one last time, take one more spin around the block, one more crazy night out on the town, just for old time's sake."

". . . ."

"I didn't think so."

The ex-nurse let out an explosive sigh of pent-up resentment as if her throat had been clogged with sand. The replacement taxi driver retreated, slid his head back against the doorframe. Inside the cab the air was hot and stuffy. Outside the rain was descending in short, violent bursts and then subsiding, like eruptions from inverted geysers.

He cracked the window, closed his eyes and focused on the jazz. He didn't know what he had been thinking. Perhaps she was right. He must have been out of his mind to call her up. But what the hell. Now he knew for certain the kid's eye was okay. That was the important thing. She would've said something if it had been really bad. So let her rifle through the kid's pockets, the suitcase. What did he care? Besides, there couldn't be much left anyway. The kid had already forked over a grand in tips, maybe more. "Sure. Whatever you say Ismene."

But she didn't respond. She had already turned her attention to the young man. With practiced fingers, she undid the young man's grip on his suitcase and slid it across the seat. She flicked it open, pushed the few shirts and socks aside, and two seconds later the false bottom popped up.

"Who the fuck hides brochures in a false bottom?" she said. And then: "Who'd you say this guy was?"

The replacement taxi driver was smiling a relaxed, unexpected smile. He was not going to get sucked in.

"I guess I forgot to mention it."

Rummaging through the young man's pockets, she seemed to exist only in a cloud of desperation. She became invisible. The replacement taxi driver stared at the shimmering darkness of the rearview mirror, but his angle was bad. He could not see what she was up to. Then he heard a sigh of scorching relief. The air inside the cab was on fire. The head of the ex-nurse shot straight up, ecstatic. He could see her head bobbing about in the darkness, a ghostly, electrified head.

"Five-hundred smackers, sweetie, stuffed in his front pants pocket. What a dope!"

For a moment the replacement taxi driver forgot where he was. He put his hands on the wheel and pulled himself up to a driving position, but he kept his eyes on the rearview mirror. He watched the ex-nurse a moment longer, her head bobbing up and down with great enthusiasm.

And then: 'Can I drop you somewhere?'

The ex-nurse smiled a soft, kittenish smile, her blonde hair now swirling carelessly about her face.

"You're such a sap, sweetie."

"No, I mean it. I've got plenty of time."

"You go ahead, sweetie. Drop this dope where he needs to go."

"You sure?"

"I'll be okay."

She began putting her things back into her bag.

And then: "You can call me any time."

Her right eye had once again disappeared behind a veil of blonde hair. She waited a moment, a gesture of gratitude, perhaps, but did not say another word. Then she slipped out of the taxi and headed towards the street. They were only a short fifteen-minute walk from the Cementerio de Cristóbal Colón. He knew that's where she was headed. She liked to walk there in the morning, especially on a rainy morning with the tombs glistening. She walked without faltering, even in high heels. He watched her until she vanished in a swirling cloud of rain and darkness. The purpose of darkness was to disfigure and obscure, he thought. He could not say what else he was thinking. After a while he started the engine and headed for the yacht club.

The sun rose in a burst of glory above the clouds, cymbals of sunlight crashing uselessly against the curvature of space, but beneath the clouds the sun was an undefinable nothingness. It was the beginning and the end of myth. Beyond the possibility of reason. The soft splattering of clocks tumbling into the mud. Then the clouds dissipated. A pale glow stretched out from the sea and infiltrated a landscape of silhouettes, two-dimensional cut-outs of leafy trees and small buildings and a few parked cars scattered about and the dark hulking behemoth of the yacht club. The silhouettes were still dripping with the moisture left over from the previous night's storm. It almost seemed as if the world had been under water for centuries.

The replacement taxi driver caught the watery glint of a car door opening, closing, a wine-colored De Soto, a beautiful car in the sunlight, but seeming different now, a ghostly, otherworldly reflection of itself. The fat stubby man appeared. He smiled a thin, fluid smile that belied a sleepless night. The replacement taxi driver had suffered a similar night and so responded with a similar smile. Moments later the two men stood outside the taxi, looking in through the window at the still slumbering young man. The atrociously puffy eye was his most prominent feature.

"What were you thinking?"

"Well I sure as hell didn't think he was going to bounce his eye off the end of a table."

"No, I suppose not."

The two men pulled away from the window.

"How long will he be out like this?"

"I don't know. I'd say a couple of hours."

"Damn Luis and his stupid games. Take the kid here. Switch taxis. Drive him there. One last night on the town. Wherever he wants to go. But not wherever. Secret envelopes. Watch out for the men with the long-barreled rifles. Cryptic phrases. 'The bull, like a castle under siege, has been eaten.' What the fuck does that even mean? Christ. Luis acts like we're living in some Hollywood movie. Only he's going to get us all killed."

The men became uncomfortably silent.

Sounds from the beach beyond the yacht club followed the light as it tunneled its way through the darkness of the trees. A few early risers beachcombing. A dog barking. The sound of a motor boat motoring slowly past the beach, the engine sputtering for a moment, a strangely suspicious sound, and then the boat suddenly speeding away.

"Where do you want me to take him?"

"Take him to Café Paraiso. On Compostela. About a block from the harbor."

"I know the place."

"And don't go disappearing. I want you to make sure he gets on that ferry."

"Sure. I'll be his babysitter till the end. You want I should spoon feed him his breakfast."

"You're a smart guy. But don't go doing anything stupid. Stay out of sight. Pull around to the alley on the side. You should be able to see the whole joint from the side door. Just stay out of sight yourself."

"Okay. Don't worry about it. I'll be invisible."

"And make sure he gets on that ferry. The *S. S. City of Havana*. It leaves at 10:30 for Key West."

The fat man handed the replacement taxi driver a set of keys.

"Give them to the kid when you get to the café."

The De Soto had vanished by the time the taxi started rolling. 'You can thank me later, fat man,' the replacement taxi driver was thinking, but he wasn't sure he would see the fat man again.

-104-

After Regla, Nerea and Immanuel headed first to Federico's estate, just to make sure, and then they switched gears and headed back towards Old Havana and the art deco tenement building. They soon found themselves motoring slowly through a crumbling, invisible neighborhood a few blocks north of Cristina Train Station. The rain had become quite severe at times, obliterating everything in sight.

Nerea had cut the other two loose for the evening. They had thanked her in Sicilian and smiled at each other with great enthusiasm for the mischief they were going to get into. They had not had a night off in a long time. But a night was only a night. Nerea had also told them to be at Café Paraiso by eight in the morning. Oscar would be there, she said. He would arrive shortly after nine. They were to keep an eye on him until she got there. He would be quite groggy from drinking the night before, so he would give them little difficulty. They did not ask her how she knew this.

After the art deco tenement, Nerea and Immanuel made their way to a small, gravel parking lot near the wharf where the *S. S. City of Havana* was moored.

They settled back in the Packard to wait out the storm.

For most of that suffocating, interminably dark night, Immanuel pressed his hand to his ear and listened with delicate intensity to the radio chatter flowing back and forth between the men in fedoras scattered all over the city. Occasionally, using a distorted, gravelly, alien voice, he spoke into a tiny transmitter that seemed to be sewn into the lapel of his jacket, but not even Nerea could have heard what he said. But in truth she did not care. By four in the morning she had all but forgotten Immanuel was sitting in the back seat. Julio Mella had returned. Nerea was almost sitting in Julio's lap. For several hours he talked about the life he had once lived. He talked in his voice of orange-blossom honey until the sun had burned away the morning mist.

The highlights of what Julio said to Nerea on that rainy, misty morning:
'Ah, yes, Tina kept her edge razor sharp.'
'. . . .'
'No, not at first. When I first met her I fancied myself a writer, not a revolutionary.'
'. . . .'
'She was a photographer. She was many things, but when I knew her she was a photographer. She wore nothing more than a simple skirt and a white blouse. Almost like a young novitiate. But her fiery, indomitable spirit gave her a beauty that no one could touch or take away, no matter how much pain she went through.'
'. . . .'
'Yes, my Nerea, you have a similar beauty, a similar indomitable spirit. You might have been sisters, or at least cousins.'
Julio and Nerea were laughing softly. Julio's lively green eyes danced with mirth. Nerea drew him close to her, burying her face in his dark curly hair, breathing in the salty smell of a windswept sea.
'Yes, she took many photographs of me. In one I am pretending to be asleep on a grassy lawn. In another I am twirling about in my fancy Texan hat, laughing and dancing on a summer's day, just like anyone. But she preferred the ones where I was the serious revolutionary. Like the photograph in the lobby of the hotel where we first met.'
'. . . .'
'No, no, my personal favorites were always the ones where I am busy at my typewriter. My typewriter was my most important weapon, and she captured the truth of this in her photographs, the truth of my idealism.'

    '. . . .'

    '"Poverty and elegance go hand in hand in this world,"
I used to tell her.'

    '. . . .'

    '"Love and death are but trials of the soul."'

    '. . . .'

'No. I was too young to understand what it really meant
to die. Yes, I had always imagined myself as the leader of a
desperate group of men, passionate even in the face of insur-
mountable odds, men whose only hope lay in the darkness of
the abyss, like those fearless and mythic Texians and Tejanos
during the Battle of the Alamo. But strangely, I never imagined myself dead. Tina photographed me all laid out in my
coffin, surrounded by flowers and candles. There was a golden
hammer and sickle on the wall. A huge red star. Do you want
to know how naïve I was? I thought my death would be held
up as a symbol of the pledge by all revolutionaries to work
tirelessly until we obtained victory for all of the exploited
peoples of the world. But we did not know how impossible
this dream would be. Symbols are incapable of doing any real
work.'

    '. . . .'

'No, no. I did not realize that I was choosing a path
until it was too late. You could say my path chose me. I was
in prison and I went on a hunger strike because they had no
reason to put me in jail. That was in December 1925. Eighteen
days I went without, and then Machado had me released.
It was a Christmas present. Of course they did not like my
politics. If Machado had let me die in prison perhaps the
world would be better off. But they did not permit a prisoner
to commit suicide. Naturally we assumed Machado was only
biding his time. That is why I went to Mexico City. Villena
was right when he declared Machado to a be a donkey with
claws. But Machado was not behind my death. I was behind
it, and Tina, and Villena, and Diego Rivera, that fat cowardly
Mexican fuck. My death put Diego in the limelight. Suddenly
the whole world was celebrating Diego and his outrageous
paintings.'

    Julio stopped talking for a moment, and in the rainy
darkness it looked like he had suddenly, but with some degree

of forethought, opened the door to a secret compartment and pulled out two books. It was like he had reached into another dimension. He gave the books to Nerea. The first book was a paperback copy of Blasco Ibáñez's novel *Los muertos mandan*. The second was Trotsky's *The Permanent Revolution*. Trotsky's book had been published after Mella's death.

Nerea paid no attention to Trotsky. Her eyes were fixated on the cover of Ibáñez's novel. There was a man with a gun surrounded by a surrealist depiction of the dead: clouds of various washed-out colors (dark faded blues, teal, tan, white) that vaguely resembled skulls, and a skeletal ghost hovering just above the man's head. Nerea had the sense that the man was a puppet of the dead. The man vaguely reminded her of Oscar.

'Trotsky believed that Communism had lost its way, and he was right. But Trotsky had been abandoned by all but those with the purest of hearts. We understood this. But we were foolish. We truly thought we could re-energize the Communist movement, that Communism would then become what it was meant to become: the beacon in the darkness.'

'. . . .'

'Do you want to know the real truth about my death? We thought we could gain more by my death than by my life. We thought my death, my assassination, would shock everyone out of their complacency. This would be the first step towards creating the paradise we had always dreamed of. Were we mistaken? Martí believed it was possible to have pure democracy and equality for all social classes. Marti dreamed of a republic "with all and for all." But there can never be political equality without economic justice. We thought my death would be a dazzling white light shining on the injustice that always thrives in the shadows.'

'. . . .'

'To calmly witness a crime is to commit that crime. How many crimes have we committed in Cuba?'

'. . . .'

'We were pretty sure Machado was going to get me one way or another. So one night we decided I would give up my life for the future of oppressed people everywhere. Truly it was the decision of people too young to know any better.'

'. . . .'

'It was Villena who concocted the story that Tina tried to sell to the press. Two assassins waiting in the shadows at midnight. Near the corner of Morelos and Abraham González. The flash of a revolver and the assassins running away. The fiery, charismatic Julio Antonio Mella bleeding out in the street. Sirens wailing in the distance, but then the sound is absorbed by the darkness all around. His one and only love staring mutely into space with uncomprehending eyes, as if the laws that governed the universe had suddenly ceased to work.'

'. . . .'

'We chose that corner because of its obvious revolutionary implications. It's symbolic relevance. González was the mentor to Pancho Villa. And Morales was the birthplace of Zapata and at the center of every revolution in Mexico since 1811. That is why we chose that corner. Only a select few would ever realize the truth we kept to ourselves, our own inner flame, the echo of courageous footsteps. Everyone else would think Machado was behind the assassination. And my death would ignite the world. But this did not happen.'

'. . . .'

'The police accused Tina. They tried to say she was working with Vittorio Vidali, that Italian pig! They thought I had been betrayed by the one person whose love for me was a tiny bright flower in the desert. An angel's love. Such a love is incompatible with violence.'

'. . . .'

'Ah, my beautiful, sweet, compassionate Tina.'

'. . . .'

'Betrayal springs from a more stringent kind of love.'

'. . . .'

'They were onto the truth of it, of course, the police. A truth of a sort. But for all the wrong reasons.'

'. . . .'

'Yes, the world is full of such ironies.'

'. . . .'

'We were men of spotless character, except for an occasional dalliance, but that is only natural. We were a creed to live by. But now we are all but forgotten, except as images of propaganda, the true meaning of our words, the vitality of our intentions twisted beyond all recognition.'

'. . . .'

'My poor, poor Tina. She was an angel who floated about, her hands taking care of many small things.'

-105-

Café Paraiso occupied the first floor of a red brick building hidden in the darkly gleaming shadows and dark green foliage of Calle Compostela, a short walk from the harbor, two blocks east of Egido and the remnants of the southeast corner of the old city wall, which was begun in 1674 and took over sixty years to build, and which the city fathers decided to tear down in 1863, but much of the wall still divided Havana, at least in spirit, even at the dawn of the twentieth century. The upper floors of this red brick building, of course, were given over to nighttime activities. This was not surprising in a neighborhood teeming with the steamy sensuality of people living on the edge, beyond the edge, pimps and prostitutes everywhere you looked, the camaraderie, true friendship and solidarity of those on the bottom rung, a neighborhood illuminated at night by the red light of moral imperfection, a neighborhood which was both beautiful and seductive in its fragility. But during the day the café was a symbol of the American dream. In Cuba there was always a great longing for anything American. The cafe promised American-style pancakes and waffles from six to ten in the morning, and a businessman's lunch from eleven until two in the afternoon. So it was bustling with activity. The tables were mostly empty, but the counter was crammed full of regulars eating hearty breakfasts and drinking bottomless cups of coffee. A middle-aged woman with thick, juicy arms glided back and forth along the counter, refilling coffee cups, appearing suddenly with plates of eggs and sausages and pancakes and waffles and heaping mounds of butter and glass jars filled with steaming hot maple syrup for the many hungry mouths

that needed feeding. The regulars all wore caps and short-
sleeve shirts and khaki work pants and muddy work boots.
Many had not showered or shaved in days. It seemed likely
that they worked somewhere on one of the nearby wharves, or
perhaps down by the train station. But they seemed to be
taking their time with their breakfasts, so it was hard to say.
Occasionally the middle-aged woman waded out into the sea
of mostly empty tables. A young man was sitting at the second
table from the door next to a row of windows. He was wearing a badly stained white linen suit and a shabby Panama hat.
He had placed a suitcase on the floor beneath the window sill.
It was clear he had had a rough night, perhaps many rough
nights. He was sipping a coffee, very black, holding his forehead with one hand, his eyes half-closed, not eyes so much as
slits, even in the absence of any direct sunlight. One of his
eyes was badly bruised, and in between sips he sometimes
touched it with his fingertips, gingerly, as if he could not quite
believe it was his eye. The row of windows afforded no view
to speak of. A building or series of buildings from the colonial
period on the other side of the street, the buildings set back
from the street, tenements, perhaps, obscured by the heavy,
wet greenery of laurel and tamarind and a few lime trees or
avocado trees (perhaps the only stretch of Compostela that
had any trees at all). A few pedestrians scattered here and
there, glimpsed through the leaves, and then disappearing
through narrow doors. Calle Compostela was a fairly
well-traveled street because of its proximity to the harbor,
though it was mostly foot traffic and bicycles out front of Café
Paraiso during the day, with only an occasional motorcycle or
car, and every now and then a truck looking to avoid the
heavier traffic on Monserrate or making a delivery, but late in
the evening there were taxis everywhere rambling back and
forth in search of lost souls. The middle-aged woman hovered
over the young man with motherly apprehension. She did not
like the look of his eye. It was an atrocious looking eye. It was
very puffy. The skin all around was deep purple in color,
almost black in places. She paid no attention at all to the two
young men in fedoras sitting three rows back from the door
along the wall. They were not interested in breakfast. They
had been drinking coffee for over an hour, cup after cup after

cup, and speaking in happy, friendly, carefree whispers, as if they had a great many jokes to tell each other, a vast number that would require many more pots of coffee but little else. They seemed friendly enough, but they were also speaking in a foreign language, she did not know which one, and she did not like the way they were looking at the young man by the window. She wondered if perhaps they had been the ones who had given the young man his black eye. It didn't matter what they had done or not done. They were trouble. That's what she thought. Once or twice she thought they were holding long-barreled rifles, but when she looked back the rifles had vanished. She wouldn't have been surprised if they had started levitating, or, conversely, if they had suddenly begun spinning like whirling dervishes, the tips of their cloven-hoofed feet (because all demons possessed cloven-hoofed feet) cutting through the floorboards of the cafe and the soft, loamy earth beneath that and the pockets of limestone, creating with their mad, unknowable desires a dark, foreboding tunnel all the way down to the black, volcanic rock that was the bedrock of the city. Yes, they were trouble, she thought. She was on the verge of asking them to leave half a dozen times, but each time the thought popped into her head it was immediately obliterated by the clamor of the regulars at the counter. There was a steady stream of regulars, as there was every morning except Sundays, and when one finished his breakfast, another would take his place at the counter. None of the regulars sat at a table. The tables were for tourists who had just gotten off a boat and wanted something to tie them over until they found their hotel, or they were waiting to board a ferry and were eating and drinking just to kill time. The regulars were talking about the storm the night before. That's all they seemed to be talking about. The storm had covered the shoreline with all sorts of detritus. Abandoned boots, shoes, articles of clothing, empty wooden crates, old tires, hubcaps, the splintered remains of boats that had capsized, smashed guitars, caps, hats, gloves, bottles of all kinds with fancy lettering blown into the glass, tin cans, water-soaked books, broken lamps, hundreds of fish carcasses (bluefin and yellowfin and ballyhoo, as well as a mixed bag of smaller fish), a smörgåsbord of dead and dying crabs, the hard-packed remains of jelly fish, an octopus or two, strands of leafy, purplish seaweed, the tangled scraps of a few fishing nets, a few juvenile marlins, and a couple of sharks. The men laughed about the sharks. You never knew what riches lay inside the belly of a shark, they said. They laughed some more. Their laughter was like a beacon in the dark. Then the conversation shifted to women and whether or not marriage was worth it, and someone said not in this neighborhood, and everyone laughed, and someone else said 'Wanted: young women with pleasing appearance to work nights, apply at Café Paraiso, particularly interested in rural girls.' The laughter became a second storm. The middle-aged woman pretended she didn't hear. Her husband emerged from the kitchen and the laughter slowly subsided, became a steady, indecent, snickering drizzle. The husband had a plate of pancakes and sausage in his hand and a steaming cup of coffee. He went over to a side door that was often overlooked. The side door was in two parts and the top part was open. The bottom part formed a counter of sorts for customers who wanted to eat outside and didn't mind standing in an alley. The alley was a grass covered alley that ran along the south side of the red brick building, the side closest to the harbor, and ended in a rubbish heap. The husband passed the plate and the coffee to someone on the other side of the half-door, a dark complected man with a gruff, raspy masculine voice. The man began to eat. The middle-aged woman didn't care who ate in the alley. The husband talked with the man while he ate and they laughed about the good old days when people came to watch them play baseball. The laughter of the dark complected man sounded a little like a flock of wild parrots whirling through the trees, screeching at the tops of their lungs. Some of the regulars wondered out loud where the parrots had come from and then they chuckled softly, knowingly, but they did not look up from their plates. Then the middle-aged woman ordered her husband back to the kitchen and the laughter like a flock of wild parrots faded completely. The two men in fedoras looked over at the man in the alley with the strange-sounding laughter but then they forgot him immediately. The steady stream of regulars continued. The conversation shifted from women and marriage to politics.

Some of the regulars were wondering how much money
Batista had stolen from the country. They guessed it was in
the millions. They did not say the name Batista, but everyone
knew who they were talking about. Someone said that it was
getting so bad that surely the Americans were going to get
involved, but everyone knew this would never happen. Then
the conversation shifted to modes of travel and the regulars
were suddenly talking like big-talkers about whether it was
more enjoyable to take a sleeping car on a train like the
Patagonian Express, which ran from Buenos Aires south to
Esquel, or a berth on a steamer, like one from the Lamport
and Holt Line, a boat that went up the coast from Buenos
Aires to Montevideo to Santos to Rio de Janeiro. The regulars
were split in their opinion, and one of them had just called
over to the two men wearing fedoras to possibly break the tie
when the front door opened and a man with a shining example of a Platt Guardsman suitcase entered the café. The man
was wearing a beige herringbone blazer, a white shirt and a
chartreuse tie, and brown and beige saddle shoes to match the
blazer. He took a seat at the third table from the door along
the row of windows, placing his suitcase on the floor beneath
the window sill. It looked like he had slept in his clothes. Or
perhaps he hadn't slept at all. He sat with his back to the
young man at the second table. The young man looked over at
the counter for the middle-aged woman, but he could not see
her. The two men wearing fedoras stared at the man in the
herringbone blazer. They were convinced they had seen him
before but they could not place him. A meaty, rollicking voice
called out from the counter: "Train or steamer, my friend?"
The regulars burst into laughter. A few applauded. But the
man in the herringbone blazer did not answer. He stood up
when his coffee arrived, staring out the window at the heavy,
wet greenery across the street, which was no longer so wet,
and the steady, throbbing, nightmarish brightness of the sun
which had burst through the clouds that very moment. He
tossed down his coffee in three gulps. Then he tossed a few
coins on the table, grabbed his suitcase and headed out the
door. Except it was not his suitcase, a discrepancy that the two
men wearing fedoras noticed instantly. The young man did
not notice the switch, or he pretended not to. He seemed

oblivious to the comings and goings in the café, except, perhaps, as one senses on an unconscious, subterranean level the
fluid tremors of a landscape always shifting beneath one's feet.
The young man's eyes were still slits. The men wearing fedoras exchanged worried glances. They bent their heads to
confer. Then one of them hurried through the door, stopping
only a moment, presumably to get his bearings, and then he
started running down Compostela towards the harbor after
the man in the herringbone blazer. Anyone who was looking
would have seen a long-barreled rifle gleaming in the fresh
sunlight. The dark complected man realized something was up
and finished his coffee and shouted a quick goodbye to his
friend. In an instant he was in his taxi with the engine running, but he did not pull out of the alley. From where he sat
he could see obliquely into the café. He could not see the
young man by the window, but he could see part of the
counter and the shadowy profiles of a few regulars, and
beyond the counter he could see the shadowy torso (like the
negative of a decayed Greek statue) of the companion to the
man who had left with his gleaming rifle. The dark complected man watched the shadowy torso with a keen intensity
that was broken only momentarily by the sound of a distant
gunshot, which was followed by a second lingering gunshot,
and then a long, eerie silence, as if the world had been a
balloon and now the air was escaping into the silent tomb of
outer space. Everyone inside the café heard the gunshots and
wondered what was happening. The young man by the
window suddenly stood up as if emerging from the blackness
of the cinema into broad daylight. At that same instant the
dark complected man revved the engine of the taxi. The
companion to the man with the gleaming rifle was distracted
by the sound and took his eyes off the young man. The young
man left a very large bill on the table to pay for his breakfast.
Then he grabbed the remaining suitcase and slipped out the
door. The middle-aged woman saw him leave and raced from
the counter, waving her arms in the air and shouting with a
strained, overworked voice, but when she saw the bill on the
table she stopped shouting. She looked out the window to see
if she could catch a glimpse of the young man in the shabby
white suit and the shabby Panama hat, who she suddenly

viewed as a supernatural being in disguise, perhaps Oggún himself, who was also known to some of the faithful as Saint Michael, but he was Saint Peter to others, and also Saint James, but the young man had already crossed over to the other side of the street and was lost in the shadows of the trees. The dark complected man saw the young man pass by the alley before crossing and took his foot off the gas. The young man tried to remain as inconspicuous as possible. He was motoring as fast as one can motor without breaking into a run. He tried to focus only on where he was going, but he saw the gleaming barrel of a rifle and could not help but look across. The rifle was heading the other way. At that same instant the man carrying the rifle looked across and saw the young man in a gap between two trees. Their eyes met. They continued walking in opposite directions, but their eyes remained locked, their heads swiveling slowly with suspicion. At that same instant the companion to the man with the rifle dashed out onto the sidewalk in front of the café. He seemed disoriented. The head of the man with the rifle snapped to attention. He saw his friend and waved and shouted and told him to get the car and started running towards the café. At that same instant the young man shoved his suitcase under one arm and grabbed his shabby Panama hat with his free hand and started running pell mell the other way. He was almost to the end of Calle Compostela. He could smell the oily, fishy smell of the harbor and the fumes from the automobiles and trucks speeding along San Pedro. He heard the low rumble of trains and a few ship horns and the ships heading out to sea and the tooting of the small ferries going back and forth to Regla and the cries of disenchanted seagulls. At the same instant the dark complected man saw the man with the rifle run past the alley. A car started and tires squealed. The dark complected man waited a moment and then hit the gas and his taxi zoomed out of the alley. The taxi smashed into a 1956 Chevrolet Bel Air four-door hardtop. The taxi was badly dented, the front grill was crumpled up like an accordion, but the Chevrolet was in far worse shape. The left side of the Chevrolet had been crushed. The doorframe had snapped from the impact and a jagged piece of metal had sliced through the driver's stomach and he was coughing and spitting up blood.

His companion was trying to open the passenger side door, but his right shoulder was dislocated so he couldn't get his arm to work correctly. He could not remember where they were or what time it was. The dark complected man was unhurt, though when he stepped out of the taxi his legs wobbled a bit. He walked over to the Chevrolet and looked with grim detachment at the two men in fedoras. The driver leaned back and looked up as if the dark complected man were an avenging angel or a deranged Orisha and smiled. Blood ran down from his gums and filled in the spaces between his teeth. The dark complected man was unmoved and pulled out a black handled Libia and shot the driver in the side of the head. The driver's companion began to panic, fumbling about the front seat with his one good arm and his one dangling appendage, trying to get his hands on his rifle, but his rifle was nowhere to be found. And then it was too late. The dark complected man had rounded the car by then. He shot the second man twice, once in the back of the neck, and the man fell to one side, his head twisting as he fell, landing on his companion's bloodied leg at an odd angle so all he could see was a narrow wedge of sunlight that came in through the open window, his eyes fish-blinking slowly, his breathing becoming shallow, spreading out like a fine mist. And then the dark complected man fired a second time, aiming very carefully, point blank, the barrel of the pistol up against the peeled eyeball of the left socket. He sent a bullet careening across the island universe of his adversary. At that same instant the young man with the suitcase was heading up San Pedro on the city side. He was no longer running. The brim of his Panama hat was pulled down, obscuring his face. But he had gone only a block or two when he was urged by a sense of mystery and unease that some would have mistaken for the voice of God to stop and turn around. The traffic was whirling past, a steady mechanical hum, then spinning around the rim of the rotunda at Desamparados. He should not have been able to see what he saw because of the trees in the center of the rotunda. It seemed as if the air was shimmering, as if he was looking down a long, narrow tunnel between two worlds. Wormhole of his devouring imagination. Refracted images of a silent movie. Echo of a fading dream. He saw a body near the remnants of the old city wall. The body was sprawled across a narrow sidewalk, a Platt Guardsman suitcase a few feet away, the contents tossed about, spilling into the street and the circling traffic. Two figures were huddled over the body, but as soon as they sensed he was watching, they stood up. It almost seemed like they were levitating. One of the figures raised an arm and there was the flash of sunlight on metal, a gun, perhaps. In the shadowy glare this first figure seemed to possess the elongated snout of a jackal or some other creature of the night guarding a forgotten tomb. But the young man was staring at the second figure, a long-legged woman with the headpiece of a shining golden sun like a halo upon her head and she had thick curly black hair and a single blood-red gardenia pinned above her right ear. She was immaculate in her blackness, a dazzling purity that took the young man's breath away. The woman put her hand to the raised arm of the first figure, a quieting gesture. The young man heard the woman speak, but he could not possibly have heard her speak or have even seen her standing there above the body of the dead man on the far side of the rotunda at Desamparados. We can let him go, my love, the woman said. She was speaking to the first figure. Come, we have done what we set out to do. The first figure lowered his arm. The tunnel began to collapse, but still the young man could not take his eyes away. The woman smiled a dazzling bright smile, as if there were a thousand jewels between her teeth. It was the smile of a goddess: implacable, relentless, murderous, beautiful and terrible to behold. It was a smile of unashamed sadness mixed with timeless, amused, irreverent triumph. It was a self-indulgent smile of privileged insight that said: that which might never have existed at all, existed once, and that makes all the difference.

-106-

The S. S. *City of Havana* was originally launched by the Newport New Shipbuilding and Drydock Company on

November 18, 1943 and was transferred to the Royal Navy
three months later and renamed the *HMS Northway*. It saw
limited action during D-Day as a transport ship for trucks
and other military vehicles, and served the rest of the war as
a hospital transport ferrying hundreds of wounded soldiers
back across the Channel to England. In 1951 it was sold to
the Suwannee Steamship Company of Jacksonville, Florida
and renamed the *S. S. City of Havana*. It provided ferry service
between Key West and Havana for eight years, until Castro
came to power. In 1962 it was sold to the West German
Navy and designated an Accommodation Ship, servicing
Bremerhaven for three years. From 1967 until 1972 it ferried
people back and forth between Antwerp and Rotterdam. The
boat was scrapped in 1973.

Oscar could not remember where exactly the *S. S. City of
Havana* was moored. He did not go down to the harbor all that
often and had forgotten the name of the wharf, but then he
saw the boat and names didn't matter.

In spite of the tenderness of his eye and the steady,
throbbing bursts of pain, he remembered everything Luis
had told him. He went down to the automobile deck and put
the suitcase in the trunk of the De Soto. A stevedore stepped
out of a hidden stairwell as Oscar was closing the trunk and
asked him what he was doing down there, all passengers were
supposed to be up in the lounge or on one of the upper decks.
The man spoke with a strange foreign accent that Oscar had
never heard before. Oscar showed him the car keys and the
stevedore nodded and made his way through the parked cars
to the other side and disappeared into another stairwell. The
boat was not yet under way, but Oscar could already feel the
steady rumble of the two steam turbines beneath his feet, and
then he heard some shouting from above and he knew that the
mooring lines had been cast off.

Oscar headed up to the passenger lounge. Near the
doors to the lounge there were several small souvenir shops or
boutiques where they sold jewelry, watches, books, magazines,
newspapers, chewing gum, t-shirts and other trinkets for the
tourists. He bought a pack of Wrigley's from a man named
Rogelio, a short, olive-skinned man with a shining bald head
and a huge, toothy smile. Rogelio was bored silly and wanted

to talk, and Oscar was too tired to resist. There were no other customers, but that was not unusual. Rogelio said he did most of his business on the trips from Key West to Havana, not the other way around. He said the owner of the ferry had put in air conditioning in 1953 to attract a higher-class clientele. The shops and boutiques had followed soon after that. And then a chef from Denmark to prepare small high-class tidbits like Danish smoked salami sausages for the passengers. Sometimes it was more than Rogelio could bear.

"But I tell you," said Rogelio, "it is very exciting work-ing here. Just last year do you know who was on this boat? Faustino Pérez was on this boat. Imagine that! Of course when we got back to Havana the police were waiting at the dock. A huge fuss of police cars with their lights flashing. Colonel Orlando Piedra, the Chief of the Secret Police himself, came on board and took each one of us into the passenger lounge, one at a time, and sat us down and asked us questions. What were we thinking, he said, to let Faustino Pérez escape like that, one of the rebels who had helped to organize the storming of the barracks at Moncada and who was now gallivanting about with Castro and plotting God knows what? What does one say to such absurd questions? How does one respond? So I said what I knew. I said a man who maybe was Faustino and who maybe was not Faustino was on this boat. He bought a book from me. An Agatha Christie detective novel named *The Secret Adversary*. Then he went into the lounge and I did not see him again. That is what I told the Colonel. That was the end of my interrogation. But I was not altogether honest. I tell you now it was definitely Faustino with his sparkling eyes full of mischief. There is no doubt. And yes, he did buy an Agatha Christie book. And what is more, he read it. I know this because I saw him one more time on this ferry. He stopped by my counter some months later and he bought this or that, and then he pulled me close and he said this book he had bought was a great book. He said it was about two Americans, a rich millionaire who carries a gun and is not afraid to use it, and his first cousin, a young nurse who works in a field hospital during the Great War and who is given a set of secret papers while aboard the *Lusitania*, just hours before the *Lusitania* is sent to the bottom, torpedoed by a German U-boat. The book depicted a world of intrigue, secret treaties between America and Great Britain, Bolshevik conspirators intent on fomenting revolution, and English spies trying to stop them. And yet it was a book every good Cuban should read, Faustino said, because it spoke the truth, even though you had to peel back many layers to get to this truth. Then he said it had been made into a movie in Germany in 1929, a silent movie, but they gave it a different name. I do not remember what it was. He said it had been directed by Fred Sauer, a great filmmaker who had eventually been abandoned by the Nazis. That is what Faustino said."

Then Rogelio pulled out a copy of *The Secret Adversary* and showed it to Oscar. The book was in English, which Oscar did not understand very well, but he bought the book anyway and headed into the passenger lounge. He ordered a mojito, but he didn't want to stay inside so he went up the stairs to the upper deck and sat down in a slatted chair looking out at the water. It was very sunny, a bright, white, burning sunshine. In the bright glaring sunlight, his white linen suit was no longer stained and timeworn, and his Panama hat was once again immaculate. He tried to read but it was too bright, so he set the book beneath the chair and sipped his drink. Four musicians — two guitar players, a bass player, and a maraca player — were playing a steamy bolero by the railing. He was sitting near the back of the boat and he could see they were already miles out to sea. For a moment he sat there listening to the music and thinking about Havana. Why had Luis headed south on San Pedro towards the rotunda and not north towards the ferry? What had happened to the two men in fedoras who had been watching him all morning? He wondered about this for a while but he knew he would never know why or what. The musicians finished their bolero and joked around a bit, laughing in the sunshine, before they started playing again. Oscar looked back at the shadowy outline of Cuba on the horizon. The harbor entrance was already lost in the shimmering brilliance of the water, but he could see a hazy, reddish-gray cloud hovering above the island. He wondered if the cloud had always been there and if you could only see it when you were miles away, or if another storm was moving in.

If Oscar had possessed a more philosophical mind, he might have concluded that his questions about the nature of the reddish gray cloud and why Luis had headed south down San Pedro instead of north and what had become of the two men in fedoras were merely symptomatic evidence that he lived within the abyss, which is where, to adopt a current popular line of thinking, we all live. But what does it mean to live in the abyss? How does one define the abyss? Is it the epicenter of infinite nothingness, a cold, lifeless void? Is it a place of unimaginable, eternal suffering? Is it something else entirely? Perhaps the answer lies in the subterranean depths of the human soul, the collective unconscious. Perhaps the abyss only seems to exist because of our inability to comprehend what is truly happening all around us and why, no matter what plausible explanations we assign to the events of the here and now, and how these events shape our hope in the hereafter. Perhaps we are like a white bird in a golden cage, an exotic, white-plumed bird like a cockatoo or a cockatiel or some other kind of white bird. And in the particular phil-osophical cage where we find ourselves, the door is always open. We may fly away at any time. Or we may stay put. It is up to us. And yet no matter what we choose to do, we are trapped inside this cage. Even when we are flying free, all we can see are the golden bars. Of course we realize that it is our own thoughts that trap us, that keep us from the truth of who we are and who we might possibly become. But what can we do? This is just the way things are. So we conclude that we can never know what is real and what is not. We can do nothing. In other words, we live in an abyss of our own making, the by-product of deluded thinking, which means that the abyss as an actual, physical place that devours the soul of humanity does not really exist at all.

But Oscar did not see the world through a philosophical lens. In fact, if he had had his way that morning, he would have drunk mojitos until he slipped into a coma (an abyss of another kind). So he sat in the slatted chair, his one good eye and his badly bruised eye closed to the unimaginably hot and yet strangely exhilarating sun and the pure sunshine burning away the features of his face, slowly sipping his mojito, listening to the four musicians and letting the music wash through him, thinking about the steamy, sensual, provocative world he had left behind, thinking about Nerea and how he would never see her again, but also thinking about the sandy white beaches of Florida and the bright lights of Miami and the nightclub he would one day open, and he already knew the name of it, his nightclub would be called La Campana, just like the one in Havana. And in this way he passed the time until he arrived in Key West.

BOOK SIX

the glory days of La Campana

The young ones have been saying I don't have many days left. They are saying I must surely be dying. Am I not afraid to close my eyes at night? I have to laugh. I am as old as any saint that was ever buried beneath the streets of Rome. But I am not that old. And I live in Miami, not Rome. But some days I feel as old as the crumbling bones that fill the catacombs of my lonely heart. These words are the truth. I stole them from Sister Faustina, but she would not mind this small theft. She speaks like that. She speaks the language of poetry. And they do fit the way I feel on some days, these words. And yet I am not distressed by this feeling of loneliness. It is a surface feeling only. A momentary pause. It is the skin of a silent drum. Beneath my loneliness, or maybe inside my loneliness, there is a great joy that refuses now to stay hidden. I think perhaps my joy is a youthful joy that I have only recently rediscovered. Or perhaps it is a joy I have never known before, but I know it now, a gift from God, a trembling sense of wonder spreading its majestic wings. I do not think there is anything at my age that could bring more joy than the gift of wonder.

I am not sure I know how to explain it. I try to explain what I am thinking to these young ones who have not yet taken their final vows, but they do not understand. So I say a word or two about God. It is easy to believe in God, I tell them. When you have seen what I have seen it is impossible not to believe in God, but that is only part of it, I tell them, and then I start to cackle and spit, and I almost choke I am laughing so hard, but they do not see the humor.

Isidora, they say, please will you tell us a few more stories. Sister Faustina will not mind. She has made us promise that we will not tax your strength, but she has given us her permission.

I have to narrow my eyes when they say that. I have to give them a very stern look. Do not be too sure, I say. If Sister Faustina heard even half of what I am telling you girls, she would send me packing. And then I close my eyes and pretend I am sleeping, but the girls persist. There are too many voices to ignore. My room is overflowing with clamoring young novitiates. What can I say?

It is not much of a room really. The walls are white and there is a narrow bed with a beige spread in one corner and a wooden desk opposite the bed with a pile of books that Sister Faustina has given me to read, but I will never read them. They are books about Mary and the lives of the Saints and the Pierced Heart of Jesus, and I probably should read them. But I have moved beyond such books now, I think. I certainly do not need them to know God. If they were poetry books, perhaps, but not books such as these. Besides, I talk to God every day. Above the desk and this pile of unnecessary books there is a wooden crucifix nailed to the wall, and whenever I want to speak to my God I look at this crucifix and I speak, whatever comes to my mouth. God listens carefully to everything I have to say. I also have a small refrigerator where I keep this and that. And I am permitted the luxury of an easy chair, because of my advanced condition, that is what Sister Faustina calls it. She is always making excuses for the open wound my life once was, but that life is no longer my life. But what does it matter? I am grateful for the chair in any event. It is a soft suede wing chair, the same color as my bedspread, with a separate footrest. It is very comfortable. The young novitiates gave me a lambswool blanket for my birthday to place over my knees in the morning or the afternoon or the evening when I am sitting in my chair. I have always liked the way lambswool feels against my skin, even on the hottest days. Emidio placed the chair by the window so I could see what there is to see. It is not much of a view, but it is not Emidio's fault.

Every so often I call Emidio by my brother's name, Emilio. Some days it is hard to know what I am saying. It is hard to tell one name from another. But Emidio does not mind. He is a good man and he does what he can for the Sisters here, and he does what he can for an old bag of bones like me. With the joy of a smuggler etched across his normally inscrutable face, he brings me many books of poetry to read and various trendy magazines and chocolate covered almonds even though I have few teeth left, which means I have to suck

on them for quite a while before I can mash them with my
gums. Yes, Emidio is very kind to me, even though I am not a
Sister. The window is a long, narrow window with a handle
that is easy to grip, so even an old woman with little strength
can let in a breeze. It is a floor-to-ceiling window that permits
me a view of a tiny sliver of the sidewalk and a tiny sliver of
the street with its parked cars and a few bungalows on the
other side and a few lime trees. I keep the window open
because there is no air conditioning. On a very quiet afternoon
I can hear the sounds of children playing in the park that is
only three blocks away. Some days the air is so still I can
almost hear the bells of the Church of the Immaculate Heart,
or the Church of Saint Jude, which is a Byzantine church,
which I went to by mistake once when I was in downtown
Miami, but it is a very pretty stone church with a red tile roof
and a few palms trees out front and some other kinds of trees
and a couple of downtown high-rise apartment buildings
nearby, looming over this small stone church, but not in a
menacing way, and they are Melkites there, which I had never
heard of before, which one of the young men standing in the
back of the church was kind enough to tell me, and he wasn't
bothered in the least that I was there by mistake, and he even
went so far as to say that there are no mistakes in the presence
of God, which I didn't quite agree with him about that, but he
was young, let him find out for himself, I was thinking, but
then, as if he had read my thoughts, he said 'God tempts us,
surely, but He does not lead us into error,' and then he smiled
a very mysterious smile, it reminded me of the way certain
saints seem to be smiling, at least the statues of those saints
whenever I stumble upon them by accident in a dark alcove
here or a forgotten park there, saints like Saint Francis or Saint
Joseph or Saint Gregory, whose own mother was a saint, if
you can imagine that, at any rate it was a very mysterious
smile he gave me, and it left me wondering about the meaning
of so many things, like why did it take so long for the universe to get where it is, and why is mankind just a tiny blip in
the grand scheme of things and hardly worth noticing, if the
scientists are to be believed, and where do miracles fit in, and
who was the last person to actually see an angel, and why are
people so concerned with how many angels can dance on the

head of a pin, which seems a ridiculous thing to be concerned
about, and how can God be one of three persons who all
express the same divine nature and so they are really just one
person, these were just a few of the questions rolling through
my brain, and for a moment I thought this young man was
going to share with me the secret of these mysteries, a glimpse
of the eternal mind of God, which God generally prefers to
keep hidden, perhaps this young man was going to share with
me a whole spectrum of secrets, oh he certainly had me going
with that smile, but he did not say a word, he just smiled his
mysterious smile, which suddenly became also quite sad,
almost forlorn, and he no longer seemed so young, he looked
rather old, like one of those old men who wander about the
beaches with metal detectors in search of treasure like they are
searching for a new beginning, and I wondered if perhaps he
had come inside looking for his son or his daughter because
he had left his metal detector at home but he had lost his keys
and his bus pass and it was getting late, and he used to belong
to Saint Jude's, which is why he knew all about their being
Melkites, but he had given it up so he could spend most of his
otherwise tranquil days searching for coins buried in the sand,
but his son or his daughter still belonged because life had not
yet bled them of their childhood faith, and then I was thinking
maybe his son or his daughter will be permitted to keep their
childhood faith without any trouble at all, what a gift that
would be, of course this would be very, very rare, *cada muerte
de obispo*, as my mother used to say, but she was always
talking about the chance of finding true love when she talked
this way, she didn't believe in true love, and this was the
source of many arguments between the two of us, but life is
difficult, as they say, and then I was through thinking, but the
young man who had become an old man had disappeared, just
like that, somewhere down a long, narrow corridor, I suspect,
a winding corridor perhaps, or maybe he just went outside.
Yes, yes . . . but where was I? Oh yes, the bells. Yes, yes, some
days the air is so still I can almost hear the bells of the Church
of the Immaculate Heart, or the Church of Saint Jude, but on
other days it might be the bells of the Church of Saint
Raymond's or Saint Peter's or Saint Paul's or Saint Hugh's,
which is a very modern church with piano concerts and a café

that serves coffee and doughnuts and a television station so
they can broadcast the Mass to those who cannot attend, or
Gesù, which was the church of my mother even before the first
of the Cuban refugees began to arrive, and it was also the
church I had hoped to be married in, but this did not happen,
or the Little Flower or San Juan Bosco, with its gleaming
golden dome and its altar of the exiles and its crazy, beautiful
stained glass windows, and my favorite window of all of their
windows is the one with the resurrected Christ like a gleaming
Spanish Adonis and two white doves flying from opposite
directions towards His outstretched hands of glory, or maybe
it is the bells of the Good Shepherd, or Corpus Christi, or Our
Lady of the Lakes, where before they built their church they
celebrated the Mass in a dairy barn, or Saint Martha's, which
started out in the Bikini Motel in Miami Shores because there
was no place else to gather, but later, after they had finished
building their church, Mother Theresa herself came all the way
from Calcutta just for a visit, or Saint Cecilia's, which had to
close its doors a few years ago but is now open again, or the
Church of Saint Catherine of Siena, who was the youngest of
twenty-two brothers and sisters, if you can imagine that, or
Saint John the Apostle in Hialeah, with its gleaming, bronze
and marble altar and a scene of the Last Supper stamped into
the metal, and behind the altar you are almost overwhelmed
by the terrifying, panoramic scene of the Crucifixion of Our
Lord and the suffering He endured, or Ermita de La Caridad,
Our Lady of Charity, the Patroness and very soul of my
mother's Cuba, which is a shrine more than a church even
though they hold Mass every day in the chapel, and you can
stand outside along the water and look out across the Bay of
Biscayne towards Cuba and pray for Our Lady's blessing,
because the same sun that bathes Cuba also bathes us, because
even here in Miami, especially here with so many exiles, yes,
yes, Our Lady protects us from hurricanes and most automobile accidents and all motorcycle accidents and the evil
designs of unsavory characters and the inevitable pestilence of
impure thoughts, or Our Lady of the Divine Providence, or
Our Lady of Lourdes, or perhaps Our Lady of Lebanon, where
they say the Mass in Aramaic, and you do not need to understand the words to know they are speaking the language of

God, or maybe it is the bells of the Church of Saint Michael, which was built in 1947, the year my brother, Emilio, was born, with its gleaming modern architecture that shines like the sun against the sky and its ghostly, glowing statue of the Archangel himself, his sword by his side, unflinching in his devotion to God. On any given day I fancy I can hear the bells of any one of the churches where Sister Faustina has been sending me these last several years. I have been all over Miami and even out to the beach and up the coast towards Fort Pierce and Melbourne, and even as far as St. Augustine. I go wherever I am needed, though it is not for me to decide when and where.

So I am sitting in my easy chair, a luxury, as I have already said. I dare not open my eyes to look out the window because I am pretending to be asleep, but the clamoring of these young novitiates is too much. Their hope that I will tell them a few stories they have already heard before and for some unfathomable reason wish to hear again is enough to break anyone's will. It is an unending hope, like the oscillating cycle of the moon. I open my eyes. I open my eyes and I smile absentmindedly and stare out the window for a moment, as if I have truly just woken up from an unexpected catnap, and these young ones laugh and clap and settle back wherever they can find room. My small deception is part of the show. It is quite crowded this afternoon and some of the girls have brought in chairs from other rooms and some are sitting cross-legged on the rug or in a monkey's row along the edge of my bed or some up against the wall. I lean my face into the warm sunshine that is pouring through the window and I feel that I am on the verge of disappearing. Then I can hear myself telling a story, and another, and so on. After a while I am barely aware of the world around me.

-108-

¡Ay de mí! To be eighteen again! I know it is a common enough wish, or perhaps it is a lament, but that does not mean the thought is in any way trivial. Yes, I know this wish is an

impossibility, at least in a world that values the precision of
clocks, especially those made in Germany or Switzerland.
But nothing is truly impossible. That is what I was taught.
That was the catechism I learned from my vanished uncles
and cousins and my long-suffering aunts, who had all died
years ago, yet still they watched over me. Not that they were
trying to teach me anything. But I listened to what they
had to say, and I listened to what was hidden in between
their words. And so I learned. I believed in the impossible.
And I was recalcitrant in my belief. Yes, that is the word.
Recalcitrant. That is how I was. Until I was eighteen I saw
the world through the hopeful, gleaming brown eyes of my
great-grandfather, Andres Ordóñez Escoraz, and through the
bright, dazzling, azure eyes of his niece, Escolástica Escoraz
Vda De Miranda, whom everyone called Tiká, and who was,
in fact, my actual great-grandmother, as some of you already
know, a secret that was kept from me until Tiká herself told
me the story. Yes, yes, but I shall leave that for another day.
Let me just say for now that we all shared the same dream,
my great-grandfather, Tiká and myself. We all of us longed
for a life where always we had fresh-cut dahlias in our hands,
always our eyes were clear and our skin pink, our lips rang
out with a laughter like the sound of wedding bells, and
always we wore the lively sandals of an early spring. Is this
not what everyone wishes for? Of course it is. But what does
that matter? It is what I wished for.

I was eighteen in 1967. That was the year I began to
lose my belief in the impossible, which some say is just a part
of the inevitable process of growing up, and which others
point to as the source of all despair in the modern age, the
disintegration of the soul. I am not sure about all that. I think
losing your belief in the impossible is almost as bad as losing
your teeth, but not quite. But it is also true that I did not
begin losing my teeth until 1996, a full four years before all
the madness in my life had settled down, so my perspective
on what is important and what is not has undergone, shall
we say, a substantial transformation. Back in 1967 life seemed
much more complicated. Back in 1967 I myself was teetering
on the edge. I was prepared to deliver myself up to the
despair of living the same loveless life my mother lived. She

had been sharing with me the secrets of her secret misfortune
for years. I think she had been hoping to gain a companion,
a friend and compatriot, a lonely confidante who believed as
she did that her misery was the only possibility among all
the possibilities of her life. She wanted to be absolved of any
responsibility for her own fate. I am sure that is how she saw
it. But I was only eighteen. What did I truly know? Little by
little I began to think that my life would become her life and
that would be that. The misery of our lives would become so
entangled that we would not be able to separate one misfortune from another. What could I do? It was foreordained. No,
no, do not get me wrong. Hers was not a bad life. But I was
struggling for breath in the sea of her disappointment, which
had, I think, also become a sea of tequila. My father made a
decent living driving a truck. He had given my mother a small
slice of the American pie. But it was never enough for her,
which was quite odd (ungrateful is the word that now comes
to mind) if you thought about it, and I thought about it a great
deal, especially late at night when the world is plunged into
silence, like the silence of an empty tomb or a sunken ship, or
the silence that envelops the world when you are staring at an
old photograph or reading various sonnets, sonnets which you
then memorize but later forget, most likely love sonnets.

My mother was born in Santiago, Cuba, but she grew
up in a small village named Cruce de los Banos, a mountain
village tucked away in the shadows of my imagination. But
then she had met my father, who was from Havana, and he
whisked her away. She never said how they met, if he had
come to eastern Cuba or she to Havana. It was a fairytale,
naturally, at least at first. During my teenage years my mother
was the first to point out that all love stories begin as fairy-
tales, enigmatic, mysterious, undecipherable, hopeful, a view
of heaven, so to speak, but then in a heart-wrenching rush of
utterly incomprehensible anguish, true love disintegrates and
the two principal actors, the young lovers (or the middle-aged
lovers, or the elderly lovers) melt away as if they had never
existed, as if they had been made of wax. But when my
mother first met my father, she didn't know what was happening at all. It all happened so quickly, she said. *En un abrir
y cerrar de ojos.* But again, she spoke of it as something out

of her control. My father had been educated at the University
of Havana and he spoke with great eloquence. He was going
to be a lawyer and then he was going to enter politics and he
was going to help turn Cuba into the paradise it was always
meant to be. He was going to bring equality to the people, just
like Marti had always hoped. Who could resist such charm?
Especially if you were a rural girl. Naturally, my mother fell
in love with him. But nothing worked out as he had hoped.
My father was an idealist in a brutal, unforgiving, intolerant
world where human frailty was an unpardonable sin. So one
thing led to another. The war started in Europe and Batista
came to power and my father joined the Navy, and then the
war was over and Grau became president and my father took
my mother to Miami.

I   My father had said he was through with Cuba, but he
never said why, though I always suspected it had something
to with the war or what he did during the war, but he never
said a word except that he had been in the Navy. But one
night he was shouting out in his sleep about some German spy
they had caught, or a whole bunch they had rounded up, and
you could almost hear the bullets flying about in his dream.
He was shouting like the whole thing was a bad memory,
something that had happened that he wished had never
happened, as if he had murdered the spy in cold blood, or he
had murdered someone in cold blood, or he had been part of
an executioner's squad, or he had killed a friend by accident.
You expect that sort of thing to happen in a war. But you don't
expect to confront it in your own family.

I   I must confess it seemed quite fantastic to me. It seemed
like it was straight out of the movies. I could not imagine
my father with a gun. I could not imagine someone dying by
his hand. But when I asked him about it the next morning
he only laughed and said 'Irse a la cabeza del toro,' which was
a puzzling thing to say, and then he headed out the door. I
remember he was grinning from ear to ear. But that was how
my father was. After a while my mother grew tired of his
strange dreams. I was twelve, maybe thirteen. My father was
always shouting out about something in the middle of the
night, and his odd, even bizarre explanations (the egotism
of a lunatic, my mother said) were almost always cryptic

pronouncements or vague warnings, song lyrics he had once
heard, or bits of poetry he had read years earlier but only
half-remembered, like 'no, no, I cannot, I don't want to be part
of these buffaloes with silver teeth,' or 'to sleep is to float,' or
'it is nothing, they are pieces of walking lava, that is all they
are,' or 'no one expects anything to survive in the desert,' or
'See, the gentleman from Paris is coming,' or something his
own mother had told him when he was a small boy in Vedado,
words of wisdom that had lost their meaning over the years,
half-truths, mixed metaphors, street slang, old wives' super-
stitions, that sort of thing, which meant that his answers had
absolutely nothing to do with the questions you asked about
his dreams and why he was troubled, at least I was unable to
make any sense out of what he said. 'Please, Papa,' I would
say to him. 'What are you talking about?' But he would only
scratch at his thin face and laugh and say, 'Hush now, Isidora,
you ask the impossible. *Pedir la luna.*'

At some point, as you might have guessed, my mother
had no more room in her tired, lonely heart for his 'unseemly
antics,' as she called them. She grew tired of his life as a
truck driver and her life as a truck driver's wife, even if her
life in Miami was far better than she could have hoped for in
her small village near Santiago. But this did not matter. He
had bought for her a tiny four room bungalow in Allapattah
so they could begin building their American dream. But my
mother no longer shared this dream. She no longer loved my
father, she said. This is what she told me. She was trapped in
a life without love with a man who was troubled by strange,
crazy nightmares. She said he would wake up drowning in
a pool of sweat in the middle of the night or early in the
morning when the dark birds were calling out to each other in
their throaty, hypnotic language of vanquished ghosts, and he
would look at her with wild, sightless eyes dripping with the
black syrup of fear, this is how she put it, as if he had just dug
out his own eyeballs with his own fingernails, which he would
only do if he had come face to face with a demon, this is how
my mother told the tale, and she said she would run to the
bathroom when he woke like this and hide in the bathtub, the
curtain drawn or wrapped around her like a shawl, fearing for
her life.

No, no, she was never in any real danger. She was a
bit melodramatic, my mother, and given to wild flights of
fancy. You have to remember that. Yes, oh she most certainly
did run to the bathroom in the middle of the night or early
in the morning. But only to pee. Which you would naturally
expect from all the tequila she drank. But she needed to give
voice to her misery, and she needed me to listen to this voice.
So that is what I did. I listened. When she talked about my
father she would often use the word *mequetrefe*, which means
good-for-nothing. Some days I agreed with her. Other days
I thought she was a great hypocrite, and I would tell her so,
but she would wave me away. But I did not truly understand.
I did not see how my father's choices had become the source
of her despair, a tree already in full flower the day I turned
eighteen, a very black tree with flowers like black orchids that
must have certainly seemed a vision of death to everyone who
knew her, but I did not see this. And I did not realize that her
despair had become the source of my own virgin lament. I was
drowning in the ignorance of youth, ready to give away my
life and the promise of love to ease my mother's heartache.
But then, miracle of miracles, I found the doorway to my very
own future and the hope of bright, sunny days ahead, which
as anyone will tell you is a glorious moment indeed and
produces a flowering tree of a different kind, even if the life
you imagine doesn't turn out as you think it will.

So one day I was walking from one place to another. I
don't remember why. But for some reason I took a shortcut
between NW 35th Street and NW 31st, a narrow alley that had
always been dirt but was now freshly paved, and there was a
sign on the corner that said La Campana Avenue, which didn't
exist on any of the city maps and never existed on any of the
maps, but there it was. I had barely walked a single block in
the glaring afternoon sun when I realized with the hush of a
thousand saints descending from on high that I had entered
the dream of my future. Is not the miracle of recognizing one's
own future a marvelous mystery? Yes, that day is forever
etched in my memory. I remember there was a great deal of
activity on that narrow street that was once an alley. Trucks
with building supplies trundled past. Men shouted at me
to get out of the way. A couple of cars went past. What was

going on? Then a few more cars. One was a black limousine.
I had never been that close to a black limousine before. I was
thrilled. I felt I could have reached out and touched one of
the taillights. Then I saw the reason for all of the hubbub.
Halfway between NW 35th Street and NW 31st, gleaming with
the pink luminescence of a coral reef, was a three-story stucco
building and a newly paved parking lot surrounded by a pink
concrete wall just three feet high. There was a set of polished
mahogany steps leading up to a polished mahogany door and
above the door there was a stained-glass window depicting
the sun and the moon dancing a sexy, symbiotic dance of
love amid a sea of stars. Next to the door there was a small
brass plaque that said 25½, and beneath the plaque, fixed to
the wall, was a tiny brass marine bell. There were also three
antique horse head hitching posts made of brass in front of
the building. I suspect the horse heads were meant to suggest
those bygone, elegant, halcyon days when the wealthy citizens
of Miami plied the streets in horse-drawn carriages, though
in truth those days never existed because Miami wasn't really
a thriving, bustling city until the 1920s when everyone drove
around in Studebakers or Chryslers or Fords, or some of them
traveled by electric streetcars, which wasn't a bad way to
travel at all, though it was limited to a few streets in downtown Miami like Flagler Street and Biscayne Boulevard and
6th Street and 12th Street, and you could also head west across
the river or east across the causeway out to Miami Beach, and
you could even head down to Coral Gables and back, which
took about an hour if you took a local car, but by the 1940s the
old electric streetcars had vanished, as everything we love or
prize beyond measure vanishes sooner or later. But I did not
care about the history of Miami and how people got around
the city and the inaccuracy of the brass horse head hitching
posts when I was standing there in front of that pink stucco
palace. I could have cared less. I had never seen such a place,
not even in my imagination. I had never even heard of such
a place. But what is more astonishing is that I could hear
the echoes of a kind of music I had never heard before, even
though no music was playing, even though there wouldn't be
any music emanating from that pink palace for many months
to come, but I heard music nevertheless, a music that flowed

on one side and an old-fashioned electric studio sign from
the golden era of Hollywood above the doors that said
APPLAUSE in bright red fancy letters when it was lit up, a
sign that my Oscar found one thunderous, rainy afternoon in a
pawn shop that existed always and only in the shadows of the
elevated highway that led to downtown Miami. My Oscar was
always fascinated by what other people would throw away or
abandon to the cauldron of eternity, that is what he called it.
The owner of the pawnshop said it was a sign from the *I Love
Lucy Show*, when Lucy and Desi, with their love of a thousand
sambas that could never be extinguished and which would
one day circle the globe, were just starting out, but Oscar was
not so gullible as that. And you did not notice the sweeping
double staircase with gleaming golden handrails and golden
edged runners, elegant staircases that curled up on either
side of the lobby to the second floor with its small intimate
ballroom for dancing competitions and a recital every once in
a while, because my Oscar loved to listen to the children play
the piano or the clarinet or the flute or the oboe or whatever
musical instrument they played, and every year the firemen
had their banquet at La Campana, or maybe it was the police,
it is difficult to remember so long ago, and every so often
there was a wedding or a reception to celebrate a first communion. And you did not notice the open archway leading to the
bar on the other side of the coat check room. What a fantastic
bar with its gleaming dark mahogany counter and the glittery,
shifting, mysterious brilliance of two crystal chandeliers like a
star-filled sky and small café tables where anyone could pull
up a chair and have a glass of brandy or whiskey or wine or a
beer, and half-a-dozen intimate booths where feuding couples
could patch up their differences after the show over Anejo
Highballs with Orange Curacao; or Green Dragon cocktails
made with Kummel Liqueur and Crème de Menthe; or marti-
nis made with Russian vodka or margaritas made with Italian
amaretto; or Harvey Wallbangers, because even though it was
the dazzling seventies with its twirling disco and handlebar
moustaches, some people thought they were still living in the
fabulous fifties; or Pisco Sours with egg whites if you were
from Peru and without egg whites if you were from Pinochet's
Chile; or a bottle of Suisse La Bleue, which even God himself

could not resist; or a bottle of Brandy de Jerez, which Oscar
said contained the magic of the Moors; or Grand Mariner over
ice, which was always my favorite; or maybe a glass of 1691
Clos de Griffier Vieux Cognac, an elixir that took us back
to our incorruptible youth, three fingers from a bottle that
Oscar had purchased on our one and only trip to Paris, our
honeymoon, a bottle which he only rarely trotted out because
it was so expensive. To tell you the truth I do not know
what Oscar thought he was doing with such a fancy bottle.
¡Ay de mí! He had purchased this extravagant bottle for the
extravagant price of fifteen thousand dollars from the owner
of a fancy restaurant a stone's throw from our hotel, which
was somewhere near Saint-Germain-des-Prés, I think, though
I cannot be sure, the streets of Paris were to me a swirling
labyrinth, and it was oh so very long ago, but I do remember
thinking that was a fairly high price for a single bottle, and I
said so, but my sweet, enduring Oscar only laughed, and the
owner of the restaurant then also laughed, and how they knew
each other I will never know, but they seemed like old friends,
like two bandits holed up in the mountains, and my Oscar
said the price was irrelevant, we were in Paris for the first and
perhaps only moment in our lives, so we should let loose our
inhibitions and our fierce, unbidden fears and smile for as
long as God would permit, and just as he said that, the words
of the great poet, Emilio Ballagas popped into my head, a
poet that my own brother had one day thrust before me since
they shared the same first name, and which he soon forgot,
as always, but the words that popped into my head that
day were just the right words to capture my mood standing
there in that fancy restaurant with the owner hiding behind
Oscar's shoulder, his eyes like two small suns hiding behind
a cloud, peering out every so often to see if he would be paid
this outrageous sum for a single bottle that could be drunk
in a single night, and Oscar ignoring my tiniest thoughts, my
trembling hands like the wings of a tiny bird or a cringing bat,
my one and only beloved oblivious to the emotions of distrust
racing through my blood, and just like that I heard the words
of Emilio Ballagas, as if the great poet himself had returned
from the scattered ashes of the dead to give voice to my
tremulous, throaty despair.

Si pregunta por mí, dile que habito
en la hoja del acanto y en la acacia.
O dile, si prefieres, que me he muerto.
Dale el suspiro mío, mi pañuelo;
mi fantasma en la nave del espejo.
Tal vez me llore en el laurel o busque
mi recuerdo en la forma de una estrella.

Was this the future that lay in wait for us? Was this the herald of that summer sadness that would plague us for all eternity? It certainly seemed so. It seemed like the future. But what could I say? Our destinies have already shaped us in ways we cannot comprehend. I have always believed this. I have always believed that when you recognize the future, all you can do is embrace it. So there was nothing I could say to warn my beloved Oscar. Besides, he would not have heard me if I had tried. Truly, the flesh is a laurel that sings and suffers, but the moment you realize this truth, it is too late. Human frailty is the natural condition of humanity. At least this is what I have come to know. Of course my Oscar was too much a part of this flesh-and-blood world to ever think so deeply. He would never listen to anyone's song but his own. That day in Paris I realized he would never truly hear me. He was riding high on the wings of success, wings which I wanted to tell him always lead to death or madness or despair or worse because they are replicas of those infamous wings that Icarus wore, but he would never believe that life could be so cruel, even though I know he had seen this cruelty with his own eyes when he lived in Havana, though he never spoke of it. But life is difficult. So I said nothing.

We stayed in Paris until we had spent every last penny of our travel money. For two glorious weeks we paraded around the city in sun-splattered finery, Oscar even bought me a fancy lace parasol for twirling, and during those extravagant, mind-bending, Parisian nights we swam in the limpid pools of our deepest desires, and we never spoke again about the price of this or that, because that is just how Oscar was when it came to money. That is just how Oscar was when it came to many, many things.

There I go babbling again. I am insufferably scatter-
brained. We were talking about the moment you stepped
inside La Campana, and there I went flying off on a wild
tangent about love and life and human frailty and honeymoons and Paris in the spring. The dreams and fantasies of an
old woman. The happiness that becomes a sadness in search
of a happiness. A wild goose chase! So let me start all over.
When you stepped inside La Campana you were dazzled by
the beauty of the coat check girls. Yes. That is true. It is also
true that you did not see the stairs going up or the doors
leading to the main ballroom or the Spanish-style archway
leading to the bar. You did not see any of that. Your eyes were
drawn immediately, with a fragile hope like tiny mice peeking
out of dark holes, to the coat check girls.

There were three coat check girls. I don't know why
Oscar needed three. They had pouty, cinematic faces with
flirty, mysterious, doleful eyes, the kind of faces you only
saw in magazines like *Glamour* or *Vogue* or *Vanidades*, like they
were showgirls or chorus girls or Hollywood starlets. God
only knows where Oscar found them.

The one I remember best was named Bonita. Was that
her name? Ah, yes, yes it was. She was very pretty. She possessed a dark, gleaming beauty that transcended all words. I
was very jealous. Every girl who walked into La Campana had
a right to be jealous. I am sure the other two coat check girls
were jealous. Funny I don't remember the names of the other
two. But I will never forget Bonita. What an extraordinary
woman she was!

Bonita had very dark hair, almost black (which was the
exact opposite of my fiery red hair), and she wore it curled
up in the back with a red rose like a Flamenco dancer, or she
might wear a gold or turquoise tortoise shell comb with her
hair twisted up, spilling out beneath the comb in braided
ringlets like water spurting out from some crazy Spanish
fountain. What a glorious, beguiling, cunning creature! She
had very long eyelashes and her lips were dripping with the

932

possibility of a kiss. A long, luxuriant kiss. You could almost
taste it.

Looking back, well, I am certain it was all a pose. I am
certain she knew exactly what she was doing. But she was
a goddess all the same! She walked on rose petals, flowers
strewn along whatever path she took, dahlias or geraniums or
gentians. She wore the shortest skirts you could imagine, silky,
slinky skirts that seemed to disappear whenever someone
opened the door and a breeze swept in and then all you could
see were two, long legs glistening in the soft orange sunset
glow of the lamps that hung from the ceiling and Bonita's
plush derriere moving slowly back and forth, a slow, sexy
samba, like an early morning caress. Every man who looked
her way, and how could they not, thought if only they could
check their girlfriends or their wives instead of their coats,
yes, maybe they could steal off to some dark corner with
Bonita, and there were many more dark corners in Miami in
those bygone, elegant days then there are now. They dreamed
of slipping away, of spending an hour or two in Bonita's
Spanish dancer arms, the starry night above them opening up,
shimmering like those ancient salon mirrors of the philosophers, mirrors which absorb all light and so become portals
to the future. They would choose to forget their wives or their
hopeful girlfriends, at least in the glare of their having walked
through the doors of La Campana, blinded by the dazzling
beauty of Bonita, dreaming that God would permit them to
curl up inside this dark-haired goddess, like returning to the
womb of creation, the men becoming invisible atoms of happy
nothingness, at peace for once in their lives, hoping beyond all
hope that the universe would collapse and their joy would be
frozen for all eternity.

What can I say? I am sure they all thought something
like that. Just as I am sure that their girlfriends or their wives
knew what they were thinking but refused to make a scene
out in public, for the women in those days were refined
beyond belief, in spite of what you may have heard or think
you know. They floated above all strife and insult on the
gentle breeze of ceremonious charm. Besides, they would not
let the tragically absurd behavior of their husbands or their
boyfriends like rusty Spanish cannons going off at midnight

ruin an evening filled with an impossible music.

It was the kind of music that swept past you like flocks of startled white ibis whirling into the air. That's what some said. It was the kind of music that sped up through the stratosphere until the air was very thin, circling round and round the face of the white-hot sun like ghostly apparitions or wayward angels in search of God's redeeming grace, and then descending hours later, absolved of original sin. That's what others said. And the patrons of La Campana drank in that impossible music without regret till dawn. And all the while the happy, drunken laughter of the men and women dancing rang out against the darkness as if the darkness did not exist, and the booze was freely flowing, vast quantities, as if from uncorked geysers, with complete disregard for the laws of physics and common decency. But you could be sure the refined gentlewomen of those bygone, mythic days, who bathed twice a day in bathtubs filled to overflowing with white gardenias or mariposa, and rubbed macadamia oil into their skin every night in the hopes of reversing the damage of the mocking, remorseless years, you could be sure these women were going to explode the moment they got home, because they were, after all, the descendants of bloodthirsty Spain and would have their honor satisfied by magic or knives or slow poison or emasculating words.

Those who were married would limit their vengeance to the bedrooms they shared with their husbands, whom they had married in the eternally mysterious and reverberating presence of God, all of them dressed in dazzling white wedding dresses that surely cost an eye from a face, immaculate dresses consecrated to heaven, but still the brides to be were reciting countless Hail Marys in the silence of their hopeful hearts as they stood before the altars of eternal bliss until the rings had been slipped onto their fingers and the churches were filled with glorious, ear-shattering applause from their families and other well-wishers. And those who were not yet married would seek their justice in the quiet corners of the various sitting rooms in their parents' houses or the screened-in sun porches or the Spanish-style foyers, which were the only rooms their boyfriends were allowed into unchaperoned (and also the dining room if they were invited over for dinner, and once in a while the kitchen, and of course the bathroom, as needed). Because all of these refined but proud gentlewomen of Spanish descent who had been born in Miami or who had traveled from the sunny shores of Cuba or Puerto Rico or the Dominican Republic or South America or faraway Spain to settle in paradise, these wives and hopeful girlfriends, they all possessed the integrity of an irrepressible heart and so refused to become strangers under other stars.

Oscar used to say that if it weren't for Bonita, we would have closed our doors after that first year. But this is not quite true. Oscar saw things as most men see things. Yes, yes, the sweaty, inconstant gentlemen of Miami returned night after night hoping to catch a glimpse of Bonita, their eyes shining like brightly polished coins, drawn by the hope of a luxuriant kiss and the possibility of more. But their wives and their girl-friends returned hoping to experience once more the ecstasy of that impossible music, a chance to fill the insufferable void in their hearts, for which music is the only cure, ever mindful that all earthly pleasures are transitory and only God knows who will find true happiness.

-111-

If my Oscar was the soul of La Campana in those days, which he most certainly was, then Bonita was its irrepressible, suffering heart. I remember one spring night the music was flowing out through the double doors right into the arcaded lobby with its freshly painted orange walls and its dazzling hanging lamps, and there was Bonita dancing like she was at the center of the universe. This was in 1972, I am pretty sure. Oscar and I were not yet married, but that is beside the point. The other two girls were leaning on the table next to the coat check room, mesmerized. The table was empty. A small circle of men and women had gathered around Bonita, who was oblivious to everything but the music. No one was wearing a coat to check. It was still early in the evening, so it was only the warm-up act. And besides, nobody would bother about

going into the main ballroom as long as they could watch
Bonita. She was a ribbon of wildfire spinning with devilish
intent in the hazy interior glow of the lamplight. She was a
delight to watch. And after a while it seemed as if we all fell
into a trance. Bonita and this ribbon of fire became two separate entities, as if the fire was a many tentacled creature of the
night and Bonita was encased within it, inside it, suspended in
a bubble of molten glass, the fire wrapping itself with greater
intensity around her tiny waist as the music soared, the notes
like tiny daggers slicing open the skin of the universe and the
bright black light of other worlds pouring in. And then all of a
sudden there was a burst of drums and then a long, mournful
saxophone and then a soaring flight of piano keys, and Bonita
flung her head back, her mouth wide open in wild, gaping
laughter, and the tentacles loosened their grip and the molten
glass began to drain away and Bonita went spinning across
the floor. But then in a motion so quick you could not catch it
with your eye, as if it were an afterthought or a young lover's
lament, she grabbed hold of the thin trailing ribbon by the
tip (which was all that was left of the fire by this point) and
pulled it after her, and so they began their wild, fiery erotic
spinning dance all over again. Sparks were flying as Bonita
and the ribbon of fire danced this way and that, unconcerned
with anyone who was watching, singeing the eyebrows of
those who were standing too close. And wherever Bonita
stepped in her feverish furry of a Spanish dancer, tiny black
heel marks were burned into the tile.

Then the warm-up act was finished on this very warm
evening, one of the warmest spring evenings of the century,
that was what the radio had said, and Oscar came out of the
main ballroom with an eager, welcoming smile, a flirtatious
smile, according to some, and his outstretched arms looking
to embrace everyone he knew, which was everyone who ever
walked through the doors of La Campana. He wagged his
finger at Bonita, whose blameless, inner smile was reflected
in the smooth, almond-colored sheen of her perspiring skin,
and she went back to the empty table in front of the coat check
room. One by one the guests chatted with Oscar. The men
shook his hand and the women gave him gentle, airy kisses
on the cheek. And all the while Oscar was a beaming proud

Papa. He was saying how they had a very special treat for
everyone that night, a young guitarist who played the electric
bass with the precision of God and the burning passion of
the Devil. *'Partirse el alma,'* Oscar said. 'This boy will make
someone's heart bleed. Yes, yes. He will make all of our hearts
bleed, I think.' And then: 'Yes, there is one table up front I
set aside especially for you.' And then: 'Yes, oh do not worry,
the waitresses will bring you whatever you like from the bar.
Whatever you can think of, whatever you can imagine.' And
that's how it went for several minutes. My Oscar stood by the
double doors chatting with everyone as they passed by until
everyone had found their seats, and then the lights in the
lobby began to flash, once, twice, a gentle reminder that the
show would begin in ten minutes or so, and then the flashing
stopped. Then for some reason, who can say why, my Oscar
walked over to where Bonita had been dancing and looked
down at the tiled floor and the black burn marks. Clearly he
didn't know what to make of them. But who could blame him?
It is not always so easy to know what you are looking at. So
he looked at the burn marks for a while, not very long, truly
it was only a moment, and then he looked over at Bonita, but
she was chatting with a young man in a ponytail. Then he
hurried back into the main ballroom.

   I did not know the young man in the ponytail, but he
and Bonita were chatting away like old friends. He was very
good looking. Dark brooding, thoughtful eyes. A deep fire
there, I could see that. I think an unquenchable fire, which
made him the perfect match for Bonita. A slightly wistful
upper lip. I was amused by their reverence for each other and
their irreverence for everyone around them. But not everyone
was amused, which you can understand. A swarthy fragment
of a man with a boxer's pug nose and a grooved chin was not
amused. I say a fragment of a man because he seemed more
like a cartoon of a man than actual flesh and blood. A comic
book villain. An eye-catching façade, but nothing of substance
beneath the surface. That is how he seemed. He was closer to
thirty than forty. He wore a black hat with a black hatband
and a black suit with a thin red tie. He wore a white shirt
with diamond cuff links, and his fingernails were freshly
manicured. In a word, he was immaculate in his appearance. I

swear I even saw glittering diamonds in the spaces in between
his teeth. He was not amused. At first glance I thought he was
simply tired of waiting for Bonita to take his coat. He was
the only person in La Campana that night with a coat to take.
But I did not wonder at this. Instead, I was caught looking at
his coat, a black Chesterfield overcoat, very stylish in another
era. The kind of coat my father would wear, but only on
a Saturday night, and only when he was younger and my
mother was still in love with him. So I was staring at this coat
and thinking of my father. I was remembering a dream I once
had about my father. In my dream my father was wearing a
coat just like the one I was looking at, but it was before he had
immigrated to Miami. It was during the war when he was in
the Navy. But he wasn't in the Navy in my dream. Or at least
he wasn't on a ship or patrolling the beaches or driving along
the coast road in a jeep. He was sitting in a dark room at a
long table. I was looking down the length of the table. I barely
recognized my father but I knew it was him. It was kind of
like looking through the wrong end of a telescope. There was
a row of strange silver machines on the table and many more
men sitting there besides my father. All of the machines were
clicking away furiously, like clocks that had gone irretrievably
mad. All of the men were wearing black Chesterfields and
radio headsets and they were listening intently to whatever
radio signals they could pick up. Their behavior seemed very
normal in my dream. They were not speaking to each other.
Every so often one of them would write something down on
a pad of paper. But nothing disturbed their rhythm. Then the
machines stopped clicking and my father got very excited.
He could hardly contain himself. He wrote something down
very fast and then tore the paper from the pad and rushed to
the end of the long table and the row of silver machines and
handed the piece of paper to a tall man wearing a glowing
white uniform. 'We've got him now, the German bastard,' the
man in the white uniform said, and he clapped my father on
the back with great joy. And then everyone in my dream was
talking all at once, including my father, but I couldn't make
sense of what they were saying except every now and then a
name would pop up out of their cloud of gibberish, Hans or
Heinz or Maximilian or Ernst or Johann or Georg or Jörge or

Jürgen or Leopold or Helmut, I could never quite tell, but I knew they were German names. That was the dream I once had. That is what I was remembering on that warm spring evening in La Campana oh so many years ago, all because I saw a swarthy man in a Chesterfield coat. Isn't it strange how memory works? And then I forgot about the dream entirely. I was standing there wondering where the swarthy man had picked up his coat and where he was from. (That is also how memory works.) He certainly wasn't from Miami. I could tell that much. The coat was draped over his arm and his arm was extended towards the empty coat check table. The other two girls had vanished. Bonita and the young man with the ponytail had stepped off to a corner opposite the table where the lamp light gave way to dark shadows, like the shadows you imagine exist at the bottom of the sea. They were cooing in those dark, fluid, watery shadows. Then I had the strangest thought. I thought by the way the swarthy man was holding his coat and the fact that it was an incredibly warm evening that he was an assassin of some sort hiding a gun. He was aiming a gun at the young man with the ponytail. Why, well, I could not imagine why. He was grinding his glittery bejeweled teeth, a symptom of dark, nervous energy perhaps, and aiming his unseen gun, counting down the seconds until he pulled the trigger. And I was also busy counting down the never-ending seconds right along with him, what else was there to do, wondering if Bonita would be next, and everyone else who was hanging around the lobby, all of us inadvertent witnesses to a most senseless murder.

But the swarthy man was not hiding a gun beneath his coat. He tossed his coat to the table and called out to the young man with the ponytail. He called him kid. He said 'Hey kid, you don't know what you're doing with a woman like that. Why don't you get lost! Leave her to someone who's got the goods.' I wasn't exactly sure if he was joking or if he was serious, but then he laughed a hoarse, rattling laugh and his meaning became clear.

Bonita and the young man with the ponytail edged over to the table. The expression on the swarthy man's face was an odd mixture of vulgar, aching lust and unacknowledged, trembling paranoia. That's as good a way to describe it as any.

I mean it is often true that words are impossible to use. They just get in the way. But what else can we do? Anyway, in the heat of the moment I remember thinking that life hardly ever worked out for him the way he hoped it would. Looking back, I guess maybe I was right, at least in this particular instance.

It was almost like watching the cinema. A dark romantic movie, naturally, film noir from the golden age of Hollywood. That is what it seems like now. Bonita took the swarthy man's coat and disappeared into the coat check room. But she did not disappear quickly. She sashayed, a slow, rhythmic twitching of her hips. I almost laughed watching the swarthy man watching her. He was stunned by her hips. The young man with the ponytail was not stunned. He had his eyes on the swarthy man the whole while. I could tell he was becoming possessive. Then Bonita returned and came up behind the young man and slipped her arms around his shoulders and kissed him lightly on the cheek. The tip of her tongue flashed in the dim lamp light. This I could plainly see. It was a treacherous kiss, if you were viewing it from a certain perspective. It was a slap in the face. An insult. It was like pulling a trigger. Of course if you were viewing it from a different perspective, it was breathtakingly beautiful, romantic, hopeful, spirited, spiritual, compassionate, an awakening, everything we hope for ourselves and for our children and our children's children and so on until the end of days.

I could not believe what happened next. As if that treacherous kiss was not bad enough. I know personally I would not have had the courage. But they did. *Frente al amor y la muerte no sirve de nada ser fuerte*, as they say. Yes, truly, they were fearless in this respect. Bonita and her lover. He was obviously her lover, but how long they had been lovers I did not know. At any rate, no sooner had the swarthy man finished digesting that most treacherous kiss, then Bonita and her lover smiled a most treacherous smile (again, as viewed from one perspective and not another).

How is it the swarthy man did not react? I swear I was about to intervene at this point, but I assumed that the damage was already done. *Ser agua pasada*, as my father would have said.

But the swarthy man did not react.

I have to admit now that I had no idea what was happening. I was standing there thinking if he did have a gun he was going to use it now, but he no longer seemed to even see Bonita. He returned their most treacherous smile with great politeness and an eager, treacherous smile of his own, even as he kept his eyes on the young man with the ponytail, a level, unflinching gaze, as if he were about to issue a challenge.

'I have heard you play before, my young friend,' he said. 'And you are quite talented, quite passionate, but your passion is no match for the passion in this woman's heart.' Then he smiled again, a smile that was not so treacherous but still quite eager, and took out a small business card and gave it to the young man. 'When you are finished tonight,' he said, 'I should like to talk with you.'

From where I was standing I could not see what was printed on the card. The young man seemed to read the words with great interest, but then he handed the card back. I do not know if Bonita saw what was on the card, but she gave the young man with the ponytail a tremendous squeeze, which seemed like a declaration of her eternal love, or at least her youthful infatuation, and then a second longer, lingering kiss, infinitely more treacherous than the first because of its panting intensity, at least this is how it seemed to me.

It makes me laugh now. I truly did not have a clue about what was going on. How little we understand what is going on right in front of our noses in any given moment. It is like we are trapped on the other side of the mirror. *Benditos sean los dulces nombres.* Suddenly the lights in the lobby were flashing once again, a furious flashing, and the young man with the ponytail had a guitar in his hand and he blew Bonita a fingertip kiss and said he would play tonight like he had never played before, the very air would bleed with the impenetrable sadness and the disfiguring joy of a thousand centuries. That is how he put it. He seemed quite pleased with himself. He was beaming with the poetry of his words as he spoke. Then he disappeared through the black leather double doors, and for a moment I could hear the tinkling of glasses as the waitresses served the last of the drinks, and then I could hear Oscar's thin, wavering voice full of a Papa's pride welcoming his new discovery to the stage, this young lion of the electric guitar, and the audience roared with their approval.

I am not sure where I went at that point. It is almost as if I became a shadow on the wall. I remember that Bonita and the swarthy man did not move from the empty table. They talked quietly for a while, a discreet conversation, the two of them bathed in the soft, underwater glow of the lobby lights, which had been turned down because of the show. It was like swimming in a tropical ocean when Oscar turned down the lights. But I am not sure where exactly I was.

Come to think of it, I might have been standing in the archway leading to the bar, a frozen moment, uncertain if I was thirsty and needed something to drink or maybe a splash of water on my face would be enough to revive my sagging spirits, for Oscar and I were in the middle of our first lover's quarrel and we hadn't spoken directly to each other in three days. Yes, I had almost forgotten that. What do you suppose we were quarreling about? We almost never quarreled. Something trivial, no doubt.

Or perhaps I was simply tired from waiting for Oscar to apologize for whatever it was he had done, so all I wanted was to lie down, though to be honest, I was probably just as guilty as my Oscar, maybe more so, which would also explain my lethargy. I do not deal well with feeling guilty. It puts me to sleep as surely as too many glasses of wine. Either way I might have been heading up the stairs to the second floor because there was a red velvet Persian sofa where you could take a nap, just around the corner from the cozy ballroom of my greatest dream, where Oscar and I would one day get married, though on that particular spring evening our wedding intentions were still only the tiniest dot on the horizon.

I confess I don't remember where I was. I might even have slipped in through the black leather double doors to listen to the young man with the ponytail play his electric guitar, yes, yes, but also to spy on my beloved Oscar, yes, I confess to that now, because Oscar liked to flirt with the waitresses if he thought I wasn't looking, especially after he turned down the lights. I suppose there are many possibilities. But wherever I was I could hear Bonita and the swarthy man talking. I could hear them quite clearly, even though they were nowhere to be seen. Their words were radio signals

shooting off into space. Their words were tiny daggers of
ice breaking off from the moon. They were talking about the
future, or more precisely, one of many possible futures.

The swarthy man said his name was Octavio or Alvarez
or Alfonso or Gutiérrez. I am terrible when it comes to
remembering names. For Oscar remembering names comes
quite easily. But for me names evaporate as quickly and as
silently as a morning mist. The swarthy man said he was an
agent for a record company in New York City. He said he had
been following the young man with the ponytail for several
months and wanted to sign him before someone else got their
hooks into him. He talked about record contracts and taking
the music world by storm and brightly lit stages and the
whirlwind of fame. He talked about the money to be made.
He said a talent like this kid wasn't so much a gamble as it
was an opportunity. But you had to strike while the iron was
hot. He'd seen talents like this come and go, so he knew. No
matter how good you were, if you didn't have the right people
in your corner you faded into oblivion. He didn't want to
see that happen to this kid. He said he would be honored to
represent this kid. He knew all of the big money men in New
York City who didn't really know music at all but who knew
all about making fortunes. He said he hoped he could count
on Bonita. Bonita said he could.

When the young man with the ponytail began to play it
was like the world had been swallowed by an ancient beatnik
darkness. The rhythm of breathing in the gutter and the rain
splattering across your face. Clouds swirling past towards
oblivion, the atmosphere dissolving into nothingness. But
then almost immediately a resurrection. The storm was over.
The soul of a dead man rising towards a hissing sun. Then a
gentle, early evening breeze and the salty smell of the sea like
a benediction cleansing away the grime of endless toiling days.
Then the staccato rippling of a car speeding along a coastal
highway, a gleaming convertible, a man at the wheel and a
girl in sunglasses by his side, windswept hair and windswept
laughter, the car surging to a stop amid a flurry of waves and
flocks of sea birds soaring into the sky and the ocean tide
roaring across the hard-packed sand, bubbling past the tires,

the two lovers disappearing in the glare of the horizon. Then night falling, starlight falling, the moonlight of a tiny sliver of a moon reflected off the shells of tiny hermit crabs scuttling back and forth in the shimmering darkness. An infinity of ghostly blue slivers. Like consciousness. Like an intimate awareness of God or the boundaries of the universe. The slivers sending shivers up and down your spine. The moonlight fading but not the ceaseless, unrepentant, rampaging shivers. Then the ghost of summer, of many summers, a strange, hollow wail. It was like leading a goat to slaughter, the sound of it. Ears dripping with the sacrificial blood of memory. A strange, mystical ceremony. Then the music changing again. The sound of the darkness swallowing itself and the sound of humanity emerging. But not quite humanity. An alternative humanity. Hollow men and hollow women with eyes like rivets, sightless eyes, shaking their naked mechanical torsos, strutting their naked mechanical legs, swinging their naked mechanical arms, screws rattling loose, pieces of metal falling to the ground, the sounds of wild parrots screaming like rusty hinges. All of this suggested by this strange, new, bewildering music. Then silence. As quiet as God's first breath. As loud as a roaring furnace. Then a steady, drumming dawning. The sun rising again, returning. Cymbals of light crashing, clashing, breaking apart. The clear sky opening up, absorbing all life. The deep bass growl of a ship's horn somewhere in the distance, a slow but steady affirmation. This is what the music sounded like.

I am fairly certain the swarthy man walked away empty handed that night. I know for a fact that the young man with the ponytail left with Bonita immediately after the show, and the swarthy man was sitting in the bar drinking mojitos with the after-hours crowd. I watched him for a while. I don't know how long. He was sitting in the bar, drowning in a sea of mojitos, as I recall, all the way up to his eyeballs and the tiny black and white and silver eels of many desires swimming in the froth. At one point, Oscar spoke to him quietly for a few minutes and then clapped the man on the back and started laughing, and then the swarthy man belched out a laugh and every head in the place turned to see who had made such a sound, it

was so loud and awful sounding like a wheezing donkey, and
then everyone went back to their own drinking. I never again
saw the swarthy man after that night. He left around five in
the morning, at that magical hour when the night birds have
ceased their flamboyant carousing and the morning birds are
searching the horizon for the perfection of the morning sun. I
also remember that the young man with the ponytail played
at La Campana on and off for the next several months. I am
sure he lived nearby. Close enough that he saw Bonita on a
fairly regular basis. Close enough that Bonita hummed with
the excitement of a love that is lived every day. You could
feel the electricity flowing through her veins when she walked
past. He was to her a godsend, a ring that has come to the
finger. But then the young man with the ponytail vanished. At
least I never saw him again, not in the flesh. But when I asked
Bonita about him, she said nothing. Then one evening she was
late for work, and when she came in Oscar was fuming, but I
could see that she had been sobbing, so I shooed my beloved-
but-every-so-often-brainless Oscar away and took the poor
girl up to the second floor. ¡Ay de mí! A woman colliding with
romance and a woman drowning in despair are mirror images
of each other. They pine away for that same tiny, rebellious
bird. Even on the brightest and sunniest of days. Yes, yes, oh
my word, yes. They receive flowers and bullets in the same
heart. That is what the poet Lola Rodríguez de Tío would say.
It is what she did say. 'Reciben flores o balas sobre el mismo
corazón . . . .' So we sat down on the Persian style sofa, Bonita
and I, and she poured out her heart of hearts that had once
grown flowers and was now riddled with gaping bullet holes.

 Bonita said those first few months when she had been
dating the young guitar player were the most invigorating
of her young life. She did not care that she was several
years older than he was. She felt like she would live forever
when she was in his arms, this is what she said, this was her
destiny. Naturally, she had been devastated when he went
away, as we all are when we have to face deprivations of any
kind. But he had told Bonita it would not be for long. He was
off to seek his fortune, his fame, but he would return to her
one day with a pocketful of stars. Those were the actual words
he had said. And she believed him with every shred that was

left of her dignity. But he had not yet returned. Bonita had
not even heard from him. But this was not the reason she
had been sobbing that day, no, no, she had convinced herself
that he would return one day, no matter how many years
would flow past in the interim, and it had already been a
few years by that point, no, no, the reason for her tears was
that she had dreamed the night before that her beloved had
died, that he had actually, truly died, a bleeding corpse on a
sidewalk in front of a nightclub somewhere many miles from
the grieving streets of Miami. And she believed in this dream.
She saw everything quite clearly. On the dreadful night of his
death he was playing at a glitzy club in downtown Chicago
or downtown Indianapolis or downtown St. Louis. This is
what Bonita said. And after he finished he went off with
some musician friends to a small, back alley dive where they
could jam for the rest of the night, a nightclub in the middle of
nowhere, but he became separated from his friends, and when
he tried to get into this club, the bouncer would not let him
in. Even when he showed the bouncer his gleaming guitar,
even when he said he was a guitar player and the musicians
inside had invited him to stop by to jam until everyone's heart
was bleeding on the floor, even after he played a few riffs on
his guitar, which he could not have possibly played because
it was an electric guitar and there wasn't an outlet anywhere
in sight, but which he did play, and then a few bricks in
the wall of this crumbling dive in the middle of nowhere
disintegrated into a poof of dust, which was a miracle any
way you looked at it, even then the bouncer did not budge.
Bonita said she could not believe the events as they were
unfolding. They were too bizarre, she said. And her beloved
would never have acted the way he did in this dream. And
yet she could not change how he behaved. Her young lion
refused to accept the bouncer's judgment, which was more
like him than Bonita cared to admit, so he tried to force his
way inside. But the bouncer would have none of it. What was
that young man with the electric guitar thinking, I wondered?
He must have been swimming in a sea of tequila and cocaine
to act with such madness, a hidden rage that flies from rafter
to rafter until the church bells strike midnight and then it is
loosed upon the world. But he stood no chance, even with

such an unexpected and cunning rage. The bouncer hammered away at Bonita's young lion and left him a bleeding, bloody pulp on the sidewalk in front of this hole-in-the-wall club in the middle of nowhere. He died on his way to the hospital. This is what she said. ¡Ay de mí! That was how he had died in Bonita's dream. It was absurd, of course. Where were the watchful eyes of the angels and the saints in this dream of hers? This is what I asked her. Where was the compassion of the Virgin Mary and the hope of the risen Christ? Where was the strength of the Holy Spirit? ¡Madre de Dios! Love stories are not supposed to end in such tragic absurdity. But Bonita believed in the power of this dream. 'If he is not already dead,' she sobbed, 'then it is only a matter of days, maybe weeks.' She was convinced that her beloved would only return to her loving arms as a ghost, an incorporeal phantom. Unless she left the familiar boundaries of Miami to search for him, to warn him, to help him escape the inescapable jaws of death. And this is what she decided to do. It did not matter if you thought, as I did, that the young lion of Bonita's heart had already become a ghost. El pensamiento no tiene barreras, as my father used to say. Bonita believed what she believed. 'If I do not find him, he will surely die a horrible death,' she said. That is why she was sobbing when she walked through the doors of La Campana that night.

Bonita left us the very next day. I do not know exactly where she went, only the general direction. And the young man with the guitar? Well, I soon forgot all about him, but then many, many years later I saw his face in the newspaper. It was his face but then again it was not his face. An artist had painted his face on a wall that was part of a park somewhere in Miami, and the newspaper had printed a photograph of this wall. I had never heard of the park. The newspaper said this young man with the ponytail had been beaten to death outside a nightclub. Just like in Bonita's dream. But he had died right here in Miami, in Fort Lauderdale, where those crazy college kids hang out, not in Indianapolis or Chicago or St. Louis. I wondered if Bonita had ever spoken to him of her dream and what he had said, but then I realized she had never found him. She had left Miami to search the world for the pieces of her heart, and he had returned at some point, or he was here all along. But he never came around La Campana looking for Bonita, which explains everything.

So there I was staring at this photograph in the newspaper, a photograph of a ghost. He was staring out at the world with those same dark, brooding, thoughtful eyes. Somehow you could feel the fire in his soul emanating from the fragile newsprint that had captured his image. An echo of an echo. Still it was a wonder the newspaper didn't burst into flames. It was a wonder I didn't pass out from the heat. He was holding his guitar with the same defiant, even liberating sense of purpose that I remembered from the sound of his music that spring night oh so many years ago. You could not see the whole guitar, just where he was holding the neck and his fingers were pressing down on the strings. I swear you could hear his music flowing out from that photograph of his face on that wall. At least I could. I remember showing Emidio the newspaper at some point and asking him if he heard this celestial music that could transport you to other worlds, and he listened carefully for a while, and then he said he wasn't sure, perhaps if he listened a little while longer, and then he started laughing, but he was very sweet about it. His laughter was a gentle, slow-rolling, lazy sound, like a single wave flowing across the sand and then retreating out to sea, dissolving. Then I asked him if he knew where the park was. He said he didn't know, but he would take me. But he never did. We were going to take Sister Faustino's station wagon one Saturday, but it was raining, and the next Saturday Emidio had too many chores to do, and the next Saturday Sister Faustino went to visit her sister in Tampa, or maybe it was her niece, and the next Saturday Emidio forgot, and the Saturday after that I forgot, and so on and so forth, and that was that. But in the months and years since I came across the photo-graph of that young man's painted face in the newspaper, I find myself thinking about him every now and then, thinking about his dark, brooding thoughtful eyes and his incredible, impossible music. And whenever I think about him I also think about Bonita and how she had dreamed of his death, but there was nothing she could do.

It is a very sad story when you get right down to it. A tragic story. It makes my heart break. *¡Espíritu de mi alma!*

But what are we to do? The church bells they are tolling. *Ya las campanas de la iglesia están doblando.* Life is difficult, as my mother would have said.

-112-

One night my mother dreamed of a fancy church wedding at Gesù Catholic Church. She dreamed I was walking down the aisle with its polished marble floor like a darkly shining mirror that absorbs all of our whispered fears. I was a bride in a fancy brocaded wedding dress, a satin gown with a full train veil lined with luminescent pearls, soft pinks and whites like the teardrops of angels, and tiny leaves made of silk, a soft ivory color, like the wings of shy, tropical birds. It was a gown which had been sewn together by a Spanish widow who spoke no English. This is how my mother described it. This was the fantastic dress I was wearing in her dream. She said I looked neither right nor left as I walked down the aisle. I kept my eyes on the fancy Baroque altars made of Italian marble and the priests standing there in their gleaming white vestments edged with gold and their eyes brimming with sacramental satisfaction.

She could not see my future husband, she said. He was obscured by the dazzling brilliance of the priests, but she was not concerned. She said this meant whoever I married was of no more importance than a passing shadow, a cloud upon the horizon. What was important, she said, was consecrating myself before the glory of the resurrected God, and also before the gleaming marble statues of Jesus and Mary and the glorified saints with their sleepy, sad, yet unimaginably compassionate eyes looking down on the rest of humanity, eyes that reflected the pain of a suffering life and the joy of putting your trust in heaven. But this did not happen, as I have already said. For my mother this dream became a recurring dream, but it did not come true.

113

My first truly vivid memory of Gesù Church begins
strangely enough with a memory of my father, who had
stopped going to church before I turned three. It is a very
long, complicated memory with many twists and turns, but
its beginning is simple enough. Every Sunday morning my
mother would admonish my father for ignoring his Catholic
duty to his children. "How will our children learn to love God
and be inspired by the saints if their own father abandons
them at God's doorstep?' she would ask. "And what will
become of them when God turns his burning, vengeful
eyes their way to exact his rightful justice for their father's
transgressions?'

Every so often my mother would say Lord Shango
instead of God, a slip of the tongue surely, but her meaning
was clear enough. But my father would only laugh a noisy,
jubilant, carefree yet big-hearted laugh, as opposed to
condescending and mean-spirited, and he would remind my
mother that it was he who had introduced her to the Catholic
Church in the first place. Had she forgotten those days when
he had found her in that ash heap of a village in the hills near
Santiago? Had she forgotten that in those days she still prayed
to Orishas trapped like genies inside clay pots or cowrie
shells? Had she forgotten that he had rescued her from the
ignorance that had kept Cuba enslaved for centuries? Then
he would flip his hat onto his head like he had seen a movie
actor once do in the movies and roll out through the screen
door.

My mother would run after him, at least as far as the
sidewalk, screaming obscenities and cursing his disreputable
family of aristocratic thieves who had never known what it
was like to bake in the cane fields under the hot Cuban sun
or suffocate in the fiery, subterranean depths of the mines.
You had only to look at my mother in those moments of her
greatest fury as she ran after my father to know that she was
capable of biting the ghosts of broken days.

Only when my father had turned the corner on his way

to the river did she return to the house, her face gleaming wet and red with the blisters of her anger, and finish getting the two of us, myself and Emilio, ready for the long bus ride to Gesù.

My mother never forgave my father for his Sunday morning blasphemy. She said he would burn in Hell along with all of the heretics and false prophets for giving up God on Sundays to play bolita. Yes, that is what my father was doing. He was playing bolita, the numbers. Every Sunday he would stroll through the sunny streets of our neighborhood, a casual walk without any obvious purpose to an outside observer, but always he would end up in the shadows of a crepe myrtle behind the Rexall drugstore one block from the river. This is what my mother said. Of course my father was not the only wayward son to make the happy trek to the Rexall. Every Sunday morning between nine and eleven the alley would be buzzing with the sounds of men waiting for their turn to play the numbers, eager to gamble away their happiness. Some had arrived by foot like my father. Others had taken cars, late model Oldsmobiles and Cadillacs. A few rode bicycles. They would gather like storm clouds and then dissipate on a gentle breeze.

Not all of them were happy-go-lucky ne'er-do-wells like my father. Some were very respectful and had only stopped by the alley for a few minutes on their way to or from church. A few even owned businesses on 14th Avenue or 22nd Avenue, bakeries or shoe stores or grocery stores or Laundromats or jewelry stores or restaurants or cafés, or one of those cheap cafeterias south of the river where they mostly served beans and rice and spicy Cuban hamburgers.

This is what my father told me. He said everyone who could afford to play bolita did so, even those who could barely afford a haircut. White, black, and every color in between, it did not matter. It was an unquenchable desire, my father said, an undying hope in the possibility of a tangible, earthly paradise that was infinitely more alluring than the promise of eternal bliss in a heaven that lay somewhere in between the upper levels of the stratosphere and the icy cold oblivion of outer space.

This is what my father truly believed.

The dark angel that nurtured this desire was a very old, very dark grandfather of Afro-Cuban descent sitting on a cinder block beneath the flowering branches of the crepe myrtle in the alley behind the Rexall drugstore. This grandfather always wore a Panama hat. And he always sat on that cinder block smoking a fat Cuban cigar. From a distance it looked like smoke was pouring out of his eyes and his ears and the gaping black hole that was his mouth, a steady stream of smoke as if from a leaky boiler, especially on very hot days.

He was very well known in the neighborhood. Every lonely soul who wandered through the alley would greet the old man by name, this is what my father said, though if they saw him anywhere else, my father added, their eyeballs would have most certainly rolled back up into their heads, for he was a dark glass to their immovable fears and secret, earthly ambitions. But it was different on those Sunday mornings. One by one they would squat down in the shade next to this husk of a huckster, this is what my father jokingly called him, and they would chat for a while, talking about sports and the agony of marriage and trading jokes. Then the men would slip a few dollar bills into the thick, padded palm of the grandfather, and the grandfather would slip the bills into a small brown pouch with a thin leather strap that he wore like a necklace beneath his crisply ironed white shirt, and then he would smile a darkly gleaming gap-toothed smile. He would set his fat Cuban cigar on the edge of the cinder block and write down a few numbers and the date and the man's name in a small notebook with a tiny fragment of a pencil, his over-sized fingers barely able to hold the stub. Then one by one the men and the grandfather would shake hands and the grandfather would take up his cigar once again and the men would disappear into the glare of their Sunday afternoons, some of them whistling, some of them singing, all of them with dreamy, syrupy, faraway looks on their faces, as if they lived on the moon.

It is a wonder to think back on all of this. What can I say? Truly the laughter of God is a soft rebuke to shame the wise and astonish the weak. Which is one way of saying that anyone who cared to observe the Sunday morning war between my mother and my father could hear God laughing uproariously. ¡Ay de mí! I can close my eyes even now and I am greeted by a dark comedy of spitting resentment, like a dark episode of I Love Lucy. But perhaps my memory has altered what actually happened. Perhaps my memory is a photographic negative of what really happened, an x-ray version of reality in which my mother and my father look forever like skeletons obscured by a darkness as fluid and inky as the ocean at night, a world in which absolution does not exist between their two smoldering hearts. Yes, perhaps that is why it seems so strange, so ludicrous and surreal, the action flipping by at supersonic speed, the ocean of everything we have ever hoped for evaporating in the sunlight, stealing away towards nothingness. Who can say? Can the world be redeemed by a kiss? Is it better to look at things with your eyes open? Perhaps it does not matter. Eu possuo apenas o que Deus me deu. I read that somewhere long ago, or maybe it was only yesterday.

Anyway, to get back to my story. The climax of my parents' Sunday morning warfare occurred in the weeks leading up to my brother's First Communion. This happened in the spring of 1954, a few months before my father started dreaming his strange, cryptic dreams. Looking back now I think everything that transpired that spring jarred loose my father's sanity and so became the first cause and inspiration of all that he later dreamed, and all the troubles that followed.

My father took no part in the preparations for Emilio's First Communion. My mother tried to convince him that at the very least he should buy his Emilio a white costume so he would be like all the other boys when they received the Blessed Sacrament, but this simple request only enraged my father. 'I do not believe in the Church,' he thundered. And when my mother did not even bat an eye he added a few lightning bolts. 'The Church believes in equality and equality is the enemy of liberty and that is why I do not believe in the Church.'

My parents did not speak to each other for several days after that, perhaps a week, perhaps longer. Perhaps never again, at least not directly. They each felt humiliated by the other. They each felt the other had been taken over by an alien presence, consumed from within, possessed by a band of roving demons for some unknown, sinister purpose. They each felt persecuted by God. (Even though my father said he no longer believed in the Church, he was not so bold or vengeful as to abandon his belief in the Almighty.)

How can anything be so tragic and yet so comic?

My father took refuge in a second-hand leather armchair he had purchased for five dollars and which he had placed near the gleaming plate glass window in the living room so he could look at the two lime trees he had planted in the front yard. He sat in his leather chair, watching the lime trees for a while, wondering perhaps why there were no limes even after three years, and then he retreated into the flimsy pages of *Diario las Américas*, the newspaper he carried with him everywhere, his gateway to a larger world, this is what he always said, this is what he believed.

And my mother, she would push her way through the swinging kitchen door, her burning gaze ricocheting about like bullets seeking revenge, and sit down at the small Linoleum table from Sears with its shiny aluminum trim and its four black and white patterned vinyl chairs, where she quickly found solace in the glamorous pages of *Vanidades*, a magazine which she devoured on a weekly basis almost without breathing, especially because each issue contained a new romance novella by Corín Tellado, who wrote novellas about nurses who left their husbands and became teachers and took vacations in the mountains, or teachers who became airline stewardesses for Pan American or yoga instructors in Barcelona and were seduced by Argentine businessmen and later testified against them in court, or waitresses who fled to Brazil with insurance agents or university professors but later missed their ungrateful children and so went back to their families and their husbands only to find that their husbands had committed suicide, which made them secretly very happy, and always these stories walked the fine line between romance and pornography, and always they had titles like *Matrimonio obligado* or *Aquel hombre* or *Profesor de felicidad* or *Tu eres para mi*, titles which maybe gave you a clue about the storyline, but maybe not. My mother lapped up every word by Corín Tellado, as if those words contained the sorcerer's key to unlocking the tucked away secrets of the universe. She especially enjoyed those stories in which the heroines lost everything early on but always managed to fight their way to happiness by the end.

Ah my blessed mother! May God care for her immortal soul. She had become a Roman Catholic because of my father, and she had embraced this new religion with a fury that amazed the most zealous priests, but she never completely abandoned her childhood faith.

She was a creature of hidden reservoirs of strength.

She was a black dry wind from the south.

She was five fish hooks arranged neatly on a small table and a lighted candle in the center.

She was a fervent altar.

But she was always afraid of the dead. She said you could not control the dead so they should be feared. She said if the dead got their hooks into you there was nothing you could do. Maybe not even a priest could help you free yourself. *¡Ay de mí!* She had some very strange ideas floating about in her head.

Then again, she was no different than anyone else. Truly, who can say why any of us believe what we believe except that we are all looking for unrestrained joy. *¡Qué alegres son las horas!* Do you know the poem? 'How joyful are the hours! Like a flock of doves wandering across the skies.' This image explains everything, I think. Yes, the poetry of Lola Rodríguez de Tío is very compelling. A sneak peek into the mind of God, who can see into every heart, even the heart of my poor, sweet mother, especially her heart. I think if you had peered into my mother's heart of hearts in those days, if you had been able to peel back the layers of flesh that tried to smother her soul in sorrow, you would have found a young peasant girl from a small village nestled in the Sierra Maestra mountains searching the skies for the doves of Lola Rodríguez, a manifestation of the Holy Ghost certainly, but also a visible sign of Obàtálá, that drunken Santería god who created humanity with all of our imperfections, because Lola Rodríguez was Puerto Rican but she loved Cuba, because she spoke for all of us, as do all truly great poets, because everywhere the sky is the sky and white doves are white doves, so that is what you would have seen if you could have peered into my mother's lonely heart in her younger days, that is how I see her even today, my mother searching the skies, an immaculate child of God forever consecrated to the mythic saint makers of Eastern Cuba.

That is why, when my father brought her to Havana, she brought the old ways of Santería with her in the form of a small Eleguá head which she kept hidden away in a lidded gourd decorated with red and black beads. I have seen this gourd. I have even seen the head. It is a head made from clay with seashells for the eyes and the mouth. It carries the name Eshu Laroyê. My mother believed that Eshu Laroyê could cause you to lose everything or gain everything and that he loved whistles and kites and marbles and he was very mischievous. Of course as you have probably guessed, my father did not know of the existence of either the gourd or the head named Eshu Laroyê, not then, perhaps he never found out, or if he did it was not until much, much later. But such is the blindness of men.

When my father took my mother to Miami, the gourd also traveled across the shimmering Straits of Florida and the terror and impenetrable sadness of the open sea, which for most, I might add, is loosely defined as the dull murmur of the ocean depths and the beckoning abyss, except if you are a poor fisherman from anywhere in the Caribbean and are used to living in small shacks or shanties with roofs of dried grass or corrugated tin, in which case the bottom of the sea is a welcome release from the blistering ache of an empty belly and the lava of vengeful thoughts. So they crossed over to Florida. They took a steamer from Havana to Miami. But the head of Eleguá remained hidden from view.

This is what my mother said.

She also said that as soon as they moved into their tiny, one-and-a-half story bungalow in Allapattah, she stuffed the gourd with the head into a corner of her bedroom closet, on a shelf very high up, so my father would never even stumble across it. She said it was surrounded by boxes filled with old shoes and abandoned jewelry and decaying photographs and other souvenirs from their days in Cuba. My mother said after they arrived in Miami she herself forget all about Eshu Laroyê.

I do not believe her. I think she was simply counting the days until she would have need of him, but that is beside the point. She also mentioned one day that there was a small bible on the shelf next to the gourd. But that was probably accidental. The bible had once belonged to my father's father, but he had died in the Great War. My mother was afraid of this bible. She said it smelled of death, and so it sat next to the gourd with the head of Eleguá for oh so many years. Why she had put it there she never said. But one can guess.

All of this my mother told me little by little. One way or another. All of this I have pieced together from many conversations and half-heard snippets, my mother muttering under her crazy, alcoholic breath or talking in her sleep, or from the pages of a small diary in which she kept letters written to herself and which she often left on the kitchen table for anyone to look at, an open invitation, which, I must confess, I accepted. I do not know the full story. I am fuzzy on some of the details, as we all are. But I know enough.

Three weeks before Emilio's First Communion, he still had no white costume, but my mother decided she would keep her anger hidden away from my father and make her case through spiritual channels. On Sunday May 23, 1954, at approximately nine in the evening, just minutes after my father had fallen asleep in his leather chair full of a truck driver's irrevocable melancholy to dream of fruit laden lime trees, my mother retrieved her decorated gourd from the top shelf of her bedroom closet and pulled out the head of the Eleguá named Eshu Laroyê.

Emilio and I were following her around that day because there was nothing else to do. But once she pulled the head out of that gourd, we would have followed her anywhere. Who knew what hidden treasures she might lead us to? Who knew what magic she might conjure? But she ignored us as easily and as completely as if we had become a suddenly aggressive night wind that could be banished simply by closing a window. But we did not mind. She took the head into the kitchen and placed it on the floor between the side door and the stove. We followed a few steps behind her. She flicked on a small lamp which penetrated the darkness as best it could,

being such a small lamp, and sat down on the other side of the
kitchen in one of the black and white patterned vinyl chairs.
We sat on the floor. The lamp was decorated with seashells
and a porcelain lampshade that looked like a small red crab.
It gave off a soft, peculiar, reddish glow because of the lampshade. If you stared at the lampshade long enough it seemed
like the crab was moving, swimming through the darkness,
assuming it was one of the species of crabs that could actually
swim, its spindly legs churning with frenetic effort, the unseen
waters flowing past. But we were not moving. We sat there
unmoved and unmovable like volcanic stones embedded in
the swirling silt at the bottom of an ancient shallow sea, or
perched precariously atop a very tall mountain and the stars
falling from the sky. I don't know which. And I don't know
how long we sat there either, but after a while it seemed like
the invisible gases trapped within the sphere of our kitchen
were about to ignite. I could see sparks forming in the air. I
could feel the heat beginning to intensify. It was becoming
difficult to breathe. I was beginning to perspire. Even my
brother Emilio could feel this heat. But my mother didn't seem
to notice. She stared at the Eleguá head without troubling
about anything around her, as if she was trying to calculate
the inner dimensions of a wandering star from a billion miles
away, or how long it would take to travel to Key West by bus
and then perhaps take a boat to Cuba.

Then she gave out a long, wistful sigh and said 'It takes
many years to understand the peculiarities of life, and even
then, nothing is clear. All that seems to be, is not, and all that
seems not to be, is.' Then she said 'Come children,' and we
went upstairs to bed.

My father slept that night in his leather chair and left
very early the next morning, an hour before sunrise. He
was on his way to Birmingham and then Atlanta and then
Jacksonville and then back to Miami. He would be gone a few
days. My mother could hardly contain her excitement as he
left, and within minutes of his leaving, the three of us were
gathered once again in the kitchen, which had been transformed at some point during the long night of my mother's
most feverish hopes into a backcountry shrine or a temple or a
small neighborhood church.

My mother set out a fish bowl with cleansing water on the table. She set out a dozen shallow bowls, jicara bowls filled with offerings she said would please Eshu Laroyê. The bowls were placed in haphazard fashion in front of her Eleguá head. One bowl contained three balls of cooked cornmeal mixed with canary seeds, another contained small candies wrapped in colored paper, another contained marbles and keys and several pairs of dice, another contained red carnations, another contained coffee beans, another contained chewing tobacco, another contained a collection of sharks' teeth of various sizes, another contained grapes and pears and unpeeled bananas that were beginning to turn black, another contained the crushed leaves of several herbs mixed together, another contained three uncooked eggs, another contained pennies and Buffalo nickels and a few old centavos and a silver peso or two from the days of the Republic, all of the coins mixed together, and the bowl in the very center contained a small coconut cake.

There were also a pair of maracas on the floor and a worn deck of playing cards and an old baseball autographed by Heliodoro Jabuco Hidalgo, a hero of Cuban baseball from the early nineteen-hundreds, and an old baseball mitt and a bottle of rum and a bottle of aguardiente and a jar of honey and a pack of Wrigley's chewing gum and three fat Cuban cigars, the kind my father liked, and the small bible that had once belonged to my father's father. All of this was being offered to the Eleguá head named Eshu Laroyê.

So we sat there the three of us on the floor of our kitchen and stared at the shadow of the head and the shadows of the jicara bowls overflowing with their offerings of an aching heart and we did not know where we were.

It almost seemed like a dream. It was still dark outside but my mother did not turn on the lamp. The birds outside were chattering away noisily, so we listened to them for a while, but it was hard to say what kind of birds they were. Perhaps they were a mixture of little brown night jars with their churring call like an engine running, and tiny yellow bellied flycatchers saying che-lek, che-lek, che-lek, which could mean anything so early in the morning, and many other birds mixed in. It was hard to tell one bird from another sitting there in the dark with only our ears to guide us. Then my mother got up and took a thick white candle from the table and set it before the offerings and she lit the candle. She retrieved the small likeness of Saint Anthony, the saint of small miracles, from his place of honor above the kitchen sink and placed him next to the Eleguá head, and in front of the statue she placed a small brown candle, a candle which she had pulled out of a hole in the darkness and which she also lit so Saint Anthony would know she was asking for his help as well. The candles possessed no scent, and yet as soon as they were lit, we could smell quite distinctly the sweet scent of vanilla and cinnamon and licorice.

My mother breathed in this sweet smell like a resurrected premonition, and then she turned to us and smiled and said she was taking no chances, the spiritual world was a world of dancing shadows and ritual magic and strange, whimsical reversals of fortune, you never knew who would be listening or how they would respond, you never knew what would work, your hopes could be gutted like a fish, so you tried everything you could think of and you hoped you didn't offend anyone. Then she started to laugh, a flimsy, insubstantial laughter like filaments of silk, but she caught herself. She wanted to make sure Emilio got his white costume, she said. Then she made the sign of the cross and knelt down on the floor, and all of a sudden we were all kneeling, Emilio and myself and my mother, the three of us now in a row like penitent spider monkeys or pink-headed vultures waiting their turn or submarine portholes at night or pearls on a string, our bodies swaying slightly before the flickering candles and our mother's glowing hope.

The likeness of Saint Anthony seemed to merge with the Eleguá head named Eshu Laroyê.

The statue and the head became a single entity.

The scent of vanilla and cinnamon and licorice grew stronger.

The birds outside grew noisier, as if they sensed that a door was opening.

The world was beginning to spin, or a second world was descending, superimposing itself over the first world.

It was difficult to tell which.

From somewhere there was the steady beating of a
drum, a soothing, calming sound, but it was very faint, as if it
were coming from inside us, from deep inside our thoughts,
trying to burst out from the darkness of our imaginations, a
darkness that did not really exist and had never really existed
because all darkness is merely the temporary absence of light,
a magician's trick, a parlor game, a leather hood pulled over a
falcon's eyes.

Then a single shaft of sunlight broke through the
window and across the floor, and then another shaft and then
another, until the world was flooded with pure sunlight and
an unassailable sense of freedom purged of all depravity and
the need for revenge.

The birds outside suddenly flew away.

We realized we had never known such freedom.

We started to forget ourselves.

Then my mother began to chant in a secret language we
did not know, and we began to chant along with her, repeating everything she said, at least the sound of it, unconcerned
with meaning. It was an ancient language and possessed a
very rhythmic sound, very soothing, mesmerizing, like the
sound of unseen drums.

We succeeded in forgetting ourselves.

We succeeded in opening ourselves up to new pathways.

Soon we were lost amid a sea of words we did not
understand, a babel of incomprehensible thoughts, the
confusion of all earthly tongues flowing together, but as we let
this sea flow through us and over us, buffeting us on strange,
towering waves, and then as we allowed ourselves to sink
beneath those waves to the bottom of this ceaselessly raging,
tormented sea where all life began and death was simply the
last of many vivid encounters, at that point understanding
came.

'*Omi tutu*,' my mother said.

'*Omi tutu*,' we said.

We could see ourselves drinking fresh water, as if we
had been traveling for days in the desert and had suddenly
come upon a small stream, a sliver of life in a barren landscape. We could feel the water gliding down our throats,
filling the hollow spaces deep inside. We drank until our

bellies became distended and we collapsed beside the stream. We drank until we fell asleep between this world and the next.

'*Axé tutu,*' my mother said.

'*Axé tutu,*' we said.

We saw ourselves waking up. We saw ourselves vigorously rubbing our arms and our legs. We could feel our vitality returning. We could feel the spirit of Eshu Laroyê rising up from our bellies, passing up along the pathways of our throats and out through our wide-open mouths. We wanted to gulp down more water but Eshu Laroyê, who was now sitting beside us, his back turned towards the sun, only laughed, as if to say that he was the only water we needed. The laughing Eshu Laroyê with his ribcage heaving looked like the black shadow of a palm tree rubbing its head against the sky. Then Eshu Laroyê stopped laughing and he vanished, poof, just like that.

'*Onã tutu, ilê tutu Água fresca, o axé é fresco, o caminho é fresco, a casa é fresca,*' my mother said.

'*Onã tutu, ilê tutu Água fresca, o axé é fresco, o caminho é fresco, a casa é fresca,*' we said.

We saw ourselves sitting beside the stream that had quenched our thirst. We were no longer so thirsty. We drank from the stream only now and then.

'*Tutu Laroyê, tutu ariku babawê, Laroyê, é fresco nossos antepassasdos assegurem que este frescor pedure,*' my mother said.

'*Tutu Laroyê, tutu ariku babawê, Laroyê, é fresco nossos antepassasdos assegurem que este frescor pedure,*' we said.

We saw many others traveling through the desert and invited them to refresh themselves with the water of this stream which was one of many streams belonging to Eshu Laroyê.

We saw the others drinking from the steam.

They were furiously gulping the fresh water.

One or two of them began pounding the ground with their fists and saying this was now their stream. There was only so much water to go around. They could not afford to share their water with anyone. They were the only ones who would be allowed to drink their fill.

We did not know how to handle this dispute. But then we once again heard the laughter of Eshu Laroyê. Eshu Laroyê was nowhere to be seen, but his laughter was everywhere. He was laughing as if to remind us that he was still the only water we needed.

Then the skies above cracked open and rain began to fall to the ground and soon the desert and the stream were part of a shallow lake, a fresh water sea. Now there was certainly more than enough water to go around so there was no longer anything to dispute, at least as far as the water was concerned. Of course now there was no dry place to sit or stretch out and take a nap, but that was another matter.

This is what the laughter of Eshu Laroyê combined with the sound of the rainstorm seemed to be saying.

Then we stopped chanting, and the understanding that had come upon us with the rising sun faded by imperceptible degrees, like a love from long ago that is one night delivered up to the wind. A few hours later my mother had cleared away all evidence of her ritual fever. Even the head of her Eleguá was back in its gourd and the gourd was back on the top shelf in her closet. That is how I remember that morning. But it was only the beginning. For seven days my mother prostrated herself before the Eleguá head named Eshu Laroyê. She offered him all manner of sweets and baked goodies because she knew that's what he liked to eat. She offered him all manner of toys and trinkets because she knew they would amuse him. And every morning she lit the white candle and the brown candle and chanted in her strange, singing bird language of hunchbacked gods and prancing, dancing, nymphomaniac goddesses.

My father had no idea what she was up to. Each morning my mother cleared away the head and the jicara bowls as soon as she was finished with her incantations. She put the candles in the middle of the kitchen table and the tiny statue of Saint Anthony back on his hook. The only evidence that anything out of the ordinary had taken place in the kitchen on any one of those mornings of my mother's furtive madness was the lingering scent from the candles.

But what am I saying? It was much more than lingering. It was as if the scent of the candles had become a living, growing thing. Perhaps not a conscious being, but living all the same. But who can say? By the end of the third day the

heady fragrance of vanilla and cinnamon and licorice seemed
to be embedded in the kitchen walls. By the end of the seventh
day our lungs would fill with a sweet rushing wind with
every breath, no matter what room we were in. And yet my
father did not notice the sweetness of the air we breathed,
except perhaps as one notices a slight drop in temperature and
with unconscious memory heads off in search of a sweater.
Yes, that is exactly how it was. On the evening of the sixth
day, my father remarked that he was suddenly consumed
with a desire for something sweet, lemon-filled pastelitos or
pineapple empanadas or a slice of rum cake or coconut cake
or cookies glazed with chocolate, what did it matter, the urge
was overpowering, he said, which was surprising, he had
never had such a sweet tooth before, but he had one now and
it was killing him, so he was going to head down to Rosario's
Bakery and knock on the door until they opened up, and then
he would buy whatever they had left. And that is what my
father did, and he came back with three bags of sweets and
pastries and a big grin on his face and we gorged ourselves
until we could no longer move a muscle.

By we, of course, I mean myself, Emilio and my father.
My mother disappeared from that evening without saying
a word, a shadow slipping into the half-light, as silent as a
broken clock. My father once again fell asleep in his leather
chair, his two unfruitful lime trees glimmering in the moonlight. He was gone before we got up. He was driving to Tampa
Bay and then Pensacola and then Mobile and then Tuscaloosa
and then back home.

But this is how it was with my parents. This is the
essence of their story. It was tragic and it was comic, as I have
said, but only if you were looking in from the outside. For
me, who was on the inside, it was oh so very sad. As lovers
they were out of tune with each other. They did not know,
nor would they ever know, that deep inside the chest of those
who sing out of tune, a heart beats softly, which is a beautiful
image I have shamelessly stolen from Gilberto's *Desafinado*.
¡Ay de mí! In English it is a very ordinary image. It sounds
oh so much more beautiful in the original Portuguese. *Que no
peito dos desafinados/ No fundo do peito bate calado/ Que no peito
dos desafinados/ Também bate um coração.* Some days when I

think of my parents I am almost overwhelmed by sadness. In my soul a flock of birds have suddenly taken wing.

On the morning of the eighth day after my mother renewed her devotion to the Eleguá head named Eshu Laroyê, she gathered up the many jicara bowls with their many whimsical and heartfelt offerings and placed them carefully inside a grocery bag, so they would not spill. Minutes later she was out the door and Emilio and I were three steps behind. We walked until our legs began to crumble, and then we rode a bus along a sunny, dusty city street, and then we were walking some more. Our long journey ended in a park, and there we stopped for a while, my mother surveying the landscape. Then she spied a few jicara trees on a small rise in the middle of the park and smiled and said 'Come children, only a few more steps.' We followed her. She knelt before one of the trees and we knelt beside her. It was a very sunny day and the branches of the jicara trees provided little shade. It was a rare thing to see a jicara tree in Miami in those days. It was not unheard of, perhaps, but we had never seen one. My brother and I stared up at the trees and the shiny green fruit. It was no accident that we were there in that park on that day kneeling with our mother before a jicara tree. We could hear birds singing from the branches but we could not see them and they were very noisy like the ones from that very first morning and once again it seemed as if they sensed that somewhere a door was opening. There was no one else in the park, which was strange, but we did not worry about this. My mother emptied the contents of her grocery bag, placing the jicara bowls around the trunk of the tree she had chosen with geometric precision. Then she took up three large silver coins that she later said she had carried with her since her days in Cuba, though why she had kept them all those years she did not say. She kissed each coin and made the sign of the cross and left them with the bowls. Then we went home.

The Afro-Cuban grandfather who ran the bolita game behind the Rexall was waiting for us when we got home. He was sitting in the metal folding chair my mother had set out in the shade of the carport next to a can for watering flowers. My mother had planted azaleas all around the house and

these needed constant watering. She was the first to notice
the darkly gleaming shadow of the old man in the chair and
she pushed us behind her as we walked up the driveway.
Emilio did not care who was sitting there so he kept his eyes
to the pavement and blindly followed our mother, but I was
curious. I did not recognize him as the man my father spoke
of. He seemed more like a dark angel who had lost his wings
in a terrible accident and so had fallen from the sky. I thought
perhaps he was being punished. I thought perhaps he had
been exiled from everything he had ever loved. Yes, certainly,
these were the thoughts of a child. But what did I then know
of the world?

The old grandfather who might have been a fallen angel
seemed to be asleep. He had pulled the brim of his immaculate Panama hat down over his eyes, but he was still cradling a
fat Cuban cigar in his fat stubby hands. He was barely holding
it, I might add. I could see faint wisps of smoke curling up
and blackened ash breaking away, dissolving in the air. I
wondered why he hadn't dropped the cigar. Of course my
mother was in no mood for a strange Afro-Cuban asleep in her
driveway. The sun was beginning to set. Already the sky had
turned a soft orange. It had been a long day and we were all
very tired. But for some unfathomable reason my mother held
her tongue. She became strangely mute, as if her voice had
been surgically removed, or she herself was only a reflection
in a darkly glowing glass and therefore possessed no voice to
begin with.

Then the grandfather suddenly took a drag from his
cigar and stood up with a sudden theatrical flourish, his
immaculate Panama hat now in his other hand, and bowed so
low that the brim of his hat swept lightly across the pavement.

'Good evening, Sweet Sister,' he said. 'I did not mean to
startle you, please forgive my intrusion.'

He did not acknowledge Emilio and myself except with
a quick glance, his eyes brimming with conspiratorial mystery
and unexpected mirth, as if he were a peasant pretending to
be an ancient god, or perhaps it was the other way around.

'Your husband is Andres Escoraz Silvestre?'

My mother still had not said a word, none that I could
hear, but with each question posed by the grandfather she

would move her hands this way and that and nod with gaping amazement, and I could see the tiny, bright shadows of many conflicting emotions flying across her face like wisps of smoke. I think now I was watching the shadows of the white doves of Lola Rodríguez flying in and out of the beams of fading sunlight.

'I thought as much.'

'. . . .'

'Your husband was very lucky this week.'

'. . . .'

'Your husband has never been so lucky. I was very surprised.'

'. . . .'

'I think that in all the years your husband has been playing bolita, he has never won even a dollar until today.'

'. . . .'

Then he reached into his pocket and pulled out a thin sliver of paper. I say he reached into his pocket but I am not sure. Was he wearing a thin linen jacket because it was almost summer? Did he reach into a pleated pocket of his pleated trousers? I do not know. I do not remember what he was wearing. It seems now as if he simply reached up and plucked the sliver of paper out of the sky. 'Sweet Sister,' he said, 'I bring you a ticket to the moon.'

Then he placed the sliver of paper into my mother's waiting hands and twirled his Panama hat once again and disappeared in a black cloud of cigar smoke. For a moment we stood there in complete darkness, as if we had suddenly gone blind or were witnessing the last total eclipse of the sun before the end of the world. Then our eyesight returned but we did not say anything. It was impossible to believe that the old grandfather had been standing there in front of us only moments before.

The sliver of paper was actually an envelope containing three one-hundred dollar bills, one bill for each of three silver coins from Cuba my mother had kissed, that is what she later said. I can see her now with her quivering lips and her trembling hands thanking Eshu Laroyê for his generosity as she was standing in line at Burdine's to purchase the white costume for Emilio's First Communion. But what is amazing, when I think about it, is that she never gave any thought to my father and how he would feel about her spending his three-hundred dollars. *Ser agua pasada,* my father liked to say. But maybe not in this instance.

I suppose I still have many questions about what happened. All I really know is that from the moment my mother opened that envelope, life began to unfold with dizzying speed. I had never before experienced the headlong rush of a future that could not be restrained or altered. I could not quite comprehend the tiniest details of what was happening let alone the big picture. I thought I had fallen into that dark abyss where everything goes sailing off the tracks and if you do survive you are permanently scarred for life. It is hard to describe how I felt so long ago, but that is pretty close. But every so often, usually late at night, I get the strangest feeling that I am back there still.

Everything is happening all over again.

A bird in motion.

The wind shifting

Patterns of thought like the syllables once uttered by soaring angels.

I am staring into the mirror of my own consciousness, a stark reminder that I am not in control of anything. I am watching my mother rip into that envelope and then stare with breathless stoicism at the three one-hundred dollar bills drifting effortlessly towards the floor, like the feathers of a bird. She scoops them up and smiles and stuffs them back into the torn sleeve and that is the last I see of the actual bills. We do not sleep at all that night. My mother pulls out her Eleguá head named Eshu Laroyê and places him once again on the floor between the side door and the stove. It was only on the other side of the door that the Afro-Cuban grandfather sat in the metal folding chair, smoking his fat Cuban cigar. My mother gives praise to Eshu Laroyê. She thanks him for his generosity, his kindness, his sense of justice. Specifically, she thanks him for standing with her against my father. She also thanks the Afro-Cuban grandfather, partially, I suspect, because she now thinks he might be the earthly incarnation of Eshu Laroyê, who walks among us now and then, testing our resolve, showering goodies on those who deserve them, pulling the rug out from under those who need to fall flat on their faces. This close to the end she is even less willing to take chances.

My mother scatters tiny glowing candles all over the house. It is dark all over except for the candles. It looks like we have brought the stars inside. The night is filled with my mother chanting and the laughter of Eshu Laroyê with his ribcage heaving and a few more stars appearing at regular intervals in the dark skies of my mother's intent.

The next morning bright and early we are on a bus heading into downtown Miami.

We are heading to Burdine's Department Store.

We are heading to Burdine's with its gleaming chrome and glass counters and gold lamé covered walls where we have only been once before.

My mother says if she had the money, Burdine's is the only place where she would shop. She says that's where all the rich tourists from Latin America shop.

I don't remember the first trip. For all I know this is my first trip.

We spend hours in the store. My mother is very particular when it comes to her purchases. My mother shops around.

She does not mind that everywhere we go people are staring. She is used to being stared at. Or perhaps she does not notice. She is so beautiful that she is oblivious to the world around her and what anyone thinks. She is very beautiful, like a movie actress. She has very dark skin, not so dark as an African, but still very dark compared to the lily whites we see everywhere in Burdine's.

At one point a man wearing a dark jacket and a thin black tie approaches us. He seems nervous. He is smoothing back the edges of his thin moustache as he speaks. He voice is as fragile as glass, ready to break. The air is too thin to hold such a voice for long. He asks my mother if we are lost and my mother looks up as if only then is she aware he is standing there.

She does not say a word.

The man with the thin moustache is struck speechless by her silence. Then he glances down at the two of us.

Emilio is hiding behind my mother's skirt. I am not
hiding. The man with the thin moustache gives us a long look,
his pupils collapsing as if they are tiny balloons that have been
pricked. He smiles weakly and retreats towards two salesgirls
behind a counter where they sell perfume and whispers
something into their ears. Then they begin to play a strange
game of whispering and staring, whispering and staring.

One of the girls is looking directly at me, and then at
Emilio. We have lighter skin than our mother. Our skin color
is like our father's, which is very light. But our beauty is from
our mother. We are both very beautiful. Emilio is beautiful like
Rudolph Valentino with dark gleaming hair. I am beautiful
like Märta Torén with fiery red hair. Many people have said
so. Many people have said we are beautiful just like our
mother, who is as beautiful as any movie star.

All the while the sales girl is staring at me I feel like a
movie star. I smile at the girl but she doesn't smile back. She
whispers something to the other sales girl and then the two of
them go off to another counter and begin rearranging boxes of
perfume. The man with the thin moustache, however, stares
at us without a break until we leave the store. He is unable to
take his eyes off us. I am certain he is blinded by our beauty.

Many years later I will finally understand why he was
staring at us. But I will not really understand why.

Then the scene shifts.

My reflection in the mirror has become strangely
elongated. My features have begun to stretch. It is almost
like the glass itself is beginning to melt, but in a way that
ignores the generally accepted laws of the universe, the center
slowly spreading out towards the brightly gilded edges of the
frame which forms the boundaries of my life. It is almost like
being trapped inside a cartoon. I hardly recognize myself. I
am sitting up in bed. It is very late, after midnight certainly.
The tiny sliver of a moon in the sky which I can barely see
through my bedroom window provides very little light. And
yet strangely there is enough light to see by, a shimmering,
sunken kind of light, the kind of light that falls like a hard
rain, swirling down the gutters, flashing in the darkness like
errant coins spinning wildly as they disappear from one hand
and appear in another, part of a magician's illusion.

Suddenly I am floating above my bed. I float out of my bedroom and then across the hall to Emilio's tiny bedroom. I can see that Emilio is not sleeping either. He does not see me floating in the air. He is busy listening to a strangely elastic mouth pouring sweet words of poison into his ear. The mouth contorts itself into fantastic shapes as the words pour out. It looks like a two-tone vintage gramophone, a black and bone-ivory orchid unfurling. Then it looks like several miles of plastic tubing coiled very tightly with a suction cup for lips. The tubing is connected to a respirator or some other piece of hospital equipment. Then it looks like a can for watering flowers, a can like my mother keeps by the side door. Then it becomes a miniature radio transmitter. It does not seem to notice that I am hovering in the air no matter what form it takes. I am inches away, if the truth be told, so close I can smell its hot swirling samba breath, or its hot antibacterial hospital breath, or its hot damp-earth breath, or its hot electromagnetic energy breath, but then without any warning whatsoever the mouth turns to greet me. It suddenly becomes more than a mouth. It suddenly becomes the Afro-Cuban grandfather. The Afro-Cuban grandfather presses an elastic finger to his elastic mouth to shush me and then resumes his experiment with Emilio's ear.

When the grandfather is finished, when he has emptied himself of words, Emilio smiles and turns over on his side and goes back to sleep.

I am still hovering only inches away.

I am frozen in the agony of my silence.

I am frozen in the mirror of anticipated guilt.

I feel like I have conspired against my brother. Or that I have conspired against somebody. Maybe myself.

I wonder what I should do.

I am almost praying.

At precisely that moment the Afro-Cuban grandfather turns his strangely elastic mouth towards me once again, as if to answer my almost prayer. But it is no longer the Afro-Cuban grandfather.

It is my very own father who has returned from his four days on the road earlier than expected.

I have many questions for my father.

For one thing I am wondering if he has found out about the money. This is actually the only question in my mind, but it feels like many questions.

This question feels very, very heavy.

I open my own mouth to ask my question but the only sound that emerges is a great swooshing sound like a great ship moving swiftly across the bay, heading out towards the open sea, or maybe it is the sound of a flock of birds taking to the air, yes, again it is a flock of birds, it is always a flock of birds, but this flock is the largest flock of birds I have ever seen (heard), way too many birds to count, the sound is deafening, the sound is earth-shattering, they must be very large birds, hawks and falcons and ocean going eagles by the way my ears are ringing.

But my father only laughs at my obvious confusion. He is laughing as if it is the most natural thing in the world for his daughter to sound like a great swooshing ship or a flock of predatory birds. It is a great crescendo of a laugh like a solar flare demagnetizing the earth's atmosphere. Then he plucks me out of the air as easily as if I am a wounded fledgling and cradles me in his arms, and when I protest, when I try to ask him my one question that possesses the weight of many questions, he simply says 'Hush now, Isidora, you ask the impossible. *Pedir la luna.*'

That is the last I see of my father for a while. The scene shifts again. It is one week before Emilio's First Communion. I am wondering how the hours can fly by so quickly.

(Many years later I will find myself wondering the same thing.)

My mother is hurrying through the side door of Gesù Church. Emilio and I are doing our best to keep up with her.

There are moments when I think Gesù looks less like a church and more like an elegant train station or bus station from days gone by. From the outside, I mean. And always there are vagrants, this is what my mother calls them, hanging around the sidewalk near the side door or sitting on the steps out front in the shade of the arched colonnade. But I do not think they are vagrants, or if they are, then we are all vagrants. Whenever I see them hanging around the side door or sitting on the steps I get the distinct impression that they are waiting for a bus or a slow-moving train to take them to a faraway destination. *¡Ay de mí!* My words are woefully inadequate to describe what I see with my heart.

So there we are, my mother, Emilio and myself. We are now sitting in a pew on the left side because that is the Gospel side of the church. We are watching the priests who are busy with their busywork. It is difficult to see exactly what they are doing at the altar because they are standing with their backs to the rest of us.

I am looking beyond the priests to the gleaming gold walls that surround the altar and the gleaming marble statues of Jesus and the saints looking down with their inscrutable smiles of glory and hidden joy, and in the domed space above the altar I can see Mary and the Baby Jesus standing in a baptismal fountain and the water pouring over the sides. They are painted into the golden background of the dome. They are very high up and I am looking at the color of the Baby Jesus' halo and comparing it to the color of the dome, which looks gold on some days but yellow on other days, and I have to strain to see Mary and the Baby Jesus, I have to tilt my head up at an odd angle, and if my mother catches me she will give me a stern shove in the back as if she is a hard piece of iron, as if she believes she is the iron stamp the Jesuits used in the old days to make the consecrated hosts. Then I am looking at the underwater glow of the hanging lanterns, and for a moment it feels like we are all under water and the lanterns are the lights of submarines moving back and forth in the frothy darkness, for it always seems dark in this church, even on the brightest, sunniest days.

I am lost in my own thoughts like this for quite a while.

I have hypnotized myself.

I hear the sound of tiny bells gurgling away and I see the priests moving about the altar, and I can see their mouths moving but there is no sound, it is like watching a silent movie, except for the gurgling bells, and then I see the faithful heading up towards the communion rail, row by row by row. I watch the faithful kneel and receive the Host and say their small prayers, like tiny fish or silver eels flashing this way and that, and then they head back to their pews.

I see my mother heading for the rail.

Then I see Emilio. He is also heading for the rail.

My mother does not realize he is two steps behind her.

Then they are both kneeling at the rail, and before anyone can say a word the priest shoves a wafer into Emilio's mouth, and it is only at that moment that my mother turns slightly, perhaps because she feels the presence of an angry, accusing God swimming in the air above her, because Emilio is a week away from making his first official communion in the presence of the Almighty, because Emilio has stolen a wafer for some unknown reason. I can see the displeasure of embarrassment, the horror of what people will think, especially the priests, creasing my mother's face. Even in the soft, shimmering, mysterious, contorted darkness of this church that is always and only lit by submarine lanterns, I can see her expression quite clearly. She has taken hold of Emilio by his ear and is pulling him along, but she does not stop at our pew. Dozens of heads have turned to see what is going on, in slow motion, of course, but they are content to leave Emilio to his fate. My mother pulls him all the way to the back of the church and out the door, and then and only then does she unleash her words of distress.

The silent movie is over. The slow-moving underwater feel from before has vanished.

Everything my mother says is in Spanish, but it is a Spanish she rarely uses. It is a dark, dangerous Spanish spoken only in the small villages of Eastern Cuba.

I wonder what possessed Emilio to do such a thing, to make a mockery of his First Communion, to make a mockery of our mother's efforts on his behalf. What will become of Emilio's white costume, I am thinking.

I do not follow them out. I do not wish to call attention to myself. I can hear the murmuring of a few nearby voices. I am certain they are talking about my mother dragging Emilio out of the church and then her torrent of angry dark Spanish, which is an assault to everyone's ears. I am certain even the ears of the priests are burning. It is a wonder the church itself did not become cinder and ash.

Then the Mass is over and the priests are trundling after their white and gold gleaming banner and everyone is following them out the doors, and I am among them, I can

hardly wait to see the sun, to gulp in a breath of fresh air
once again. I am wondering what has happened to Emilio. I
am wondering what my mother will say on the long bus ride
home. But when I reach the steps I realize Emilio and my
mother are long gone.

At first I am not sure what to do.

I sit down on the steps and lean back against one of the
pillars holding up the arched colonnade.

A few of the faithful are lingering in front of the pillars,
chatting with the priests, but then one of the priests hurries
down the steps and the conversation slowly withers away. It
is a bright sunny day, and it is very hot. But I do not mind the
heat.

For a while there is no one around. Then I hear the
heavy church doors open and then close with a heavy,
hollow-sounding thud, and the echo sends a chill up and
down my spine. A younger priest runs past me and then stops
and turns. He asks me what I am doing there. I tell him I am
waiting for my mother. He nods and smiles and then runs
away.

I do not know how long I am sitting there.

I watch the traffic flow past and the pedestrians going
one way or another. I think about the vagrants waiting for
their trains or their buses. Gesù Church sits on a fairly busy
street. There are many people on their way to many different
places. Then I see a small shadow approaching. The shadow
grows larger. It is my father.

'Hallo little one,' he says. 'Have you been crying?'

But I have not been crying.

My father is all bright eyes and gleaming white teeth
when he sees me. He does not say anything about Emilio. He
does not say anything about my mother. I want to ask him
if he was the one who was whispering into Emilio's ear and
what he was whispering about and if he was the one who told
Emilio to steal the consecrated host. But I do not say anything.
What can I say in the presence of my father? So I smile happily and he laughs a happy, hearty, meaty, uncompromising
laugh and scoops me up and we head for home.

114

The days and weeks that followed my brother's impetuous dash to the communion rail were a return to the wild, unruly, irrepentant passion of my mother's childhood. What can I say except that life is an explosion of competing impulses, some carry us forwards, some carry us backwards, always when we least expect it. For my mother this suddenly meant that her longing for her childhood days, which she had never quite abandoned, became a vital, visible, unstoppable force which impacted the lives of everyone around her. It was a late summer hurricane. It was a tidal wave. It was as if we had suddenly been swept across the Straits of Florida to an earlier moment of history and were now trapped in the mythic mountains west of Santiago, Cuba. When my mother woke up in the morning we heard the rattling cry of a solitary hook-billed kite as it sounded an alarm. When she went out into the yard to water her azaleas we heard the mythic Torocoro with its mantle like a cape the color of the ocean at sunset crying *toco toco tocoro tocoro*.

Every afternoon we could smell the sweet invigorating scent of wild mariposa growing in the invisible forests of our deepest desires. The lush, moist smell of ferns and magnolia and kapok and palm trees invaded the pores of our skin. In the evenings we could smell the earthy, metallic scent of sacrificial blood and the stench of decaying animal carcasses sprouting weeds mixed with the gun powder and hot, dry choleric breath of determined revolutionaries lost in the jungle, this odd mixture of smells drifting through the humid, Floridian air like pollen on the wind. And every night near midnight we were startled awake by the heady perfume of incense burning and strange, guttural, chanting voices knifing through the stillness of the long Cuban night that lay ahead.

My mother rarely spoke about her childhood. She said her village was a village of peasants, descendants of Indians and slaves and criminals and the lonely survivors, mostly deserters and defeated captains, of the many rebellions and wars of Independence that had plagued the island of Cuba over the centuries.

This was her narrative. This is all she would say.

Whenever she discovered she was on the verge of revealing more, she would simply stop. But in her most unguarded moments, most often after she had just polished off a bottle of tequila, she was plagued with an inability to keep her mouth shut. In those moments we saw a darker side to my mother, a darkness that enveloped first my father, then Emilio, and finally myself. Where did this darkness come from? Who can say? It lived within her like a smoldering fire. But what could we do? What could anyone do? Peace almost always eludes us. Some days all we can hope for is redemption. *Que Dios nos saque de penas y nos lleve a descansar.*

The darkness that enveloped my mother and my father was the easiest to ignore because it was always vibrating just beneath the surface. It became for us just background static. Radio signals from another planet. My mother said she had given herself to my father in marriage in the hopes of altering her destiny, but she knew deep down it was doomed from the start.

'We are not permitted to change the course of our own ships,' she liked to say. She said she knew this from the words of an old woman who had lived and perhaps still lived in the greening shadows of the forest near Cruce de los Banos, a mountain slope which my mother roamed at will when she was small. She said the old woman wore the costume of a slave from the nineteenth century, a woven skirt and a turban, and that her sagging, wrinkled breasts were bared for all to see. My mother said it was often difficult to understand this old woman because she spoke in a strange, guttural fashion, her mouth completely closed except for a thin line to let her hissing breath escape, her words often sounding like they had been turned upside down, as if her teeth were falling out as she spoke and all she could do to keep them from falling to the ground was press her lips together. On some days she went by the name Cachita Tumbo and she wore a slave's woven skirt and a turban and her breasts were bare, but on other days she preferred the name Mamona or Guimazoa.

My mother said one day she encountered the old woman after a drenching downpour that evaporated as quickly as it had begun, and she went with the old woman to a small

stream hidden in the underbrush near a small cave high up
in the mountains where even the clouds might lose their way,
thinking they were bumping into a reflection of the earth on
their journey from west to east when it was the earth itself.
My mother and the old woman sat down among the ferns
and unnamed flowering bushes along the stream and listened
to the birds calling out to each other and the swiftly moving
water for a while. The old woman said her name for that day
was Cachita Tumbo. She asked my mother if she wanted to
know the future, and my mother said yes. She asked if my
mother was afraid she might see something she did not like,
and my mother said no, she was not afraid. She asked my
mother if she would accept whatever she saw and not attempt
to change her future, and my mother said she would let her
life unfold as it was supposed to unfold, and more than that,
she said she would let her life flow through her as swiftly and
as brightly as this tiny mountain stream was flowing through
the forest all the way to the sea, and of course Cachita Tumbo
was pleased with my mother's enthusiasm.

    ¡Ay de mí! Who can penetrate the dark hood of the end-
less Cuban night? Who would not be filled with unyielding
despair at the thought of dying alone? My poor, poor mother.
She did not share all of the details of the dark vision of the
future Cachita Tumbo shared with her on that hazy, smoldering afternoon oh so many years ago. But she did say the old
woman predicted that on three separate occasions she would
be betrayed by the people she loved the most in the world.

    The first betrayal, of course, was the betrayal of my
father. No, he did not sneak off with a wayward woman. He
did not possess an uncontrollable libido. He was not like that.
No, my father's betrayal was much more devastating for my
mother. It was a betrayal of the spirit of love, though perhaps
such betrayals are inevitable. I think my father simply grew
too old. 'Romance is a game for the young,' he would say.
Instead of losing himself to love, my father lost himself in his
books and his world of ideas and in driving his truck, and
after a while he forgot my mother even existed.

    The second betrayal was Emilio stealing the Communion
wafer. My mother could never look at my brother after that
without wagging her finger and reminding him of the incredi-

bly long and unforgiving memory of Eshu Laroyê.

But the worst betrayal was mine. In my mother's eyes it was the worst possible betrayal one could suffer. My father's betrayal was a betrayal of the past, a past which she, too, had abandoned, so she really lost nothing. My brother's betrayal was a betrayal of the present, which carries less and less weight with each passing day, so in the end that too was nothing. But my betrayal was a betrayal of everything she had ever hoped for. Mine was a betrayal of her future, and so it was always fresh in her mind.

But what else could I have done? On the day I stumbled past the palatial pink stucco extravagance of La Campana, I traded her future for mine. That was the day I first beheld my beloved Oscar. He was standing in the radiant bubble of his own ambition, watching with studious appraisal the efforts of the men working to bolt the movie-house style marquee to the side of the building. It was a beautiful moment. And though he took absolutely no notice of me that afternoon, I knew without any doubt whatsoever that one day we would be married. It was simply a matter of destiny. So I ask you again, what else could I have done?

-115-

My mother was not the only one who secretly (or not so secretly) wished to steal my future. My dead relatives, my happy band of wayward angels, who had been lingering in between worlds for years, suffering from varying degrees of disbelief but watching over me all the same with their unvar-nished, saintly vigilance, they were all, with one exception, eager to substitute their own dreams of the future for mine. (Never mind that on that day when I first mentioned my dream, bubbling over with adolescent enthusiasm, my Oscar could hardly have asked for my hand in marriage since he had not yet even noticed me.) I never had to seek out their advice. They occupied a small alcove next to the upstairs bathroom, where my mother had arranged a small, brightly colored love seat and three brightly polished walnut chairs with a few vintage magazines laid out on a small coffee table. It was the perfect spot to waylay an impressionable young girl.

The only one who filled my beleaguered heart with the faith of the chosen was Tiká. Whenever she was present, the others kept their tongues in check. She would occupy the love seat and the others would gather around her and sit where they could. Whenever she was absent, the seating arrangements were as follows:

My great-uncle José Ignacio would sit in the middle of the love seat, tearing open small brown packages of analgesics and popping the tiny white tablets into the gaping black hole of his mouth with unthinking regularity, an addiction he had acquired, he once told me, during his days working in a cordage warehouse in Havana just after the Great War. Dozens of empty packages littered the floor at his feet, and yet there was always a crisp, new package in his eager hands, and even more tucked away in his pockets. Uncle José Ignacio possessed a seemingly inexhaustible supply of tablets, though why he needed so many and how he was able to procure them in the invisible, metaphysical limbo of the in-between he never said. Naturally my great-grandmother (and here I mean my great-grandfather's wife, for even though I now know the truth of my family tree, I will always think of Tiká as my cousin, and I will always and forever think of the second to last Ana Silvestre as my great-grandmother) would sit beside him, on one side or the other, pouring bittersweet words of unassailable regret into his glowing red ears, as only a mother born over a century ago would be tempted to do, and every now and then my uncle would sprinkle a few tablets into her withered, wrinkled, trembling hands.

My great-grandmother's one and only daughter, an adopted daughter it is true, but a daughter nonetheless, the very last of an incredibly long line of Ana Silvestres, if by name only, would sit across from the love seat in one of the walnut chairs. She paid no attention to either my great-grandmother or my uncle and his tablets. She was always embroiled in an overly enthusiastic yet decidedly bitter battle (a lot of arm waving, hands tracing arcane patterns in the air, finger

pointing, that sort of thing) with her sister-in-law, Nuria
Barruti (the second walnut chair), a dazzling beauty who had
grown up in El Cobre, Cuba, and who had been arrested at
the unlucky age of thirty for using *brujería* magic to seduce
the husbands of several wealthy women from one of the fancy
neighborhoods of Santiago. Tia Nuria had mysteriously died
in prison before her case could be heard, an unequivocal
tragedy in the modern age that was immediately and unani-
mously proclaimed the will of the resurrected God.

It was very difficult to argue with Tia Nuria. Every once
in a while when I looked into her eyes of a Santería priestess, I
could see the fractured, bluish light of long dead stars where I
should have seen two reasonably steady black pupils. I swear
this is true. It was almost like the universe was contained
within the ghostly jelly of Tia Nuria's eyes. There is not much
one can say in the presence of such a strange, alien light. It is
like being lulled to sleep by two cat's eyes. It is like staring too
long into the void of a lunar eclipse. So Tia Nuria won most
of her arguments without uttering a single word. But this was
not the case when she argued with my grandmother, though
to be fair, they only ever argued about the circumstances of
Tia Nuria's strange death, which appealed to my aunt's carefully concealed vanity, for it gave her a shining platform from
which to tell her own sad story.

My grandmother believed Tia Nuria had angered the
Virgin of Caridad del Cobre, the patron saint of love and
lovers, but Tia Nuria said that was absolute poppycock, she
had strictly adhered to the wishes of the loving and compassionate Saint with every spell she had cast, every ritual she
had performed, she had heaped all manner of honors on the
altar of fervent hearts in the hope that the sister of Yemaya
would bless her accordingly, and she had been exceedingly
blessed in matters of love, and in other things, no, no, Tia
Nuria said, her strange, unexpected death (the coroner could
find no physical manifestation of illness or any signs of foul
play) was simply a case of Yansá, the goddess of unexpected
hurricanes and the caretaker of drowned sailors and crumbling cemeteries on the verge of disappearing forever, anticipating a death when no death was upon the horizon. It was a
mistake such as anyone might make, that was all. The battle

between my grandmother and Tia Nuria had been raging in this manner for years.

The last two faces I would see would be those of José Luis the estranged, beleaguered husband of my aunt, and José Luis their happily indigent son, who had died in 1966 and was thus a recent participant in these impromptu family gatherings. The two José Luis's would be crammed into a single chair (the third walnut chair). They were both short, frail men with wiry arms and the long slender fingers of pianists, though neither had ever played. They possessed dark complexions from too many hours playing baseball. And their rough, leathery skin still somehow smelled of tobacco from years of incessant smoking. (They had only ever smoked thick, leafy cigars which they rolled themselves.) Curiously, they had both died of sunstroke at the age of thirty-five, so they looked more like brothers than father and son. They were also embroiled in a battle of their own, but they spoke without venom or hysterics or even ego, expressing themselves in low, desiccated whispers, trying not to draw any undue attention to themselves, their conversation punctuated now and then by bursts of sweet, endearing laughter like the sound of a salt water breeze rattling a set of wind chimes, or the unrivaled poetry of the tiny Torocoro, a bird that would become suddenly mute when caged and die the slow, withering death of inconsolable sadness, but in the wild it sang with an uninhibited and undiminished joy that only the angels could match. My great-grandmother often remarked on the similarity between the song of the Torocoro and the laughter of the two José Luis's. She used to say that when she was a young girl she would wake every morning and fall asleep every night to the Torocoro serenading the world with its sweet, happy song of absolute freedom and unburdened love. The laughter of the two José Luis's had the same sweet sound, she said. And so it did. The two men would laugh with a regularity like clockwork even while they were debating who was the greatest Cuban baseball player who ever lived. It was in fact a very comical debate, for they were constantly changing their minds, suggesting new players without the slightest provocation, swapping their claims on older ones without remorse, going through the entire pantheon of Cuban greats again and again

and again, even those players who had only played in Cuba
for a single season. This battle, an exact opposite of the other
on so many levels, had begun as you might have guessed as
an innocent game between a father and a son when both were
still alive.

I can say this now, looking back as I am with a faint,
blushing but unashamed smile, that on those hot, sultry
days and darkly oppressive nights when my dead relatives
surrounded me like silhouettes cut from black cardboard, the
kind of silhouettes used to frighten birds, I often wondered if I
had not gone mad.

It was as if I had become the inspiration for a line of
poetry by Julia de Burgos. *'La locura de mi alma vive en el
silencio del librepensador, que vive solo.'* What could I say to
them? I was willing to gamble a love as freely flowing and
relentless as water against everything that is inhuman and
unjust. This was the feeling in my heart. But I did not yet
possess the words to make my feelings understood. And they
did not wish to see me suffer, a sentiment that was magnified
by their own vanished intimacies and keen sense of loss. But
they knew as well as I, even at the tender age of eighteen,
that suffering was the price we pay for love. *¡Ay de mí!* What
young girl does not know this truth? All of which is to say
that they were not stringent or resolute in their hypocrisy. I
think my dead relatives just wanted to raise their voices to
the tornadic winds that obliterate all earthly desires and lay
waste cities that have stood for a thousand years and send
futuristic spaceships hurtling through the dark tunnel that
we call the void, and when they (the occupants within those
shiny, elliptical vehicles from the future) reach the other side,
they find they have crash landed in the frozen, snow-covered
Andes of centuries ago, so they flee the scene like cannibals on
the verge of starvation, or detectives in search of a high profile
crime, or young, restless, relentless lovers who have suddenly
and irrevocably gone blind, all in a mad dash to speak their
minds before God claims the right of final judgment. This is
why I think my dead relatives spoke as they did.

On the day I first beheld my beloved, my great-grandmother, the second-to-last Ana Silvestre, was the first to speak
among the dissenters. She had already seen the darkness in

the mirror, she said. She was quite poetic as she spoke. She spoke with the murmur of the ocean's millenary waves, at turns soothing, cajoling, and then provocative, unsettling. A strange hush fell over everyone. She spoke with the voice of my great-grandfather as much as her own, a voice that she had carried in her head from the day he had died until she had joined him in the in-between. What she said was a warning, and yet it was not a warning.

Yes, I see the two of you strolling into the lobby of your fancy Parisian hotel, a soft glowing golden light bouncing off the walls, a hall of mirrors, twelve, thirteen, twenty, an infinity of mirrors, the light now bending in peculiar ways, giving you plenty of opportunity to change direction if you choose. But you do not change direction. You walk arm in arm with death, that impertinent lover who whispers only bitter stories. No, you and your beloved are unaware, you are laughing carelessly, heedless of the future that will one day arrive. You are caught up in your luxurious surroundings. The décor is vaguely Romanesque with blood-red marble pillars edged in gold, pale green walls. Maybe not Romanesque. Minoan. Yes, that's it! The pillars and the walls suggest the island of mythic Crete. The ancient Minotaur trapped in an underground labyrinth. It has the feel of bygone elegance and dangerous depravity. But you do not notice. You are absorbed in thinking about the paradise of your surroundings while your beloved is signing the hotel register. The clerks and bellhops are chatting away happily, garrulous fellows. One of the clerks leads you from the lobby to the dead center of an art deco atrium with a glass bubble at the top. The narrow walls of the atrium are a whitish yellow for the most part, but near the bottom they are a deep, vibrant, volcanic orange. The bellhop tells you to look up and so you do. You feel like you are looking through a slender telescope manufactured in the age of marvels. You are looking at the white-hot center of the sun, that is the impression you have. You grow dizzy. You almost faint, but the bellhop catches your falling arm, and then your beloved makes a small joke about too much wine for so early in the day. Then the bellhop points out with mock enthusiasm an inlaid marble pattern on the floor. It looks like the corona of an indelible black sun, and at the very center is a bronze medallion that looks something like an eye. Perhaps it is an Egyptian eye. Or the one eye of the

Minotaur. Yes, you are reminded again of the Minotaur and the labyrinth. But this eye does not blink or fade. It stares at the white bubble of the sun oh so many miles above for all eternity. The one bellhop encourages the two of you to stand directly on top of this darkly polished, eternal sun, this unblinking eye. The bellhop asks you what it most resembles, a sun or an eye. You decide it looks more like an eye. Again, the bellhop presses you to stand directly on top of this iconic work of art embedded in the floor. He says he will take a photo of the two of you. You realize it is a bit of a cliché to pose for posterity's sake in this manner, but you do not mind. You are willing. Everyone who stays at this fancy hotel stands upon the eye. The famous writers who lived here and died here. The writers who wished to die here but died instead in their sleep in their own homes after returning from short, uneventful trips to Denmark or Belgium or Lebanon or Spain or the islands of Honduras. But not just writers. Everyone. The honeymoon couples stretching back to the dawn of the twentieth century and even earlier. And other couples as well, older absent-minded lovers, petulant lovers, criminal lovers, slap-happy lovers, homosexual lovers, lesbian lovers, generals and courtesans, painters and poets, a gourmet chef and his ex-wife, two young besotted philosophy students, indifferent to the passing years, who later become two middle-aged lovers stung by the pain of jealousy and the force of circumstances, twosomes and threesomes and foursomes, a man in a bandana playing a Spanish guitar, singing an ancient Iberian love song to a green moon and a demon lover hiding out in a balcony. All of them surreal caricatures of themselves, as we all are.

You and your beloved stand on the eye in the center of the atrium, but only for a moment, because your beloved is uncomfortable with the scrutiny of so public a display of affection. So he begs off, laughing sheepishly. You realize there will be no photograph, but you forgive him instantly. The idea of recrimination is not even a thought in your head. It is your honeymoon, such as it is. Then your beloved slips the bellhop a bill and the bellhop scuttles away clickety-clack on all fours, crab-like, to see about your luggage. Your beloved lingers only a moment more, giving you a curious backward glance before heading in the opposite direction and disappearing through a gauzy blueish-green curtain.

During the two weeks you are in Paris this curtain will remind you on a visceral, unconscious level of the color of the Caribbean Sea. It will be the sensation of a feeling lost in the gap between neurons rather than a specific thought or a re-created memory. During the years to come, this image of the curtain will haunt your dreams. You will begin to think of it as a symbolic reminder of that curtain through which we must all pass on our way to the grave. But on that bright sunny day in Paris these later more sinister interpretations will not occur to you. But you do not follow your beloved through that curtain, you remain standing on the darkly gleaming inlaid eye for a few moments longer, perhaps many moments, the precise number is difficult to gauge, and while you are standing there, your own eyes half-closed, immersed in the delicious swirl of romantic possibilities and the swirling white light from the neon sun of your imagination, the ghost of Marguerite de Valois whispers something impertinent into your ear. Yes, Marguerite de Valois, the promiscuous French queen who took her many lovers, an infinity of irrepressible lovers between 1589 and 1599, to a small stone house on the very corner where your luxury hotel now stands, a house which was known ever after as the 'Pavilion of Love.'

The ghost of this passionate yet staunchly unrepentant queen whispers into your ear the very same words she whispers into the ears of all the guests who stay at the hotel. You hear her voice quite distinctly, and yet there is a transient, ephemeral, faraway quality about the sound, as if the air has become suddenly quite thin. It is like swallowing in a single gulp the exhilarating, indescribable joy of the Sacryn bells during the Catholic Mass. The ghost of Marguerite de Valois tells you that lovers are not criminal in the estimation of one another ('Che la forza d'amore non riguarda al delitto'). You are so startled that you turn in a complete circle to see who is talking, but she vanished years ago, centuries ago, so there is no one there, not even one of the bellhops, not even the clerk from the front desk. Only the irrepressible joy of Marguerite de Valois' libido remains. Yes, my darling granddaughter, it is quite a romantic hotel your beloved will pick. It is your hotel. It is 'the' hotel. I cannot reproach him for that. The two of you will stay in an elegantly furnished room, a sunny soft orange color on the walls, softer than the orange

of the lobby, and thick drapes, a burnt orange color like a dying
sun. The art-deco furniture is covered with mirrors, the relics
of a once popular French singer, a legend of the Follies Bergere
with a sweetly despairing pouty face and fulsome lips who was
desperately in love with a Brazilian diplomat, and even bore him
a son, but they never married. But you are the first in the room
on this day. Your beloved has vanished within a few hours of
your arrival in Paris but you do not wonder why. You are not
troubled. You are surrounded by your own joy.

Wake up, my darling, wake up! Your youthful naiveté
is sweetly inspiring, but tragic, as Isolde's love for Tristan was
tragic, oh so very tragic. Do you not see this? Do you not feel the
tremors of what is happening, the tremors that will inevitably
lull you to sleep if you are not careful? Your beloved has not one
room in this hotel; he has taken three. In a second room, he is
keeping his mistress of the week, a young slip of a girl he met at
the airport while you were freshening up in the ladies' room. No,
there is no need to tell you what she looks like. She is the flavor of
the day. But her room is so extravagantly decadent. That should
tell you all you need to know. He is keeping his eager mistress
in a boudoir from the 18th century with a view of a cobblestone
street, a gloriously shameful room in honor of the notorious
Madame de Merteuil, complete with gold wallpaper and gilded
mirrors, and a damask baldaquin to keep prying eyes from seeing
what goes on in the bed. How can you not smell her treacherous
perfume on your beloved's skin when he comes to bed each night?
How can you not register the smallest flicker of irritation and
resentment when he whispers her name in the middle of a dream?
Ah my sweet, enduring granddaughter, what is to become of
you? Why are you sacrificing your love? Do you wish to live
as his concubine? Just one of many? And yet if it was only an
occasional dalliance with a young girl here, a restless, lonely
housewife there, or even many dalliances, he could be forgiven. If
he were sleeping with his own sister, he could be forgiven.

Wake up, my darling, wake up! Open your eyes to the
world around you. ¡Andar por las nubes uno se olvida del suelo!

In the third room, your beloved is keeping a peacock of a
young man who owns a small restaurant known to some as Café
de la Trois Pommes, but to others it has been known for years as
Chez Jules. It is a fancy restaurant for very fancy crowds just a

few blocks away on Rue Mazarine. It is a gathering place for the recalcitrant.

No, no, I will not describe to you what unseemly aberrations will take place in the peacock's room. The scandalous nudity is almost more than I can bear. But even this indiscretion could be forgiven, for such is humanity, such is weakness, such is love. 'Echar un palo,' as the old ones in Cuba used to say.

You see, my darling, I am not without compassion or understanding. I know we are bound to each other only if our love is freely given, as yours is. I know that if you have become love, you do not need to consciously forgive any sin because love is the incarnation of forgiveness. I know that every breath a lover breathes brings absolution.

Yes, I can see all this in the mirror as well. But what of the deception that is unforgivable? Your beloved has lied to you through his extended silences and his mysterious disappearances. He is trying to whitewash his depravity with words, which only God has the power to do.

No, no, I have no advice to give. I cannot see what happens after Paris. The mirror grows very dark after Paris, as dark and frothy as a wine-colored sea, as the poets say. The mysteries of your future quickly become impenetrable. But this is just as it should be. Perhaps there is nothing to worry about. Yes, my darling granddaughter. Life is never finished until it is finished. All prophecies are simply an artist's sketch of a moment, an evolving work of the imagination, the mind of God interpreted, and then reinterpreted. No one can look at a sketch without making a change, a subtle shading, an added detail, and wallah! the prophecy is altered.

Yes, my young invincible heroine, in spite of my warning, I must acknowledge that there is always hope. The mind of God is a tricky labyrinth indeed. Perhaps you are right in your unrestrained enthusiasm for this man. Perhaps the purity of your heart will carry you through. Perhaps I have no right to question you in this manner. I might as well ask you which has the saltier or sweeter waters, the Caribbean Sea or the Straits of Florida? No one can answer this question for another. It is a matter of personal taste. And so it is with you.

The last thing I see is the two of you dining at the small restaurant owned by your beloved's Moorish paramour. You

have already polished off a plate of veal and carrots flavored with
jasmine and are waiting for dessert.

The owner stops by your table with a warm, welcoming
smile, a tad over-friendly, you think, but the smile is for you as
much as for your beloved so you smile back. The owner is talking
with rapid-fire enthusiasm. His eyes do not betray his feelings,
but he is nervous nevertheless. His palms are sweaty. He seems
to be waiting for something. Then a waiter appears. The owner
tenses but then relaxes. It is only your desserts. Your desserts
have arrived. A lemon and raspberry dacquoise for each of you.
You take a bite and the taste overwhelms your senses. For a
moment it seems like the world is spinning. Then the owner leans
close to your beloved. He puts a hand to your beloved's shoulders
and whispers something in his ear. You are not sure what you are
seeing. The owner is gently massaging your beloved's shoulders
as he whispers. The two men laugh softly like conspirators with
no fear of discovery. Then a second waiter appears out of nowhere
with a bottle of Cognac. He presents the bottle to the table. It is
a very fancy bottle. It is a gift, of course. No money exchanges
hands. And yet your beloved leads you to believe that he is going
to spend an extraordinary sum on this single bottle. You will be
paupers for the rest of your honeymoon.

Why does he lie to you? What is the point of such a trivial
and yet monstrous deception? One can only guess. Perhaps he
cannot help but lie to you. Perhaps there is a better reason. Then
the two of them are laughing some more, but it is a different kind
of laughter. They are now laughing away like hyenas, their teeth
snapping at the empty air. You are staring at them with broken
wings. You are suffering on a cross of silence and ashes. Then
the mirror turns black.

-116-

My grandmother, the very last Ana Silvestre, was much
more direct in her words of warning. She believed that if I
married this Oscar, he would meet a sudden, savage, premature death. She said he would die amid the terror of a battle at

sea, a casualty of a brutal and ultimately inconsequential war. Then she reminded me of her own tragic love affair with my grandfather, Emilio Valentín Menoyo.

My grandmother met my grandfather one sunny after-noon in Havana in April 1916 at the age of fourteen (though she could have passed for a fulsome twenty-two) while she was strolling down the Paseo del Prado, admiring the many beautiful homes and listening with half an ear to a sultry bolero drifting on the silky currents of a spring breeze. She never admitted exactly how they met. She never said what my grandfather looked like or where he came from or how he made a living. All she would say is that from the moment they laid eyes on each other, the past was forgotten and the future was hungrily spent tangled up in each other's arms. My grandmother was certain that the love they shared would be the subject of sonnets for centuries to come. Oh, to be so lucky! Sadly, their love was not to be. History intervened. One year after my grandparents met, Cuba declared war on Germany, and President Menocal instituted a draft. But Cuba never officially sent any troops to Europe during the conflict, though the Cuban government issued Victory medals all the same at the conclusion of the war. But that is beside the point. My grandfather was among the many eager draftees who trained in earnest in secret training camps in Oriente and Camagüey provinces under the expert tutelage of retired United States Army colonels. It was no one's fault that the war ended before a single Cuban soldier crossed the Atlantic. God was determined to preserve the life of every single Cuban soldier. And yet my grandfather, Emilio Valentín Menoyo, died a casualty of that war all the same.

'He was an idiot,' my grandmother often said. 'He was not a soldier. He was a farmer, a musician, a poet, a grocery store clerk, an insurance salesman, a race car driver, a pharmacist. He was like anybody else. What did he think he was doing? Did he not realize that I was waiting for him to come home to me? Did he not realize that even my father had warmed up to him? I did not mind him traipsing about Cuba for a summer, pretending to be a soldier, flirting with the girls in Jiguani or Santa Rita, or even Bayamo, when they had a free weekend, not if that would make my Emilio happy. Besides,

I knew the girls in those towns, so I was not afraid of any dalliance. I was not afraid of anything that might take place on the island of Cuba. But why did he not come home to stay as soon as that summer was over? What made him seek out this war on the other side of the world? What excuse could he make to me? What madness came over him? What demon was whispering in his ear, requiring his blood? Oh, I wish that we had never met. How could my heart have been so deceived? Did he not see the beautiful life that was waiting for him? Oh why oh why did we not get married before he went off to the war? Was that too much to ask?'

This was the great betrayal of my grandmother's life. My grandfather had grown impatient with Cuba's war effort. After that first summer he realized the Cuban troops would never be ready to join the fighting. So he decided he would head for Brazil, because the Brazilians were hot for revenge. The Germans had sunk several Brazilian freighters bound for Spain, several more bound for France, and a steamer heading for the Caribbean, which meant, according to my grandfather, that there was a better chance of getting into the war if he went to Brazil than if he remained in Cuba. He told my grandmother of his plans on the last Saturday in September 1917. It was cloudy and very warm that day, so they decided go to a desolate beach some miles west of Havana. They had ridden their bicycles (because it was either that or walk).

All that afternoon they chased after each, splashing in the surf and then running along the beach and then diving beneath the waves, their naked skin glistening with foam and the incomparably resilient athleticism of youth, their laughter glistening with their nakedness. They made sweet, delicious love with the water lapping at their toes, without a single thought to the future. ('I did not realize how young I was until much later,' my grandmother told me. 'It was my first and last transgression of the flesh.')

It was a most romantic scene. As the sun began to set, as if on cue, it began to rain, so they grabbed their clothes and took refuge beneath an overturned fishing boat that had most certainly seen better days. My grandmother said it was quite a ferocious storm. She said it rained with a torrential intensity rarely seen even in the tropics. But she was not afraid. They spent the rest of that evening and the night that followed hiding beneath the boat. My grandfather wrapped his arms around her and began to whisper into her ear. The last thing she remembered hearing before she fell asleep was the rhythmic drumming of the rain on the hull mingling with the plangent sound of my grandfather's voice. He was telling her about his plans to leave for Brazil and fight in the Great War, how he would be at the forefront of many great battles and return a conquering hero with a chest full of medals, and then they could get married and live out their happy days in Miramar, or wherever she wanted to live. She had the crazy impression that she was lost in a dream.

Years later my grandmother realized with a strange mixture of incredulity and reverence that the beach where they had made love (and where my father was conceived) was the very same beach where centuries earlier the very first Ana Silvestre had made love to her secret husband, a lonely soldier of fortune who could not stop his feet from roaming and so had gone off with Hernando De Soto in search of cities of gold in 1539. Every Ana Silvestre for five hundred years dreamed with her eyes squeezed shut that she would be the lucky one to escape the bloody catacombs of the past. Not even my grandmother was able to escape those catacombs, in spite of the fact that she had been adopted. The next morning, she woke up to a crowd of ancient, weather-beaten faces surrounding her like a net, which was God's way of playing a joke, she later said, because she herself was stark naked except for a torn fishing net draped across her legs. In fact her legs had become tangled up in the net, which was attached to the boat, which is perhaps why the storm had not swept her out to sea. The vagaries of fate are strange indeed.

The weather-beaten faces belonged to a cluster of dirt-poor fishermen who dressed in rags (which does not matter when you are out in a boat). There was also a strange, courageous light in their eyes, and the expressions on their faces ranged from concern to paranoia to incredulity to an almost uncontrollable excitement. Some were making the sign of the cross and looking up suspiciously at the sky, as if they thought my grandmother was an angel that had been struck by lightning and had fallen to the sandy earth, a blistered, burning heap. Others were looking out at the unusually tranquil water that morning with great longing and wondering about the miracle of the sudden, ferocious squall that had come up from the south the night before, and then wondering why this young girl had not perished in the storm, and then their heads turned slowly in unison, following a trail of reddish seaweed back to the overturned boat, as if they thought my grandmother was perhaps a mermaid who had lost her tail but still possessed great magic. All of the men were whispering, though my grandmother later said it sounded less like whispering and more like the droning of insects hiding in the vegetation along the side of the road.

It took my grandmother several minutes before she realized that my grandfather had vanished, and several more before she could break through the hood of superstition that covered the understanding of the fishermen. When they finally understood that she had spent the night with her betrothed beneath the boat, and when they finally understood, on this glorious morning with the beach littered with all sorts of refuse coughed up by the sea, that her betrothed was nowhere to be found, they laughed with unembarrassed delight and then launched into a furious conversation with hurried, high-pitched voices, trampling over each other's words, and then one of them said 'Lobos de una camada,' which was followed by more laughter, which was followed by a moment of embarrassed silence when they realized my grandmother was listening to them with great apprehension.

Then one of the men squatted down by the boat so he could look directly into my grandmother's eyes. 'Excuse us Senorita,' he said. 'We have meant no disrespect. We can clearly see you have been through an ordeal. Forgive us. We are brainless, as you have surely guessed. Our heads are no bigger than the heads of falcons or ferrets.'

It was a strange thing to say, but my grandmother only nodded and smiled a blank, vaguely hopeful smile, which the fishermen took for a sign that their rustic version of an apology had been accepted. Then they laughed some more and helped my grandmother to her feet. One of the men, after some searching, located her bicycle half-buried in the sand. There was no evidence of a second bicycle. Then they gave her a damp blanket to wrap around her bare, glistening hips, and off she pedaled towards Havana.

My grandmother never saw my grandfather again.

Near the end of July the following year she received a letter that he had sent from Rio de Janeiro. The letter was signed 'your brave and true Emilio, a moth to the eternal flame that is our love,' but she was still angry that he had abandoned her beneath the boat and refused to read it for almost a year. But eventually, as you most certainly have guessed, she read it every day, and then twice a day, before she abandoned it utterly to the ash heap of her despair, because it was the only letter he ever sent. It was dated April 29, 1918. It was a naively optimistic letter, the kind one expects from a young man going off to war, which skillfully avoided sentimental excess by avoiding the topic of love altogether, except by implication.

What my grandfather's letter said:

My Dear Sweet Ana, How I miss you. I arrived safely in Brazil on a very cold Monday. I have been staying with a kindly couple that I met down at the fish market. Their names are Adelita and Sagueo. Adelita grew up in Brazil and has never been anywhere else. Sagueo is from Mexico. He fled his country when Carranza came to power. He cannot stand Carranza. He calls Carranza all sorts of names. He says he is a very fat frog in a very small puddle. He calls him a thief and a liar, an overstuffed brigand, a buffoon, a lizard, and the name of another reptile I had never heard before, a hideous monster with jaws of iron and poisonous breath that roams the forgotten deserts of Mexico in search of unwary travelers to feast upon. He is exaggerating, of course. Can you imagine such a reptile? Carranza sounds just like any other politician. But Sagueo cannot wait for him to die so he can take Adelita to Mexico City. Sagueo says his family owns a very beautiful home there in one of the suburbs, a gleaming white palace of a home in a prosperous suburb where the sky is always a crisp, clean azure and rumors of murder always turn out to be propaganda created by those who are envious. He wants to take Adelita there as soon as possible. You would like Adelita, but I am not so sure you would like Sagueo. He has a very quick temper and has gotten me involved in two nasty brawls already.

Who knows? Maybe you would like him after all. You cannot imagine how it was when I first met them. You cannot imagine what a joy it was to hear the lovely sound of Spanish being spoken after so many weeks of Portuguese. I do not know how the Brazilians can speak their language. It is so very different from Spanish. It is very challenging. Adelita is teaching me Portuguese bit by bit, enough so I can get by. She has the noble temperament of a sweet saint (as do you, my love). She would need to possess such a temperament to teach a brainless wolf like me. Sagueo has no patience for teaching. He has no patience for anything that does not involve copious amounts of alcohol or the raw, mind-numbing images of symbolist poetry. He is always reading a French poet who died years ago. Some of the images are very strange indeed. In one of his poems a partially bald woman is rising up out of a bathtub that resembles a zinc green coffin. In another, packs of ferocious wild dogs in heat are eating the bandages of those who have gone insane from pleasure. Horrific images, some of them. Sagueo thinks it is a waste of breath to learn Portuguese. He says I should learn French. But it is not a waste of breath. I have no use for French. Portuguese is for me the language of war. I will teach you Portuguese when I return if you like. There is no rose without thorns, as they say. Do you remember that night beneath the boat? It is a most fantastic memory. I know this memory will sustain me on the many long and lonely nights when I am at the war. Everyone here is excited about avenging the honor of Brazil against those barbarian Huns. Everyone is talking about the perigo alemão, the German danger. Sagueo says it has been a topic of conversation in the cafés and smoking rooms for years, but now this danger seems just around the corner. The government declared war back in October, but the level of excitement is still very high. You would not believe how much the Brazilians hate the Germans. It is a lacerating, visceral hatred, especially in the south. Every day in the newspaper there is a story about this German couple whose shoe store or deli or music shop or leather goods shop was ransacked, or that German couple who was murdered in their sleep by drunken patriots because someone found out they were actually saboteurs. A riot broke out at a German cigar factory somewhere in Bahia, just north of Rio, and the manager was beaten to death with clubs. The government had to send in troops to restore public order. Here in Rio a mob set fire to the grand hall of the Pan-German Association and the building burned to the ground. Of course the anarchists are not happy. They are hoping to expand the perimeter of violence beyond those of German descent. But the rest of Brazil is unified in their hatred. Every German school in the country has been closed and the teachers sent to internment camps. The German banks are all closed. The doors to every German magazine and newspaper have been locked. Even the great German books of ages past have been removed from the shelves of every library. If you are German, it is better to head for Argentina or Paraguay or even Chile than to remain in Brazil. Every German face you see is suspect, and that is the truth! So Sagueo and I have joined the Navy. Adelita was quite unhappy, and for three weeks she refused to serve us anything to eat except feijoada, a very hearty black bean stew, even for breakfast. It is a delicious stew, and Adelita packs hers full of spicy sausage, but one can grow tired of anything if one overindulges by predilection or dint of circumstances. But we forgave her. Adelita does not understand the importance of our decision. We have been assigned to a very great ship with a very great name. I am not supposed to say which ship, but I will tell you anyway, our beautiful ship is called the Laurindo Pitta. Yes, just to look at her is enough to take your breath away. We will be part of a flotilla of great ships given the great task of patrolling the waters off the coast of Africa. I am not supposed to speak of our mission, but I will tell you, my love, so you will not worry. And so you will know what a brave hero your betrothed has become. We will be hunting down German U-boats. We will also be sweeping the coastal waters from Dakar to Gibraltar for mines. Ah, my love, the treachery of the Germans knows no boundaries. Oh, the atrocities they committed during the invasion of Belgium. And it is the same everywhere they go. It is very great work we will be doing. We are very lucky to have been chosen. Of the thousands and thousands who wished to fight the Germans at sea, only nine hundred will do so. School children will one day read about us. It is almost like destiny. 'Through the sufferings and delusions to which the war has given rise, a new and better world will be born of liberty.' This is what our Captain said to us, and I, for one, believe him. I will write more when I am able. I do not know when that will be. But do not worry. Dry your eyes. For now,

I am a wanderer, a cloud with a hidden purpose drifting across the ocean, a circumnavigating bird without a nest. But I will be home before you know it. Lo prometido es deuda!

-117-

One cannot appreciate how utterly your life, with the diabolical cunning of the insanely jealous, can abandon you until it does so. And so it was with my grandmother. After my grandfather vanished, she became a pilgrim unto herself. Confounded by the chaste symmetries of the universe, she avoided the bright spaces that represent the unfolding of our lives and became a creature of plummeting darkness.

Ah, my poor, poor grandmother! She all but gave up looking after her young son, my father, Andres Escoraz Silvestre. She had given birth to her son in her own childhood bedroom in the great house in Miramar, and there she had remained, shrouded in the mystery of her own despair while her son spent most of his waking hours chasing after the dreams and memories of his grandfather (my great-grandfather). Young Andres usually fell asleep just before midnight in the arms of my great-grandfather, usually in the library with its dark mahogany floors and its row after row of history books and volumes of poetry and dictionaries in several languages (Spanish, English, French, Turkish) and various atlases, and its single shelf devoted to the three Cuban philosophers. My great-grandfather's deep musical voice filled every corner of the house as he recounted to my father with immeasurable pride that unsurpassable evening when he had listened to Enrique José Varona himself tell the tale of a mythic bullfight in mythic Mexico and the sea of weeping women dressed in white who had prayed for the deliverance of the bullfighter. But such is life.

Then one day, long after the Great War had ended, my grandmother received a small package. It did not arrive by regular post. She later said that it seemed to materialize right out of thin air one dark, hazy evening when she was

sitting by her open bedroom window, hovering on the edge
of consciousness, listening to the sound of a distant bolero
floating across the Almendares River. She could not quite
hear what the bolero was about, but it brought tears to her
eyes nonetheless, and she was groping about her nightstand
and then her dresser for a clean cloth to dry her eyes when
her fingers found the package instead. The package was from
Mexico City.

She opened it immediately. She said the thought briefly
crossed her mind (and it was a welcome thought, which will
give you some indication as to her emotional state) that the
package might contain a small explosive device or a tiny pistol
with tiny golden bullets or an exotic and fast-acting poison
derived from the secretions of the golden poison arrow frog
found only in the wilds of Colombia or on the western slopes
of the Andes, bizarre, potentially lethal possibilities that
excited her growing pathological sense of urgency.

Instead, the package contained one official looking letter
and one official looking telegram, both from the Brazilian
Navy, a brown jeweler's box containing a bronze colored cross
fixed to the end of an orange ribbon with three black stripes, a
second precisely typed letter from my grandfather's Mexican
friend, Sagueo, and a small bible.

The official looking letter had originally accompanied
the box and explained in official language that the bronze
cross adorned with a ribbon was a Campaign Medal that had
been awarded in the spirit of undying gratitude from a hopeful and forward thinking nation to Emilio Valentín Menoyo, a
native son of Tubarão from the province of Santa Catarina, for
his dedicated service to the Brazilian Navy during the years
1917-1918. The letter was dated November 1922 and embossed
with the Brazilian Navy's official seal.

The telegram, which bore the date 16 June 1919, came
in a yellowed envelope that had been forwarded again and
again, first from Rio to Natal, then from Natal to Paramaribo,
then from Paramaribo to Caracas, and finally from Caracas to
Mexico City. It was almost unreadable. The author of the telegram had used an uneven bold-faced type, and there were so
many misspellings and words misused or missing altogether
that the telegram had to be decoded to be understood, as if,

my grandmother said, it had been produced by a drunken chimpanzee trained by Russian circus clowns.

The telegram announced with an understated gravitas that Emilio Valentín Menoyo, a seaman of exceptional patriotism aboard the ocean going tug the *Laurindo Pitta*, had been lost at sea during a skirmish with a German U-boat in the dark waters off the coast of Africa near the city of Agadir and was presumed dead. A search had been initiated after the battle had concluded, but was called off a few hours later due to inclement weather. No evidence of Seaman Menoyo's body was found during the search. At the end it said that the precious name of Emilio Valentín Menoyo would appear on a bronze plaque commemorating those sons of Brasil who fell during the Great War. The plaque would be located in a grand park in Rio de Janeiro known as the Passeio Público. It would bear witness to the heroically deceased for generations to come.

The letter from Sagueo contradicted the telegram both in its tone (Sagueo's words were filled with remorse and nostalgia) and in its detailed account of the death of my grandfather. My grandmother never forgot Sagueo's words, which she said took refuge in the dark empty spaces of her heart like so many blue scorpions hiding from the sun.

-118-

The letter from Sagueo Ruedas:

Dear Miss Ana Silvestre, my name is Sagueo Ruedas and I knew your betrothed, Emilio Valentín Menoyo. He stayed with me and my wife, my beloved Adelita, for almost a year when he was in Rio. But after that, well, how can I say this? They are both gone. In its own way the war took them both. My Adelita suffered an aneurysm shortly after we left for the war, a condition I am sure was made infinitely worse by my absence. And your sweet Emilio died a few months later while we were at sea. I am so sorry I did not write sooner. I was not up to the task. No, that is a lie. I have been distracted by the absence of my Adelita. I write to her every day. The truth is I could not stay in Rio. Everywhere I went I saw my Adelita. So I returned to Mexico in 1921. That is where I was born. But even this did not help. I was utterly consumed by my Adelita, so to relieve the tension I began to write to her. The writing helped. I was able to control my grief. I was able to gain a foothold in the world once again. Those were dark days. But I must confess that in all those years I did not once think about Emilio. That is why I did not write any sooner. And I am only writing to you now because the other day his medal arrived from Brazil, and the day after that the telegram with the news that he was missing at sea. Imagine that, the telegram arrives almost eight years after his death! It is absurd. The whole thing is absurd. The Brazilian government. The Navy. The war. All of it. So there it is. I have been living in Mexico City and have not thought about Emilio once in five years, and then the medal and the telegram arrived, and after that, of course, I could think of nothing but Emilio and his beauty and his courage. What can I say? If the Brazilian government knew Emilio the way I had known him, they would have sent him a dozen medals. But they didn't know anything about him. They didn't even realize he was from Cuba. Then again how could they know something as elemental as that? Life is what it is, after all. When we signed up in those bright, happy days after Brazil declared war on Germany, I told Emilio to say he was from Tubarão. That is a small coastal town in the south, an impossible journey from Rio if one travels overland, which is why Adelita and I always traveled by steamer. A great many Germans settled in Tubarão before the war, but after the sinking of the Rio Branco everyone started to hate the Germans. It was incredibly bad in Tubarão. My wife was from there, so she told Emilio a little bit about growing up in case anyone asked him, but no one asked him anything. No, no one cared where he was from. There were too many men who were eager to take a crack at the Germans. It was all the recruiters could do to take down names and addresses. Ah, yes. Cada cual hace con su vida un papalote y lo echa a volar, as they say. But it is enough to crush one's heart. It is a very great irony, yes, it is a tragic irony, my wife and Emilio, a daughter and an adopted son of Tubarão, a city of Germans, both dying from the war against Germany. Some days how I wish I had traded places with Emilio, for I was not there

*when my beloved Adelita died. This burden is difficult to bear.
I should have been there with her. I never should have left. But
what is one to do? It is as sad and tragic as any of the great fados
they used to sing years ago. But I was there when your sweet,
courageous Emilio died. And that is another reason for this letter.
He did not die the way they said. The telegram says we were off
the coast of Africa near the city of Agadir. But we were much
further north than that. Our fleet had already pushed through
the Straits of Gibraltar. We were supposed to keep to the Atlantic,
but then a German U-boat fired upon us. I don't know which
ship, but the torpedo missed. Then our ships started dropping
depth charges with a mania I had never seen before, and the sea
exploded with fire and dead fish. I remember the shockwaves from
all those explosions were so great I could barely breathe. Then we
started chasing the sub. The whole fleet was chasing after this
phantom German sub which maybe had never existed at all. How
does one catch a ghost? But we were chasing him just the same,
and every ten minutes we dropped more depth charges, just for
good measure. It looked like the sea was a lake of fire. Of course
our boat was not really part of the action. The Laurindo Pitta
was a Navy tug. Our job was to help the big ships get in and
out of port, so wherever they went, we went. I was watching the
whole damn show from the rail, and I remember how exciting it
was. It was like watching one of Toscano's movies, except I could
smell the burning diesel and I could feel the cooling spray of the
saltwater as we rushed this way and that. It was exhilarating, to
tell you the truth. Emilio was not there at first. He was sleeping
below. He had taken sick with the Spanish influenza and had not
left his bunk for three days. Our boat had already lost three men
to the flu and everyone thought Emilio was going to be next. But
that night he crawled out of the belly of the ship and then there
he was, standing at the rail with the rest of us. At first I thought
he was delirious. He seemed to be having a conversation with
an unseen entity hovering three feet above his head. Then I took
a step towards him. I was going to help him back to his bunk.
But just at that moment he turned and smiled a most becoming
smile, as if to say he was through the worst of it. I can still see
him quite plainly. The moon was very bright that night and lit
up every inch of the deck. Then Emilio turned back to the rail and
the boat pitched and Emilio was gone. The sea had swallowed him*

in a single gulp. That is how he died. I called out to the watch
that a man had fallen overboard and they took up the cry, but the
boat did not stop. We just kept following the other boats. That
was it. Later, before I returned to Mexico City, I received my
own letter from the Brazilian government. The letter said that
the government was going to put a plaque in the Passeio Público
in Rio to honor all the seaman who had died during the war.
But this was also a lie. There is no plaque. I visited the Passeio
Público on many different occasions before I returned to Mexico
City, always searching for this mythic plaque, but there was no
plaque. So I hold Emilio in my heart, along with my beloved
Adelita, and all the rest who died during those years. It is the
only thing I can do.
    With great sorrow and eternal regret, Sagueo Ruedas

-119-

I am no fool. I am not dimwitted. I knew from the
beginning that my love for Oscar was stronger than his love
for me. But I did not mind. Nothing Oscar ever did or might
do could surprise me. I knew he still held a torch for the
Afro-Cuban goddess he had left in Havana. (Whatever else he
left in Cuba he never said.) I knew he chased after the girls in
La Campana. He was heroic and compassionate in the manner
of the ancient Greeks and loved men as much as women. I
knew he swung from chandeliers. But all that did not matter.
And even though there were many days in the years before
we were married that I almost gave up all hope (and during
those most trying days the criticisms of my dead relatives all
but vanished into the abyss of their contented hearts), I knew
with a knowledge that goes beyond knowing that one day
we would be together the way I had imagined from the very
beginning. My heart became a mirror of God's forgiveness.
The beautiful spirit that was Oscar leapt through me like the
sea. I was a ship of seagulls resting on the waves of his joy. He
was light and I was shadow. And then one day, as fantastic as
it sounds, what was true for me was true for him. He swam
to me without question in the madness of loving me. And I to

him. *Único hombre que ha besado en mi alma al besar en mi cuerpo.*
That was how it was. That is how I choose to remember it.
And the day Oscar realized that I was the only woman who
kissed his soul when she kissed his body, on that day he asked
me to marry him.

The story of that day began at Sunny Isles. It was the
only place we ever went. A retreat into the glory of a separate
sphere where no one bothered Oscar. He could become a
spectator, a happy ghost with no name, a child once again
with all of his choices before him. Oscar liked to walk out on
the pier and chat with the fishermen. He did not fish himself,
but the fisherman reminded him of the old men he had known
in Baracoa or along the Malecón in Havana. The waves, the
indomitable waves crashing on the shore, reminded him of
days gone by. That's what he said. Of course I was not so
much impressed by the sound of the waves or the fishermen
on the pier in those days. I possessed a restless, relentless,
energetic spirit. I was afraid of all of his ancient regrets. I
wanted bright lights and dazzling sambas. I wanted to feel
lightning bolts coursing through my veins. So we stayed at
a fancy resort on an island all to itself, just across from the
ocean. It was called Castaways, which is just how we felt.
My beloved Oscar started taking me to Sunny Isles in 1969.
He asked me to go so I went. I gave in to the urgency of the
moment and did not imagine the disorder of my heart that
was to come. But this, too, is life. That very first night we
stayed in room 227. And after that, well, somehow we always
ended up in room 227. *¡Ay de mí!* Those were good days.

Oscar proposed to me on Monday December 6, 1976 at
two in the afternoon just after we crossed the bridge to Bal
Harbour Beach. It was a most amazing day. We had left the
resort just before noon and driven north for a while, maybe
an hour, before Oscar turned the car around and headed back
towards Miami. We drove along the water the whole way.
It was very sunny, and we were driving with the top down
and Oscar had turned the radio on. The radio was blaring,
which meant that neither of us said a word while the car
was moving. To be honest, we did not speak even while the
car was stopped at a traffic light. In fact, we had not spoken
two words to each other since the previous afternoon when

Oscar was making love to me like a madman in the bed of
my dreams, but all he was saying at that point was 'move this
way baby, that's it, oh my God, that's fucking incredible, oh
baby, your legs feel so good, yeah, keep them just like that,
Papa is on his way to sugar town, don't move, don't move, oh
my God,' which wasn't the kind of romantic pillow talk a girl
hopes for, and it certainly wasn't much help in deciphering
his mood that afternoon or the next day, but what is a girl
supposed to do?

I like to tell myself that my Oscar was silent that morning because he was trying to come up with precisely the right
words to express his undying love. He wanted to write my
name in heaven. Our love would be a blazing constellation.
He wanted his words to come gushing forth like the fountain
of creation and take my color away. *¡Sacar los colores a alguien!*
He wanted a blushing bride. But this is pure fabrication on my
part. A balm to soothe a troubled heart. To be truthful, and I
am wholly committed to the truth these days, I must confess
that I do not know why he chose that day as opposed to any
other day to propose to me, or why he even proposed to me
at all, especially given his lingering, devastating silence on the
ride back. I know what I said. The day Oscar realized that I
was the only woman who kissed his soul when she kissed his
body, on that day he asked me to marry him. But that is also a
fabrication. I have been lying to myself about what happened
for years. But that is not unusual. Who does not engage in the
odd bit of retrospective sleight-of-hand now and then? To be
blunt, I had no idea what was going on in Oscar's heart and
soul that afternoon. His thoughts, which were normally easy
to decode because they rarely varied from one moment to the
next, were cavorting across the suddenly tormented landscape
of his brain with dizzying, almost supersonic speed.

-120-

So here is the truth of what happened and why it happened as best as I can piece it together.

We didn't get to the resort up at Sunny Isles until late Friday night, December 3, 1976. I went into the lobby with Oscar. He chatted with the front desk clerk for a while and I went over to a parrot the management kept in the lobby to entertain the guests. The parrot had been a part of the lobby as long as we had been going to the resort. His name was Herman, though a lot of people called him Schwartz.

Oscar and the clerk were talking about baseball.

I was talking over matters of the heart with Herman. I asked Herman if this was going to be a good weekend, and he said 'That's a stupid question,' which is how he responded to most questions, and then he broke into a fit of screeching, raucous laughter. Then Herman stopped laughing and I could hear a scratchy rendition of "Yellow River" pouring out of the speakers in the ceiling of the lobby. Herman grew suddenly very quiet, morbidly quiet, and started swaying slightly to the music. I don't know what kind of parrot Herman was except that he was very clearly a German parrot.

Oscar came back with the key and an irrepressibly lopsided smile and said he was going to have me out of my clothes by the end of the night, but I could leave my hat on. Suspicious minds would have thought the worst of my beloved. But it was really quite a sweet thing to say. I was wearing a tight-fitting pair of black and white zebra capris that showed off the curves of my derrière (which Oscar liked to say was an arrow that went straight to his heart), a ruffled white blouse held in place by a single lace strap, shiny black boots, the kind that Nancy Sinatra wore, and a rather chic looking black beret, all of it a gift from Oscar.

You wouldn't guess it to look at me now, but I was very beautiful in those days. I daresay I even caused a car accident or two just by walking along the sidewalk.

I can laugh about it on a day like today, but back then, well, back then was a different story. I thought I looked like a Parisian countess in my ridiculous go-go-dancer's outfit, which was silly, as you are surely thinking to yourself, because a Parisian countess wouldn't have been caught dead in such wildly provocative clothes. But what did I know at such a young age. My imagination was very vigorous. I felt like a countess, and I was very happy (ecstatic is more accurate) that my Oscar wanted to get me out of my clothes. I was Oscar's pussycat. What else were my clothes for but to have Oscar rip them to shreds in the desperate frenzy of a mad, passionate love affair? I would have stripped to my skin in the lobby if he had asked me.

The next few hours went by in a blip, and then it was seven in the morning. We slept all day and went to dinner at six. You can decide for yourself if we got any sleep at all that first night.

I don't remember what we ate for dinner.

The next thing I remember is the two of us sitting at a small table in the sunken ship nightclub drinking tequila and listening to a crazy mad guitarist jamming on the stage. I don't remember the guitarist's name. I didn't know it then. But Oscar seemed to know him. Oscar knew pretty much everyone in the music business in Miami.

I don't actually see myself in this memory. It is like a movie flashing across a giant movie screen. The movie is in Technicolor.

We were sitting in the front row, and pretty soon Oscar and the mad guitarist were trading swigs from a bottle of Jack, and all the while the guy was playing his crazy mad guitar. He played until three in the morning. He was blitzed out of his mind, but nobody seemed to care. Everyone was going wild for him. When he finished he sent his guitar spinning across the stage and it smashed into a stool and the stool toppled over. Then he invited the whole club to join him for some pancakes and we all headed across the street to a pancake house and ate pancakes. There must have been a hundred people crammed into those tiny blue booths. The crazy mad guitar player said he would pick up the tab, but when the bill came he confessed that he was flat broke, which precipitated a mad dash for the door. The poor waitress never stood a chance and she knew it. She shrugged a resigned shrug and moved to the tables on the far side of the cash register and began wiping up the tiny pools of syrup that remained. When she finished the first table she looked up, an odd, sort of whimsical, half-expectant expression on her face, as if she had just woken up from a long, troubling dream filled with dark clouds and false promises.

The crowd had vanished by then. But not my Oscar. My beloved Oscar was waiting by the register, his face glowing with the same silly, lopsided grin he always wore when he thought he was being courageous or clever or unspeakably kind. The waitress and Oscar looked at each other for a moment. I suspect she was hypnotized by his immaculate good looks. He was immaculate the way a movie star is immaculate in his white linen suit and his thick dark hair slicked back like Rudy Valentino and his thin, carefully combed moustache and the scent of fresh mint lingering on his skin and his happy, dancing, mischievous brown eyes. He wasn't very tall, my Oscar, but his lopsided smile made up for that. You felt yourself swooning whenever he smiled at you.

I suspect the waitress was about to swoon. She was trembling slightly, a leaf in a gentle breeze.

Then my beloved Oscar peeled off a pile of cool, crisp one-hundred dollar bills from his money clip and pressed them into the girl's hand. Then he peeled off a few more, half a dozen, just for good measure.

Then we went back to our room. But Oscar did not stay. He kissed me goodnight and said he needed to speak with the mad guitarist. I knew what he was planning. The mad guitarist had gone back to the club and was jamming away. You could feel the vibrations of his guitar strings in the air. It was a shimmering, fluttering kind of sensation like an agitated pulse rushing up and down the many public and private corridors of this resort on the beach. Like the world was hyped up on amphetamines. I knew my Oscar just wanted to be part of the scene. He didn't play any instrument. He just wanted to hang out with the mad guitarist and be seduced by the vibe of an electric guitar and drink and laugh. He wanted to turn back the clock. So Oscar headed to the sunken ship and the jam session that was most definitely happening even though he did not play an instrument, and I curled up in bed and fell asleep.

Truly, I was not the jealous type. Whatever made my Oscar happy made me happy.

He came back to the room a little after eight in the morning, reeking of whiskey and someone else's perfume, and crashed into his pillow. He seemed to be dreaming delicious dreams, and I wanted to be a part of those dreams, but I did not wake him. He slept until four in the afternoon, and then he woke up just like that, as if he had heard my soul calling out to him. We made sweet, delicious love for two hours. Then he showered, shaved, and put on his fancy white slacks and a white linen jacket, an outfit which he only wore on very special occasions, and a Panama hat that he had worn for years without even thinking about what was covering his head, a grand, shining, immaculate Panama hat from his days in Havana oh so many years earlier. I asked him where he was going and he just tossed me a cavalier, lopsided smile and said I possessed too much curiosity. Then he laughed and said he'd be back in an hour or so, the mad guitarist had agreed to play at La Campana, he'd be there for two straight weeks beginning in May, it was a done deal except for signing the contracts.

Up till that point it had been a glorious weekend. I thought about the question I had asked Herman, the parrot. Yes, I said to myself, it had been a stupid question. I remember wondering how the parrot could know so much. Then I remembered that Descartes once said that the reason parrots appeared to possess the gift of speech was that they were possessed by the Devil. I don't know if Descartes actually said such a thing. It was just something I had once read or heard someone else say. But then Oscar returned and I was forced to revise my estimate of Herman, the parrot, and the mental acuity of parrots in general. You see Oscar had only been gone ten minutes, but when he came back he was not himself, not in the least. He motioned for me to get dressed, so I did, but he paid no attention to my flashes of nudity, which was quite a shock to me. Oscar had never before treated me with such alien indifference. He always asked me to adopt a leisurely pace when getting dressed and undressed, especially late at night with the lights blazing away, so he could sit back and watch. I enjoyed catering to my Oscar's every whim. But he was not interested in my nudity on that day. So I got dressed. What else was I supposed to do?

Then we went to dinner. We went to the teahouse, one of the most popular restaurant at the resort with its gleaming crystal lanterns and fake cherry blossoms. I asked Oscar if something had happened with the deal, but he refused to answer. He refused to even look at me. He only bit his lip and turned his shoulders with a sudden declarative swiftness so he could look out the window (we were at a window table). I noticed that his lips were bleeding slightly. He seemed kind of jittery. But whatever was troubling Oscar he wouldn't say. Our waiter came and went. Our food arrived. The couples all around us were laughing while they ate and then getting up to dance to one or two songs before running back to their tables to stuff a few more bites of some expensive and therefore popular seafood delicacy into their fat, slobbering, untroubled mouths. But Oscar and I ate in trembling, exhausted silence. I was confused, as you would expect. I was enveloped in a fog of chaos and spiritual decay. I did not understand my beloved's strangely steep silence. But what could I do? How could I perforate the impervious bubble of his inattention? I decided there was nothing I could do. I let my beloved's strange silence like a sea flow through me. His silence became an exploding current of tiny wriggling eels and silver fish and other small rustling creatures of the night trying to avoid exposure. And then the current was gone. The sea shrunk and became a cluster of birds. The explosion became a vague restlessness. I realized I was part of the world again. I drank a glass of wine in a single gulp and then I drank another, with more relish, less speed. I immersed myself in the fast-moving eddies of worldly noise swirling all around our table, listening carefully, methodically, to the buzz of dozens of conversations from every corner of the teahouse. I suddenly possessed superhuman hearing. It was a minor miracle of sorts, a transcendent moment. I could even hear the waiters whispering to each other as they waited by the kitchen doors.

In my experience one rarely questions miracles when they are occurring, especially if one (meaning me, naturally) has been weaned on the chicanery of priests. But oh, my poor, poor Oscar! Slowly I realized that the trouble that had plunged my beloved into the abyss of silence had become part of the eternal memory of the resort. Everyone in the teahouse was talking about this trouble as if it were their own. It was on everyone's lips, how the mad guitarist from the night before had been found dead by his agent that afternoon, how the preliminary findings suggested that the guitarist had died from alcohol poisoning, which did seem odd because clearly the guitarist drank like a fish, an ability which he had most likely possessed for years, which is perhaps why the police were making a thorough investigation, just in case a more sinister cause of death could be identified and a criminal apprehended.

Ah those gossipy lips with their irreverent, even ludicrous, but still crippling innuendo! But how else would we have known that the guitarist's girlfriend, a voluptuous blond named Nikki, worked at the resort? She was a wild, slightly perverted and therefore dangerous go-go dancer, some said, impervious to envy and gossipy speculation, but others said she was a waitress in the Seven Seas Lounge who barely made enough to get by, and one voice declared she was a low-life cashier in the gift shop who had been skimming from the receipts for years. But no matter what she did, no matter what crimes she had or had not committed, all the voices agreed that she was a double-dealing opportunist, a Jezebel of the worst kind, willing to pit one frustrated lover against another in a no-holds-barred struggle to the death. The lips said as much. The lips said the girlfriend was also seeing a lifeguard who worked at one of the resort's seven pools, and how she was often seen in the company of insurance salesmen or lawyers or corporate executives who wanted to get away for a fast weekend, no questions asked, and how she had an ex-boyfriend who rode a Harley, and whenever he roared into town, which was only once in a while when he was running low on cash, he threatened anyone who gave her even a sideways glance, because the girlfriend was definitely stacked. To hear everyone talk she was built like a brick house. This was the gossip that had taken hold of the collective imagination of the tearoom in the chaos of the unexpected death of the mad guitarist, obscuring the facts most assuredly, but it gave the police detectives who had arrived on the scene plenty to think about, plenty of grist for the mill, plenty of leads that would lead nowhere, but they didn't mind, they were busy exploring every possibility, very busy.

It was hard to comprehend what was actually happening.

I wondered if God was listening as intently as I was to the frantic voices that were swirling about the teahouse, voices of shock and overwhelming sadness and paranoia and downright gossipy glee (because people love to talk about the death of someone else). Then I was thinking that perhaps God's attention was focused elsewhere.

I am certain now that my poor, distracted Oscar was worried that he would be grilled by the police. He was sick to death with worry. He feared that the police would see in his Cuban face a face of introspective guilt. He was always afraid he would be discovered. He even confessed to me once that he had used the name of Luis Sarabia when he bought the property that would become his nightclub just so he could hide behind a fictitious name. But that night I think he was staring straight into the abyss.

He admitted that he and the mad guitarist had polished off a bottle of something in fifteen minutes flat, and then they had had a few beers, and then he had lost track. He also had a vague memory of the girlfriend suddenly materializing out of a beam of sunlight. She was waving her arms in the air and her mouth was moving, but Oscar couldn't make out a word she said. It was all garbled, muffled, as if she had become detached from her voice and her voice was now trapped at the bottom of the sea. Then the mad guitarist smiled and opened his wide, welcoming arms and the girlfriend crawled into his lap.

Oscar didn't remember where they were at that point. Maybe they were in the mad guitarist's hotel room. This is what my beloved Oscar said. So he had been an accomplice to the mad guitarist's drinking, nothing more. And even if he had crawled into bed with the mad guitarist and his girlfriend, what of that? The man had been sleeping peacefully in the arms of his girlfriend when Oscar left at eight in the morning. That fact alone was his alibi. But Oscar was certain the police would disregard the plain facts and probe instead the depths of his perpetually guilty Cuban face of a possible drug lord and discover by chance that he had arrived in Key West in 1957 with a forged passport, that he had cavorted with gang-sters while living in Havana, that he had escaped the dark paradise of Cuba with a suitcase full of stolen money, that he had used that money to build his nightclub, that he had never registered his actual name with the government, that he paid no taxes.

It seemed to Oscar a very long list, an endless litany of subversive crimes, unspeakable crimes that would be his undoing. He was certain that once the police began their basement questioning the truth would come tumbling out. He could see the whole scenario unfolding with rapid-fire precision before his suddenly world-weary eyes. The mad guitarist's girlfriend would find herself in hot water and spill the beans. His name would surface and the police would come calling. They would drag him to the police station in irons if need be. Perhaps they would take him for a spy or a saboteur. Who knew? Their questions would be delivered with angry enthusiasm. They would pound their fists on the table. They would certainly blow cigarette smoke in his face. Perhaps they would hook him up to a series of electric cables and throw the switch for a minute or two, just to make sure he was being honest. When they were finished grilling him in this manner, they would drag his almost lifeless body to a damp, rat-infested cell and toss him like an unwanted stone to the cold tile floor. It would be a communal cell, the kind of cell where they kept rapists and pedophile priests and secret agents and rabble rousers and revolutionaries, all of them streaked with dried blood, because the first thing the police did to criminals of that sort was beat the hell out of them. And who could truly blame them? Oscar saw this future path unwind at the speed of light with incredible, ruthless clarity. He would spend two or three days in his communal holding pen while they processed his deportation papers, suffering such indignities of the heart and soul that would leave God himself on the verge of tears. Then they would send him back to the darkness that was Cuba, a broken man. This is what my Oscar was thinking. This is what he saw. It was a fate worse than death.

Fortunately for my Oscar, the mad guitarist's girlfriend did not remember who was with her boyfriend the day he died. Of course I can say this now, looking back. But we weren't sure what was happening when it was actually happening. By eight o'clock Monday morning everyone in the resort had heard the rumor that the girlfriend had been

interviewed by the police. What were we to believe? One
rumor among a river of rumors. But a few apparently well-in-
formed whispering lips provided a play-by-play transcript
of the interview. It was almost like watching it on television.
There were minor differences between the competing versions
of what had happened, as is always the case with stories that
linger in our collective imagination, but the essential details
remained the same.

The interview had taken place in the lobby from ten
o'clock to just after midnight. The girlfriend had been sitting
on a red chaise lounge while the detectives plied her with
drinks, listening carefully to every word that slipped out of
her mouth, occasionally writing something down in their
police report notebooks. Herman the parrot was a constant
source of amazement during the interrogation. Some of the
detectives began noting which questions Herman thought were
stupid and which he ignored. The girlfriend told the police
that one of her boyfriend's musician buddies had been in the
room that morning, that if the police were thinking foul play,
that was the guy they should be hammering away at. But she
was unable to elaborate. She wasn't sure which of the dozens
of possible musician buddies it might be. She didn't remember
his name. Amnesia is like a desert, she said, and then she had
started giggling. Apparently the police were not amused, but
they thought they might be onto something so they plied her
with a few more drinks. She liked amaretto on the rocks. Then
completely out of the blue she said she thought this mysterious unnamed buddy played the trumpet, or maybe the drums,
but she couldn't be sure. The detectives were happy with this
new detail. They were scribbling furiously. The girlfriend said
she had gone to the room at about seven in the morning and
there were the two of them, her boyfriend and this other guy,
the drummer, they were in bed, sleeping or whatever, and she
had crawled in between them, and after a while the drummer
left. One of the detectives scribbled down the phrase 'ménage
à trois' followed by the word 'homosexual' with a question
mark followed by the phrase 'jealous lover' followed by a note
that said 'jealousy is as good a motive as any.'

The girlfriend was oblivious to all the scribbling. Yes,
she said, he was a drummer, a very famous drummer, if she

had her facts straight, at least as far as other drummers were concerned. But she only paid attention to drummers if they were extra-special famous like Ringo Starr. This guy wasn't famous like that. But other drummers would know him. She said he was probably long gone. This is the tale she told the police, a tale she later repeated (without the aid of the amarettos and with only a few topical alterations to make a good story even better) for the newspaper reporters who descended upon the hotel the next day without any restraint whatsoever in search of a bombshell, which naturally they found in both the sexy, oversexed girlfriend sitting on the red chaise lounge in the lobby, and in the gritty, suggestive truth that lay behind her words.

Oscar became more paranoid than ever when he heard that the police had spent two hours raking the girlfriend over hot coals. Yes, I know the image of the police raking someone over hot coals is something of a cliché. But I am sure this was the exact image that raced through the corridors of my Oscar's troubled brain on that day. His imagination had been shaped by watching too many gangster movies from the 1940s. He believed the police would do anything they could to gain the upper hand, and it didn't matter if there were witnesses or not. The police didn't care who saw what. They would simply whitewash the truth. They were absolutely without scruples.

This is what my beloved Oscar believed. He became an alternative version of Humphrey Bogart in *To Have and Have Not*, trying his best to avoid the big sleep, weighing his options, counting down the seconds until the only choice he had left was to make a break for it. One could say he was trapped by the net of a very long night. For over an hour he behaved as if he had stumbled into a lunatic city, pacing about the room in socks and underwear, occasionally pulling back a corner of the curtain and peering cautiously out the window to the parking lot below. He became a dark space, a ruined landscape filled with smoke and piles of rubble, a hungry heart, silent and carnivorous. *Callado y carnicero.* And all the while he was muttering to himself and laughing hysterically by turns.

At one point I heard him say 'it's just a riddle that neither one of us knows the answer to,' but he did not say if this cryptic comment was meant for my ears or for someone else, a government agent, perhaps, recording our most intimate secrets with a micro transmitter tucked away inside the brand-new radio alarm clock that sat with conspicuous brilliance on the table next to the bed.

At ten minutes to ten he rang the front desk and asked for a bellhop to pick up our luggage.

At ten o'clock on the dot he rang the front desk again and asked where the hell the bellhop was.

At ten-fifteen the bellhop arrived and carted away our luggage.

At ten-thirty he poured the last few ounces from a bottle of rum into a tumbler and drank it just like that.

At eleven he put on his white linen suit and his immaculate Panama hat, but he did not bother looking into the mirror as he usually did to see if he was presentable.

Then we started for the lobby. We took great pains to avoid the probing eyes of the police. My poor, sweet, suffering Oscar. But who can blame him? The hotel was literally crawling with plainclothes detectives and state troopers. ¡Ay de mí! The detectives were wandering around in pairs, stopping hotel guests at random to ask a few questions in their low murmuring monotone voices, frisking those who looked suspicious, writing down names and addresses. The troopers, looking for all the world like overgrown Boy Scouts in their crisply ironed, beige uniforms and darkly glowing dark green Stetsons, were stationed at random intervals along the ever-expanding labyrinth of hotel corridors. It was not altogether clear what they were doing. They were chatting away happily in small groups of three or four, commenting on the unseasonably warm, sunny weather, making witty, suggestive remarks about the girls in bikinis heading without even a backward glance to one of the various resort swimming pools. All of the troopers were wearing dark sunglasses. They were scrutinizing with unruffled scrutiny every guest who passed beneath their stiff, robotic, collective gaze.

We made it to the lobby just before noon. It makes me laugh now. But we were not laughing then. The lobby was crammed full of newspaper reporters from every newspaper in Florida. They were off to one corner, a single, pulsating

entity like an alien creature from another dimension, listening
with unrestrained glee to Nikki, the girlfriend, retelling her
tale. She was back on the red chaise lounge, talking a mile
a minute, her breasts jiggling uncontrollably as she spoke, a
deliberate act of manipulation. The reporters could not resist.
It was almost comic. They gave in to the hypnotic tremors
of her soothing voice. They were slobbering all over her,
writing down everything she said, every word, asking her if
she wanted her photograph taken for this newspaper or that
one, asking her if she wanted to pose with Herman the parrot
for a few celebrity shots and Herman saying 'That's a stupid
question!' and then everyone laughing, and then the flash
bulbs flashing and Nikki showering the mob of reporters with
her own giggly, flirty, sensuous laughter and blowing them all
pouty, frivolous kisses that suggested a whole lot more than
any of them would ever receive. Yes, it was quite a show. It
was a virtuoso performance. Which meant, of course, that no
one paid any attention to my beloved Oscar in his dazzling
white linen suit and his immaculate Panama hat, an outfit
which he had worn since his days in Havana and which had
become an integral part of his enthusiastic, affable, loving
persona. Even the front desk clerk, who only three days before
had chatted with Oscar like an old friend about baseball,
paused just long enough to collect the room key and grab
the cash that Oscar laid on the marble counter before losing
himself once again in his unimpeded view of Nikki and her
jiggling breasts.

So what was my beloved Oscar thinking as we left the
resort that day? I truly do not know. He was vulnerable,
yes. His fears of the police and of deportation were not
unfounded. And I am certain he was shaken by the death of
his new friend. He was visibly shaken. My poor, sweet Oscar.
Truly, our happiness quickly becomes a sadness in search
of a happiness. I suspect his silence was born of the need to
digest this unwelcome truth. I suspect he was wondering how
many years of happiness he would have before he joined the
saints in heaven. I also suspect he was thinking about the last
conversation he had with the mad guitarist, how one minute
the two of them were riding high on the glorious promise
of better days, and the next minute death had entered the

picture. And then his thoughts had turned to me.

Oh, I don't know when precisely he began thinking of me. I am certain he was thinking about how to avoid the police in the future while we were driving north along the coast, just as I am certain that the image of the dead guitarist crossed his mind when we passed by the resort on our way south, for he shuddered as we drove past the glistening pink pagoda rooftops. But I also think that on some subliminal, spiritual level, my Oscar realized that I had been a comfort to him on both the long drive north and the longer drive south. He realized that we were traveling a darkly gleaming river of uncertainty, but that it was better to travel this river together than alone. That our souls were tethered to each other in some mysterious, unfathomable way. That we were each God's gift to the other. This is what I had always believed, and that day my faith was rewarded. Once we crossed the bridge to Bal Harbour Beach, I knew that his fears had been eradicated. He was his old, smiling self again. That's when he pulled off the highway and we got out of the car.

'Come on,' he said. 'Let's walk on the beach.'

And that's what we did. We left our shoes in the De Soto and walked along the shore. There were very few people out there on that day. A few lonely-looking fishermen. A few tourists from up north. From somewhere there was the sound of a radio, a salsa as light and bouncy as a summer morning. We watched a cargo ship heading south for Miami. We watched a fishing trawler going the other way. We watched the seagulls flying about. Then Oscar kissed me. It was a gentle, airy kiss. His lips barely touched mine. But it was electric all the same. The sea began to glow. Cherry blossoms suddenly blanketed the beach. The strangely luminous waves exhausted themselves against the sky. The air began to vibrate. Then my Oscar leaned close and whispered into my ear, and I whispered back. Yes, my beloved, yes. The fragrant phosphorous of his words illuminated the darkest corners of my imagination. Yes, my love. I will marry you. I knew without any doubt whatsoever that my Oscar was holding the round key of the universe. There was nothing I could do but say yes.

So what was I talking about? Yes, yes, I remember,
the day my Oscar proposed, the beginning of my tragedy,
and that is certainly one way to look at it. Perhaps if Oscar
had loved me more, or I had loved him less. But that is a
cliché, isn't it? Perhaps if my mother, God bless her tortured,
unhappy soul, had not tried to tangle me up in her net (yes,
I know, another cliché). Perhaps if she had not said what she
said. But she meant well (and yet another). Perhaps she was
simply joking. Of course if that is true, then my beloved Oscar
played up to that joke, took it as a truth to win my mother's
vacillating heart, and in so doing, sealed his fate (yes, yes, I
am filled with clichés this morning, but on some occasions
there is no better way to say a thing). Naturally, I do not
blame my mother. And I do not blame my beloved Oscar.
We are all of us tangled up in a labyrinth of compromise and
secret liberties, so it is next to impossible to see precisely
where we are headed, where we will end up, when we will
breathe our last. So we all deserve each other's forgiveness.
Truly, *de illusión también se vive*, as they say. Now and forever.
Even so, what my mother said was actually quite unbelievable,
even for her.

A week or so after I told her I had agreed to marry
Oscar, she waltzed herself in through the doors of La
Campana and cornered my beloved Oscar in the coat-check
room. My mother was in a rare mood. I know this because
there were several witnesses.

There was Herminio Arréllaga, a Paraguayan refugee
who tended bar for Oscar, and who was there early to receive
a delivery, several cases of smooth, dark Demerara rum
imported from Venezuela, and several cases of *El Presidente*.

There was the guy making the delivery.

There was a union electrician standing on a surprisingly
rickety ladder, working intensely (or perhaps it was sporadically, his mind on other things) to fix the **APPLAUSE** sign,
which had not worked properly for several years.

There was a younger couple waiting in the lobby to see
Oscar about purchasing two advance tickets. I never knew

their names. They wanted to see who would be playing on a certain date in July because they would be celebrating their first anniversary. They were staring down at the floor while they were waiting, contemplating with visible amazement the black marks that Bonita had once burned into the tile.

There was the taxi driver, the same one who was always at La Campana, who had driven my mother from Allapattah to Burdine's downtown and then to the Cathedral and then to La Campana. He had come inside to have a quick drink even though it was only two-thirty in the afternoon because my mother apparently had two more stops to go and he hadn't realized just what he was getting into on that particular day.

And there was a new coat-check girl who saw everything. What she was doing in the coat-check room in the middle of the afternoon she never admitted. But she did say she felt incredibly lucky that my mother didn't see her skinny, white, trembling legs protruding suspiciously from beneath a dark overcoat hanging in the darker shadows near the back. She said she had never before felt so afraid for her own life. She was all gooseflesh.

So my mother burst through the doors and saw my beloved Oscar, a fractured statue trying desperately to piece itself back to together again, a torso oozing dampness, partially illuminated by the naked bulb of the coat-check room, his arms and hands submerged in the oily darkness of another dimension, his legs (hips to ankles) splashing about in the dim light of the lobby, his feet and head missing altogether.

Fortunately for my beloved (and also, perhaps, for the tremulous-as-a-tiny-bird coat-check girl, her short, raspy breaths filling the air like so many plucked out feathers), my mother's voice preceded her entrance by a solid twenty seconds. Her voice echoed with the insatiable, uncomprehending rage of a fighting bull in the throes of death. She paid no attention to what she was seeing, to what was directly in front of her nose, because she was trapped in the cephalic bubble of a thirsty purpose.

'How dare you think you can marry my beautiful daughter in this dingy hovel of gangsters and thieves!' my mother shouted. 'She deserves better than that. She deserves a fancy church wedding. She should walk down the aisle of a cathedral, a floor made of darkly polished Italian marble like a dark mirror. She should be wearing a fancy brocaded wedding dress, a satin gown with a full train veil lined with luminescent pearls, soft pinks and whites, like the teardrops of angels. Heaven itself should proclaim her the most beautiful bride in the history of brides. What kind of a man are you anyway? Do you know anything of love? I can see you know nothing. I can see you think love is a game, a passing fancy. It is all I can do not to spit in your face. May the laughing spirit of Eshu Laroyê, who has the power to grant every wish and condemn every folly, may he be the lightning bolt of God's eternal justice.'

And just like that my mother apparently whirled on her heels in a motion so fluid and unexpected that everyone who was listening to her nearly lost their balance, but then she stopped and turned slowly, an overripe fruit bursting with deceit.

She stared at my beloved for a moment, her eyes brimming with an unexpected flash of sunlight from the bar, where the delivery man had finished unloading the last of the cases of El Presidente and Herminio had signed the receipt.

'But perhaps I am wrong,' she said. 'Yes, yes, I can see you are willing to entertain the notion that I am an addled old woman descending down the long tunnel into dementia and then death. Yes, yes, perhaps you wish to prove yourself. Perhaps you wish to prove that you possess a heart of pure gold. Is that it? Well there is one way. The priests might call it an act of selfless charity, proof of a higher reality. But who can say until the deed is done?'

It was at this point that the stories of the witnesses began to diverge. They all agreed that Oscar moved quickly away from the disfiguring glare of the light bulb blazing away in the coat-check room and stepped towards what looked like a shadowy ball of hissing alley cats, all except the delivery guy, who thought this shadowy ball or whatever it was looked like a smoky moon on the verge of exploding.

They all agreed that my mother lowered her voice in an effort to perhaps create an atmosphere of mystery, which made it exceedingly difficult (but not impossible) to hear what she was saying.

But they all disagreed about what they actually heard.

Herminio heard my mother say there were a couple of hoodlum boys, brothers, perhaps they were even twins, who lived in Coral Terrace near the park, a neighborhood plagued at all hours with the sound of crowing roosters, and these boys needed a good job or they would surely take a deviant path, or if not a good job, then they needed to be beaten to a bloody pulp. They needed one or the other. It wasn't clear if they were teenagers or if they were older.

The younger couple heard my mother say she had a friend who was in some trouble and this friend lived in a strange, dilapidated, disemboweled (disemboweled?) neighborhood in South Miami, but whenever she went for a visit she feared for her safety, so she asked Oscar to accompany her once a week until the trouble her friend was having had passed, at which point she wouldn't need to make the journey quite so often.

The coat-check girl heard my mother ask Oscar if he had ever been to the Church of the Epiphany on SW 57th, but it was clear by the expression on Oscar's face that he wasn't a church-going sort.

The delivery guy said all he heard was an incoherent babbling that could have been the sound of water running down a drain or seagulls fighting over scraps of garbage at the beach, and he decided at that moment he had better get his ears checked.

The taxi driver heard my mother ask how long it would take to get to Pinecrest and back during rush hour.

The electrician heard my mother say it was a matter of electricity. When there was too much energy flowing through the circuit, blam, the whole world went black. When there was too much resistance, for whatever reason, well, you could not swim against the current forever. The electrician wondered where my mother had picked up her knowledge of electrical circuits.

The younger couple heard my mother describe the incredible pain a burn victim must endure on the road to recovery. They could not tell if the trouble her friend was having was related to surviving an everyday housefire or a violent chemical explosion of some sort, but whatever the cause of her burns, she had endured (barely survived) the incredible suffering of extensive skin grafts and several rounds of antibiotics to treat sepsis, and she was home now, but she was having difficulty moving room to room.

The delivery guy listened intently to the sounds of the seagulls fighting for scraps. Then he wondered if perhaps they were roosters. He could not believe his red-glowing ears. Then the seagulls (or roosters) morphed into the sound of a lonely train whistle even though the nearest railroad crossing was two miles away, give or take. At that point the delivery guy decided that he needed a drink more than a hearing test. Herminio gave him a bottle of *El Presidente* on the house.

Herminio heard my mother ask Oscar if he would at least speak to the boys, but he did not catch their names or when or where they were to meet Oscar because he was digging out a bottle of *El Presidente* from one of the cases.

The taxi driver heard my mother ask how long it would take to get to Coral Terrace and back on a weekend with very little traffic.

The younger couple heard my mother say that there had been a string of daylight robberies committed in South Miami and a few cases of suspected arson. The police had originally assumed the crimes were being committed by a roving gang of juvenile delinquents.

The coat-check girl heard my mother tell Oscar that the trouble with musicians was they were all alike. She could not tell what Oscar said in reply, but it seemed to her that he was shaking with embarrassment, or perhaps he was suffering from a fit of nervous chuckling.

The delivery guy ordered another beer and Herminio gave him another *El Presidente* on the house, and then another, and so on.

The electrician heard my mother say that a charge in a parallel circuit will only pass through one resistor.

The taxi driver heard my mother say maybe it was better to take a bus.

The younger couple heard my mother say that the police had quickly revised their earlier assumptions about who was committing the crimes. The police were now looking for two humorless young men, identical twins with black leathery, crusted-over skin and a reputation for unprovoked violence. The police believed the youths lived in Corral Terrace with their grandmother.

Herminio heard my mother say it was shameful about those boys, the twins, some said they were homosexuals, or they were refugees from Borneo or Sulawesi or Sumatra, some third-world country on the edge of that whispering fraud we call oblivion.

The coat-check girl heard my mother say 'huevo del Diablo,' but it was unclear just who she was talking about.

The electrician heard my mother say in a series connection, the entire charge passes through every individual resistor.

The younger couple heard my mother say that the police also believed the two young men in question had two older cousins or two brothers who had once lived in Coral Gables.

The taxi driver heard my mother say only someone with a pure heart would get on a bus without knowing where it was going.

Herminio heard my mother say only someone with a pure heart would take two slippery devils like that under his wing, so to speak.

The coat-check girl heard my mother say only someone with a pure heart could tell the difference between a child of God and a child of the Devil.

The younger couple heard my mother say only someone with a pure heart could stomach looking at a burn victim because it was very difficult to see the essential humanity of someone, anyone, beneath even a single layer of charred, cracked skin, let alone someone who had felt the fat of his (or her) subcutaneous layer bubbling away. It was like looking at a deeply depressed paralytic artist's depiction of a demonic alien life form intent on destroying the Earth.

The electrician heard my mother say only someone with a pure heart would realize that we are all atoms of light seeking a path to each other.

The delivery guy was too drunk to hear anything beyond the soft swooshing sounds his inner ear was making. It was an immense attic of sound from which he had no desire to escape.

A few days later my beloved Oscar hired the Velázquez brothers, and after that my mother was no longer so vocal in her criticisms. Was this a coincidence? I do not think so. And yet I do not think my mother was entirely to blame. I seem to remember that Herminio was also involved. Perhaps he had persuaded my mother that Oscar needed help (not that she truly needed persuading), and then maybe he had said that most likely the Velázquez brothers weren't criminals or charity cases so much as they were misunderstood. Yes, I think it was something like that. I can see my mother lapping up every obsequious word spewing out of Herminio's mouth, delighted that she might be able to bend Oscar's will in this matter, grateful for Herminio's behind-the-scenes support, eager to have some say, however small, in the world that Oscar and I were trying to create for ourselves. Herminio and my mother were co-conspirators. No other explanation makes any sense.

-122-

It is funny looking back, but deep down I think I knew that the day I married Oscar, I was in symbolic terms as well as in practical effect moving from defeat to defeat. To begin with, let's look at the day itself. Dawn or near enough. Well, to be precise, it was ten o'clock in the morning. Except that numbers on a clock do not tell the whole story. The sun had already crashed through the dark portals of the petrified, pre-Adamite sky. But the light did not come up over the horizon as it usually does, slowly seeping up and over the dark, forbidding line and pouring itself across the plateau of reality, inviting color to join memory and recreate a symphony of strange noises and reinvigorated smells. It came instead as a lightning bolt of retribution or a laser beam from an alien spacecraft set on incineration. The color of that strange light that morning was the color of burnt hair or skin (but not a surface burning, it burned much deeper than that, a burning away of everything down to the waxen core) and eyeballs dripping with mascara and Kabuki ink stains of rouge eating

like a cancer into the flesh of soft, white cheeks as white as
the underbelly of dead fish or white ribbon eels, but it wasn't
just the color of the visible world, it was also the color of
sounds and smells and passing thoughts; it was the color of
the musty, mustardy smell of freshly plowed, rumpled earth;
it was the color of the incurable seeping paranoia (insanity?)
that accompanies chronic betrayal, that bohemia of a thirsty
soul; it was the color of the sea salt smell of toilet soap and
the convulsive withering noises of trampled insects with
wings like cellophane beating frantically for a few seconds
and then disintegrating as easily as if life were just a cruel
trick invented by a deranged mechanic or a demented Syrian
demigod, a brusque, godless demise; it was the color of the
penetrating acrid, cleansing smell of midnight jazz, even
though it was the middle of the morning; it was the color of
dark, smoldering thighs wrapped in lace lingerie wound a
tad too tight and the crystalline purity of love's deceptions
and the raw, overwhelming, incomprehensible sadness of
inaction, a paralyzing, blinding flash; it was the color of
disordered silence, yes, disordered silence is so accurate; it
was the color of the geranium pots that had been placed on
steps and in courtyards all over the city, dripping with dew or
droplets from an overnight shower like so many tiny mirrors
reflecting (refracting?) the trauma of earlier days (though to
some I am sure those droplets looked like hippie strings of
metallic beads crisscrossing the cosmos, each bead containing
within its sphere a miniature replica of this bubble we call
the Earth); it was the color of the traffic whizzing by on NW
36th Street; it was the color of those excitable birds that one
could only hear from the steps of La Campana, what were
they? warbling warblers? or mutinous martins? or a covey
of covetous chickadees? or yellow-billed cuckoos or yellow
orioles? or furious swallows? or is it infuriated? or were they
neurotic parrots or parakeets, those lucky birds that are the
augurs of life and death? or a flock of *chachalaca* originally
imported from Central America or Mexico or even Texas for
hunting club hunting purposes but then they escaped? 'shut
up ¡chachalaca!' you might hear someone say while listening
to those birds, and then others might say, as if in response,
'boom Shaka-laka-laka!' boom Shaka-laka-laka!' and then they

would laugh and prance about to their booming boom boxes and vanish into the glare at the end of the street and the sly sky would break into a harmonica solo, or perhaps those elusive feathered creatures were the physical manifestation of the birds that sleep in all good wines, as the poet says, but whatever genus and species (*Setophaga coronata coronata, Dendroica coronata, Progne elegans, Poecile carolinensis, Myiarchus tyrannulus, Coccyzus americanus, Icterus nigrogularis, Tachycineta bicolor, Melopsittacus undulates, Amazona tucumana, Amazona collaria, Alipiopsitta xanthops, Ortalis ruficauda, Ortalis vetula,*) those invisible birds on that particular morning were roosting and chattering away across the street from La Campana like paranoid idiot savants or drunken game show hosts in the limelight of a few lime trees or a few transplanted Paraíso trees (also called Cape Lilac or Persian Lilac) with their purple gleaming blossoms like baubles for a queen and their poisonous even deadly yellow fruit that falls to the sidewalk without warning.

That is a fairly accurate description of what the color of the light was like, but I was the only one who noticed. What was everyone else looking at? Did they notice that the dream of my wedding took place in the smaller, second-floor ballroom of La Campana and not in a church? Did they wonder that there was no reception, no wedding cake, no musicians? Of course I myself am partly to blame for how my wedding turned out. When my beloved Oscar told me he didn't want a church wedding, I told him neither did I. And when he told me that he didn't want a big fancy wedding with photographs in the newspaper and a seven-tier wedding cake and guests flying in from New York City and Chicago, celebrities, musicians, politicians, athletes, I suggested the second-floor ballroom. It would be the perfect place, I said. And my Oscar agreed.

Normally, that is to say on most occasions, the second-floor ballroom was an elegant retreat from the hubbub of the world, but on the day of my wedding it was a disaster. You see two weeks earlier, my Oscar had rented the ballroom for a somewhat rousing Bar Mitzvah, but no one had bothered to clean up afterwards. In the corner opposite the only door in or out there were a small upright piano, an unplugged speaker, and two microphones still fixed to their stands with their cords trailing across the floor like abandoned snake skins. There were also several long narrow tables shoved up against the row of narrow windows overlooking the parking lot. The table linens were stained with crescent moons of red wine. Dirty wine glasses, many of them toppled over, were everywhere. The floor was littered with shreds of paper confetti. And again, I was the only who noticed. Not even my mother spoke up.

Then again, did any of that truly matter? Why not revel in the fact that it was a beautiful, sunny day in late February (in spite of the strange color of the light and the chaos in the ballroom) and I was getting married to my beloved Oscar? Could I have been so divorced from the reality of that moment oh so many years ago? Oscar was my dream come true. I could not have possibly anticipated the end when I was only at the beginning. Yes, yes, I know what you're thinking. Truly, one eye sees and the other eye feels. Perhaps that is why we never truly understand what is happening to us in our lives or why. My beloved Oscar proposed in December, but we did not get married right away. We waited, as all serious couples should. Besides, January was too cold. In fact, that January it snowed in Miami, the first and only snow in the history of Miami. For four days there was ice on the roads all the way across the state from Miami Beach to Labelle. I am sure the tangerine crop was destroyed, and the tangelos and temple oranges as well. Who could believe it! Oscar said maybe he should move back to Cuba, but he also said I was more than welcome to tag along. Then he said maybe the freak snowstorm was an omen of things to come. Maybe we should not get married at all. But he was not being serious. Then the snow melted, the warm breezes and the sun returned, and we were married. We were married on Sunday, February 20, 1977, a fairly warm day for February, bright and dry and sunny. Still, I must confess that my wedding day was not quite what I had hoped for. Would that my Oscar had been able to speak sweet words of poetry to me, words that the whole world might hear. But my beloved, it seemed, told very few people about our wedding, let alone the world. My wedding was what you would call a secret wedding. Yes, I was disappointed. But I am certain my Oscar felt he had no other choice. He was still afraid of being deported. That is why he chose to marry me while the world was looking the other way. What other reason could there possibly be?

So the guest list was very small as you can imagine. You could even say there was no guest list at all. There was my brother Emilio and my mother, and that was it for family. Oscar had no family in Miami or anywhere else. And my own father had died eleven years earlier. My brother had found him sitting in his five-dollar armchair in front of the plate glass window in the living room. His head was angled oddly so that it appeared he was staring with uncompromising expectation at the two lime trees in the front yard that had never borne any fruit in all those many years, neither before nor since. He was only forty-eight, and he was fairly slim and he did not drink to excess, and I am sure he had given up his Cuban cigars, but who can say. I do not think he chased after young girls, though I must admit he had plenty of opportunity after my mother abandoned the dream of their love.

I remember the doctor speaking with my mother in the kitchen that day, and then she had said something that made him laugh and then they were both laughing and then they swallowed their laughter because such behavior is always a sin in front of the newly dead, and they knew this. Then the doctor left without saying a word, without even a second glance at my father, who was still sitting in his leather armchair. My mother took us into the kitchen and sat us down at the table and looked at us with two heavy, dull eyes that seemed like rivers choked with silt. She told us there was no earthly reason why our father had died. She told us it was God's doing. Or perhaps the mark of the Devil had been on my father's soul for too many years to count — my mother firmly believed this — so the Devil, not wishing to give my father a chance to repent, had come calling. My mother said she could not tell for sure, but it was one or the other. God or the Devil. That was all my mother said.

So the guests at my wedding included my brother Emilio and my mother, the Deputy Clerk who married us (a middle-aged chubby fellow named Schofield or Stovall or Torres, something like that, from the Marriage License Bureau in downtown Miami), a stenographer from that same office who would have been the official witness if no one else had shown up, a couple of new girls working at La Campana, a hung-over musician from Saturday night who had spent the night in one of the booths in the back of the bar, a taxi driver Oscar had known for years, who hung out in La Campana's fabulous bar on Friday and Saturday evenings waiting so he could drive home the drunks, and the strangely ubiquitous Velázquez brothers, Bull and Horse, who had been working for Oscar for over a month by that point.

I remember thinking that morning that my marriage to Oscar would never last because my father would not be there to give me away. I remember worrying about this up until Oscar and I exchanged vows, and even after. I remember thinking these ridiculous thoughts even as Oscar was slipping the ring on my finger. I remember the Deputy Clerk was jabbering away but I could not concentrate on what he was saying.

I was praying as feverishly as I had ever prayed. I was asking God to send my father back to earth for just a single hour so he could give me away properly.

There were tears streaming down my face.

Then the Deputy Clerk stopped speaking and everyone was waiting, and some part of me buried deep inside knew they were contemplating my river of tears, and they all thought, or I assumed they thought, that I was shedding tears of joy when in fact I had never been so far from joy in my life. I was drowning in a joyless sea. I could not breathe. I was on the verge of passing out. But then I suddenly heard my father's calm, fatherly, compassionate voice eclipsing all reality. 'Hush now, Isidora,' I heard my father's voice say. 'You ask the impossible. *Pedir la luna.*'

And so my father's calming words returned me to myself. I began to breathe more easily. I heard my own voice saying 'I do,' and then my beloved Oscar kissed me. And just like that I was married.

The trouble with secret weddings is they usually beget secret honeymoons. And so it was with ours. Yes, we went to Paris. But Oscar pretended he was going on a business trip and that he had invited me to tag along, an expression he was quite fond of, at the last minute. I am sure he fooled no one. Certainly not the girls who worked at La Campana. Certainly not Emilio nor my mother nor the taxi driver waiting for the drunks nor the strangely ubiquitous Velázquez brothers, who always seemed to be watching my every move when I entered a room with these idiotic expressions on their faces that left little doubt about what they were thinking. Then again, Oscar did take me to Paris. That is not a trivial gesture. We arrived Tuesday, May 17th and left one week later. The warmest day was Friday, when the temperature hit 77 degrees Fahrenheit. I think it rained once or twice, but only late at night or early in the morning. A very light drizzle. The days were very dry, which the Parisians we met said was unusual, but not extraordinary.

Let me just say three things about my honeymoon.

First, we did indeed stay in an elegant, boutiquey hotel that stood on the very corner where a small stone house belonging to Marguerite de Valois once stood, a house where she transported her myriad of lovers to an ephemeral plane, and what is more, the ghost of Madame de Valois whispered into my ear one night that lovers are not criminal in the estimation of one another. 'Che la forza d'amore non riguarda al delitto.' Just like my great-grandmother, the second-to-last Ana Silvestre, had said would happen.

Second, we did indeed return from Paris with a very rare, very expensive bottle of 1691 Clos de Griffier Vieux Cognac, but it was not a gift, as my great-grandmother had said it would be, my beloved Oscar purchased the bottle from a strange little man, the owner of a small restaurant on Rue Mazarine, and no, I do not think he was a Moorish paramour, as my great-grandmother suggested, but yes, clearly, he and my beloved Oscar treated each other with an astonishingly intimate familiarity, so I am sure they knew each other, but I

do not think they had ever been lovers, how would they have
accomplished this amazing feat, to achieve such closeness
in only a few days, no, no, what I think is that each man
recognized in the other a kindred spirit, a lover of life, a lover
of love, man or woman it makes no difference, and the bottle
of Cognac was simply a vehicle to commemorate that moment
of recognition. That is what I think.

Third, the night before we left Paris I did not sleep well.
What I mean to say is that I dreamed a strange dream. It was
not so much a dream as a reordering of the world. It was as
if I had fallen into a deep well where light did not penetrate.
No, no, that image is not quite right, is it. No, it was more of
a, more of a dark mirror that swallowed all light. Yes, that is
what it was. And yet I could see well enough in this strangely
dark world, so there must have been some light. I could make
out the dark contours of our art-deco room with an art-deco
chair at the foot of our art-deco bed and another one near
the door, and there were mirrors everywhere, on the walls,
the ceiling, even the dresser was made of mirrors, all of them
refracting the darkness of the world, a darkness that was at
once both a gleaming brightness and a swirling void. To be
honest, I could see just fine. But everywhere I looked, well, it
was like looking at things from the inside out. The angles of
existence had been reversed, as if I had suddenly become my
exact opposite, a flawless reproduction of my normal self but
condemned to imitate in a most obscene fashion the life and
mannerisms of someone else. I was a puppet on a string, as
they say, at least this is how I remember feeling that night. I
now know there is nothing at all obscene about experiencing
life from an opposite vantage point. Such a gift is rarely
received. But that night I was quite beside myself.

At any rate, there I was, a puppet trapped in the darkly
gleaming glass of this nether world, when I became aware
of two voices whispering furtively, furiously (furtiviously?)
in the darkness. I could not see where they were. Briefly, I
wondered if perhaps I was merely reconstructing a memory
of an earlier conversation between my normal self and my
beloved Oscar, but that thought soon evaporated without a
trace. I focused instead on the sound produced by these two
invisible voices, and I did so with a dispassionate almost

scientific interest because I could not understand a word they were saying. It was all gibberish to my ears, what some would call an epic giglamesh, and what others would call a sweet, musical *glíglico*. And yet in spite of my inability to break the code of their private love language (yes, it was clear to me from the start that they were speaking a language of shared intimacy, the dots and dashes and daggers of a love invented by two people who, for one unassailable moment, shove themselves into the tiny box of a single soul), the tragic beauty of what they were saying bled itself across the sky, if you will excuse a rather odd and certainly lame metaphor, but I do not know how else to describe what I heard in this dream. I did not understand a single word, but the order of the sounds themselves conveyed a depth of anguish and regret, the suffering of those who love with a pure heart in an impure world, that was too strong to ignore. It was a swirling, tornadic tide of emotion eroding the shores of every sentimental delusion I have ever possessed. So I had no choice, really. I let this tide sweep me away.

What the two voices said, word for unintelligible word:
'My slithy borlis, my belooped and strumming dagma, your tendermuzzle gurgling gizma are flappodoodling like the wind. It is a sleepspackling sound that frackles my ears and sweams with the glorígoro, yes, my ears are redrendering with ostriperation, but I'll not regurgamaze, nor will I glú glú de la ele! No, no, you cannot deniflate this either, the spalmy swave, the strumpeting of your tierno la le li lo lu, your sly nun-ogling, which is all the spizmo gism of the infinite anyway, so what else can I do, I can do nothing else but obscinilate, it is now but a swilly smote to say we are grunfeathered,' said the first voice. It is such a flurious glorígoro my swofty swizzle. Libre, suelto, saltarín. Regaggle the swashsnaggling of this vitriolized spiro-undulating,' said the second voice. 'Ah my belooped you are fenilated. Enough of your unresipient silly stingle-stangling. I'll not have any more. I am too far smuckered for such drivalizing, sodomodulated sodoshyte. Visage me nightingale to nightingale for once, if you will. Fill your eyes with asmocardisiac farts, as the Quevidian says. Tell me you are not just about the dilly-dally,' said the first voice. 'Oh no, baby, no, my swofty swizzle

sweeter than the nectar of Olympianus. Do you not hear the swunclocking of the swailing swankles? The limit of all our petty slobberdigging? Partilejos elífera alamabe. Partilejos, partilejos! Frenteliris de muerte girófora,' said the second voice. 'Nadasada, oooh my swilly, swailing astrobelooped, nadasada,' said the first voice. 'But I am not just about the dilly-dally. I will remicile our evollé,' said the second voice. 'Ala olalúnea, my belooped,' said the first voice. Partilejos elífera alamabe. Partilejos! Partilejos!,' said the second voice. 'Ala olalúnea,' said the first voice.

-124-

It is always difficult to pinpoint the exact moment when a subtle change becomes an inevitable force. Probably this is because we are too distracted by the world, engulfed in the obscenities of empty pleasures, swimming in the febrile soup of the long, fermenting night, inventing demented lullabies to soothe our twisted, glassy-eyed reflections, lullabies that have less in common with the simple, unrehearsed joys of small children running about barefooted and more in common with the millenary murmurings of Medea, who for no good reason murdered her brother Absyrtus (a Greek name which initially meant 'brother of Medea,' but which inevitably morphed into the Latin word *absurdus*, which means out of tune, which is a rather elegant way of calling someone or something irrational or ludicrous, which is the meaning of absurd in the modern sense); and then because her father was now hot on her heels to avenge the death of Absyrtus, she flung her brother's dismembered body into her father's path so he would have to stop and pick up the bloody limbs of his dead son, which he did, and Medea got away scot free; and then later she murdered Glauce, the daughter of Creon, who was having an affair with her husband, Jason, but that wasn't enough to stop the voices that the poet Euripdes had put into her head so she killed two of their (hers and Jason's) three sons and ran away to Thebes; and then it is hard to say what happens after that because there are too many competing versions

from other poets through the centuries, not to mention how
her story was taken up and transformed (transfigured?) by
various Europeanized painters, for you can go into many
an art museum in Europe and America and see Medea
wandering through the imaginations of dozens of painters,
like the reformist, Pre-Raphaelite imaginations of John William
Waterhouse or Frederick Sandys or Evelyn De Morgan, or
the French Romantic imagination of Eugène Delacroix, or the
strange, mysterious, rebellious imagination of Paulus Orlando
Bor, that Dutch madman who could see beneath the surface
layer of things no matter what he was looking at (rivers, bowls
of fruit, laundry women, oblivious nobles; a woman with what
seems to be a dragon; an archangel informing a startled and
clearly dismayed Mary that she will soon die; the three kings
gathering around the infant Christ; a nude woman taking a
bath; an old hooded woman whose sole possessions appear to
be a string of onions, a tiny snarling, miscreant of a dog and a
money bag; a twelve-year-old Christ lecturing in the temple),
and so each of his paintings provides a glimpse of that savage
paradise that awaits us all.

Who can point to the calendar and say 'this date here,
yes, this is when the glory days of La Campana began,' and
then flip through the pages for a while and then stop and say
'and this day over here, yes, this is when they ended.' No,
no one can say such a thing. Life is not so cut and dried, as
they say. And yet by the same token, it was equally clear to
me what was happening, as it must have been, as it should
have been clear to anyone in those days who had two eyes
to see with, especially Herminio, what a two-faced bastard
Janus he turned out to be, *caco, cabrón, chabacano pendejo,* if
you'll excuse a momentary lapse of good manners. *¡Ay de mí!*
You think I am joking! You think I am telling an old woman's
story! But I am not joking. I have simply learned to hide my
face. Yes, yes, of course it was a matter of survival. That is true
of all deceptions, even those that go badly.

So I wore a carnival mask, *larva* not *volto,* yes, yes, children, *larva* in every sense of the word. Oh my God, all I have
to do is think of how Herminio abandoned my poor beloved
Oscar to the treachery of those evil twins, truly those who bed
down with wolves will learn to howl, and there wasn't a thing

anyone could do about it, not even the police, it was as if my Oscar had never existed at all, my blood begins to boil over at the thought of what happened, look at me, I am shaking, look at my hands, my fingers trembling like carnival wind chimes and it was years ago.

'. . . .'

No, no, I still have much to learn. *¡Dios dame fuerza!* Truly, we feed upon sorrow with deep spoons. Let me just say that four or five years after the Velázquez brothers began working for my beloved Oscar, the glory days of La Campana had become a distant memory.

'. . . .'

What do I remember? Is that what you want to know?

'. . . .'

Yes, yes, *quien bien ama, tarde olvida*, as they say. But you must have patient ears. I remember the music changed. That is the first thing that struck you if you hadn't been to the club in a while and then one night on a whim you went back because there was a warm, sultry breeze blowing through the streets of Miami, a taste of the ocean with its pulsating sensuality only a few miles away, and you remembered the wild, frenetic music from when you had first gone to La Campana, you remembered drinking smooth mojitos or jazzy highballs like bolts of indiscriminate lightning or beer imported from the Caribbean or Mexico or Central America, a happy, intoxicated state, and the girls were running back and forth between the auditorium and the bar even during the show with order after order after order, their lithe, shadowy curves wiggling through the glistening disco darkness with such vulnerable bounciness that every man in the audience was immediately erect, and all the while you were in this happy, bewildering, intoxicated state, you were listening to that glorious, impossible music like flocks of startled white ibis or ghosts or angels seeking God's redeeming grace, yes, yes, so you wanted to dive back into the froth of those memories which appeared to you out of the blue on that warm breezy night like the fuzzy light of the corona during an eclipse, so you went back to La Campana because you wanted to re-live those salad days when you were electrocuted with the electrifying energy of Willy Chiron (before he got big), or mesmerized by the joyful, soulful beauty of Gwen McCrae, who was bubbly even when she was plagued by sadness, and on occasion she sang with her husband George, and those two had a silky sound you could not ignore in those days, or Rick James, who once made a surprise stop at La Campana on his way home from Europe to sing about his mama, or Jimmy Bo Horne playing the big tease, singing "You Get Me Hot," and it was all so slick and chic and cool and funky, parapapa papapa paraparapa, and my beloved Oscar's booming, soothing voice echoing beneath it all with eternal delight, the anchor of our universe, the pride of a proud Papa, and he was always saying '*Partirse el alma*. This boy will make someone's heart bleed. Yes, yes. He will make all of our hearts bleed, I think.' And then: 'Yes, there is one table up front I set aside especially for you.' And then: 'Yes, oh do not worry, the waitresses will bring you whatever you like from the bar. Whatever you can think of, whatever you can imagine.'

Many people asked me what had happened to the music, but what could I say? It was clear my Oscar no longer cared who was playing or what they sounded like. This was in 1981. For some reason that I have never understood, the Velázquez brothers started booking musicians. What was my Oscar thinking? It was like giving two small boys a stone for killing birds in a cage. They did not know a thing about music. Well this was obvious! For one thing they hired bands with shitty names, names like *Polvo Blanco* or *Blitz* or *Hermana Menudo* or *¡Hace un Frío del Carajo!* or *¡Mala Suerte!* What kind of crazy names are those? But what could we do? You could not say anything to the Velázquez brothers. They were very dangerous men. I know, I know, some people say that the bull that gores you throws you to a better place. But when is this ever true? Besides, the Velázquez brothers were truly evil. They reeked of vengeance and smoking guns and the narcissistic stupidity of men who believe they are in control of their own destinies, their frog eyes bulging in ludicrous anticipation of the deaths of countless victims, unsuspecting men and women walking along the street, hailing taxi cabs, inhabiting the cafes and restaurants and movie theatres and dance clubs where we all go, all of their victims chosen at random, in as much as God had turned a blind eye, a staggering number. The Velázquez

brothers were nocturnal creatures who spread their leathery
wings to blot out the sun so their eyes could shine like bullets
or the blood-thirsty moon. They were the dogs of Anubis
patrolling the edges of a crumbling, soon-to-be-forgotten
cemetery, their mouths open slightly, drooling, such sinister
grins. They were bright butcher's knives with ivory handles
for slicing through the bone. They were bright rivers of molten
lead converging, clogging up the arteries of the world.

So just like that La Campana was overflowing with
bands with shitty names, and the music of these bands, my
God, it is a wonder the very walls did not disintegrate with
the clawing, scratching, unnatural sound produced by broken
guitars and tin-can drums and the wailing, diseased voices
of chainsaws mocking the profound simplicity of true love. It
was the sound of raw sewage spilling into the air, the odor of
disgust. Yes, yes, it was the smell of death, but not the heavily
perfumed, hermetically sealed in sealing wax oleander smell
of a proper send-off. It was the rusty, bloody-earth smell of a
bestial death of ritual slaughter, the dark fragments of ancient
skulls scattered about, the heady wine of fermenting corpses,
a field of mutilated onions in flames. It was as if La Campana
had been transformed into an abattoir, a dazzling modern
temple to honor the gods of murder and despair, those ancient
gods who are always with us. There was even a small article
about it in *The Miami Herald* (page twenty-six, stuffed in
between an ad for toothpaste and an ad for a cream to remove
penile warts) with a headline that said: What Happened to La
Campana?

Naturally, the sweaty, inconstant but cultured gentlemen
of Miami and their insufferably beautiful and emotionally
volatile wives and girlfriends stopped coming to the club.
They were replaced by a different clientele, gritty, unwashed,
unshaven, ageless men, like mannequins or robots or worse,
always seeming to be destitute of funds, and yet always
wearing fancy black hats and black jackets that were always
buttoned to conceal shoulder holsters with ferocious looking
revolvers which they would whip out at a moment's notice,
empty sockets where their eyes should have been, as if their
eyeballs had recently been dug out with pocketknives, this is
how it seemed to me, blood running down the sides of their

ashen-colored cheeks like mascara, like gangsters in a Mexican vampire movie. The gangsters would come and go throughout the evening.

There was no need for a coat-check room since no one checked their coats anymore, so the coat-check girls joined the waitresses, who still scurried back and forth between the bar and the auditorium. Except the role of the waitresses was also evolving. If you happened to wander into the auditorium at any point past nine o'clock, as I did on a few occasions – I don't remember why, it wasn't to check up on Oscar, I know that much, because he was usually sitting on a stool at the end of the bar closest to the lobby, a drunken figurehead rotting away – but if you happened to pass through those black leather doors to the main ballroom, as I did once or twice, you would be greeted with a sight of extraterrestrial dimensions like a drug-induced dream. Strange flashing neon purples and blues would stab at your eyes and drive you to the edge of unconsciousness. Your nerves would begin to tingle from the terrible music. You began to wonder if you had gone suddenly deaf and if that terrifying ringing in your ears was actually the sound of blood rushing along the fragile (disintegrating?) arteries of your inner ear. You would notice strange, floating platforms at various heights, like alien spacecraft descending or taking off. There were fewer tables. The tables were illuminated by a weird, pulsating candlelight like tiny meteors exploding and then coalescing and then exploding again, the light spreading out with inevitable precision like the fumes of regret. The tables reminded me of miniature ocean liners lost in the vast empty spaces of a dark ocean. And everywhere you looked (the strange floating platforms, up along the stage, straddling the darkness that surrounded the tables) you would see weird ribbons of shadow twisting and gyrating, rotating slowly then speeding up, a cacophony of unexpected movement. The movement of these ribbons was fascinating, weirdly seductive, indescribably beautiful, and you would stare at this movement for a while. It was almost like you had been hypnotized. Yes, truly, it was like you were a puppet and you could feel someone pulling on your strings but you did not mind. And then you would realize that these weird, gyrating ribbons of shadow were in fact the waitresses, who had all but given up serving drinks and were instead performing various lewd acts for the various vampire gangsters that had gathered in small groups of two or three in the hazy, shimmery, neon-streaked darkness.

To be honest I had no idea what was happening until Herminio took me aside one evening and told me. I was looking for Oscar but he was not in the bar. There was only Herminio. He was standing behind the counter, but he was not drying the same shot glass over and over again or creating crystalline pyramids like you would expect. No, he was standing there in the frail light of the afternoon reading a book. Up until that point I had thought Herminio was only an illiterate slob from Paraguay who had narrowly escaped death by firing squad. But there he was reading. It was a Spanish novel by Pérez Galdós. He said it was pretty interesting, a bit outdated, a bit of romanticized slapdash about a war in Spain in the 1800s, there were many bloody battles, yet he couldn't quite tell what was happening, it was fluid like water, it was full of a crackling energy just beneath the surface, yet it was also very, very dull. He was baffled by the seeming contradictions contained within the book.

'I am looking for Oscar.'

'Yes, of course you are. But as you can see, he is not here.'

I don't remember what I said to that. I caught a distinct whiff of insolence in his reply, and I am sure I became angry and was about to hurl a dagger or two his way, but he had already plunged himself back into his very dull book.

I stared at him.

I was teetering on the edge of an insatiable silence like a great sadness about to take wing.

I was falling into the funnel of a sky that rejects all imitations.

Then Herminio spoke without looking up from the pages of his book. It seemed as if he were reading a speech that had been prepared just for him, for precisely this moment, by a long vanished Spanish novelist from a century ago.

'Do not be sad,' Herminio said. And then: 'It is the inevitable way of the world. Everything that has fulfilled its function disappears. Oscar is not here now but you will see him later, such as he has become. But do not be too hard on him. *Á muertos y á idos, no hay amigos,* as they used to say. I am certain he was only thinking of the future.'

I had no idea what Herminio was talking about, but suddenly I was very nervous. I was sitting at the bar by that point, and I suspect Herminio felt my nervous energy. He pushed his book to one side and lowered his chin to his tremendous chest and began squinting like a newcomer.

'What was he to do?' he said. 'Was he to go around planting trees and various shrubs around the edges of tennis courts? He was not so seditious. And besides, he had no money for trees or shrubs. Every dime he got his hands on, he sunk into this monstrosity, and for what? He paid the musicians too much, and he charged too little for the greasy *gamberros* of Miami and elsewhere who came every Friday and Saturday evening to bask in the comfort of this elegant palace and enjoy Oscar's unbounded generosity.'

Herminio looked at me as if he expected some sort of reaction, a nod of understanding, recognition, anything, but I said nothing. What could I say? I was taken completely by surprise. Then Herminio shook his head and reached into a small refrigerator beneath the counter. He pulled out a tin of sardines and some goat cheese and some brown bread and we ate while he talked.

'You did not know this?'

He passed me a plate and I was suddenly very hungry.

'Oscar spent vast sums just to keep this place afloat.'

Herminio paused a moment, as if he was about to share a secret message that only he had been able to decipher.

'But where did this debilitating obsession spring from?' said Herminio. 'And how did Oscar have so much cash to give away in the first place? Even the walls of La Campana were whispering these questions. Idiot! Losing money year after year becomes an invisible habit until the magnitude of what you have lost becomes all too visible. I am sure he thought the Velázquez brothers were a godsend. Yes, anyone would have thought as much under the circumstances. But such unexpected gifts are often costly in the end, and this is especially true when the Velázquez brothers are involved. *La paloma es la ralea del halcon.* Do not be too hard on him. It is the same old story. First we dream a dream. Then we are seduced by the dream. And then we are sacrificed in the name of the dream.'

And then it seemed that Herminio was finished with what he had to say. We finished the sardines and cheese in a silence that was both familiar and uncomfortable. But when he was cleaning up he began speaking again, but the tenor of his voice had changed. What is more, he did not even move his lips while he spoke. It was a hissing, guttural, unnatural voice I heard. It was almost like I was listening to a radio tucked away in the crevices of my imagination. Perhaps this is true. Perhaps Herminio said nothing more after the sardines.

Then again, I know what I heard.

'Do not trust these Velázquez brothers,' Herminio said. 'You are an indestructible passionflower, and they sense this about you, so they will most certainly try to destroy you. Just as they are in the process of destroying Oscar. No, he did not know what he was getting into. They are sly wolves who now deal in cocaine, but Oscar did not know this. But now it is too late. They have turned La Campana into a cocaine den. Surely you have wondered what goes on here. But you must not look too closely. Every evening these two cocaine gangsters enter-tain guests in the second-floor ballroom. You must never again go up there, Isidora. It has become a palace of fragile peace until the deals are struck, and afterwards, which is to say after the money exchanges hands, well, then we are too busy serv-ing drinks to take much notice of what happens. These guests, these vampires, they drink to wash away the fear and nervous anxiety that accompanies all transactions that take place in the shadows after dark. And then they head into the main ballroom and listen to that strange raging symphony of the devil, and they masturbate right there in front of the dancing girls, barking at the girls in a demonic, guttural Spanish that does not come close to sounding like the pure Spanish we were born with, but the girls seem to understand their meaning anyway and so they begin to strip, and these vampire gangsters laugh with unrestrained glee, wolves howling at Quevedo's blood-red moon, though even Quevedo did not imagine such gratuitous depravity, so they laugh some more and probe these girls with their fingers and then lick their fin-gertips, still laughing, and order more to drink, and the girls

are trembling in their sudden objectified nakedness, their eyes
glowing with a vulnerability like a shallow sea, too terrified
to run away, hoping their juices will begin to flow freely so
they can avoid a sudden beating, and maybe these vampires
take hold of a slender wrist and drag a young, nubile body
into one of the empty rooms backstage to satisfy their lusts,
yes, my innocent Isidora, there are now several empty rooms
backstage for just this purpose. Remember, to find oneself
between the horns of the bull is to be in the greatest danger.
Not even Oscar could save you if you wandered into the main
ballroom. Especially not Oscar.'

And it was true. It was all true. Everything Herminio
said about La Campana and about my beloved Oscar was
true. Of course I did not want to believe. I cursed the name of
Herminio for filling my empty girlish head with such vitriolic
distortions of reality. But everything he said was the truth.
What could I say? What could anyone say? So I said nothing.
And every evening after that, at seven o'clock on the dot, I sat
down in a small forgotten chair in a corner of the lobby and
I watched my beloved Oscar wander through the dream of
his demise as if he were hanging onto the delicate, cellophane
wing of a blue bottlenose fly. Every evening at seven o'clock
my beloved Oscar retreated to the bar and Herminio served
him drinks until he was too drunk to even stand. He sat at
the bar, unmoved by the horde of vampire gangsters whose
very presence had caused the sanctity of our little world
to collapse, suffering without horror the vengeance of that
terrible music that was the absence of music. And he drank
and drank until the alcohol ran out of his ears. And every now
and then he would wave at someone traipsing through the
lobby on their way up the stairs to the second-floor ballroom
of my dreams and the bright dazzling, sacrilegious purity of
mountains of cocaine, or down the stairs to the main ballroom
and a table of what was for most men a volcanic eruption
of lascivious delight, and then he, my beloved Oscar, would
plunge himself back into the self-annihilating liquid gold of
his bottomless glass. Or he would wave at the dark shadows
dancing on the walls, shadows he had mistaken for those
who had once filled each night with the glorious joy of their
appreciation but who had in the end abandoned La Campana

to her misery. Or he would wave at the ghost of Bonita, a fiery
whirling dervish spinning like mad, retracing the scorched
path of her footprints that would never fade. Or he would
wave at the image of his own tiny fractured self reflected in
the glass of his ambrosia, which was itself a strange reflection
of his other self trapped inside the antique glass of that darkly
gleaming mirror which oh so many years earlier, an infinity
in the dreaming, had been anchored with an unshakeable
purpose to the wall behind the bar.

-125-

Truly, one must always be ready to suffer.
'In the window of a hotel a face like a clown's grimaces
behind the glass. The shadow of a dove rubs up against the
excrement a dog leaves behind.' I remember reading these
lines somewhere. I do not remember who wrote them, but
that is unimportant. What is important is that I remember the
images. We use images such as these to hide our suffering.
We use these images to distract us from the incomprehensible
nature of what we truly feel, what we are truly experiencing.
What is more, we knowingly embrace such linguistic theatrics,
the poetic deceptions that allow us to sleep comfortably at
night, the bricks we use to plug the holes in the wall, because
we know deep down in that place we call the soul that every
experience is a singular, virtually unrecognizable, untranslatable event. Every experience damns the language we use
to describe it, but what choice do we have. Yes, yes, we can
avoid the nasty topic altogether by embracing the immediacy
of the experience as the only thing that matters, as if we were
being absorbed directly into a painting by Chardin. But we do
not truly believe that a momentary distraction is a window
to enlightenment. We do not wish to be mistaken for those
dreadful, vagabond bums who are always distracted by one
thing or another, *el papador de moscas*. We do not wish to be
fooled by the anti-sunlight and the anti-shadow of fruit on a

table, peaches, pears, apples, grapes, a bottle of wine, a small cup, a knife for cutting bread.

So the cynical world will begin to whisper over our shoulder, casting spells, mocking our naiveté. 'This anti-reality you perceive is nothing more than a delusion created by your intellect,' the cynical world will say. 'It is a sham, a mask to hide behind.' And we will believe the cynicism of the cynical world, but our belief (or unbelief) will also be tested. Inevitably we will try to remember that moment oh so long ago when we were directly absorbed into a painting. We will wonder what happened to the fruit, who we were eating with, how much wine we drank, and so on.

But then we will begin to confuse wagon wheels with wafers, just as the cynics in the manner of prophets might have predicted. We will decide we need to grow a second set of eyes to decipher what is really going on. But this will be of no help. The two sets of eyes will cancel each other out. We will not be able to see a thing. We will become blind, irrevocably blind, and we will wallow in the provocative terror of this blindness. We will take note of a shuddering, sinking feeling that begins in our ancient reptilian brains and shoots down our crumbling spines to land with a hollow thud somewhere in the steamy, vegetative darkness of our stomachs. And in the growing despair that results, as resilient as any black hole, we will crawl back into our mother's womb, whimpering with or without shame and yet thoroughly disgusted with the way our puny lives have turned out, begging God or some reasonable facsimile to have mercy on us and send us a witness like an avenging angel who will listen in rapt amazement to what we might have to say. No wonder our memoirs and our histories and our fictions and our poetry, and even our letters and our postcards and our private notebooks and our teenage diaries, are filled with wave after wave (or wafer after wafer, or wagon wheel after spinning wagon wheel) of nauseatingly imprecise images, a pastiche of empty clichés, failed metaphors of every ilk.

The image of an old sea wolf drinking from his bottle of gin, his face tanned by the Brazilian sun, thinking vaguely about misty, faraway islands and violent typhoons in the South China Sea, the creation of a courageous poet pursuing a form just out of reach.

The image of an elderly couple who have exhausted all of life's possibilities, except somehow they are still madly, even passionately in love with each other, they have murdered each other with their love, but this does not stop them, their corpse-like bodies are relentless in pursuing the physical release of their necrophiliac passion, the expulsion of all doubt, or at least hers, and in the indescribable, indestructible ecstasy of the moment they become a wheat field, which suggests, perhaps, that they are engaged in the process of separating the chaff from the pure grain, a noble endeavor, but in the haste of their passion (or hers), the wheat field goes up in flames anyway.

The image of two men playing chess in a bombed-out café in a city of ticking clocks and shattered glass and the swirling dark clouds of infallible pigeons who know exactly what they're doing, to steal half a line (and mutilate the meaning of that line) from that loveable, whineffable wheccentric who whonce whandered wherratically about the sun-streaked streets of Chillán, whondering whimsically wherever whe whent.

The image of two connected spools of thread, or copper wire, or Hollywood celluloid, the one spool unwinding as quickly as it possibly can, the other spool taking in all that the first spool has to offer in a madcap, mechanical, sprockety but uniform dash towards the future, that fraudulent dream that lingers on every horizon.

This is as close as we can get to explaining the pain we feel. The images we select. The parables we tell. And if we are trying to explain the whappiness whe feel, whell, that whill quickly and whinevitably whorph whinto pain, so whit is whall the same thing whin the whend.

¡De illusión también se vive! as my grandmothers used to say, but what they really meant in their heart of hearts was that if one lived by hope, one would die a slow, withering death.

-126-

I remember quite vividly the very last night I saw my Oscar. I remember everything with a cinematic clarity that resembles the ringing of church bells to announce a papal decree (otherwise known as a papal bull), or the stratosphere fifty kilometers up with its unimpeded view of the curvature of the Earth, as much as it (the cinematic clarity of my memory) resembles the malleable (we are but clay in the hands of our maker) delusions of a self-proclaimed, self-medicated schizophrenic walking hand in hand with the three Fates, the apportioners, what the Greeks called the Moirai, now firmly committed to whispering over my shoulder (or, alternately, from the shadowy creases of the ever-increasing shadows), casting aspersions as well as spells with every roll of the dice. I still do not understand what happened or why. My mind is a sieve when it comes to understanding. But I remember every last bizarre, inconceivably absurd detail, from the strange book Herminio was reading (I was still struck by the incongruity of seeing that coward Herminio reading a book) to Emilio's determination to watch a boxing match on television (my dear sweet Emilio, who had always preferred poetry to pugilism). My memory of that evening is impeccable.

-127-

A madwoman's third-person catalogue (collage, montage, litany, chronicle of sleepless nights, diary written in fresh blood, surrealist painting, anti-surrealist painting, Cowleyan ode, Baroque cantata, dodecaphonic symphony, a day in the life) of every fleeting image that traversed the empty spaces of her (my) brain on Friday evening the 21st of August 1981, from about six-thirty in the evening, when she (I) headed into the bar to talk to Herminio about my beloved Oscar's deepening despair, until there was nothing left to talk about:

She considers the possibility that she is traveling the path of an endless spiral, a true descent into madness, a nether world illuminated by the faint orangeish glow of Satan's cauldron, this is how she imagines the end of the road she is taking, for she realizes she is heading in a generally downward direction, and always she can see her beloved Oscar two or three levels below, but the moment she catches up to where he has been, he is long gone. Her mother's own preoccupations were by way of contrast incurably frivolous, the darts thrown by an adventurous heart, the false anguish of an irrepressible soul with a flair for drama, the tantrums of a sugar plum fairy, the irresistible shadow cast by a carefully pruned crepe myrtle, the exotic artificiality of a decorated gourd from a half-remembered dream. She suddenly finds herself inside her mother's dream, a dream of forgotten Cuba, a beam of sky-blue light descending upon the faithful, absolving everyone of original sin. But she is interrupted by the weary, impatient voice of Herminio, that prophet of eclipsed moons, who is tending bar.

'He does not know what it is like to be married,' she thinks, 'the pain and the confusion and the irrepressible joy.'

And yet she has sought out Herminio precisely to save her marriage. She is sitting on a barstool directly opposite Herminio, whose eyes are two, puffy slits the color of crushed violets, at precisely six-thirty in the evening, thirty minutes before her beloved husband who has forgotten what it means to be married will take his now customary seat at the bar in La Campana and proceed to get rip-roaring drunk.

She wants to ask Herminio if he has noticed the strange aberrant malaise that has descended upon her Oscar, a sudden unwillingness to take her to bed, to make wild, passionate love to her, to participate in the rife with life world around him that is his for the taking, if only he would take it. It is a malaise as thick and loamy as the rust-red musty earth that will one day cover us all.

She wants to ask if Herminio has noticed this heart-wrenching transformation on the way to the grave. Then she hopes to ask him how to re-ignite the raging rocket that was once Oscar Garcia Raimundi speeding effortlessly from one end of the universe to the other, and so re-ignite her own flagging passion for living.

She does not see Oscar emerge from the gleaming darkness of the lobby, a nocturnal creature escaping from a culvert made from corrugated galvanized steel. He is sitting along the edge of the gleaming, mahogany bar for several minutes, maybe longer, drinking glass after glass of sweet Demerara rum before she notices, for she is heavily immersed in the heavy words she takes for wisdom that are spewing forth with frothy regularity from Herminio's mouth. Then she hears Oscar laugh into his glass as he drains it and she realizes just how drunk he truly is.

Once her mother had discovered her father drunk at the kitchen table, his head flat against the wall, an empty bottle of wine on the table, on its side, a puddle bright as blood on the floor, an occasional bubble from a drop falling. Her mother had hurled the empty bottle into the sink, shattering the glass with the impact, a great crescendo of sound lacerating the air itself, and her father woke in an instant, but he was not yet himself, he had no clue that he was still in the kitchen, trapped as he was in a culvert of his own making, and when he saw the puddle on the floor, he panicked, thinking he had somehow injured himself and that he was bleeding copious amounts of blood and was on the verge of death, and so he had run out the kitchen door and then out into the street, thinking perhaps that he could flag down a wayward ambulance or some such nonsense, at least this is how her mother had always told the tale.

Naturally, this madcapped dash into the cool night air had immediately restored her father to himself. He had realized he wasn't dying, so he had gone back to his kitchen chair and leaned his head against the wall, a gesture of imminent defeat, and it was then he had seen my mother standing only a few feet away, a beautiful almost angelic vision in the sacrificial glare of the tiny recessed light above the sink, laughing silently at his idiocy, but it was a smoky, smirky, detached kind of laughter, at least this is how her father had always painted the scene, her mother's eyes tiny and hard like two weathered plum pits or cherry pits, her mother's features already blossoming with the stony, blackening orchids of disdain.

(She whonders for a moment if her father was simply defending himself whin the whelling of the whale from his point of view, a vigorously poetic defense, against the vague whinsinuations of her mother's laughter, as any father might do when a whondering child whonders what is going whon, or was he recounting with mock sincerity the tragedy of his whown absurd marriage, whor all marriages.)

Then the memory of this story of two authors fades and from somewhere Isidora hears the sound of someone chanting, faintly at first, a strange, guttural voice like a bolo knife cutting through the now verdant, leafy, jungle darkness of her imagination, but then she has the distinct impression that she has been absorbed by the sound, that it is all around her, that she has become this sound and is now spinning violently through the air, as the sound of any chanting voice would be spinning if that voice were trying to project itself across the yawning abyss of the centuries, that gaping mouth that will one day swallow itself, so she takes this leap, why not? (although even as she does so she realizes she is taking a leap in reverse) and lands in a cool moist place high atop a mountain. She sees a strange old woman on this mountain top (the source of the original chanting, obviously), an old dark-skinned woman wearing a slave's woven skirt and a bright blue turban and her saggy breasts are bare. The old woman is squatting beside a swiftly moving stream. Who can say what she is doing? Not Isidora. Isidora's mind is perplexed. It is filled only with questions. Her neurons are firing like mad. Who are you? How did I get here? Why are you squatting beside that stream? Were you thirsty? Did the fins of a swiftly-moving fish catch your eye? And just like that, as if to answer all of Isidora's silly questions with a single swift stroke, the old woman stands up, her bright blue turban shining like a newly birthed sky, and waves her hand in the air with a violent gesture of ultimate finality, and Isidora finds herself back in the bar, staring vacantly at Herminio, who has sort of clammed up now that Oscar is sitting right there. Herminio has become a mountain of silence.

Then quite unexpectedly Herminio says there is one thing he is at liberty to say, and he is casting sideways glances in the direction of Oscar (but he is blushing as he does this, a deep violet color like the tail end of a sunset, almost as if he is ashamed for keeping to himself even the most trivial of secrets), and then he says it was Oscar who had suggested that he pick up a copy of the Galdos book, El amigo manso, which he has read not once but twice because it is a very wise book. Herminio says that according to Galdos, some of us love in a Petrarchan way with a cold, intellectual sentimentality that might allow us to write a few fiery love sonnets, but is that all we really want from love. It is not clear if Herminio expects an answer, but then the moment for answers is obliterated by a peeping-Tom voice piping up from the lobby.

The voice, which belongs to Isidora's brother, Emilio, says that today is the long-awaited boxing match between Wilfredo

Gómez and that tenacious Mexican, Salvador Sanchez, for the
junior featherweight boxing championship of the world. This fight
of the 'Little Giants' will take place in Caesar's Palace in Las Vegas,
Emilio says, but it will be beamed to all corners of the planet, this
pale blue dot, via satellite television. Emilio has been working at La
Campana for several years now, various odd jobs like a sailor adrift
on a shallow blue-green sea, and popped his head into the bar to
say 'hi' on his way to the main ballroom. Isidora does not remember
when Emilio began to show an interest in boxing.

Oscar says he likes boxing in general but he doesn't give a
damn about this particular fight, though he's not talking to anyone
directly, perhaps his own wavering, watery reflection in the mirror
behind Herminio.

Oscar says he is embroiled in a fight of his own, in case
anyone (his reflection?) is (was?) interested, a fight to the death,
he says, but he doesn't elucidate. He downs another glass of sweet
Demerara rum, that amber ambrosia of the gods, and wipes his
mouth with his sleeve and then leaves the bar, a shadow in search of
a beam of bright sunlight.

Isidora is about to follow, but the precise moment she starts
to slip off her barstool she hears her mother's voice from beyond the
grave. Her mother's voice becomes an impenetrable barrier.

Isidora settles back onto the barstool.

She does not remember exactly what her mother died of, only
that she died a few years earlier in Jackson Memorial with dozens of
slender tubes pumping various liquids into a body that was already
bloated and covered with purplish bruises like the phlegmy flesh of
rotten, half-eaten plums. The voice from the darkness beyond simply
says 'whoever you marry is of no more importance than a passing
shadow, a cloud upon the horizon,' and Isidora falls swiftly into a
reverie of contemplation and loses sight of her beloved. Truly, who
can penetrate the dark hood of the Cuban night?

Herminio pulls out the Galdos book and thumbs quickly and
decisively through the pages until he comes to a well-worn spot that
has been marked up with a pen (a purple Bic, probably the only pen
that was available, a pen that was leaking, or at least the flow of the
ink was uneven, to judge by the look of the smudges on the page).

Why did my father stay locked in a marriage without love,
Isidora thinks, a marriage that was slowly bleeding him dry, so
much so that he looked like a strange Kabuki mannequin in the

months leading up to his death, except for a faint hint of red around his lips, a forlorn, disenfranchised puppet which her mother, on any given night, might pull apart limb from limb. Why would anyone stay in such a marriage? Are these the sacrifices we must make in the name of God just because we believe He is watching our every move, the ritualized castration of the bull to honor the mythology of our creation and then all we can do is stand back in horror and watch the dark red blood running through the streets of our despair? Who said so?

Slowly her metaphysical questions dissolve, and for a moment there is nothing but the image of her father floating effortlessly in front of her memory like the rarely seen blue moon of those ancient Cuban kings who roamed the Caribbean in search of prophecies.

Then Herminio begins reading from the Galdos book: 'The same perverse friend who had brought me into the world took me out of it, repeating the same magic words he'd said way back then, and also the diabolical sorcery of the bottle, the drop of ink, and the burnt paper which had preceded my incarnation.' Everything you want to know about God and love and marriage and foretelling the future you can find in this little book, he says with an air of exaggerated mystery.

What in the world are you talking about, Isidora says.

I am talking about the peace that eludes us, Herminio says, and then he laughs a hearty laugh that defies interpretation. Que Dios nos saque de penas y nos lleve a descansar, he says, after he has stopped laughing, his eyes narrowing in clichéd fashion, his air of exaggerated mystery returning. What do you even know about the sacrifices that go along with marriage, the perpetual suffering, Isidora says back to him with her eyes, but he has already gone back to his book.

The world becomes a 1910 vintage gramophone, the kind with an elongated funnel like a mouthpiece to the stars. A scratchy record from years ago begins to play, the music from an unknown singer spiraling through the darkness, but then the unknown voice of this unknown singer is suddenly replaced by Oscar's sweetly singing voice. 'Baby, go over there, turn on the lights, come back here and stand on that chair and then take off your shoes, yeah, Baby, now take off your dress, yeah Baby, that's it, wave your arms in the air, just like that, let the suspicious tongues keep on wagging, they don't know what love is, yeah, Baby, take it all off, that's it, take it all off, *except you can leave your hat on.' Yes, she knows it was an absurd bit of erotic playfulness, words in all probability that her beloved Oscar had stolen from a forgotten song on a forgotten album from 1972 and had pretended were his own, but it was a game the two of them thoroughly enjoyed, a game they would play all night until their skin was bathed in the absolutely pure, tangy, orangey glow of a sexy, sticky, marmalade sunrise.*

Then her mind shifts gears and she is once again thinking about her mother. Why was her mother so set on a church wedding when she believed more in the dark mystical powers of an Eleguá head named Eshu Laroyê than she did in the collective might of the pantheon of Catholic saints? Did she know what she was doing when she challenged Oscar to demonstrate the purity of his love for her only daughter? Isidora is wallowing in resentment. What a hateful, cynical thing to do! How Isidora hates her mother and her mother's Cuban heritage, but even as she voices these feelings to herself, an acknowledgement of the suffering we can never subdue, she knows she is being absurdly overdramatic. Her mother is not the reason Oscar hired the Velázquez brothers. It was Herminio. He is the reason.

Then Herminio himself breaks into the bubble of Isidora's inner dreaming with yet another passage from the Galdos book, but Isidora is unable to decipher the suddenly obscure language of this novel from a century ago (it is as if she is squinting to read a page right beneath her nose but which seems a million light years away because her once pristine eyesight is failing her). Only poetry can transcend the unforgiving years and capture how I truly feel, she thinks, and it is a thought that gives her tremendous satisfaction, it is almost as if her finger is poised on the trigger of a loaded gun, though where she might aim this gun, who she might wish to do in, well of this she is not sure. 'La locura de mi alma vive en el silencio del librepensador, que vive solo,' she says to Herminio, who is once again absorbed in the pages of his book.

Emilio returns from the main ballroom and takes the seat that Oscar had vacated. 'Turn on the television,' he says to Herminio, 'the fight is going to start shortly.' Herminio closes the Galdos book and turns on a small television on a small diagonal shelf in the corner above the cash register, but clearly it is the wrong channel because a well-groomed man sitting behind a pale blue desk is saying that today in Miami federal investigators discovered massive amounts of fraud in how the city has been managing the food stamps program.

Wilfredo Gómez, who is also known as Bazooka Gómez because of the power of his punch, was born in the crumbling Las Monjas neighborhood in San Juan, Puerto Rico, and later lived in Hato Rey, a stone's throw from the Martín Peña bridge, an art deco landmark that Gómez took whenever he was going to Santurce, which he did on a semi-regular basis because his mother and grandmother had belonged to the Church of the Crab Sellers (Iglesia San Mateo de Cangrejeros) on the corner of Calle San Jorge and Avenida Eduardo Conde, a quick five minutes (without traffic) from the bridge.

Before Herminio can turn the channel, the well-groomed man clears his throat and says that Pan Am is going to sell the Intercontinental Hotels Corporation (which can trace its roots back to the William Bass Brewery, which opened its doors in 1777 in the town of Burton in East Staffordshire, England, which the well-groomed man does not say) to another company headquartered in England, Grand Metropolitan Life (which will turn around five years later and sell the hotel chain to a Japanese group, having decided for financial reasons to focus on fast-food franchises like Burger King instead of hotels, which the well-groomed man could not possibly know, but which somehow Isidora has intuited, or at least she later imagines that she had), then click.

Oscar had never permitted anyone to watch television in the bar between the hours of seven o'clock and midnight, though there was one notable exception to this rule. He said it was bad for business. But Oscar wasn't there. Isidora's mother, on the other hand, was a fanatic when it came to television, and would show up at La Campana at eight, nine, ten in the evening, especially on a Saturday when it was busiest, and she would demand that Herminio put on a show, so what else could he do, not even being threatened with the pain of death could have altered the outcome. Her favorite show was The Love Boat, but to tell the truth she didn't care what was flickering away on that tiny little box in the dark corner like a window to the fifth dimension (that's what Oscar called it) above the register as long as she was there to see Oscar come storming in, for she knew that no matter where he was in the building, he always seemed to know if someone had turned on the television (it was usually Herminio, who loved to watch a ballgame or two); even

*if the volume was turned down to practically nil, Oscar somehow
sensed a disturbance in the equilibrium of the universe and would
come storming out of the darkness, an avenging god who existed
only in the spaces in between interjections, ready to pop a vein in
his neck just to test his immortality, but then he would have to
choke back his bluster, his face contorting into a weird grimace of
self-loathing when he saw that Herminio had only been the hapless,
helpless victim of a sinister plot to undermine his authority. So
Oscar would drift aimlessly about the lobby for a while, a man of
confounded purpose, a tad unsettled still, checking to make sure the
coat-check room was secure, or checking to see if the potted plants
in the lobby needed watering, or taking a peek outside to see if there
were any latecomers hustling in from the parking lot even when he
knew he would only be greeted by the steady, mechanical whine of
insects hidden away in the darkness of the trees, and then he would
quietly shut the door and slink as shadows slink along the edge
of the wall, slipping swiftly, gratefully (one might also have said
expertly) through the black double doors on the far side of the lobby
into the main ballroom and the euphoria of a world light years away
from the ruthless mischief of his mother-in-law.*

*Isidora begins to wonder if Oscar ever existed at all, or if
he was a pagan of lust-filled days and nothing more. She stares at
the mahogany bar, at the mirror behind the bar and the row after
row of shimmering bottles stacked against the glass, deep reds and
burgundies and ambers and light oranges, the bottles catching
the rays of television light beaming from that black hole above the
cash register. Everywhere she looks she is looking for some sign
of her Oscar, a lingering scar of his passing that has somehow
been impressed into the very molecules that make up the air she
breathes and which will remain miraculously visible no matter
how many breaths she takes. Yet she sees nothing. There is no
sign of her beloved Oscar, no miracle unfolding before her bleary,
watery eyes. She stares at the mirror as easily as if she is staring
into an abyss of her own making. The beaming, television light like
sulphurous vapors leaking through a tear in the fabric of reality is
now projecting images of the fight between Gómez, the favorite, and
Salvador Sanchez, his Mexican challenger. Gómez is doing poorly.
He was knocked down in the first round. He has been repeatedly
rocked by Sanchez, who has stunned the world with the incredible
speed and accuracy of his combinations, a flurry of pumping fists,*

the symbiosis of unimaginably profound artistry and unspeakably degenerative violence. It is the end of the third round and Gómez has a severely damaged eye. His eye is beginning to swell. There is nothing his corner can do except cut it with a razor. But Isidora is oblivious to this flickering reality. The boxing match does not yet exist for Isidora, except perhaps on a subliminal level, an ironic bit of mental dexterity given that Oscar now exists only in Isidora's subconscious mind. She continues to look for the lingering scars of his presence with an air of scientific detachment, hoping against hope to reverse the inevitability of her madness as she imagines one might theoretically (but not instantaneously) reverse the polarity of the Earth with a flip of a magnetic switch. But even while she is searching she accepts the futility and foolishness of the search. Gómez returns with a vengeance in the seventh round and literally lifts Sanchez off his feet. But Sanchez does not fall down. He rubs his chin. He shifts his protruding jawbone back and forth, as if to make sure it is in working order. Some of his teeth are loose, but he is undaunted. Suffering is the only way out of his predicament. Isidora is confronted by her own complicity in Oscar's continued absence. She is suddenly overwhelmed by the thought that to look for some proof that her beloved once existed and continues to exist outside her never neverland imagination is to profane the memory of that very existence, which is in all probability a sin against the act of creation. But the seventh round proves to be the last gasp for Gómez, his last chance for victory. Both of his eyes are swollen now. Isidora wonders if God will punish her for her sin and if this punishment will fit the crime, and then she is sure this will be the case. She is given the gift of brutal clarity. Everything coincides. Gómez staggers out into the middle of the ring at the beginning of the eighth round, but he is unable to zero in on Sanchez. All he is able to see are strange, flickering shadows dancing deliriously on the periphery of his awareness. He wonders if he has gone insane. He wonders what will happen if he takes one more punch. He wonders if his already swollen, bulging eyes will explode. All he needs to do to test this hypothesis is to lean into a left hook by Sanchez. Gómez leans into a left hook by Sanchez and he feels the explosion, a sensation of light fragmenting and then sudden darkness. He feels strangely vindicated, even though he knows he has made a serious mistake. Then he feels the sensation of his eyeball jelly oozing out over his bruised, bony sockets, trickling down his cheeks, but he is

*not altogether sure what he is feeling. (Later, during an interview
with a Mexican reporter, he admits that he was having some
difficulty distinguishing the eyeball jelly from the blood.) Herminio
and Emilio are stunned. From the television one can clearly hear the
chanting Mexican fans at ringside. They are shouting '¡Olé! ¡Olé!,
¡Olé!, ¡Olé!' with every volley of punches. Isidora has convinced
herself that the only just punishment for her sin is to be deprived of
her beloved. How she came to this conclusion she cannot say. It is
a feeling more than a rational thought, a physical sensation like a
soft caress that turns into a snapping of a slender neck. She does not
even consider what life without Oscar will look like if in fact this is
the punishment the gods decree. She only hopes she is mistaken. But
nothing is what it appears to be. Gómez is sent to the canvass by a
terrific Sanchez smash. Never mind that Gómez had no idea what
was coming because he was virtually blind. Still, champion that he
is (was), he beats the count, but the referee steps in and the fight is
over. A new legend is born in Mexico. A boxer has become a bullfighter. It is a fight for the ages, the history books, the newspapers,
the tabloids. This is the price we pay for our human folly, our frailty
which is the by-product of countless centuries of evolution. By any
other name, the robust violence we are witnessing is what we call
the psychedelic transmogrification of our immortal soul. Isidora no
longer remembers what the rollicking laughter of her beloved sounds
like. But neither does she remember the hissing insistence of his
despair these last few months, these last few days and hours, like
the hissing, leaky-balloon sound of the Earth's atmosphere escaping
through a hole in the ozone layer. Instead she hears the sweet
invigorating cry of the Torocoro with its mantle like a cape the color
of the ocean at sunset. She has not heard the lingering cry of the
Torocoro in many years, though to be honest, she has never heard
the sound of that mythic bird except through the inverted funnel of
her imagination spitting out its contents like so many gentle, airy,
poofy kisses that quickly evaporate in the ether some fifty miles up.*

128

From the notes of a failed linguist, Nicholas Ruedenberg,
a doctoral candidate at the University of Greifswald,
Greifswald, Germany, discovered among some papers stuffed
into an empty flower pot in his tiny fourth-floor apartment
shortly after his suicide in 2026:

'Some stories end. Others do not. But it is next to
impossible to distinguish one kind from the other. But what is
a story to begin with? And once we decide upon a definition,
who will do the dishes? Is the random sequence of narrative
events a cohesive story? No, story is not sequence. That is
an illusion, the gift of the magi, the darkness that follows a
swarm of phantasmagorical taxis. But what if these sequences
are logical, predictable, causal sequences? That is more of the
same, a rabbit hole. Straight lines or a frenetic zig-zagging
motion, it makes no difference. We plant a seed in the ground
and we water the seed and care for it, and if there is plenty
of sunlight and warm temperatures and we have planted the
seed in good ground to begin with, then the seed begins to
grow, and from this we infer causality. But we recognize that
our understanding is a surface understanding, so we say to
ourselves, perhaps we have not gone deeply enough. We set
up expeditions to plumb the depths. But sadly, no matter how
deep we go (up to our armpits, wallowing in it, up to our
necks in it, then our eyes disappearing, our bodies subsumed
entirely by the seething darkness below, our minds consumed
by an irrational need to control the chaos of the world, our
souls vanquished by seditious dichotomies, not even a net
can save us now), we can always dig a little deeper. This is
the lesson of quantum mechanics, which is also the lesson of
philosophy, which is also the lesson of religion, of chemistry,
of biology, of sociology, of history. It is the lesson of every
snobology. So sequence, and causality, which is the wicked
stepbrother of sequence (or at least a deranged cousin), are
merely anachronistic structures we superimpose upon the
bizarre, incomprehensible images that bombard us daily in the
vain hope that we might extract some meaning. We will invent

a sequential, causal structure in order to sustain this hope. But meaning does not exist. Beginnings exist and they are replaced by new beginnings. It is the same with endings. But there is no meaning to connect the two, and so any meaning we invent will sooner or later, inevitably, just slide off the page. So what then is a story? I must accept the fact that I can never know. All I can know is that one door opens and another door closes. The labyrinth extends beyond the limits of my imagination. I am unable to process the riddle of the mandala. I cannot appreciate the dizzying heights of the Yggdrasil, the tree of death and life, which towers above all creation. Even the first branch is beyond my reach. Some stories end. Others do not. And so it goes.'

129

From the personal field notes of Miami Police homicide
detective Àngel Andreu, which served as the basis for a formal
report concerning the death of Oscar Garcia Raimundi that
was filed on September 14, 1981, (which was, incidentally,
only twenty-four days after Wilfredo Gómez lost the junior
featherweight title to Salvador Sanchez):

"**August 23, 1981. Sunday, 9 AM**. I am at my desk. Why
the hell I came in on a Sunday morning to tackle that mound
of paperwork I can't really say. I mean I know why well
enough. Let's just say the wife wanted to go to church and I
didn't. Fair enough. Let me just add to that: fuck paperwork!
Better delete that last part. So a fucking call comes in. 9 AM
on a Sunday morning for Christ's sake! Why couldn't this call
have come in say five hours earlier before the Saturday night
homicide boys went over to Julian's for a bite to eat. Christ! So
a call comes in. There's a dead body in Coral Gables, somewhere along US 1. So what I say, there's probably lots of dead
bodies in Coral Gables along US 1. The guy on the other end
just blows past my little joke like I didn't say a word. Some
kids found it at a playground in Washington Park, he says,
and I'm thinking Washington Park isn't anywhere close to our
jurisdiction, but the guy on the other end keeps blabbing. The
officers who first arrived on the scene said from what they
could tell the dead guy was from Allapattah. Allapattah is in
our jurisdiction, which is why they called it in. The guy on
the other end says the officers on the scene will wait till I get
there, assuming I don't take too long, it is Sunday morning,
after all, they probably have wives waiting for them. Then he
hangs up. Yeah, it's fucking Sunday morning, all right, wives
or no wives. So I have to go down to Coral Gables. Which
actually doesn't bother me, to tell you the truth. Then I see
Ramirez. Ramirez is straight out of a television crime show.
He's the light-skinned Latino that pushes the boundaries of
diversity but doesn't alarm the mostly white audience. He
is walking in as I am heading out the door and I say you're

coming with me pinhead, and he gives me a blank look like
he always does, but he knows I'm just messing with him. How
the fuck they got the number to my fucking desk in the first
place I'll never know. Fucking fate, I guess."

   "**August 23, 1981. Sunday, 11:30 AM**. It took us a while
to get down to Washington Park. It's a pretty nice little park
for the kiddies I have to admit. A little bit of green space, a
place to toss a ball around. Not the kind of place you'd expect
to find a dead body. But what the fuck. Dead bodies are
everywhere. That's a simple fact of life. So we got there late.
There wasn't anybody in the park when we pulled up, but
there was a Coral Gables squad car parked six inches from
the curb near the Northwest side of the park. It was a very
precise parking job. A very Coral Gables kind of parking job.
Two officers got out as we pulled up. I pulled in right behind
the squad car. My car is a 1965 dark blue Pontiac Bonneville
two-door hard top coup. I mean it really stands out. But it's
also a state-of-the-art cruiser with a Motorola two-way and
an engine that really kicks. Needless to say, the Coral Gables
guys knew who it was right away. They were pissed. Wives
or no wives, they were pissed, but what the fuck. Me and
Ramirez stopped for a bite to eat on the way down. I mean
who said we had to starve. Screw that. So the two officers
got out and we chatted a while and one of them gave me a
clipboard with the log of everyone who had visited the crime
scene: the two officers who greeted us, two more who stopped
by at 10:15 just to have a quick look, an inspector named H.
Miller, and right there I'm thinking are you kidding me, 'H.
Miller?' why not Henry Miller or Hank Miller or Harry or
Hamilton or Hamoelet or Harlan or Henley or Hermes or
Hariman or Huldiberaht or Herwin or Heyward or Hal or
Harpo or Hadrian or Hagrid or Hiram or Haji or Hieronymous
or Hervé or Hamon or Hanes or Hany or Hardie or Howard or
Hrorek or Herrick or Hewitt or Horatio or Hitch or Hobbard
or Hubbard or Hulbard or Humphrey, or even Heinrich, for
Christ's sake, all randomly assigned monikers to be sure,
providing no clue to the essential character of the named, but
not the pitiful, purposely vague and therefore morally bank-
rupt signature of 'H. Miller,' who probably didn't even get

out of his car because then the eyes of the world would have
been upon him (that blustery, fat Aryan fuck) and he would
have felt unavoidably (inevitably?) duty-bound to investigate
(though it probably would have been a sham of an investigation, you can bet your ass), in which case they never would
have called me, so he sent a lieutenant to do a quick walk-thru
to see if there was any way to pawn off the dead body, some
pasty-faced, snot-nosed lieutenant most likely, and so the last
guy listed in the log (until me and Ramirez showed up) was
that very same pasty-faced lieutenant picked by the invisible
H. Miller. There were a few preliminary comments by the
lieutenant. His name was Lieutenant Beckert (another German
name). I read over the comments but it was like reading a fifth
grader's seven-sentence summary of the *Movie of the Week*.
Fucking fifth grade handwriting too. Pretty much illegible.
I wrote my name in the log and asked him if he wanted the
clipboard back. He said no. I signed a receipt. More fucking
paperwork, every step of the way. He seemed satisfied. He
seemed like he couldn't wait to hand off this mess to someone
else and get back to his regular Coral Gables police-type
duties. I asked him if he was Beckert and he said he wasn't.
He said it was Beckert who had figured out the dead guy was
from Allapattah. 'How did he manage that?' I asked him. 'It
was easy,' he said. 'He looked in the guy's wallet and there
was a card that said La Campana, some nightclub up there,
and the guy's name.' 'And that was enough for Beckert.'
'Sure.' 'And the guy's driver's license?' 'There wasn't any. Just
the card with the guy's name on it.' 'But that was enough for
Beckert.' 'Sure.' 'Right, and the crime scene?' 'Over there.'
The one guy was pointing past a clump of crepe myrtles. You
could see some playground equipment through the branches.
You could see they had tried to surround the playground
equipment with yellow tape to keep the neighborhood away.
They had tied one end to the crepe myrtles and then looped it
around the playground and then back to the beginning. They
were trying to close the loop, as they say. But it was a pretty
sloppy job. There was a bit of a breeze blowing through the
crepe myrtles and it was staring to drizzle, just like it's been
doing on and off for what has it been, two weeks now, two
weeks of fucking rain and no end in sight. Anyway, the yellow

tape was flapping like mad. I mean you knew it wasn't going to keep anybody out for too much longer. Then the one guy started up again, but he wasn't looking at me. He was looking vaguely at the crepe myrtles. 'Beckert didn't call the coroner,' he said, 'you know how those guys are,' and he gave me one of those polite, mealy-mouthed German beerhouse smiles like I knew the same exact guys he knew. 'He figured you'd want to have a look around first.' 'Sure, thanks.' The one guy nodded but the other didn't even look at me (still pissed, I guess). Then they got in their squad car and drove away."

"**August 23, 1981. Sunday, 11:45 AM**. Fuck this rain. I love Miami and I love thunderstorms and I love walking on the beach in the rain and all that romantic shit. But two fucking weeks is more than enough."

"**August 23, 1981. Sunday, 11:46 AM**. We did a walk-thru of the crime scene. The playground equipment is a sort of jungle gym rocket ship with a rocket tower for climbing at one end and a slide at the other. The dead body was hanging head down from the rocket ship tower. The feet were tied to the jungle gym bars. The arms were pulled out to either side and tied to a fucking two-by-four laid across the guy's back. Like a gleaming white inverted crucifix. From a distance it looked like the dead guy was smiling, an inverted smile to be sure. The two-by-four was tied to the lower posts of the rocket tower, I guess so the guy wouldn't flap around or dangle. The guy's hands were nailed to the wood. I mean the killers had actually hammered a nail through the middle of each of the guy's palms. Maybe not a hammer. Maybe they used a nail gun. Something with a little kick to it. They had it in for this guy whatever they used. Cause of death uncertain. Once we got a little closer we could see quite clearly that the guy's throat had been cut, I mean ear to ear, a very clean, precise cut, very methodical, a very professional job. Still, no matter how clean a cut like that, it's a hell of a painful way to go. But no idea if this was the cause of death or not. Could all be for show. Like hanging the body upside down. Have to wait for the coroner to be sure. I said to Ramirez the guy looked like a dead shark or something pulled out of the sea. He laughed and said the killers were obviously playing around with Catholic symbolism. 'You mean like Christ on the cross,' I asked him. 'No,' he said. 'I mean like Peter the Apostle. He was crucified upside down by the Romans. Just like this guy here.' 'What the fuck does that mean,' I asked him. 'I have no idea,' Ramirez said. 'It just looks pretty symbolic the way he's laid out. But it's pretty fucked up symbolism all the same.' I didn't know what to say about that. Ramirez can get pretty hyped up by all that Catholic mumbo-jumbo. But the dead guy did look like a shining example of everything that's wrong with religion. He was wearing a white linen jacket but no shirt. The jacket looked like it was about to fall off but it had got stuck around the guy's armpits and then the corners had folded themselves around the back of the guy's neck. It sort of looked like wings that had been partially sliced away. The dead guy was also wearing white slacks tucked into his socks, but no shoes. At least the killers weren't perverted, I mean they were clearly sick fucks with a sick sense of humor, but at least they left the guy the dignity of his pants. He was also wearing a white Panama hat, which we couldn't figure out why gravity didn't do its thing at first, but then we saw that the hat was nailed to the top of the guy's head, right through the cranium. It seems obvious now they were using a nail gun. The white slacks were stained with blood and the rain, but strangely there were no blood stains on the jacket. No visible signs of blood on the playground or the rocket tower. Which means maybe they killed the guy somewhere else. Then again, the whole crime scene had been scrubbed pretty clean by the rain. And there was no telling how long the body had been there. That was another item for the coroner. I checked the inside pocket of the guy's jacket for his wallet and there it was. No driver's license, just like that pasty-faced Lieutenant Beckert had said. And there was the card with his name, Oscar Garcia Raimundi, the poor dumb fuck, and underneath the name was the name of the nightclub, La Campana in glittery letters, and then a raised line in italics that said from 'dusk till dawn,' and beneath that the address: 25½ La Campana Avenue, Allapattah, Miami, Florida. It was a very fancy card. I mean they don't get much fancier."

"**August 23, 1981. Sunday, 12:15 PM.** Took pictures of everything noted above. I hate taking photographs almost as much as I hate fucking paperwork. They give me a state-of-the-art unmarked police cruiser for cruising the streets, but they give me a piece of shit Minolta for taking pictures. Rain started to come down harder."

"**August 23, 1981. Sunday, 1:30 PM.** The guys from the evidence collection unit pull up. Crime Scene Investigators Randy Graeff, just out of college (The University of Miami, what else), Martin Lorenz, who's been doing this for more years than he cares to count, and sweet little Natalie Henderson, who takes an awful lot of shit from everybody, but you should see her strut around in a skirt. And she's always wearing skirts. Man, she knows what she's doing, you better believe that. Better delete that last part. Anyway, right behind Natalie and her two bookends comes the coroner, Leon Vallejo, along with Bob Nordyke, the Chief Death Investigator, and Andrew Havlik, whose area is forensics, or maybe pathology, or maybe both. We've been waiting in my car for over an hour. We give everyone a quick briefing and then they go to work. They don't say what kept them and we don't ask. Not even Leon comes clean, but then it was probably his fault to begin with. Every Sunday Leon takes his family to the brunch at Denny's. Everybody had probably been waiting on Leon to get back from brunch. So anyway, the rain has sort of halted by now. It's still pretty cloudy so you know it's going to start up again. But we're good for a while. Ramirez says it's God's doing, meaning the break in the weather, so Leon can get the body into his van before any more of the dead man's dignity is washed away. I say what the fuck are you talking about Ramirez, but he just laughs. Ramirez sweats religion. I mean you can smell it pouring out of his pores. Like gardenias or something. I don't know. Maybe the way he smells has something to with what he eats. Or maybe he's always running late so instead of showering he douses himself with his wife's perfume. Maybe that's why he's always running out to the mall to pick up a bottle of Chanel or Yves Saint Laurent. I don't know. But it smells like religion to me. Anyway, we talk with Graeff and Lorenz for a while

over by the playground equipment, but we're really trying to
catch a glimpse of Natalie. She's climbing up into the rocket
tower but you can't really see her because of the dead guy.
She's looking for clues. But every once in a while you catch
the curve of her hip and your jaw just drops. Graeff is saying
the way the killers laid out the body clearly indicates they are
at the very least sociopaths with little regard for social mores
or human dignity. Lorenz says you mean psychopaths like
in *Psycho*? Graeff shakes his head and says he doesn't think
so, though there is certainly an elemental psychopathology in
the explicit symbolic messaging of the crime scene. It is very
theatrical. It is almost as if they were presenting a short play
in which the brutality of murderous violence is not shown,
only its aftermath, much like the great German movie director
Fritz Lang did in his 1931 thriller, *M*, but without the sexually
deviant overtones of a child predator. Yes, says Lorenz, but
what does all that mean? Graeff laughs and says it means that
one could argue that these killers are borderline psychopaths
because on one level this murder seems to be a textbook
example of their need to exercise their creative imagination
in a vain attempt to control their environment without any
concern for who gets in their way, though one could argue
just as persuasively that they are mere sociopaths (which is
to say they are not yet robots without any compassion for
the human condition), whose murderous impulses are in
reality unconscious, conditioned responses to certain as yet
undetermined social stimuli, what in the vernacular we would
call triggers, which made this particular murder necessary,
even inevitable. What kind of triggers says Lorenz. Graeff
says it could be anything, an unwillingness to go along to get
along, a crooked smile, a disagreement over religion, which
would certainly make sense given the obvious anti-Catholic
symbolism, but it could be anything. Then Graeff's eyes light
up. Hey Ramirez, what was the dead man's name? Ramirez
blinks stupidly for a moment, like he is trying to wake up, like
his eyes are tiny mouths gasping for breath. He was probably
lost in that fantastic labyrinth of intellectual gobbledygook
that Graeff has been leading us through. Then Ramirez
shakes free of the cobwebs and says Raimundi, Oscar Garcia
Raimundi. Graeff says, there you have it, Raimundi, a name

which could mean the Light of the World, though it could mean many other things as well. But suppose this Raimundi was an associate of our killers, a man who held some position of authority over them, a man who was seen by others as a light in the darkness, so to speak, and then suppose his death was the result of some power struggle, as is the case with many of the deaths in gangsterland, and suppose our killers are slightly psychotic, or even robustly psychotic, so they slit his throat and nail him to a cross and hang him upside down to make some explicit comment about their role in assuming the mantle of the dead man's power, they have extinguished the old Light of the World and in the process have become the New Light, a new order for a new day. Everyone who knew the dead man and who knew the killers would realize that a new order had been created. Yes, it could very well be something like that. Lorenz doesn't know what to say. Neither do I for that matter. Graeff is smiling like the fucking cat that ate the canary. He's into all that psychological crap. Lorenz says okay, sure, but that really only tells me why they hung him upside down. It doesn't come close to revealing their motives for killing him in the first place, other than some vague insinuations about this mythical power struggle. What exactly was the trigger? Why did they kill him? Graeff doesn't say anything for a moment. His face begins to contort in odd ways, as if he is experiencing a sudden change in air pressure. Then he says he doesn't know for sure and bites his lower lip. It's like a forced confession. Like Lorenz is a priest from the days of the Inquisition flaying the skin off Graeff to get at the truth. Graeff's face has taken on a sour look. Apparently he doesn't like confessing. I get it. No one likes to appear weak, especially in front of their peers. Maybe that's the reason why the killers killed Oscar Garcia Raimundi. They didn't want to appear weak in front of their peers. Maybe it was as simple as that. But I don't say a word. Then sweet Natalie flashes her hips and the conversation is over."

"**August 23, 1981. Sunday, 4:30 PM**. Everybody's pretty much finished. Leon left with the body at 3:45. Nordyke and Havlik followed in their car. Natalie and Graeff and Lorenz left at 4:00. Me and Ramirez are sitting in my car. It's rained

on and off the whole afternoon, but after a while rain is easy
to forget. Leon won't be finished with the preliminary autopsy
report until maybe Tuesday, and even then it'll be inconclusive
until we get the results of the tox screen. The others probably
won't be ready with their reports till Wednesday. But me and
Ramirez already have three leads to track down. The first is
the nightclub up in Allapattah. The second is a newspaper
article from *The Miami News* that was folded up and stuffed
in a slot in the dead guy's wallet. The article is about an
offshore speedboat race that is going to be held up at Sunny
Isles over Labor Day weekend. The article says the race is not
sanctioned by the American Powerboat Association, so the
racers won't get any points like they could with sanctioned
races. But the event organizers are expecting over a hundred
racers and over a thousand spectators. The article goes on
to say that the primary purpose of the race is to showcase
the speed and versatility of the new cigarette boats that are
taking the speedboat world by storm. Miami resident Pepe
Nuñez, a self-proclaimed speed freak, won the Pelican Harbor
Trophy Race in 1980 with one of these cigarette boats, a boat
that had been manufactured by Pantera, a company which
Nunez had founded with his wife Linda in 1974. Another
South Florida resident, Joey Ippolito, won the Bacardi Race
this past May with a cigarette boat manufactured by Wellcraft
Boats of Sarasota, Florida. The writer of the article can not
praise these boats enough. The third clue is a receipt from
The Miami Skyways Motel out on Le Jeune Road. The receipt
was for Friday night, a one-night stay. It's a great place right
across from the airport. Nice restaurant. Swimming pool.
Striped yellow and white umbrellas to keep the sun off your
back. A comfortable lounge with anything you'd want to
drink. I met the owner four years ago, Manny Melamed, an
eccentric sonofabitch, but a nice guy. Always smiling. Really
dark hair, and a wild looking Fu Manchu moustache. I don't
know about his taste in clothes, though. I mean when we first
met he was wearing a crazy, artsy silk shirt with these weird
geometric patterns, dark blue rectangles, aquamarine circles
or triangles or something, and a light blue paisley jacket and
bright sky-blue slacks. I mean the whole outfit hurt your eyes.
I met him at a downtown luncheon for something or other and

he invited me to come out to the lounge to hear Sonny Rollins
play his saxophone. He must have seen the blank look on my
face because he started to laugh. I'm not really into the music
scene. I don't even listen to the radio. And I sure as hell had
no idea who Sonny Rollins even was. But he wasn't half bad.
So anyway, me and Ramirez are heading up to the Miami
Skyways Motel to see if anybody remembers our dead guy.
It's only twenty minutes away. Head straight north. I mean
it's an absolutely straight shot, no turns or deviations of any
kind. Now all we gotta do is figure out what connects these
two dots on the map other than SW 42nd Avenue."

   "**August 23, 1981. Sunday, 6:35 PM**. We drove into the
parking lot of the Miami Skyways Motel. The rain had picked
up again, a steady, annoying, roaring, smoky downpour, but
you could still see the orangeish neon lettering of the motel
flickering. We parked directly beneath the overhanging marquee sign and headed straight into the lobby. Manny Melamed
was nowhere around, so we talked to the night manager. His
name was Charlie Perrine. A nice enough guy. Balding, a
slightly distracted look that not even the wire-rim glasses he
was wearing is able to correct. Charlie said he remembered the
guy with the Panama hat because nobody wears Panama hats
anymore. 'Yeah,' Charlie said. 'And he was wearing a white
linen suit that had clearly seen better days.' Charlie said the
guy asked for room 227 but he didn't say why. No visitors. No
phone calls. He paid in cash. He went out for about an hour
or so and came back with some Carvel ice cream. 'I remember
because he came into the lobby just as the Gómez/Sanchez
fight was about to start, and I asked him if he wanted to
watch with us, I mean there were a dozen of us, maybe more,
crowded around that the television over there.' (At which
point Charlie pointed to a brand-new wall-mounted color
television on the other side of the lobby with a couple of sofas
and chairs scattered around and a coffee table with magazines
and some potted ferns for atmosphere.) 'But he said he wasn't
interested in the Gómez/Sanchez fight, he wanted ice cream,
he wanted to know if there was a Carvel ice cream store
anywhere around. I told him the nearest one I knew was
down on Kendall, which is about twenty minutes away, and

he said good enough and headed out the door. To be honest
I don't remember just when he came back or if he came back
at all. After the fight was over I had some work to do back in
my office.' Charlie showed us the register where the guy had
signed. Oscar Garcia Raimundi, a very flamboyant signature,
but for his home address he had put down Havana, Cuba,
which we thought must have been a fucking joke. 'Don't you
check these things?' Ramirez asked Charlie, but Charlie only
smiled a sheepish smile and shrugged. Then he took us down
the hall just off the lobby and up a small flight of stairs and
let us into room 227. He said there hadn't been anyone else in
the room since the Panama hat, and then he left us to go back
to the lobby. I don't know what we were expecting. I mean the
room had already been scrubbed clean. I mean it looked like
any other airport hotel room waiting for a few out-of-town
suckers. Ramirez checked under the bed and in the bathroom
and in the closet. I went over to the window and pulled back
the drapes. Poolside. A balcony with a wooden railing. A view
of the pool and the rain pelting the pool with a merciless rage
and half a dozen pool umbrellas folded up and the tables
they normally protected from the sun getting hammered by
the wrath of God. Then Ramirez motioned for me to have a
look at the room safe. A typical hotel room safe on the floor
of a typical hotel closet next to an ironing board. A safe that
anyone could crack with a screwdriver. 'Look at this,' Ramirez
said. He pulled out a small satchel made of imitation leather
and set it squarely on the small table next to the bed. He
undid the buckle, slowly, as if to heighten the importance
of his discovery. I remember thinking that if this had been
a fucking movie there would have been suspense music in
the background and I almost broke up laughing. Then just
like that we were staring at ten-thousand smackers neatly
stacked inside this cheaply made brown satchel that looked
like it had been purchased at K-Mart. I remember thinking
what the fuck was this guy doing with ten-thousand dollars
in cash, and then I was thinking why was the money still
here? 'Drug money?' Ramirez said. 'Maybe,' I said. 'Maybe
it was a drug deal gone bad and that's why he's dead?' said
Ramirez. 'Maybe,' I said. 'But if it was about drugs, then why
is the money still here? Why would the killers leave that much

cash behind? Didn't they think to check the safe? Were they fucking idiots? It doesn't make any sense.' Ramirez stuffed the cash back into the satchel and then we headed back to my car. We moved uneasily back down the steps and then down the hall. There was nobody in the lobby when we got there. The television was still on but there was no sound coming out of it, which was really odd. I had the feeling like we were either walking into a trap or we had just narrowly escaped. We headed out past the strange, blueish glow of the strangely muted television as if suspicious eyes and ears were following our every move."

"**August 24, 1981. Monday, 11:00 AM.** The sun has come out and the rain has stopped. It is almost surreal. I keep look-ing up at the sky expecting it to cloud over all of a sudden. Ramirez says I shouldn't tempt fate, and by fate he means God. We head out to the Carvel ice cream store on Kendall and speak to the manager. The store looks brand-spanking new, as close to perfection as an ice cream store can get, all white counters and dazzling chrome and a white-tiled floor. The manager's name is Ralph Hernandez. Ralph is not happy to see us. His eyes are dancing about randomly, like bullets about to explode. He thinks our visit is about some unpaid parking tickets. He tells us he is a Vietnam vet. He bled for his country. He points out several photographs hanging on the wall behind the ice cream counter. They are all Vietnam photos. One is of a younger Ralph standing on a gunboat on some river. He is holding an M60 machine gun. Sunlight is glinting off the gun barrel. There are two other guys in the photo, one on either side of Ralph. One of them is holding a grenade launcher. They are all dressed in green fatigues with floppy green hats like fisherman's hats and smiling like idiots. The date on the photo is August 1967. Ralph says the guy holding the grenade launcher was a cracker named Sam Tennyson from Birmingham, Alabama. He bought it one month after this photo was taken. An ambush on the Ba Rai River southwest of Saigon. A hellacious gunfight. The official body count was three American sailors and seventy-seven wounded. But Ralph says he knows for a fact that over twenty guys got killed on the Ba Rai River that day. The other guy's

name is Danny Madsen. He and Ralph still keep in touch
even though Danny lives in Houston. They almost never talk
about Vietnam, so as the years drift by they have less and less
in common. We assure Ralph we could care less about minor
infractions of the traffic code. We tell him we are trying to
track down the whereabouts of a person of interest and that
we had information that he bought some ice cream at this particular location this past Friday night at some point between
the hours of seven and nine in the evening. Ralph is visibly
relieved. He gives us each an ice cream cone. He says he was
not at the store Friday evening, but his assistant manager, Eric
Valera, he was working. Eric will be in from four till ten."

   "**August 24, 1981. Monday, 2:40 PM**. Finally, we pull up
to La Campana. We only found it by accident. La Campana
Avenue doesn't exist on any map we looked at. I called
Dispatch for a little assistance, but Stacey Guglioha, who has
been sitting at that desk since before I was born, got all crazy
bent out of shape. I'm probably the only bozo in the whole
department who bothers Stacey for directions because he's
too lazy to ask a gas station attendant or a bus driver. Why
she tolerates my deviant departures from protocol I haven't
a clue. She could care less that I'm a detective. 'You better
get your lazy derrière off this channel, mister' she said. But I
didn't, of course. I started arguing with her. We were parked
at a Chevron on NW 36th Street maybe three blocks from
the high school. I was telling Stacey that I was looking at the
guy's business card and there it was plain as daylight, 25½ La
Campana Avenue. I guess I was pretty vocal about it. But she
was pretty damn feisty herself the way she was shouting back
at me, saying there was no such avenue, and she should know,
she had the comprehensive list. Stacey likes to say she is all
fire and that fire is the source of all beauty. So I was yelling
at her and she was yelling at me, and then she said 'Stand
by!' and then just like that, whammo, nothing but static.
Beautiful Stacey. Anyway, I was just about to track down a
gas station attendant when it got really quiet all of a sudden,
and it wasn't just the radio. I mean it was a strange, kind of
eerie but absolutely peaceful silence. It was like I had died or
something. I mean I couldn't hear a thing, not the birds, not

the traffic whizzing by, not a siren, not the sound of a distant train. I hung up the mike and looked over at Ramirez but he was dozing. Then an old but agile voice leaned in through the window of my car and grabbed me by the collar. Now under normal circumstances I would have been startled. I'd have been out the car door and on the pavement in an instant. I might even have pulled my gun. But this did not happen. For one thing, the voice was a peaceful voice, in keeping with the mood that had descended all around. I guess that's the only thing, the only reason. The voice exerted a calming influence on me. 'Are you looking for La Campana, the nightclub?' the voice asked. 'Yeah, yeah, that's the place,' I said. 'It's a few blocks that way and hang a right,' said the voice, and I followed the voice to the arm that was attached to it and nodded with unconvincing enthusiasm. 'You'll be there in a jiff,' said the voice. 'Thanks,' I said. And then the voice moved away from the car and became an old vagabond, one of those retiree-types who walk around with a metal detector in search of lost keys and old coins and bottle caps. I watched him as he crossed to the other side of the street, where he boarded the J bus heading west, and then the bus disappeared into the glare of the sun. 'Did you see that guy, Ramirez,' I asked. But Ramirez was just waking up. He laughed. 'You must have been dreaming, same as me,' he said. He hadn't seen a thing."

"**August 24, 1981. Monday, 2:45 PM**. We can hardly believe our eyes. How is it we have never heard of this pink stucco palace, this behemoth that would look more at home on a slice of beachfront than tucked away amid the grime and perpetual poverty of Allapattah? Even from the parking lot you are overwhelmed by the looming, faded elegance of the building. It is almost surreal, the impressions I am getting, strange, conflicting images, an endless parade of world class musicians, the wealthy, cultured, refined citizens of Miami in the audience, but also a vagabond collection of murderers and drug dealers and thieves and international spies, all of them cutting loose to the groove, the booze flowing freely, vast quantities of booze, a truce between opposing layers of society, at least for an evening. Ramirez stops a moment to admire the brass horse head hitching posts. I am already up

the steps, but I have also stopped. I am lost in a labyrinth
of idle thoughts and pointless conjecture. I am staring at the
stained-glass window above the door, a sun tangled up with
a moon amid a gallery of stars, and suddenly I feel as if the
door in front of me is a doorway to another dimension. I am
struck by the incongruity of La Campana. That it even exists
at all seems to contradict everything I know about reality.
Then Ramirez breaks my reverie with a hearty slap on the
back, a little jovial laughter, the camaraderie of two explorers
stumbling about in the dark, and we push our way inside. The
lobby is dimly lit, a weak, syrupy light. The source of the light
is impossible to pinpoint. Ramirez gives a low, appreciative
whistle, though just what he is appreciating he doesn't say.
Then we head over to the bar. The lighting in the bar is better
than in the lobby. It seems impossibly bright by comparison.
A steady stream of sunlight is pouring through the windows
along the far wall and bouncing off the mirror that runs the
length of the mahogany counter.   There is a fat man behind
the bar and two unsavory characters sitting at the counter,
drinking shots and trading jokes with the fat man."

  "**August 24, 1981. Monday, 2:52 PM.** The fat man's name
is Herminio Arréllaga. He is standing at the elbow of the bar
near the entrance, about twenty feet from the two unsavory
characters. He says he has been tending bar here since 1979.
Then he asks if we are thirsty. Ramirez smiles and lays the
card of Oscar Garcia Raimundi on the mahogany counter.
Ramirez asks Herminio how well he knows Oscar. Herminio
picks up the card and scrutinizes it. He holds it up so it
catches a beam of sunlight and then shrugs a shrug of indifference and hands it back to Ramirez. 'I know him well enough,'
he says. 'But I did not know he had such a fancy looking
card.' It is at this point that the two unsavory characters get
up from their barstools and walk over to us. They do not seem
surprised that we are there. They do not seem anxious. If
anything, they seem relaxed, as if they had just received good
news after a long drought. They are talking as they walk, a
rapid machine-gun volley of words slicing through the air.
'So you have brought news of Oscar? We thought that's why
you might be here. Where did you find him?' says the one.

'Yes, and how did you find him so quickly?' says the other. 'Was he holed up with some floozy? Or did he get stopped by some traffic cop?' says the one. 'Yeah, how did the dumb fuck give himself away?' says the other one. 'Well, serves him right whatever the circumstances. But what were we to do?' says the one. 'You're damn right, ten-thousand dollars is a lot of money,' says the other one. 'Did he confess yet?' says the one. 'I hope you guys throw away the key,' says the other. 'If he needed the money he could have asked. We would have loaned him whatever he needed,' says the one. 'Maybe my brother would have loaned him the money. But I'm not so sure I would have been so compassionate,' says the other one. 'Brother, Oscar has been with us since we opened our doors. La Campana wouldn't be La Campana without Oscar. Besides, he's family. You don't just abandon family,' says the one. 'Yes, Brother, but to steal from the hand that feeds your mouth. That is very difficult to digest. I do not think I will be able to forgive him as easily as you have,' says the other one."

"**August 24, 1981. Monday, 3:30 PM.** The two unsavory characters are Héctor and Miguel Velázquez, brothers, obviously, they might even be twins. They are not pleasant to look at. They have dark, leathery, crusted over skin, as if they were the victims of some diabolical experiment conducted by the CIA. Ramirez thinks they are ex-military. He thinks they took part in covert operations in Nicaragua, Chile, or Bolivia. I'm not sure where he comes up with this stuff. They are not bad fellows once you get to talking with them. And yet there is something about them that strikes me as off-center. I can't quite put my finger on it yet. But I get the feeling that Héctor is one step away from being locked away in an insane asylum. He is cheerful enough on the surface, happy-go-lucky, robustly happy, but just beneath this thin veneer of ultra-normalcy there lurks a menacing, uncontrollable rage. This is the sense I get. I think if it weren't for Miguel, Héctor would have died in a hail of bullets long ago. So anyway, we talked for about half an hour. Héctor said Oscar managed the club for them. They had bought the property in 1978 from a man named Luis Sarabia, a Cuban exile. Oscar was already working at the club as the manager so they kept him on.

Oscar was also a Cuban exile, but he had entered the country illegally. He had an appetite for fine dining, pretty women, diamond rings, and fast cars, the lifestyle of a gangster. He was unrestrained in his appetite, so he was always in debt, always in need of money. Okay, so much for background. I asked them when they had last seen Oscar. 'About three o'clock Friday afternoon,' Miguel said. 'We wanted to speak to him about Friday night.' 'What about it,' I said. 'Normally you can't get a seat at La Campana on a Friday or Saturday night,' said Miguel. 'I mean we really pack them in. But for some reason we never do very well when there's a boxing match on television. So there was no show on Friday night. We cancelled it as soon as we knew about the Gómez fight. I don't remember how we found out. I guess that was about three months ago. We were going to keep the bar open anyway, just in case someone from the neighborhood wanted something to drink. But we told Oscar he could close up shop whenever he felt like it. I mean there's no sense in staying open if nobody comes in.' 'Okay, okay, so what were you doing Friday evening?' I said. 'Well, we rarely get away on the weekends, so we decided to head down to Little Havana,' said Miguel. 'A friend of ours just opened a small pizzeria on West Flagler. It's called Eduardo's.' I nodded. I had heard of the place. It had only been open a few months, but the guy made really good pizza, even *The Miami Herald* said so. 'Where'd you go after Eduardo's?' I said. 'We came back here,' Miguel said. 'We got back about midnight. I went into the bar and started chatting with Herminio. My brother went upstairs to the office. I asked Herminio where Oscar was and he said Oscar had left a few minutes before seven. Herminio didn't know why. Then my brother came running into the bar. He said somebody had broken into the petty cash strong box and cleaned us out. Ten-thousand dollars. We called the police and reported the stolen money. The next morning an Officer Andersen showed up and took our statement. He didn't look too happy. He had been driving around for thirty minutes trying to find this hellhole. That's the exact word he used. Hellhole.' I looked at Ramirez and we both shook our heads. We both knew Andersen. He's a pussy and a tight-assed prick rolled into one. 'By that point we were fairly certain that

Oscar was the culprit,' Miguel said. That's pretty much all the
Velázquez brothers had to say. We didn't tell them that Oscar
was dead. I guess we were being cagey. We asked them if
they had a photo of Oscar. We said we didn't like to use mug
shots for the newspaper guys unless we had to. Miguel pulled
out a photo of Oscar and some red-headed floozy like he was
just waiting for us to ask. The photo was taken in front of La
Campana on a summer evening with the neon lights flashing.
It was a publicity shot. Miguel handed me the photo and said
we could keep it. We told them to stay in town for the next
week or so, just in case we had any more questions. Héctor
asked us if we had found the money. We told him yes, but the
money had been impounded as evidence, this was standard
procedure, but they'd get it back once the investigation had
been concluded, but that wouldn't be too long, this was a
fairly routine case. We told them the same tired shit we tell
everyone else. I mean the words just came pouring out like we
had no control whatsoever. We were like two degenerate and
prodigal parrots spewing out this fucking river of sewage."

   "**August 24, 1981. Monday, 6:30 PM.** We head back
out to the Carvel ice cream store on Kendall to speak to the
assistant manager, Eric Valera, to see if he remembers seeing
our dead guy buying an ice cream cone. Eric Valera is a trip.
I mean he's a fucking fruitcake of a kid and he looks like a
stoner to boot. Ramirez thinks I should cut him a break, that
he's just a wide-eyed dopey kid like any kid. Okay, maybe
so. But it's hard to believe he's the assistant manager of
anything, and after the story he tells me and Ramirez, even
Ramirez agrees. The kid says he remembers 'the suspect in
question.' That's just how he puts it. Like he's reading lines
for a goddamn TV show. He says he remembers the guy
because he never before met anyone wearing a white linen
suit and a white Panama hat. Okay, so I have to give him that.
He says the guy ordered an ice cream cake and slapped a
hundred-dollar bill on the counter and said Valera could keep
the change, and then he asked that Valera bring it out to his
car. Not one of the ice cream girls. The guy wanted Valera,
which the kid admits was kind of weird. The kid says he was
thinking maybe the guy wanted a blow job or something right

there in the parking lot, but he didn't wink or smile or show
any emotion whatsoever when he made the request, so then
the kid figured maybe his first impression had been wrong. So
the kid brings the ice cream cake out to the car. He says it was
a purple color kind of car, a really old model. He says with
the way the lights from the ice cream store were shining on
the hood it was sort of glowing like some kind of purple star.
He says the guy was sitting behind the wheel just staring out
through the windshield like a zombie or a robot or something.
Then he says when he gave the guy the cake, he realized there
were two figures sitting in the back seat. 'I couldn't see them
very well from the glare of the lights,' he says, 'but I could see
well enough.' But then his story loses all touch with reality.
He gets very quiet and starts speaking in a soft, feathery,
whispery voice. 'You're going to think I'm crazy when I say
this. But the two creatures in the back seat weren't even
human. They were two enormous dark shapes sucking up all
the light, like something out of *The Twilight Zone*. That's why
I couldn't really see them. I'm pretty sure they were demonic
angels with their wings folded over, and they were speaking
in this strange, screechy, whistling, clicking language, like
dolphins or porpoises or killer whales. All I can say is I was
shitting in my pants and I couldn't get away from the car
fast enough. I ran back inside and looked back to see if they
were coming after me, but they didn't get out of the car. Then
the guy you're looking for drove away. But here's the really
strange part. The two demons weren't there anymore. I mean
I could see clearly at that point into the back seat and the
back seat was empty. I don't know, man, I was pretty weirded
out. But I wouldn't hold my breath waiting on that guy to
show up. I'm pretty sure those two creatures had their hooks
into him pretty good. They probably sucked out his brain or
something.' That's what the kid told us. Eric Valera. His eyes
were bulging with every ludicrous word, like tiny supernovas
about to burst. But you could tell he was dead serious. He was
sincere. I thought Ramirez was about to bust a gut. What a
fucking load of crap."

"**August 24, 1981. Monday, 9:30 PM.** Some home-brew
kind of café on 8th Street in Little Havana. I don't even know

how we got here. Ramirez says they serve pretty good food, and anything you want to drink. So that's where we are. Ramirez orders some spicy beef hash and fried potatoes and a bottle of beer and I order the same. Our waitress is pretty sexy. She's wearing a light breezy chiffon skirt, and when she walks by you can see the cheeks of her brown ass wiggling to beat the band. She's flaunting the kind of ass you just want to reach out and grab. It's still pretty crowded for a Monday evening. The beers come first. We probably have three or four before the food comes. Then we begin to eat, and in between bites we start talking about Eric Valera. Ramirez agrees that the kid is stark raving mad. He agrees that it's going to be next to impossible to sift through what actually happened when our dead friend, Oscar Garcia Raimundi, headed off in search of an ice cream cone and what the kid at the ice cream store remembers. But then Ramirez says the oddest thing. He says we only see the madness of Eric Valera from our own perspective. Yes, it seems to be as debilitating and profound as the madness of any inmate in any asylum. Then again, not everything is what it seems to be. I try to get my two cents in. I try to tell Ramirez he's full of shit. But his voice just rolls over mine. He asks me if I know what day it is. I tell him of course I know what day it is. I'm not that drunk, not yet. But Ramirez only laughs, as if I've already given him the wrong answer. He asks me if I know the significance of this date, the 24th of August. I tell him I could give two shits about the significance of the date, but he ignores my vitriolic response. He says August 24th is the day when that great literay madman don Quixote enters the cave of Montesino, falls into a dream-like trance, and comes face to face with the dark secret that caused his madness in the first place. You mean the guy in the book, I say. Yes, he says. Then he says August 24th also marks the third day of Leonora Carrington's own battle with madness. I say who the hell is Leonora Carrington. He says she was an artist, a surrealist painter. I say it figures. He says in late August of 1940 she left Paris to go to Spain in an effort to escape the Nazis. She had to leave her lover behind, a German painter named Max Ernst, another surrealist. She crossed over the border on the 22nd of August. She later said she saw dead bodies everywhere. Some were hanging from the branches of trees like icicles dripping. Some were draped over rocks and the wheels of overturned vehicles like so many carelessly forgotten overcoats. Others were sticking straight up out of the ground like pins from a pin cushion, pale yellow, twisted faces, rigid in the deformity of death. By August 24th she was certifiably mad, at least the Spanish authorities thought so, so they had her committed to an asylum on that date. No wonder, I say. She sounds certifiable. But Ramirez just smiles. Do you know the writer Julio Cortázar, he says. I say I don't know him. Ramirez doesn't miss a beat. According to Cortázar, he says, August 24th is one of the three days when the earth opens up to the cosmos, to God, if you will, and in those moments it is possible to slip into another dimension or another level of consciousness. Cortázar doesn't say what the other two days are, but he is definitely on the money about the 24th of August. This is what Ramirez says. I'm just shaking my head. I don't know how to respond, and Ramirez realizes I don't know how to respond, so he stops eating his spicy hash, rinses his mouth with a little beer, and then looks me squarely in the eyes. 'What I'm trying to suggest, my unbelieving friend, is that Eric Valera may have tapped into the mind of God on this day the 24th of August, which means that everything he said was the absolute truth.' Some days there is just no way to adequately respond to Ramirez.

   "**August 25, 1981. Tuesday, 10:30 AM.** I didn't get much sleep last night. I should have gone right to sleep. I was drunk enough. But I kept thinking about what Ramirez said about Eric Valera's madness. I mean for once Ramirez sounded like he actually knew what he was talking about, especially that part about the cosmos and God. Anyway, I kept thinking about what Ramirez said the whole night. Pretty damn depressing when you don't believe in God. Then at 6 AM it started raining again. Fuck that. Fuck a lot of things. I guess I'm in a sour mood. I just spent an hour with Leon Vallejo going over his preliminary autopsy report. Bob Nordyke was also there. Leon began his autopsy 10 PM Sunday evening. He worked through the night and finished about 4 AM. He's a strike while the iron's hot kind of guy. But the report doesn't really help all that much. I mean there's no smoking gun.

Still, it gives a pretty good indication of what happened to poor Oscar Garcia Raimundi. To summarize Leon's findings: the dead guy was of average height (68 inches) and weight (roughly 155 lbs, hard to be precise after a guy's been dead for a couple of days). Age somewhere between 49 and 54. Brownish gray hair, slightly wavy. The eyes are wide open, brown doe eyes, like he didn't see it coming until it was too late. The pupils are 0.4 cm. The corneas are cloudy. There are ligature marks on the guy's ankles and wrists. The marks on the guy's ankles are more pronounced and show significant bruising (what Leon calls petechial hemorrhaging), as if the guy had been hung upside down. The marks on the guy's wrists are less pronounced but also show signs of bruising. So the guy was tied up before he died. Oddly, there are no defensive injuries on the forearms, which means the guy didn't put up a fight. There are patchy bluish-black discolorations (what Leon calls *post-mortem hypostasis*) on the backs of the arms and the upper back and shoulders, which suggests that the body had been hanging upside down for quite a while. The small intestine contained remnants of a partially digested semi-solid mass, so death occurred maybe five hours after Oscar had eaten his last meal. (It was not clear if this last meal contained ice cream.) Rigor mortis has already passed. The skin has already taken on a marbled appearance. Blowfly larva are present in the moist cavities of the dead body. Leon says the guy died between 10 PM Friday and midnight. Leon says the guy was killed somewhere other than the park and then his body was moved. There is a deep gash in the guy's neck. I ask Leon if they cut the guy's throat and then tipped him upside down so that his blood would drain out. Leon smiles and says he only reports facts. He says interpreting facts is my department. Good old Leon. The incision in the dead guy's neck cuts through the skin, the superficial fascia, the sternocleidomastoid muscle (both left side and right side), the carotid artery (again, both left and right sides), and the trachea. I mean it's a monstrous incision. The length of the gash is 14 cm. The width is 4 cm. The depth is 5 cm on the left side and 4 cm on the right side. It's a hell of a gash. But there is a lack of hemorrhage along the incision, which according to Leon means that the guy's throat was cut several hours after

he was dead, which means that his blood had already begun
to pool, so even if the killers had tipped him upside down,
very little blood would have made its way to the incision
point. The puncture wounds in the guy's hands (dead center
of each palm) and through the top of the guy's skull also show
a lack of hemorrhage. There are some signs of asphyxia: a
slight (Leon says very slight, easy to miss) bruising of the lips
and around the mouth, the eyelids are dotted with petechial
hemorrhages, there is a slight swelling of the lungs with
scattered areas of *atelectasis* (Leon's word), which means some
of the tiny air sacs in the lungs had collapsed. But the signs of
asphyxia are inconclusive, at least in terms of fixing the cause
of death. Leon is a perfectionist. He says the only thing he
is waiting on is the preliminary toxicology report, which he
hopes to have by Friday."

"**August 26, 1981. Wednesday, 11:00 AM.** Another
drizzly morning. I am meeting with the Crime Scene
Investigators, Martin Lorenz, Randy Graeff, and sweet little
Natalie Henderson, to go over their preliminary report. What
a fucking waste of daylight, even if it is raining. They know
it. I know it. But we gotta go through the steps. Of course it's
nobody's fault. The killers, whoever they are, didn't leave
behind a damn thing. Lorenz says they bagged everything
that looked promising (they were very hopeful) within a
thirty-six-foot radius of the rocket tower. The stub of a Cuban
cigar, a silvery looking cigarette case with the words *Cuba
Libre!* on it, blue cloth fibers they plucked off the dead guy's
jacket, several strands of hair (also from the dead guy's jacket),
green bottle glass fragments they found scattered about, as if
someone had smashed a bottle or two against the rocket tower,
a couple of empty, unsmashed green bottles of *El Presidente*,
a pool of some sort of cream-colored, viscous fluid, obviously
diluted by the rain, that they found beneath the rocket tower,
a couple of mangled tube socks, a plaster cast of a footprint,
and a plaster cast of a muddy skid mark of a tire track they
found in the grass over by the crepe myrtles (the only bit of
potential evidence they identified outside the bubble of the
thirty-six foot radius). An analysis of the evidence didn't
reveal much. The Cuban cigar could have been purchased in

Little Havana or on the street or by someone who had recently
been to Cuba. The silvery looking cigarette case is not even
silver plate. Martin calls it German silver. He says it is a
mixture of nickel, copper and zinc. It is the kind of junk item
you can buy in any drugstore at the beach. The phrase *Cuba
Libre* is actually a decal. Parts of it had already rubbed off.
There are no fingerprints on the cigarette case. The blue cloth
fibers are polyester, probably from a suit, but it is impossible
to be definitive. The strands of hair are from someone with
long red hair. There is nothing else to say about the hair. The
green bottle glass fragments are probably all that is left of
two bottles of *El Presidente* beer, which makes sense given the
proximity of the two unsmashed bottles. There is no way to
tell where the beer had been purchased or if it is in any way
connected to the death of Oscar Garcia Raimundi. There is no
telling how long the bottles and bottle fragments have been
in the park. There are also no fingerprints. The cream-colored
viscous fluid was identified as human fecal matter mixed
with mud. No telling how long that degenerate deposit has
been hiding in the shadows beneath the rocket tower jungle
gym, waiting for our Crime Scene Investigators to scoop it up
and bag it as evidence. The mangled tube socks were actually
filled with cotton wadding, obviously damp from the rain. The
socks are covered with bite marks from what are most likely
canine teeth. Probably a dog's chew toy that had been lost or
abandoned. The footprint is very small, a child's tennis shoe
or sandal or Mary Jane. It is next to impossible to tell with a
child's shoe. The skid mark was only four feet long, which
they said made it difficult (meaning impossible) to determine
the direction the vehicle had been traveling. And there was
only a single skid mark anyway, as if it had been made by a
motorcycle. But it wasn't a motorcycle tire, and it wasn't the
kind of tire you'd find on a motocross bike either. The width
of the track was eight inches. The tread was an 'S' pattern
tread. It is the kind of tire you find on a golf cart. So maybe
the killers used a golf cart to transport the body to the rocket
tower playground. But why would they stop at the crepe
myrtles? It could just as easily have been a gardener using a
modified golf cart as a utility truck, a gardener who had some
business with the crepe myrtles. Except neither Miami Dade

Parks maintenance staff nor the South Miami Parks maintenance staff use modified golf carts. They drive around in small
utility trucks. Maybe it was some guy from the neighborhood
with a golf cart who just wanted to whack around a few golf
balls, just to kill a few hours, and Washington Park was the
closest bit of green. Who the fuck knows? Maybe it was a kid
with a Big Wheel."

"**August 28, 1981. Friday, 3:30 PM.** The rain has finally
stopped. Not even the inconclusive results of the toxicology
report can dampen my spirits. Oscar Garcia Raimundi was
fucking out-of-his-mind blitzed. Leon says he's lucky he didn't
die of alcohol poisoning. But that was it, just the alcohol.
There were no other chemicals in his bloodstream when he
died, no mysterious poisons, nothing, so the precise cause of
death is still a mystery."

"**August 31, 1981. Monday, 7:00 AM.** I woke up at 5:30
and it was drizzling, but only a little, and by 6:30 the skies
had cleared. I don't usually get up so early. I am more likely
to go to bed at five in the morning then get up with the sun.
There were only a few other guys on the second floor when I
got to the station. Just my luck the Captain was one of them.
I ran into him in the hallway outside the can, but it was not
an accident. The Captain was looking for me. I knew he had
already read Leon's preliminary autopsy report and the CSI
report and the preliminary toxicology report, and he knew
that I knew. He asked me how long before I wrapped things
up and moved on to the next case. He said there were plenty
of cases to keep me busy. I said I was almost finished. I told
him I needed to drop by a pizzeria called Eduardo's to check
out an alibi, and he gave me a sort of noncommittal nod. Then
I told him about the article in the dead guy's wallet, but I
could see he wasn't convinced. He asked me if I really thought
I was going to pick up the trail of the killers by going to an
offshore speedboat race at Sunny Isles on Labor Day Weekend.
I told him that you could make any theory seem ludicrous
if you wanted to. I told him I wanted to head up there on
Saturday and ask around, see if anyone knew our dead guy
before he was dead. I told him if nothing panned out then the

final report would be on his desk the following week. He gave me a strangely sympathetic look, but he didn't say anything right away. He was just regarding me. Then he seemed to slip through a door to another dimension. 'Sure,' he said. 'Go to the beach on Saturday, but don't drink too much on the Department's dime. And make sure you take Ramirez along.' Then he walked away. Fuck that. That's what I was thinking. Fuck the Captain. But I didn't say a word."

"**September 2, 1981. Wednesday, 1:30 PM.** Me and Ramirez head to Eduardo's pizzeria. The shop is on West Flagler, a few blocks from the John Bosco Catholic church. It's a two-story corner building painted yellow with orange trim and a plate glass window facing the street. Part of the window is decorated with a happy pizza chef with a white chef's hat and a phone number to call for delivery. An orange awning runs the length of the window. The telephone number in the window is also on the awning in huge block numbers. You cannot miss the telephone number. We stand in the shade of the awning before we go in, peering through the window. It is a hot sunny day with a bright blue Miami sky and the place is packed. Every table is occupied, and there is a line at the counter that extends out through the door to the sidewalk. Eduardo is by the register shouting orders to a kid working the pizza oven. The kid is a flurry of motion, shoving uncooked pizzas in with a giant wooden spatula, sliding the cooked ones onto trays or into boxes. A couple of girls take turns delivering the trays. Eduardo is in charge of the boxes. It seems like Eduardo needs to hire more help. I slide up to the register and flash my badge discreetly. Nobody seems to notice me except Eduardo, who looks me squarely in the eyes and smiles like we are old friends. 'Come, come,' he says. 'I have been waiting for you.' Eduardo is a fat, happy, mid-dle-aged man, about the age of our dead guy, happy brown eyes, thick, curly black hair, a thick moustache. A stereotypical figure behind the counter. He shouts something into the roiling, doughy atmosphere of the pizza shop. One of the girls materializes out of a cloud of flour dust and takes over the register. Eduardo ushers us into a tiny backroom office which doubles as a bathroom, which is probably a health code violation, but I don't give a fuck. He wipes his hands on his apron and then shakes our hands vigorously. His hands are slightly damp from perspiration. We tell him we're investigating a string of robberies in the neighborhood. We ask if he was in his shop this past Friday night. He smiles a broad, confident smile and says he was in the shop. He is always in the shop. It is his shop, after all. Where else would he be? We ask him if anything unusual happened Friday evening. For a moment his body tenses. He looks suddenly bewildered, as if he is trying to remember a speech he has spent hours rehearsing, or perhaps he is being bombarded by a series of seemingly pleasant images from the past that when seen as a whole reveal some sinister truth. Then he relaxes and says 'Sure, Friday, that was the night of the Gómez fight, we were watching the fight. I set up a tiny television right here on the counter. It was a slow night, not as busy as it is now. I let everyone else go home. But my friends were here. Héctor and Miguel Velázquez. They own a club up in Allapattah so I almost never see them. But they came for a visit on Friday night. They showed up around six-thirty. We watched the fight and drank and talked. They will vouch that I was here. They left a little before midnight. After that I closed up and went upstairs to bed.'"

"**September 5, 1981. Saturday, 2:15 PM.** Finally, a weekend full of sunshine. Seems like it's been forever. The speedboat race at Sunny Isle's Beach is in full swing. All of the motel parking lots along Collins Avenue are jammed full, from the pier all the way north to 183rd Street. We park in the lot of the Sahara Motel and walk the mile and a half to the Newport, which is the official race headquarters. I don't mind the walk to tell you the truth. It's bright and sunny and hot, and everywhere you look there are babes bouncing around in the skimpiest bikinis you'd ever hope to see. And of course there are vendors all over the place selling everything from beer to barbecue to racing souvenirs to sunglasses. It's a hell of a party. A couple of steel drum bands here and there. Or maybe the same one. Music blasting away from every hotel along the beach and from the jukeboxes of every restaurant and hotel bar and hole-in-the wall dive along Collins Avenue and the steady droning buzz of the speedboats and people shouting

and laughing and joking around and sirens in the distance. We
don't get to the Newport until after four. We talk to a few
racers hanging out with a beer vendor up by the pier and we
show them a photo of Oscar, but they don't know him. But
they tell us to talk with a guy named Frankie Dennis. They say
if anyone here knows this guy it's Frankie. He's one of the big
shots with the Offshore Power Boat Racing Association. They
were the guys that put this race together. They have a trade-
show tent up by the hotel with posters and pamphlets and '*I
Love Speedboat Racing*' buttons and a VCR hooked up to a
small color television so you can watch footage of old races.
We talk with Frankie for a while. He's got curly brown hair
and he's wearing khaki shorts and a yellow and green
Hawaiian shirt and he has a tan that won't quit. He's passing
out pamphlets right and left and talking up a storm about
speedboats in general and Miami in particular. He's also
wearing a 24K gold chain and is flashing a Rolex, so you know
he's pretty well fixed. He's the kind of guy you'd think would
be sporting a motorcycle moustache, like Tom Selleck in
Magnum P. I., but he isn't. Frankie takes a long hard look at
the picture we show him, but then he shakes his head like he
is truly, sincerely disappointed with his poor memory and
says if he ever met the guy he doesn't remember. Then he
shoves a pamphlet and a couple of buttons into my hands and
goes over to talk with a bevy of half-naked Miller Lite girls
who have been admiring Frankie's watch from afar. The
Miller Lite girls are so excited as Frankie approaches that
several of them bounce out of their tops. We talk with a few
more racing types down by the makeshift grandstand set up
on the beach. One of those aluminum jobs. Then we head back
up to the pier and we go all the way to the end to watch the
boats for a while. I don't know how long we're there. Maybe
an hour. At some point we put on the buttons. All the while
we're watching the boats we're drinking beer. Then all of a
sudden Frankie is standing right beside us. The boats have
stopped racing. The Miller Lite girls are long gone. Frankie
invites us into the hotel for a drink and we oblige him. It's not
much of a bar, but it'll do. When the drinks arrive (whiskey
sours) Frankie starts right in talking about organizing a race
between the Keys and Cuba. He says the Bureau of Cuban

Tourism is working tirelessly to promote such a race. They say
it would be a good thing for Cuba. 'You mean a good thing for
Castro,' says Ramirez. But Frankie isn't interested in talking
politics. He nods politely, expertly, without any hidden
agenda whatsoever, and says he thinks the race will happen
within a couple of years. 'You wait and see,' he says. Then he
smiles a reassuring smile and orders another round of whiskey
sours. It is eight o'clock before we start back to the Sahara.
Neon lights are everywhere. Purples and oranges and aquamarines. All of the motels are lit up like postcards. And that is
that, as they say. It looks for sure like my theory about the
speedboat race is a bust. It's like a door closing. But on our
way back the door is all of sudden thrust wide open. We
haven't gone more than half a mile when we realize how
hungry we are, so we stop in at a glitzy diner called Wolfie's
Rascal House. We grab two seats at the counter. We are sitting
where the counter curves so we have an excellent view of the
front door. I order the fried scallops and Ramirez orders a
Halibut steak. We are just about to dig in when we hear a
familiar voice say 'Will you look who's pounding the pavement at the beach? What are you doing so far from home,
Detective?' followed by a robust hearty laugh, which is followed quickly by a hearty (the word meaty also comes to
mind) clapping of a hand on my back, and I turn and look up
and there staring at me with a happy, friendly, confident smile
is Héctor Velázquez himself. For some reason I am not surprised. Then I realize that Héctor is not surprised either. He
sits down next to me, right at the elbow of the counter so
whenever I look up I can't help but see his happy-go-lucky
disfigured face, and orders beef tongue with creamed spinach.
He says it's the best thing on the menu. He says whenever he
eats beef tongue he feels like an Orisha god at the receiving
end of an African ritual. It is hard to tell if he is serious or
not. He doesn't give anything away, at least not for free. That
is the impression I get. Not unless he wants to. A few minutes
later his brother Miguel joins us. Miguel doesn't say a word,
but it is clear he is not happy with Héctor. But it is just as
clear that Héctor is the man in charge. Miguel takes a seat next
to Ramirez. We are like three prisoners sitting on death row,
me, Ramirez and Miguel. Miguel broods heavily over the

menu for a while and then orders a corned beef sandwich. It is
a bizarre dinner on many levels. For one thing, the buzz I have
been enjoying for the better part of the evening evaporates in
an instant. I have rarely if ever been so alert. Naturally the
conversation focuses on speedboat racing. Apparently the
Velázquez brothers have been racing for years. Héctor says
they got their start in 1965. They were just kids. They were
just twenty years old and they didn't know shit. They were
working for Southern Air Transport in those days. I look at
Ramirez, but he's not really listening. I realize the coded
nature of this conversation is sailing right past his young
Hispanic ears. What a fucking pinhead. It's common knowledge, at least if you're in law enforcement in Miami, that
Southern Air Transport has been a CIA front since the 50s. So
either the Velázquez brothers had once worked for the CIA, or
maybe they are still on the company payroll, or they want us
to think they are. I catch Héctor giving me a thoughtful look
as the words come spewing out of his mouth, as if he is trying
to gauge my reaction. But I don't react. I just let him talk. But
I am committing every word to memory so I can go over it
later. The Velázquez brothers own three boats, a 38-foot
Bertram and two Cigarettes. They didn't do as well as they
had hoped today. They finished seventh. But they don't mind.
They just enjoy being out on the water. They don't even finish
every race. Three years ago they sank within sight of the
finish line during the Pelican Harbor Challenge. 'That was a
hell of a race,' says Héctor. 'Surreal, that's what it was. The
course was littered with floating coconuts, and then for some
reason my brother here tried to fish one out with a net. We're
going full speed and he's trying to get a coconut. Why there
was a net in the back of the boat I don't know? Anyway,
Miguel lost his balance and flipped into the water, so naturally
I had to retrieve him. What else is a brother supposed to do? I
wasn't going to let him drown. But he was lucky he didn't
break his neck, and I told him so, but he just said get back
behind the wheel. Well, we were pretty much out of the race
by that point, I mean we were fucked, but what the hell, I
thought, so I gunned it, I mean I really let her rip, and by God
if we didn't close the gap, but then the engine overheated, and
then it blew sky high, and just like that our chances of even

finishing dropped to absolute zero. Yeah, it was surreal. We
were twenty-five yards from the finish line, but we were
drifting the wrong way. The drunken bastards in the grandstand were going wild. Somebody yelled out for us to grab a
paddle, like we were in a fucking fiberglass canoe. Then just
like that we sink. The explosion that took out the engine had
also opened up the bottom of the hull. We started taking
water, only we didn't know it at first. And then it was too late.
We sank like a fucking cannonball.' I have to say Héctor tells a
pretty good story, with just the right balance between action
and narrative commentary, even if the whole sinking at the
finish line climax sounds fairly implausible. Then the dinner is
finished and me and Ramirez are heading towards the register. Héctor turns in his seat and calls out to us. He is only ten
feet away and yet he calls out like he is standing on a distant
shore. He says in his robust voice of a self-indulgent maniac,
without any apology for disturbing the dinners of the other
patrons, that they are out on the water at least once a week,
usually in the afternoon. He says their boats are faster than
the Coast Guard, faster even than the drug runners coming up
from Cuba. Some day we should come out on the water with
them just to experience the extraordinary speed. Money can't
buy that kind of pleasure. Money can't even come close. It is a
blatantly manipulative thing to say. Everyone in the joint can
hear him clear as a bell, and yet oddly, everyone keeps their
faces focused on their own plates. Then Héctor turns back
towards his brother, who has moved two seats closer, and
suddenly it seems like me and Ramirez don't exist at all. We
are just dust particles dancing in a stray beam of starlight. I
pay the bill, but at the register I notice a souvenir rack of
silvery cigarette cases. The cases all say Cuba Libre. It is an
odd coincidence, but perhaps not so odd. I buy one just for the
hell of it. $5.99 plus tax. Then I follow Ramirez out the door.
Only then do I realize that we are still wearing those idiotic 'I
Love Speedboat Racing' buttons. I feel as if we have barely
escaped from someone else's dream."

"**September 9, 1981. Wednesday, 12:45 PM.** I met with a
friend of mine from the FBI, Special Agent Edmundo Lagunas.
I've known Lagunas for years. We trade favors back and forth.

He's a very clean-cut looking guy. Dark hair, almost black, and very short, almost military style, and a squared-off jaw. He's always wearing a light tan suit, a white, crisply pressed shirt, and a thin brown tie. In a word, he is fastidious. I had called him up first thing Monday morning. I said I needed whatever background he had on two unsavory nightclub owners with an interest in speedboats. I almost never give Lagunas the straight dope right off the bat, so I didn't say who exactly I was talking about. I wanted to gauge his mood first. He got very quiet, as if he had withdrawn into another dimension, and I thought, oh, well, he's not going to be much help. But then his voice returned to the line with a manipulative vigor. He asked me if I was talking about Héctor and Miguel Velázquez. I said I was. He asked me what made me think he knew anything. I said nothing in particular. They just seemed like the kind of characters the FBI would know something about. He asked me about the nature of my inquiry. I said it was part of a murder investigation. He retreated again after that. He was silent for a full five minutes. Nothing but the breezy wind of static. Then the line went dead. Fifteen minutes later my phone started ringing and it was Edmundo. He didn't identify himself. It actually sounded like he was trying to disguise his voice, which is fucking hilarious. He said 'The Marine Stadium. Noon. Wednesday.' Then once again the line went dead. The Marine Stadium was an odd choice for a meeting. Mostly the stadium was for boat races or concerts. I saw Loggins & Messina at the Stadium. But in the middle of the week there wouldn't be many people around, a few tourists maybe, a few office workers from downtown sitting in the grandstand, eating a bag lunch, looking out at the water, but not many. If anyone were watching us, well, they could draw their own conclusions. I got there at noon on the dot and climbed three-quarters of the way up towards the top. I sat down in the shade in the dead center of the grandstand. There were a couple of tourists sitting halfway down in the sun, and some old guy in the front row wearing a fisherman's hat. He was pulling a bottle out of his backpack every now and then and taking a swig and putting the bottle back. There was a nice breeze blowing through the stadium, and if I hadn't come with a purpose I would have kicked back and taken a nap,

which wouldn't have been too easy since those stadium seats
were a little tight, but I was pretty tired. As it was, I watched
the boys from the Miami Rowing Club for a while, and then
they left, and then I watched the two tourists head up and
then out the back of the stadium, and I was just about to
abandon this wild goose chase myself when the wino from the
first row sat down beside me, only he wasn't a wino. He was
Lagunas. He laughed at my initial confusion, a goofy grin on
his face, but then he got right down to business. He reached
into his backpack and pulled out five large manila envelopes,
each of them stuffed with documents. He carefully placed the
envelopes in his lap.

"'I shouldn't even be talking to you, Andreu,' he said.
'But Abrahms didn't want you snooping around where you
didn't belong. He thought you might get yourself killed, and I
guess he didn't want that on his conscience.' And then: 'Don't
look at me like that. You know me well enough. I wouldn't be
here if I had a choice. But for some reason Abrahms likes you.
So here I am. I am officially unofficially here.'

"Then Lagunas opened the first of the manila envelopes
and took out several photographs, but then he paused and
gave me the oddest look. It didn't actually seem like he was
looking at me at all. It felt more like he was looking past me,
over my shoulder, as if he had just caught the flash of something sinister. Then he blinked and the trance was snapped.

"'All of this begins in Cuba,' he said.

"His voice possessed a grave, gravelly kind of authority
that you could not question. It was almost like he was narrat-
ing a documentary of events that he himself had personally
witnessed.

"'In 1936, responding to an increasing threat to our
national security from the rise of the Nazis in Germany, the
FBI created a German anti-espionage team. In those days
everyone believed the Germans would go through Cuba to
get to the United States, so we sent a lot of agents to Havana.
But when war finally broke out in 1941, the War Department
appropriated most of our funds for what they said were more
pertinent activities. Sure, they kept a few Naval Intelligence
officers in Havana to keep a lookout for German subs, but
mostly it turned into Batista's show. By 1942, virtually all

anti-espionage activities in the Caribbean came through the OSS, but Hoover wanted to keep a skeleton team in Cuba nevertheless, and Hoover did what he wanted. It was a challenge to say the least. Havana was a hotbed of German spies and Spanish Falangists in spite of what Naval Intelligence reported. What made the situation even worse was that Cuban politics was itself corrupt. You could buy the acquiescence of any Cuban Minister for a price. For a larger sum you could ensure his complete cooperation. And we were short-handed. So we had no choice, really, but to enlist the aid of the mob in keeping an eye on any suspicious activity, anything that might pose a threat.

"'In hindsight, of course, this was stupid. When the war ended, the Mafia had become an integral part of the degenerate honeycomb that was Cuban politics. In other words, we could not simply pick them up and toss them in jail. Certainly not without the help of the Cuban government. Besides, we didn't want to expose ourselves. Then in 1947 the CIA was born, which further complicated an already tense and complicated environment. We were directed to begin transitioning our anti-espionage activities to their oversight, though we did not comply right away. For one thing, the number of ex-Nazi agents in Cuba had increased, and we were the only agency who had maintained a presence there. And anyway, Hoover didn't really trust the bozos that Truman had put in charge. So we kept doing what we were doing. Then in 1950 things changed and we began recruiting a Mafia underboss named Luis Sarabia, who worked for an old-school don named Giuseppe Federico DiCarla.'

"(Here Lagunas passed me photographs of Sarabia and DiCarla. Both men looked like Hollywood movie stars from the 1940s. Sarabia sort of looked like Peter Lorre but without Peter Lorre's pouty smile. DiCarla looked like a clean-cut version of Boris Karloff.)

"'We never really understood exactly what DiCarla's role in Cuba was. We knew he was a childhood friend of Mafia Boss Salvatore Maranzano. They had both grown up on the streets of Castellammare del Golfo, in Sicily. There was some speculation that DiCarla had helped Lucky Luciano with the hit on Maranzano, but this has never been substantiated. At any rate, DiCarla was in bed with numerous Cuban politicians and government and union officials, and Sarabia was his right-hand man. Then in 1952, DiCarla's operations took a big hit when a warehouse building he owned in Havana burned to the ground. The warehouse was on San Pedro directly across from the harbor. It was the center of DiCarla's operations. Afterwards, Sarabia began what must have been a relentless pursuit of the men behind this act of sabotage, and by 1956 he had amassed quite a lot of information. He began to send us coded letters. Each letter contained a piece of the larger picture.

"'Sarabia believed a group of renegade anarchists was responsible for the destruction of the warehouse. He said most of these renegades were ex-Nazis seeking revenge, but there were also a few disgruntled Sicilian mercenaries, a few Jewish anarchists from Eastern Europe, a few home-grown Communists, and some Cuban radicals, national purists who believed that the only way to permanently secure a free and independent Cuba was to eradicate all foreign influence. It was an impossible collection of competing ideologies. You would have assumed that whatever promises had brought them together would have dissolved at the first sign of dissension. Quite frankly, these men had virtually nothing in common except for the desire to inflict great violence upon the world at large. No wonder we knew nothing about this group until Sarabia started his digging. No wonder they slipped beneath our radar. Sarabia said the ringleader of this mob of anarchists was a man named Immanuel Király, a German of Hungarian descent. He said Király had worked for the Nazi propaganda machine during the war and that he had arrived in Havana in 1947. He had even brought over some of his movie-making crew from Germany. Their purpose was to film bigwigs in compromising situations and then blackmail the poor saps. That was apparently how Király funded his entire operation. Sarabia told us that Király had only one aim: to destroy the Cuban people's faith in the Cuban government, in the Cuban political system, in the dream of Cuba itself, and so drive Cuba to the brink of absolute collapse. Király, he said, also wanted to offer up the United States as the villain in what the Cuban people would come to believe was the crime of the century. According to Sarabia, Király's people were the ones behind the Supervielle scandal. Supposedly they had managed to produce a pornographic film starring a big-shot named Manuel Fernandez Supervielle in bed with some unknown floozy. Supervielle had been elected the Mayor of Havana in 1946.'

"(At this point Lagunas handed me a photo of Supervielle, who did not, I might add, look like a movie star. He more or less resembled a clean-shaven albino walrus, which made it difficult to imagine that he had been the star of even the shoddiest of pornographic films, whether he knew he was being filmed or not. Lagunas kept right on talking.)

"'The film was discovered among Superveille's papers and personal effects shortly after his suicide, and did in fact cause quite a stir among the Cuban political establishment, though it was not widely known beyond that small inner circle.

"'Sarabia also believed that Superveille's well-publicized suicide was not a suicide, though he had no actual proof. But he became suspicious when he learned that Superveille had been killed with a Kongsberg Colt pistol. According to Sarabia, many of the men who blindly followed Király owned Kongsberg Colt pistols. Besides, Superveille didn't even own a gun. Not that he couldn't have procured one, but a Kongsberg Colt would have been an odd choice. It was just a matter of putting two and two together, that's what Sarabia said. But we were skeptical. The whole ex-Nazi, German anarchist angle sounded pretty far-fetched to us. Naturally, we didn't believe Király was involved.

"'We had first heard about Király in 1945 when our guys entered Berlin. His dossier was just one of the many dossiers of Nazi underlings that we were able to secure. From 1935 through the end of the war, Király had worked for the Department of Film, part of Germany's Ministry of Propaganda, under the direction of Karl Neumann (a photo of Neumann, who seemed to be wearing pants that were a little too tight). In other words, he had indeed been employed by the Nazi's well-oiled propaganda machine, as Sarabia had discovered. But we didn't think Sarabia knew what he was talking about. Why would Király even be in Cuba? It didn't make any sense. We thought someone was feeding Luis false information.

"'Király was brilliant at what he did. In 1936, he was attached to Colonel Wolfram von Richthofen's staff. (Photo of Richthofen, narrow face, eyes set close together, a very sour expression.) The Colonel had taken a field command with the Condor Legion, a group of volunteer German pilots, to support Franco's nationalists in the Spanish Civil War. (No photo of Franco.) Király's job was to capture the bombing of Guernica on camera. Then in 1938, after receiving a commendation from Goebbels himself for his 'unparalleled ability to capture the stoic heroism of German aviators during the battle of Guernika,' he was back in Berlin, where he worked with a variety of movie directors to produce dozens of Nazi propaganda films over the next six years. From 1938 to 1944 he worked with Karl Ritter, Gustav Ucicky, Boleslaw Barlog, Wolfgang Liebeneiner, Karl Anton, Leni Riefenstahl, Wilhelm Stöppler, the great Werner Klingler, and Max Kimmich, among other prominent Nazi directors.'

"(Only three photos, one of Riefenstahl, who had hawkish, unfeminine features and sort of looked like an angry librarian, one of Klingler, a pensive looking man with finely chiseled features who reminded me of a tax collector, and one of Karl Anton, slicked back hair, a monocle, and a bowtie.)

"'In spite of his accomplishments, however, as the war progressed, Király became less and less efficient, and his behavior became more and more erratic. There were some reports that even suggested Király was a borderline schizophrenic. He once proclaimed to a senior Nazi Party official that he was in direct communication with an alien civilization that was seeking the assistance of the Nazis to colonize the Earth. He told this official the aliens would assume the form of ancient Merovingian kings. Initially, of course, his madness was passed off as an aberrant sense of humor. But during the filming of the movie *Die Degenhardts*, which was a film about a family surviving the Allied bombing of the city of Lübeck, Király crossed an invisible line. In February 1944 he had the actors imprisoned in an abandoned bomb shelter near the Blohm & Voß shipyards in Hamburg.'

"(A photo of Hamburg after an Allied air raid.)

"'Both the shipyards and Hamburg had been practically leveled during the Allied bombing raids in 1943 and had remained the object of repeated attacks. Király left the actors in the bomb shelter for seventy-two hours, from February 19 to February 22, but he only left them food and water for two days. Coincidentally, or perhaps Király had secret sources of information and knew what was coming, Hamburg suffered through six hours of intense Allied bombing on the 20th of February, and though the objective of this raid was to smash the German aircraft industry, the shipyards were certainly fair game for any bomber that was forced to deviate from its original course. 4,200 civilians were killed during the raid. Hundreds were burned alive in inadequate bomb shelters. And while Király's actors escaped serious injury, all of them suffered from dehydration and psychosomatic stress. One said he lost his hearing as a result of the thunderous explosions. Another one later went mad and committed suicide, though probably not as a result of the air raid experiment. Király defended himself by saying the only way to be true to reality was to subject yourself to reality. But the Nazis had had enough. In spite of the success of the film, which opened to rave reviews in Lübeck on July 6, 1944, Király was sent packing. Supposedly he went to live with an uncle in Freiberg after that, but when the war ended, Király had vanished. Everyone, even his uncle, thought he had fled to Argentina. Argentina is where the ex-Nazis went. No one suspected Király had opened up shop in Cuba. It just didn't make any sense his going there.

"'In retrospect, it is quite clear that Sarabia had tried to warn us. But we ignored him. We were pursuing what we believed was the best long-term strategy for dealing with both the threat posed by this strange group of anarchists who had torched DiCarla's warehouse in '52 as well as the looming menace of the Communists. In January 1953 we began pressuring DiCarla, with the help of Sarabia, to move his operations to Miami. We were relentless with our pressure. We believed that we could use DiCarla and his Cuban contacts as a tool to sow disunity among the Communists, who always seemed to be on the verge of a coup, and to keep this mismatched collection of anarchists at bay. But we also believed that we needed DiCarla in Miami so we could keep him on a tight leash. Unfortunately, the whole thing backfired. We never realized that once DiCarla began to seriously consider moving to Miami, once he raised the issue among his inner circle, he would begin to alienate the very people we wished to connect with. This is precisely what happened. By 1956 there was a significant amount of dissension among DiCarla's people, which somehow, according to Sarabia, the anarchists took advantage of. Then in January 1957, Castro and his ragged band of revolutionaries achieved their first strategic victory when they overran the garrison at La Plata. (A photo of a young Castro.) The eastern half of Cuba was soon embroiled in a guerrilla war between Castro's forces and the army. Castro's success pushed the anarchists into a corner, which meant that they were a powder keg ready to explode. Sarabia tried to warn us of this as well. In July 1957 he sent a letter that stated in unequivocal terms that Király and his group were mobilizing for some last ditch effort to put themselves at the forefront of the political upheaval that was engulfing Cuba. He wasn't sure what they had in mind, but he also said they were underestimating the impact that Castro was and would continue to have. Of course he levied the same criticism at us. He also said the hotel where he lived was crawling with Király's men. He was certain that his phone was tapped and that he was being watched by more than one set of eyes. He had even begun to suspect his girlfriend, but that was all he said about her. He never told us who she was or why he suspected her in the first place or if he had confronted her. Sarabia only shared with us what he wanted us to act on, and clearly, the girl was off limits. My guess is he had a soft spot for this girl and wanted to protect her. But by the same token, he knew the clock was running out. You would have to say in hindsight that he knew exactly what he was doing. He must have known. He said he was certain that when Király made his move, he and DiCarla would be at risk. He said he was going to beat Király at his own game.

     "'Once again we failed to take Sarabia seriously, even though we knew without any doubt whatsoever that he was not given to sudden bouts of paranoia. By all reports, he was the coolest customer you could imagine, no matter how tight the circumstances. But we did nothing to help Sarabia. We just let the events unfold. Then in September, Sarabia wrote that DiCarla had finally agreed to move to Miami. In the first week of November he sent word that he, DiCarla, and Sarabia's protégé, Oscar Garcia Raimundi, would arrive in Key West on the *S. S. City of Havana* on Thursday, the 14th of November. We had no idea that anything had gone wrong until the boat arrived and only Raimundi was on board. (A photo of a young Oscar Garcia Raimundi, very handsome, dark hair, clean-shaven, a more pristine version of his white linen suit and Panama hat, a slightly bewildered look about him.) We later learned, although the details were somewhat sketchy, that there had been a bloodbath the night before Sarabia's boat was to depart. Apparently Király had chosen that particular week to move on DiCarla and his other targets, targets which were scattered all over Cuba, because it coincided with a weeklong celebration in honor of the Feast of San Cristóbal. It was never made clear to us why that madman chose that date or what he thought he was going to achieve. Perhaps he thought the whole country would be inebriated as a result of the festival, so he would be able to assume complete control with little resistance. Perhaps he thought he was paving the way for the Merovingian kings he believed in. Anyone who might have known is dead by now. In any case, he miscalculated. After November 1957, Király and his group fell off the face of the earth, literally. They were never heard from again. It was almost like they had never existed at all. Castro and the Communists assumed total control in 1959 and everyone else was out. But the night of November 13, 1957 was an incredibly brutal night. Thirty-three people were killed in Havana in a span of twelve hours. What a number! And that was only thirty-three we knew of. We also began to get reports of dozens of others being killed in every major city in Cuba. All of the murdered men were in some way involved in politics or with the unions or with organized crime or with all three. All of the women had close personal ties to the men. Király and his gang of anarchists even targeted children. It was incredible, the bloodshed, almost surreal.'

"(Lagunas stopped for a moment to catch his breath. He pulled out a bottle of water and took a swig and pulled out another bottle and gave it to me and I drank half the bottle without a second thought. It must have been ninety degrees, even in the shade. We looked out at the water for a while. I think Lagunas was trying to recover his voice. Then I was looking at the photos once again and trying to digest everything he had said. Then he opened the second manila envelope and pulled out another pile of photographs. They were mostly crime scene photos of the people murdered in Havana. Shocking, grisly photos. The faces of death, the various twisted poses. As Lagunas went through the names of the people who had been killed, he would hand me a photo to look at. Thirty-three photos in all. Not once did he look at the photos himself.)

"'Both DiCarla and Sarabia were killed,' he said. 'Here's a photo of Eladio de la Campa, a rising star of the Electrical Workers Union who had once worked for Prio. He was found in one of the city parks that looked out upon the Straits of Florida. His throat had been cut. Here's one of Eugenio Castellanos, Treasurer of the Gas Workers Union. He was found floating face down in the Almendares River. Here's one of Eugenio's entire family, his wife, a daughter, and twin boys. They were also killed, murdered in their beds and then their house was torched. Antonio Billiteri, a gangster who had himself been charged with the murders of dozens of Cuban citizens on his rise to the top but none of the charges had ever stuck, had apparently been bludgeoned to death with a base-ball bat and his body had been deposited among the jagged rocks along the Malecón. He had been staying at the Gran Inglaterra Hotel. There were two naked girls in their twenties in his room; both of them were maids who worked for the hotel; their throats had been slit and their bodies dumped in the bathtub. The body of Ruperto Medino Borges, a former editor of *Diario de la Marina*, was found in an alleyway a short walk from the Marina building. He had been strangled with an Argentinean bolo whip. There was a lifeless body sitting slumped over in a third-floor hallway of a building in the 200 block of Calle Obispo. The man had been shot in the chest at close range with a revolver and was sitting in a pool of his own blood; the killers had also disfigured the guy's face and cut out his tongue. Just down the hall from the disfigured guy, in an office that was a front for DiCarla's operations, a thin

wiry clerk was found leaning up against a window next to a
water cooler, his kneecaps smashed, a single bullet through
his left eye, the wall smeared with blood where his hands had
reached out to grab hold of something, anything, before he
died. The building, a magnificent example of Spanish Baroque
architecture, belonged to DiCarla. A Hungarian cinematog-
rapher named Georg Vertov, who had worked with Király
in Germany, was found dead in his penthouse apartment, a
single bullet to the forehead. Vertov's sister, Elsa, was also
found in the same apartment. She was found practically
naked, crumpled up on the floor of the bedroom. She had
been shot at point blank range. The gun had been shoved up
against the bottom of her jaw and then boom, a third of her
skull had vanished just like that. In Regla, a heavy-set woman
named Jaqueline Berroa, a friend of DiCarla's, was found dead
in a second-floor apartment above a neighborhood café, a café
which she had owned for twenty years. DiCarla's body was
found in a back room of that same café. Apparently his face
was twisted in a strange, maniacal grin, as if he had glimpsed
some greater reality at the moment of his death. DiCarla's
orderly, Ramón Salgado, who had worked the night shift at a
small hospital for the criminally insane known as Mazorra, a
Dante's *Inferno* if there ever was one, before he began working
for DiCarla, was found dead in the alleyway just outside
the Regla café. His head had been blown away. In Vedado,
Armando Portuondo, the owner of a small garage and taxi
cab company, whose clients often included several notable
members of the Mafia, was found stuffed into a garbage can
in the alleyway behind a drugstore on Linea with a plastic bag
taped over his head and his throat slit for good measure. Two
taxi cab drivers who worked for Portuondo were also casualties. The first was Jacob Taoi Amadi, a Nigerian immigrant
who had tried out for the Havana Sugar Kings baseball club
in 1954 but had failed to make the final cut. The second was
Efrain Jaramillo, a second-year law student at the University
of Havana who had grown up in Cienfuegos, the City of One
Hundred Fires, and had within three months of his arrival
in the capitol joined the FEU, an intensely militant student
organization, though whether he was spying on the FEU or
he was a committed activist is unclear. Both men were found

slumped behind the steering wheels of their taxis. They had
each been tapped just behind the ear. Their taxis were still
running when they were found. There were also five German
nationals who died that night. They did possess diplomatic
papers, but when we later brought these papers to the German
Embassy for verification, we were told they were forgeries.
According to the forged papers, the men were all supposedly
between the ages of thirty and fifty-two and had arrived in
Cuba on various dates between 1949 and 1953. Supposedly
their names were Ernst Slovogt, originally from Cologne,
Heinrich Hombach, originally from Neustadt, Detlef Kirstetter,
originally from the town of Gundelsheim, Nils Dissinger,
originally from Birkweiler, and Udo Geiszler, originally from
the small town of Klingenthal, on the border between what is
now East Germany and Czechoslovakia. The German nationals
all carried Kongsberg Colt pistols. Finally, there were seven
undocumented, unidentified and probably unidentifiable
Sicilian immigrants, Mafia soldiers most certainly, who were
also found dead at various points throughout the city. The
Sicilians all carried long-barreled rifles. The bodies of two of
the Sicilians were found in the front seat of a 1956 Chevrolet
Bel Air four-door hardtop that belonged to DiCarla. The
two had apparently been injured quite severely in a head-on
collision in front of Café Paraiso on Compostela with one of
Armando Portuondo's taxis. (A photo of the accident, with
Café Paraiso in the background.) But according to the patrons
of the café, they might have survived had not the taxi driver
walked over to their vehicle and shot them dead. No one
knows what happened to the taxi driver after that. Sarabia
himself was gunned down only a few blocks from Café
Paraiso, about half a mile from where the *S. S. City of Havana*
was moored.'

"(A photo of the *S. S. City of Havana*.)

"'To tell you the truth, we have no idea what really happened that night, or why. I am not sure we will ever be able
to untangle the net. There are so many unanswered questions.
Who was working for whom? Why were so many people from
so many various backgrounds targeted? Why did the family
of Eugenio Castellanos have to die? Were some of the victims
just in the wrong place when the bullets started flying? What

the fuck happened in Cuba that night? This is what we were asking ourselves.

"'Naturally we had a lot of questions for Raimundi when he arrived in Key West, but we did not pick him up right away. We watched him for a week. He stayed mostly downtown. Mostly he didn't leave Duval Street. He rented a room in the Southern Cross Hotel and took his meals at a tiny café a block away. Turtleburger sandwiches and coffee and a piece of apple pie for dessert. After lunch he would buy a pack of peppermint gum at Kress's dime store. Every evening he went to a nightclub called The Bamboo Room to listen to jazz and have a drinkie-pie or two or three. There was a small stage behind the bar where three guys put on quite a show. The stage contained a piano, a sax, and drums, and the guys played everything from calypso to Dixie to George Gershwin. After The Bamboo Room, Raimundi would head down to one of the waterfront dives so he could watch the strippers strut their stuff. That's how he was spending his days. We didn't know what he was waiting for. It didn't seem like he had a clue about what had happened in Havana, so we picked him up. We told him about the bloodbath. He already knew some of it. He had seen Sarabia's body. But he practically collapsed in a heap right there in the lobby of the Southern Cross when he realized that his entire world had vanished. Everyone he had ever known was gone, and if he went back to Cuba he would surely be killed. He was ripe for the plucking. We told him that if he worked for us, he could stay in the U.S. If not, we'd have him deported. We'd ship his ass back to Cuba. This is what we told him. Then we confiscated his suitcase. You wouldn't believe how much money he had in that suitcase. The poor, untutored sap.'

"(At this point Lagunas descended into an uneasy, thoughtful silence. I knew he wasn't finished. I knew he had a lot of ground to cover. I also knew he didn't like being put on the hook. It was close to three by then. It was a lazy, mojito kind of afternoon. We heard the whirring sound of speedboats from somewhere, but we couldn't see them. The sound of the speedboats was like a premonition. Then Lagunas took hold of the fourth envelope. He handed me a series of photos showing Oscar Garcia Raimundi at various locations in the Keys. Even

though he was working for the FBI, they were still taking
surveillance photos.)

   "'Initially we set up Raimundi in Key West. We knew
there were going to be a lot of Cubans coming over, particularly with the success Castro was having. And we knew that
as soon as Castro took control he was going to start sending
spies to keep tabs on any counter-insurgency activities that
might be taking place here in Florida. We wanted to keep tabs
on everyone coming over, and we thought Raimundi would be
an ideal point man. We thought he would be able to sniff out
genuine refuges from the implants. We thought the fact that
he had worked for DiCarla would work to our advantage. Of
course we didn't throw him into the deep end without a net.
We had men all over the Keys. Here's how it was supposed to
work. Raimundi would hang out down at the port whenever
a ship came in and he would mentally sort through the new
arrivals. If he thought there was someone we should keep
an eye on, he was supposed to engage them as if he were a
co-conspirator. He was to say if they were ever in need of any
assistance, or if they had any questions about anything Cuban,
they could count on a man named Jorge in the AerovisasQ
ticket office in the 700 block of Duval on the east side.'

   "(A photo of the ticket office with a smiling Cuban
family on the sidewalk out front on a very sunny day and a
series of beautiful panoramic photos of the Havana skyline
in the window and a sign to one side that said Fly to Gay
Tropical Havana in 30 minutes for $10 plus tax.)

   "'If these potential persons of interest smiled and
seemed pleased with that tidbit of information, Raimundi
was to press a ten-dollar bill into their hands and say if
they needed any prescriptions filled they should head to
the Oriental Pharmacy on the corner of Duval and Truman
and ask for a man named Nilo. Finally, if Raimundi spotted
someone who looked like they might have some information
we could use or who might be able to help us in any way
possible, he was to give them a coupon for one free night at a
dump called the Blue Marlin Motel on Simonton.'

   "(Photos of The Blue Marlin and the Oriental Pharmacy.
The photos of the Oriental Pharmacy were so grainy that it
was difficult to determine what exactly you were looking at.)

"'If he wasn't sure what to do or if he himself was having any difficulty, he was supposed to go to the Flagship Restaurant and sit outside if it was sunny or stand at the counter if it was raining. He was to order a fish sandwich, a Coca-Cola, and a piece of Key Lime pie, and when his order arrived he was to ask if Amos had gone home for the day.'

"(A photo of the Flagship Restaurant, which looked more like a walk-up diner than a restaurant, and it didn't resemble a ship of any kind in spite of the owner's attempt to create a little ambience by placing an obviously fake ship's smokestack squarely on the flat roof.)

"'We thought Raimundi would do quite well for us. He had a regular talent for chatting people up. But he had no talent at all for discerning the hidden motives of others. He was just as likely to send one of Castro's agents to the Blue Marlin as he was to send a disenfranchised refugee to the Oriental Pharmacy. We should have pulled the plug sooner. We knew by '62 that he wasn't going to pan out as a ferret, but some things just take longer than you expect. We didn't pull Raimundi out of Key West until 1966. One year later we had set him up in a glitzy nightclub in Miami. All the action was in Miami by then anyway. The club was called La Campana, but then you already know that, don't you.'

"(At that point Lagunas handed me a recent surveillance photo of me and Ramirez going into La Campana. I realized I had been tagged long before I called him up. But Lagunas didn't rub it in. He kept right on talking.)

"'We told Raimundi we wanted La Campana to be the kind of club that everyone from Cuba would frequent. I don't know whose idea it was in the first place, but we purchased the property in the name of Luis Sarabia to remind Raimundi who was actually in charge. Then we gave him access to a bank account and told him to run the club. We used the money from the suitcase to set everything up. We wanted him to be the gracious host, shake everybody's hand, and keep them coming back. That was all he had to do. The bartender worked for us. Not the guy that's there now. Ours was a guy named Eddie Cardona. He used to run a bolita game in Allapattah until we got a hold of him. We also had a couple of taxi drivers working the club. They hung out at

La Campana on Friday and Saturday nights in case there was
a patron too drunk to drive home, and there were always
plenty of drunks. Our taxi drivers were supposed to keep their
ears open for any political chit-chat that might give us a clue
about what Castro's boys were up to. We were desperate for
intel. In '67 we were scared shitless that Castro was trying to
destabilize Florida on behalf of the Soviet Union. There was
even some locker room talk that the Cubans and the Soviets
were planning an invasion to get us back for the Bay of Pigs,
even though we knew that was utter nonsense. But there was
a lot of talk floating around in those days, so getting the dope
on Castro's boys became a priority. Then Carter got elected
and Cuba was off the table and the drug cartels became the
issue of the day. I can tell you right now a lot of guys down
at the Bureau swore off the Democrats when that happened.
Fucking Carter. So we pulled Eddie Cardona from Raimundi's
nightclub and put him to work on a drug task force down
in the Keys. If my memory serves, he started bartending at a
real hellhole of a place on Stock Island called The Boca Chica
Lounge. Every other night somebody was getting shot up or
knifed in that joint, or out in the parking lot. They were open
all night so they picked up all sorts of riff-raff in the wee
hours of the morning because the bars in Key West closed
down at four. Anyway, we were done with Cuba, but somehow Raimundi slipped through the cracks. Nobody picked
him up. Nobody shut down his bank account. He was running
La Campana as if he owned the joint, but there was nobody
running him, and that's when the CIA got wind of Oscar
Garcia Raimundi.'

"(Lagunas began rummaging around in his backpack
at this point and retrieved a couple of candy bars and gave
me one. We ate the candy bars. We looked out at the water
while we ate. Another group of tourists had materialized
seemingly out of thin air and they were walking along the
narrow path in front of the first row of seats and one of them
was pointing to the band shell on the other side of the water
and then making wild gestures in the air with his hands. It
was clear he was talking about a concert he had once attended
at the stadium. We watched the guy for a while. Then Lagunas
opened the fifth manila envelope.)

"'Jack Hendershot was the CIA fucker who contacted our office. He wanted to know what kind of game we were running with Raimundi and why his office didn't know a goddamn thing about it. He was quite vocal in his displeasure. After that there were a number of closed door sessions between Abrahms and Jack's boss, a guy named Robert DeFoor out of Washington, a real spoon-fed prick if you ask me, so don't get me started. But just like that the CIA took charge of everything associated with La Campana. This was in 1977. That's when Héctor and Miguel Velázquez, your two suspects, come into the picture.

"(Lagunas paused and gave me a very hard look.)

"'Are you sure you want to hear this?'

"(I nodded.)

"'Well, okay then. It's your funeral. Apparently the CIA had been working with certain government officials in Cuba to create an international information network that would give them an inside track on any political developments in any Latin American country. This had been going on since 1970. The backbone of this network, the means of paying the bills, was and is the World Finance Corporation. The role of the WFC is to launder money earned from the trafficking of drugs into the United States. Most of the drugs now come from the Medellín Cartel out of Colombia, which routes most of its shipments through Panama and then Mexico. Seventy percent of the cocaine coming into the United States is coming from Colombia. But the Gulf Cartel out of Matamoros, Mexico is also a key player. Since García Ábrego took control, they have become quite clever in how they transport drugs across the border. But there has also been a lot more seemingly random, collateral violence in both the border towns along the U.S./Mexican border and in the streets of Miami as well. We believe Ábrego is getting help from corrupt officers in the Texas National Guard, but we have been unable to catch anyone just yet with their hand in the cookie jar.'

"(Lagunas forked over several black and white surveillance photos of drug smuggling activity. Some of the photos had the phrase Gulf Cartel scrawled in black marker on the back. One of these showed a chubby, thirty-year-old Ábrego eating at some restaurant. There was one other person at his table. An elderly gentleman in a white Stetson who seemed to be instructing Ábrego while he ate. Ábrego looked like a Latino Orson Welles after he had passed the point of no return. Another photo showed the elderly guy after he had been gunned down. The other photos were of the Medellín Cartel. One of these was a photo of Juan David Ochoa, Germán Castro Caicedo, Carlos Lehder, and a clean-shaven Pablo Escobar sitting around a small white patio table with a white fringed umbrella rising up out of the middle for shade. Ochoa seemed bored, or detached, as if he was formulating his own plans. Caicedo and Lehder seemed to be trading jokes. Only Escobar was looking at the camera. It seemed as if he was posing for the future. All of the photos seemed to be clichés, depicting rough looking, unshaven Latinos with machine guns or speeding away from some unidentifiable warehouse pier in speedboats or enjoying drinks at a swanky café or nightclub, surrounded by beautiful, half-naked girls.)

"'The CIA has been turning a blind eye to the drugs coming from these cartels for years and then skimming money right off the top to finance covert operations in Nicaragua and elsewhere. What a nest of Machiavellian vipers! We aren't sure how La Campana fits into all this. We know that the nightclub has become a haven for all sorts of drug dealers. We suspect the CIA simply wanted to create a safe haven for the drug lords they were working with to facilitate the flow of both cash and information. Simple as that. Still, it has been difficult to determine who is sleeping with whom. The WFC is a case in point. The WFC was founded in 1971 by Guillermo Hernández-Cartaya, a former Cuban banker who doubled as a CIA operative.'

"(A photo of Cartaya sporting wavy hair and a crooked, gin-and-tonic kind of smile.)

"'Yet Cartaya is also a friend of Castro.'

"(A photo of Cartaya and Castro having coffee at a sidewalk café, a bright sunny day.)

"'He was instrumental in helping the Colombian government secure a one-hundred-million-dollar loan from Cuba through the aegis of the WFC. To complicate an already complicated scenario, Cartaya is at this very moment working with René Rodriguez-Cruz, an official of the Cuban

intelligence service and a card-carrying member of the Cuban
Communist Party, to secure a drugs for arms deal to support a
counter-revolution in Nicaragua to oust the Sandinistas.'

"(A photo of Cruz, a psycho with a receding hairline
and glasses that seemed to magnify his eyes, which seemed to
be glowing with the ruthless, irrepressible, primordial joy of
an executioner.)

"'In April of this year, several high-ranking CIA officials
went to Panama to meet with Cartaya, Cruz and a charismatic
Nicaraguan leader named Edén Pastora. The purpose of
the meeting was supposedly to discuss how to finance the
counter-revolution. Pastora became disenchanted with the
Sandinista revolution when the Sandinista leaders began
moving into elegant colonial style mansions in an exclusive
suburb of Managua.'

"(A photo of Pastora in a black beret and green army
fatigues with grenades clipped to a shoulder strap. He was
holding his rifle in the air and smiling with confidence.)

"'And that brings us back full circle to La Campana
and Héctor and Miguel Velázquez. They grew up in Coral
Gables. (A photo of the Velázquez brothers standing outside
a small cinder block home in Coral Gables in 1960.) They
were basically juvenile delinquents. As teenagers they were
always getting arrested. (A photo of the Velázquez brothers
getting arrested across the street from a high school.) But for
some reason they always skated. (A series of mugshots from
the years 1961 through 1964, the Velázquez brothers grinning
these ridiculous grins in every photo.) Then in 1965 they began
working for Southern Air Transport, which is why you called
me in the first place. Let me just say that not everyone who
works for Southern Air Transport is CIA. Just so we're clear
about that. But the Velázquez brothers were different. Their
potential, shall we say, was noticed almost immediately. They
have been working for the CIA ever since. They spent ten
years down in Central America, and another two in various
hot spots around the globe. (Several photos. The Velázquez
brothers standing in front of a Jeep Wrangler somewhere in
one of the jungles of Central America. The Velázquez brothers
drinking coffees at a café in Granada and an unknown man in
sunglasses looking on. The Velázquez brothers and a group of

Nicaraguan rebels riding on top of a Route Four bus traveling
from Granada to Managua. The Velázquez brothers standing
next to small green tank parked on a city street. The letters
FSLN are painted on the front of the tank using white paint.
The Velázquez brothers with several Colombian rebels in the
jungles of Venezuela. The Velázquez brothers watching a
freighter passing through Miraflores Locks in Panama. The
Velázquez brothers standing in front of a disco called Habana
Panamá and then leaving that same club several hours later,
each with a couple of half-naked girls draped over their arms.)
In 1977 they were put in charge of whatever was going on
at La Campana. Whatever is still going on. Their interest in
speedboats began as part of their cover, but they really get off
on the speed. (Photo of the Velázquez brothers in a speedboat
moored at the Fontainebleau Resort Marina in Miami Beach.)
And most importantly, they are untouchable. Besides, they
are very, very professional. They do not leave any evidence
behind, which you probably already know. I am certain they
killed Raimundi. What's more, they are psychotic bastards,
which means they probably enjoyed it. I am just as certain that
they killed him because he was becoming a liability. But you
will never be able to prove a thing. Nothing sticks to these
guys. My advice to you is to stay away from them. Close the
case. Bury it in a filing cabinet. You'll be signing your own
death warrant if you don't.'

"(Lagunas stopped talking and we regarded each other
for a moment. It was close to five o'clock and you could hear
the comforting hum of rush-hour traffic like a warm breeze.
We were both tired. Lagunas stuffed the manila envelopes
back into his backpack and then slung it over his shoulder
college style and started sidling down the row towards
the stadium exit. The persona of the wino from before had
evaporated, as had the personas of the cynical bureaucrat and
the worldly spy, but just before he disappeared down the
ramp, he turned and gave me a profoundly thoughtful look.
It was a very strange look. It was like he had more to say but
he could only communicate with his eyes. But the strangest
thing about that look was that I thought I heard his voice, like
I was reading his mind. *One more thing,* he seemed to be
saying, *the bartender that's there now, Herminio Arréllaga,*

*he was also CIA. He began working at the club in 1979. Prior
to that he was working in the field in Panama, and before that
he was in Nicaragua. In August 1978 he was part of a rebel
group that stormed the Nicaraguan National Palace and took
several high-ranking members of the Nicaraguan Congress
hostage. They also killed nineteen palace guards. The leader
of that rebel group was Edén Pastora.'* And then just like that,
Lagunas was gone.)"

"**September 10, 1981. Thursday, 4:35 PM.** La Campana.
Another rainy day. I didn't tell Ramirez about my meeting
with Lagunas. I was sick to my stomach thinking about it,
but there wasn't much either of us could do, so why ruin his
day. Besides, Lagunas was right about the evidence. There
wasn't any. At least there wasn't any evidence that made any
sense. I've never seen such a case. It was impossible to connect
the dots even knowing that the Velázquez brothers were the
killers. So at two o'clock I took the ten-thousand dollars out
of the evidence locker and got in my car and headed over to
La Campana. I have to say now that the Velázquez brothers
acted as if they knew I was coming. Héctor met me at the
door. He gave me a tremendous bear hug and then roared and
roared for his brother to come see what the cat had dragged
in. The next thing I knew I was having drinks with Héctor
and Miguel Velázquez. Herminio was pouring. At some point
one of the brothers signed the receipt for the ten-thousand
and then the money was whisked away and Herminio put
another drink in my hands. I don't remember if we talked
about anything at all. We were just drinking. The last thing I
remember is Héctor reaching for a bottle on a small diagonal
shelf above the register and his brother calling out to be
careful, he had better not drop that bottle. It was a bottle of
1691 Clos de Griffier Vieux Cognac. Héctor said it had cost
them five thousand smackers from some Islamic fucker, but
it was probably worth ten. Those were Héctor's words. They
had bought it years ago on a trip to Paris, their one and only
trip. They didn't say why they went. Then Héctor poured a
glass for everyone, even Herminio. Then we raised our glasses
and Miguel said something I didn't catch but Héctor started
roaring, and then we drank the Cognac. I think we drank the

whole goddamn bottle, but I could be mistaken. That's the last thing I remember.

"**September 14, 1981. Monday, 9:55 PM.** I had told the Captain I would have my report on his desk no later than Friday afternoon. Last Friday. Well fuck that! I wasn't in the mood to write the damn thing on Friday. I wasn't in the mood today either, to tell you the truth, but what else was I going to do? At five o'clock I grabbed a mushroom burger at Julian's, a mushroom burger and two glasses of whiskey to be precise, and I felt a little better after that. I went back to my desk just after eight and sat down to type. I gave the Captain just what he wanted, a report containing only facts and direct observations, a report which highlighted only the relevant eyewitness testimony, and kept erroneous opinion to a minimum. I left out all of my suspicions. I did not interpret. I focused on what we could prove. The report was three pages long. I slunk into the Captain's office like some kind of thief and laid it on his desk. Then I went out to get rip-roaring drunk."

-130-

From the medical chart of Isidora Escoraz Calzada, August 12, 2000, 11:00 PM, as noted by the attending ED physician, Andrés Huerta, Jackson Memorial Hospital, Miami, Florida):

"Initially the patient walked into the Emergency Room Ambulance Bay but appeared disoriented. When two EMTs asked her if she was lost, she started babbling incoherently and then collapsed. The EMTs brought her into the Emergency Room and she was placed immediately in an ER bed. Her initial vital signs were generally good, except for her blood pressure reading, which was 183/106. Patient is 50 years old. Her DOB is 12-26-49. I examined her at 11 PM. Her BP was still elevated. Her pulse rate was 92 with no arrhythmias. Her lungs were clear. Her abdomen was soft. Bowel sounds were present in all quadrants. Her left eyes showed evidence of recent trauma. There was visible blood in the anterior chamber of the eye between the cornea and the iris, which is consistent with a diagnosis of hyphema. The patient did not remember injuring her eye, but she did indicate that she was experiencing some pain and a mild sensitivity to light. On a scale of one to ten, she said her eye pain was a five. Her skin showed no signs of any rash or petechiae, except for her face. There is a five-inch scar on her left cheek which shows significant fibrosis. The patient said the scar was the result of an injury she had sustained in 1986. Upon initial examination, the scar tissue was a bright red color. After a brief consultation with Dr. Simon Geist, a physician of Geriatric Medicine at Jackson Memorial, I gave the patient 0.5 mg of Ativan intramuscularly to treat her anxiety. I also put steroid drops in her left eye to reduce the level of eye pain and placed a patch over the eye until she could be seen by an ophthalmologist. After thirty minutes the patient appeared to be in a calmer state. Her BP was down to 156/92. She also said her eye did not hurt as much. After an hour, her scar tissue was a darker brown color. The patient said this was the normal color of the scar tissue. BP was also in the high normal range. By 2:35 AM the patient was in generally good spirits and was well enough to be discharged, but upon discussing this with the patient, she indicated that she could not go home with her eye the way it was. There was no one there to look after her. She lived alone. After a thirty-minute consultation with Dr. Geist, we contacted Dana Peterson, a social worker who is on staff at the Homeless Assistance Center in downtown Miami and is part of their on-call Emergency Team. Dana indicated that the patient would receive short-term housing assistance, three meals a day, basic health-care services, and counseling services as warranted. We discharged the patient and transported her to the Center at approximately 3:30 AM."

-131-

From the Case Management Report for Isidora Escoraz Calzada (August 13, 2000 to October 30, 2000), Miami

Homeless Assistance Center, Hannah Grajek, Case Manager,
filed November 6, 2000:

"Isidora came to us from the Emergency Room at
Jackson Memorial Hospital early Sunday morning, August
13, 2000. She was immediately placed in a private room. It is
clear from her physical appearance that she has had a difficult
life. She is only fifty years old, but she looks like she is in
her seventies. On the Monday afternoon following her arrival
she was seen for follow-up care by Dr. Sandra Gutiérrez,
one of our staff physicians. On Tuesday she was seen by an
ophthalmologist for treatment of hyphema in her left eye. On
Wednesday she met with one of our counselors and provided
significant information about her life and her current situation.
On Thursday, she and I met for several hours. I, for one,
expend more effort than most trying to understand the people
who come to us for help. I believe the more I know about
a person's life, the more I can do for them. I go over every
detail of their stories, however seemingly insignificant. I listen
carefully not only to what they say, but how they say it. And
I verify every fact that can be verified. Naturally, I do not
delve in the life of anyone without their permission. I do not
wish to invade anybody's privacy. And some people are more
open than others. Isidora was perhaps more open to talking
about the personal details of her life than any other person I
have ever met. She wanted her life to be an open book. And
whenever I pointed out that something she said didn't jive
with reality as I knew it to be, she would only smile softly,
without getting defensive, without exhibiting a judgmental
attitude of any kind, and say, 'Yes, yes, that is to be expected,
God reveals to each of us only what we must know, and only
when we are ready.' Isidora talks like that a lot. She has been
a joy to be around.

"So to begin. Isidora has been living in her parent's
house, a tiny bungalow in Allapattah close to the river. Both
of her parents are dead. Her father passed away in 1966. Her
mother died three years ago. Her parent's house is the only
place where she has ever lived. However, she is at this point
actually squatting on the property. She told us that the City of
Miami had sold the house this past May due to several years
of unpaid property taxes. Isidora said the city engaged the

services of 21st Century Reality to sell the house, but so far no one has shown any interest, so the house, which is actually something of an eyesore, remains vacant except for Isidora. She also had one brother, Emilio, who also lived at the house until his death in 1986. The circumstances of her brother's death were suspicious, but no charges were ever brought. Isidora believes two small-minded thugs, two brothers known to Isidora as Bull and Horse Velázquez, murdered her brother. She said the Velázquez brothers had also murdered her husband. She had heard them talking about it afterwards. Her husband was a Cuban immigrant named Oscar Garcia Raimundi. He owned a small nightclub in Allapattah called La Campana. Isidora said her husband had opened the nightclub in 1967 and that she had started working at the club as a hostess in 1968. She said she and her husband began dating in 1969 and got married in 1977, but she then said their happiness together was short-lived.

"According to Isidora, 1977 was also the year that the Velázquez brothers began working at the club as bouncers, and within a few years they turned the club into a haven for drug dealers and thieves, which her husband didn't notice right away, and neither did she, because they were both focused on the joys of marriage, and she could not fault him for that. When he finally did open his eyes in 1981, he tried to get rid of the Velázquez brothers, but he did not anticipate how dangerous they were. They were very dangerous. Isidora said they murdered her husband without even a second thought and took over completely. She said she wanted to go to the police, but she changed her mind when she saw the detective who was investigating her husband's death drinking with the Velázquez brothers. When she saw that she decided to keep her mouth shut. She didn't remember the name of the detective. She said she stayed on at the club because she had nowhere else to go.

"From a completely objective perspective, Isidora seems to have some difficulty separating fact from fiction. But it is next to impossible to look at Isidora with an objective eye. For example, we checked with the Miami-Dade County Clerk of the Courts and we were told that in 1967 a man named Luis Sarabia had filed a deed for a newly constructed nightclub

called La Campana, and then in 1979 he had sold the club to
Héctor and Miguel Velázquez. The club went out of business
in 1992. A company listed as La Campana Enterprises is the
current owner of the property, which has fallen into disrepair.
There is no record of an Oscar Garcia Raimundi associated
with the nightclub. There is no record of such a person living
in Dade County between 1960 and 1990. We also checked
with the Miami Police Department to see if Mr. Raimundi had
in fact been a victim of foul play in 1981. Detective Michael
Delarosa told us that in 1981 there were 622 murders in Dade
County; the names of all of the victims were known; the name
Oscar Garcia Raimundi was not on the list. But when we
presented these facts to Isidora, she merely smiled sweetly and
said we were mistaken. In spite of her delusions, and in spite
of the trauma she has clearly experienced in her life, she is an
incredibly loving and compassionate person. It is impossible
to separate her persona from what she tells us. It is like being
hypnotized. Every word she says has the ring of truth, even
when what she says cannot possibly be true.

   "So to continue. Isidora said after her husband had
been murdered, her brother Emilio, who also worked at the
club, started to keep a diary of all the people the Velázquez
brothers had killed, beginning with Oscar Garcia Raimundi.
Emilio wanted to keep their memories alive, she said. Then
in 1986, he was killed. Isidora blames herself. She said by
1986 the club had become a private club where negotiations
among those trafficking in drugs took place. The girls who
had formerly worked as waitresses now entertained the drug
dealers once business had been concluded. Isidora was among
these poor unfortunate girls condemned to entertain these
men. She said she suffered through those days the best she
could, but one sunny afternoon in late September of 1986, she
allowed her emotions to get the better of her. On that day,
the Velázquez brothers had given her to three Panamanians.
She was to entertain all three. She became inebriated and was
raped repeatedly, and then she fell asleep. When she woke up
several hours later she discovered that one of the Panamanians
was passed out on the couch. He was naked. She didn't know
where the other two were. In a fit of madness, she said she
took a knife and cut off the sleeping man's penis and his balls,

and then she opened up an artery, she didn't say which one, and he started bleeding profusely. He bled to death right there on the couch while she watched. Then, not knowing what else to do, she went to her brother Emilio and told him what had happened. Emilio told her not to worry. He told her that he would take the blame for the death of the Panamanian. He said he would tell the Velázquez brothers that the Panamanians had gone beyond simply enjoying the afternoon with his sister. He would tell them they had violated her in every conceivable way, they had raped her until she was bleeding from every orifice, and that as her brother he could not stand idly by and let such things happen. He would tell them it was a matter of family honor. She said the Velázquez brothers were very angry with Emilio and took him to a small getaway house they owned just off NW 22nd Avenue and tossed him from the roof. Later, they brought Isidora into their office and told her what had happened to her brother. They asked her if she had had anything to do with the death of the Panamanian. But she didn't say a word. She just sat there in a chair across from the Velázquez brothers, but she wasn't really there. She said she was remembering a day many years earlier when she and her brother had accompanied their mother to Burdine's in downtown Miami. Then the brother named Bull pulled out a knife and began to carve out pieces of her face. She said she didn't say a word even then. She didn't cry out. She just sat there. She said her neck and chest were dripping with blood. Then the brother named Horse grabbed the other one by the wrist and said enough, it is best not go on a killing spree today, and the brother named Bull put his knife away and told Isidora to go home. She said she tried to clean out her wound as best she could. She did not seek any medical attention. Nor did she call the police. For Isidora, the temporary pain of having a maniac carve up her face was a very small punishment compared to the gravity of her sin, and by sin she did not mean the death of the Panamanian. She meant her role in bringing 'death, that impertinent lover who whispers only bitter stories, to meet her brother.' That is exactly how she put it.

"After Isidora's brother was killed, she said she took over his diary. But her intentions were not as pristine as those

of her brother. Emilio had once told her that every person the
Velázquez brothers murdered seemed to vanish completely. It
was as if they had never even existed, he had told her. This is
why Emilio had kept the diary. He wanted a visible reminder
that these poor murdered souls had once been alive. He
wanted to honor their memories. But Isidora said she wanted
vengeance. She wanted to document every gruesome detail of
the crimes committed by the Velázquez brothers and then turn
over the diary as evidence. She wanted to send them to the
electric chair. She wanted to watch the Velázquez brothers fry.
She said she hoped their executions would be botched so they
would die inconceivably horrible deaths. She also said she
was uncertain whom she could trust with her brother's diary,
but she did believe that one day the Archangel Michael would
appear with his fiery sword and show her the path to God's
justice. So she added to Emilio's diary. From August 1981 to
September 1986, Emilio had made one-hundred and fifty-seven
entries with names, dates, and details about the lives of the
victims. From October 1986 to June of 1994, Isidora recorded
the stories of another three-hundred and seventy-five victims.
She said the burden of so many deaths weighed heavily on her
own soul. It was an unbelievable number of murders. It was
incomprehensible. When I asked her why she stopped keeping
the diary, I expected her to say that it was because having the
reality of so many murders right there in front of her eyes
was too much for her to take, that she was slowly, inevitably
going mad. But she did not say this. Instead, Isidora said she
stopped keeping the diary in July of 1994 because she saw a
billboard with the face of a local news anchor, Eléna Montaño.
Eléna Montaño was a local girl who had graduated from the
University of Miami in 1977. She had been hired by Channel
Ten in 1990 as an investigative reporter. In May of 1991 she
became the weekend news anchor. Isidora said when she saw
Eléna's face up on that billboard with those dark, inquisitive
Spanish eyes and that bright, beaming smile, she knew imme-
diately what she was going to do with the diary. She knew
Eléna Montaño belonged to Gesù Church in downtown Miami.
Gesù had been her mother's church. So she prepared a short
letter, though she did not sign this letter or reveal her identity
in any way, and then she placed the letter and the diary in a

shoebox and went to the Church. She said there was only one priest in the Church when she got there. He was coming out of the confessional as she was heading up the aisle, and he had called out to her, asking her what she wanted. She told me it was as if God had been directing her footsteps. It was very dark inside the church. She could barely distinguish the priest in his dark clothes from the hazy darkness that surrounded them both. All she could really see was his glowing head and his strange eyes like the eyes of a frog or a bloated sea creature. But she was not afraid. She told the priest she had some information for the investigative reporter, Eléna Montaño, but she didn't know how to get in touch with her. The priest said he knew Eléna. He said he had known her since she was a small child. He would make sure she got the shoebox. Isidora said that she was suddenly full of hope. But one month later she saw on the news that Eléna Montaño had been killed in an auto accident. She had no idea what had become of the diary.

"As horrific as Isidora's story was, there were only two verifiable facts in the entire account, at least as far as I could determine. First, Isidora's brother Emilio died on Saturday, September 20, 1986. His body was found the following morning by pedestrians on the sidewalk next to a smoking shop on NW 22nd Avenue. His skull had been fractured, presumably as a result of falling or jumping off the roof of the cigarette store. In his report, the coroner noted that he couldn't say if Emilio had committed suicide or if his death had been accidental or if somebody had pushed him. The coroner also noted that he had ruled the death an accident because there were many more efficient ways of committing either suicide or murder. Not everyone who fell sixteen feet died from their injuries. Emilio had just been one of the unlucky ones. Second, news anchor Eléna Montaño was in fact tragically killed in an accident on the evening of Sunday, July 17, 1994. According to newspaper accounts of the day, she had been driving back from Bahia State Park down in the Keys and had apparently lost control of her vehicle while crossing the Seven Mile Bridge. She swerved into an oncoming truck and was knocked off the bridge, disappearing into sixteen feet of water. The current in the channel was approximately two knots. Her car, a Custom Club De Soto convertible, was recovered the next day. Ms. Montaño's bloated body washed up on Little Pine Key a week later.

"With the death of Eléna Montaño and the mystery surrounding the whereabouts of the diary, Isidora said she fell into a deep depression. She continued working for the Velázquez brothers because she had no other alternative. Since her face was disfigured, she was no longer asked to entertain the drug lords. She became instead a thief, a snitch lurking in doorways, a stalker of lonely hearts, a backdoor spy, a purveyor of half-truths and outright lies. In short, she became a stooge, and she remained employed by the Velázquez brothers even after they closed the club. She did whatever they asked her to do. Of course this new role took its toll on Isidora's psyche. She had all but given up hope that her tormentors would ever be brought to justice. And yet she did not completely abandon her faith in God. Every morning when she woke up, and every evening before she went to bed, she prayed that God would send her a sign, a divine message, so that she might escape her predicament.

"Isidora believes that she did receive just such a divinely inspired message from God in May of this year, though she is the first to admit that she did not recognize the nature of this message right away. In May of 2000, the Velázquez brothers asked her to keep an eye on one of her neighbors, a young man she knew as Broken Bike. Apparently Broken Bike had worked for the Velázquez brothers for a number of years, a fact which Isidora had not known. But he had fallen out of favor with his employers in the spring of 2000. At first, Isidora was simply to keep an eye on him and report on his activities every other day or so. She did this. But by the beginning of July, Isidora realized that the young man's life was in danger. She did not know the details of his disagreement with the Velázquez brothers, but she did know about their volatile hostility. Then she learned that Broken Bike's Christian name was Malachi. She was floored by this revelation. Malachi was the twelfth minor prophet in the Bible. The name Malachi meant Messenger of God. Isidora said that up until that moment she had been waiting for God's message, and then all of a sudden she was confronted with God's messenger in the flesh. It was almost more than she could believe. She said she became more vigilant in keeping an eye on Malachi after that, but her goal at that point was to protect him from the Velázquez brothers so she might learn what God intended. She also said this was not as easy as it sounded. The Velázquez brothers were angry, determined men. Their reach never seemed to exceed their grasp. Then on August 12th everything came to a head. Isidora saw Malachi at a parade and tried to warn him that the Velázquez brothers were going to shoot him on sight. She knew she was not the only one who was supposed to report on his whereabouts, so she took him to the ruins of La Campana. She said she thought they could hide out in La Campana until she could figure out what to do next. She said the Velázquez brothers never went there anymore. What she hadn't counted on, what she did not expect, was that Herminio would be at the club. Herminio had been the bar-tender at La Campana for years. Isidora said she and Malachi waltzed into the bar of the club and there was Herminio watching cartoons. She wasn't sure what to do. She said it was like two destinies colliding. She remembered feeling a wave a nausea roll through her, and then she heard herself tell Malachi her name. She said she knew Herminio would call the Velázquez brothers at the cartoon break. Then she realized that there was nothing she could do. Her fate, Malachi's fate, everyone's fate was in God's hands. So she left.

"When I asked Isidora what had happened to Malachi, she smiled and said Malachi was very, very lucky, and then she laughed and said even though there is no such thing as luck. When I asked her how she knew this, she said she was watching from the shadows. She said she was filled with great remorse after she had abandoned Malachi, so she hid herself in the empty shell of an old car in the lot next to La Campana. She said she could see everything from where she was hiding. She saw Herminio leave through a back door. Ten minutes later a young man she did not know pushed his way through the front door. A few minutes after that the Velázquez brothers went into the club through the side door Herminio had used. Herminio returned. A few moments later Malachi came out the front door. He was flying down the street. Then there was some shouting and a few muffled gunshots from inside the club. Then the Velázquez brothers ran out into the street. They were turning around in circles, but they had no idea which way Malachi had gone. They headed off, but it was in the wrong direction.

"Isidora said she later spotted Malachi sitting on a bench on the elevated platform of the Allapattah Metro Station. Malachi sat there until after the sun had set and then he headed off into the darkness. Isidora said she followed him to a club called La Mamacita's, but she did not go in herself. She said an international film star named Salma de la Prada was holding court inside and that Malachi was hoping to speak with her. Nevertheless, she said the place seemed strangely vacant for a Saturday night, and the thought crossed her mind that perhaps the Velázquez brothers were lying in wait and that as soon as Malachi went in he would be killed. Then a black SUV pulled up and the Velázquez brothers got out and ran right past her. She said they had seemed oblivious to the world and everything that was good. A few minutes later the unmistakable sounds of gunfire erupted inside La Mamacita's. Windows were shattered. Bullet holes appeared in the exterior walls and the flat, warehouse-style roof, and the front door was completely blown away. A cloud of tiny fragments blew into her face and that was when she injured her eye.

"After the commotion had subsided, she went inside. She said she saw men dressed in body armor clearing away broken glass and bits of rubble, the remnants of what surely must have been a hellacious gunfight. The men were speaking a strange, guttural language she did not recognize. She saw a giant of a man attending to Malachi, whose arm appeared to be broken, but otherwise he was unhurt. The Velázquez brothers were nowhere to be found. It was as if their bodies had merged with the hazy darkness of the night sky, which was now visible through the holes in the roof, a darkness which seemed to be descending, filling in all of the empty space inside La Mamacita's. This is exactly how Isidora described the scene. Then she saw two beefy men carrying Salma de la Prada to a limousine that had suddenly pulled up to the club. She was an immaculate vision, Isidora said. Her feet never touched the ground. Then the limousine drove off. Then there was a steady procession of men in body armor climbing into several vans that had also appeared as if by magic. The vans followed the limousine. Isidora said that by that point she could hear the sounds of sirens floating through the night air. It was like a choir of invisible angels, she said. Ten minutes later two ambulances arrived. Malachi was loaded into one of the ambulances and an old man into the other. She said she knew Malachi was all right, but she went to Jackson Memorial just to be sure.

"Isidora said she was excited beyond her ability to comprehend. The terror that was the Velázquez brothers had been eliminated. God had finally answered her prayers.

"Of course based on her incredibly complicated tale of woe, we decided Isidora might benefit from speaking with a psychiatrist. She said that would be fine. She had been to a psychiatrist one summer as a young girl. In fact, she had been to three. She was not afraid of them. Two days later we had her evaluated by Dr. Samuel Quintana, a psychiatrist who has been on the staff at Jackson Memorial for years. Dr. Quintana said Isidora was as sane as you or I. She had a few nervous tics, a few paranoias, and she harbored a few illusions about what had transpired over the years. But who among us is immune to the vagaries of life? Dr. Quintana conceded that Isidora might benefit from continued counseling, but he felt quite strongly that she would benefit far more by finding a safe, stable place to call home, and by making a few friends. Dr. Quintana also suggested that given her abiding faith in God, she would probably find immense satisfaction from connecting with one of the dozens of Catholic churches in the Greater Miami metropolitan area.

"As luck would have it, though I can hear Isidora herself saying that luck had nothing to do with it, we were able to secure accommodations for her with a community of nuns up in Hialeah. I met with the Mother Superior of the convent, Sister Silvia Faustina, and their Director of Spiritual Life, Sister Nadia Saenz. We spoke about Isidora's situation, her need for stability, etc., and they agreed to drive down to the Center and meet with her. After the meeting, they were bursting with excitement. They assured me that Isidora had found a home with them in Hialeah. She would be well cared for in their convent. They were certain the story of her life would inspire their young novitiates. They were amazed that she could have endured so much and yet possess so strong a faith. She had, they said, followed the excruciatingly rocky, narrow path of the saints. They also thought she might enjoy talking with young women in need of spiritual guidance. There were plenty of churches in the Miami area hungry for speakers with Isidora's gift. Isidora was an example for us all. Three days later, at one in the afternoon on Monday, October 30, 2000, Sister Faustina and an older, gray-haired gentleman named Emidio Peralta (who possessed a well-worn but kindly face) pulled up to the Center in an old station wagon. Emidio helped Isidora into the back seat. He was very polite and she was very gracious. Then they left."

-132-

From a forty-minute interview with Emidio Peralta as part of the University of Miami Oral History Project, conducted by Nathalia Ibarra, a Senior at the University of Miami, and recorded by Tomás De Aguero, a Junior, at the Otto G. Richter Library from 3-5 PM on Sunday, October 26, 2008:

[**Interviewer's comments:** Emidio moved to Florida from Maracaibo, Venezuela in 1976. He was thirty-two when he arrived in Miami. He said his childhood years were unremarkable. His father worked for a large industrial chemical company along Avenida San Francisco. His mother worked as a surgical nurse at the Surgical and Maternity Hospital of Maracaibo. He did not see much of his parents. He was like every other teenage boy growing up in Maracaibo in the 50s and 60s. He graduated in the middle of his high school class. He played soccer in the streets. He stayed out of trouble. His life was dull, he said. Later, he hoped to go to work in the petrochemical industry, so in 1973 he enrolled in the University of Zulia to study Petroleum engineering and make this dream come true, but he dropped out of the program after two years. His father had died from complications due to emphysema, which Emidio said was fairly common among the men working at the chemical factory, so there was no money to pay for his education. Emidio never did earn a degree. He has no children. He never married, though he has been in two long-term relationships, one in Maracaibo and one in Miami. After his mother followed his father to the grave in 1976, he came to the United States and found factory work with a company called Dolphin Boats, located in Homestead, Florida. He spent sixteen years building fishing boats. In 1992 he went to work as a janitor for the Servants of the Pierced Hearts of Jesus and Mary, a religious order of mostly Hispanic nuns in Hialeah. He has been there ever since.]

[This excerpt begins at the **18:21** mark.]

Nathalia: Why did you decide to work for the Servants of the Pierced Hearts of Jesus and Mary after sixteen years of building boats?

Emidio: It is not always so easy to say why one does one thing and not another. I was tired of building boats, that is for certain. I worked as a fiberglass laminator to create the hulls for custom built boats. Most people don't know all the work that goes into building boats. When I started, we were building boats with sold hulls. We built very good boats. I was proud of every boat we built. Then one day we began building boats with cored hulls. This was in the mid-80s, I think. We wanted to be very high-tech. We used foam for the core. We even used a vibrating machine on the hull to make sure the bonding putty was spread out evenly throughout the core and that all the seams were filled, but this didn't always work. But foam was the thing, even though it caused a lot of problems. I remember one year we started using a new kind of foam called Airex. It was supposed to be stronger and lighter. A hull made with this material was supposedly less likely to absorb water. What the salesmen who sold us Airex didn't know, and what we found out later, was that the foam would soften at high temperatures. Then the hulls would blister, and then they would start to come apart. So we stopped using Airex. But when the next new thing came along, we jumped right on that bandwagon just like every other small boat manufacturer, and hoped for the best. I guess that's when I became disillusioned with building boats and I started to wonder about the future, my future. I realized I needed to do something different. This was in 1991. August maybe. Or September. I was very worried about this. There were many nights I did not sleep. Then on All Saints Day, and I remember this like it was yesterday, I knelt down before Mass and started to pray, and I heard my voice, only it didn't sound like my voice, it sounded very far away, a small, thin voice, like my father's voice when he was dying of emphysema, but not mine, and yet I heard the words distinctly, clearly, like the tolling of a distant church bell. I was saying, 'God, I do not want to die in a boat factory. Tell me what I should do?' And just like that the answer came. God asked me to come work for Him.

Nathalia: But you did not leave the factory right away.

Emidio: No. I did not want to believe God was calling me to work for the Church. I pretended that God was calling someone else.

Nathalia: What made you change your mind?

Emidio: Well for one thing, God is very persistent. Whenever I began to pray, he would interrupt me within the first minute or two to ask me when I was going to quit the boat factory. This went on for three or four months. That kind of pressure takes its toll after a while. So one day I asked Monsignor Guidera what I should do. He suggested I work for the nuns up in Hialeah. They had only been around a few years. They needed a janitor. I went up to Hialeah and met Sister Faustina and she hired me on the spot.

Nathalia: What was the transition like?

Emidio: It was not so bad as you might think. There are many moments when you are building a boat that feel like praying. You are at peace with the world. You are living outside yourself, as if you have left your body and are looking down from somewhere, watching, and in that same moment you are deep within yourself, like a seed that has been planted. I found the same to be true working for the Sisters of the Pierced Hearts, though maybe not right away.

[At the **21:27** mark the tape recording became unintelligible and remained unintelligible for twelve minutes and six seconds. The remainder of this excerpt picks up at the **33:33** mark. During this segment, Emidio talks about his relationship with an elderly woman named Isidora, who stayed at the convent from 2000 until 2007. It is not clear from the interview if Isidora died or moved away.]

Nathalia: Had you ever met anyone like Isidora?

Emidio: There was no one like Isidora. She was beyond my imagination. She was an extraordinary woman.

Nathalia: What made her so extraordinary?

Emidio: There was not just one thing. She was filled with joy, and for those of us who have grown old, to be filled with joy is a tremendous gift. She also did not judge you. She took the Bible to heart in this. And she loved poetry. She would ask me to bring her books of poetry. Old poets, new poets, she read them all. I must confess to you that I never bothered with poetry until I met Isidora. I do not remember the names of the poets, but whenever I brought her a new book she would ask me to sit with her and she would read some of the poems out loud. It sounded to me as if she had written the poems herself.   I did not tell her this, but she had the voice of an angel.

Nathalia: Was your relationship with Isidora a romantic one?

Emidio: No, it was not romantic. But I truly loved her. Everyone loved her. If you had known her, you would have loved her too.

Nathalia: What is your favorite memory of Isidora?

Emidio: I do not think 'favorite' is the right word. I have so many memories of Isidora. I remember one day Isidora showed me a newspaper article about a guitar player, a young man with a ponytail, who had been murdered in Fort Lauderdale. He had been a great guitarist, and after his death, a Miami artist had painted his face on a wall in some park I had never heard of. A photo of the face on the wall accompanied the article. I remember staring at the face, and then all of a sudden I could actually hear guitar music, as if the young man with the ponytail were playing his guitar right there in Isidora's room. I don't know what kind of expression my face registered. But then Isidora asked me if I could hear him playing. Did I hear any music? I was so startled by the question that I didn't say anything right away. I remember thinking either she heard this ethereal music the same as I did, or I was going completely mad. The next thing I remember I started laughing. I guess in my heart I was trying to tell Isidora that whatever she heard, I heard too, whatever secrets she wished to share, I would guard them with my life. I was trying to tell her all this, but I was incapable of speech at that moment. Then the music stopped and Isidora and I decided we would seek out this wall with the face of the young guitarist who had been killed. I didn't know the park in the article, but we would find it, I told her, the two of us. But this never happened. We never went out in search of that park. Not even once.

[36:26.]

The story continues in *The Mad Patagonian: Part Three: An Elegy for a Dream Once Dreamt*